REMNANTS

on the

TIDES

OF TIME

Book Three of the Adrift Series

TRINITY DUNN

Copyright

Cover design by Twisted Plum LLC

I dedicate this book to my sister.

You are my real-life Cecelia and Lilly wrapped into one amazingly inspirational human being. You are my rock, my laughter, and my favorite.
I love you.

THE ADRIFT SERIES BOOKS
(IN ORDER):

Book 1: More of Us to the West

Book 2: Feathers Floating Through Ember

Book 3: Remnants on the Tides of Time

Book 4: A Reflection of the Sky on the Sea

(Coming Winter 2022)

PART I

The weightlessness of forgetting.

Chapter One

I attempted, despite my trembling body, to remain standing while Fetia pinned the last pieces of gaudy red silk to the stays she'd tied entirely too tight. Juan Josef had excused himself from my room hours prior, instructing me to stay put as he left me alone with my babies and a racing mind.

Hours passed, and as the sun began to lower outside my small window, my anxiety was at its peak. With Zachary and Cecelia less than a day old, I'd tried to focus exclusively on them; feeding, changing, swaddling, and holding them; memorizing their little faces in the event something might happen to me. I tried to forget I was a captive and Jack and the others were *'detained'* somewhere.

Despite my best attempts to keep my mind occupied, constant movement on the other side of the bedroom door indicated there were others in the house with me, and I couldn't help but torture myself with the possibilities of what might happen when someone came through it.

Could I run? Would I be able to fight whoever filled the doorframe, somehow get to the ship, and save the others with two newborns wrapped in my arms? How much did Juan Josef's spy tell him about us? Might it be possible that they left out the names of some of our people? None of us ever spoke to Phil, so it was possible he was still roaming free. Although he'd have no reason to save us, and was the last person I wanted to find coming to my rescue, I held onto hope that, if he was still out there, he might try something just to save himself from being left alone in Tahiti. Was Kyle with him? Kyle and Fetia had been romantic with each other. If Fetia was the spy, and if she felt a connection to Kyle in some way, she might've refrained from offering him up.

Fetia. It was hard to believe she was capable of turning us in to Juan Josef. She was so young and timid, and she'd been with the captain for almost a year, spending every day with us since our arrival in Tahiti. She wouldn't have had time to form an alliance with Juan Josef, so I had to assume it was her family that was behind our capture, and she was merely a pawn in a game she had no control over.

Rallying back and forth between feelings of hopelessness and attempts to formulate a plan to escape, I'd jumped when Fetia came through the door, red silk fabrics draped over her petite arm. She hadn't spoken, but lit the lantern and candles, appearing just as shaken as I was when she'd motioned for me to stand and allow her to dress me.

I hadn't fought her. I was terrified of fighting anyone for fear of my children being punished for it. Juan Josef scared me in every way, and if she was a pawn in his game, I would respond to her with the same compliance I would him. When he'd stood over my babies, I had been more frightened than I'd been during the plane crash that brought us here; than I'd been when I'd looked out at the ocean and felt the helplessness of being stranded with no rescue; than I'd been when Chris informed us we'd traveled back in time.

The way he looked at me made my soul cower. I'd never met a man that radiated wickedness quite the same way he did, and I had been unable to prevent my words from shaking during my encounter with him.

I stood and let Fetia work. As she added articles of clothing, I tried to communicate with her. I pleaded for answers; begged her to tell me where the others were and what was going on outside my room. With the language barrier, I hadn't expected much of a response. If she understood me at all, she did not give me any indication, keeping her eyes focused on her hands as she added more and more layers of silk.

When she circled around to place a ruby necklace at my neck, her hands were trembling. She was afraid too, and I wondered if it was Juan Josef that frightened her, or if she was terrified I might strangle her for the role she played in our capture. There was a part of me, the part that imagined Jack and the others locked in a cell somewhere, that desperately wanted to wrap my fingers around her small throat and squeeze.

Not that I was physically capable of violence in my state. Having given birth just one day prior, the simple act of standing seemed like it took every bit of strength I had. My insides burned, my breasts were tender, and my muscles felt like lead against my bones. My knees shook beneath the layers of fabric she'd wound around me, and mentally, I was drained. I didn't think I would be able to keep my eyes open, let alone deal with whatever Juan Josef had in store that required me to be dressed in such a way.

Fetia motioned to the chair near the door, touching her hair to communicate that she needed to style mine. I maneuvered awkwardly, unable to walk or bend naturally from the weight and tightness of the clothing.

I sighed once I sat, looking down at my breasts where they were squeezed and pushed by the stays like a half inflated balloon inside a tightening fist, threatening to pop with even the slightest addition of pressure. And pressure was something that was building by the minute. I would need to feed the babies again, *and soon*.

I stared at the closed door while Fetia pinned my curls to the top of my head. What was on the other side? I could hear shuffling; items being moved around the living room; glass clanging against glass, and furniture scraping against the bamboo floorboards, but I couldn't hear voices. Was it Juan Josef on the other side, or would I find Jack and the others unharmed and waiting for me?

Although I knew, deep down, it wasn't my people on the other side of that door, I wondered if I wouldn't be even more horrified to face them if it were. I'd shared everything I knew about the possible way back through time with Juan Josef. I'd given him dates, times, and the coordinates willingly. Giving the coordinates and dates could allow Juan Josef and his men to go through time instead of us. I knew only three could go, and if he inserted his people in place of Anna, Chris, and Maria, we would be forced to wait until March.

With a lingering brain injury from the plane crash, we didn't know how long Chris might be able to go without treatment. And Anna had spent the past year and a half concerned her abusive ex-husband might be granted custody of her young son.

By giving away everything I knew about how the time-portal worked, I'd potentially stolen Chris's deteriorating mind from him, and had taken even more memories away from Anna and her son.

I thought about Juan Josef's revelation to me. For him, twenty years before the date *we'd* come through had been 1977. Twenty years before that date for the rest of us had been 1997. This meant time was moving slower on this side of the portal. Six months in the 18th century would be one whole year in the 21st. Anna hadn't lost a year and a half of her son's life during our time away. She'd lost three. Assuming we could outwit Juan Josef and then manage to find the way back, Liam would be eight by the time she got to him. If we couldn't get through as a result of my spilling my guts to Juan Josef, I would've taken yet another year of his life from her.

Now that I'd held my own children, I couldn't imagine losing even a second of their lives. I hadn't had five years to grow the kind of bond with them she had with her son. I'd barely had 24 hours. And yet, I would sacrifice Anna's friendship, Chris's mental health, and do just about anything to keep those two tiny humans beside me. Maria had called me selfish, and I supposed I was, because there was no amount of information I wouldn't give to make sure *my* babies were safe; no length I wouldn't go to in order to make sure Juan Josef wouldn't separate them from me.

I peered over the baskets once more, needing to make sure both were still breathing, and I felt my pulse ease a little when I could see the subtle movement of their lungs filling and expelling air without any need of assistance. I had two healthy babies; two babies the world had told me I'd never be able to have. Those two children and Jack were my whole world now, and no amount of obligation to anyone else would make me put their lives second. If that made me selfish, then so be it. I'd wear that title proudly for them.

I squeezed my eyes closed as Fetia pulled the last of my hair up into pins. I was almost ready. What would come next? After labor and a night spent awake to feed and dote over my twins, my thinking was cloudy at best. I had to get my wits about me if I was ever going to get us out of whatever this predicament was.

What *was* this predicament, anyway? He already had all the information he needed. What more could he want? While I'd tried to negotiate with him—promising him money and a partnership between our groups—he hadn't given any indication that he was willing to take me up on that offer before he'd exited the room. If his mind was made up that he would go instead of us, why was he having me dressed? And why in such an elaborate garb?

I cringed as I considered that he might want something physical from me—why else send a fancy red dress and jewelry?—but I dismissed that notion almost immediately. Swollen from labor, and disheveled in every possible way, I would've been the least attractive woman in our group. If it was physical, he'd have had Maria, Lilly or Anna dressed instead of me. Unless… he was already doing that very thing? Were they out there dressed similarly? Were they alright?

I hadn't gotten a look at the rest of his men when we were in Eimeo. I'd only seen the two he'd sent to guard us and had paid them very little attention in my search for Chris. Was there a much more sinister reason for my getting dressed in such a way? Would I and my friends serve as an offering to his men before they shipped out? If they were anything like the men aboard the Resolution, it wouldn't matter that I had just given birth. I only needed the parts they lacked.

Fighting with nausea from both the nerves and the tightness of the corset, and feeling my palms sweat as I imagined what his men might be capable of, I almost fainted when the door opened and Juan Josef filled its frame.

"Come," he said.

He was taller than I'd remembered him being when we'd come across him in Eimeo. His beard was thick black with bits of grey, and there was a hint of green in his eyes I hadn't bothered to notice before. He might've even been attractive were it not for the darkness that emanated from him. He stared at me in such a way that made me feel as if I were naked before him; like he could see through the dress, and even through my skin, to the deepest parts of me; the parts of me that trembled and curled into themselves by the sheer nearness of him. From the look on his face, it was evident he knew what kind of effect his reappearance was having. The corner of his lip turned upward in a knowing smile as if to say, *'I dare you to fight me now.'*

I rose from the chair and began to reach for the babies when he held up his hand.

"Leave them. Fetia will stay."

"No," I said, planting my feet. "I have done everything you asked. I will continue to do whatever you want, and I won't fight you, as long as they remain within my sight."

He tilted his head to one side, a strand of his long black hair falling over his forehead as he flashed his teeth in a daring smile. "You won't fight me, anyway. Leave them."

I shook my head, feeling my voice tremble and hating myself for being so weak. "I can't. They'll need to be fed again soon."

"When that time comes, I shall return you to this room. We will only just be there." He pointed toward the living room where I could see a small round table and two chairs set out in front of the lit fireplace. A white tablecloth had been laid over the tabletop, and dinner was served on two place settings, surrounded by lit candles. I didn't see anyone else in the room; no soldiers or guards or signs of my own people. What would he do once he'd gotten me alone in there?

I looked back toward the baskets, Zachary and Cecelia both still sleeping inside each. "Can I leave the door open?"

His eyes lingered on my breasts where my nipples were just barely covered by the corset, and I had to close my eyes to hide my disgust. "If you wish for the door to remain open, then I shall keep it open. Now come. Dine with me. I am not a patient man, and it would not bode well for you to continue to defy me throughout the evening."

Opening my eyes, I swallowed, and looked down at the dress he'd picked out for me where the candlelight reflected on its shimmering red surface. "And this?" I asked, waving my arm over the rich fabrics. "What is this for? What do you intend to do with me now that you've dolled me up like this?"

He took a deep breath and rolled his eyes. "I am a lot of things, madam, but I am not a man to force myself upon an unwilling female. It would be uncivilized to expect you to dine in only your shift." I watched his fingers flex and curl into fists, "Now, I have already asked you several times to join me, and I shan't ask you again. I have considered your offer and wish to speak more about it. I presumed you would be hungry after giving birth, and so I offer this conversation over dinner. We needn't be unpleasant to one another." He offered me his arm. "Come."

I didn't take his arm, but moved alongside him toward the living room, feeling every inch of distance my steps took me from the twins. I scanned the dimly lit living room and listened for signs of men either in the house or posted just outside. There were none.

"Sit," he instructed, pulling out my chair for me. "I daresay you shall be delighted that I've had red meat prepared strictly for this occasion."

I sat awkwardly in the dress, the sleeves of the jacket pulling taut against my arms as I positioned myself so I could see the other room through my peripherals. What would I do if Fetia made a sudden movement? Would I be able to get to them?

On my plate was a giant slab of glistening steak with buttered boiled potatoes, cheese, wine, and bread. Having gone so long without the taste of any of those things, I would've otherwise been falling over myself at the promise of a meal I had spent the past year and a half craving. As it stood, the only thing my eyes could focus upon was the knife sitting at the side of it all.

He took a seat across from me, unfolding his napkin to lay it across his lap before he picked up his wineglass and held it near his lips. "I had my only cow slaughtered just for you, and I spent the day overseeing its butchering so I could offer you the finest cut. Please, rid me of my anticipation and take a bite so I may enjoy the fruits of my labor by seeing your reaction."

I stared at the knife, trying to dream up some kind of way to use it to get out of the situation. He was toying with me, I knew, and as a result, my nerves were wound too tightly to have any kind of appetite. "Where are the others?"

He sipped his wine and calmly set it on the table. "Was I unclear when I informed you I am an impatient man? I have expressed my eagerness to watch you enjoy this meal I have spent the entire day preparing for you, and yet I am met with resistance and mistrust. If you were a man, I should shove the steak into your mouth and force you to chew. Make no mistake, it is not beyond my character to do that very thing to a woman. Eat. *I* will ask the questions at this table when I am ready to do so, and you will answer them. Do I make myself clear?"

I nodded, picking up the fork and knife and cringing as I watched my hands quiver beyond my control while they cut into the steak.

I wanted to be so many things at that moment. I wanted to be defiant, to refuse him answers and remain silent and insubordinate until he'd released my people; to play the unwavering badass who would not be intimidated. I wanted to feed into his evident attraction; to flirt with him and give myself some sense of power over him. I wanted to be the heroine; to use the knife in my hand to deliver him one deadly jab to the throat so I could run off and search his ship for the others.

But I was none of those things. With two babies so far away from me, I couldn't help feeling intimidated, defeated, and meek as I took a bite I couldn't taste, and forced myself to chew.

He enjoyed this kind of power, and he knew what he was doing. Purposely refraining from posting guards in the room or inviting anyone else to dine with us, he wanted us to be alone;

wanted me to know he didn't need help to overpower me; wanted to instill in me the knowledge that he, without any assistance, could throw me down and do as he pleased, toss me into a prison alongside the others, and steal my children away if I defied him.

He'd dressed me to make me uncomfortable, to humiliate me, and to assert his dominance over me. He'd chosen me because I was the weakest; because I had more to lose than anyone else and I would obey. Despite my early attempts to play it cool and appear unaffected by him, he'd seen through me. Whatever I offered him as a means to offset his power, he would simply take. He would not negotiate with me. He didn't need to.

He smiled and picked up his own utensils. "Was that so difficult?" He sliced a large strip of meat, stacked a potato onto the fork alongside it, and shoved both brutishly into his mouth, not waiting to swallow to initiate his interrogation. "So... this plane crash. What argument could you make that would entitle your people to a settlement of any substantial means? It is not the fault of the airline the plane traveled through time. Why would they have any reason to compensate you for it?"

I chewed slowly, begging my upset stomach to accept the food and not vomit. "One of the men with us is a lawyer. He said it wouldn't matter what caused the airplane to go down. The airline would have to compensate us for pain and suffering, regardless of the cause."

Plucking his wineglass up from the table, he sipped loudly, washing the enormous bite he'd taken down, and expelling an audible exhale after he'd swallowed. "And the lawyer... he's one of the ones you wish to send?"

"No." For as much as I wanted to lie, I couldn't. I had no way of knowing who he had detained or what he already knew about us. I didn't want to risk putting anyone in harm's way as a result of being caught in a lie. I had to tell the truth. "He has no attachment to our group, and couldn't be trusted to come back for us. If we can make it to the future, we'd have much better luck hiring a lawyer there to work the lawsuit."

His eyes lingered on my neckline. "And so you intend to send three of your people to travel to the future, sue the airline, and return here in March to willingly give me a share in their reward... Is that right?"

"Yes." I hated how small my voice sounded.

"Why three? Why not one or all? I feel as though you are holding something back from me. You know something more about how it works. The math. You mentioned the possibility of a percentage. I had six on my boat, and three came through. That's fifty percent. You were in a commercial airliner. Surely there were more than thirty on your flight?"

I nodded. I didn't want to give him all the details; had tried to dance around the knowledge that only three would be able to cross through in September, but what was the point? That theory wasn't concrete. Nothing was. For all I knew, we would navigate to the coordinates and nothing would happen. There'd be no storm and no portal, and then what? Would he think we'd tricked him? There was no reason for me to hold back any information, since none of it was certain. If I offered up what I knew, maybe this man's own experiences could solidify our theories, or shed light on details we hadn't seen. I sighed. "Originally, we thought it might be fifteen percent because that aligned with our numbers and the notes we found in the journals, but then you showed up with fifty percent. I think it may be that only three can cross in September, and fifteen in March... maybe."

"What year did the man in the journals come through?"

I poked at a potato with my knife. "1928."

"Eat." He ordered, pointing at my plate with his fork as he rose from his seat. He grinned at me as he set his napkin on the table. "I'd almost forgotten..." He hurried to a table near the door where, much to my surprise, an antique gramophone sat. It was old. The wear on its surface was indicative of at least a hundred years of time since its creation, meaning it'd had to have come back in time alongside him. I was pretty certain nothing like it would be invented for some years still, and with that kind of wear, it certainly didn't belong in 1774.

He leaned to one side, glancing out the window before he laid a record on its surface, winding it for a while before he lowered the needle and a soft jazzy bass filled the room.

I hadn't heard music in so long I almost forgot I was his captive. As the piano joined the bass, the music sent a chill down my spine that forced my eyes closed.

"A gift from my wife." He said, pulling me back to reality to find him still standing near the door watching me. "I never liked the sound of an 8-track, and she bought this for me on my twenty-fifth birthday to take with me on my boat." He smiled. "Said it was so I could bring my music wherever I went. What she didn't realize was that I then had to buy custom copies of my records so I could actually play them on it. I didn't mind." He let out a long breath, closing his eyes as a single trumpet joined the mix of piano, drums, and bass to identify the player as Miles Davis. "It was almost like she knew just how far I would go... I hadn't thought so then, but it is the best gift I could've ever received."

"What was her name?" I asked, hoping, with the addition of music, he might reveal some softer side of him that could place us on more even ground.

"Gloria." His lip curled upward as he said the name.

"Is she why you're so desperate to get home?"

His smile disappeared, and he frowned at me, turning his head to one side. "No. My reasons for going back have nothing to do with her."

"Well, you obviously have strong reasons driving you, otherwise you wouldn't need to go to such extremes to ensure you got there. What's so important that you would threaten the lives of my babies, imprison my friends, and work so hard to intimidate me into telling you everything I know?"

He crossed the room and sat back down in his seat, observing me for a moment through narrowed eyes. "I was a very rich man," he said, stabbing into his steak and slicing another large chunk off. "I left behind an estate worth hundreds of millions of dollars. I had riches you could only dream of; yachts and mansions and airplanes and servants... *and women...*" He smirked. "So many women to choose from that if I told you a number, you would think I was lying." Again, he pointed at my plate with his knife. "Eat."

He waited until I'd taken a bite to continue, leaning back in his chair as he chewed to one side. "I had respect. Everyone knew my name and lined up to dine at the table of Juan Josef." He huffed. "Here, I have spent twenty long years wasting away on a ship full of filthy savages for a crew, being snubbed by society, and looked at like I am no one. I am *not* no one and I am sick and tired of being treated as such. I want the life that has been stolen from me. I want to be the man I was destined to be."

I sat up straighter, keeping one eye on Fetia where she was looking down on Zachary's basket. "But if you went through now... it's been forty years... No one would believe you are you."

"Depending on how we go back, I would not need to be Juan Josef Sr., my dear." He raised an eyebrow as he brought his wineglass to his lips. With his attention momentarily pulled from me to the wine, I discreetly slid my knife into the sleeve of my jacket. "I have a son who bears my resemblance," he continued. "He escorted you to your friend that day on Eimeo. I am forty-seven years old... The same age he should be if he were to return."

I stared down at my dinner. Offering him any part of our settlement wouldn't help me negotiate the release of my people, not when he already had a claim of his own. Our promise of money wouldn't give me the leverage I needed, so, feeling a bit more relaxed with the soft jazz in the background, I tried a different approach. "Look, there's no evidence of anyone ever making it to the future. You would think, if someone had made it, they would travel back and forth through time. There would be some indication in these parts—stories or legends—to prove it was possible. We have been searching for a year for those very stories and have come up with nothing. What if we sail to that location, find the storm, and the people that go through find themselves even further back in time? What if it only goes backward? If you go through now, what would you have in the 16th century? There'd be no riches, no respect, no notoriety, and possibly no ship. You'd have to start all over again. If time moves as slowly there as it does here, you would be that much further removed from the people who know your name. That thought terrifies *me* enough I don't ever want to go back to that storm. Does it not frighten you?"

"*That* thought is why I am considering your offer," he said cooly, extending his palm toward me. "Come. If you will not eat, dance with me."

"No, no... I'm eating." I hurried to plunge my fork into a potato, mortified at the idea of his hands on my body.

"That wasn't a question," he assured me, rising to his feet. "Come."

I stared at his offered hand; the steak rising up to sit in my throat as I surrendered to take it. "I really shouldn't... so soon after giving birth... My body is in no condition—

He jerked me to my feet, pulling with enough force that my body was driven to press against his. I saw the menace in his eyes as he observed my cleavage from such an angle, and I swallowed the bile that rose in the back of my mouth as a result. With the cool metal of the knife against my forearm, I wondered if I could stab him. Did I have it in me? Was the blade sharp enough? Would I be strong enough to drive it into his throat or would it simply graze him and agitate him further?

"Here is my offer," he said, holding me in place against him. "I will allow your people to go ahead of me, but I must have confirmation that they have indeed made it. I cannot trust them to return for you, and so I shall send one of my sons along with them."

He took my right hand in his left, winding his other arm around my back to lead us away from the table and sway to the gentle piano and trumpet.

"We shall follow along with your original strategy; keeping a distance from the vessel we send through to watch as they pass." He spun me with the growing tempo. "I shall then return us all here to wait for their arrival in March." He brought his face closer to mine; basking in the tremors his nearness sent through me.

"You know I am afraid," I said, wincing as my burning abdomen protested with the movement. "Why continue to prove you have power over me by making me uncomfortable? You know I won't fight you. You have all the power. What do you want from me?"

"You remind me of Gloria." He bit his lower lip, rocking us slowly as the drums came in. "You have that same look about you. But this…" He squeezed my hand where it was locked in his. "This is not about power, my dear. This is about trust."

"Trust?" I laughed haughtily. "I'm supposed to trust you after you've taken us all captive? After you continue to threaten my day-old children? After you've just sat there and commanded me to eat as if I were your dog?"

He pulled me closer. "This is not about you trusting me. It's about my ability to trust you. You think I did not notice your knife has gone missing?"

I stiffened, and he held me tighter still, grinning mischievously down at me as he continued the dance. "Where exactly did you intend to stab me? The chest?" Keeping his hand on my back to hold me in place, he released my hand so he could run a thumb up the crease between my breasts. "The neck, perhaps?" He smoothed his calloused palm up the side of my throat, and I squeezed my eyes closed as his fingers gripped my hair and jerked my head backward. "Come on then, do it," he hissed against my neck. "Pull the knife out and stab me with it. See if you can kill me."

"No," I breathed, trying to turn my head against his grip to see into the bedroom.

"You hid it for a reason. Go on and do it." He let go and stood with his hands held out at his sides. "See if you can make it stick. Go on, stab me as hard as you can. I dare you."

I shook my head. "I can't. It was a mistake."

The trumpet grew stronger, seemingly attempting to interrupt us, and his voice increased a decibel as a result. "Where is it now?"

"Here." I hurriedly pulled the knife from my sleeve, letting it drop to the floor and clang against the bamboo floorboards. "I shouldn't have done it. I don't know what I was thinking."

His eyes darkened and he licked his lips. "And what will you do to regain my trust? Eh? After you have so evidently betrayed me, how will you prevent me from punishing you? From separating you from your children who, by the looks of things, are getting hungry?"

"Anything." I looked toward the room to see Fetia pulling Zachary against her shoulder. "I'll do anything. I'm sorry. I won't fight you. Whatever you want… please. It was a mistake."

"Anything?" He stepped closer, his hot and heavy breath moving over my lips.

Disgusted, I swallowed. "Anything. Just please don't take them from me."

"So then it is safe for me to assume you are *not* an unwilling female anymore?" He ran his finger over my lower lip and I recoiled.

Once again, I was trembling. "If…" I looked back toward the room where Zachary was starting to fuss. Tears welled in my eyes as Fetia rocked him softly, but I blinked them away and stood straighter. "If that's what it'll take to keep them, then I won't fight you."

He leaned in closer—so close I could almost feel his lips on my own. "I shall remember that, then," he whispered, stepping away from me to bow, "for when you are *in the condition*." Straightening, he smiled. "I gave you my word you would be returned to your children when the need should arise. Go."

I frowned, looking between the bedroom and him. I had so much more I'd meant to discuss. I needed to negotiate; needed to find out what he intended to do with the others. "The others… where are they?

"They are being served steak and potatoes on my ship as we speak. Go and tend to your babies, then we shall join them to work out the conditions of this arrangement."

Chapter Two

Fetia wrapped a long white fabric around me, securing both babies against my chest in two makeshift pouches supported by my shoulders. She'd re-tied the corset, but had added the wrap in place of the jacket that was once pinned to the stays. While the fabric and the babies added to the weight of the already too heavy dress on my fatigued muscles, I was grateful for the feel of their little bodies against mine. So long as they were attached, I could protect them.

Juan Josef had lingered at the door throughout, watching while I'd fed, burped, and changed them; always careful to look away when I asked him to. He'd refrained from speaking, and I wasn't sure if I would've been more or less uncomfortable if he'd chosen to talk.

He'd looked at me like prey while he'd danced with me, but his behavior was inconsistent when the babies were in my arms. Over dinner, he'd been callous and intentionally fearsome, making every effort to see me cower. In the room, however, both during the morning and that evening, he'd been respectful enough to turn his head whenever I'd requested it, and had even been thoughtful; handing me linens to change them with and assisting Fetia while she tied the sling.

He removed the lantern from the wall and presented his arm to me. "Shall we join the others?"

My legs protested as I stood; the bones and muscles like jello as I took a wobbling step forward. Everything beneath the dress was either trembling with fatigue and anxiety, or burning as though a hot poker had been shoved inside me to sear my organs and muscles. Taking a deep breath, I pushed the pain to the back of my mind and slowly joined him at the door. I would rest when I'd gotten us to Jack.

I was anxious to get to his arms. Even though he was just as much a captive to Juan Josef as I, in my mind, I knew, if I could just get to him, we'd be safe.

Juan Josef took my arm and wrapped it around his own, tightening his grip on me when I attempted to withdraw it. "It is a far distance to walk in your condition," he said, pulling me alongside him through the living room. "You will need my assistance. Do not let your distaste in my touch place unnecessary threat on your children. Should you stumble along the way, you could harm one of them in your fall."

He was right. I was just barely keeping my feet beneath me as it was, and although every part of me wanted to separate my body from the side of his, I leaned into him, allowing him to support me as he opened the door to the cool night breeze, and I took my first breath of fresh air in days.

We stepped out of the house, the dried leaves beneath our feet the only sounds on a completely desolate beach. All the natives had fled, and even his own men had returned to the ship. It was only the two of us hobbling down toward the sand.

"What are their names?" He asked softly, holding the lantern out so I could see where my feet were going. "The babies?"

I covered their heads with my free hand, feeling suddenly defensive of their identities. It was one thing to have them anywhere near this man. It was another for him to speak their names as if he would play some kind of familial role in their lives. I focused on the ground at my feet, opting to remain silent rather than answer the question.

He laughed to himself. "Fair enough."

As our feet sank into the cool sand, he slowed his pace to match mine. "Tell me *your* name then."

"Why?" One foot slid with the loose sand and I lost my balance. As I began to fall forward, he caught me by our joined arms, steadying me almost instantly.

"My dear, if we are to spend the next several months in each others' company, I would prefer to address you by your name. You know mine. Is it not only fair I know yours?"

"Alaina." I grumbled.

"Alaina," he echoed, an icy chill crawling down my spine at the sound of it. "I do not wish for us to be enemies over these months we must endure alongside each other. It is my intention to keep you *rather close* during our time together. Let us not begin our relationship as foes." He squeezed my arm in his. "Tell me, Alaina, did you inform the English captain of how you came to be in this time and place?"

"No," I said cautiously. "Why?"

"Curious is all." He loosened his grip as we reached the water's edge, and he placed the lantern inside a sloop positioned on the sand. He took my hand in his and assisted me inside, pushing the small boat out into the water before he climbed in and took the oars. "You've one of his men with you. Forster... Tell me what reason this man has for remaining among you while the English captain has sailed ahead?"

He slowly pulled the oars, the lantern on the floor shining up on his face and casting shadows over his features to make him appear that much more sinister.

"He figured us out." I said, smoothing my hand over Zachary's tiny head, smiling at the softness of the little bits of blonde hair against my palm. "He found a driver's license. He's interested in helping us find the way back. Do you have him, too?"

"I have them *all*, my dear." He grinned.

I curled my arms around both babies as the breeze softly kissed my skin and sent a shiver through me. "What do you want, then?" I asked, closing my eyes. "You mentioned *'conditions of our arrangement.'* What'll it take to let them go?"

"You will remain at my side; take your breakfasts, lunches, and dinners at my table. You will converse with me as you would the English captain; see me as the same sort of man as him—a man to be respected; a man that you can *look in the eyes*. I will allow you to spend time with your people. I would advise you spend that time convincing them to offer me the same respect I shall come to earn from you. Once I am certain I can trust you, I give you my word they may walk freely among us."

I opened my eyes. "I don't understand. We ran from you because we thought you wanted Maria for a bounty. Now that we know you're one of us and not just some pirate... now that we know you want the same things we do... we wouldn't run or fight you. You have no reason not to trust us."

Our boat reached his ship, and he stood to attach the ropes that would pull us up to the top deck. In the darkness, I hadn't been able to make out the enormity of it, but as I sat in the sloop staring up at the towering wooden monster, I felt tiny. Tripling the size of Captain Cook's ship, this one was adorned with rows of large windows; the orange glow from inside each dancing over the elaborate wooden carvings encasing them. Floor after floor climbed higher than my eyes could see, and I was once again terrified as the sloop was hoisted upward.

He sat back down in his seat across from me. "When you've been around as long as I; seen the things I've seen, you recognize a look in people that warrants mistrust. You have it now. Right now, you are attempting to find a way to deceive me. If I gave you and your people permission to do as you pleased, you would flee. You would abandon me here. It matters not that we want the same things. I am not one of you, nor shall I ever be without forced intervention, and you would leave. I have learned in my time on this earth that it is only the man who takes what he wants that will ever accomplish that which he sets out to do. I have set out to return home, and it has taken me more than twenty years to find the way. There is nothing I will not do or take; no man I will not kill; and no length I will not go in order to get there."

He leaned forward, running a single finger over Cecelia's head before I could turn my upper body away from him. "Do not deceive me, Alaina." He repositioned his finger at the side of my jaw, sliding it down to rest beneath my chin. "I do not wish to harm your children... but I will do whatever I must to see my life restored to what it should've been."

I let out a breath when his hand returned to his lap, and I held both babies tighter against me. I hated him, and the idea that I would be forced to withstand his company for any length of time made my stomach turn. Maria would've been better suited to play this role. She could flirt and manipulate him to believe she was riveted by his company, where I had never been able to fake interest in anyone. I hadn't been popular in school because I could never prevent my face from exposing my distaste in people's behavior. I had been kept away from Captain Cook because I was the worst liar among us. As the sloop rose higher, I could feel my facial expression exposing my disgust, and I battled the muscles in my face to adjust themselves. I wouldn't be capable of faking the respect he wanted from me, and so I would need to work hard to find something respectable about him.

If I'd felt tiny at the side of the ship, I felt microscopic on its surface. As Juan Josef assisted me out of the sloop, I stared up at the masts and sails, the light of the multiple burning lanterns climbing up to where they towered so high, they disappeared into the night sky.

Around us, men busied themselves, paying no regard to me or the captain as they secured the sloop, cleaned the deck, mended sails, and conversed in small groups around lantern light.

"This way." Juan motioned me to follow him. Purposely turning his back to me in a show of security among his men, he led us to a covered stairwell that disappeared into the shadows of the lower decks.

I followed silently, both arms wrapped around the sleeping bodies tied to my chest, making a mental note of the two sets of stairs we took to the corridor, and the number of doors we passed until we stopped at one at the end of the long hall.

Posted outside the door were two men. Each was armed with a rifle against their shoulder and a large sword at their hips. They bowed their heads at Juan Josef before one inserted a key into the door they guarded and opened it.

With a hand at my back, Juan gently pushed me into the candlelit room. "I shall return to collect you in the morning," was all he said before the door closed loudly behind me.

An onslaught of female voices overwhelmed me, all speaking at the same time.

"What happened to you?"

"Where's Kreese?"

"Have you seen Jimmy?"

"Where are the others?"

My heart sank as I took in the faces suddenly surrounding me. Magna, Anna, Lilly, and Maria circled me. Izzy laid on a white tufted sofa just behind them. I scanned the room to find no additional occupants, and my ears muffled their words as they continued to ask questions. Jack wasn't there. Where was he?

"Oye, what's going on?" Maria grabbed my shoulders and turned me toward her. "Where were you all this time?"

"I…" I noticed every one of the women had been dressed similarly. They all wore elaborate silk gowns in various rich colors; blue, emerald, and violet reflected the room's candlelight beneath the glistening jewelry fastened at each of their necks. "I was at the house. I woke up and everyone was gone. Juan Josef and Fetia were the only ones there… What happened to you?"

Lilly's eyes were full of tears. "They took them. Jimmy and Grandpa, Bruce, and Kyle… they all tried to fight his men… but there were so many… and they grabbed us and brought us here, and we didn't see where they took the men. We assumed they were holding you wherever they took them."

Maria nodded. "They came for us at Fetia's parents' home. I don't know how long they'd been there, but they were waiting for us. They covered my eyes with a blindfold. I could hear Kreese and Jack trying to fight them, too. I don't know where they took either of them. What do they want? Why are they doing this to us?"

I frowned. "He didn't tell you?"

Lilly sniffled. "No. They sent a woman to dress us. They took us to a dining room and gave us food, then brought us back here. They won't tell us anything!"

"He's one of us," I said, looking around the room at the lush furnishings. In the center of the tall ceiling hung a large chandelier lined with lit candles. Beneath it was an embroidered rug, over which sat two matching white sofas and two crimson wingback chairs. There was a fourposter bed tucked away to one side with thick red and gold velvet curtains pulled open. "He's from our time. He and his sons came through more than twenty years ago and have been trying to get back."

"He's what?!" Maria shouted. "If he is one of us, why is he doing all this?"

"He wants us to take him to the portal," I said dazedly, turning in a circle to observe the rich mahogany paneling that lined the room. "He doesn't trust us to tell him the correct place to find it, nor does he trust us to take him there without being forced."

"Why would we?" Anna asked. "He can't take us prisoner and expect us to help him!"

I sighed. "We already have. I told him everything."

"YOU WHAT?!" Maria shrieked. "What do you mean, *everything*? You told him where it is?"

I nodded. "I told him where it is, what dates we think it opens, how long it would take to get there, and how we had planned to go through. Only three of his six came through in September, and so I told him only three can go... told him about the journals and the plane... I told him everything." I looked at Anna. "I'm so sorry. He was going to hurt the babies, and I had to."

She swallowed whatever anger wanted to surface and took a deep breath. "It's alright—

"It's not alright!" Maria growled, spinning to pace the room. "How could you do this? Are you stupid? You just offered up every single bit of leverage we could have had over him! Why would he hurt the babies if he knew they could be used to bargain?! We have nothing left to offer! Now he will kill our men and kill us the minute he finds what he is looking for!"

"Maria," Anna attempted to reason. "No mother would willingly offer up her children to a madman."

"We do have something to offer," I said, feeling deflated as Maria proceeded to glare at me. "He's afraid to go through time himself; afraid of what might be on the other side. He's agreed to let two of ours go with one of his sons and wait with the rest of us for them to return for confirmation that it worked. He swore he won't hurt any of us if we go along with his way of doing things."

"*Two* of ours?" Maria stopped pacing to place both hands on her hips. "And who will we send now? Eh?"

"Chris and Anna."

I knew as I said the names, an explosion would come in response to her name not being among them, but I hadn't been prepared for the extent of it.

A barrage of Spanish obscenities spewed from her lips before she switched back to English. "And just who do you think you are, Alaina? You think you can speak for all of us? Offer up whoever you want to this man to be slaughtered?! No. No, Kreese will not be a part of this. I was supposed to go with him. *I* am supposed to be beside him to show him what is real. He cannot go with damage to his brain and be able to judge for himself. You cannot use us as your bargaining chips! You are not the only one whose life he is threatening! You are so selfish to—"

"SHUT UP!" Lilly exploded. "Will you please, for the love of God, just shut up?!"

"Lil," I tried to neutralize the situation, placing myself between them. "There's no need for us to argue. We can talk about this. Calm—"

"No," she huffed. "Don't tell me to calm down! I'm so sick of her pushing everyone around! You haven't been stuck in here all day listening to her run her mouth." She peered around me to narrow her eyes at Maria. "You know why women don't like you, Maria?"

"Lil, please—

"Women don't like you because, unlike men, your exterior doesn't distract us from seeing into your absolutely rotten interior! You walk around here judging everyone and everything to take the spotlight off yourself. You get some kind of satisfaction out of making her feel bad about herself; never forgetting to remind her that her failed marriage was *her* fault; kicking her at every opportunity she is down. Look at you! You're so much worse than the things you accuse her of! She's barely able to stand up after giving birth and has had to endure that man for hours to try to find a way to keep her children safe, and you dare to call her selfish? Everything you say is either a judgment, a contradiction, a demand, or complete bullshit! You're the selfish one!"

"Lilly. Stop it." I insisted. "She's just upset."

"No, I will not stop anything. I have held my tongue long enough." She met my eyes. "Stop sticking up for her. And for the love of God, stop listening to her! She's not some saint that deserves your friendship. She's an asshole, Alaina. And a bully. And a woman who clearly spent a year trying to seduce a married man, and then has had the audacity to blame you for it. Befriending her is more toxic for you than trying to hold on to a man who couldn't even be bothered to kiss you, let alone love you!"

Anna, behind her, nodded her head in agreement.

Lilly refocused her tirade on Maria. "You can't bat your eyes at a woman and erase the awful person you are, Maria. That's why we don't like you. You can't flirt your way into *a woman's* heart while you insult and degrade us out of the other side of your mouth. Does insulting the people around you make you feel better about yourself? You make up lies about your life in the hopes that we'll all think you're so interesting, but what's really in there that you're trying so hard to prevent us from seeing? Is there any humanity at all; any bit of sincerity beneath the bullshit you spout, or are you just completely horrible?"

"Lilly, that's enough." I placed my hands on her shoulders. "Come on, this isn't the time or the place, and you don't mean that."

"Oh, but I do." She shook free of my grip. "I don't know what happened in your life that has made you this way, but you are a mess, Maria. And if you want women to warm up to you, you'll stop projecting that mess on the people around you; stop attempting to hide that mess by flirting with every single man—

"Ay, Princess…"

All of us jumped and turned toward the door where Jim stood, his face lined with cuts and bruises and his hair disheveled and standing on end.

"Jimmy!" Dropping whatever point she was about to make, Lilly rushed to leap up into his embrace, her arms and legs winding tightly around his torso as she covered his mouth with her own.

"Thank God you're alright," he said breathlessly, his forearm tightening around her waist as his fingers combed the hair from her face. "Are ye' hurt?"

She shook her head. "No." Squeezing him tighter, she kissed him again and again.

"Come on now," he said, not making any physical attempt to fight her as she continued to kiss him between words. "Let me get a look at ye.'" He scanned her face, running his palm over her cheek. "He made ye' dress up like this?"

She nodded, her hands moving hurriedly over his face and up into his hair as she continued to press her lips over his cheeks, eyes, and nose.

"Did any of 'em put their hands on ye?'" He took her face softly in his grip, searching her eyes for signs of abuse.

"No, Jimmy." She pressed her forehead against his, smiling as she finally let out the tears she'd been holding in. "No one's hurt us."

"I'm so sorry." He breathed, smoothing his thumb over her lips. "I didn't want this for ye.' Everything's so Got damn cockeyed since we left that island… These men… Dressin' ye' up like this… it ain't without some kind of darker reason. We gotta' get yuns out of here. We've all been talkin.' Jack thinks we can—

"Jack?" I straightened. "He was with you?"

Noticing the rest of us waiting patiently for answers, he wrapped both arms around Lilly and rested his chin on her shoulder to look out at us. "Yeah. They got us all held up in a room downstairs. Me, Jack, Bud, Bruce, and Kyle. Ain't seen Chris, Phil, Johann, or 'em other two, though."

"You think they might've escaped?" Maria asked, her voice full of hope.

He ran his fingers over Lilly's spine, closing his eyes as she held him tighter. "No. They took Chris same time they took Jack. I think they're keepin' us locked up separate to prevent us from fightin' 'em. It's what I'd do."

"Are they alright?" I asked. "Jack? Is he hurt?"

He blew out. "He's fine. Kyle's in the worst shape. Didn't know when to quit. He'll be alright, though. We've all been worried sick about yuns and tryin' to figure out what in the hell they want with us."

"He didn't tell you, either?" I asked.

"Tell me what?"

"You might want to sit." I offered. "All of you... There's more."

One by one, everyone found a place in the center of the room, Lilly refusing to let go of Jim as he sat down in one of the wingback chairs with her body still wrapped around him. I took a seat on one of the sofas, laying the babies across my lap to relieve my shoulders as I walked them through everything that had happened to me since I'd woke that morning.

It was Anna that spoke first once I'd finished. "So... if he's telling the truth, time is moving faster there than here. And we've been gone for... three years?"

I nodded. "I think so."

I could see her working out the math in her head; envisioning all her worst nightmares of Liam's father being granted custody. I watched her struggle to contain the devastation those images implanted in her as she straightened. "We can't afford to lose any more time. If they know how to get there and when to go, we'll have to go along with this plan. We can't risk one of us not being among the three to go through."

Jim shook his head. "No. We ain't stayin' with these lunatics. We'll have to figure out a way to escape and get there first."

"We can't." I said. "No scheming, no escaping, and no more lies. I don't like it anymore than you do, but whatever we have to do so we all get out of this together, we need to do. All he wants is to go back to his time, and I believe him when he says there's nothing he won't do to make that happen. If we can get him there, and do so without a fight, we might make it out unscathed. If we fight him, he could kill us all."

"*Unscathed?*" Jim balked. "Woman, ye' think he wants to keep you close to him because he enjoys the company? Has yer cheese fallen completely off yer cracker? Ye' know damn well what he intends to do dressin' ye' up like 'at. We ain't lettin' that man touch none of yas."

"I don't think that's what he wants, Jim. Not right now, anyway. Dressing us up is a tactic to assert dominance over us. He enjoys having power. He wants to feel important, to know he is feared by the people who surround him. But he's also not a complete monster... He could've overpowered me easily in the house if that's what he was after, but he didn't. And he looked away when I fed the babies... A monster wouldn't have done that. I've been thinking about this... He was on a yacht with two very young sons when he went through time, but there were three other people on that boat that didn't cross through with him. What if the other three were family? What if he had more children? His wife maybe? What if losing them made him the way he is? He said I reminded him of her... maybe he intends to keep me close as a way to make up for that loss..."

Jim raised an eyebrow. "And if he is? How long before he expects his replacement wife to warm his bed?"

"I'll cross that bridge if I get there." I folded my arms over my chest. "We can't very well fight him."

"Hell, I'd rather fight than let him do what it is he intends to do with ye'!"

"And then where would we be?" I huffed. "Dead probably. And who would raise these babies? Who would take care of Izzy? Who would go and find Liam to make sure he was alright if we're all dead? No one. Juan Josef was not a part of our plan, but he's here now, and the only way we're getting to that portal—if it's even out there—is on this ship along with him. If we can get him to trust us... if we can understand what makes him feel the need to imprison us... Maybe we can get there in one piece."

Jim clicked his tongue. "Woman, there's people out there that's just evil for the sake of bein' evil. Ye' cain't try to understand 'em cause there ain't nothin' to understand. They enjoy bein' evil. I'm sure he does want to go home, but I'm tellin' ye,' I looked that man in the eye, and there ain't no good to be found in him. He'll spend evra' minute of our time gettin' there inflicting that evil on us cause he enjoys it."

Magna cleared her throat, petting Izzy's hair where she was snuggled against her side. "We have a few weeks before we need to set sail. The woman who dressed us is a native Tahitian. I could ask her when she returns to send a message to Tu. Juan Josef may have weapons, but he is gravely outnumbered if Tu's people would help us fight."

"Please." I begged. "Give me a few days to feel him out. We have time before we need to start plotting. Maybe he's evil, or maybe there's a side to him we're not seeing. Maybe there's a reason he feels the need to use force instead of trusting us. He's been here a long time. Who knows what he's endured? I have to try things his way first. If I don't..." I combed the hair on Zachary's head, a lump forming in my throat when his little eyes opened for a fleeting moment. "He could hurt them. He could hurt Izzy or one of us..."

Anna cut Jim off as he moved to argue. "I agree. We have to do things his way. We've worked too hard to get this far; spent too much time lying and scheming and plotting... we can't let it be for nothing. We're no good to anyone if we're dead." She looked toward the door and back at Jim. "Why do you think they let *you* come to us?"

He kissed the top of Lilly's head where she'd curled into his chest, letting out a long breath as he surrendered his argument for the moment. "Don't know why he picked me, but a big ole' behemoth of a man opened up the door and unlocked my chains and—

"Chains?" Lilly sat up straight, taking his wrist in her hand to pull it up to eye level. "They had you chained?"

He grinned. "Like I said, that lil' summbitch Kyle didn't know when to quit. And since Kyle was still throwin' punches with his one good arm, the rest of us wouldn't be able to call ourselves men if we didn't do the same. If they didn't want us to keep fightin,' they had to chain us. Anyway, they come in a little while ago and let me loose. Didn't tell me where I's goin', just led me to your room and tossed me inside. I don't know how long before they'll take me back — if they plan to take me back at all."

"Do you think they sent you here to see what we'd do?" Lilly asked, looking back toward the door. "Like a test? You think they're listening right now?"

"I would be if I's him." Jim followed her gaze. "Seein' who I could trust and who I could turn against who. Wouldn't need to watch ye' to know that, though. I could hear yuns hollerin' from halfway down the hall." He interlaced his fingers with Lilly's. "Didn't I tell ye' not to go startin' fights ye' got no business startin'?"

Lilly rolled her eyes and laid her head back against his chest. "If I'm going to be locked up with her, it needed to be said."

The corner of his mouth twitched as he looked up at Maria. She was seated beside me and had avoided eye contact with everyone in the room since their earlier encounter. "Now ain't the time for none of it. That goes for you, too, Firecracker."

Maria looked up at him then, seemingly appalled that he could include her in the guilty party after she'd suffered through Lilly's reprobation.

"*You* quit insultin' people. And you…" He squeezed Lilly's hand. "Quit lettin' yourself get offended on other people's account.

If freckles ain't mad, there ain't no reason for you to be. Got it? We need to stick together now, all of us."

"I'm not apologizing." Lilly said, looking over at Maria. "It's not *me* that should be sorry for the things that were said today."

Maria, never one to shy away from an argument, kept her head down—much to my surprise, and waited until the others had slipped into more casual conversation before she turned toward me. "I'm sorry," she whispered. "I shouldn't have said those things."

I smiled. "Maria, really, it's alright—

"It's not alright. I am all those things she said I am. I have always been this way. And I am terrified I will lose the only person who understands those things about me... I am so afraid he will lose his mind before he gets back... and no one will ever know me again." She gently placed her pinkie into Cecelia's palm, watching as Cecelia's little fingers curled around it. "None of that is your fault, and I'm sorry for blaming you."

Cecelia opened her eyes and smacked her lips, and Maria couldn't help but smile when her eyes met hers.

"Do you want to hold her?" I offered.

"You'd let me hold her after everything I said?"

I raised Cecelia from my leg to place her into Maria's cradled arms. "What, you think you're the first person in the history of the world to find fault in your boyfriend's ex-wife? That fault didn't just show up there without some additional assistance." I adjusted Cecelia's wrap, then pulled Zachary to my shoulder. "He's not the only one who will ever know you, you know." I glanced over at Lilly, who had moved on to focus her attention on the bruising under Jim's eye. "We've all got our issues, and we've all found a way to love each other for them. We'd love you too, if you let us."

Chapter Three

I laid in the bed, Zachary and Cecelia's squirming bodies placed between myself and Magna where we both stayed awake, listening for signs of Juan Josef.

Maria and Anna had each taken a couch, and Lilly and Jim laid out a pallet on the floor, placing Izzy between them. After hours with no signs of Juan Josef's return, we'd all helped each other undress down to our shifts. Where Anna and Izzy fell asleep almost immediately, the rest of us remained on edge, whispering through the night; everyone dreaming up their own various escape plans while I continued to thwart them.

It wasn't as if I didn't desperately want to get away from a man like Juan Josef. I did. But I'd spent enough time with him to be more afraid of getting caught than they had. I'd seen the promise in his eyes as he'd said the words, *'I will do whatever I must to go home,'* and I believed him. I believed him, and I was far too terrified of him to make any attempt to defy him.

I'd only ever been terrified of one other man in my life, and that man had a similar wickedness in him. His name was Yiannis, and he was the owner of a Greek restaurant down the street from where I grew up. He was also my first boss.

I came to realize later in life that Yiannis only hired young and timid girls so he could assert his dominance over them. He never left the restaurant, and would sit at a table in the corner to watch our every step, waiting for an opportunity to correct something one of us might've done wrong. Ketchup bottle half-empty on a table? Yiannis would yell. Forget to add *'no mushrooms'* to a customer's order? Yiannis would yell. Customer not happy with the food none of us had cooked or had any control over? Yiannis would yell. He enjoyed making girls like me quiver with his sheer presence. It gave him power, and he loved that power.

One would think a young girl would simply find another job under those kinds of circumstances, but he was just manipulative and attractive enough to keep most of us working there for far too long. When he was in a mood, we'd tremble, but if he was happy with one of us, he had a smile that made you feel like a God… at least, that's how it felt for timid young girls who hadn't the life experience to know what he was.

It was strange to think back on my sixteen-year-old self and recognize anything familiar in her. I was so naive and carefree then, excited about life and love and opportunity; completely undamaged by the defense mechanisms I'd formed after years of reacting to a painful world. I didn't realize he was a monster back then. I really thought he just wanted a well-run business and we were all lacking in our abilities to give it to him. Years later, I wondered if he wasn't the first person to create a bit of my damage; if my desire to please him by not making mistakes as a teenager wasn't a reason I overthought everything I did as an adult.

Juan Josef got the same enjoyment out of watching me tremble, but I wasn't a sixteen-year-old girl anymore, and I wasn't going to give him the satisfaction I'd once given Yiannis. I wouldn't let him see that I was afraid of him. Instead, I'd try to get to know him; try to understand some part of him so I could give him the trust he was searching for from me. He'd looked away when I'd asked, which was something I couldn't imagine Yiannis doing in a similar position, and even though his words made me tremble, that one little detail gave me hope that he wasn't *all* bad. If I could figure out a way to relate to him, maybe by the time we reached that spot on the ocean, we would not be his prisoners, but his friends. I would not be some meek woman quivering in his shadow, but his equal; both of us simply working toward a similar end goal.

The sun started to rise outside our bay window when Fetia finally came into the room. She held an emerald green dress folded under her arm and pointed at me as she spoke softly to Magna, careful not to wake the others who'd only recently fallen asleep.

"He wants you to join him for breakfast," Magna whispered, sitting up in the bed. "You and Zachary and Cecelia."

I covered both babies with the blanket, hoping to shield them from the world just a little while longer, and joined both women at the mirror in the far corner. Fetia continued to speak to Magna as she lowered a slip over my head. Anger sitting heavy in my chest, I was unable to look at her.

Juan Josef had been at Fetia's parents' home waiting for us. He'd known I'd given birth, and had known Maria and Chris were headed there. There's no way he could've been in such a specific location without her involvement. I wasn't sure I could keep myself from strangling her if I made eye contact.

"She says she didn't do this." Magna frowned as Fetia continued. "She says she knows we think she did, but neither her or her family was involved. They didn't know he was there. They're holding her father captive downstairs and forcing her to work in exchange for his release before we leave."

Fetia looked around the room cautiously before she pulled a small piece of paper from her dress and handed it to me.

"She says none of the Tahitians were involved in our capture. They want to help us."

I looked at her then, trying to find some evidence of deception in her perfect features. "Someone knew where Maria and Chris were going. If it wasn't the natives, who was it?"

Magna translated while Fetia tied the first skirt around my waist.

"She doesn't know, but it wasn't them."

I unfolded the little piece of paper in my hand. Written on its surface among several large globs of dripped ink were the words:

'We have a window in our room. Kyle is loose from his chains and working on ours. I will be there soon. -J'

Jack. I smiled down at his scribbled handwriting and felt that much closer to him. The letter was as comforting as if he'd wrapped his arms around me, and for a moment I felt safer than I'd felt since I'd woken with Juan Josef looking over me. Knowing he was alive and well enough to write that letter made my heart flutter.

I glanced out our window. Would I find him climbing through it later that night? And what would happen if he did? What would Juan Josef do to him if he found their room empty?

"I need something to write with," I said, staring at the letter. "I have to get a message back to him before he gets himself killed."

Magna nodded, turning to rummage through the vanity.

"The rest of them," I started, "Chris and Johann... Jacob and Michael... Has she seen them too? Are they alright?"

Their conversation continued, the only words I recognized being the men's names as Magna opened the drawers of the vanity and explored their contents while Fetia answered.

"Yes. Chris, Phil, Jacob, Michael, and her father are in a room together on the opposite end of the hall from the other men... She says Johann is the only one she hasn't seen."

A tingle of excitement shot through me at the idea of Johann being free. "That must be why Juan Josef was asking about Johann... He must've gotten away. Do you think he could be out there working on a way to rescue us?" I grunted as Fetia wrapped the corset around my torso, pulling the stays tight. Where I'd been sore and fatigued the day before, I was now on fire. Every pull of the laces to bring the corset's bones tighter against my ribs felt like a vice squeezing my organs out of me.

Painfully aware of the fact that the pressure would amplify the amount of bleeding I'd experience, I waited until she was finished to grab a few of the cloth diapers from the side of the vanity. Hiding behind Magna's wide frame, I secured the fabrics beneath the slip in a makeshift pad before returning to let Fetia continue adding layers.

Magna smiled. "It could very well be that Johann is attempting to catch up to Captain Cook in Huahine. Huahine isn't far at all.

Johann could get there on the cutter within hours." She presented me with a small round tin, inside which was a shimmering pink rouge. "Can you make this work to write a message?"

I nodded. With all that had happened since he'd left us, I had forgotten that Captain Cook intended to stop on the nearby islands. He was within reach and Johann had sailed alongside him long enough that he would know exactly how to get there. I couldn't help but smile as I imagined Captain Cook and his men storming the ship to demand our immediate release.

I waited until Fetia had finished attaching the padded skirt supports before I moved to the vanity and plucked a hair pin from its surface. Inserting the pin into my mouth and the rouge repeatedly to create a paste, I scribbled a message on the back of Jack's.

'Don't fight. Stay put. Johann is free. Cook is nearby.'

"How long before she can get this to them?" I asked for Magna to translate.

"She's supposed to bring them breakfast soon. Maybe an hour at most."

Fetia continued to talk to Magna as she tied the shimmering green petticoats around my waist.

"She says Juan Josef let her go back to shore last night. He knows she'll come back since he has her father. She doesn't think Hitihiti has been taken. If she's allowed to go back again tonight, she'll ask him to speak to Tu on our behalf. She says Tu is afraid of Juan Josef but might be willing to attempt a trade." Magna frowned, tilting her head as Fetia spoke more rapidly. Her response was more argumentative in tone than I'd ever heard from Magna and it made me frown at both of their reflections.

"What?" I demanded.

"She says... Kyle is her husband now?"

"Her husband?!" I matched Magna's quizzical look. "He's barely seventeen!"

Magna slowly shook her head. "Maybe I'm misunderstanding. The language is a little different.... Whatever the meaning, she doesn't want to leave the ship without him. She asked if we'll teach her some English to help her negotiate his release."

"If they keep us all separated, it'll be dangerous to send messages back and forth on paper," I said, hoping she'd misunderstood and brushing off the idea that Kyle might actually be married to the girl. "If she can speak a little bit of the language, she might be able to communicate between us without evidence being left behind. Do you think Hitihiti would be willing to go to Huahine? We can't just sit and wait for Johann when we're not even certain he's out there."

Magna translated and Fetia nodded, speaking softly as she gazed out the window toward the island.

"She says she is certain he will help however he can. She will ask him… if she's allowed to go back to the island again tonight."

"Ay." Jim whispered, standing slowly from the floor and stretching his back. "What's the plan?" He tiptoed over Lilly and Izzy's sleeping bodies to join us at the mirror.

"Johann is loose." I said. "Captain Cook is still nearby. The plan is to wait and see if Johann or Hitihiti returns with him. He'd be outnumbered and outgunned if Captain Cook returned for us. He'd have to let us go."

"I don't like this." Jim huffed, inspecting the dress. "It ain't right the way he's dressin' ye' up to use ye' for his amusement. It should be one of us… Me or Hoss that he's talkin' to… not you."

"Jim, we went over this last night. I'll be fine. With Johann free, I have a feeling we all will be alright very soon. He'll know how close the captain is. He'd go to him. And assuming we were still going along with Juan Josef's plan, there'd be too much to prepare for to assume I'd be in any danger today. We'll need to figure out what the people going back will need, how we'll explain their disappearance and the sudden reappearance of not only our people but his son as well. Even if he's evil, he wants to go back more than he wants to mess with my head. There's too much to talk about today."

I watched Fetia in the mirror as she began to pin my hair. "And someone was keeping him informed. He knew where to find Chris and Maria, and he knew the moment I'd given birth. We'll have to figure out who betrayed us if it wasn't her. Did Kyle say anything to you about being *married* to Fetia?"

Jim snorted. "No! Why?"

I raised an eyebrow.

"Noooo...." He examined Fetia, shaking his head slowly. "Although, I wouldn't put it past the little summbitch to go and do somethin' like 'at. You dangle a woman in front of him, and his elevator don't exactly go all the way to the top, if ye' catch my drift. That kid's got it bad... Real bad. Been yammerin' on about her since they locked us up."

"You don't think *he* could somehow be involved in our capture, do you?"

"No. Not by choice. He ain't the sharpest tool in the shed, but he wouldn't turn on us unless he was backed up against a wall." He sighed, looking toward the door. "Are ye' sure you don't want me to whack ole' Juan over the head with somethin' when he comes in here for ye? If I could knock his ass out, ye' might be able to take 'em babies and get a runnin' start. If Johann's on his way back with the captain, ye' could get to the safety of his ship before Juan can lay a hand on ye.' He ain't gonna' kill the rest of us for it. He needs us to get to the future."

"No, Jim. I'll be alright. We just need to wait it out. I'm not afraid."

As if on cue, the door opened, and a large man filled its frame. "Alaina," he said with a deep, thick voice, "the captain is ready for you now."

I swallowed, feeling suddenly sixteen again and about to step foot in Yiannis' office. I *wasn't* afraid. I was horrified.

I was ushered into the great cabin to a seat at a large wooden table. Much like our room, the great cabin was immaculately decorated with rich wood paneling on its walls, two chandeliers, and thick velvet tapestry pulled to each side of its large bay window. The table was lined with fruits, breads, meats, jams, and cheeses with assorted candles and fresh flowers sprinkled throughout. This room felt like a dining room fit for royalty instead of a cabin on a pirate's ship.

To one side of my seat, they'd placed a wooden bassinet. Its dark wood shined with the daylight streaming in from the window and its rounded rocker base swayed gently with the movement of the ship. Inside, fresh white linens and pillows presented a surface comparable to a modern-day crib, and, needing to relieve my shoulders of their weight, I pulled Zachary and Cecelia from the makeshift sling to lay them inside.

"I had that made for my grandson," Juan said behind me, forcing me to jump as he made his way to the head of the table. "He and his mother traveled with us for a time. I hope it is to your liking."

"It's nice, thank you."

He was just as finely dressed as he'd been the first time I'd seen him. His red coat showed not a single wrinkle or sign of wear, pristine beneath the shining brass buttons that lined each breast. Under the jacket was a white shirt, its collar sat high over his dark throat without a hint of discoloration. "Sit," he said, motioning to my chair at the side of him. "You must be hungry."

I did so, obediently, watching as his eyes once again undressed me. I held my chin high with the knowledge Johann was still free, holding onto the hope that this was temporary, and I would be rescued by the British navy at any moment.

"The green suits you better." He said, inspecting my dress as he reached for the silver teapot and poured out two cups. "*Much* better. Sugar?"

I cleared my throat and straightened my back, folding my hands in my lap. "Yes, one please."

He added a cube of sugar from a porcelain bowl, dropped a spoon into my cup, and placed it in front of me before sitting down to sip his own. "Did you sleep well?"

I shook my head. "No. I am a prisoner to a man whose motives I don't understand. I didn't sleep at all."

He laughed heartily, snapping his fingers to the two men standing near the door to instruct them to serve us. "Well, we can't have that. Tell me, my dear, what information can I offer to ease your mind?"

I watched as a man loaded my plate with meats and bread, my stomach grumbling at the smell of pork. Gathering what courage I could, I unfolded my napkin and placed it in my lap. "You've been in this time for more than twenty years... Why not build an empire here? It would be easy to do with all we know about the past. You could've had all the respect and authority you wish for. You could've been even more powerful and rich than you were in your own time. Why play the pirate? Why not give up and build something here with your sons? This is where they grew up. Why not stay with them? What's so important in the future that you'd go through all this to get there? It can't just be money."

He flashed his teeth in a smile, bright white beneath his thick salt and pepper beard. "I could ask the same of you. What's so important in the future that you insist on sending your people through? Why not stay and use your knowledge of the past to your own advantage?"

"Family," I said, "for some... Modern medicine for others..."

"Ah," he said, waiting until the servants placed our plates down in front of us before continuing. "What makes you think I do not have the same motives?"

I knew his sons were with him so I had to assume he was speaking to the latter part of my statement. "Are you sick?" I asked, sipping my tea and letting it warm my trembling body.

"Do I look sick?"

I shook my head.

"And do I look like a man who has not spent the last twenty years building my own empire here?"

I looked around the room at the extravagant furnishings that surrounded us. "No..."

He took a piece of bread from his plate and smeared jam across its surface. "I could stay in this time and live comfortably if I so choose... I have created the means to see that my sons are taken care of, but this is not my place. This is not where I belong. I had things I set out to accomplish in my life. Being pulled through time to steal and claw my way into society was not one of them. I've plenty of years left and I intend to use those years to live the life I was destined to live."

He offered me the bread and I took it, placing it on my plate as he took another for himself. "You had your sons with you, but there were three other people on your boat... Who were they?"

He tilted his head to one side. "*That* is none of your concern."

"Isn't it?" I picked up my fork and knife to cut into a piece of sausage. "Let's say we find the storm... if my people are going to the future with your son, we'll need to know your story. It's one thing to make up identities in this time where nothing can be verified, but in the future, it won't be so cut and dry. You can't just make up a name and have people there believe it. What will he do when border patrol pulls up to find him with no identification? He'll have no country to return to, and no money should he manage to get past them. My people can explain their three year disappearance and will be returned home. How do we explain a man who has been missing for forty years? Where will he go?"

"I have his passport and no small amount of cash to send with him in my safe."

"A passport issued in the 70's for a twenty-something year old man who has been missing for forty years? The passport would raise more questions than it would if he had nothing. And cash? A man can't just show up in the 21st century with stacks of cash and not seem suspicious."

"Can't I?" A man asked behind me.

I turned to find two men, both dressed in similarly immaculate attire, entering the cabin. One of them was the image of a younger Juan Josef, his long dark hair pulled back at his neck to highlight piercing dark green eyes and a menacing smile. He didn't have the beard his father wore, but kept a small bit of dark growth around his lips. The other had lighter features, and his hair fell in waves around his face. Where his brother had black hair, his had a hint of auburn mixed in, and his light green eyes seemed kinder—almost familiar—above his short beard.

"Alaina," Juan Josef rose from his seat to wave his arm out toward them in presentation. "My sons. Juan Josef Perez Hernandez Jr., and Dario Fernando Perez Hernandez."

Juan Jr. peered down into the bassinet as he passed. "Twins... Really, father?"

"Come and sit, Juan. Alaina is our guest. We wouldn't want to make a poor impression by acting untoward during our first visit."

"Oh, no," he balked, "we certainly wouldn't want to make a poor impression upon the woman we've taken hostage, now would we?" Rolling his eyes, he plucked up a piece of bacon from a tray as he circled around the table with Dario to take a seat across from me. "Are you quite comfortable, madam, in your prison?"

Dario elbowed him in the rib, smiling at me as he placed his napkin in his lap. "Ignore my brother's foul manners. He is most unpleasant in the mornings."

Juan Jr. smiled. "She does look like mom, though."

"Enough, Juan," his father warned him, returning his attention to me as he sat back down. "We were just discussing plans for how we will explain Dario's reappearance in the future. Alaina doesn't believe he will be able to return so easily."

"Why not?" Dario asked, spreading jam over his bread. "I am who I say I am... Sure, I may look younger than the forty-five year old man I should be, but people age differently."

I shook my head. "But you have been missing for forty years. And you've got a passport with a child's face on it. And you're going to show up with people who have been missing for three years. The appearance of my people will be difficult enough to explain... Them showing up with *you*? That's impossible."

"We were vacationing in Hawaii when we disappeared," Dario said proudly, his light green eyes dancing between me and his father. "Would it not be possible that we might've stayed there and that I had simply been out on my boat when I came upon your friends?"

"The odds of you and them resurfacing at the same time... It's too unbelievable. They'd have so many questions..."

Juan Josef held up one hand to silence us. "Who's to say *they*, whoever *they* may be, would even be looking at him? Perhaps he was just out on his boat fishing when he found your friends. He wouldn't have any identification on him if he didn't think he would need it... Wouldn't *they* be much more interested in your people and less concerned with the fisherman who found them?"

I frowned. "If the intention is to return to the United States, the U.S. border patrol would have questions for him and eventually those questions would lead to: *'where are you from, what's your name, how can we reach you?'* How will he answer that?"

"I live in Hawaii with my father. I was out sailing when I found them."

I blew out. "And if they pull out their computer and find no evidence of a Dario Hernandez living in Hawaii? If they check your old passport and find the man you claim to be has been missing for forty years?"

Juan Jr. smirked. "See, little brother, I told you it would not work."

"But I haven't been called Dario in a very long time." Dario smiled. "My father is in hiding and he changed my name years ago. I'm sure one of your friends could know of someone who lives in Hawaii whose identity I could borrow."

"I have no way to find out since you're keeping us all apart." I moved the food around my plate with my fork. "And why would your father be in hiding?"

Juan Jr. looked at his father. "Oh, but didn't you know, madam? Our father is the infamous Juan Josef Perez Hernandez, the man who was wanted in several countries for supplying most of the world its cocaine in the 70's." He raised an eyebrow, his lip curling slowly upward. "We weren't vacationing. We were fleeing. Isn't that right, father?"

Juan Josef calmly sipped his tea. "We weren't *fleeing*."

"Still..." I said, biting into my bread and waiting until I'd swallowed to continue. "For two people who had been missing for three years to show up with the son of a missing drug dealer on a very old boat… it's too much. You'll raise even more eyebrows, and no one will be able to accomplish anything once they are there. It'll be impossible for any of you to get through customs or be allowed to roam free so you could return here."

Dario pursed his lips in thought as he mindlessly poked at his breakfast. "Well then, what if I am not the one to find them? You have a raft with you. We could bring it, put them out to sea to travel one direction and be rescued while I travel the other. I could sneak into Columbia or Mexico to wait while they go about their plans in the United States. Surely, there'd be some way for me to stay connected with them? Our father has told us about telephones. Could we not use them to remain in touch; to form a plan to come together at sea when it is time for us to return?"

I reminded myself none of this would matter. Captain Cook would get to us long before they could ever reach the portal. They had the coordinates, but we could send our people in March or the following September if we had to. I just needed to get through the next couple hours. "Or the internet." I said, biting into my sausage. "You can find just about anyone with social media… but that's all assuming we can even find the portal."

"Why wouldn't we?" Juan Jr. asked.

"Because everything we know is just a guess based on coordinates we found in a very old journal." I shrugged. "For all I know it only goes one way… or we could very well sail to that spot and find nothing there."

Juan Josef smirked. "For your sake, I hope that is not the case."

His tone sent a chill over my spine and I had to straighten against the chair to prevent myself from shivering. "Why?"

He smiled as casually as if we had been conversing about the weather. "Because then I will have no use to continue feeding and supporting fifteen additional guests on my ship. I'll have no choice but to throw you overboard."

I slowly shook my head. "But we haven't promised you anything. We didn't ask for you to feed or support us by taking us captive. We could've supported ourselves and led you there on our own cutter if you'd given us the opportunity. We still can. We're not your enemies, Juan. Threatening to kill us all is not going to get more out of me when I'm giving you all I have now. My people want to go home too. I have no reason to hold anything back if you're the one taking us there."

"It's not a threat to get more from you," he assured me, sipping his tea. "It's what must be done. Taking fifteen people captive is not a convenience to me. Releasing them after I've done so would be irresponsible to the men of this ship. If you are not my enemy now, you will be before this is over, and I will not have my men looking over their shoulders for signs of your revenge."

Juan Jr. laughed an airy laugh as he shook his head and tossed the bread he'd been buttering back onto his plate. "Such a noble man, my father is." He stared at Juan Josef with a sarcastic smile. "To pluck up women and children and use them to get what he wants, instilling a sense of doom should they not be able to provide… You confuse me father. One minute she is your precious Gloria returned from the dead, *with twins no less*, and the next she is to be a slave to your purpose? Disposable when it is done?"

I cleared my throat. "You mentioned the twins before when you came in the room… why do you say it like that?"

He leaned back in his chair. "Shall I tell her father, or would you prefer to do it?"

Juan Josef cleared his throat, flashing his oldest son a glare before returning his attention to me. "Dario was a twin. Why my son feels there is any significance to that fact remains a mystery."

"She was his favorite." Juan Jr. berated. "His little perfect Dahlia. Of course there is significance to a woman who looks like our mother with male and female twins sitting at our breakfast table. Hoping she'll give you one of them, father? Or are you just attempting to pick up where you left off should Dario not return with what you're searching for? Start a new family with these three since your sons were ruined after we crossed through that storm?"

"Juan," Dario cautioned. "Stop it."

Juan Josef dabbed the corners of his mouth with his napkin and placed it back into his lap before picking up his utensils. "Forgive me, Alaina. I'd hoped my son would show some civility in the presence of a guest. I have poorly misjudged his character. I have no intention of *stealing* your children from their father."

"But… you already have…" I said, feeling emboldened by Juan Jr.'s defiance. "They need their father as much as they need me. You must know the torture he's in being kept separate from us."

Juan Jr. laughed haughtily. "Madam, you mistake my father for a man who has a heart. He is incapable of empathy."

I could see Juan Josef was struggling to remain calm. Each of his son's words were driving a knife through his thinning patience and he was on the verge of losing his temper. There was truth to what his son said about me replacing his wife. I'd had the foresight to see what he wanted with me before I'd even sat down at the table, and I needed to use that to buy time. I needed to see Jack to make sure he wouldn't attempt an escape while we waited for Johann. I needed to establish some kind of trust with this man in the event that Johann didn't return.

"I don't believe that at all." I said, forcing myself to smile at Juan Josef. "Your father's not a monster, I can tell that much. He's just doing what he feels he needs to do to get back. I wouldn't trust us either. Not after a life spent looking over my shoulder. I hope I can change that."

Juan Jr. grinned as he bit into a piece of bread. "Wow, she speaks just as sweetly as mom did too… think she means any of it or is she *exactly* like mom?"

Juan Josef laid his napkin on the table and took a deep breath. "I'm afraid I've lost my appetite." He rose from his seat and snapped his fingers toward one of the men guarding the door. "Mr. Gil, please escort our guest back to her chambers." He offered me his hand and I took it, standing bewildered alongside him. "I shall work out the details of the trip with my sons before I call for you again. Please remain dressed for tea this afternoon. I would be most devastated to see you changed from this exquisite dress when I've not had the proper amount of time to admire you in it."

I shuddered as he brought my hand to his lips and kissed it, the slight bit of moisture left behind on my knuckles feeling like a brand against my skin. "And Jack? I can keep him from fighting if he's allowed to see his children; if I can talk to him for just a minute. I can't guarantee he won't retaliate without my persuasion, and I wouldn't want you to throw anyone overboard before we've even had an opportunity to search for the portal."

He kept my hand in his, looking defiantly toward Juan Jr. "I shall consider it."

Chapter Four

Mr. Gil did not escort me back to the room I'd been in before. Instead, he led me down the hall from the great cabin and through a single door that opened to a smaller room. A single fourposter bed sat in its center with a large bay window to one side. The furnishings in this room were just as rich as the others, but void of any additional occupants, this one made me much more uncomfortable.

Across from the bed was a small vanity where a basin sat next to a man's shaving kit. The razor sat unfolded beside a black bristled brush.

Was this Juan Josef's room? I looked back toward the door, my arms tightening around the sling that held Zachary and Cecelia. And now that I was not an *'unwilling female'* what would he do with me inside? I backed into the room to stand at the window and look out at an empty sea—no signs of the captain's return anywhere in sight.

'Please let him come for us.' I prayed.

What if Johann wasn't free? What if he was being held separately? What if Juan Josef only wanted us to assume someone was out there to come to our rescue as a means to keep us from fighting him? And what if Fetia really was the spy and she was only planting the seeds of our complacency on behalf of Juan Josef?

I looked back toward the vanity at the unfolded razor, its blade glistening in the morning sun. Had he intentionally left it there to see if I would grab it? And what if I did? Juan Jr. didn't seem thrilled they'd taken us captive. None of Juan Josef's men even paid him the respect to acknowledge him when we'd come onboard. If I slit his throat and ran, would anyone left alive even care, or would I be doing them all a favor?

Juan Jr.'s words played on repeat in my mind. His father was evading capture when he'd gone through time. Why would he want to risk being detained and punished for his crimes by going back? It didn't make any sense. Juan Josef was not a stupid man. There had to be more to it. Perhaps it was Dahlia he wished to go back for. If she'd been on the boat, maybe he needed to return to make sure she was alive. Or maybe he was afraid he might die too soon in this time. Maybe he was starting to feel the effects of aging and wanted to return merely for the sake of living a longer life... Or maybe his grandson had something to do with it. Was the grandson sick?

I'd always been able to read people's characters; find a way to relate to them to make sense of their behaviors, but Juan Josef was unreadable. One minute, he was a monster threatening to throw us overboard, and the next, he was just a man trying to establish authority over his ungrateful son in front of company. He'd threaten and intimidate me in one sentence, then compliment me in the next. He'd looked at me like I was a piece of meat to be devoured, then blinked and I was a long lost treasure to be cherished and adored.

What did he really want? And which was he? The man or the monster?

Zachary whimpered in my arms, and I could feel the weight of my breasts getting heavier with the need to feed them. The lack of sleep was also setting in. My entire body felt like lead as I sat down on the edge of the bed and sank into its heavenly soft surface. After going so long sleeping on straw and bamboo, this mattress was begging me to give in to my fatigue.

I watched the door as I fed them one at a time, very much aware that Juan Josef could barge in and find me exposed at any moment. Relieved once I'd finished and returned my breasts to their uncomfortable position smashed inside the corset, I laid down and wrapped an arm around my two babies.

I hadn't had the time to fully soak in the joy of being a new mother before he'd shown up to rip that precious time away from me. I should've been spending those first hours counting fingers and toes with Jack, not fearing for their lives. I should've been in bed with their little bodies rested against my skin, falling in love with them, instead of attempting to understand the thought processes of a dangerous man.

I watched them both as they tried to focus their little eyes on their surroundings. It was amazing how they'd already begun developing separate personalities.

Zachary was the curious one of the two. He moved his eyes a lot more than Cecelia, always seeming like he needed to know what was happening around him. He was even starting to lift his head, like he was just too excited to experience the world to wait for the muscles to develop. For as much as he was curious and determined, he was also impatient, and never shied away from letting me know he was hungry the instant his eyes opened.

Cecelia, on the other hand, was complacent. She would look at whatever was in front of her, often going cross eyed before she gave up and closed her eyes. Where Zachary woke up and demanded to be fed, Cecelia would wiggle patiently, knowing the food would come. As a result, I'd been able to feed him while she waited her turn, and that was a relief because attempting to feed them both at once was a juggling act I hadn't been able to master, particularly when it required both arms and a great deal of effort to get Cecelia to latch on.

It seemed surreal, now that I had them, that it had only been two years since I'd sat in Dr. Moore's office and she'd told me I'd never be able to have a child of my own. I remembered feeling empty to my core in that moment; like I'd somehow failed as a woman. I'd wanted to be a mother more than I'd ever wanted anything; more than becoming a successful songwriter; more than building a graphic design career; more than living in a perfect house. I was born to be a mom.

I remembered feeling so completely selfish when she handed me a pamphlet from an adoption agency for the second time. To be told you'll never have your own and then offered someone else's in the same sentence was like an exclamation point; like, by taking the pamphlet, it was somehow made final that I would never know the children I'd dreamt of.

And I'd dreamt of them endlessly. It was always a boy and a girl. I'd named them several different times in my mind throughout the years, and had known them after years of watching them grow up in my dreams. They were a little bit of me and a little bit of Chris; creative, thoughtful, and full of life. Taking that pamphlet in my hands felt like I'd killed them both.

I wasn't opposed to adopting, I just hadn't been prepared for that to become my only option the day it did.

My eyelids grew heavy as I admired the children I'd once given up on having, and I echoed Cecelia's yawn with one of my own, desperately needing to sleep but fighting it so I could continue to stare at them just a moment longer.

Slowly, consciousness drifted away from me, and I slept for a while, meeting those two children who now had names in my dream, noticing they were still a bit of me and a bit of Chris but now Jack was mixed in as well. They were perfect in every way, and it was hard to pull myself from their five-year-old faces when the sound of the door brought me back to my body.

I remembered I was in Juan Josef's room. Paralyzed with the fear of what he might do, I didn't open my eyes. If I pretended to be asleep, maybe he would leave me alone. Maybe the kinder side of him would let me rest for a while before he shifted back into the monster to frighten me into submission. If he wanted sex... what would I do? What *could* I do?

I could hear him moving closer and I suddenly felt more vulnerable than I'd ever been. Squeezing my eyes shut, I tried to prepare myself for his hands on me; for his face over mine; for his lips against my skin. I attempted to calm my racing heart from beating out of my chest as I felt the mattress dip with his weight at my back.

'It'll be over soon.' I promised myself. *'I'll keep my eyes closed. I'll try to think of something else... Everything will be alright. I can do this... As long as the babies are okay...'*

"Red..."

One whispered word was all it took for every bit of anxiety to melt immediately away. I opened my eyes to find Jack sitting on the bed looking down at me. I sat up and wrapped both arms tightly around his neck, tears of relief rendering me speechless.

His hand pressed against the center of my back, instantly assuring me I was safe, while the other curled into my hair and pulled me tighter against him. "I shouldn't have left you," he breathed, "not for a second."

"I'm alright." I half-laughed, half-sobbed, clinging to him as if I would never be able to do so again. Tucking my face into the crook of his neck, I breathed in his familiar scent, basked in the warmth of his body against mine, and wept with the knowledge that he was there, and no matter what I would need to endeavor from that moment on, I was safe.

Realization washing over me, I pulled away. "How'd you get here? Did he let you out or did you escape?"

"A few of his men brought me to you." He smiled, brushing the hair from my face. "I got your message."

"He wasn't after Maria. He was after us. He's from our time and—"

He placed his finger against my lips to silence my rambling. "Jim told me everything this morning." Slowly he scanned the green silk I was dressed in, and I watched as his jaw hardened. "Has he touched you?"

"No," I whispered, closing my eyes as he smoothed his thumb over my cheek.

"Red, I have to get us out of here before he does. You know that."

"But Johann…" I argued. "He's out there somewhere, and he could be trying to catch up to Captain Cook. Fetia's going to ask Hitihiti to find the captain too. We're outnumbered without them. We can't fight. Jack, he's not a predictable man. He could hurt our babies. We can't risk their lives for our own. We have to play along."

He smiled down at Zachary and Cecelia where they laid beside me. "And what if Johann's not out there? What if Hitihiti can't get to the captain? We can't just go along with this. We'd be stuck with him for months. Red, *I* can't risk my family falling victim to that man. I have to do something. There's a window." He motioned to the glass beside us. "We can climb down, swim to shore, and make a run for it."

"And Chris and Maria? Kyle and Izzy? Jim and Lilly? Magna, Anna, Bud, Bruce? You'd risk all their lives just to save ours?"

He took my hand in his and kissed it. "Alaina, I'd risk the lives of everyone in this time and our own to see that you and our babies are safe. Come on." He pulled me toward the edge of the bed. "We have to get you out of here."

I pulled my arm away. "No, Jack. He will catch us. He's a smart man and he's probably listening to us right now… trying to validate his mistrust in us by discovering us in an attempt to escape. He will catch us and he will hurt us far worse if we deceive him than if we just go along with his plans. All he wants is to get back to his time. All we have to do is get him there."

"LET HIM KILL ME," he said loudly toward the door. "I don't care. I'll die willingly before I stand aside and let him touch MY FAMILY. It doesn't matter that he's from our time or that he just wants to get back if he intends to use you for his amusement while we travel there." He searched my eyes for some sense of understanding. "Red, please. You can't stay here."

I shook my head. "No. Even if it were possible to climb down this ship with two newborns and swim to shore—*and it's not*—I've seen the darkness that's in him, Jack. He won't make a threat he doesn't intend on seeing through should we disobey. Whatever it is he's trying to get to in the future is worth far more than any of our lives. This isn't a movie. It's real. We can't be heroes in this one. There's only one way out of this if the captain doesn't return. Look at them." I turned his head toward Zachary and Cecelia. "He will take them if he senses the slightest bit of deception. There is nothing I won't do or take to prevent that from happening. It's not your job to keep me safe anymore. It's *our* job to keep *them* safe now."

I saw his shoulders slump in defeat as he sat back down on the bed to pull Zachary up into his arms. He smiled in surprise as Zachary's eyes popped open. "I don't even know which one I'm holding," he said, shaking his head. "I don't know my own children. How can I keep them safe if I am kept in chains? How can I call myself a man if I just let him do what I know he intends to do with you?"

"That one's Zachary," I informed him, leaning against his shoulder. "You can tell by the hair. His is lighter than hers." I sighed as I watched him brush his palm over the top of his son's head. "Jack, I asked Juan Josef to let you see them, and here you are with your son in your arms. Maybe this is a sign of his willingness to work with us? The man is unstable, but I don't think he's a complete monster. I think he's lost faith in people. He wants to go home, and the only way he knows how to ask for our help is by forcing us to take him there."

He rocked Zachery gently. "He wants you, too… Will he force you the same way?"

I shook my head. "He would've done that already. It would've been him coming through that door instead of you."

He looked over at me then. "I'm so sorry. I never should've left you. Not after you'd given birth… And not when we found out you were pregnant either. If I hadn't left the island, and if I'd killed Phil, we could be safe there still. The captain never would've found us. We never would've been brought here for Juan Josef to discover us. What I wouldn't give to go back to that island with you."

"None of us could've known that this is where we'd end up. None of that is your fault." I smiled. "Oh, but what I wouldn't give to have one more night alone on the summit… dancing beneath the stars to the sounds of the ocean in the distance…"

He softly kissed my lips. "Do you think we'll ever have that kind of peace again?"

I nodded. "We'll take whatever time we have together to create that kind of peace until we have it again for good." I grinned and stood up from the bed, motioning him toward me. "Come on, Volmer. We're together for now, let's not waste it. I can still hear the ocean in the distance. Dance with me while I have you. Give me that moment of peace to look forward to."

Gently, he laid Zachary back down beside Cecelia, and stood to wind his arms around me. He sighed as I rested my cheek against his chest, kissing the top of my head. "I love you so much, Alaina."

I closed my eyes as he swayed us softly. "And that is why we'll get through this. We have each other, even when we're out of reach. You will always take care of me, and I will always take care of you. And we'll both take care of them. Let me take the lead here, however hard it might be. If I tell you to stay put and not fight, trust me that it's with our best interest in mind. Now, I'm done wasting anymore of my moment of peace talking about him. Tell me something else… Tell me how Kyle got out of his chains."

He chuckled. "I have no idea. I looked over and he was loose, talking about climbing out the window to search for Fetia. Did you know they were married?"

I groaned. "Fetia mentioned it but we were all hoping we misunderstood her. There's no way I'm letting that kid stay married at seventeen. And to Fetia of all people! She says they weren't involved, but Juan Josef was there with her family when he took you, Chris, and Maria. They *had* to have a part in this, right?"

"I don't want to waste our moment talking about Juan Josef either, but there's one other person that knew where I was taking them. John Edgecumbe. He suggested the location."

"Why would John turn us all over to Juan Josef? He might hand Chris over, but not all of us. Especially not Maria."

He shook his head. "Don't you find it odd that Juan was conveniently landed on an island within a few miles of the only other time travelers in this world? John did mention he'd dined with the man once before. Perhaps there was more to that dinner conversation than he cared to inform us of."

"You think John knew what Juan Josef was searching for all along? You think he sent word?"

Jack shrugged. "Seems much more likely he knew and sent word to him once he'd discovered the truth about Chris and Maria than for Juan Josef to just coincidentally be in the vicinity. John's interest in Maria could've been a tactic to keep them close until we arrived here. His jealousy and sending Chris to that island could've been a message to Juan that we'd arrived. It would explain how he was so close and why he took such an immediate interest in our group."

"It *is* fishy that he was right there... And John hasn't exactly been a friend to us... But what about that whole story of him searching for Michael? He said he found out about us after he'd spoken to Uati."

"You forget I spent two months with Uati. He is not a man who makes deals with sailors, no matter the trade. I think John could've told him about Michael and Uati to cover up his own involvement in our capture."

"So if Johann or Hitihiti goes back to Captain Cook and runs into John first?"

"He's proven himself capable of violence before in preservation of his own interests, I can't see why he wouldn't do it again. Although, Johann is a smart enough man that he'd probably have drawn similar conclusions by now. He's more determined than most of us to find the way back, and he would be cautious of John."

I pursed my lips. "Jack, we've put a lot of faith in this very roughly thrown together concept of Johann's. I mean, none of us have even talked about what we would do if we got to the coordinates and nothing happened. You really don't think we're going to sail out and this magical portal through time is going to appear, do you?"

I felt his chest move in a soft laugh. "No, but you seemed so set on finding it I assumed you did. I didn't want to ruin that for you."

I sighed. "Honestly, to this point, I've gone along with it for the sake of Anna. She needed hope, and I was willing to sail out there for her, just to see what might be there." I looked back toward the bed as Zachary's legs began to wiggle. "But that's all changed now. What happens if the captain comes to our rescue? Do we really want to risk running into Juan Josef out on the water in search of something so far-fetched? Or should we just face the fact we're stuck here? Stop searching for a way back home and *build* a home here? We'd been planning to stay anyway."

He took my hand in his as he turned us, gently separating himself from me to meet my eyes. "Let's say we get out of this, where would you want to go? Where should home be?"

I shrugged. "I don't know… We can't go to America with the war approaching. And with our connections to the captain, England could be just as dangerous. You'd risk being expected to join the fight. Where's there the least amount of war right now? Ireland, maybe?"

He playfully tugged on a strand of my hair that had come loose from its pins. "You'd fit right in there." He smiled. "Have you ever been?"

I shook my head. "No. My great grandparents came from there. I always wanted to see it, just… never got the chance."

"I've been there a few times." He placed his finger beneath my chin to tilt my face up to him. "And I could see you there, that fiery red hair blowing against an endless green backdrop… Zachary and Cecelia playing outside a small house tucked away in the hills." He kissed my lips and pressed his forehead against mine. "Anna would never give up, you know. We'd have to say goodbye to her and, most likely, Bruce too. They'd spend their lives searching for a way back."

I hated the idea of any of us separating, but it was only a matter of time before we'd have to. I wasn't willing to cross through that storm with the twins, and neither was Jack. I nodded. "I assumed we'd have to at some point."

He smiled. "Just because you and I haven't discussed the plausibility of not finding a way back doesn't mean it hasn't been discussed. Everyone has their doubts about Johann's theory. We were all willing to give it a shot, but now... If we can escape, I think we should give it up... for a while anyway. Jim was considering waiting things out in England until the war's over and then settling in America, but I like the idea of Ireland for us. We could start over. Live simple... Develop fun Irish accents as we get older... Can you imagine Jim slowly developing an Irish accent?"

"I can barely understand him as it stands. But I want that life for us... As much as I'll miss my family, I never fit into that world. I think I might fit into an 18th century Ireland."

"I'll do everything I can to give it to you."

"No, Jack. *We'll* do everything we can to give it to ourselves and our family. Starting now. Whatever's waiting in the future for Juan Josef is just as important to him as Liam is to Anna. He's not going to give up, and I believe him when he says there's nothing he won't do to get there. We can't fight him, but we can try to understand him. He'll use us against each other if we try to outwit him. He'll use our babies against us if we attempt to fight back. Let me spend some time feeling him out. I really don't think he's going to hurt me. If I can earn his trust, maybe I can convince him to let us go in the event that the captain doesn't come for us. His son didn't seem to agree with our being imprisoned. Maybe, if I can't convince Juan Josef, I can convince his son to let us go. I need you to trust me to handle this. If I feel myself failing, I'll hand it over to you to do things your way."

"But if he tries to hurt—"

"Then I'll hand it over to you, I promise."

Zachary began to wail, putting an end to our moment, and I let go of my grip on him. "We have about sixty seconds before he increases his volume to a level that is ear piercing."

He laughed as he escorted me back to the bed. "How are you so sure he won't hurt you?"

"Because I just know," I said, hurrying to pluck Zachary from the bed before he woke up Cecelia. "He mentioned that I reminded him of his wife. His son echoed that observation this morning. There's something sentimental there, buried deep down. He throws out words and threats to intimidate me, but then he looks at me with this sort of familiarness… like he sees her in me. And I think he loved her… in his own sort of way. Maybe she was the only person he ever loved. And I just know he won't hurt me because of that."

"I don't like that any better."

I grinned. "Don't worry. I only have eyes for you." I glanced up at the clock. "How long do you think they'll let you stay?"

"They didn't say." He reached behind me to loosen my stays and Zachary wasted no time latching on the minute he had access. "Oh wow. Does that hurt?"

"Yes." I yawned. "It's strange… like my body needs to do it and it's a relief when they start, but at the same time it hurts like hell. My skin is raw and I'm all veiny and leaking from everywhere, and that little thing I used to have somewhere deep inside that made me feel feminine; that gave me any sense of being the slightest bit sexy, is just gone. I am a dispenser now…"

He chuckled, sliding into the bed behind me to rub my shoulders. "You're a sexy dispenser. And you're really great at this whole motherhood thing. It's been what? Two days? And you're already a pro. Motherhood looks amazing on you."

I rolled my head back as he worked the knots around my shoulder blades. "Ugh, well maybe it's new motherhood that's got me obsessing over Kyle. I can't stop thinking about him. When did he even marry Fetia? How did none of us know about it? He's been with us for a year and a half. You and Jim are like father figures in his life… Why wouldn't he talk to us first?"

"Because he knew damn well none of us would approve. Apparently, he told Chris."

"And Chris let him do it?! Jesus, brain damage or not, he should've stopped him! What was he thinking?"

Jack smirked. "I imagine he wasn't overly concerned about a boy's 18th century Tahitian marriage ceremony while he was plotting a way to get that same boy back to the 21st century."

"Still... *he* should've told us. He's changed a lot this last year and a half. I hardly recognize him anymore."

"Don't do that." He worked his thumbs lower, reaching beneath the corset to massage near my spine.

"Do what?"

"Don't demonize him just because he and Maria are doing it to you. You had your reasons for loving him, and you had your reasons for choosing me. Neither of those had anything to do with him being a bad guy. I know what he's doing to you hurts, but he's a guy, and we need to blame our hurt on the people that hurt us before we recognize the faults in ourselves that led them to do it."

I exhaled heavily. "She called me selfish again last night... Lilly laid into her pretty hard; called her all kinds of names. I felt sorry for her. I know I should hate her, but it's not her fault he blames me for everything... She's Maria and she's ridiculous and she has these nonsensical outbursts she can't control. It's him I want to hate for putting those thoughts in her head. After all we went through... After all this... Why can't he drop it? Why can't he just be happy that we're both happy?"

He laid a kiss against my neck. "He's a guy."

"That's not a good enough excuse."

He kissed my neck again, moving lower. "He's a brain-damaged guy."

I laughed, closing my eyes as his lips moved toward my shoulder.

"And he loves you..." He said softly, resting his forehead against the center of my spine. "When he found us, he was beside himself when I told him you were alive. He cried. I've never seen a man cry like that... It took us a whole day of sailing to get to you, and he spent that entire time standing on the bow of that ship staring out at the ocean for signs of the island. He didn't eat or sleep or speak to anyone once we set sail. His excitement to get to you ate away at me. It ate away at Maria, too. I think, watching him stand there like that, it instilled in both of us this sense that whatever we meant to each of you would be gone forever once you were reunited. He loved you entirely. For you to choose me after all that… I know that hurt him. I saw it that night we fought. And for him to choose you, well, that hurt her too. It's not going to be easy for him *or her* to just drop that. There's a lot of pain there. Pain I wouldn't be able to let go of if you'd chosen him over me. And it's hard for me to believe you have dropped it so easily."

I hadn't dropped it at all.

Chapter Five

The grandfather clock in the room read 2:30 when Mr. Gil appeared at the door to summon me once again. "The captain has requested your company on deck for tea. He's asked that you leave the children with their father, and he assures you Mr. Volmer shall remain unbothered with the children inside this room while he awaits your return."

I saw the panic wash over Jack's features and wondered if he was more afraid for me to be alone with Juan Josef, or for him to be alone for the very first time with the babies.

"They just ate." I reminded him, glancing down at their two sleeping bodies in his arms. "You'll do fine, and so will I. Trust me."

He nodded, his eyebrows raising in a show of helplessness as I stood from the bed to straighten my skirts. "You're sure you're alright?"

I took his chin in my grip and kissed his lips. "I promise, I'll be fine." Surprised by my own lack of anxiety, I kissed each of the babies' foreheads, and turned my attention to Mr. Gil. "Will someone come to fetch me if the babies start to cry? They need to be fed every hour or two right now."

Mr. Gil bowed. "Madam, you have my word that you shall be swiftly returned the moment the children are in need of their mother."

I looked back at Jack and forced a smile. "It won't be long before I'm right back here beside you. I'll beg him to let you stay with me. He's shown me kindness before when I have asked. Hopefully, he will continue to do so."

"I hate this."

"I know." I adjusted the sleeves of my jacket. "It'll all be over soon. It's just tea on the top deck. He won't do anything there. I'll be fine."

"Just... be careful, okay?"

"I will."

I was unable to pull my eyes from the image of his massive arms cradled around our two tiny humans. How heartbroken and helpless he appeared as he watched me leave. I stared all the way to the door and out until it was closed behind me and I was forced to turn forward.

I wasn't afraid as we walked down the corridor and began climbing the stairs. Maybe it was Jack's effect on me, or maybe it was the lack of control Juan Josef had during breakfast, but there was a part of me that was almost looking forward to tea. I was intrigued by Juan's interest in the future, and my inability to read his character was a challenge I wanted to overcome. Hatred sat heavy in my chest, and I wanted to understand him so I could sleep without the weight of that emotion forcing my eyes open to check my surroundings every few minutes.

We ascended the stairs into the bright afternoon sun, a warm breeze blowing softly against the bits of skin left uncovered by the layers of green fabric.

Juan was seated at a table near the railing, and he stood to remove his hat as I joined him. His dark eyes moved down to take in the dress, and he licked his lower lip, the gesture implanting the anxiety back into the pit of my stomach.

"Sit," he commanded, before turning his attention to Mr. Gil. "Leave us."

As I sat and watched Mr. Gil return to the stairs, I noticed the silence around me. The deck was empty of its crew, and far off on the shoreline, the beach was abandoned. There were no boats in the water of native fishermen, and no ships far out on the horizon coming back to our rescue. I was sure the top deck would be safe when I'd left Jack, but now, being completely alone in the vacant open space, I felt more threatened than ever.

The giant sails above our heads were rolled for docking, but bits of their fabrics hung loose to crack with the wind. They towered high above my head and added to the smallness I felt being alone with such a man.

He remained standing as he poured two cups of tea, dropping a sugar cube into one to place it in front of me.

"I have given you what you asked for," he said as he lowered himself down into his seat. "Are you not content with the time you have been granted?"

"I am," I said, cursing my voice for shaking. "How long will you let him stay?"

"That all depends on him, my dear." He sipped his tea.

I stared down into the amber liquid in my cup, watching the small leaf particles dance and settle at the bottom. "What do you mean?"

"You were quite confident that, should I give you time with this man, you could convince him to trust me. In our absence, we shall test his trust in *you*."

"I don't understand. I asked him not to fight, and he has agreed."

He smiled. "You are an intelligent woman. You cannot pretend you did not notice the item I left upon the vanity. I was delighted to find that you, yourself, refrained from taking it. If Mr. Volmer can show the same faith in you that you've shown in me, you shall remain together during our travels. If, however, upon our return, the item has gone missing, I'm afraid I'll be obliged to return him to the other men."

The razor.

I closed my eyes. Would Jack see it as a test, or would he see it as an opportunity? Would he trust me to handle this like I'd asked him to, or would he pocket the blade in case he needed to play the hero? Part of me knew the answer and dreaded returning to the room.

"Now," Juan Josef straightened, his ominous expression melting away to a more human-like casualness. "We haven't much time to prepare for our journey. We'll need supplies for the ship as well as for the travelers. I've my men working to stockpile food and water at this very moment."

He leaned back in his chair, holding his teacup just beneath his face as he studied me. "You should know that Dario is not being sent to the future to watch over your people once they arrive. They shall part ways long before they are discovered. While your people sort their own affairs in the U.S., he shall be sorting mine in Columbia. He will need their assistance to navigate a time he is unfamiliar with. You said something this morning about a way for them to remain in touch. The internet? Tell me how this works."

I walked him through modern day technology in depth, all the while, my mind remained on the image of Jack in the bedroom. I saw him staring at the razor, could hear his thoughts as he laid the babies on the bed to move to the vanity and take it in his hand. As I detailed the use of social media, I cringed at the outline of the razor protruding against the fabric of his pocket. I knew Jack, and I knew he was going to take it. Juan Josef knew it too, and as he listened to my account of how our people could use the internet to communicate, I could see he was delighting in the same images that plagued my mind.

He was a smart man, and this test of trust could drive a wedge between me and Jack; a wedge that he might be able to slide between. How many of these tests would he use on us? How far would he go to pull me away from Jack? Had Juan Jr.'s assessment been correct? Did Juan Josef intend to start over with me and my babies at his side? I shuddered at the thought.

"Juan," I took a deep breath, "I meant it earlier when I said it's unlikely that we'll find anything. This whole idea of the equinox and time travel... it's not concrete by any definition of the word. It's a very rough hypothesis we came up with as a means to give ourselves some bit of hope we might return home. I mean, we barely remember anything about our own accident, and we came up with this idea pulling at strings from a hundred-year-old journal. You have to be prepared for that, too."

"Do you think me a fool? I have been searching for more than twenty years. Long ago, I'd accepted the likelihood that there was no way back. But your appearance has given me a small bit of hope I might escape this world, and so I must make an attempt."

"And if there's nothing?" I asked. "Are you really going to throw us overboard? Leave us for dead in the ocean? With children?"

He nodded. "To release you all could place my own men in danger after having imprisoned you... And my men would turn on me if I so willingly put their lives at risk. Let us remain hopeful, for your sake, we come upon this time portal."

I sipped my tea, reminding myself that he'd turned his head when I'd asked... and a man that would do that wasn't going to kill us. There was a heart in there somewhere. He had to be bluffing. "Let's say we find it. It's been forty years. If you were evading capture, how do you know there's anything left of the life you had before? They could've confiscated it all by now. There could be nothing there for you... Or worse, you could be identified as Juan Sr. and imprisoned for the crimes you committed forty years ago."

"Again, I say, Dario is being sent to sort out my affairs." His eyes lingered on my neck. "He shall inform me, upon his return, as to what is waiting for me there."

"Or who..." I added, immediately regretting the words as they struck the chord which prompted him to morph back into the monster.

His brows furrowed as he leaned forward over the table. "Do not let my son's disregard for my authority tempt you into forgetting your place, madam. He is my blood and his life cannot be ripped away from him the way yours can you."

"I'm sorry. I didn't mean it."

"Do not lie to me either. You did mean it. You're hoping to find some weakness in my character that can be used against me to give your people power. I assure you, you shall find none."

I could feel my ears reddening, the heat from the sun at my back suddenly becoming unbearable. "I'm sorry. It won't happen again."

"The lawyer," he said calmly, changing back into Dr. Jekyll. "You mentioned before he could not be trusted. He put his hands on you once, yes?"

I frowned. How could he possibly know that? None of the Tahitians knew about my encounter with Phil. Only my people knew. My people, and John Edgecumbe, that is.

John had been asked to keep Phil away from us, and an explanation as to why was required for him to do so. Jack's theory about John's involvement *had* to be correct. There was no other way for Juan Josef to possess that knowledge. Phil certainly wouldn't have offered up that information of his own volition.

Slowly, I nodded. "Yes."

His nose twitched in response. "He has made many appealing offers to assist in our endeavor to secure my position in the future. It is his wish that I send him in place of one of your people."

I shook my head. "You can't trust him."

"Trust is a funny thing." He leaned back in his chair and sipped his tea. "We think we know who we can and can't trust until that trust is tested."

He was talking about Jack. He knew it was eating away at me, and he was fanning the flames of my own mistrust to accentuate his point.

"But like I said, I'm no fool." He looked down into his teacup. "To bestow my good faith on a man such as he would be reckless. I could not trust him to follow through on his promises when he's revealed such a distasteful character." He set the cup down on its saucer and tapped his fingers against the edge of the table.

"However, given your doubts this morning about Dario's ability to implant himself in the future, I must reconsider who we send alongside him. If Dario is detained and unable to return, who among you has the most to lose by abandoning the voyage back to this time?"

'Jack...'

Panic swept over me. Doubtful as I'd been we would actually find a portal, the concept became infinitely more concrete when faced with the notion that Jack could potentially be sent through. "No. Please. Chris has Maria. He wouldn't abandon her. He'd kill to get back to her."

Juan Josef raised an eyebrow. "Would he? A man who has lost his mind might be convinced, upon treatment of his injury, to doubt that time travel had happened to him at all. Or he may be hospitalized for being delusional; unable to make his way back to the ocean. And the nurse certainly could not be trusted to return when she is so anxious to be reunited with her son. A mother could not be so easily pulled from her child." He turned the teacup back and forth on the saucer. "I considered the lawyer for a time since his own son is here among us, but I think perhaps Mr. Volmer would be much more inclined to get back to his family... Or... You."

"Me?" I shook my head. "The babies wouldn't make it without me."

"Mothers die in childbirth every day and their children survive on milk provided by other women or goats. There is no shortage of goats or nursing mothers in Tahiti. Our very own Fetia should begin developing milk any day now with the child that grows inside her."

Fetia was pregnant... Of course, Kyle would marry her. I wondered if her parents had forced him after they'd found out, or if he'd done it out of pure chivalry.

Juan Josef grinned. "So, you see, I *could* send you... and I could send Mr. Volmer... and I would be able to rest assured, knowing someone *would* come back."

"Juan, please." I begged. "*If* there's something there, we know nothing about how it works. You could be sending us away from our children forever for all we know. I'll do anything to stay with them, and so will he. Anything you ask, it's yours."

He reached across the table and took my hand in his. "My dear," he ran his thumb over my palm, "you will do anything I ask, anyway. Come."

He rose from his seat and pulled me up against him, winding one arm around my back to bring me closer. I attempted not to recoil as he cupped my face in his hand and tilted it up toward him. "Are you not curious to find out just how much trust Mr. Volmer has in you? Perhaps you may be more willing to send him away should you learn he has such little faith in you."

He leaned down, his breath brushing over my lips as I trembled and squeezed my eyes closed. "I am not the lawyer, Alaina, and I will not force you. It will be you that comes to me."

Releasing my face, he wrapped my arm in his and led us toward the stairs.

My heart raced as we walked down the corridor, and I replayed his words over and over again. Did he want me to come to him, offer myself in exchange for one or both of us to remain in this time? And if there was no way back? Would I need to offer myself in exchange for the rest of their lives?

What did he mean, and how soon would it be before I would need to make that offer?

Down the stairs, I stared ahead at the set of double doors. Jack would have the razor in his pocket. I knew him, and I knew he would take it and save it for a time when he might need to use it. "Juan, if he took it, it would only be so that—"

"Unlock the door please," Juan called ahead to the two guards standing on each side. One man inserted the key and turned it while two additional guards appeared at our backs from the opposite end of the hall.

"Please," I begged, "he won't use—"

"Open the door."

As the double doors were pushed open, I didn't look toward the bed, but stared at the vanity's surface—at the empty space beside the basin where the razor had once been. My eyes welled with tears as Juan pulled me inside, and I froze in place as the guards moved ahead of me to take Jack back into custody.

"I hope you have enjoyed your time with them." Juan Josef said cooly. "Unfortunately, that time has run out and I'm afraid you must be returned to your quarters."

"What happened?" Jack demanded, noticing my tears. "Alaina? What is it? Did he do something to you?"

I took a deep breath, looking up at him where he was attempting to wiggle free of the four guards that were struggling to keep his arms held behind his back. I shook my head. "Not to me. To you." I stood on my tiptoes and kissed his lips one last time, reaching into his pocket to pull out the razor. "He was testing you…"

Juan Josef stepped to my back and laid his hands on the skin that shone at my collar, tauntingly moving his fingers over my throat. "And your failure to listen to your fiancé, Mr. Volmer, shall not go unpunished."

I stared into Jack's eyes, pleading with him not to attempt to fight as I felt Juan Josef's breath hot against the nape of my neck. "I have learned a lot about punishment in my years at sea." His nose moved up my cheek to my temple and I tensed as he slid one arm around my waist. "Beat a man who defies you, and it will only cause him to rise up again." His palm moved slowly up the bodice of my dress. "Take away that which the man fights for, and he shall fight no more." He pressed his lips against my temple. "I wonder if she will taste as sweet as she looks?"

Jack attempted to lunge toward us, but was held tightly by the four massive guards, and could only writhe against his restraints. "I swear to God, if you touch her—

"What?" Juan teased, running his palms down the sides of my arms. "You'll kill me? Try it."

"Jack," I begged. "Please… stop."

"Return him to his chains." Juan ordered, placing his hand on my back and pushing me toward the bed, pinning me against one of its posts with his full weight at my back. "I shall see to his punishment straight away."

I heard the shuffling of kicking feet against the floorboards, and the heavy breathing of a struggle as Jack attempted to fight.

That sound gradually led out into the hallway, growing further and further away.

Slowly, Juan Josef released his grip and pulled away, clearing his throat as I straightened and turned to face him.

He grinned. "As I stated before, Alaina, I will not force you... however, the illusion of force will have the same effect. Let him think that I have. And let us see how obedient you can keep your men now that they understand who will pay for their crimes. Gather your children. I shall escort you back to your room now."

Chapter Six

Chris

'The women are locked in a room at the end of the hall two floors down from the deck. 1 guard outside their door. Room has window facing the island. 2 guards outside our room. Alaina in trouble. When? -J'

Chris stared at the small scrap of paper, then back up to Fetia, where she busied herself setting out bowls of stew for each of them and conversing in her own language with her father.

He and Jack, using Fetia as a vehicle to deliver messages between the two rooms they were held in, were gradually forming a plan to escape. They'd been able to deduce that they were held on opposite ends of the same floor, with the women one floor up. With the most recent letter, he now knew there were four guards in total that stood between the two rooms and that the women's room was just above Jack's.

They had to get off this ship… tonight.

Juan Josef was unpredictable. For as long as they were within his reach, the women and children would remain in trouble. He was terrified for them all, but, surprisingly more than he'd been prepared for, he was worried about Alaina.

Since they'd found each other, he'd been numb in the areas of his mind that had to do with her. She'd chosen Jack, a practical stranger in comparison to her years with him, and the blow to his pride had been too hard to process. He'd let himself stop feeling anything toward her—sadness, anger, jealousy, love; anything—he went numb and kept his distance, putting every bit of his energy into loving Maria.

Until that single line jumped off the paper. *'Alaina in trouble.'*

He was in love with Maria, and as a result of loving her, it had been easier, distracted as he was by it, to force himself to feel nothing for Alaina. Maria made him happy. She was everything he ever wanted... but so was Alaina once, and he hadn't been fair to her or himself in turning his emotions off the way he had. They hadn't given their relationship the closure it deserved.

There were things she'd wanted to talk through with him and he hadn't let her. There were things he needed to say to her too, and he hadn't let himself. Now, trapped in chains in a room full of strangers, knowing she was in trouble, he couldn't help but relive every moment of coldness he'd shown her in their time since the island. He couldn't help but worry that whatever trouble she might be in would prevent him from ever having those conversations they both needed to have.

He couldn't turn his mind off... not when the world was so quiet. In the quietness of his imprisonment, his thoughts were constantly moving; questioning, doubting, and fearing everything around him.

It was a strange thing to possess the knowledge that he was losing his mind. Before he'd been informed he could have brain damage, he'd always been able to identify what was real and what wasn't, and the fact that he'd heard voices or seen images at all hadn't felt like anything abnormal when framed as a vivid dream. He certainly had never felt disabled by it.

He'd felt like a man. He'd even been proud of the type of man he was becoming; one who could swing a sword and stand up for the things that meant something. He'd earned the respect of the men around him and been followed by them. Their respect had given him a sense of purpose in his life, and he felt more himself than he'd ever been.

But that all changed when Anna said *'brain injury.'*

Everything after that moment—every sound, image, and thought—was suspect. Even the grandfather clock that sat near the door of the room was questionable. Was it even there? Was the constant ticking sound that grew louder by the second real, or was he hallucinating its existence altogether?

He hated feeling disabled, and hated being treated that way even more. In the few months between returning from Eimeo and being captured by Juan Josef, the others had all looked at him differently. They didn't see the man anymore, just a fading mind. But it didn't feel like his mind was fading. Sure, he heard things sometimes; saw them vividly from time to time, but he knew what was real. Didn't he?

He'd been too afraid to ask; to recount events or conversations he was sure had been real for fear the answer might confirm the disability he was positive he didn't have.

"What does it say?" Phil asked, his chains clanking loudly as he attempted to get a look over Chris's shoulder. "Is Kyle with them? Did they get our first message? What's the plan?"

Chris looked back down at the scribbled letters. Had Phil spoken? Was Phil even in the room? Being locked up with four men he barely knew, he was constantly self-conscious about his actions. He cursed Anna for making him feel so suddenly crippled in his own mind. What he wouldn't give to return to the time before she'd diagnosed him, where he'd been blissfully ignorant of his injury and capable of having a conversation without second-guessing everything.

"They're on the opposite end of this hall. I need the pencil."

He slowly looked up from the paper and sighed in relief to find Michael, Phil, and Jacob all searching their surroundings for the missing writing utensil. The letter was real.

They'd all been brought to a small room, shackled to the wall with about three feet of chain to move around. They'd each been provided a cot, and so far, meals were brought in regularly. Having been imprisoned before, he and Jacob hadn't panicked the way Michael and Phil had, and Fetia's father had only shown concern when Fetia would come in to deliver their meals. He remained otherwise silent.

Phil and Michael were pulling drawers from a small side table, noisily shuffling against their chains as they searched in the dim lantern light for the pencil Chris had had in his back pocket when he was captured.

Tick-Tock…

He shook his head. He needed to use whatever was left of his brain to get them out of there. The knowledge of his disability couldn't keep him paralyzed while Maria, Alaina, and the babies were locked up on the ship somewhere in trouble. He'd only caught a glimpse of Juan Josef when they'd captured him, but he'd seen enough to know the man could easily overpower any one of the women if he hadn't done so already. That thought enraged him. He needed to find a way to get out of his chains and to the end of the hall tonight, brain damage or not.

For as much as he'd once loathed Jack, he'd grown to trust him more than the others. That didn't mean he liked the man, but he knew if he could get to him, together they might be able to reach the women and escape. He'd sent a message with Fetia earlier that morning—hoping she wasn't the traitor—for anyone she could get it to. It'd been simple and to the point.

'Where are you? I will come. -C'

There was too much noise.

He watched the door, wondering how long before the guards would grow suspicious. "Shhh! Everyone stop. Fetia," he touched his hair, "can I have a pin from your hair?"

The others froze and watched the exchange. Fetia frowned, touching her hair in response and then, clarity washing over her, pulled a small steel pin from her dark hair.

The steel was bent like a U and thick enough, he could use it to attempt to unlock his shackles after he'd finished his own message.

He dipped the pin into his stew and painstakingly wrote on the back of the same paper:

'4 guards total. Will overpower and come tonight. We go together. Swim in dark. Huahine is close. -C'

He handed Fetia the letter, illustrating for her to be careful not to smudge the wet lettering.

She carefully wrapped it in a piece of fabric and tucked it into the breast of her dress before turning to tap on the door for the guards to let her out.

"What's the plan?" Phil whispered, sitting down beside him. "Is Jack coming?"

Tick-Tock…

Chris frowned at the little U pin as he twisted it around itself and stuck it into the small keyhole of the lock on his shackles. "I don't know yet."

He wiggled the pin around, listening for the sound of the locking pins releasing.

"Is Kyle with him?"

Chris concentrated harder on the lock, bending the pin inside. "I don't know."

"Well, what did the note say?"

Ignoring Phil to concentrate on the lock, Chris envisioned the two men posted outside the door. They both had rifles and broadswords. If he could work all their shackles loose, they could pretend to still be locked in their chains the next time the door opened.

They'd come to take Phil once before for a meeting with the captain. Phil had assured him the meeting went well, and he was confident he might be able to get the captain to agree to let him manage his legal affairs. Perhaps they would come to take him again before the day was over.

Tick-Tock…

He was bigger than one of the two guards, and confident he could ambush him long before the second guard would be able to use the rifle or pull his sword. That would allow Michael, Jacob, and Phil the opportunity to tackle the bigger man. Chris would pull the sword away from his man and he'd have to kill both of them, arming himself and Jacob with their rifles and swords before the two guards from the other end of the hall reached them.

Tick-Tock…

He glanced up at the clock and back down at the lock on the shackle, squeezing his eyes closed in an attempt to drown the deafening sound out.

The rifles would make too much noise. There were only four guards on this floor. If they didn't want to attract more, they'd have to take them down with swords.

"What did the note say?" Phil repeated, growing increasingly agitated.

Tick-Tock...

"It said they're on the opposite end of the hall and the women are just above them. We need to get to them tonight. Now be quiet. I need to concentrate."

"You're not seriously considering trying to get to them, are you? You realize how unstable Juan Josef is, right? He'll kill us all."

Chris glanced at the door. "Keep your voice down. They're listening."

"Think about what you're doing." Phil hissed, sitting back to take his bowl of stew into his lap. "There are too many of them. I counted at least thirty when they brought me up."

"Thirty is not that many." He whispered back, closing his eyes as he moved the pin at a different angle and heard something release inside. "Not if we do this right." His mouth fell open when the padlock pulled loose, and he grinned at Phil as he pulled it from his shackle.

"I want no part in this." Phil said, taking a bite of his stew. "I don't want to die on this ship."

"They told me you were a coward." Chris narrowed his eyes at him as he jerked Phil's wrist into his lap and shoved the pin inside its lock. "She was my wife, you know... That day you forced yourself on her, she was still my wife. And you *will* die on this ship by *my* hands if you don't do exactly as I say. I am far more unstable than Juan Josef."

Chapter Seven

I sat on one of the two sofas in our room, a feeling of defeat sitting in my throat. Juan Josef had enjoyed testing us. I'd seen the satisfaction in his face; the sense of accomplishment after he'd painted the picture of what he would do when Jack left the room. He'd assumed what he'd done would deter Jack from retaliating further, but I knew it would only enrage him more. Somewhere beneath us, Jack was coming up with an escape plan I was helpless to prevent, and Juan Josef was looking forward to it.

Hours passed, and as the sun began to set, I wondered if Juan Josef would come to collect me again for supper. Did I have it in me to do this every day? I'd been intrigued by him earlier that morning; determined to find something human about him, but now I was just disgusted. I didn't want to know him; didn't care to understand a man who got so much enjoyment out of our unhappiness.

I'd told myself he wasn't a monster earlier that morning, but after seeing the joy on his face after Jack was hauled off, I doubted that judgment more and more. On the one hand, he hadn't raped me, and had only wanted Jack to think he would. Did that mean he only wanted us to think he would kill us to keep us in line but wouldn't actually do it? Was it all for show?

On the other hand, he had promised me I would *'come to him'* and I couldn't help but cringe as I thought of all the possible ways he might force me to do it.

A tap on the glass of our window shook me from my dazed state, and all of us looked toward it to find Kyle balancing awkwardly against the frame outside.

Lilly rushed to the glass, unlatching the lock to pull the window open and drag him quickly inside. "Kyle!" She pulled him into her arms and squeezed. "Are you alright?"

"I'm fine." He wiggled out of her grip, peering across the candlelit room to focus his two blackened eyes on me. "Jack sent me. He had to know if Juan Josef—

"He didn't touch me." I assured him, crossing the room to join him at the window. "He just wanted him to think he had. I'm alright. But you…" I touched his face where he'd been beaten nearly unrecognizable. His cheeks and eyes were dark shades of purple, yellow, and blue, and his lip was busted and bright pink. "Jesus Kyle, you look terrible. They'll beat you worse if they find out you're missing. You have to go back."

He scanned the room. "Fetia just brought our dinner. They won't come back into our room for a while—if they come back at all. Has she been here yet?"

"No." Lilly placed her hands on her hips. "When were you going to tell us she was pregnant? And does that have anything to do with how we got here? Don't you *dare* lie to me."

Kyle shook his head. "Lilly, she's not involved, and neither is her family. She's a hostage, too. They have her father."

"How do you know they're not involved?" Lilly hissed. "She doesn't speak a word of English! You don't know anything about her or her family."

He stood taller, his jaw hardening in defense of his new wife. "I know *everything* about her. You don't always need words to know a person. We can argue about this later. We're getting out of here… tonight. Magna, will you help me get a message to Fetia?"

"What do you mean, tonight?" Maria frowned at him. "How? And where will we go?"

"Huahine," he said, facing Magna. "Juan Josef will send Fetia back to shore tonight after she is done with her duties on the ship.

Tell her to get her father's boat ready. We will meet her there and sail to Captain Cook."

"What about Kreese?"

"He and Jack put this whole plan together," Kyle assured her. "We'll wait for Chris before we come for you."

I frowned. "How will we get past Juan's men?"

He shook his head. "Last night, after dinner, they didn't come back into our rooms until the following morning. Jim said it was the same here. Chris has a plan for the guards on our floor. Once they're disabled, Jack will come for you the same way I did. We'll climb down and swim to shore. They won't see us swimming in the dark if we spread out. Not from the top deck."

I glanced at the window, trying to imagine climbing down and swimming to shore with Zachary and Cecelia in my arms. Could I do it? And which was more dangerous? Staying put, or attempting to escape with two newborns?

Kyle motioned to the shadow of land through the window, speaking faster as he laid out their plans. "Once on the shore, we'll run inland. Fetia's boat is in an inlet on the far side of the island. If they don't catch us in the water, we'll have hours to get to the boat and head for Huahine before they discover we're gone. If Hitihiti went ahead of us to the captain, we may run into him along the way. Either way, we'll be safely onboard the Resolution before Juan Josef can catch up to us."

Anna crossed her arms over her chest. "But if we join the captain, how will we get to the portal?"

"We won't," he said, adjusting his tone as her eyes began to water. "Not now, anyway. We'll come back when it's safe."

"But how do we know the captain's still in Huahine?" I asked. "What if he already left?"

"Then he will be in Raiatea," Maria noted, nodding her head slowly. "He planned to stop in both and spend at least a few days with the people there. We can still get to him if we leave tonight."

"You do what you want," Anna said, holding her hand up, "but I'm not leaving this ship. I don't care if he's crazy. I don't care if he wants to tie me up and torture me the whole way there. I have to get to my son."

"Anna," Lilly attempted to reason, "we can't leave you behind. He's—

The sound of a key being inserted into the door's lock silenced us all.

"Hide," I whispered to Kyle. "And close the window."

Kyle hurried to crawl under the bed as Lilly closed the window and I took my seat on the sofa, every inch of my body suddenly trembling.

Where I'd expected to find Mr. Gil coming through the door to summon me, I instead found Dario entering the room, Fetia behind him with a tray of food. He held a finger to his lips to instruct us all to stay quiet as he closed the door behind her.

"Where's the boy?" Dario whispered, peering around the room.

Lilly carefully shielded Izzy with her body and stood taller. "What boy?"

Dario took a deep breath. "This is not a time for games. You are lucky it was I that was listening and not my father. The boy needs to go back before my father catches him. Your escape plan will not work. He knows what the men intend to do and is prepared to counter their attack on his guards. The boy must go back and stop them before it is too late."

"Why would you warn us?" Anna asked, glancing back toward the door to be sure no one else would follow. "And how does he know about their plan?"

"He is listening."

He crossed over to the bed and tapped on the post several times with the toe of his boot. "Come out of there… *quietly*. We're all listening. That's why he sent one of the men up yesterday. He wanted to see what you would do; how much you would plan. We can hear every whispered word. He knows about their plan to escape, your hopes for the captain's return, and what each of you is most afraid of. I warn you because I need you, and I don't want to see you punished…" He looked toward me. "…I don't want to see *her* punished."

"Me? Why me?" I stood, slowly joining him at the side of the bed. "And you need us for what? Why's he doing all this? We would've helped him without force."

Dario took a deep breath, cautiously watching as Kyle slithered out from beneath the bed. "My father trusts no one, and will go to great lengths to ensure those he does not trust will bend to his will. You said he is not a monster, but he can be if he is crossed. He has no intention of returning to his life in the future so soon—not in the way you might think, that is. I am being sent to retrieve something he is in need of, and I fear I shall never be able to navigate such a foreign world in search of it without your assistance. Should you attempt to escape, he will surely have you punished, or even killed. And I do not wish to travel through time with those who would begrudge me for my father's actions. I will need your help to find what it is he is sending me for. I cannot return without it."

"I won't be able to get a message to the men in the other room," Kyle said, watching Fetia until her eyes met his, boyish grin forming on his lips as he continued dazedly, "they've already brought dinner and won't return again until morning."

"Stop the ones in your room, then. I shall send word to the others." He grabbed Kyle's shoulders to turn his attention to him. "Look at me. This is not a game. I give you my word that I will make sure my father does not harm her or any of the women here, but I cannot do so if you defy him. Captain Cook will not return for you. No one is coming to save you. I am your only hope of leaving this ship. You must do what I ask of you."

He turned toward me, leaving Kyle to wrap his arm around Fetia and whisper sentiments she wouldn't understand. "And you." He ran a hand over his auburn hair, his expression softening. "I'm afraid your role is far more complicated. My father saw you on the beach that day and, recognizing the strong resemblance to my mother, was determined to have you for his own. He's even called you by her name on occasion. He will stop at nothing to have you, and he intends to send your betrothed to the future. He has no desire to see him return, and has asked me to do everything in my power to prevent it. I would not be so hasty to betray my father in warning you of this were it not for the fact that I, too, am mesmerized by your likeness to her. Your face is so much like the woman I remember…"

He tilted his head to one side as he looked over my features. "Impractical as it may sound, I am terrified you might somehow *be* her, and I cannot bring myself to betray a woman I have dreamt of for so long. I won't hurt you, and therefore I will not hurt Jack, but I cannot promise my father won't if you do not show some sign of returned affection toward him… If you *are* her, or anything like her, I know that is the farthest thing from what you want, but… Please, try… just until I've had time to find what it is he is searching for."

Anna crossed her arms over her chest. "Just what is it he's looking for, anyway?"

Dario sighed, looking back toward the door. "The explanation for what it is he seeks will take time, and I promise to give it to you when we are not obligated to join him in a timely manner. You and I will travel together, so I will be granted an audience with you soon to allow for us to plan." There was a hint of flirtation in his voice as his eyes met hers. "I assure you, I shall hide no detail of his plan from you."

He turned back toward Kyle. "I have been asked to retrieve Alaina for supper, and if I do not return swiftly, he will surely grow suspicious. I beg of you, return at once to your cabin and make no move to rise against my father at this time. And you," he smiled at me, "please, let us not keep him waiting. He's asked that you bring the babies as well. My brother and I won't allow anything to happen to them."

"Magna," he continued, while I slowly slid the sling over my shoulders. "I shall tell my father I have discovered a rat on board the ship and insist he send Fetia around to collect the dinner plates before she is dismissed for the night. Can you ask her to memorize the words: *'abandon the plan'* so she can relay that message to the men in the other room? Tell her to say it loud enough that the men outside may hear it."

Magna hurried to translate while Dario offered me his arm, still staring at me with the dewy eyes of a boy who recognized his long-lost mother.

"I'm not her, you know," I said as I secured the babies in the sling and took the offered arm.

"I know that." He opened the door for me, ushering Fetia out ahead of us. "You just… you're so much like how I remember her. And I cannot help but see her when I look at you." He slowed his pace as we began climbing the stairs behind Fetia.

"I was five when she was murdered, but the love I felt for her then was powerful. I have never let go of it, and for reasons I can't explain, that love for her is pushing me to help you. It is hard to remember it all, but I remember she wanted to leave and he would not let her. My father's idea of loving a person is holding onto them so tight they cannot breathe and beating them if they attempt to escape his grip. I do not wish to see him hurt you the way he did her. Please, do not give him a reason to."

I tightened my grip on his arm, stopping midway up the steps. "Murdered? By your father?"

He shook his head. "No. Beating her was one thing, but he would never kill her. He loved her… in his way."

I frowned. "Dario, let's say we navigate out to that spot and somehow find a way through time, unlikely as I think that is… We can't just stay with him for six months waiting for your return. My people won't sit back and let themselves serve as his entertainment. We may not *live* for six more months. We haven't even been on this ship a full day, and look at where we're at. The rest of them don't even know that he's threatened to kill us if we find nothing, and they all want him dead."

He made a move to speak, but I cut him off. "The coordinates I've given, they're the truth. You don't need us to get there. I didn't lie. You could help us escape, and you could still go and find whatever it is he needs."

Dario shook his head. "I'm sorry. What my father seeks in the future is important to me as well. I will need the assistance of your people to find it."

He began to climb the stairs, but I tightened my grip and held him in place. "If you tell me what it is you're searching for, perhaps I can tell you where to find it. Please." I looked down at Cecelia and Zachary. "I can't put them at risk."

He took a deep breath and glanced upward to be sure no one else was on the stairs. "It is not *'what,'* it is *'who.'* I don't know anything about telephones or cars or this internet thing you so casually speak of, but I know I'll need to use them. I'll need your people for that. I'm sorry, but I cannot say more at this time. Nothing on this ship goes unheard. Come. We mustn't keep him waiting."

I blew out as we came out at the top of the stairs and made our way down the corridor. Who was he searching for? If I found out, could I use that to my advantage?

Mr. Gil was standing in front of the doors to the great cabin and bowed his head as we approached, hurrying to push the double doors open for us to enter. The gramophone had been set up in the corner of the room, and the perfect vibrato of Edith Piaf washed over me as I entered.

Juan Josef was seated at the head of the table, a knowing smile plastered across his dark features as he rose. "Alaina, my dear, you grow more beautiful by the hour. Please, sit." He motioned to the same seat I'd taken that morning beside him, the wooden cradle still positioned where it'd been next to it. "I've arranged for some entertainment while we dine this evening."

With one eye on him, I placed Zachary and Cecelia into the cradle and took my seat, my stomach growling as I eyed the stew that sat in front of me. Carrots, potatoes, and juicy chunks of red meat emitted a glorious aroma that beckoned my tastebuds.

He sat, as did Dario, in the same seat across from me he'd been in during breakfast.

I couldn't help but notice the absence of his brother. Juan Josef caught my eyes landing upon the empty seat and grunted. "Have you taken a liking then to my eldest son? Worry not, my darling. He shall be joining us soon enough. We needn't wait for him to eat.

He's not a very punctual man, and I wouldn't want your supper to grow cold."

He dipped his spoon into his own stew and held it over his bowl, waiting patiently for me to do the same.

I picked up my spoon, noticing an uneasiness in Dario across from me as I took a bite. His eyes danced nervously from me to his father, to the door, and back. Something was wrong.

"Perhaps it is my youngest son you have taken a liking to, eh?" Juan Josef teased through a mouthful of stew. "Don't you think him a bit young for your taste?"

Unwilling to play any more games with him, I stared down into my bowl as I dipped the spoon back inside. I was starving, and I knew it was only a matter of time before I would lose my appetite. Whatever twisted game he had in mind to serve as *'entertainment'* would certainly turn my stomach at any moment. I focused on eating, letting the beautiful music whisk me away as I did so. I needed the sustenance for the twins.

"My Dario has a certain way with women..." He continued playfully. "It's a wonder he's not settled down yet. He certainly could have had his choice in fine women the way they all fall over themselves when he enters a room."

He sucked in air dramatically, forcing my eyes upon him as his face lit up in a playful grin. "But what would Mr. Volmer say? I knew my test upon him would play to my advantage, however, I did not think it would happen so quickly. I daresay, madam, you certainly do not waste your time. Pray tell, how long *exactly* did it take for you to move from the husband I keep in one room to the fiancé I keep in the other? I dare say I might be doing you a favor in keeping them apart."

I rolled my eyes and looked back down at my bowl, depositing a large chunk of meat into my mouth so I was unable to respond.

"Dario, my boy, you must teach me how to enchant women the way you do. I fear my own methods of flirtation result in their unwillingness to even look me in the eye." He noisily slurped his stew. "Oh, but perhaps it is not my flirtation at all that turns their heads... For my own son will not look at me either. What has happened in my absence that has caused you both to be so fascinated by this rather dull stew?"

"Forgive me, father." Dario sighed, "I've warned them."

Juan Josef laughed loudly. "Of course you have!"

I looked up then, watching as Juan Josef wiped the corners of his mouth. "Alaina, my dear, my youngest son wishes nothing more than to be as ruthless as I, but he is quite incapable. From the moment he was born, he was as wholesome as they come." He shook his head in laughter as he shifted his focus back to Dario. "Tell me, what exactly have you warned them of?"

Dario straightened. "I told her you knew about the men's plan to escape. I encouraged her to stop it. My apologies, father, but I do not wish to see anyone harmed, particularly if I am to travel with them."

Juan Josef smiled warmly. "My son. Such a good heart... just like your mother."

Before he could say more, a loud creaking noise emitted from far beneath us, and the ship's sudden movement had me gripping the cradle and the table to prevent myself and the babies from falling over. "Why are we moving?" I asked in a panic as we continued to rock with the momentum of the turning ship. "We still have weeks before we need to depart."

Juan Josef calmly sipped his wine as Dario and I exchanged confused looks.

"We haven't enough provisions yet," Dario said, frowning at his father, "for so long a journey. We would surely starve upon our return voyage!"

"We shall have to make do, won't we?" Juan Josef grinned. "For so long as we sit idle on this shore, we risk losing our only hope of returning to the future. I'll not wait for another escape attempt tomorrow or the next day... How would I possibly get any sleep?" He chuckled proudly. "No. Once we are out at sea, there is nowhere to escape to. We may lose a few crewmen with a lack of stock to serve them, but we will make up for the loss once we have achieved that which we've set out to do."

"But father—

Juan Josef held up his palm. "The decision to leave is final, Dario. Let us not spoil the rest of the evening by beating a dead horse." He turned toward me. "Alaina, you are looking quite pale. Eat."

I shuddered. Suddenly, the air felt colder with the knowledge that we would no longer be anchored in Tahiti; the promise of a possible escape no longer within reach. We would not see the Resolution coming to our rescue, and even if we did somehow manage to sneak off the ship, there would be nowhere for us to go; no way for us to navigate back to land once it was lost on the horizon.

Mr. Gil opened the double doors, rushing to the head of the table to lean down and hand Juan Josef a small slip of paper. He glanced suspiciously toward me, then back to the letter. He nodded, placing the paper into his pocket, then spoke something in return that sent Mr. Gil back out of the room in a hurry.

As the doors closed behind him, I saw a sinister excitement return to his expression. Whatever he'd read on that paper roused him in the same way threatening me or testing Jack had earlier in the day. He tore off a piece of bread from his plate and dipped it into his stew. "Alaina," he started, barely able to contain his anticipation, "I'm growing rather weary of instructing you to eat. I'm afraid I may have to find a wet-nurse to take care of your children if you will not take better care of yourself."

My throat felt heavy as my stomach rolled with the momentum of the ship. "We can't leave yet. We have medicine at the house still—medicine we may very well need... and all the clothing that fits the 21st century... we can't send people through time in these clothes... and the raft... and—

"Eat," he said again, with a growing sense of aggravation. "I shall send someone with instruction as to what items must be retrieved. You and your people will not return to the shore. I needn't tell you why."

"Can you really blame them for planning an escape?" I demanded, my anger with the entire predicament pouring out of me as my hormones caught up. "I mean, you've taken us prisoner and you continue to toy with us... After what you did this morning, of course they would plot! Who wouldn't? How can you expect any of us to simply comply when you're acting like a complete madman? When you're keeping the men chained to a wall or giving the impression to them that you will punish their defiance by forcing yourself upon the people they love? Of course, they will make every possible attempt to defy you. How could anyone blindly trust a man who does such things? Wouldn't you do everything in your power to escape the very same circumstances if it were you in their shoes?"

He twirled his spoon around the surface of his stew for a moment, contemplating his response, before looking back up at me. "You know nothing of my own shoes, madam. If you did, you would understand that the things I do are what I believe must be done for the sake of my own children. Trusting anyone who isn't blood is not without its costs upon one's character. People will betray you for the sake of themselves, more so than they won't. You will learn that lesson over time."

The corner of his mouth twitched. "Your fiancé was right this morning. It is no coincidence I found myself within reach of the only other time travelers in this century. Would you like to know how I came to be in such close proximity at just the right time?"

I straightened my back against the hard wood of my seat. I already knew that answer. "John Edgecumbe."

He shook his head. "No, madam. Johann Forster."

My heart sank as he said the name. Johann had played such a large role in our lives and in the formation of our theories and plans. For someone like him to have betrayed us felt like a knife through my already torn heart. The wound cut so deep that I felt the need to crumple into myself. How could he, of all people, hand us over to such a man?

He watched my throat move as I swallowed his revelation.

He smiled. "When he sent his correspondence from Queen Charlotte Sound, there were only two of you. I hadn't been prepared to take in so many. I knew, after our encounter in Eimeo, you wouldn't come willingly, so I had to make arrangements to keep you all separated. Chaining them was never a part of the plan. However, they would not submit, and I had to do whatever was in my power to preserve the best interests of my sons and my men... I cannot have a group of men plotting the death of anyone under my authority. It will not go unpunished. Surely, you must know this by now."

"You speak of punishment as if we are insubordinate children in your care. We are adults who only want each other's safety. We are not owed punishment by attempting to keep each other safe. If you showed any bit of civility—"

"Civility?" He said the word back to me as if it tasted sour in his mouth. "I offered you civility in Eimeo and you would not receive it. You fled. I said nothing to indicate my intentions were anything but earnest. You made an assumption without ever knowing who I was, and so I, in turn, had to make the assumption you would flee again should the opportunity arise."

"So you're just going to, what? Sail out and float on the ocean for a month, waiting for the storm as punishment?"

He sipped his wine with one dark eyebrow raised high on his forehead. "That is not the only preventative measure I intend to take, my dear."

As if on cue, the doors opened, and he placed his wineglass on the table with a loud exhale. "Tonight's entertainment..." He waved his arm in presentation as several of his men escorted the thrashing tied bodies of Jack, Chris, Jim, Fetia, and Kyle into the cabin.

My stomach turned in knots as I observed the nooses dangling loose from each of their necks, the shackles keeping each of their hands secured tightly behind their backs, and the ominous gratification that swept over Juan Josef's features as he rose from his seat.

"A game of choice, if you will..." He beamed, leaning on his forearms against the back of his chair. "I warned you any act to rise up against me would not go unpunished and these five have done just that. You said you could control your men, and I've given you ample opportunity to do so. Now, I'm afraid your failure to keep them in line will result in the punishment of one... But... which one?"

He casually crossed the room with his hands folded behind his back, stopping first at Kyle. Where the other men's wrists were shackled behind their backs, Kyle's single arm and shoulder were held by a guard. "This young fellow was caught climbing down the side of my ship. Very impressive for a boy with one arm. Should I punish him?"

I could feel my body begin to shake as Mr. Gil tossed the loose end of Kyle's noose up over a rafter in the ceiling. Was this a tactic to assert dominance or did Juan Josef really intend to hang one of them?

Dario stood from his seat, the piece of bread he'd been preparing to butter before the doors opened still in his hand. "Father, please. This isn't necessary. I had it under control."

Juan Josef spun to face his son. "Did you?" He turned back toward Kyle, his hands still folded reservedly behind his back. "Tell me, Kyle, what was on the letter you slipped to Fetia just before she left the room?"

Kyle held his chin high and did not respond.

Juan Josef turned back toward Dario. "The letter said, and I quote," he pulled out the piece of paper from his pocket, "'*Attack now. Do not wait.*'"

He paced past Kyle to stop at Jack. "This man stole a razor blade, and coordinated an attack upon my guards with this man." He placed a hand on Chris's shoulder as Mr. Gil flung the ropes hanging from each of their necks over the rafter alongside Kyle's. "They were determined to escape tonight with all of you. Imagine my devastation to find your people conspiring to leave me behind when I only endeavor to make it back to the same future they intend to return to... What was it you said to me, Alaina? I believe it was something to the effect of: '*If you'd said so, we never would've run from you. We can help each other.*' But here we are, less than 24 hours later, and these five have done little else *but* conspire to run from me."

He strolled past Chris and Jack to stand in front of Jim, grinning as he watched Jim's rope fly over the beam. "And this one…" He narrowed his eyes at Jim as Jim spat on his boot. "This one managed to sneak a dagger on board with him and armed his wife with it when he visited her room last night. He instructed her to stab any man who laid his hands upon her." He smiled and turned back. "Mr. Gil, were you able to retrieve the weapon?"

"I have, sir." Mr. Gil grinned as he presented Juan Josef with the dagger I'd seen Maria carrying in Tahiti.

"Ye' better kill me dead, because so help me Got, I'll murder evra last one of yas if ye' turn me loose!"

Juan Josef smirked, taking the blade and pacing with it held behind his back. "Oh, I don't doubt that, sir." He stopped at Fetia, who was shaking with tears, her dark eyes wide with fear as her own rope was thrown upward. "And this one…" He clicked his tongue. "She carries the messages between them all, setting the whole plan in motion… like her father means nothing to her."

He looked at me. "Decisions, decisions, Alaina. One of these five must pay for their crimes. Which one will it be?"

I shook my head, staring at Jack while he fought against the men holding him in place. How could I possibly sentence one of them to death? "Please, Juan, stop. You've made your point."

"Which one will it be, Alaina? You certainly don't want *me* to choose." He curled his fingers around Jack's rope.

"Wait… please." I trembled, looking from Kyle to Jack to Chris to Jim, and finally stopping upon Fetia. I reminded myself she was pregnant… but how could I possibly choose anyone else? I couldn't let Juan take Jack from me… or Chris… or Jim or Kyle.

Kyle read my mind and immediately stood straighter. "Me. I'll take the punishment. It was my idea to fight. I got loose, and I wrote the letters. I climbed out the window. It was all my plan. I'll pay for it. Let them go back. Let Fetia go."

"Shut yer mouth, Kyle," Jim said. "He ain't got sense. None of this was his doin.'"

"It was *all* my doing." Kyle insisted. "It's my crime, and I'll pay for it. Let them go and don't hurt anyone else for what I did."

"Shut up, Kyle." Chris hissed. "This isn't the time to be a hero."

"No, it is not." Juan Josef agreed, placing the dagger on the window ledge to trade for a small whip, several knotted threads hanging from its tightly wound handle. "I assure you, boy," he said, brushing the claws of the whip against his palm, "this is not a punishment you shall soon forget. Are you sure?"

"I'll take it," Kyle said. "And I won't fight."

"You certainly won't." Juan Josef said, waving the others off as he stood in front of Kyle. "And I hope you will encourage the others to reconsider should they attempt to rise up again."

"Please," I begged. "There has to be something else… some other way… Something else you want more?" I cringed as I heard his voice in my head assuring me, *'you will come to me.'*

He smiled mischievously back at me as the guards holding Chris, Jack, Fetia, and Jim all began to loosen the ropes at their necks.

"Not him," Juan said, placing a hand on Jack's chest to stop them from releasing his noose. "He stays."

Jim and Chris set their feet and fought to remain in the room as the guards pushed them closer to the door. Both shouted in protest, pleading with Juan Josef all the reasons why they should be the ones punished.

Juan Josef kept his eyes on me, though. He moved a little closer, apparently intrigued by my outburst. "Tell me, Alaina, what else could I possibly want more than to see these men punished?"

I pressed my palms against each other to stop my hands from shaking. "Me…"

"No." Jack and Kyle said in unison, both understanding the offer and refusing it on my behalf.

Kyle stood tall and set his jaw. "Leave her alone. I will take the punishment. I'm not afraid."

Juan Josef grinned as he spun back toward them. "*Very* impressive. Dumb, but impressive." He looked over his shoulder at me. "Alaina, come and do it then."

I swallowed. "What… what do you mean?"

I could hear the other men protesting and Fetia sobbing loudly as they were dragged down the hall. My mouth grew dry and the world around me was muffled by the sound of my pulse filling my ears.

"You did not think *I* would whip the men you promised to control, did you?" Juan said. "You will flog this man for betraying you when you instructed him not to fight."

Suddenly trembling, I shook my head. "No… please, I can't. He's just a boy."

Juan Josef motioned toward Mr. Gil, who took hold of Jack's rope where it hung loosely from the rafter and pulled it tight. "You can and you will."

"Please—"

"Do it." Kyle insisted as he was turned around violently by a guard and his shirt ripped open to expose his back. "I can take it."

"Alaina, it will be you who whips this man." Juan Josef instructed as I slowly inched toward them. "Or I shall have Mr. Gil hang Mr. Volmer. Is that what you would prefer?"

"No."

"Father, this is madness." Dario offered. "You cannot do this. It is cruel."

"Cruel?" Juan Josef scoffed. "Cruel is promising I could trust them to help us when we have spent twenty long years trying to get back to our time only for them to betray that promise by attempting to abandon us. This is not cruel. It is necessary. I told you we could not trust them. Let this be a lesson to you, Dario. If you want something, you must take it."

He held the whip toward me. "You want your men to listen to you? Take this and whip him with it."

I took the whip from him, its braided claws dangling against my arm.

"It's alright, Alaina." Kyle assured me. "I'll be fine. Just do it."

"Do it hard." Juan Josef said, joining Mr. Gil at the end of Jack's rope. "The harder you strike him, the sooner this will be over with."

I stared down at the whip in my hand and swallowed. "I…"

And then there was a creaking sound that sent a chill through my veins. I looked up to find Jack flailing as Mr. Gil and Juan Josef pulled the rope to take his feet out from beneath him. "You had better hurry." Juan teased.

Kyle spoke, Dario argued, Juan teased, and Edith Piaf's heavenly voice continued to sing, but all I could hear was the struggled gurgling choke emitting from Jack, and the air between his legs as he kicked them wildly to survive.

That sound, within only a few seconds, conjured up the last happy image I'd had of him; sitting in bed with our two tiny babies wrapped up in his large arms.

I couldn't lose him. Not now.

"I'm sorry," I sobbed as I pulled the whip back, every part of me aquiver, then launched it forward across Kyle's exposed and tensed back muscles.

I knew he cried out, but all I could hear was Jack struggling to breathe.

"Again." Juan Josef instructed somewhere far in the distance.

I brought the whip back and forward, harder this time, as Jack choked and urgency filled me.

"Again!" Juan shouted, and I obliged, noticing streaks of red where the whip cut into Kyle's flesh.

I didn't wait for Juan's order, but heard the rope creaking where it was still pulled taught, and struck Kyle again and again in desperation, unable to see the damage I inflicted through the tears that filled my eyes.

"Enough!" A new voice ordered, and at long last, after what had felt like an eternity, I heard the sound of Jack being released, his body collapsing onto the floor where he gasped for air.

Suddenly, Edith Piaf was louder than ever as the cheerful music, a stark contrast to the reality around us, continued to pour from the gramophone's horn.

Dropping the whip, I wiped my eyes to find Juan Jr. pressing his father's back against the far wall, his fingers wound tightly in his jacket as he plunged him harder and harder against the wood.

"It is you who should be in chains," he said through gritted teeth. "You know that? You have lost your mind!"

"Let him go," Dario shouted behind me. "Stop it! You're hurting him!"

Knelt down beside them, Jack was attempting to catch his breath, choking and gasping audibly. I fell to my knees, loosening the noose that was still digging into his throat.

"Coward!" Juan Jr. released his father to turn his fury on his brother. "Are you really so spineless to just stand there and let him nearly murder this man?"

"They intended to escape; to murder our men..." Dario said defensively. "He was just doing what he thought he needed to."

"Let that boy go." Juan Jr. said to the guard still holding Kyle. "And all of you leave us."

The men followed his order, making it clear who was really in charge as they hurried out of the room. As Kyle collapsed against the wall, I could see the damage I'd inflicted lining his back in long red streaks that dripped down over the bits of his torn shirt and tan breeches, and I hated myself; hated Juan Josef for what he'd made me do.

"I did this because it was necessary." Juan Josef argued in his defense, launching himself off the wall to glare at his son. "They will not make another attempt. We needed to do it if we're to stand a chance at fulfilling our destiny. Have you forgotten I am doing this for you?"

"You're doing this for me, are you?" Juan Jr. scoffed. "I did not ask for *this*." He forced a hand hard over his hair as he shook his head at Kyle's back. "It should be you who is whipped; tortured... This..." He pointed to Kyle and then to Jack. "This was not for me. You did this for your own demented enjoyment."

"None of it will matter," Juan Josef said. "You won't remember any of this, nor will he... or I. We won't have to be the beasts we've become in this life. We'll be different men, you'll see."

"...water." Jack managed, and I leapt onto my feet and hurried to the table, ignoring Juan Josef's stare as I plucked my water glass from near my seat and rushed back to his side.

"Forget?" Kyle asked breathlessly, turning slowly around and wincing as he lowered himself to sit on the floor. "How will we ever forget any of this?"

Juan Jr. held up a finger, then quickly crossed the room to the doors, leaning outside them and instructing the guards to leave the hallway before he closed them and turned back to us. "I lost—"

"Don't." Juan Josef warned.

"Your way is not the *only* way, father." He grabbed a glass bottle containing an amber liquid from the table, took a swig, and knelt beside Kyle to offer it to him. "Perhaps we shall be lucky enough to forget, but on the day of our judgment, we shall surely be reminded. I will not risk eternal damnation to erase *my* pain. If this is all for me, then I shall have a say in how it is done."

He looked back at Kyle. "This life... this time... it is as much a curse to you as it has been to us. We are not supposed to be here. None of us. We have tainted God's plan for us, and so God will take everything good from our lives until we are returned to the path he intended for us." He watched me while I tipped the water glass to Jack's lips. "He'll separate you from the people you love... take your children from you with plague. You shall suffer nothing but heartache and loss until you are returned to your destiny."

Juan Jr. looked up at his father. "The man who killed our mother—"

"Brother, this is not the way," Dario warned. "They will try to stop us if you say more."

Juan Jr. ignored him. "His name was Richard Albrecht, and he is the same man that turned us in to the authorities, forcing us to take to the ocean that day and run into the storm. My father believes that, by erasing Richard Albrecht's existence, we will all somehow wake with memories of the life we should've lived and no recollection of the events or the pain that happened in this time. We have spent many years seeking out anyone with the name Albrecht in the hopes that if we killed the right one, that may have been our only way home. But now, with your coordinates and date, we might be able to cross through time where we will have access to records detailing the real lineage of that man. With that information in hand, upon my brother's return, we can seek out the ancestors of Richard Albrecht and kill the correct one."

I shook my head. "But... it can't be that simple... there's twenty years of time that would just... be erased? All the life you've been through to this point would've never been lived?"

He raised an eyebrow. "It would've been lived differently and we all would feel its existence just as much as we feel our existence now. And if that is the case, you and your people never would've been captured by us. None of this will have happened to you, and you'll have no memory of whatever has to happen between now and then. If you help me, it'll help all of you."

Suddenly, I felt even more on edge. If time really was that fragile, then anything we did could affect the course of our own lives. If I bumped into the wrong person and prevented them from meeting someone else, I could just as easily wake up beside Chris, having no knowledge of Jack, our children, or the lives we lived here.

What if the ancestors of Richard Albrecht played some kind of role in the events that brought us through time? What if Juan Josef killed them and erased everything that had happened to us, the island, and all that we'd come to discover of each other here? No matter how difficult our time on this ship might become, I wasn't willing to risk erasing my family to prevent it from happening.

The last notes on the record played out and a steady thumping scratch played on repeat from the gramophone, hypnotizing us all as we contemplated the theory.

"Look at me." Juan Jr. said, focusing on me from his place next to Kyle. "You're cursed too. You just don't know it yet. This is not the life you're supposed to live. You will see nothing good come of it. You, too, must reverse your path... Or I assure you, you'll find yourselves, in twenty years, unrecognizable as the people you once were. Turned into monsters by the torment God will place upon you for diverting from his plan." He sighed. "My father was not always evil... it is God's wrath upon him that has made him this way. And now, with an opportunity to erase his wickedness, I fear he is loathed to enjoy what is left of the beast before he is once again made a man."

I swallowed, running my palm over Jack's back as he slowly recovered his breathing. "So, what happens now? Will you send us back to our prisons? Keep us separated while we wait to see if we can cross through? Let your father do as he pleases with us and hope none of us will remember after you see your plan through?"

He shook his head. "I do not wish to hurt you. You and your people are quite possibly the only way for us to be returned to the paths God intended for us. But I fear I don't quite know how to reverse the damage that is already done. You would not stay willingly and we need you."

"I will help you. Just let us stay together," I begged. "You can listen and guard and keep us confined to a room on this ship, but let us stay together. We won't fight you if we don't have a reason to. He needs a nurse... Both of them do. Let me take them to our room. Please, don't keep us apart. I'm begging you."

Juan Jr. looked toward his father. "I am not yet the captain of this ship, as you never fail to remind me, father. It is not my decision to make, but I must inform you whatever response you give her in this moment, the judgment I render as a result of it shall never fade from my memory whenever you are present. If you show some semblance of humanity in the form of mercy, I shall know you are still the father I once admired. If you do not, I fear I shall see you as only the wickedness you impart and no longer the man I once loved so dearly."

Juan Josef adjusted his jacket where it was crinkled from the altercation, sliding his hands down the red fabric until it sat smooth against his chest. Collecting his normal authoritative posture, he moved to the gramophone to remove the needle from the spinning record.

How heavy the silence in the room suddenly became.

My hand was still resting on the small of Jack's back, Dario still stood with a piece of unbuttered bread in his hand, and Juan Jr. stood at the side of Kyle, all of us watching Juan with bated breath as we awaited his reply.

"Mercy, you say…" He shook his head, folding his hands behind his back as he casually strolled back to his seat at the head of the table. "And if I am to give them this, how would I ever again be a man worthy of respect? After they have witnessed my very own son placing his hands upon my person with no retaliation from me. After that same son has had the audacity to tell me what I should and should not do on a ship under my command? What's to stop them from turning on us all now that they have seen our weaknesses? What's to prevent them from an ambush? From turning you even further against me? From fleeing?"

"We are moving," I reminded him. "There is nowhere for us to flee to. Whatever your weaknesses, you are in control. We are very much aware of that fact. None of us wants to see a repeat of today's events. Let us stay together where we won't need to wonder about the safety of the people we love. If these men know that their women and children are safe, they'll have no more reason to plot an escape."

He sat down in his seat, looking as if we hadn't all just gone through what we had, as he took a sip of his wine. "Very well then. You haven't given me much choice, Juan. If I am proved right by granting this, the ramifications of any uprising attempt shall fall solely upon your conscience. Do you understand?"

"Yes, father."

"Take them away then."

Chapter Eight

Dario escorted Jack, Kyle, me, and the babies back to the large room containing the other women. Shortly after our welcome, the rest of the men were brought in by Juan Jr.

The entire room was alight with embraces and tears of joy. Maria grabbed hold of Chris and didn't let go for a good long while.

Much to my surprise, when she finally did release him, he turned to me and wrapped his arms around me, holding me in an embrace that was filled with love I hadn't felt from him in a long time. As he unwound his arms, he placed a familiar kiss at the center of my forehead.

"I'm sorry," he said softly, tilting my face up toward him. "I mean that. I was worried about you... and so very sorry I didn't come to see them." He smiled at Cecelia in Bud's arms, then at Zachary, where Jim rocked him against his shoulder, refusing to let anyone take him away. "I should've had all the conversations we both needed to have to put closure to ten years of marriage, but instead I let my pride put a wall between us that was impenetrable. I've been unfair in my treatment of you. I won't be anymore."

I was taken aback by the gesture. I knew I'd hurt him, and I'd surrendered to a fate where we lived as strangers alongside one another, silently observing each other's happiness while restraining the desire to be more than an onlooker in one another's lives. To love someone for so long and then be completely cut off from knowing their heart and mind when they are living beside you is a daunting task. It had come with a weight I hadn't realized was there until that moment when it was lifted from my shoulders and I felt I might float away with the freedom from it. I smiled and nodded because if I would've spoken, the words would've cracked with the relief that sat in my throat.

I could feel Jack's eyes on us, watching with curiosity... Maria's, too. Hers felt less curious and more territorial. He felt them as well and wisely took a step back, smiling as his eyes met Maria's for a fleeting moment. "I cannot tell you how difficult it has been to be locked away with my thoughts. There are things you and I need to say to each other. Perhaps we can talk at some point now that we're all together?"

"I would like that."

Behind us, the group had gathered around Juan Jr. and Dario as they prepared to explain who Richard Albrecht was and how he tied into their motivations for reaching the future.

"You should listen in on that," I said, turning toward Jack as he moved to the far corner of the room. "We'll talk soon."

With both our babies safe in the arms of people who loved them, I took the opportunity to disappear into the shadows where Jack was waiting. It was the first time we'd been truly on our own since I'd given birth, and I immediately sank into his chest the moment he reached for me.

The warmth of his breath rolled over my neck and shoulder as he bent into the embrace, tightening his arms as he let out a long exhale.

This is why I'd chosen Jack. There was something so effortless about being with him. He knew exactly what I needed when I needed it, as did I for him. We held each other and didn't require words to say everything we each were going through in that instance. We could feel it all radiating off the other.

Jack didn't need to prove his love by building things or buying things. It was just there, and I felt it even when we were apart; this overwhelming sense of him. That was the best way I could describe it... I felt him everywhere.

Loving him was unavoidable. I'd been pulled to him almost the instant I'd laid eyes on him. I needed to be loved by him, and he needed to be loved by me, and that need was like a magnet drawing us a little closer with every day that passed on that island. I'd tried to fight it, so did he, but it was impossible not to love each other. It was as if we'd been made together, two pieces of a whole existence pulled apart and unaware of our own lacking until we'd finally come back together.

"He didn't touch you?" He asked against my shoulder, his voice choked and hoarse from the swelling in his throat muscles.

"No. He only wanted you to think he had." I held him tighter than I ever had, feeling his sense of failure and needing to assure him our predicament was not his doing. "I'm alright," I whispered. "Are you?"

"I am now," he said so softly it was barely audible.

"You should probably try not to talk for a while." I released my death grip on his waist to slide both palms up to rest on his chest and get a good look at him. It was dark—both outside and in the room. The candles on the chandeliers didn't reach this corner and I could only see a hint of their reflection in the moisture of his eyes.

I didn't need to see his face to know the way he was looking at me. His fingers were featherlight as they swept along my cheek to tilt my lips up to his.

The kiss was tender and careful, as if he was attempting to keep himself from shattering. It was apologetic, guilty, and lost in surrender to our circumstances.

We weren't surrendering. We were surviving. I curled my fingers into his shirt and pulled his kiss deeper, a desire in me I wouldn't be able to subdue so soon after giving birth, taking over our mouths. I pulled him closer, harder against me, needing to let my senses be momentarily filled by only him; needing more to let his feelings of defeat be replaced by the complete appreciation I felt for his lips upon mine.

He understood, letting go of his restraint to take a firm grip of my hair and match my nearly bursting desire for him. I forgot to breathe, forgot who I was, and was whisked away from the room and the world for that tiny moment we shared before we both were pulled back into reality by the raised voices in the main living area.

"That don't make no sense, whatsoever!" Jim said hatefully. "If this ain't the path God intended for ye,' you wouldn't have ended up on it. Ye' cain't just erase everything ye' done for the past twenty years."

As the kiss was inevitably cut short, I pressed my forehead against his. "I disagree with what they want to do... I think it's dangerous... but I can't bear another day like today, so we'll go with it... until we can make a move. Got it?"

He took a deep breath, disconnecting our joined foreheads to push the hair behind my ear. "Got it."

I looked over to the seating area where they'd gathered. Jim was sitting beside Anna on the floor, both of them tending to the cuts on Kyle's back. "And if this is all *your* plan, why ain't you the one goin' through time? Why send your brother?"

Juan Jr. sighed. "Because my father believes that every action he takes now shall be erased the very moment we have killed Richard Albrecht's lineage. There is no end to what that man might be capable of if he believes everything he does from now until then will be stricken from existence. Especially to a group of people he knows cannot be linked to his own heritage. My brother cannot control him the way I can. If time is as malleable as we believe it to be, then we cannot risk him changing the course of it by harming anyone else in this century. He could inadvertently, through his desire to inflict pain, set us even further off our destined course."

"What if *this is* your destined course, though?" Jim dabbed a damp fabric over a deep cut on Kyle's back while he pursed his lips in thought. "If the good Lordt didn't intend for ye' to cross through time, he'd have prevented it from happenin' altogether. I believe we all was meant to come here. I believe the things we do here is what makes the future the way we know it. We were destined to find each other. You go on and kill whoever ye' need to, but I'm pretty damn certain you ain't gonna' wake up and forget what ye' done."

"I have to try," Juan Jr. said simply. "If there's any chance I could wake up and not know the things that have happened here, I'll take it. I am sorry for what my father has done to you today. I sincerely hope those memories will soon be removed from your minds and the scars vanished from his back…" He bowed his head. "I must return to him now to make amends. What I have done for you is no favor to you. It is a necessity for me. Make no mistake, I am no less wicked than my father after spending so long in this time. My intentions are for the good of myself, and should you prove him right by attempting to abandon us, I fear I shall do far worse than he to get to my destination. Come, Dario."

Dario bowed his head and obediently followed his brother out the door.

"What if he's right?" Kyle asked after they'd left. "What if we're all cursed for leaving our time?"

He was walking proof of a curse if I'd ever seen one. Missing an arm, beaten unrecognizable with bruises lining his face and swelling his eyes, then whipped until he bled, he'd hardly had any kind of happiness in the life he'd lived in our short time in this century.

"We ain't cursed," Jim assured him. "We didn't go through that storm on purpose." He patted Lilly's knee. "And we certainly cain't erase what happened to us."

"Why not?" Anna asked. "Let's say, for the sake of argument, *we* found Frank's lineage… If he hadn't been the pilot, a different pilot might not have flown into that storm. We wouldn't even know this life had happened to us. There'd be nothing to miss about it. We'd just… go on with the lives we'd been living, ignorant of it all. How could we possibly remember it if it never happened? Why not erase it and go back?"

"Because we ain't supposed to. We was put here for a reason, and goin' out and *killin'* someone to change it, well, *that's* goin' off God's course, not the other way around." He softened his tone. "I know this ain't been easy on ye' darlin',' and I'm sorry, but we cain't just erase what's happened to us." He interlaced his fingers with Lilly's. "We cain't take this away."

Anna's sudden interest in formulating a plan just as outrageous as Juan's had my heartbeat racing. Jack and I slowly rejoined them, taking a seat together on the floor across from Kyle.

"But we've been gone for *three years*," she argued. "What if Liam's father has done irreversible damage to him in that time? I have this horrible feeling something's gone wrong. If anything has happened to my son and it is within my power to change it back, I will dedicate my life to making sure I never make it to that airplane."

"We're getting way ahead of ourselves." I said, very much aware that many of us, myself included, would be dead if Anna hadn't made it onto that airplane. "We don't even know what's out there on that ocean or what we'll find if we somehow make it through. Let's not start talking about changing the future before we know what future awaits us, okay? One thing at a time. Anna, if anything has happened to him, we'll *all* do what we can to change that. I promise."

Phil smirked from near the window. "No, you won't. None of you care about the lives any of us had before that crash. You don't care that she missed three years of her son's life or that Kyle and Izzy could be living out normal childhoods without being deaf, crippled, or estranged from their mothers... You don't care that Magna could've spent this time beside her own family or that Chris's brain might be restored to healthy... It doesn't matter what future you find, you're not going to let her change anything. You're too selfish."

Magna, seated in one of the wingback chairs with Cecelia asleep in her arms, cleared her throat. "Do you hear what you're really saying? Do you understand what altering the future would entail? You would have to kill, not just one person, but an entire lineage of innocent people to alter your *own* timeline."

She clicked her tongue. "You would not just kill one of Frank's ancestors. You would kill every single person and event that derived from them. You'd kill these babies too. That's selfish. This is not who we are. We have only been on this ship for two days. Do not let the evil hearts of these men taint your own. This is the life we've been given. It has been harder on some of us than others, but it is what we have. We are not murderers. Anna, you least of all. We have been blessed to be together in this room. Let us appreciate, that much more, the blessings we are granted when we are granted them."

Phil motioned toward Kyle's back. "You call that a blessing?"

"He is in this room, surrounded by people who love him very much instead of chained to a wall. I call *that* a blessing."

Chris leaned forward on the sofa to rest his elbows on his knees. "He is right about one thing. We don't belong here. Not them or us. I hadn't thought about it this way before, but Magna, you're right. The smallest act here could eliminate any one of us. I could have a conversation with a man in this time that prevents him from meeting what should've been his wife and, all of a sudden, one of you could disappear. Jack, Bud, and Maria have all killed people in this time… For all we know, there could've been more of us that came through time, but we've forgotten them after bumping into the wrong person. Same for Juan Josef and for the men in those journals. There's no certainty around any of the numbers we've come up with around crossing through because there's no way to know what their presence in this time has changed from one day to the next. We all need to go home and stay there before we can do real damage to each other here. And we need to make sure they go too and can never come back."

Ten years of marriage had apparently given us very like minds. He echoed the same thoughts that had been racing through my own head. I imagined he might've been just as terrified to wake up in bed beside me in our old life, tiptoeing around our issues and living a life alone together.

"You don't look so good," Kyle said, looking over at me. "Are you okay?"

Taken aback, I blinked. "Am *I* okay?" I shook my head as I patted his knee. "Honey, I'm fine. It's me that should be asking you that question. I'm so sorry for this. Are you alright?"

He shrugged and presented his arm where the bottom half was missing. "I've been through worse." He grinned. "I'll heal."

Anna finished applying a bandage to his back and frowned over his shoulder at me. "He's right. You don't look good at all. Are you feeling okay?"

I sighed. "I'm just exhausted and sore."

"And it's no wonder, the way you've been pulled every which way." She rose up on her knees, pressing her palm against my forehead. Noticing her hand felt like an ice cube against my skin, I wondered if the fatigue I'd been feeling throughout the day was from a fever instead of just exhaustion.

"You're burning up." She clicked her tongue. "With your condition, there's no way to know what kind of damage might've been done to your insides, and you're not in the clear yet—not by a long-shot. Lilly, knock on the door and see if one of the guards will call for Juan Jr. or Dario to come back. The antibiotics are still at the house and she's gonna need them. Come on." She extended her hand to me and stood. "Jack, help me get her undressed. She'll need to stay in bed for a while. Juan Josef will have to pick someone else to torment for a few days."

"Really, I'm alright," I assured her, proving it by standing on my own.

"That may be," she said, looping her arm through mine to escort me toward the bed, "but we're not taking any chances."

Jack made a sound as if to speak but choked on the words against his swollen throat. In the candlelight, I could just see the rope burns, bright red on his neck beneath his shirt collar, and shook my head. "You should rest too, you know."

He nodded, placing an arm at my back. "I will," he whispered.

The room was filled with conversation as Anna setup the screen behind which she and Jack could help undress me. I heard Lilly speaking to the guards, insisting Juan Jr. be called back to us. I listened closely as the door closed and she joined the debate around destiny and lineages.

"...but what if that *is* the way back?" Phil asked. "None of us can know for certain there's anything out on that water. It's naïve to assume we'll sail to that spot and find a storm waiting for us. What if the only way to get back home is to prevent the crash from happening altogether? Bud, consider the life you might've had with Bertie these past few years. You might've had more time... Kyle would have an arm... Anna would have her son... Lilly, you would have your career, and Jim, you'd be rich beyond your wildest dreams. Think of what we've been through... we've killed people and done things we never thought ourselves capable of. Are we not monsters already? None of us, no matter what you might feel now, is a better person for being here."

"That ain't true," Jim said. "Ye' don't know what kind of person I was before this... Hell, ye' don't know who none of us was 'cept yourself. *You* may be a monster, but not all of us."

"No?" Maria asked. "We lie to good men to keep ourselves alive. We are knowingly corrupting history—*important history*—by having James Cook return to Tahiti for us. We have killed and we continue to hurt the people around us by extending their torture in this place... and for what? Fear of losing a life we'd never know we had? I think maybe Anna is right. It's not like Frank was a good man... If we erased him, we'd erase the crash, and then we would not be changing history. Kreese would not be losing his mind... Everyone would be better off."

"How can you say that?" Chris scoffed. "After all we've been through?"

She huffed. "If you and I are truly meant to be together, then it will happen in another time and place where we would not be changing history to do so... where your brain would not be damaged. What if you only love me because your mind is broken? Eh?"

"My brain is working just fine, thank you," he growled. "We're not killing anyone."

As Anna moved to untie my petticoats, I shyly placed a hand over hers. I knew I'd been bleeding consistently and had definitely bled through the fabrics of my makeshift pad. I was afraid of what I might look like beneath the cover of the skirts with Jack beside her to see it and potentially panic.

She met my eyes and, acknowledging my anxiety, turned toward Jack. "There'll be blood. Bleeding is normal for a woman who's just given birth. Can you bring that water and basin over so we can get her cleaned up?"

As he hurried to oblige her, she leaned in. "When was the last time you were able to check it?"

I blushed. Being on the ship with bedpans instead of closed-door restrooms made it difficult for me to have the privacy I'd need to merely use the bathroom, let alone change out a pad, and as a result, I'd gone almost the entire day without checking the damage. I knew I'd bled through the fabrics; could feel it on my legs, but had no clue just how much. "Sometime this morning..."

"Your brain is working fine, is it?" Maria raised her voice. "That is only because it is busy at the moment! What happens when you are content in this place? When there is no escape to plan or nothing to build? Will you wake up one morning so far gone that you do not recognize me at all? You are too great a man to lose your mind, and I would rather lose you from my life than to watch your greatness slip away from you."

"That's not fair," Lilly argued. "You don't get to play righteous when you're talking about murdering entire generations of people —not to mention stripping a mother of her two newborn babies!"

"She wouldn't even know she'd had them," Maria attempted to reason.

"Grandpa, please... talk some sense into this delusional woman!"

Bud cleared his throat. "Kyle... what do you think?"

"Me?" Kyle asked, clearly dumbstruck that his opinion in such a complex debate should be asked for.

"Yes, son, you," he said calmly. "You've had the hardest time out of all of us here. What do you think of this whole thing? Do you think God put us here for a reason, or that he is warning us to return to a path he intended?"

I held my breath as Anna worked the ties of the skirts. I'd been through this once before, but because of how early Evelyn had come, the bleeding had been minimal. This time, it felt like my insides had been seeping out all day, and I wasn't sure if I should've been concerned by it. I focused on her face, waiting for a sign in her expression to indicate normalcy.

As the skirts fell, I didn't find the comfort of normalcy in her expression, but concern instead. "You're going to need to stay in bed. You can't be up moving around and wearing these corsets."

"Well..." Kyle started, drawing my attention away from the blood dripping down my legs. "I don't really know if there's a God or not... but we are here, aren't we?" He paused. "If we weren't supposed to be here—if Frank wasn't supposed to be piloting that plane... he wouldn't have been. If I was meant to have my arm, I'd have it. Same with Anna and her son. I don't know about destiny or paths or whatever, but I do know what's happened to us and I don't think killing people to erase it sounds like the right thing to do. You don't get an *'undo'* button for the life you've been given. That doesn't seem right."

"Smart lil' summbitch, ain't he?" Jim joked.

"Jack," Anna said softly, "grab a new shift out of the trunk over there."

I shivered as I stood naked behind the screen, both from fever and from the anxiety the debate was giving me.

As Jack turned toward the chest, she leaned in to whisper while I pushed a washcloth over my body. "This may be the only opportunity I have to say so, and although I know it's the wrong time, I'm saying it, anyway. I know you don't agree with changing things, but something is wrong. I know it. You're a mother now. You'll know this feeling someday. One of those twins will be out playing and you'll just get this strange intuition... and you'll run outside, and there one of them will be with a broken arm or a bloodied knee. There's no explanation for it, but it happens. I always knew the minute Liam got hurt. And I've had this feeling for months now. I know how crazy it sounds to want to kill entire generations of people to change my own history, but... as a mother, it is my job to protect him. If that's the only way I can do my job, I will do it. And you would do the same if it was one of yours."

"If you prevent the plane crash, I will never know the feeling." I whispered back. "You would kill my children to save yours... and I won't let that happen."

Jack returned with the shift to cut the conversation short, but there was an understanding in her expression as she worked the clean shift over my head. Neither of us wanted to be the enemies we'd been when Jack had left the island, but we would be in this if one of us didn't back down from our stance.

"A conversation for another time," she said, motioning toward the bed. "Both of you need to rest for now. We'll look after the babies for a few hours and we'll try to send someone for the antibiotics before the ship moves too far away. If we can get those in you soon, you'll be just fine in a few days. Endometriosis is not uncommon after a birth in this time. Jack, you're going to need to let your throat muscles relax. Lay down with her and try not to speak."

Jack climbed into the bed and gently pulled me in alongside him. He curled one heavy arm over me to pull my chilled body against his warmth as Anna dragged the velvet curtains that framed the bed closed. Returned to his arms, I felt my anxiety ease and buried my face in his chest.

"Don't respond," I whispered, "but we can't let them keep talking about this as if it were something any of us could consider. It's bad enough we have to worry about Juan Josef. Now half of our group is arguing reasons we should murder people to prevent the past year and a half from even happening. I won't let them take this from us. You and Zachary and Cecelia... you are everything to me. As hard as this may be for Anna, I can't risk never knowing this life with you."

He swept his palm over my hair and nodded softly, saying without speaking, *'I won't ever let that happen.'*

Chapter Nine

I woke to find Jack missing from my bed. It was dark, and I could hear a sound just beyond the curtains that lined the bed. I crawled down to the foot of the bed toward where the sound was coming from. Just as I reached out to open the curtains, I recognized the sound I was hearing was a panting... it was a man's panting... a *familiar* man's panting... and the floorboards were creaking beneath him at a steady rhythm.

I pulled my hand away from the curtain and sat perfectly still, listening to his breathing grow heavier. Beneath his sounds, there was a second set of lungs expelling heavily into the air and they blew through vocal cords that were distinctly female... occasionally making a low ecstatic hum as the floorboards creaked more consistently.

'Jack...'

I crumbled into myself, pressing my hand over my mouth to prevent the sob from escaping it. I knew it was him—recognized his breathing—and couldn't believe it.

I tried to rationalize it; told myself I was being crazy and Jack would never do such a thing to me. But then I remembered who Jack once was before I'd met him—the tabloids and the rumors of multiple women—and my heart broke in two because suddenly my life was over.

Since we'd been together, we hadn't had to go through any length of time where we weren't intimate. Could he really be the type of man who couldn't wait a few weeks for me to heal after birthing his children?

I cried as I tried to make out her sounds… who was it that laid beneath him? Did I want to know? If I didn't see it for myself, could I pretend it didn't happen? Could I convince myself that the panting—panting I knew with all my heart was Jack's—could be coming from the lungs of someone else?

Or maybe it wasn't that sort of panting at all. Maybe whoever else was with him was in trouble…

If I didn't look, I couldn't be certain… and needing some sense of certainty, I placed my shaking fingers on the curtain and began to pull it back…

Then I woke up.

I had never been so relieved to wake up in all my life. I sat up in the bed, clutching my heart as I caught my breath.

'It wasn't real. Thank God.'

The pain of the dream lingered in my chest. My entire body ached, actually, and I realized I'd been sleeping for quite some time.

The last time I'd had a fever, I'd lost an entire week and my bones ached similarly. I hadn't lost time in quite the same way with this round of illness; I recalled feeding the babies—sometimes at night, sometimes with bits of sunlight shining through the gaps in the velvet curtains that hung around the bed, but I'd lost moments. The time between feedings was hazy, and I wasn't sure if I'd interacted with anyone but the babies for days.

It was light out. I could see a warm glow coming through the curtains indicating a setting sun, and, feeling relieved that what I'd just experienced hadn't been real, I crawled to the foot of the bed to peek out through the curtains in search of my faithful fiancé.

The room was empty save for one male body lying on the sofa.

Had they attempted an escape again? Was there a new punishment being administered in the dining room? Had Juan Josef decided to separate us again? Where were my babies? Who the hell was on the couch?

With no regard for the fact that I was wearing only a shift and had spent what I assumed was several days in it, I leapt out of the bed to the seating area. The sudden movement made Chris sit upright on the sofa with a jump.

"Where is everyone?" I asked, my eyes moving across the room in search of my children.

"Dinner," he said calmly, running a hand through his hair to smooth it where it stood on end. "It's alright. They're alright. They'll be back soon. Jack hasn't left the bed in days and I volunteered to stay behind with you and the babies so he could eat something. They're there." He pointed to the wooden cradle that had been in the dining room and I could see their outlines under the white blankets they were tucked under.

I let out a long exhale. "How long have I been out of it?"

"A few days in and out. Anna said you needed the sleep. We got the antibiotics in you before we sailed off. Your fever's been gone for two days. I think you were just tired."

He pulled the blanket that he'd been wrapped in from his body and offered it to me. "How are you feeling? Are you hungry?"

I draped the blanket over my shoulders, pulling it closed to hide my lack of clothing, and sat down beside him. "Not at the moment." In truth, I was starving, but was still too shaken from the dream to eat. "What have I missed? Juan Josef... has he...?"

He shook his head. "He's sent for you every day, several times a day, but with Anna's insistence you needed the rest, he's been relatively absent. It's been quiet. They brought Fetia in to stay with us, which has made Kyle and her father very happy. The rest of us have just been waiting... Today, Juan Jr. arranged for the others to join him and Dario for dinner in the cabin. He said there was no need to keep us locked up all day now that we are out at sea. He figured they could use the change of scenery lest we all go stir-crazy. No one has tried to defy them. You made us all promise we wouldn't during one of your half-awake feedings."

I smiled at that. "So no one's been beaten or hanged or any manner of awfulness Juan Josef can come up with?"

"No... he doesn't seem interested in any of us. Just you."

I rubbed the sleep from my eyes and let my spine rest against the tufted back of the couch. "Thank God."

He forced a smile, an evident mountain of words lingering inside his throat. "Al," he picked at a piece of loose threading on his breeches. "There's something I've been meaning to ask you... since we have a minute alone... Do you find me very different?"

I frowned. "What do you mean?"

"I mean..." He blew out. "Do you think I'm losing my mind?" Nervously, he continued just as I opened my mouth to speak, pulling at the loose thread while he rambled without pause. "Because I don't. But I can't help but not trust my ability to make that call. I don't trust anything that has gone on in my head since Anna suggested it... or even after the crash. It's like I'm imprisoned by this damn diagnosis, forced to question and doubt everything I've done since, and I can't stand it any longer. You know me better than anyone here. Do you think I'm crazy? Do I seem crazy?"

I shook my head, laying my hand over his to stop him from fidgeting. "No, love. Well, maybe a little crazy at the moment, but no. You are different... but different in a good way, not crazy at all."

I watched the tension immediately melt away, and he sat back on the couch, his shoulder resting ever so slightly against mine. There was a comfort in having physical contact with someone I'd spent so much of my life with. I suddenly felt home in a way I hadn't for some time.

He squeezed my hand. "I still love you. You know that?"

I would normally tense at words like these when I was clearly in love with another man, but this wasn't some passing fling confessing his undying love for me after only a few months of knowing each other. This was Chris, my husband. There was nothing uncomfortable about the statement. In all honesty, it felt good to know he felt anything toward me at all after months of avoiding me. I'd been mortified by how quickly he'd been able to turn off all attachment to our lives. I hadn't been able to, and I was glad to see him opening up to me. I squeezed his hand in return. "I know. I love you too."

He looked taken aback. "You do?"

"Of course I do, Chris. I never stopped."

A quizzical look remained on his face, and I sighed. "Do you remember that morning after we brought you back from Eimeo? When it was just the two of us and you told me you stopped knowing me after Evelyn?"

He nodded.

"Well," I covered our joined hands with my other. "What I wanted to say to you that day... what I *should've* said to you that day was that you knew me just fine and my unhappiness at the end had nothing to do with you. Not really. You brought up seeing the gun clip on the vanity that day, and I never got a chance to explain it. And I need to explain it... for the sake of both of us."

I turned my body toward him. "The truth is, no matter how much time passed, I couldn't look at you after Evelyn and not relive the moment she stopped breathing. That wasn't fair to you, nor was it fair to our relationship, but it's just how my mind worked. No matter what I tried, when I looked at you, I saw her lifeless body in my arms. Everyone kept telling me I needed to let go of it—that it had been long enough and I needed to get past it, but I couldn't. I pushed you further and further away because I couldn't see anything but her in you. Of course, our perfect relationship became strained after two years of me avoiding all physical contact with you. My expectations for you to immediately return to the man you'd been before all that were unrealistic and unfair. I broke my husband and ruined a perfect marriage, and because of what I'd done; because of my own unwillingness to let go of that anger and be the wife you needed, I wanted to end the miserable life I kept myself inside of."

I met his eyes then. "That clip had nothing to do with you, Chris. It wasn't *you* that made me unhappy, it was me. I couldn't let go of Evelyn and all the things I'd done after. And it was selfish of me to even consider it that day."

I stared down at our hands, squeezing his softly. "I chose Jack —not because I ever stopped loving you or because you weren't enough, but because I could love him without the shadow of Evelyn and all the horrible things I'd done reflecting back at me through his eyes for the rest of my life. Life with him was like stepping entirely out of who I was to be someone else. I could touch him without the reminder of all the hurt I'd caused him, and he could touch me and I wouldn't forever feel the loss of a child I couldn't give him. I chose Jack because the moment his arms wrapped around me, I forgot about Evelyn for the first time since it'd happened and I wanted more than anything to feel the weightlessness of forgetting every single day after. I never stopped loving you, and I never will. And I will always look back on the marriage you gave me and remember it as a happy one."

It was always strange to see Chris get emotional. That's not something either of us had ever been good at showing each other, but he did so freely, letting the tears roll down his cheeks. "Would it be weird if I held you for just a minute?"

I shook my head and reached for him, pulling him against my shoulder as he wound both arms around me. We stayed like that for quite a while, both of us squeezing tightly as we finally put an ending to our marriage.

"I'm so sorry, Al." He whispered against my shoulder. "For all of it. It's nobody's fault we lost her, but what I wouldn't have given to be able to save her for you; to save both of us from everything we put each other through after. I should've known my wife's heart better. You shouldn't have pushed me away, but I should've fought harder. I should've helped you get past Evelyn instead of expecting you to do it on your own; instead of running to that woman's bed. I should've stayed in Minnesota for as long as it took to get you back... because the wife I loved was worth getting back. I'm so sorry I didn't. I told you before, I'm happy you're moving forward, and I mean that. I told you we wouldn't be strangers and then I became one to you. I'm sorry. I shut you out because I couldn't understand that we don't have to be husband

and wife to mean something to each other... And you will always mean a great deal to me."

"You mean a great deal to me as well." I clung to him for a moment longer before I let him pull away. "Being married to you was a wonderful chapter in my life. Thank you for it."

"Thank *you* for it." He wiped his eyes and let out a long breath of air. "And I love Maria very much, you know... I don't want you to think I don't because I said I still love you."

I grinned. "I know you do. I can see it when you look at her. I gotta tell you though," I smirked, "you couldn't have chosen someone more my opposite. I'm so glad you did. She loves with the same ferocity you do. You deserve that."

"She's not always been nice to you... I've heard some of her remarks on occasion."

I sighed, rising from the sofa as Zachary began his small crackling sounds that generally prefaced a screaming, hungry meltdown. "I don't take them personally." I hurried to the cradle to scoop him up before he could wake Cecelia. Turning back toward the sofa, I bounced him softly against my shoulder. "She loves you and needs to defend you from time to time. I know it's not malicious. Not really."

I sat back down beside him, laughing to myself as he looked every which direction but at me while I positioned Zachary at my breast. It always seemed strange for a person who'd already seen another person naked to look away as if they hadn't. Mindful of his own discomfort inside the situation, I adjusted my thinking, covering myself with the blanket. "You can look now, the boob is hidden."

He blushed when he looked back at me, acknowledging the absurdity of the two of us and bursting into laughter.

"Sorry." I chuckled. "I don't even look at my body that way since I became two tiny humans' food source. I forget it's probably awkward to have a woman pulling out a boob beside you."

He waved it off, looking toward the cradle as Cecelia made soft whimpering noises. He glanced over at me. "Do you want me to get her? Is that okay?"

"Of course it is." I touched his cheek. "You're her family too."

He walked to the cradle, slowly leaning over it to look at her. I watched him as he gently pulled her to his shoulder and rocked her from side to side, smoothing his giant palm over her tiny back. The image of him holding her struck a nerve as I was reminded, once again, of the daughter we lost... How wonderful he would've been as a father.

He saw everything I'd been thinking in my expression. "You were right to choose him. I'll always remind you of her."

I nodded. "I would've given anything to save her for you, too. You would've been the best dad anyone could've asked for."

"Well, I can still be a pretty damn good uncle." He grinned at Cecelia as he pulled her from his shoulder to his cradled arms. "Unless that would be weird for Jack?"

"Not at all," I assured him, patting the sofa beside me. "Now, before they get back, tell me, how do you feel about this whole Richard Albrecht thing? It's insane, right?"

"Very." He sat, adjusting the position of his arms and the blanket several times until he was sure Cecelia was comfortable before he leaned in to whisper. "I think it's a dangerous thing to trace the lineage of a person and attempt to rewrite the course of events. Who else is linked to that person? Am I? Are you? Part of me wants to prevent it from happening altogether... which would mean killing Dario—a man I have no desire to hurt—before he can come back with that information."

"It's strange the way we talk about killing people now, as if it's as simple an act as brushing your teeth."

"Do you see any other way to prevent them from doing it?"

I shrugged. "Juan Jr. said they'd been hunting and murdering Albrechts for years, hoping for the same outcome. Would they not be doing far worse if we left them to guess?"

"But do you really think it could be possible they'd wake up in a different life? And if it is, how many different versions of our lives do you think we might've lived as a result of the things they've already done here? What if I only exist as a result of them killing an Albrecht? Or you? What happens if they erase it all from happening and never cross through time to murder those men?"

I blinked heavily. "That's a whole lot of information to attempt to process after coming out of a three-day nap…"

He laughed at that. "Sorry… my mind has been spinning a little uncontrollably with this whole thing and no one really listens to me now that they all think my brain is damaged."

I clicked my tongue. "They don't?"

He shrugged. "Maybe they do, but I just get the impression they're all thinking, *'here we go again… Chris is having another one of his episodes.'*"

"I doubt they're thinking that. It's not like what you're saying isn't valid. You're extremely intelligent and people recognize that. It's why people always gravitated toward you in every place we ever went. These people notice it too. They're all drawn to you. Even Jack. Not one of them has ever mentioned seeing you as less because of a *potential* brain injury, that, in my opinion, is nothing more than a few lucid dreams, nothing to feel all handicapped about. Here, trade." Zachary had finished, and I carefully pulled him away without uncovering myself. I held him out to Chris, who looked confused as to how we'd make an exchange with his arms already filled by another tiny human.

I laughed, balancing Zachary against his shoulder as I pulled Cecelia into my arms. "You're not going to break them, you know."

"You sure?"

"Well, you won't break him, that's for sure. Just tap on his back a little until he burps or poops." I moved Cecelia beneath the blanket, sliding it craftily to the other shoulder and juggling her until she grabbed on. "What are we going to do about Anna? While the rest of us seemed to feel the same about the Richard Albrecht story, she started planning a version of her own. One that Maria seemed onboard with."

He smoothed his palm over Zachary's back, turning his head awkwardly to try to get a look at his face. "Don't worry about her. She has no concept of inner thought. The woman just spews out whatever goes on in her mind without thinking about what she's saying or who might be affected by what she has to say. She would never do anything that could separate you from these babies. And Anna... I don't know her well enough to know what she's capable of, but I imagine, if I'm to go through time with her, I will know soon enough. Don't worry, Ally. Nobody's taking this life away from you. I won't let them."

I laid my head against his arm, perfectly at peace with the life we'd both ended up in together. "I won't either. Do you really think we'll sail out there and find a storm that will magically transport you home?"

"I do."

There was comfort in his sureness; comfort that made me think about my family with a nearness I could almost touch. "I know we can't tell my family where I am, but... could you find some way to let them know I love them all very much?"

I could hear the smile as he spoke. "I promise I will. Do you think, if we go through safely, you and Jack will go back with the babies at some point?"

I sighed. "I don't know yet. That'll be kinda strange for our families, won't it? For both of us to come back to life after being thought dead for so long with entirely different lives?"

"If you and I were able to navigate it and come out better for it, they will too."

I watched Zachary's eyes grow heavy as Chris smoothed his hand over his back. "Still... I don't know that I'm willing to take the babies through that storm. I was growing used to the idea of staying in this century... finding someplace quiet to raise them without all the politics and technology and craziness of the 21st century."

The doors opened, and our people, full of smiles and casual conversation, poured into the room. I couldn't help but laugh out loud when I spotted Jack. While I'd grown accustomed to seeing everyone else in 18th century attire, Jack had refused to change out of his beloved blue jeans and button-up shirt.

Apparently, while I was napping, he'd given in. He entered the room in black breeches with white stockings and a ruffled white shirt. Upon my continued uncontrollable laughter, he narrowed his eyes at me. "Shut up."

"You caved!" I shook my head as I took in the attire. "What made you change your mind?"

He rolled his eyes. "Zachary puked all over me yesterday. I had no choice." His expression softened as he met my eyes. "How are you feeling? You look so much better."

"I feel like I slept for days." I smiled at Chris. "And the weight of the world has been taken off my shoulders."

Chapter Ten

Chris

Chris curled up on a pallet on the floor at the side of Maria. After his time with Alaina, his mind felt more at peace, and he was able to feel honest about his relationship with Maria, having finally closed such a large chapter of his life left open for too long.

Maria had been amusingly suspicious of him all night, offering side-eye glares in his direction since she'd returned to find him seated all-too-comfortably beside his former wife. Her anger wouldn't last long, particularly after she'd had a chance to interrogate him, but watching her play the outraged and jealous girlfriend for the few hours before bed was far too entertaining to cut short.

He dared not touch her when he laid down beside her, but propped himself up on his elbow to smile down at her. The moon was shining in through the window, illuminating the scowl on her face in a cool blue hue that made even her frown look flawless. "What are you smiling at, Superman? You know I am angry at you."

"Honey, there's not a person in this room that doesn't know you are angry at me." He playfully tugged on her hair only for his hand to be swatted away. "Oh, come on, you know that was nothing. Are you going to let me explain or do you want to stay huffed up all night thinking the worst?"

"Finding you snuggled up next to the wife you love so much is nothing?"

He chuckled. "I wasn't snuggled up to anyone and you know it. I was sitting next to her... having a very important conversation."

"Her head was touching your arm, and the other day, I saw the way you held her... the way you kissed her on the forehead... I am too jealous and insecure not to notice and feel hurt by these things when I know you still love her."

He gently brushed the hair away from her forehead. "You know, I'm tempted to just leave it alone and let you scowl at me all night. You're gorgeous when you're mad at me."

"Don't you dare try to fix this with compliments, estúpido. I have said you still love her twice, and twice you have failed to correct me. How am I supposed to feel?"

"I love *you*, Maria," he said, hovering over her lips with his own. "I want you and only you." He slowly reached beneath the blanket to slide his palm over her arm. "You've got nothing to be insecure about. That part of my life is over, and the best part—the part with you in it—has only just begun. Come on, don't be angry right when we've gotten to the best part."

"You are so cheesy. You know that? Do you enjoy listening to yourself talk this nonsense?"

He lowered his face a little more, waiting patiently for her to close the gap between their lips as he felt her anger slipping away. "You love that I'm cheesy."

"Do I? How do you know what I love when you are so busy snuggling with other women?"

He let his palm glide up her shoulder and along the side of her neck. "So you're going to stay mad at me all night for sitting next to her?"

She narrowed her eyes. "That wasn't just sitting. Don't make me out to be ridiculous for noticing it."

He grinned, lifting the blanket so he could slide his body against the side of hers. "I love that you're being ridiculous. I love that you're jealous and angry with me. No one has ever loved me enough to be jealous."

She huffed. "Tell me what this important conversation was about, then?"

"It was everything we both had left to say to put an official end to our marriage. I needed that so I could look at you without feeling like there was something left unfinished. I've spent these past few months feeling like I wasn't authentic enough; like the love I've been so sure I feel for you was lacking, like there was a shadow hanging over the words each time I said them, and there was... because I hadn't had that conversation. Now, lying here with you after getting it all out, I've never felt more secure, more sure of the words *'I love you.'* That chapter of my life is officially over, and it's given me the blank slate I needed to write all my new chapters with you."

"All your new chapters?" She was trying to appear angry, but he could see the hint of a smile beginning to form on her lips.

"I want to spend the rest of my life arguing with you."

Maria rolled her eyes. "Are you going to kiss me or are you just going to hover there listening to yourself say cheesy things the whole night?"

"I'm going to hover," he bit his lip as he glanced down at her mouth, "until you kiss me."

"Ha! You are going to be waiting a long time, then."

"I doubt that... You can't resist me when I'm being cheesy."

Her eyes darted to his lips and back. "You really are brain damaged if you think, after all this time you have known me, I can just stop being angry that easily."

"Don't say that." He stiffened.

"Say what?"

"I know it was a joke, but I want to be seen as a man and not as a brain injury anymore. I'm not crazy and I'm tired of feeling like I am. Every time someone says *'brain injury'* I feel further and further away from the person I thought I was. Let's not use those words anymore."

Her frown returned as her hands gripped each side of his face. "Oye, who told you that you weren't a man? Eh? Who says you are crazy or any less a man because of some stupid brain injury? Of course you are a man. You are the greatest man I have ever known. Tell me who has made you feel like less and I will kill that person."

He turned his face in her grip to kiss her palm. "I have. Ever since those words came into my life, they have played on repeat, forcing me to question every conscious thought my brain has conjured up since. I have felt like less and made myself out to be crazy. We are all damaged in some way... I can live with that, but I can't live with being the only damaged one. I don't want the pity or the *'poor buddy'* side glances while you all are off in conversation. I want the same respect I had before those words were spoken... so I can feel like the person I was before she said them."

"Then those words will never be said again, mi amore. I will make sure of it." She pulled his mouth down to hers and put exclamation to her statement.

That was the thing about kissing Maria. Just as she left no room for inner thought in her words, she left nothing unsaid in the way she kissed him.

This kiss did not tease. She did not start slowly to build anticipation, but instead devoured his mouth the instant it covered hers. This kiss dared any woman to come try to take him; warned him she would fight for what was hers. This kiss assured him he was a man worth every ounce of fight she had in her. God, he loved kissing her.

He loved it too much, he realized, as both their bodies were awoken by their mouths and the floorboards beneath them creaked loudly, a painful reminder that they were in a room full of people.

She groaned as he pulled back, blowing out with as much frustration as he felt. "Tomorrow," she said, "I will ask Juan Jr. to give us our own room to sleep in. We can stay here throughout the day, but there are too many of us to sleep comfortably at night. He likes me. I think he will do this if I ask him."

And suddenly Chris was the jealous one. "What do you mean, he likes you? What happened at dinner?"

She smirked as she snuggled into his chest. "Juan Josef wasn't there, just his sons. It was nice. They played music, and we ate pork roast—I think I'm going to suggest they bring Bruce into the kitchen. He's bored with nothing to cook and he cooks so much better than the chef they have down there... Anyway, Anna and Dario seemed to hit it off. They were off in their own little world talking about the trip to the future while the rest of us talked about our experiences in this time. Did you know they have homes in California? Apparently, the west coast is full of either Spaniards or Indians. They plan to take us there while we wait for you to return. They say it's very beautiful. I wish you were coming with us."

"Get to the part where you said he liked you..."

She laughed out loud. "Jealous, mi amore?"

"Extremely."

She kissed his chest and rested her chin there as she looked up at him. "After dinner, they took us up to the top deck. It was nice to feel the sun on my face. He came and stood next to me. Out of nowhere, he started telling me about his wife and their children... how they got yellow fever after sailing to the east with Juan Josef and died on this ship... He told me that's why he has remained on the ship searching for a way to reverse it all. He says he feels closer to them by being in the place they died. Men don't share intimate details like that with a woman if they don't feel some kind of connection to them. He likes me... and I'm going to use that to get us our own room."

"Careful there," he warned, running his fingers through the hair near her temple. "We don't know what these men are capable of."

"Juan Jr. is not a bad man... Not like his father. Whatever wickedness might be in him stems from pain and anger, not evil... I know how to tell monsters from men. He is not a monster and he won't hurt me."

"What about his brother?"

"Dario is a different story. At the core, he is good—kind and sweet—but I think he wants his father to love him as much as he loves Juan Jr., and that makes him dangerous. It's very obvious his father favors Juan Jr. over him. Dario will do anything Juan Josef asks him to in order to earn some of that favor... including becoming a monster, if he thinks his father would love him more for it."

"You said you would ask Juan Jr. for a room tomorrow... does that mean we have been invited out of the room again?"

"Yes." She laid her head back down against his chest. "They've invited us to lunch and tea on the top deck. I think they feel guilty about what their father did to Kyle and Jack and they're trying very hard to reverse our opinions of them while Juan Josef waits for Alaina to recover."

"Seems to be working... you almost sound excited about lunch and tea."

"Mi amore, I'd be excited if they invited me out of this room to shovel manure if it meant I'd get another few moments in the sun."

"What do you mean, *'while Juan Josef waits for Alaina to recover?'* What's he planning to do with her when she does?"

She sighed. "I don't know. He didn't appear even once while we were out. Juan Jr. said he's waiting for her... but he wouldn't say more. I'm not sure he even knows what his father wants with her."

"From the sounds of it, he gets a kick out of intimidating her... Some twisted enjoyment out of playing the dominant male to a helpless female—using her children and the people she loves as a threat to get her to quiver beneath him. We'll have to keep her in bed when they come... try to extend her recovery for as long as possible."

She propped herself up on her elbow. "Did you talk about me during your important conversation with her?"

He grinned, running his thumb over her chin. "Of course we did. She said you love with the same ferocity I do and she's happy I have you."

"Hmmf." She adjusted the collar of his shirt. "And did she tell you all the things you did wrong to end your relationship? Did she blame you for all of it?"

"No. She told me how wonderful and perfect I was and how she just couldn't look at me without seeing our dead daughter in her arms. She said it was her fault for pushing me away, and I told her it was mine for letting her. In the end, we both stopped beating ourselves up for a relationship neither of us meant to ruin, and we both can move past it now and look back on it as a good memory instead of a bad one. It's not her fault, and it's not mine... Life happened and put an end to a marriage that was great once, but that could never be great again."

"Oh..." She swallowed. "I guess I can't be angry at her for letting you know you are wonderful and perfect, can I?"

"Are you?"

"You know me, and so you know I want to be. I want to blame her for the hurt I watched you go through... Ridiculous as it may be... It's hard for me to just accept that life did that to you and not this beautiful woman with the *'hair for days'* that chose the handsome actor after only a year apart from you."

"I loved you after only a year apart from her," he reminded her. "And if you're going to hold on to my descriptions, you should hear the way I describe you."

She laughed then and pressed her lips to his once more. "You are so cheesy."

Chapter Eleven

I'd managed to remain in bed for another week before Juan Josef inevitably came to the room to see my condition for himself. He'd grown weary of our excuses that prevented him an audience with me, and insisted he inspect my condition with his own eyes.

Throughout the week, the others had been granted more and more freedom to roam the ship. They'd joined Dario and Juan Jr. frequently for breakfasts, lunches, and dinners, and Maria had even negotiated private sleeping arrangements for herself and Chris. Bruce had been invited to join the kitchen staff and, after a few very successful dinners, had been offered a position as head chef.

Izzy was coming out of her shell. Dario had a dog, and all she wanted from the moment her eyes opened was to go up to the top deck and play with it. All she ever talked about was that dog. We hadn't come up with a sign for dog on the island and it took us a while to figure out what she was trying to illustrate. Magna eventually put it together, and we came up with a gesture suitable —a gesture she made more frequently than anything else.

From what they told me, Dario didn't seem to mind sharing his dog. He enjoyed Izzy's company, *particularly when she was accompanied by Anna*, and had even taken the efforts to learn a few of her signs.

Life on the ship almost felt normal were it not for the fact that Juan Josef was onboard somewhere.

No one had seen him until that morning when he barged through our double doors to stand over my bed.

It was the first time I'd laid eyes on him since that awful evening in the dining room. He seemed different as he leaned over the bed to look at me. Beneath his tidy beard and flawless attire, he appeared more desperate, lonely, and genuinely concerned for my health; not at all like the villain I'd experienced during our last encounter.

He *was* the villain though, and as soon as he knew I was faking a fever I'd recovered from a week ago, he'd return to the head games he enjoyed playing so much. I had spent the week preparing for just that.

I felt fine, aside from a bit of seasickness from the constant motion of the ship. It'd gotten particularly bad the night prior, as the water had grown more choppy. I prayed my skin was still lacking in color after a night of vomiting. Now that he stood above me, I wasn't as prepared as I thought I'd be.

"What do you want from me?" I asked as he laid a palm over my forehead. "Why do you insist on only conversing with me and not the others?"

He frowned as he removed his hand. "You seem well enough to have breakfast. Fetia," he motioned toward her, disregarding my questions. "Come and get her dressed."

He said nothing more, but spun on his heel, folding both hands behind his back as he strolled proudly away from me, his guards following at his heels.

"You can't do this." Jack hurried behind them. "She is my fiancé. The mother of my children. You can't storm in here and summon her as if I don't exist... as if she's your personal plaything."

Hearing the anger in his voice, I rushed out of the bed to Jack's side just in time to catch Juan Josef turn toward him and cock his head to one side. A grin slowly spread across his lips as he met Jack's eyes. "Oh, but I just did."

Not waiting for Jack's response, he continued past us, turning back once he'd reached the double doors. "Alaina, my dear, please do get dressed quickly." He scanned my body where I stood in only my shift, making sure he did it with so much intention that it would not go unnoticed by Jack. "I'm afraid I'm quite ravenous."

Jack tensed and made a move for him, but I took his hand in mine and pulled him back. Jim, too, had observed the interaction and placed himself between them with a hand on each of Jack's shoulders. "He ain't worth the fight, Hoss," he whispered. "Not yet. There's too many of 'em. Come on now. Ye' got them babies to think about, and she's gonna' need ye.' He'll get what's comin' to him soon enough."

Jack's chest was heaving when the double doors shut. While Jim tried to calm him, Lilly appeared at my side with Zachary asleep in her arms. "I really thought that part of it was over... Like he felt guilty after what he did to Kyle and we wouldn't see him anymore. I'm so sorry, Lainey. This isn't right."

Jack spun around, cupping my cheek in his palm. "You don't have to do this," he whispered. "You're not his entertainment. I'll do whatever I have to..."

"It's alright," I lied, looking between all three of them. All I wanted to do right then was collapse into Jack's chest; to cry out, *'I want to go home,'* and let him be the protector he wanted so desperately to be. That wouldn't do anyone any good and I had plans of my own, so instead, I motioned for Fetia. "It won't be much longer until we get to that spot. If there's no storm and no way to get to the future once we arrive there, I'd feel a whole lot better if he sees us as friends and not people he needs to dispose of. I can handle myself so long as you all keep going along with it."

"If he puts a hand on you..."

"You'll do nothing unless I ask you to. I can handle breakfast, even if he's hell-bent on tormenting my mental health all the way through it. Just don't do anything to give him fuel. And you take the babies. I'll feel much better if they're further away from him."

"I'd feel much better if *you* were further away from him." He squeezed my hand as I attempted to move to the mirror. "Red, I'm serious. Is there really nothing I can do?" I could see the helplessness in his eyes as they met mine. "He can't expect me to say nothing when he comes in here to collect you like this."

I touched his cheek. "It's all a part of his twisted game. He wants you to feel that way. He wants you to do something about it so he can play the monster he's dying to play and punish us for it." I raised up on my toes, pulling him toward me to rest his forehead against mine. "We won't give him the satisfaction, Jack. We won't play his game. The best way to fight him is to be unaffected by him. I know it's hard, but it's all we can do right now."

"I'm going to kill him," he whispered. "Not today, but someday when we're not trapped on his ship, I will find him and I will kill him for all this. I swear it."

I sighed. "I never want to hear his name again once we are free of him, and I'll be damned if I'm going to let you go out looking for him. Let someone else kill him."

'Like me.'

In the time I'd spent in bed, I'd relived the scene in the dining room over and over again. Each time I replayed the events, Edith Piaf's voice sang sweeter, the feel of the leather whip in my hands grew heavier, the slices on Kyle's back bled darker, and the wind on my face from Jack's flailing legs was colder than the most frigid Chicago winter I could ever remember. After what Juan Josef had done, I couldn't look at him as anything but the monster. I could never unsee Jack's flailing body in that noose. I didn't know if he would carry out his threats to kill us if we found nothing, but I wasn't going to wait to find out. Nor was I willing to spend months alongside him, allowing him to torment us while we waited for their return. I was going to kill Juan Josef and I wouldn't feel any remorse whatsoever.

I'd planned out exactly how I was going to do it, too. Just as he assured me I would, I would *'come to him.'* It wouldn't be immediate. I'd need to spend the next several weeks warming up to him; getting him to believe I was beginning to care for him. Once I was sure he believed it, I'd wear the green dress, take his hand in mine, and touch his chest lightly in the spot over his heart that indicated true affection. I'd let him kiss me, and I'd make damn sure I kissed him back the same way I kissed Jack—which meant I'd have to convince myself that I was kissing Jack. He would lead me somewhere private—he was too orderly a man to be seen by any of his men without his clothing. I would undress him, make him feel like I was the only person in the world he could be vulnerable with, and once he was at his most vulnerable state, I was going to slit his throat.

Maybe Juan Jr. was right. Maybe we didn't belong in this time and we would all be made monsters by it... And maybe some of us had already become monsters... because I killed him over and over in my dreams and felt nothing.

A half hour later, I was seated at the side of him in the dining room as two servants filled our plates with eggs, sausage, bacon, bread, and cheese, and I waited patiently for him to begin the conversation when they left the room.

I wasted no time biting into my bacon, and I reached toward his side of the table to grab a glass jar of jam and began spreading it on my bread. He would not need to instruct me to eat. I would do what he wanted and I would do it happily because I knew I was going to kill him. Nothing he did between now and then could frighten me the way it once had. I felt more powerful than I'd ever been.

"It's good to see you eating," he said, watching me with his hands frozen in place over his own utensils. "I'm certain you must be starving after being ill for so long."

"Ravenous," I echoed his word back to him as I scooped up a bite of eggs.

"I did not mean for the events that took place to cause you that illness. I hadn't considered your fragile condition so soon after giving birth. I only meant to prove a point."

I looked him in the eyes then. This was something I was going to need to be capable of doing more often, and I'd need to do it without showing him how repulsed I was by him. "And what point did you prove, Juan?"

Saying his name was also something I'd need to get used to. I could see the way his name on my lips invigorated him. He liked it. He wanted to hear it again... I would give him that. I would give him so much more than that.

He picked up his fork and knife, but held them at each side of his plate, attempting, I assumed by the confused look on his face, to decipher my mood. "That you are just like me. That you would do horrible and unthinkable things merely to save the people you love most."

I took a sip of my tea. "And here I thought you were punishing them for plotting to escape."

"Two birds, one stone." He moved his utensils as if he were going to dig into his meal, but paused to look at me. "Are you pleased with the freedom I've granted them to spend time on the top deck and dine with my sons?"

I tilted my head to one side, pretending to be grateful. "You did that? I assumed it was Juan Jr."

He frowned. "I am the captain of this ship, not he. It was my decision to take them out of the room on occasion. I promised you I would grant them freedom if they were kept in line. They have made no move to rise against me since the last time I saw you, and so I thought I would show my gratitude by allowing them more room to roam."

I sliced into my sausage, holding it near my lips. "Now that we are further away from land, will you give us more room to roam? Actual freedom? Treat us as guests on the ship instead of prisoners? There are too many of your men for us to attempt anything and even if we did, not one of us knows how to sail a ship like this or which direction we'd even need to sail in to get someplace safe. We need you and your men if we're ever going to see land again, so there's no point in us fighting now... not that there was ever a point in fighting then, particularly when I told them not to." I pointed at his plate with my knife. "You should eat."

He twisted his lips, not looking down at his food. "You're... different this morning."

I chewed the sausage thoroughly, taking a deep breath as I did, and waited until I'd swallowed to continue the charade. "That's because I'm angry."

"I do not wish for you to be angry with me Alaina, I only meant—

"Not at you." I shook my head. "At them... for proving you right in your inability to trust us." I set my utensils on my plate, turning toward him. "I asked Jack not to fight. Begged him to trust me... and he didn't. Instead, he plotted behind my back with the others... And I'm angry. I'm angry that you, a man I've only just met, could see that a man I loved and thought I knew so well, would so quickly betray me."

And there it was. I'd planted the first seeds of distrust in my relationship. I could see a flicker of delight cross over his eyes as I said the words. The more I could nurture that and grow it into complete detachment in Juan Josef's mind, the better I could keep Jack safe from him. If he assumed I was falling out of love with Jack to fall in love with him—something he knew me capable of with both a husband and a fiancé locked up down the hall—maybe he wouldn't feel the need to hurt him once we'd reached our destination.

I cleared my throat. "I'd like you to give us the freedom to roam the ship because I need to be able to get away from them— from him. It's hard to be cooped up together with the people who forced my hand... Listening to all the excuses why they felt they needed to. The more time I'm stuck in there, the harder it is for me to look any of them in the eyes. I thought I was angry at you for making me punish them, but I've realized during my time stuck in bed, I was angry it had to *be you* who made me see what little faith any of them have in me and my ability to handle a situation on my own."

It was easy to make that sound believable because there was a part of it that was true. I knew Jack's instincts were to protect his family, and while I wasn't angry at him for it, I was disappointed he hadn't given me a chance to handle things when I'd asked him to. I was frustrated that, as a result, I'd been forced to watch him hang, to whip a boy I loved dearly and leave scars that would never go away. I loved Jack with all my heart, and I understood why he did it, but that didn't mean I wasn't hurt that he did.

Juan Josef observed me for a moment, looking for some sign of deception and finding none. He poked into his egg, letting the yoke slide over his sausage as he cut into a corner of it. "Then you shall have it. The freedom is yours. I'll pull the guards from your door during the day, and I shall let my men know that you and your people are free to roam the top two decks to do as you please. We'll have to keep your door locked at night, though."

I sighed. "Thank you. I can't promise you they won't try anything because, well, I was so sure they would listen to me the first time, and we both know how that went. I have no desire to punish them for their crimes again. They seem to respect your sons... perhaps they will listen to them instead of me. And if they do, let it be one of them that punishes them next time."

"I'd not been expecting you to feel so strongly," he said softly. "I know what it is to be betrayed by someone you hold dear. I'm very sorry, my dear. I can see how this pains you."

I needed to have some semblance of the woman he knew me as, lest I give myself away too soon, so I let him see the disgust in my eyes as I looked at him this time. "But you're not sorry at all, are you? You wanted me to feel this way about him. Are you satisfied?"

He shook his head, dropping his utensils to place his hand over mine on the table. It took all of my willpower not to recoil at his touch. "Your unhappiness could never satisfy me."

I looked down at his hand over mine. Had I placed it on the table knowing he would do just that?

"Do you still plan to kill us if we don't find the storm?" I asked softly, raising one finger to lightly brush against his palm before lowering it. I could see all the emotion that one simple touch brought him; watched him attempt to hide it behind an adjusted posture.

"I'm afraid I don't have a choice," he said, avoiding my eyes. "I've given my word that I would, and I am nothing if I'm not a man of my word."

I watched his hand as it retreated from mine to return to the side of his plate, and I cleared my throat. "Why do you wait for me and not spend any time with the rest of them? I have nothing to offer you if I am to die so soon."

He took a deep breath and sliced into his sausage. On the surface, he appeared collected. I might've even considered him unaffected by my presence were it not for the white knuckles against his knife as he held it tightly in his grip, a clear indication of an inner battle he was struggling to keep contained. "I like talking to you," he said evenly. "I have no interest in conversing with the others."

"It's more than that." I hinted at flirtation while still keeping a great deal of prisoner's contempt in my tone. "What is it you want from me? I can see by the way you look at me, it is more than just companionship. Why did you wait for me? Why did you show me how little faith Jack had in me? What do you really want?"

He was... uncomfortable. I'd seen Juan Josef wear many different faces in the little time we'd spent together, but discomfort was never on any of them. This was new and uncharted, and I wondered if I should continue or cower away. He was unpredictable, and if he didn't like that I was making him feel this way, he might turn sour... he might begin to suspect me... But what if he did like it? What if he was drawn to me because I had acted more fiercely that morning he'd first come to me? Did he want a woman that was unafraid to speak freely? Did he want to feel exposed and vulnerable by a woman? To be dominated in private while he dominated everyone else in public?

He did not look at me, but stared at his eggs. "You know what I want."

That was enough for today. I couldn't act upon those words; couldn't show any hint of returned interest. He knew it wasn't there yet, and if I said anything more, he was intelligent enough to see through me. I swiftly shifted back to our earlier conversation. I needed to build the interest slowly by asking questions about his life. "You said you wanted to prove I was like you... that I would do awful things to protect the people I love most. Who are *you* protecting, Juan?"

Again I saw the satisfaction it gave him for me to say his name, and a part of me wondered if I wasn't exactly like him in more ways than one, because simply knowing I was fully in control of such a powerful man was more satisfying than I'd liked it to be. It frightened me that I was enjoying his discomfort. It frightened me even more that deep down inside me, every time his eyes met mine, a little voice echoed, *'I'm going to kill you,'* and that voice gave me pleasure more than any sex I'd ever had.

I *was* going to kill him, and that was a secret I held close to my heart; a promise to myself that if I could just get through these next few weeks, I would have that reward.

Killing him wouldn't feel like murder because I didn't see a man in front of me. Juan Josef wasn't a man. He was the boar circling, waiting for that moment to dig in its tusk. He was the ocean attempting to swallow me, and the steep muddy cliff I slid down with no way to stop myself from falling over its edge. He was the pneumonia in Jack's lungs, the threat of death looming over my pregnancy, the distance between me and my husband. He was my death if I let him be; the death of my children and the man I loved if I let him be. I was sick of death lurking; fed up with being a woman that cowered away from it to let someone else come fight it for me. I was tired of him and this ship and this place where the threat of death felt affixed to my shadow. He was not a man but a purpose, and I was not Alaina, but his own death staring back at him... I would not let him be the death of us, and the power I felt in being the only one of us that knew that made me smile.

He sat back in his seat, holding his teacup near his lips, the steam rolling up over his beard to leave small bits of shine on its black surface. "I'm protecting my son."

"From what?" I asked, leaning back in my own seat to sip my tea.

'I'm going to kill you.'

"From himself."

I tilted my head to one side. "What do you mean?"

He inspected me for a moment, then tossed his napkin onto his plate and stood. "Will you walk with me?"

I nodded, and I took his hand without hesitation when he offered it, standing as he assisted me out of my seat. I let my shoulder brush against his as he curled my arm into his forearm and escorted me out of the dining hall and up the stairs to the top deck.

Unlike the others, I hadn't been outside in almost two weeks, and the air in my lungs was heavenly. I closed my eyes and let the breeze fill me, feeling every hair on my body come alive at the softness of its squall.

Juan Josef escorted me to the railing, and I looked out at the infinite sea, a straight blue line on the lighter blue sky in every single direction. Tahiti was gone, and we were the only blemish on the ocean as far as the eye could see.

"Juan Jr. is my heart," he said, letting go of my arm to place both his palms on the railing and look out at the water. "My whole heart... And he was good. He was good the moment he was born. He loved with that goodness and I envied him for how his wife loved him back that much more for it... For the way his children looked at him with the same kind of adoration."

He looked down at me where I was watching him intently. "Juan Jr. never wanted to go back to the future. *I* could never let go of the future, though. I had unfinished business I was determined to get back to... and that determination led to the death of his wife and their two children."

He gripped the railing tighter.

"You see, when I couldn't find a storm in the Pacific, I thought I'd try the Atlantic... maybe search for the Bermuda Triangle to see if it was somehow related. I realize that sounds ridiculous, but so does running into a storm at sea and ending up in the past. Juan Jr. and his family had never been to the Atlantic, so I asked them to join me. The children were old enough that they could make a longer journey, and it would serve like a vacation for them. I treated it as such, stopping on the various islands and spending time with them on the beaches."

He paused and swallowed, his knuckles tightening against the wood railing. "I never knew what yellow fever was... didn't know the symptoms when his wife and both children developed them... and we were in the middle of the Atlantic with nowhere to take them when they got worse. They died, and they stayed dead on this ship for days until I could get back to land. That's when my heart —my whole heart—stopped beating. Juan Jr. wasn't good anymore. All that goodness was sucked out of him. He tried several times to join them in death... It was so bad I couldn't trust him to be alone because he *craved* death. And standing there, holding the son I love most in my arms to prevent him from leaping off this ship for the fifth time, I came up with the plan for Richard Albrecht. If I could change it all—prevent all of this life from happening, Juan Jr. would forget the pain... he'd live a life without any of that weight hanging over him. His wife would be alive and living out a different life somewhere where the yellow fever could never touch her. He'd *want* to live again. And that promise is the only reason he is still here. If I cannot find it, he will take his life, and my heart will be gone forever. So you see... I will do anything, kill anyone, sail anywhere for as long as it takes to keep my heart still beating."

'I'm going to kill you.'

The words didn't feel as good now that I knew a piece of the man beneath the monster. I almost felt sorry for him had he not been the same man who'd placed that whip in my hand the last time we'd been together; had he not ensured me he would kill us all if there was no storm.

'I'm going to kill you.' I thought again, and I raised my chin in defiance of my own empathy. I would not empathize with this man. I didn't care what made him evil. I didn't care about the pain he'd gone through to become who he was. He was the boar and the ocean and the cliff and the pneumonia and I was going to be his death.

Chapter Twelve

I was obsessed. More than obsessed… I was bordering on the edge of psychopathic. In the week that passed, my thoughts grew so consumed with the act of killing Juan Josef, there was little room for anything or anyone else in my mind.

I fed my babies and, instead of delighting in the act of providing for them, I fell into a trance, thinking of all the ways I would lure Juan Josef into the submissive state I needed in order to do it.

Entire conversations played out in my head. I planned for different scenarios where I might be exposed. I dreamt up lie after lie and told them so many times in my mind that they almost became true.

And they were partially true. I came up with the lies using a rule I'd always lived by in songwriting. I couldn't remember who had said it, but when I had first started out, someone told me that if you write a song, it has to be rooted in some sort of truth in order to feel authentic. As did lies. I knew myself, and I knew my face would give me away if I couldn't feel whatever words I was saying. I would need to be as authentic as possible, and if I needed a lie, it would have to be rooted in some form of the truth.

If I wasn't planning conversations and reactions, I was considering the final act and the events that would lead up to the knife slicing his throat. Would I let him touch me in those moments right before it happened? Would he be the first to do so after the birth of my children? I hadn't been able, nor would I be for several more weeks, to be intimate with Jack... Would the knowledge of what I would do to Juan Josef immediately after be enough for me to allow him to be the first to touch me there? And if it was, would I ever be able to scrub the feel of him off my skin? Would I ever be free of the guilt that would come with the allowance of his touch or would that touch linger to form a barrier between me and Jack? Like the memory of Evelyn's death had for Chris and I, would the feel of Juan Josef's hands upon me drive us apart?

It hadn't even happened, and I felt disconnected from him. It was no wonder I felt far away. I was holding onto a secret I couldn't share with him, spending days on end thinking of little else but that secret, and he was an outsider to my thoughts, trying desperately to squeeze himself back in.

I knew he felt it too because every night he held me a little tighter than the one before. He sat closer, always touching me in some way, as the others helped Chris and Anna plan for a potential trip through time, discussing all the things they would need to do if and when they got there.

I didn't want to be so obsessed; wasn't doing it intentionally. I made several attempts to be present, but their voices always became background noise to a scene that played uncontrollably in my head—a scene where Juan Josef was half naked in his bed, choking for air while he clawed at his open throat...

It was a scene that should've been disturbing, but it wasn't. Each time I tried to be disgusted by it, I would look at the rope marks on Jack's throat or at the bits of scarring on Kyle's back that peeked out of the collar of his shirt and felt vindicated. Juan Josef, covered in his own blood, was a scene that meant the safety of the people I loved most; it meant the safety of my children. Killing him would ensure none of us would ever be tormented by him again. The scene did not disgust me; it comforted me. It told me we would go on living without ever being afraid he could reappear again.

I considered the consequences that might come to us if his sons or his men decided to retaliate. The more time we spent among them, the less I worried about that. Juan Jr. was disconnected entirely—from his father, from us, and from life in general. I'd never seen a man so disinterested in living. He hadn't the will to retaliate. If I killed his father—*when* I killed his father—I doubted he would be affected at all.

Dario did concern me a little, but he had a good nature, and he still looked at me as if I were his long-lost mother. If I told him his father attempted to force himself on me; if I convinced him I was remorseful and only did what I had to in self defense (it was self defense after all), maybe he would be understanding. Maybe all of us, Dario included, could finally get on with our lives without the dark shadow of his father looming over us.

The clock in the corner read 2:50. It was almost time for tea. Being given the freedom to roam as we pleased meant that I was no longer summoned, but expected. I wiped Zachary's mouth, tucking my breast back inside my corset, and handed him to Jack as I stood and straightened the light blue folds of my dress.

I hated that I was anxious to get there. The obsession was unhealthy. Every bit of me looked forward to continuing on with my plan, and I couldn't wait to get it over with so I could return to something a little closer to human.

"I have to go up for tea," I said, as if he hadn't been dreading it since I'd returned from lunch.

"I know." He didn't look at me as he pulled Zachary against his shoulder.

"I won't be long," I assured him, hoping he would look up for just a second so I could show him a part of me was still there.

He didn't, and I couldn't blame him after I'd been so distant. I would have to tell him something to make things right. And lying to Jack wasn't an option... I'd have to find some version of the truth that would suit us both. He couldn't know the extent of it. No one could.

I had just stepped outside our doors when Bud grabbed me by the elbow and pulled me a few steps down the hallway. "I hope you know what you're doing," he warned, keeping his voice low.

I frowned at him. How could he possibly know what I planned on doing? I hadn't told a soul.

He softened his expression, the fine lines around his eyes fading as his facial muscles relaxed and he scanned the corridor for anyone who might overhear. "I know the look of a person who is working up the courage to kill another. It is not my place to tell you whether or not you should do it. I'm only warning you that it will stay with you forever if you do. Are you prepared for that?"

I took a deep breath and nodded. "Very." And I was. I was more concerned about the events that would take place before I killed him than the actual act of killing him.

"And have you told Jack?"

"No. He'll try to stop me. I'm the only one who can get Juan Josef to put down his guard, and that makes me the only person who can put an end to this."

I saw the understanding in his features indicating he knew exactly what I had planned, and I was glad not to see any accompanying disappointment. "When will you do it?"

"It depends," I said, feeling a little relieved to not be the only person carrying the secret. "...on whether or not Chris and Anna go through time. If we get there and we don't find a storm, I'll have to do it then... Before he can kill us first. If they make it, I'll have to wait... possibly when we reach his home in California... or maybe when we return for them? I haven't worked that out yet."

"That's a long time to keep it from Jack. You're going to have to do a better job of hiding it, sweetheart... He knows something's wrong."

"I know." I glanced toward the stairs and back. "And I'll give him a bit of the truth, but not all of it."

"Be careful." He laid his hand on my shoulder. "That man up there is no fool. One wrong step and he might kill you first."

That's precisely why I've been obsessing,' I thought to myself as I nodded and headed for the stairs. I'd played out several different conversations and scenarios, placing myself in Juan's seat to question the authenticity of my role. I needed to be very careful with what I said and how I said it. Everything I did—every touch, laugh, smile, or scowl needed to be thought out and strategic. I'd prepared for every possible reaction. I had to. My life, Jack's life, all of their lives depended on my ability not to screw this up.

When I ascended onto the top deck, I found him near the railing, sitting at a small table with two place settings for tea. There was a deck of cards in between them. The result, I assumed, of my telling him the day before that I used to play Rummy with my grandmother.

I had surprised myself with how natural it became to play the Alaina that had a growing interest in him. Due to my obsession, I did have a growing interest, and I'd rehearsed the role in my head so frequently, it felt almost real. I imagined I might've even made for a decent actress, assuming obsessing and isolated one's self from everyone around them was a part of the job.

"I didn't know you had cards," I said sweetly, waiting as he stood to pull out my chair for me.

"They're a little worn," he smiled, and in this particular smile, I found the vulnerability I was looking for; there was hope and a desire to please that went beyond a subtle crush to pass the time. He hurried back to his own seat and poured out two cups of tea, dropping one cube of sugar and a spoon into mine before he handed it to me. "My sons stopped traveling with me when they were old enough to make that decision, and so I had to do something to pass the time."

"That doesn't sound like much fun. No one to torment. How *did* you survive?" I grinned to assure him I was making light of our situation and beginning to accept him for what he was. Nothing I did was accidental. "How long did you travel without them?"

He began shuffling the cards, their frayed and brown ends showing the wear from being dealt so many times. "A couple of years. How are you?"

Again, his vulnerability shone in the way the word *'how'* seemed more sung than spoken. The note dragged downward as if his next breath relied entirely on the answer being in his favor.

I shrugged. "I don't know... Maybe it's postpartum hormones, but I can't seem to shake this anger."

Versions of the truth...

"My mind is caught up in it. It's consuming and exhausting to be this angry at a person. I've never held a grudge before... not like this. And to make matters worse, the only person I can talk to about it is the one person I have sworn to loathe for all my life... You."

He laughed at that as he divvied up the cards between us. "He's never betrayed you before?"

"Didn't really have a chance when we were isolated on that island. If anything, this has made me realize how little I know him in the real world. And that terrifies me the closer we get to it."

"I must warn you," he said, stopping mid-deal, "I have no idea how to play Rummy and am just dealing cards with no clue as to what I'm doing. How many should we each receive?"

"Ten," I said, folding my hands around my teacup. "You mentioned you know what it is to be betrayed by someone you love. How did you get past it?"

He set the deck down on the table, looking at me for instruction as I picked up my cards. "Turn the top card up."

He followed my instruction, then picked up his cards and began to sort them. "As you can imagine, I didn't respond well to being betrayed. I fear the answer to that question might place a stain upon the good opinion I'm certain you have of the one person you've sworn to loathe for all your life."

I picked up a card from the pile, the two of diamonds, and I placed it back on the table face up. "Was it your wife who betrayed you?" I held my palm to my mouth and shook my head as if the words had slipped out—of course, they hadn't. "I'm sorry. Don't answer that. I shouldn't have asked you that when it's none of my business."

He picked up the two of diamonds and placed three twos down in front of him, seemingly unaffected by my question. "It was."

I glanced at the set in front of him and raised my eyebrow. "You don't seem like you've never played Rummy before." I picked up another card, stuck it into my hand, and discarded another. "Since you answered... can I ask what she did?"

He looked over his cards at me, a tinge of suspicion in his eyes. "Why do you want to know?"

I'd played out this conversation several different ways. This could be a pivotal moment or an air disaster. I took a deep breath and did my best to read him as I navigated carefully. "We're not born bad. Not any of us. But everyone, even the best of people, develops into worse versions of themselves every time they get hurt. It's pain that ultimately makes us who we are, and..." I made eye contact with him, praying I looked sincere. "It's very difficult for me to spend this much time with you and not want to know why you are the way you are."

It worked. Thank God. I could see his guard melting away to expose the need inside him to share who he was with the one woman he wanted to really know him. He pulled a card from the deck and discarded it, frowning down at his cards as he said, "I found her in our bed with another man."

I laid my cards face down on the table in front of me, offering him my full attention as I rested my chin against my palm. "What'd you do?"

He laid his own cards down and picked up his cup, staring off some place further away than I could see. "God, I wanted to kill him... I wanted to kill them both for the pain in my chest when I walked through that door. I thought she loved me—I really did. She'd never given me any indication she didn't—not a single sign that her heart was ever not in it."

I waited patiently for him to continue, not daring to touch my cards or my tea while I had him exposed.

He was lost in memory for a moment, but continued without looking away from a spot on the horizon. I wondered if he even remembered I was sitting across from him. "It wasn't just any man she decided to bring to my bed. It was Richard Albrecht, the cop who'd been stalking my family for two whole years before that. If I killed him, everyone would know it was me that had done it. But I couldn't very well let him go. I had no idea how much she'd told him in their time together. She knew everything... How the business worked, who was involved, where the money was... And with no idea how long she'd been laying with him, I couldn't let either of them out of my sight. So... I separated them, locked him in a room in my basement, and had my men question him around the clock. I questioned her for three days and she wouldn't say a word. Then..." He looked at me then, his vulnerability hardening into what felt like a warning. "I beat her. I beat her so hard and for so long, I was sure I killed her. And I wasn't sorry for it. When I saw she was still breathing, I was angry I *hadn't* killed her."

I stared at him, playing the scene out in my mind and forgetting I was still putting on a show.

He straightened and picked up his cards, adjusting his expression as he released the memory. "Whose turn was it?"

I blinked back into reality, unable to shake the image of a woman who looked enough like me to have both Juan Josef and Dario in awe of my face being beaten almost to death while locked in a room and unable to flee. "Mi-mine, I think."

"Do you think me less for beating her?"

"It's hard to say," I admitted honestly. "It's easy to say that a man should never hit a woman when you've never had a woman rip all your dignity away."

"I never got over it," he said. "Not even after she died. To be honest, I wanted to beat you just for looking like her... I considered it that first night when you slid the knife into your sleeve."

I swallowed as I picked up a card from the deck. "Why didn't you?"

"Because for as much as I wanted to hurt you, I wanted to kiss you more."

'*Shit.*'

It was far too soon for him to perceive me as someone who would respond kindly to that statement. I needed weeks, maybe even months, before I could fake a blush and flirt back with him. I wasn't there yet. He shouldn't have thought we were there yet. He was too smart for that assumption. Was he toying with me? Did he know I was toying with him and attempting to expose me?

I realized I was staring dumbfounded back at him with my mouth partially open, and wondered if that was exactly the right response to that statement.

I hadn't been entirely unprepared for this. There was a lie I wasn't looking forward to telling if I was truly exposed; a lie I had reserved only for an emergency. "Juan," I stuttered, "that's not... this isn't what this is."

"No?" He tilted his head to one side, picking up a card and not even looking at it. "Then tell me, Alaina, what exactly is this? What's with your sudden interest in me, eh? Where's the defiance? How is it that you are suddenly angry beyond forgiveness at a man you loved merely for defending your honor? Do you think me a complete idiot?"

"No." I said softly, letting my cards fall onto the table. I was exposed and I would need to play the one card I didn't want to play. I took a deep breath and prayed that what I was about to say would result only in the outcome I intended. "My interest in you... well, it's just..." I bit my lower lip. "I don't have anyone else to turn to right now."

I could see the spark of intrigue momentarily light his dark features as he raised his eyebrows to encourage me to elaborate.

I sighed, running my pointer finger over the rim of my teacup. "Jack was famous back home... I'm sure you know this already."

He nodded, gripping his chin as he leaned forward. "I'd heard."

"Well, he was notorious for sleeping with *multiple* women. Had you heard that?"

He frowned and shook his head, leaning ever so slightly closer.

"I never believed it—*wouldn't* believe it—not my Jack... *My* Jack would never do anything like that... Not to me... At least, that's what I believed before we were locked together in a room with several other women whose bodies are capable of doing things mine can't do so soon after giving birth." My hands were shaking, but I let them as I briefly met his eyes. "He's not the man I thought he was."

I stared down into my teacup, conjuring the dream I'd forced myself to relive over and over to make it believable; to make myself and my circumstances something he could relate to. "I woke up one night while I had the fever and he wasn't in my bed. I was terrified to look out and see where he was... because deep down, I knew what I'd find and didn't want to see it... Didn't want to know which one he was with... Oh, but I could hear it... just beyond the curtains... on the floor beside the bed. I could hear all of it and I knew it was him. He couldn't be bothered to wait just a few goddamn weeks."

I had either become a great actress or was starting to believe my own lie because my nostrils burned and my eyes filled suddenly with tears as I relived every emotion I'd felt during that dream. "You're not an idiot, Juan. I hate you for what you made me do, but right now, I hate them more." I looked up at him then, letting the tears keep streaming down my cheeks. "I don't know which one of them I heard that night, and I don't know who else knows about it. I can't even look at them, I'm so angry. And the only time I don't feel completely pathetic is when I'm with you. You, the fucking monster keeping us captive." I growled and wiped my eyes. "I am stuck in this time with two babies from a man who can't be bothered to stay faithful for a few weeks... and somehow I still love him. I love him too much to jump in the ocean like I want to... love his children too much to ever abandon their father like I need to... but not enough to keep myself from looking to you with the hopes of making him feel the same amount of pain."

I'd come to him... And I was terrified of what would come next. There were only a few options. He could laugh in my face for being a horrible liar. He could agree and take me to bed right then and there when I wasn't prepared for it... He could run downstairs and kill Jack to defend my honor... or... he could feel sorry for me... He could relate to that kind of pain after what his wife had done and he could let me guide what happened next.

He laid his napkin on the table and slid his seat backward. "Come."

"Where are we going?"

"If you want to hurt him, we'll hurt him, but I won't risk him stepping out on this deck to find you here crying over him. He doesn't deserve your tears. Come on." He pulled a kerchief from his pocket and handed it to me as he gently pulled me from my seat and into his side. "We'll go someplace more private. I won't do anything untoward. Not until you ask me to."

The vulnerability was back in his voice. He was hopeful, apologetic, and anxious to play the comforting caretaker. I leaned against him and let him lead me across the deck.

Before we could reach the doors, a sailor pushed through them, bolting to the railing to vomit over the edge.

Mr. Gil hurried out behind him to greet us. He scanned my tear-swollen face for a moment before he focused on Juan Josef. "Some of the men have grown ill, Captain."

I could feel Juan Josef tense beside me. "How many?"

Mr. Gil ran a hand over his reddened face, slowly shaking his head. "Appears to be confined to the lower deck, sir. So far, only five of them have symptoms." He regarded me, raising an eyebrow high on his forehead. "But *she* was sick just last week and I'm concerned, now that we've given her people freedom to roam, we have exposed the men to an illness that could take down the ship."

I shook my head. "My fever had to do with being up too quickly after giving birth. No one else from my group has been the least bit ill."

Mr. Gil was panicked. I could see his chest moving heavily beneath his jacket and I realized, in this time, even a small stomach bug could be a very dire situation. I cleared my throat. "I could send Anna to check on them. She'll know what to do."

Juan Josef looked down at me, then back to Mr. Gil. "Take that man back down and keep the sick isolated. We'll send the healer down straight away to inspect. Make haste. I can't have a sick ship, Mr. Gil. Not when we are this close."

Mr. Gil bowed. "Aye, sir." He walked with purpose to the sailor bent over the railing, careful not to get too close as he encouraged him to join the others.

Juan Josef led me down ahead of them toward my room, but he stopped short at the bottom of the stairs and took me by both shoulders to face him.

He looked down the hallway toward our double doors. "Do you think your nurse will help us? After everything?"

I nodded. "She wants to go home to her son; wants it more than any of us. She'll help for the sake of getting there."

I began to turn away, but he took my hands in his, whatever heart he had fully exposed then.

"I know what it's like to feel pathetic," he whispered. "My wife handed me over to the man she was sleeping with. She destroyed everything my family worked for generations to build. She destroyed me... And even now, I still love her. *You* are not pathetic."

His words were hard to shake when I laid in bed that night beside Jack. We left the curtains around the bed open and bits of moonlight shone onto our faces through the window. Anna hadn't returned, and I laid awake, worried about where she might be and what might be happening on the lower decks. I turned onto my side to face him, unwilling to hide from him after the day I'd had... after the lie I'd told.

He curled a piece of my hair around his finger and smiled as my eyes met his. "There you are," he whispered. "Where have you been?"

"Stuck in my head." I pressed my palm against his cheek.

"Will you tell me about it? Or do you want me to keep assuming the worst every time you're up there?"

I nodded against the pillow. I couldn't hide this from him. It was too big, and I was tired of lying. I wanted to tell him all of it because I couldn't stand feeling so far away from him any longer. "I'm going to make Juan Josef fall in love with me."

He froze. "Why?"

"So I can kill him."

He slid the few inches between us so his nose was almost touching mine, and he swept his hand down my hair. "No, you're not. That's my job."

"No love, it's mine. You can't get close enough and I can't afford to risk losing all of you if he's true to his word about killing us if we don't find the storm. I believe him when he says he will."

He gently shook his head. "You're not a killer."

"No, but I'm a mother. And I will do whatever I need to do to protect them."

"How, exactly, are you going to kill him?"

I laid my hand over his where it rested against the side of my head. "Please don't make me answer that... and please don't treat me like a child that doesn't know what she's saying."

"How, Red?"

I exhaled heavily. "I'll make him think I don't love you anymore... that you've hurt me and I'm running to him for comfort. I'll spend the next few weeks making him trust me... making him feel there's something between us and then..." I closed my eyes because I couldn't look at him when I said it. "I'll get him alone... with no weapon to defend himself... and I'll slit his throat."

"No." He said simply. "You won't."

"Jack—"

"You'll get him alone with no weapon to defend himself, and *I'll* slit his throat."

I opened my eyes to stare into his, relieved he was willing to help instead of attempting to talk me out of it.

He smiled. "What will I do to hurt you enough that you'd run to him?"

"You've already done it."

"And what did I do?"

"You slept with one of the women in here."

He half-smirked at that. "Which one?"

"Don't know. I only heard you from inside the curtains... it was just outside, on the floor beside the bed, and I was too afraid to look out to see it... afraid to know for sure it was you."

"Jesus, that's dark."

I sighed. "It was an easy lie because I'd lived the pain in a very, very realistic dream. He believed me."

"What the hell's going on in your head to give you dreams like that?"

I smiled. "Hormones... the fact that I can't be intimate with you... it does all kinds of crazy stuff to my head."

"But you know I would never do anything like that, don't you?"

"Yes. I know... it's just the hormones messing with me."

He slid his hand down to my cheek and tilted my lips up to his. "Are you sure you want to go through with this?"

"No," I whispered against his mouth. "But it's too late to change my mind."

He covered my mouth with his, rolling me onto my back to kiss me deeply, his fingers winding into my hair as his breath rolled over my cheek.

"What are you doing?" I managed when he moved to my neck.

"Preventing you from having another one of those dreams. Be quiet before someone hears us."

I laughed as he slid one hand down the side of me. "Wait, I can't... not for another few weeks."

"Shh..." He covered my mouth with his palm as his other hand pulled my legs apart. "There are plenty of other ways to be intimate, Red."

Chapter Thirteen

"Will ye' quit that?" Jim hissed from the pallet on the floor near the foot of the bed, making it clear that Jack and I weren't the only ones with intimacy in mind that night.

It was still dark, and I'd woken hours prior, the day's events sitting heavy so my mind was spinning and preventing me from going back to sleep. I was grateful for the distraction. It had felt like ages since we'd been on that island where I frequently overheard Jim and Lilly as they attempted—*poorly*—to whisper in the night.

I loved getting brief glimpses into their relationship. There was always something so honest and pure about the way they interacted. They bickered frequently because they were so entirely opposite in personality and upbringing, but neither of them ever attempted to alter who they were to suit the other. They were complicated and yet so simple in the way they loved each other. I didn't ever intend to eavesdrop, but I didn't necessarily ignore them when I got an opportunity to peek into their little world.

"Oh, come on Jimmy, everyone's asleep."

'*Not everyone,*' I thought, a little ashamed to be listening in on what I assumed she was trying to accomplish.

"Your grand-daddy ain't but ten feet away. And there's kids in here. Quit it."

She sighed heavily. "Fine..." I could hear the floorboards creak beneath them as she adjusted her position.

Silence...

As much as I hated intruding on them, the silence was a disappointment. My mind had been in need of anything to pull it away from that room; from Juan Josef's watering eyes as he held my hands and fully sympathized with a lie I hated myself for telling. From—

"Jimmy?"

"...yes, Princess?" Even in his whisper, I could hear his aggravation. He wanted to sleep—much as he'd wanted to so many times on the island when she'd whispered his name in that way— and we both knew she was about to keep him up for at least another half hour. I smiled and laid still.

"I want to have a baby with you."

"Christ, woman, it's the middle of the dang night. Cain't we talk about this in the mornin'?"

"No. I want to talk about it now. We've never talked about children... and if I'm your wife, that's something we need to talk about. Don't you want a baby of your own?"

He blew out. "Get yer hand someplace else and quit. We ain't makin' one now."

"Why not? You're so good with Izzy and the twins and Kyle..."

"Get. Your. Hand. Someplace. Else. Woman. We ain't conceivin' on this damn ship..."

"When then?" She huffed. "You're getting older and I want to have them while you're still in shape to keep up with them."

"*Them?* How many ye' thinkin' we're bout' to have?"

"Four."

"Four?" He laughed. "Woman, you done lost yer damn mind. I ain't havin' *four* kids."

"Oh yes you are, Jim Jackson."

He groaned, realizing he wasn't going back to sleep anytime soon. "Sugar, we don't even know where we're gonna' end up yet. Where we gonna' raise your four kids?"

"We'll raise them wherever we are... Maybe it's in this time... or in Ireland like Lainey's talking about. Maybe it's in our time...

we could go anywhere we wanted between my money and yours... We'd give them a great life either way."

"We don't even know if we're gonna' make it off this dang ship. Did ye' forget about the lunatic down the hall? The one threatenin' to kill us all if we don't find the storm?"

"Jimmy, we're not gonna die on this ship and I'm not gonna wait until my eggs shrivel up to start building our family."

Again, the floorboards creaked as one of them turned. "Look at me, darlin. Now, I love you, and I mean this in the nicest way possible, but you are out of your Got damn mind thinkin' now's the time to get started. Go to sleep. We got bigger things to worry about than the heathen offspring you and I would create."

"There's never going to be a right time, not with us. On the island, it wasn't right because we were stranded. In Tahiti, it wasn't right because we were going to look for the storm. Here, it's not right because there's a lunatic... What's the next excuse? And the one after that? When's the right time?"

"Lillian—

"James."

I heard his neck crack as it so frequently did when he rolled his head backward. "I don't know when the right time is, but I can sure as shit tell you it ain't now. We ain't even technically hitched yet. Now quit."

"You haven't mentioned our wedding even once since you asked me. Marriage suddenly matters that much to you?"

"It does if I'm to put a baby in ye.' I've already got one bastard child out in the world somewhere... I won't do that to another child. And I ain't talked about the wedding because I know what kind of wedding you deserve and it ain't one I can give to ye' here."

"You know what? You *are* an idiot."

"I told you I was when ye' was chasin' after me." He chuckled.

She didn't laugh, and there was a long silence then, long enough, I noticed the cadence in Jim's breathing begin to fall into the steady rhythm of sleep.

"You really think I care about *where* I get married?" I covered my mouth to prevent the laugh stuck in my throat from escaping. If Lilly was anything, she was relentless when she had her mind made up about something.

He let out a long sigh as he was pulled from the edge of sleep once again. "Yes ma'am, I know you do. Especially if we make it home. You'll be invited to your friends' hoity-toity weddings and you'll always look back on ours and think it wasn't enough. And then you'll start to wonder if our marriage is enough... and I'm not sacrificin' what we have over one stupid ass day. I know all about the wedding you've dreamt of... You talked about nothin' else for a month on that island. One way or another, that's what I'm gonna' give ye, and then, after you've had your dream wedding, we'll start makin' your *four* babies."

"One *stupid ass day*? Is that how you think of the day we get married?"

"Lordt help me," he muttered, "I've angered it. All them words I just said to ye,' and them's the ones ye' hold on to? That stupid ass day will be the single greatest day of my whole life and you know it... I want to give you a wedding that's suitable for a day as important as that day will be to me. One that ye' can look back on and remember the same way I will."

"Don't I get a say in it?"

"Honey, whether or not you get a say in a thing has never stopped you from sayin' so anyway. Lordt knows ye' gonna' say now, ain't ye?"

"I am," she said proudly. "And you don't know me at all if you think I will look back on our wedding day and notice anything but you standing across from me. I'll get married to you right here, right now, on this floor and remember it just as fondly as if we were getting married at the Plaza. I don't care about what's behind us when we say the words to each other. I just want to say them and live my life with you."

"What do you want me to say to ye? Ye' want me to marry you on this ship tomorrow? Is 'at what ye' want? Get ye' pregnant here and now while we're sailin' through storms and tryin' to get away from a mentally deranged person? If that's what ye' want, fine. I'll give it to ye' so long as you let me go back to sleep."

"Okay, fine." She said sharply back to him. "Let's do it. Let's get married on this ship tomorrow, smartass."

"Lilly," he blew out, "go to sleep... and for the love of Christ, get yer hand someplace else."

Several hours later, the sun began to seep into the room, little bits of dust particles dancing in the rays that stretched from the window to the floorboards. I straightened my limbs in a stretch, and Jack's arm tightened around my midsection. I closed my eyes and smiled as he kissed the nape of my neck. "I don't want you to do it," he whispered against my skin.

I turned in his arms, curling into the sleepy warmth of his chest. "I'm not going to. You are."

"Not that..." He kissed the top of my head. "Everything before it..." He rested his chin on my crown and ran his fingers gently down my back. "I've never been a jealous man, and I know how absurd it is to feel this way when we're plotting to kill him, but I can't stand the thought of him believing you love him. Can't bear the image of your hand touching him in any way... of his touching you... even if it's innocent. I don't want you to do it."

I wound my arm around his waist, squeezing him tightly. "I don't want to do it either... but it's too late to stop now."

"What if it's all for show so we'll help him find the storm? Is it possible he might let us go the minute we do? Couldn't you just say you were wrong about what you heard and then we'll bide our time until we get there? Keep our heads down until he gets what he wants from us?"

"After what he's done already? He promised to kill us all if there's nothing there... Zachary and Cecelia, too. And I believe him. You and I both know it's much more likely we'll find nothing than a storm that'll take us through time. I can't give him that chance."

"But Juan Jr. and Dario are both much more rational than their father. Surely, they wouldn't let him kill any of us. Let me talk to them."

I shook my head. "Dario stood and did nothing to stop him when he hung you from the rafters. And Juan Jr. won't care enough to stop him if we don't find that storm. With no way to prevent the tragedies he's suffered, Juan Jr. won't want to keep living this life. Why should he care if we do?"

He pulled me away from his chest to look into my eyes, and I could see all the jealousy he was trying to contain beneath them. "Couldn't we get it over with now? Not spend weeks working up to it? Could you just get him to a room and let me do the rest?"

I shook my head. "I need you all to keep spending time with his sons so they can see that we're good; so they can see that we only want what's best for each other. I need a better feel for his men. Aside from Mr. Gil, the sailors on this ship seem to respect Juan Jr. more than they do his father. If Juan Jr. knows us to be good, maybe he can keep them from retaliating."

"What if he tries to kiss you? Will you let him?"

The question broke my heart because I could tell he'd been imagining it all night and I knew that image, if it were me in his shoes envisioning him kissing another woman, would destroy me.

"He won't. Not unless I give him the impression that I want him to."

"And will you?"

I took a deep breath. "Only if I absolutely have to in order to get him alone… and even then, I'll try everything to avoid it." I ran my thumb over his lower lip. "I never want to kiss anyone but you for the rest of my life… The thought of that man's lips anywhere near mine makes my blood boil… but if I have to do it to keep our children alive, I will squeeze my eyes closed and try my hardest to convince myself I'm kissing you."

"Don't you dare picture me."

I frowned. "How else am I supposed to get through it?"

His expression was dead serious as his eyes shifted from my left to my right eye. "I don't know, Red, but not like that. I won't have any association between my kiss and his. I won't live the rest of our lives wondering if my kiss is a reminder of him. You'll know it's me and not him when *I* kiss you. So you'll picture anything—*anyone but* me if you must do it."

"Alright."

"And you'll tell me if you do it. I won't be able to live with myself if I have to wonder every time you come back."

I wanted so badly to wake up and find ourselves on that island or in Tahiti without any memory of Juan Josef ever coming into our lives... without Jack knowing I'd ever even considered kissing this awful creature. And then I wondered... what if I could? What if we killed Richard Albrecht's ancestor and all of it went away? For as much as I'd opposed the idea, I wondered now if it was the only way we'd ever survive... both physically and mentally.

Chapter Fourteen

"I've an idea," Juan Josef said, smiling at me.

We'd just finished an awkward breakfast alone in the dining room. We'd said very little as we ate. I, because I couldn't bring myself to ask him questions about himself when I was so determined to kill him. The more I learned about him, the harder it was going to be to go through with it. Just the act of him taking my hands in his and tearing up on my behalf made me doubt my own intentions.

He remained quiet, I assumed, because he was suddenly shy about what I'd asked of him. The fact that I wanted to use him to hurt Jack was something that appealed to him, but deep down, he hoped it might turn into something more. I think he was afraid that if he said too much, I might just change my mind, and he'd never get the opportunity.

"What idea?" I asked, avoiding eye contact as I sipped the last of my coffee. Now that Bruce was making the coffee, I was delighted to sip something that resembled the taste of the coffee I remembered back home.

"The others are on the top deck," he said, "Jack is among them... You and I could go up... maybe walk together for a while... make sure he sees you laughing at something I have to say... It wouldn't hurt him quite as bad as he hurt you, but it would have a substantial effect... it would leave a door open for what's coming to him. Besides, we could all do with the fresh air with sickness lingering in these walls."

I cringed at the thought of Jack seeing me laugh at anything Juan had to say, particularly after our conversation that morning. I knew he would be jealous, despite his knowledge of it. I couldn't come up with a reason not to, though. It made sense to agree to it, given the plan Juan Josef assumed we were developing, and Jack would know what we were doing up there. He'd know, in the end, it wasn't real. Hesitantly, I nodded. "You think that would work?"

"Oh, I know it will. I was always devastated when Gloria would laugh with another man... even if it were only her brothers." He stood and offered me his arm. "It'll be fun, and more importantly, it'll be harmless. You deserve at least small bits of revenge, don't you think?"

I took his arm and stood, forcing myself to lean into him slightly. "Does it even matter?" I asked. "Every day we get closer to those coordinates, I get closer to death. I don't think we're going to find your storm, Juan. And you have promised you'll kill me if we don't. Does making him jealous even matter if none of us are going to live much longer?"

"We'll find the storm if you're telling the truth about the location." He escorted me out of the room. "I know it's there."

"And if it is?" I asked. "Who's going through? And what will we do while we wait for their return? You said yourself that we don't have the provisions for a return trip... a return trip to where?"

He patted my arm. "You're very grim this morning, my dear. Let your heart not be troubled. Not when we're about to have so much fun exacting your revenge. I won't send you if that is your concern. And I won't let you starve either."

"And Jack?" I asked, stopping on the stairs to look at him. "Will you promise not to send him?"

"You want a man like him to stay and torment you night after night?" He sighed. "Of course you do... You are a fool to still love him."

"I am and I do and I can't help it." I planted my feet as he attempted to move us along. "Promise you won't send him."

"Are you ordering me now?"

I squeezed his arm where it remained wrapped around mine. "I'm begging you."

"You want me to send the nurse and the ex-husband and expect them to come back instead?"

"Yes."

He shook his head. "What reason could I possibly have to send either of them? Particularly when I've sick men and your nurse is the only one among us that can assist in their recovery?"

"My happiness."

He narrowed his eyes, glancing up the stairwell, then back to me. "Was it the nurse you heard that night?"

I hadn't thought about blaming Anna as a means to ensure she could be sent through time, but it couldn't have been a more perfect plan. "I can't be certain," I said, feeling guilty about including her in my twisted lie, "but I think it was. She's the only single woman among us…"

"And what about the other one? Why do you insist on sending him?"

Now I would need to make Juan the jealous one. "Because he told me he still loves me a few days ago… because technically we are still married and he could use that to force me to stay with him. He'll come back." I met his eyes. "He won't ever let me go."

"I thought he was paired up with the Cuban woman?"

I shrugged. "For a few months… But he spent a year searching for a wife he'd been married to for ten years. He sailed across the ocean and back to try to find *me*. Do you really think he's going to cross through time and not come back for the one person he's spent so long looking for?"

"And you've no wish to be reunited with him? After what Mr. Volmer has put you through?"

I shook my head. "I could *never* go back to being his wife."

"I will consider it." He tugged me as he began climbing the stairs. This time I followed. "You are not at all the happy family you'd made yourselves out to be when I came upon you."

We stepped out onto the top deck and, as luck would have it, Jack and Anna were kneeling down together, Izzy between them, all three of them scratching the belly of Dario's white and tan dog. Dario leaned against the ship's railing, observing the interaction with a smile.

"The nerve of that man," Juan said under his breath, pulling my shoulder against his. "I should have them both hanged if I didn't need her."

"No," I said much too quickly. "It'll hurt him more if he has to live the rest of his life regretting it."

"She's rather plain in comparison," he noted, observing Anna. "I cannot fathom what would possess him to choose that one over you... Shall we walk or would you prefer to remain in sight and have a game of cards?"

Something on the horizon caught my eye. Far in the distance there was a speck of grey indicating land. I considered how long we'd been traveling and the direction we'd been traveling in and couldn't help but feel my pulse race as I put it together. I pointed toward it. "How close are we to the Devil's Islands?"

"You've a rather keen eye," he grinned, escorting me away from the others in the direction of it. "I do believe that's one of them."

I began to ramble. "The island we were stranded on... it's one of the three. It was vacant and appeared to have been vacant for a very long time. There are plenty of supplies there and we have weeks before September... Maybe we could stop there? With the sick, we could spread out until they are healthy to prevent more of the men from contracting it."

He shielded his eyes as he looked over the ocean. "Those islands are quite dangerous. Are you sure you were alone?"

"Positive."

"And was yours the one with the large volcanic mountain or one of the flat ones?"

My heart beat a little faster with the idea we might return to a place that was more home to me in this time than anywhere else. "The one with the mountain."

"A keen eye indeed," he laughed. "That's the mountain you're seeing. What kind of supplies might we find there?"

I was all but shaking with excitement. "Boar," I grinned, "lots of them... and the fishing is good. You can see all the way to the bottom... there may still be Kolea. They taste like chicken... and tons of fruit. Guava, breadfruit, F'ei bananas, and these roots that can be ground into flour... and spaghetti algae."

He looked confusedly back at me. "What in the world is spaghetti algae?"

I laughed loudly at that and I could feel Jack's eyes upon us as I did. "It's this algae full of nutrients. Vitamins your men could use to prevent them from getting sicker. It has a texture kind of like sauerkraut - tastes a little like it but not really sour..."

He tilted his head to one side as he looked down at me. "You're very excited about returning to it. Why?"

I smiled up at him. "It's the closest thing to a home I've got. I could show you where to find the boar. Help you gather fruit... I could help treat the men. It'd be a nice break from the ship while we wait. We're not far from the portal if we're already here."

Excited as I was to see it, I wondered if I might be ruining our island by allowing Juan Josef's feet on its shores. His presence could ruin every good thing about that place. I didn't want him anywhere near my summit, my cave, my waterfall.. I didn't want to ever think back on all those beautiful places and taint the memories Jack and I had made with an image of Juan Josef in their place.

On the other hand, I could kill him there. I could kill him and make it look like an accident. He could fall into one of the pitfalls... He could find himself down there with a boar like I had... I knew, from experience, no one would hear him scream. Hell, there might be a boar or two in those pitfalls waiting.

He could slide down the cliff face that overlooked the waterfall, just as I had... and if he was able to get a grip on something to stop his fall over the edge, I could be there to push him over...

He could get trapped or crushed by crumbling rock in the caves near the summit...

He could fall over the side of the summit...

"He's looking at us, you know."

My eyes were pulled away from the horizon. Juan Josef was staring at my mouth. He smiled and his eyes flickered toward Jack and back at my lips. "If you want him to regret what he's done... to really hurt him... I could—

"No." I could feel my body beginning to shake. I didn't like the way he was looking at me and suddenly I didn't want anything more to do with my plan... not if the plan meant he would continue to look at me with that kind of desire for the entire duration of it. "I can't."

He sighed and leaned against the railing. "He doesn't deserve you."

"I know..." I stared out at the spot on the horizon.

'I could kill him there.'

He followed my gaze. "You really want to go there? To the place you spent so much time with him?"

I nodded, almost catching the sweet scent of the flowers that grew on the summit, and without a second thought as to what I was saying, my lips formed the words, "What better place for him to catch us in but the one where he proposed?"

He laughed at that, loud enough to make sure Jack noticed. "And here I thought I was the wicked one among us. I'll have the men turn the ship. We should be there by nightfall."

Chapter Fifteen

Chris

"She's up to something," Maria said, narrowing her eyes in the direction behind Chris as he stood at the bistro table and poured himself a second cup of coffee.

"Who?" He asked, spinning around to follow her gaze.

"Your wife."

He rolled his eyes. "I wish you would stop calling her that. She's not my wife anymore, Maria."

She leaned in so the shipmen around them couldn't listen. "Look at the way she is smiling at him... Right in front of Jack... She's definitely up to something."

They watched her for a moment and then she laughed, placing a hand on Juan's forearm as she did. Alaina was flirting with Juan Josef, which meant she was most definitely up to something.

He looked over at Jack, where he was kneeling down by the dog, watching them. If Alaina was planning to make a move, Jack had to be in on it.

"Oye, do you see? She's going to get herself killed... or all of us, for that matter!"

He sipped his coffee and turned to observe the rest of them. Did they all have a scheme going? They'd spent more time together and had a bond that he and Maria were on the edge of. It was possible they might've been planning a move all along and failed to let him in on their secret.

Bud was watching her too… as was Jim. If they had a plan, they weren't doing a very good job of hiding it. "Wait here and don't say anything." He walked hurriedly toward Jim and Lilly at the opposite railing.

"Ay beanstalk." Jim raised his own coffee cup in greeting. "Ye' gettin' any sleep in that private room yuns finagled your way into? Thanks for considerin' the rest of us while you was workin' out your deal… I don't mind sleepin' on hardwood floors every night. My back's just fine, thank ye' for askin."

Chris smiled, but he didn't have time for small talk while there was no one around them to overhear. He tilted his head in the direction of Alaina. "What's she up to? You guys got a plan I'm not privy to?"

Jim shook his head. "I's just tryin' to figure that same thing. She damn sure looks like she's up to somethin,' don't she? Carryin' on like 'at… She ain't the type to flirt with the enemy. Hell, she ain't the type to flirt with nobody."

"She's not very good at it," Lilly said, her eyes following theirs. "…if that's supposed to be flirting."

Chris sighed. "Oh, that's definitely her version of flirting. You think Jack's in on whatever she's planning?"

Jim sipped his coffee, narrowing his eyes at Jack as he swallowed. "If he ain't yet, he's about to be… He's been watchin' her like a hawk this whole time."

"So are we," Lilly noted. "If she is plotting something, we might be giving her away."

"If she's plotting something, we should know about it." Chris turned his focus back to Jim. "If it goes wrong, that could affect all of us. Juan Josef isn't exactly a level-headed person."

"Oh, you can bet yer ass I'm gonna' get to the bottom of it." Jim looked over Chris's shoulder. "Hush now. They're comin' over."

Chris turned to see Alaina, a smile spread from ear to ear as she approached with Juan Josef at her side. The smile appeared natural, and he couldn't understand what would possess her to smile like that with such an evil man attached to her side.

"Lilly!" she called, breaking free of Juan's arm to hurry toward them while Juan split off toward the quarterdeck. She grabbed Lilly's shoulders and spun her toward the direction she'd come from, pointing ahead of them. "Do you see that speckle of grey on the horizon?"

Lilly squinted. "Yeah…"

"That's *our* island," she said, hopping with excitement. "…and we're going to it!"

Both Chris and Jim turned to look out in search of the spot on the horizon. Chris had his closure with Alaina and felt better, but he still didn't like the way she said *'our island'* as if it was a sanctuary for all the best moments in her life. It's also where she'd forgotten him and ultimately let him go. It shouldn't bother him, but he didn't like it nonetheless.

More so, he didn't like the idea that she was plotting secretly behind their backs. If she was about to make a move on Juan Josef, they all were in this together, and she should include them in any major decisions. She couldn't insist they avoid fighting him while she did it herself.

"That's really our island?" Lilly's eyes watered. "How long will we stay?"

Alaina smiled. "We have a few weeks before September. I imagine we'll stay at least two weeks there. We need to gather some supplies for the ship anyway… and with this size ship, we'd only be a few days away from the coordinates. Juan Josef is—"

"Ay…" Jim scanned their surroundings. "What are you gettin' at with him?"

Her immediate fidgeting was a dead giveaway. "What do you mean?"

"Don't you dare play dumb, Lainey," Lilly reprimanded, crossing her arms over her chest. "You are up to something and everyone can see it. Whatever you're planning to do, we should know what it is."

"I'm just trying to look out for us. If I can get him to like us, maybe he won't torture or kill us in the next couple of weeks. That's all."

"That don't seem like all," Jim said, sipping his coffee loudly. "The way you's carryin' on over there, I'd say you're lookin' to get him to do more than just *like* you."

"And what if I am? What if the only defense I have for my children is to get that man to care about me enough that he can't bring himself to kill me or those babies when the time comes? I have to do something, and this is the best I've got."

"Hoss know what yer up to?"

"Of course he does." Her eyes were a warning. Chris knew the look well. It was a look she'd given him many times in social situations when he was about to say something she didn't want anyone else to hear. She needed to put an end to this conversation lest someone overhear it.

"How soon will we get there?" Chris asked, moving the conversation elsewhere. "To the island?"

"He says we should be there by nightfall." Her shoulders relaxed as she looked back toward it. "Maybe we can spend tonight on the beach... Tomorrow we can go put flowers on Bertie's grave... maybe take a trip up to the summit."

"That sounds lovely," Chris said, cutting her short as he noticed Maria making her way toward them. "I think Juan Jr. was hoping to talk to you - his father's been taking up all your time and I know he wanted to check in on you... maybe you should go and find him." He flashed her the look that she would know meant *'someone you don't want to talk to is coming up behind you.'* Ten years of marriage had at least given them their own silent language. That could come in handy while they were stuck with these men.

"Right." She said, acknowledging the look. "I'll talk to you all in a bit. I thought I saw him go into the dining room." She hurried off toward the stairs just as Maria joined them.

"Well?" she demanded, avoiding eye contact with Lilly. "Was I right? Is she up to something?"

"Nothing so grim as an attack," Chris assured her, not entirely convinced of it himself. "She's just trying to get him to care about her so he won't hurt her or the babies."

Maria rolled her eyes. "She is the only one who has access to him. He won't even talk to the rest of us. Why isn't she planning to kill him? If it were me, I'd be flirting my ass off until I could get him alone and undressed so I could slice him open from one end to the other." She made a slicing motion with one hand. "Like a fish."

Jim raised an eyebrow in Chris's direction, once again lifting his coffee cup toward him. "Ye' know what? I don't feel so bad about the room now... You probably need it more than I do... Lordt knows, if I's you, I'd be sleepin' every night with one eye open."

"Do you think that's what she's planning?" Lilly still had her eyes on the horizon, and she spoke dazedly without looking away. "To get him to fall in love with her so she can get him defenseless and try to kill him?"

Chris couldn't imagine the woman he'd known for ten years to be capable of thinking up such a thing, let alone doing it. He shook his head. "No, I don't think so. Al could never kill anyone."

"No, but he could..." Jim nodded toward Jack, who was now standing near the dog saying something to Dario. "...all she'd need to do is get him defenseless."

Lilly shook her head. "Lainey couldn't do that. She has too good of a heart to want to kill someone."

Maria's head turned sharply toward her. "I killed someone. Are you saying I don't have a good heart?"

Jim straightened his back and peered down into his cup. "Welp, I'm gonna' go fix myself another cup. It's too good not to. Best of luck to ye', beanstalk."

He watched Jim walk away and wondered if he shouldn't have found a reason to follow him as he stood between Maria and Lilly. The sudden tension in the air was thick enough to cut with a knife. This was not a situation he wanted to be in. He'd almost prefer to be locked in chains in the bottom of Captain Cook's ship... at least he'd be safer there than in the middle of these two women.

Lilly kept her chin held high. "How's your room?"

"It's fine." Maria matched her cool tone.

"How'd you get them to give you your own room?"

Maria smirked. "I flirted with Juan Jr. and he gave it to me."

"Figures."

"What, like it's a bad thing to use your powers as a woman to get the things you need?" Maria's head was moving with each word like it might swivel off and roll away. It was amazing to him that so much attitude could be pent up inside such a tiny person. "It's not like I slept with him... It is not my fault men are easily persuaded by pretty women... and I'm not a bad person for using that to my advantage. You can judge me all you want with your nose stuck up in the air like that, but I sleep on a bed now while you sleep on a floor."

Lilly looked up at Chris. She had it too... the same pent up attitude in her tiny body... only her head didn't swivel. It was still. It was her eyes that gave her away as they pierced into his soul. "Doesn't it bother you, the way she flirts with every man that looks at her?"

Chris put both hands up in surrender. "I want no part in this."

"No, it does not *bother him* because he knows who I love. Men are built a certain way. We acknowledge their strengths and celebrate them for it. We have strengths too, you know, and women like you make women who use them feel like less for it... With *my* strengths, I can take a man down easier than he can. So can you if you used them... so can Alaina."

Jim grinned at him from his place near the bistro table, his eyes flickering from the woman to his left to the one on his right. He mouthed the word *'sorry'* and joined Jack and Dario against the railing.

"Alaina is not going to kill anyone," Lilly said proudly, crossing her arms over her chest. "Like I said, she's got too good of a heart."

Maria's hands were curled into fists at her sides. "And women who are capable of killing a man don't."

"No." She didn't look at her, but kept her eyes focused on the island as the ship slowly turned toward it. "I'm just saying Alaina couldn't do it... even if she wanted to."

"Could you do it?" Maria asked, with slightly less venom in her voice.

"In a heartbeat."

"Really? You, the one with her nose in the clouds? You could kill someone? Wouldn't you be too worried about getting blood on your shoes?"

Lilly smiled. "If it were me that he wanted an audience with, I would also flirt my ass off, get him naked, and kill him... I'd just make him buy me new shoes right before I did it."

Chris wasn't sure if he was relieved that the two of them had found some common ground or more terrified than ever. He'd never thought about murdering someone in such a coldhearted way. He'd only ever thought of it as something he might have to do to defend himself or other people... Were all women this ruthless?

Maria laughed loudly at that. "Maybe someone needs to tell your husband *he* should sleep with one eye open, too."

Lilly joined her in laughter. "Oh, he sleeps with both eyes open."

Feeling like it was safe to leave them to their sinister devices without either of them ripping the other's head off, Chris took the opportunity to cross the deck and join Jim, Jack, and Dario in what he hoped would be a much lighter conversation.

"Sorry 'bout that, buddy." Jim smacked him on the back as he took a place at his side. "Didn't mean to leave ye' to the wolves."

"Wolves would've been safer."

Jim chuckled. "Don't I know it? Both of them women scare the hell out of me."

Chris smiled back toward them, where they appeared to finally be settling into comfortable discussion. "I don't know which one is more terrifying... Yours seems so sweet on the surface... but she didn't mind letting me know she could rip a man's throat out if she wanted to."

"That's my girl, alright." He tipped the coffee cup to his lips while he watched her. "She's as sweet as pie until she ain't. And when she ain't, you better grab your ass and run cause' she'll take hold of ye' and turn ye' every which way but loose."

Chris laughed, setting his coffee cup down on the table. "I wonder if they know we're terrified of them?"

Jim nodded slowly, watching them. "Oh, believe you me, both them women know we're scared shitless... Worth it though. If ye' ain't a little scared, ye' ain't living."

Izzy motioned for Jim to pick her up, and Jim pulled her up into his arms, leaving an opening for Jack and Dario to step a little closer. "What about you, Hoss? You scared of Alaina?"

He frowned. "No... Why? Should I be?"

Jim laughed. "You'd know better than me, buddy. Ye' hear we're headed for our island? It's just there." He pointed ahead of them. "We'll be there by nightfall. Gonna' spend the next few weeks holed up there."

Jack's face lit up as he followed the direction of Jim's finger. "I didn't think we'd ever see it again."

Jim rocked Isobel to one side. "Neither did I."

Again, Chris felt on the outside of whatever bond they'd created on *their* island. They all viewed it with a sentiment he couldn't relate to. He wondered where they might be if he and Maria had been able to get on the raft. Would he, too, view it with so much nostalgia?

Dario looked out toward it. "I'll be glad of the solid ground beneath my feet for a few weeks."

Jack nodded in agreement. "It'll be nice to spread out a bit... Do you think your father would let us roam freely? It's not like we can escape anywhere."

Dario shrugged. "It's hard to say what he would and wouldn't do on any given day."

Jack propped his forearms on the railing. "Alaina's asked him several times if he still intends to kill us if we can't find the storm. You know him better than any of us. When he says he still intends to, does he mean it?"

Dario exhaled loudly and ran a hand over his auburn hair. "He's never made a threat that he didn't follow through on. Not once in my life."

"We'd put up a fight if it came to that," Jack assured him. "You know that. What would happen if the result of that fight didn't end up in his favor? Does the threat end with him?"

Dario knelt down to scratch the dog's ears. "If you're asking me whether or not I shall forgive you for killing my father, I'm afraid the answer is no. But I am not the one in line to assume command of this ship if you are asking if we shall retaliate. My brother is the one the men would look to, not I."

Chris knelt beside him, smiling as the dog licked his face. "What's his name?"

"Her," he corrected. "Luna."

"Hi Luna." He scratched the top of her head. "Dario, I know he's your father, but you have to understand we have just as much desire to live a better life as you do. None of us will just lay down and die... and none of us want to fight."

Dario nodded. "I know that. I realize the bizarre predicament we find ourselves in - all of us attempting to be civil while his intention for you lingers beneath every spoken word. You must know I am not without a heart, and I would not be so callous about his actions if I did not truly believe in his mission. I feel sorry for him for what he's become in this time. And I believe wholeheartedly that everything he does from now until we complete this mission shall disappear from your existence. You won't remember this conversation or the things he has done. If you are killed, you shall be revived... You will all live a better life... a life he will never have been a part of... the moment I get that name."

"Don't you worry about your own existence?" Chris asked as they both stood. "What if one of the descendants of the man you kill is somehow related to your birth? An introduction, an interruption... the slightest action has a million tiny reactions that shape the world we know. What if you kill that man and suddenly none of you exists because one of those tiny events doesn't happen and prevents your father's parents from ever coming together?"

"We've discussed that." Dario looked toward the quarterdeck where Juan Josef stood. "And it's a risk we're willing to take... if we stopped existing, we wouldn't even know it, would we?"

Jack tilted his head a little. "If you believe so much in this mission... if you believe everything that happens between now and then will be erased... why not let us fight him? Let me save my future wife from him. You can see the way he looks at her... you know what it is he wants from her. Let me fight him. If he dies, he shall be revived, right? I would stay and help you find the storm... all of us would help you to erase what we did so you could have that life with the father you want him to be. I would love to forget everything that's happened since he came upon us... to know he'd never laid a hand on her. I'll help you. Please, let me help her."

Dario frowned. "I know how hard this must be for you, but if the mission should somehow be unsuccessful, neither me nor my brother would willingly take the risk that would come from turning the other cheek."

Chris crossed his arms over his chest. "Then lock him up and let your brother captain the ship... we won't have to fight and nobody will have to die. We will help you get to the future and we'll wait for your return. Hell, I'll kill the ancestor myself if you'd like. And if it falls through, we'll have a chance to get away... Don't answer now. Think about it. Talk about it with your brother. We don't need to figure this out right now. We have a few weeks."

"I'll consider it. And I'll talk to my brother, but it is a dangerous thing you're doing, plotting behind his back. If he catches you, I needn't tell you what might happen."

"Will you turn us in?" Jack asked.

"No. Nor will my brother. But speak no more on the matter, especially when you are in your rooms together. Nothing you say to each other on this ship goes unheard."

Chapter Sixteen

I'd been anxious to get back to Zachary and Cecelia with the knowledge I'd be returning to the place they were both conceived. I'd hurried back down to our room to find the cradle pulled up to the side of one of the wingback chairs where Magna sat with a watchful eye. Fetia was seated in the chair on the opposite side of her, Kyle between them on the floor. I watched from the doorway as Magna served as both translator and teacher.

It was a casual conversation; one about their favorite childhood memories, but Magna used every translation as a way to introduce the English words to Fetia, encouraging her to repeat each word after she said them.

I admired her patience and hoped I could one day learn the kind of natural maternalism that radiated off of her. She was so instinctively nurturing in everything she did or said; it was hard for any of us not to view her as a mother-figure in our lives... even Bud, who was almost old enough to be her father, looked to her when all felt lost.

I imagined her daughter, wherever she was, had to be feeling Magna's absence, maybe more so than anyone else we'd left behind. I sometimes missed her when she was just in another room. I could only imagine what someone who'd grown up with this kind of mother must've been going through. No, Juan Josef couldn't take her away from the daughter that was waiting for her. He wouldn't touch her. I wouldn't let him.

She smiled at me when she noticed me standing in the doorway, giving me the familiar nod that communicated *'the babies are fine.'*

"She seems to be picking up the words quickly," I observed as I joined them in the seating area.

Kyle smiled proudly. "She's very smart."

"She's got a good teacher," I said, noting that Magna tapped on her temple and pointed at Fetia after Kyle had said the word *'smart,'* inviting her to repeat the word.

Fetia smiled a wide smile, her bright white teeth a stark contrast to her Sienna complexion. She really was beautiful, and it was no mystery why Kyle had taken an interest in her. She had eyelashes that were likely the reason modern day women wore eyeliner, dark black and thick to make the whites of her eyes seem almost fluorescent where they housed her caramel eyes. Her skin was smooth and uninterrupted by blemishes or freckles where it encased a slender nose that led down to lips that pouted without effort. She was naturally slender, but with all the right curves, and she held a youthful wonderment in her expressions as she experienced life—even under the circumstances we were stuck in. Around all of that, she glowed... I'd always heard about the "pregnancy glow" in books and television shows, but I'd never seen it before her. She was radiant with it.

Kyle, when observing him as the father of the child inside her, no longer looked like the boy I once knew so well. He was still young at seventeen, but he wasn't a child anymore, and I felt as though I were looking at a stranger in the man I suddenly recognized across from me.

Where his skin had once been spotted with acne, it had smoothed as he grew out of puberty and he'd grown a short wheat-colored beard around a mouth that had grown to fit teeth that once appeared too big. Even outside of his matured features and improved skin, his eyes were older. Through those eyes that were no longer innocent, he looked at Fetia, not the way a boy lusts after a girl, but the way a man looks at a woman and recognizes her as his whole heart.

"We're headed back to our island," I said, unable to pull my gaze from Kyle now that I'd really noticed him. "September is still several weeks away. We're going to stay there while we wait… gather supplies."

Kyle, unlike the others, didn't seem at all excited about the prospect of returning to a place we all had spent so much time in. He merely nodded in acknowledgement. "Alaina, can we talk for a minute? In private?"

"Of course we can." I motioned toward the hallway, and he stood to lead me out into it. I followed behind, sensing the tension in his shoulders and anxious to find out what might be wrong.

"You don't approve," he said, not waiting for me to even fully exit the room to get started. His single arm was held defensively across his chest where he gripped the remaining upper half of his other.

"Of you being married at seventeen?" I scoffed. "Of course I don't approve. You were just a boy when that plane crashed. Can you blame me?" I sighed. "Your mother's not here and I can't help feeling like we all failed her by not protecting that boy from the world so he could take his time growing up."

He drew his eyebrows together, releasing his arm to run his hand through his hair. "But I'm not that boy anymore, am I? We've all had to grow up after that plane crashed. Even you. You might think I'm being naïve or that it's some passing fling I'll regret when I'm older, but you're wrong." He looked over my shoulder into the room. "I love her. With all my heart, I love her. And even if I'm wrong about love, she is carrying my child and I won't ever be the absent father mine was to me. She's my wife and my family now, whether you like it or not. Wherever I go from now on, she will be by my side. If we get out of this, I want so badly to go wherever you go; stay wherever you end up staying; learn to be the man I want to become from Jack and Jim and Chris and Bud; the parent I want to become from you… but I won't go where my family's not welcome."

My heart sank in my chest. Disappointed as we all might've been that he'd made such a hasty decision to leap into adulthood without informing anyone, who were any of us to treat him like a child now that he had? Who was I to judge anyone after the things I was planning to do? I could barely get a handle on my own emotions. I was in no position to tell him what he could and couldn't feel. "Of course, your family is welcome, Kyle." I wrapped my arms around him and wasn't sure if I was comforting him or if he was comforting me. "Of course they are. I'm sorry if I made you feel like they weren't. We will love her and your baby just as much as we love you, I promise."

I could feel the relief pouring from him as he tightened his arm around me. "Are we really going back to our island?"

I nodded against his shoulder. "Yes."

He pressed his cheek against mine and whispered so quietly I barely heard the words, "the gun is still there."

I thought about those five words as the day dragged on. It was naïve to assume I was the only one with a plan, and keeping it from the others might be more dangerous than telling them. One of them could try something before I had a chance. Once we were a safe distance away from the ship, I would tell them all about our plan for Juan Josef. They needed to know we weren't just waiting for Juan Josef to decide our fate. We were taking it into our own hands.

I found myself counting the seconds through lunch and dinner, staring out the windows of the ship as the summit became more distinct; as the trees that climbed its side grew more green, eager to step foot on the sand of my home. I could almost feel the warm sandy dirt beneath my feet and felt somehow safer for it.

I hadn't given it a proper goodbye when we'd left with Captain Cook. Between Jack and Chris and the awkwardness of making the decision to leave one for the other, I hadn't had the chance to comprehend what it meant to have that island at my back.

I had died on that island, and I had woken up with a new life; a life surrounded by family. It had washed away the grief I'd carried and introduced me to sides of myself I'd never known were a part of me. That island gave me strength. It gave me peace. It gave me love and joy and children. Silly as it seemed to have mourned the loss of a plot of land in the middle of the ocean, I had, and I was grateful for the opportunity to touch it one final time.

I'd wrapped the babies in a sling and stood at the bow of the ship, watching beneath a bright blue moon as the black shadow of the summit came within reach to loom high over the ship. Jack stood behind me, my back pressed against his chest as he gripped the rail on each side of my arms.

I sighed as the ship slowed and prepared to anchor, laying my head against him and closing my eyes as the wind sent wisps of hair to tickle my eyelids. We were home, with all its familiar smells and sounds. Home. It didn't matter what we'd need to do while we were there or what Juan Josef's death might mean for the rest of us. We were home. I didn't worry about what Juan Josef might think seeing us standing on the bow together like we were. It didn't matter that the threat of death or murder was growing closer by the second. At that moment, there was only Jack's solidness behind me and home in front of me.

"I may have found another way," he whispered softly against my temple. "A way to avoid all of it."

"How?"

He rested his chin on my shoulder. "We don't need to talk about it now... not here... But I wanted you to know that before we step onto that island. I'll tell you when I know it's certain... when we aren't on this ship with men attempting to overhear us."

He released the railing with one hand to brush it over the top of Zachary's head. "Are you ever afraid of me, Red?"

I laughed softly at the way his mind shifted from one thought to another. "No. Why?"

"Even though I killed someone?"

I leaned my head against the side of his. "Not at all. Why? Did you think I was?"

He shook his head slightly against mine. "Jim and Chris asked me earlier if I was afraid of you... they were joking about how terrified they were of Lilly and Maria. And that made me wonder if you were afraid of me for what I did. I'd never thought to ask after I returned."

I smiled at the thought of both of those large men being afraid of the two smallest women among us. "No Jack, I'm not afraid of you. I *am* curious what you said to them, though. *Are* you afraid of me?"

I could feel his smile against my temple. "I said no, but I'm maybe more afraid of you than anyone I've ever met."

"Me?" I chuckled, laying my hand over his on Zachary's head. "Why?"

"Honey, if you could just spend a few seconds in my head, seeing all the ways you could completely destroy me, you'd understand."

I laced my fingers into his, pulling his hand up to my lips. "I would never do anything to hurt you. Not ever."

"I know, but that doesn't mean you still can't destroy me."

"How so?"

I felt him take in a deep breath of air. "I could disappoint you... that look you gave me the last night we were here when I told you I knew someone had gone into the bathroom on the plane... The disappointment in your eyes was unbearable. You could give me that look again and destroy me."

I reached back to run my knuckles over his cheek.

"You could get hurt. God help me, I can't help myself from thinking of all the ways that man could hurt you every time you leave with him... and sitting on my hands, making small talk as if that threat isn't there all day every day while he hurt you... that would destroy me."

I let my hand fall from his cheek to glide down his forearm where it was wrapped around me and our children.

He kissed my temple. "Or... worst of all, you could wake up one day when we're older and realize I'm not enough... you could fall out of love with me, and that would kill me."

I turned my face so I could see his. "You can worry about me getting disappointed or hurt all you want, but don't you dare worry that I'll ever stop loving you. It's your breath in my lungs that keeps me breathing, not mine. Remember? I ran out, and you gave me yours. To stop loving you would be like holding my breath and waiting for my body to shut down. It's impossible to do."

He relaxed and let out an airy laugh. "Who's the rehearsed one now?"

I grinned. "It's not rehearsed, just front of mind... especially now that we're here where it all happened."

He pulled me closer against him. "Dario said they'll want to send the men ahead in the morning before the rest of us to make sure we're alone. If Uati found it—

"If he did, he'd have found it empty and gone home. If he didn't, maybe Uati can take care of our little problem for us. I'm not afraid now that we're here... For the first time since I woke up with Juan Josef in our room, I'm looking forward to tomorrow."

Chapter Seventeen

I'd been staring out the window, unable to sleep, when Cecelia woke the rest of the room with an ear-piercing cry I'd never heard from her. She vomited twice and would not be consoled. I'd bathed her and rocked her and bounced her and rubbed her back for an hour in an attempt to relieve her of the stomach ache that had her screaming at the top of her lungs.

Along with the rest of us, her sobbing kept Zachary awake too. Not to be outdone by his sister's screams, he howled even louder. As one hour turned into two, and neither Jack nor I nor Magna or Lilly could console Cecelia, I sobbed alongside them.

I couldn't fathom what was hurting her. Magna suggested colic, but as all her suggestions failed to quiet her, I assumed something far worse was going on. Was she in pain? Had she caught whatever sickness was working its way through the sailors below deck? The thought of something bigger tormenting my daughter had me seeking out Anna's medical advice, only to find the couch where she slept vacant.

My heart sank at the sight of the blanket thrown back on the sofa. Anna wasn't in the room. Of course she wasn't. She would've come to my aid if she had been and I'd have realized that if I wasn't so so sleep deprived. She couldn't have left without someone coming to retrieve her since they kept our doors locked at night, and I wondered if the sickness downstairs had gotten worse.

"Dario came for her," Bruce informed me from the opposite sofa, his tone heavy with contempt. She'd been spending all her free time away from the sick men with Dario to discuss what they would do once they reached the future. Every day, it became increasingly evident that there was an attraction blossoming between the two of them that Bruce had hoped to have for himself, and he made no attempt to hide his jealousy. "When I asked him where he was taking her, he said Juan Jr. had symptoms and he needed her help."

"I need her…" I cried, bouncing with Cecelia as she worked up to another scream. "Something's wrong and I don't know what else to do. What if she's got what the other men have?"

"Let me see her," Jim said evenly, his back cracking loudly as he stood from his pallet on the floor and stretched.

Willing to try just about anything, I handed her to him and hovered over his shoulder as he sat on the edge of the wingback chair and placed her on her stomach over his knees. With one hand cupped under her cheek to keep her head supported, he bounced his legs in small motions, subtle but quick and comparable to vibration. Her cries wobbled with his movement but gradually became quieter until she was completely silent.

"How did you know to do that?" I whispered, feeling like a fool that I didn't as I watched him expertly run his free hand up and down her back in rhythm with his legs to lull her to sleep.

He shrugged. "Seen my cousin do it when hers was fussin' like 'at. Figured I'd give it a shot. Lordt knows you tried everything else."

"Was something wrong with your cousin's baby?"

He shook his head and smiled up at me. "Sometimes babies just get sick, darlin. Everything's new to 'em and their bodies are just adjustin' to it. It's probably a little indigestion, is all. We'll get it figured in the mornin.' Go on and lay down for a while. She ain't goin' nowhere."

I looked out the window at the dusk that was beginning to lighten the sky and give color to our island. There was no way I was going to sleep. I was traumatized. "It's almost morning… You think they might let me go find Anna? Just to be sure there's nothing major happening that could cause her to cry like that?"

"With the lungs these two got on 'em, I doubt anyone's left still sleepin.' Go on ahead and knock on 'at door. I'll keep an eye on her."

I stared down at her where she'd passed out beneath Jim's hand. I couldn't shake the feeling that she was in pain, and I was reminded of Anna's warning that one day I would just know when one of them was hurt. I'd spent hours trying to get her to stop crying, but now that she was silent, all I wanted was for her to make noise again for fear she wouldn't ever wake back up.

"You should sleep," Jack said softly, and I noticed he was standing beside me with Zachary tucked into one arm. I wondered how long he'd been there and if he felt as frantic as I did.

"No," I insisted, turning toward the doors. "I'm gonna try to find Anna. Something's wrong with our baby, I know it. You stay with them."

"I can go find Anna," he placed his palm on the center of my back. "You should rest. You're exhausted."

"They're not gonna let *you* roam the ship." I moved away from his touch and hurried toward the doors. He followed behind me and stood to one side as I beat frantically on them.

"She's alright, Red. Calm down before you give yourself a heart attack."

"Don't tell me to calm down, Jack. That cry is not her normal cry. She's in pain. I can't lose her."

The door opened, and Mr. Gil stared at me through bloodshot eyes.

"I need you to take me to Anna," I ordered impatiently. "Something's wrong with one of the babies."

He took a deep breath and gripped the bridge of his nose tightly. "I surmised as much, given the incessant screaming."

"Dario came for her. He mentioned something was wrong with Juan Jr. Do you know where I might find them?"

Mr. Gil peered into the room, then back down the dimly lit corridor. "Aye, come on then. I'll take you to his room. *Only* you."

I didn't even look back as I rushed out into the hallway and hopped from toe to toe as Mr. Gil took what felt like a small eternity to shut and lock the doors.

He escorted me four doors down the same hallway and rapped lightly on the door. If Anna was in a room this close, she had to have heard Cecelia crying.

I heard movement inside but no voices and took an instinctively defensive step backward as Juan Jr. jerked the door open. "What?"

Even in the dim light from Mr. Gil's lantern, I could see his eyes were bloodshot, but they softened from the glare once he noticed my presence. "My apologies, Alaina. I didn't see you there. Is something wrong?"

I nodded, unable to control the tears that seeped out of my eyes. "I don't know what it is, but something's wrong with my daughter. I'm scared she might have what the other men have. I need Anna."

"She's not among you?"

I shook my head. "Dario came for her at some point in the night. He said something was wrong with you. I assumed she was here?"

He rolled his head back and let out the breath of a laugh. "Dario…" He offered an apologetic look. "I assure you, I am quite well. I cannot say the same for my lovesick brother. Mr. Gil, you may return to your post. I shall see to it that they both are returned."

He tightened the belt of his robe and placed a hand on the small of my back, ushering me in the direction of the stairs as he closed the door behind him.

"I heard her crying," he said softly as we began climbing. "My son cried like that not long after he was born. He cried all day and all night for almost a week straight before we were able to identify what ailed him."

"What was it?"

"The milk."

"What was wrong with the milk?"

There was sorrow in his expression, and I remembered we were talking about a son he no longer had. "I don't know," he said, "but for whatever reason, my wife's breast made him ill. It was my father that recommended we give him goat's milk. The same night we gave it to him, he stopped crying… and she didn't put him back on her breast again after."

"Do you have a goat onboard?"

He yawned as he escorted me up the second set of stairs. "We've eight of them. After we find your nurse, I'll take you down to collect a bit until we can go ashore. We may have a few bottles in the kitchen still from when…" He trailed off, unable to continue the statement.

Could that really be it? Was my milk making her sick? Suddenly, I felt a wave of guilt wash over me. Getting her to latch on had been a struggle since the first day. She always fought me. Maybe somehow she knew it was poison to her and I had been forcing her to drink it, anyway.

Juan Jr. smiled down at me as we came out to the cool early morning air on the top deck. "My brother has never met a pretty woman he didn't fall in love with." He extended his arm. I followed it, seeing the smallest hint of the sun's rays far off on the horizon, and just beneath them, on the floor of the ship, two silhouettes seated side by side in conversation.

Her head was rested on his shoulder, bits of her thin hair blowing with the breeze, and I could see one of his hands rested behind her back as the other pointed outward in illustration of whatever words he was speaking.

There was a part of me that wanted to turn away and give her the rest of the morning with him. Cecelia was asleep after all, and Anna hadn't had a second of happiness since our plane crashed. I didn't want to pull her away from this moment. Not after all she'd done for us. If anyone deserved to have a romantic moment away from reality, it was her. She so rarely smiled, and while I couldn't see her face, I knew she was definitely smiling.

"Should we interrupt them, then?" Juan Jr. whispered.

"I wish we didn't have to."

He grinned. "This will not be the last time my brother comes for her in the night. Dario is far too romantic to sit alone under the stars."

Despite myself, I laughed at that. Even if Dario was only looking for a short-lived fling, Anna could use one. I didn't feel so bad when their heads turned toward us at the sound of my laugh and Anna hurried to scramble onto her feet.

"What are you doing up here?" She asked, straightening the folds of her skirt as she joined us. Dario calmly folded the blanket they'd been seated on and strolled up behind her.

"I'm sorry," I said, "I didn't want to interrupt. It's just… Cecelia's been crying all night. Nothing I do helps. It's not a normal cry… she's screaming. No one's slept, and I didn't know what else to do."

"Probably colic…" She smoothed her hair self consciously. "Has she thrown up at all?"

"Twice. Jim finally got her to sleep, but I'm terrified something's wrong with her. She's never cried like that."

Juan Jr. cleared his throat. "My son was the same way. I suggested goat milk. We've got several down in the hull."

Anna pursed her lips. "That might help if she's colic… so would catnip tea. I saw a few cats onboard. Do you have any?"

Juan Jr. shrugged. "I'm not sure. The cook will be up soon. I can inquire if you'd like?"

She smiled at him. "Yes. Thank you."

"Catnip?" I asked, feeling defensive after I'd already poisoned her enough with my milk.

Anna nodded, and I noticed her hidden smile as Dario purposely brushed her fingers with his at their sides. "I know it sounds odd—it's part of the mint family and safe for humans, too. It's actually very good for colic and nausea and upset stomachs. You just need a small amount in boiling water. We'll strain it and give her a bit whenever she gets like that. How did Jim get her to sleep?"

I sighed. "He created a vibration in his legs by bouncing them softly. He laid her on her stomach over them and that was the only thing that helped."

She touched my cheek. "It's colic, honey. She's gonna be fine. And if she's asleep, you should take advantage of the chance to nap while you've got it. You look like you haven't slept in days. We'll give her goat's milk for a while and if we can rustle up some catnip, we'll make her a tea for when it gets bad. Don't worry. She'll be back to normal in no time."

"Are you sure it's not something else? I've never heard a baby scream like that... it couldn't be something wrong with her insides causing her pain?"

"Gas is quite painful," she assured me, "and if it were something more severe, she'd still be screaming. I'll come down and give her a thorough exam to be certain."

"Wait." Dario placed his hand on my shoulder to prevent me from heading back toward the stairs. "While we're alone up here... There's something we should all talk about."

I was anxious to get back to the room, but I didn't contest as he motioned for us to follow him out to the railing.

He looked cautiously around us before he turned to Juan Jr. "Tell them."

Juan Jr. put his hands into the pockets of his robe and sighed. "We cannot imprison him and your people cannot kill him. The men may respect me, but not enough to stand with me should I make a move against their captain. The men do not know what it is we hope to accomplish by going to the future. His death or capture would not be something that could be undone in their eyes, and therefore they would retaliate against me, my brother, and all of you. There are too many of them to fight."

"How many?" I asked.

"Thirty-five. I could possibly convince a handful to stand behind me, but not enough. We would still be outnumbered. I'm afraid I cannot do what your husband has asked."

I bit my lip. "But you would not retaliate? If something were to happen to him?"

Dario tilted his head. "Did you not hear him? It wouldn't matter. The men would see justice served."

I shook my head. "If it were done by one of my people, the leadership would fall into your hands... I'd rather be imprisoned by you than killed by your father."

Juan Jr. sighed. "I cannot give you permission to kill the man who raised me. I'm sorry. I know he is cold and heartless, but he is still my father." He ran a hand over his face and looked out over the ocean. "But I can't let him kill you either... I won't have that on my conscience. So I must help you escape."

Anna held up her hand. "But I have to go through time. I have to get to my son. I can't escape... I have to see this plan through."

Dario took her hand in his. "We're escaping with you, my love. You and I will still go through... the ship will be empty and free for the taking. The men left behind shall be servicemen—kitchen staff and waiters—and they won't fight us. They don't care who orders them. We'll sail away while our father is on the island. You'll all be safely out of his way before we return for him."

"But who will come back for us when we return from the future?" She asked.

"You all survived on this island for a year. He and his men will be fine while we wait for you in Otaheite."

I frowned. "Won't he be furious when you do finally come back for him?"

Juan Jr. grinned. "I'm looking most forward to that very thing." He offered me his arm. "Come, let us tend to your daughter first. We have more than enough time to prepare in the coming days. Anna, if you're quite confident in your diagnosis, perhaps I shall escort Alaina down to collect some goat's milk and check the kitchens for catnip while you check in on the baby?"

Anna smiled as Dario curled her arm into his. "I think that's a great idea. She won't sleep long and it'd be nice to have the supplies ready for when she does wake up."

I felt an enormous pressure in my heart release as I took Juan Jr.'s offered arm. How on earth Juan Josef managed to raise two decent humans when he was so evidently disturbed was a mystery. Their mother must have been a saint.

"You two go ahead." Juan Jr. stopped me mid-step. "There's one more thing I wish to discuss with Alaina before leaving the safety of the deck."

I watched Anna and Dario disappear into the stairwell before turning toward Juan Jr. His expression was painted over with concern. "This game you are playing with my father is a dangerous one. He may be deranged, but he is far smarter than you may give him credit for. He will find you out if he hasn't already. For your sake, I pray he is still so disillusioned by your likeness to my mother that he is unable to see what I can see."

"I won't have to now," I assured him. "Not if you're going to help us escape."

"We won't escape tomorrow, you know. You'd do best to stay away from him until we can. Use your child's illness as a means to avoid him. Keep her crying if you must before he can see your real intentions."

"And what intentions do you think I have?"

He offered a knowing smile that was meant more as a warning than it was anything else. "For the man who has threatened to kill your children and everyone you love so dearly? I should think you intend to kill him first. My father is no fool. He is wise enough to be suspicious of the very same thing. There is no other reason—not even the revenge upon an unfaithful lover—that a woman like you should warm to him. I beg of you, find any excuse to stay away. I cannot protect you from him otherwise."

Chapter Eighteen

The sun had risen by the time Juan Jr. and I returned to our floor with goat's milk, a bottle, and catnip from the kitchens. They'd unlocked all the doors and removed the guards, and Juan Jr. left me on my own once we'd reached his room. I could hear both Cecelia and Zachary crying even from his doorway and didn't stop to thank him as I hurried toward the double doors. I had a hand on the handle of my room when Mr. Gil's deep baritone called out from the stairs. "There you are. The captain has asked that you join him in the dining room straight away."

"My baby is sick, Mr. Gil. He'll have to find someone else this morning."

"No, he won't," he said sharply. "He is impatient that you are not there already. He wishes to discuss plans for your stay on the island and the treatment of the men. I'm afraid he insists."

"Do you hear her screaming? I can't leave her today. I'm sorry."

He continued down the stairs toward me, the determination on his face making it clear he would not be returning without me. "You can and you will. Whether or not you go willingly is up to you. I've been instructed to use force if I must."

My entire body cringed as he grew closer. "Fine. Wait here. I'll just drop these things off for Anna and be right out."

"Make haste. The captain is in a mood this morning and will not wish to be kept waiting much longer."

I rushed through the doors to find Magna bouncing a screaming Cecelia while Jack paced with Zachary. From the bloodshot eyes of everyone staring back at me, I gathered I was not the only one on the verge of a complete meltdown that morning.

"I'm so sorry. I had to go down to the kitchens and wait until the cook came in for the—

I frowned as I scanned the room. "Where's Anna?"

Lilly tilted her head to one side. "I was going to ask you the same thing. Isn't that who you went looking for?"

I set the supplies on the table and hurried to Magna's side to peek over her shoulder at Cecelia. "She hasn't been here? I was with her on the deck. She and Dario were going to come straight to the room to check on her while I got the tea and milk."

Magna shook her head as she continued to bounce, one hand tapping gently on Cecelia's bottom. "She never came. Cecelia woke up about five minutes ago. I'm pretty sure this is colic."

I laid a hand over Cecelia's head, relieved she wasn't feverish. "That's what Anna said too. She suggested catnip tea and switching to goat's milk for a while. I brought both."

"He's hungry," Jack said behind me, wincing as Zachary raised his volume by several decibels.

The lack of sleep was catching up to me. My mind was spinning as it searched for which direction it needed to go. Mr. Gil was waiting, Zachary was hungry, Cecelia was sick, Anna was missing, Juan Josef was growing suspicious, and everyone was waiting for me to do something.

I reached for Zachary. "Give him to me. I'll have to take him with me."

"Take him where?" Jack demanded as he surrendered him to me.

"Mr. Gil is seething outside that door because I'm not at breakfast... he intends for me to go one way or another... I'll need you to handle Cecelia until I get back. Take a little of this catnip and make a tea out of it. Let it cool down to lukewarm and give her a bit at a time. It'll help relieve the stomach ache. I don't know about the milk... maybe we should wait a little while before giving it to her? Anna didn't say... Where the hell is Anna?"

I was growing increasingly frustrated. So was everyone else as the babies continued to scream over us. I was angry at Anna— assuming in my clouded mind she and Dario had made a stop on their way to the room to finish whatever they'd started on the deck. I was angry at myself for taking so long when I knew both babies would need to be fed. And I was angry at Mr. Gil and Juan Josef for the fact that I was going to need to feed Zachary in their company. Everything that had happened and was happening in that moment felt like it was suddenly too much.

"It's alright," Magna said softly, acknowledging the breakdown I was teetering on the edge of. "Go. We can handle this."

I snagged the small nursing blanket, draping it over Zachary's head as I turned a circle, wondering what else I should do before I abandoned them with his screaming sister. "Are you sure?"

Magna held Cecelia against her shoulder with one arm as she poured out bits of catnip into a teacup with the other. "It's a crying baby, not an apocalypse, honey. We'll be fine. We don't want him coming down here if he grows impatient. I'll handle her."

I flashed Jack an apologetic look just before I hurried back toward the door with Zachary's screams muffled against my shoulder. In that fleeting bit of eye contact, I could see he was feeling just as overwhelmed and helpless as I was, and I wanted nothing more than to stay at his side and work together to treat her.

Where the hell was Anna in the single moment we really needed her?

I didn't look back again before I stepped out of the double doors to hurry past Mr. Gil and down the hallway. I couldn't stand the sound of either of them crying, and the least I could do was feed my son as soon as possible.

I could hear Mr. Gil's footsteps as he followed, keeping a safe distance behind me to save his ears.

Juan Jr.'s warning to stay away from his father sat at the forefront of my mind, and I prayed as I passed his door that he'd heard Mr. Gil's earlier insistence and had already made his way to the dining room ahead of me. There was a sense of security when it came to Juan Jr. after his involvement in the previous altercation and his ability to take command. If he was in the room, I was sure his father wouldn't hurt us.

I took the stairs two at a time, bouncing and speaking softly to Zachary the entire way to the dining room. I didn't even look up when I let myself in, and rushed to my seat near the head of the table. "My daughter is sick and I need to feed him. I'm going to need to spend most of the day with her." I sat and covered myself with the blanket, fumbling to move fabrics out of the way so he could finally latch on and quiet.

Only then did I look up at the table around me. To my right, in his normal seat, Juan Josef sat silently observing me. To my left, Juan Jr. sat at the opposite end of the table. Across from me, Anna sat beside Dario, both of them painted over with concern.

I frowned. "What are *you* doing here?"

Juan Josef sat back in his seat, folding his hands beneath his chin. "Imagine my surprise to come across your nurse holding hands with my youngest son on the way to breakfast this morning. I thought it only proper, since they were both awake and dressed for the day, that I ask them to join us for breakfast this morning." He inspected the blanket. "Pray, what is the matter with your children that has kept them crying through the night? Have they grown sick as well?"

Before I could answer, Anna straightened. "I didn't want to say anything before I knew for certain, but I think we should clear the ship as soon as possible. I think it's typhoid fever. If the babies have it, it could spread through your men like wildfire. You could lose most of your crew if we don't get ahead of it. The sooner we can all get on land and spread out, the better."

"Typhoid?" He leaned forward in his seat. "How can you be sure?"

She shrugged. "I can't, but the symptoms are there. Racing heartbeats, vomiting, abdominal cramps, and lethargy. The men have it and now one of the babies has it too. Whatever it is, it's contagious. We have some antibiotics left and if we can spread everyone out and isolate the sick, we won't lose anyone."

Suddenly, my limbs felt weak, so weak I could hardly hold on to Zachary. Typhoid fever? My baby had typhoid fever? I couldn't remember the history of it, but I was pretty damn sure it was deadly.

Juan Josef stared at her for a long moment, undoubtedly trying to find some sign of deceit, before he rose from his seat and crossed over to the doors. "Mr. Gil," he called down the hallway. "Gather the men and start disembarking immediately. Separate the sick. They'll need to be transported in their own sloop. Put the prisoners in with the sick, but keep your distance."

"Yes, sir. Right away, sir."

Juan Josef closed the door behind him, and a chill ran over my spine as he stuck a key into it and turned the lock. Meandering back to the table, he crossed his arms behind his back. "I imagine it is too late for the rest of us, given the amount of time you've all spent together this morning." He strolled to his seat, his eyes moving to each of us as he did so. "And I've questions I should see answered before we join them on land."

He pulled his chair out and sat down, picking up his fork and knife and cutting into the ham on his plate. "First, Dario. Tell me what reason you had for retrieving Miss... I'm sorry dear, what is your name?"

"Anna," she said shakily.

He smiled his sinister smile and looked back to Dario. "What reason did you have to retrieve *Anna* so late in the night and keep her into the early hours of morning? I've been told neither of you were on the lower decks to assist the sick."

"We're going to the future together," Dario said, looking down into his cup where he held it just beneath his lips. "I wanted to spend some time with her away from everyone else... Get to know her a little better."

"Get to know her better?" Juan Josef repeated sardonically. "By holding hands and whispering in the dark? You understand she will not exist to you in a matter of months, don't you? We are on a mission, and getting to know her a little better can do nothing but dilute that mission. You understand?"

Dario took a deep breath and nodded. "I know she won't exist to me, but while I'm here—

"*While you're here,* you will remain focused on the mission we have worked so hard to perfect. I cannot have you falling all over some whore and forgetting what's important!"

"She's not a whore," Dario said defensively.

"Oh, but she is." He looked over at me. "Isn't that right, my dear?"

All the eyes in the room were suddenly on me and my cheeks burned for it. I didn't answer—*couldn't* answer because of the betrayal Anna would surely feel for being excluded from plans that had included her name in such a way, so I looked down at the blanket and shifted Zachary in my arms.

"Tell me, *whore*," he continued, disregarding Dario entirely. "How will you treat the infected?"

She was still staring at me as she answered meekly. "Keep them a safe distance from the others—out in the fresh air. We have antibiotics onboard for the ones who get it the worst. There's not much left though, and we'll need to spread it out to only the most severe cases. For the less severe, catnip tea will help relieve the symptoms, and there's fruit high in vitamin C on the island we can collect to boost everyone's immune systems—even the ones who aren't sick. It can help prevent them from getting infected. Bruce knows the fruit well. He can turn it into a dessert so they don't get worried."

"Anything else?"

She shrugged. "The ones who are sick are going to need to stay off their feet. The sunlight, tea, vitamin C, and antibiotics should have them feeling better and able to join the rest within a week or so."

"Very well," he said and then there was a motion—a flash of movement in his arm as quick and swift as the flick of a wrist.

I couldn't process what was happening as his arm returned to his side and Anna's throat sprayed out across the table, covering the food, the blanket, and my face in her blood. Her wide eyes stared at mine and she made a clicking somewhere beneath her open throat as she struggled for a breath she'd never again be able to take.

"What have you done?!" Dario shouted, placing both his hands over the wound in an attempt to stop the bleeding.

"Is this not what you wanted?" Juan Josef asked somewhere far in the distance; far, far away from the vacant eyes staring back at me.

I was unable to comprehend the question, frozen as I was in time, staring at her as she stared back at me, neither of us able to respond to the world around us.

Juan Jr. was out of his seat. So was Juan Josef. There was scuffling and swearing and an evident fight going on just behind my head, but I stared into her eyes as she clicked.

"I'll fix this," Dario promised, moving his hands at various angles against the blood gushing from her neck in an attempt to stop it. "I'll erase this. You'll be fine. I promise. You'll never meet us... This will never have happened to you. You'll see, my sweet sweet girl. You'll be fine. Please... I'm so sorry."

"I'll find Liam." That was all I could say. That's all she would care about, and what she would've asked for if her clicking could've been translated into words. Slowly she fell forward and Dario caught her, pulling her over into his arms with no mind to the blood that covered him.

The clicking stopped.

He wept, and I stared as the blood spilled red over her light blonde hair. Unable to move or speak, I stared until my vision blurred and I could no longer make out the distinct shapes of their bodies. In the blurred lines, I only saw the quick motion of Juan Josef's arm and the spray of her blood over and over and over again. My face felt cold, and the chill had frozen me in place. I couldn't even feel Zachary in my frozen arms; forgot he was even in them.

Anna was dead.

Anna was the best person among us. She'd sacrificed everything for us. She'd saved all of our lives and we hadn't saved hers.

Anna was dead.

Anna, who only wanted to get to her son… who'd stitched us and treated us and waited patiently beside us… who'd rushed to the aid of the men holding us captive… who'd forgiven us over and over for putting our own plans ahead of hers… was dead.

"ALAINA!" Juan Jr. shouted, and I dazedly looked over at him. His father was unconscious on the floor at his feet. "Did you hear anything I just said?"

Slowly snapping out of hypnosis, I shook my head. "Is he dead?"

"No," Juan Jr. assured me. "But you need to get out of here before he wakes up. All of you. Get to the island. Use the blood as part of the sickness they think is onboard so no one will come near this room. Dario, send me any of my men if you see them. The ones we can trust."

Dario was just as frozen in time as I'd been, squeezing her lifeless body against his. "We have to bury her."

"For Christ's sake!" Juan Jr. pulled me out of my chair and into his side. "Dario, lock the door and take his key. Keep him here."

Dario stared down at Anna's lifeless body in his arms.

"Dario! Lock the door and take his key and do not let him out of this room until I come back. Tell me you hear me!"

"I hear you."

Juan Jr. fumbled with the lock, then rushed out of the room, shielding my blood covered body with his side as he hurried down the corridor. I clung to Zachary as the emotions welled inside me.

"What's happened?" Mr. Gil demanded from somewhere in front of us.

"Stay back!" Juan Jr. warned. "It's contagious. Where are the other prisoners?"

"They're at the boats, sir. Where is the captain? Is that blood?"

"We're exposed to it now. I'm afraid it's much worse than we thought. Gather whoever you can and get the hell off this ship before we all die of it! I'll bring the captain when I can determine if he has been infected or not. Go! Now!"

Several pairs of boots ran up the stairs, and we followed up behind them.

I could feel the sun against my closed eyes but couldn't bring myself to open them as Juan Jr. led me across the deck. I could hear the shipmen shouting and running, panic overruling logic as they all hurried to leave the sick ship.

"What's happened? Is she hurt?" Jack asked, and I felt his hands on me in inspection.

"Are you all accounted for?" Juan Jr. asked.

"All but Anna... Whose blood is this?!"

"Get in the boat. I shall lower you down. Get to the shore and take her someplace safe. I will join you soon."

Jack pulled me into his arms and I broke down then, sobbing uncontrollably. Someone took Zachary from me as he scooped me off my feet and held me tightly against his chest.

I kept my eyes squeezed tightly shut for fear that if I opened them, I'd see him slice her throat again. I felt us step out into the sloop and buried my face against his chest as we were lowered down.

"What happened?" Lilly asked.

"Is she stabbed? Is the baby alright?" Chris asked.

"Where's Anna?" Bruce demanded.

"Red," Jack whispered, his fingers running frenziedly over my body. "You have to tell me what happened. I need to know what's going on and where to look for a wound."

Slowly, I pulled my face away just enough to look up at him and shake my head. "It's not my blood," I whispered. Then I faced the others and took a deep breath. "Anna's dead."

PART II

It's not goodbye.

Chapter Nineteen

Everything felt like a dream. The world had a static haze around it as I stepped onto the shore I'd been so anxious to return to. I was on *our* island, and yet, nothing about it felt familiar without Anna. The lack of her presence was like a black hole, sucking everything that had once been beautiful about the island away to cast a dull grey hue over all of it.

Anna was dead. And I'd done nothing. I'd sat and stared and I'd done nothing to stop it.

'Is this not what you wanted?' Juan Josef had asked, and I heard those words over and over amid the fuzz that filled my ears.

Anna was dead, and not only had I done nothing to stop it, I had essentially been the one to kill her.

I killed Anna.

My ears were just as silent as they'd been during the plane crash that had brought us there. My face was cold and my legs felt like they might give way beneath me; like I might sink down into the sand with all the weight now stacked on my shoulders.

I killed Anna.

'I killed Anna... Is this not what you wanted?' Those words repeated over and over, my voice and his bouncing off each other as they volleyed for attention until they formed a steady static in my pulsing ears.

It was Cecelia's crying that cut through the static, and I turned to reach for her, recalling the words *'typhoid fever'* as two of the last words Anna had spoken.

Magna handed her over, and I pulled her against me, rocking her gently. I didn't know what typhoid fever was or how to treat it. Without Anna, I didn't know how to keep my baby alive. I killed the one person who could keep my daughter alive.

'Is this not what you wanted?'

I sat down in the damp sand on my butt and cried alongside her. Would I lose this daughter too? Didn't I deserve to lose everything after what I'd done to Anna?

'You are a selfish woman,' Maria's voice joined the growing crowd in my mind. And I was. I hadn't thought through what I was doing in that instance on the stairs when I confirmed his suspicion of her. How could I place her in danger? How could I have been so reckless when I knew him to be the monster he was?

Jack sat down in the sand beside me while the others silently made their way further up the beach. He kissed my shoulder and tucked my hair behind my ear.

"Juan Jr. was right," I whispered. "We don't belong here."

I could see his head slowly shaking in my peripherals while I stared out at the ship on the ocean. I could feel him trying to think of the right response, but there wasn't one.

"We're going to lose Cecelia too." I held her tighter against me as she continued to cry. "And probably Zachary since they've been kept so close together... Maybe everyone."

"Don't say that." He slid closer, forming his palm into the nape of my neck and pulling my temple to his lips. "We're not losing anyone else."

I blew out, pulling Cecelia away from my shoulder and against my bent knees to look down at her. "Yes, we will. The men are sick and so is Cecelia. Right before she died, Anna said the sickness is typhoid fever." I met his eyes then. "Jack, we're gonna lose everything we love... just like Juan Jr. said we would. We've already lost Anna and Bertie, and Cecelia is getting worse. He said we'd be made monsters for our time here, and we already are. It was my lies that killed Anna... not Juan Josef. We don't belong here."

I watched his expression then, and for the first time since we'd met, I saw a man without an answer; a man who was feeling just as defeated and helpless as I was. "We're not losing anyone else," he whispered again, but I could feel the lack of confidence around those words just as much as I was sure he did. He looked down at Cecelia, placing his finger into her grip, and he watched through somber eyes as she squeezed it to relieve the pain I could see all over her scrunched and tear-swollen face.

I rubbed her stomach gently, hoping to offer some kind of comfort, but she kicked her legs in protest and continued to cry.

Magna knelt with some effort on the opposite side of me and handed me the porcelain bottle. "The tea helps," she said softly, urging me to take it. "It'll settle her stomach so she'll stop crying."

I hadn't noticed how badly my hands were shaking until I took it from her, nearly spilling the little bit of liquid inside all over Cecelia.

Jack placed a hand over mine on the handle to settle me. "I'll give it to her," he said softly. "Thank you, Magna. Where's Zachary?"

"Lilly has him. He's alright." She kept her eyes on Cecelia as Jack pulled her from my legs and into his arms. "She'll be hungry. It's been several hours since she's eaten. Maybe we can give her a small bit of the goat's milk once she's settled?"

Jack nodded. "We'll give it a shot. Do you mind keeping Zachary for a little while? She's still in quite a bit of shock."

"Not at all, baby." She swept her palm down my hair. "You take as much time as you need."

Throughout the course of the day, Juan Josef's men set up camp far down the beach from where our people were reconstructing our old beach shelter. Five of their sick had been grouped with us on the sloop and were huddled under a tree about fifty yards down the beach. The rest wouldn't risk coming near any of the *'infected.'*

I kept the babies apart too, holding out hope that Zachary hadn't caught it, and I clung to every second I still had with Cecelia in a spot down the beach from the others.

I only held my son to feed him and kept him under a blanket so I didn't breathe on him. I wasn't even sure if typhoid fever was a viral infection, but I prayed it wasn't something that could be passed through my milk.

"Bruce mixed up some kind of natural immune booster with some of the fruit and algae," Jack whispered, sliding behind my back to wrap his arms around us. "He said any bit of vitamin C will help. He and Mr. Gil are giving it to the sickest now and then they're going to administer it to the healthy. Do you think we should give her some?"

I shook my head, looking down at Cecelia's tiny sleeping body in my lap. "She's too little still, I think... maybe if I take it, the vitamins can pass on to her... If she can even take my milk. God, I feel so goddamn helpless."

He kissed my temple. "We'll ask him for some when he's back. Our immune systems are strong and theirs are too. She's gonna be fine. They both will be... We'll all be alright."

"He slit her throat, Jack..." My mouth was suddenly dry. "He did it so fast... I didn't even know it had happened. There was no warning... He just..." I shook my head. "It was less than a second... And I just sat there staring at her... trying to figure out why her throat was making that sound; why blood was pouring out of her. I didn't realize she was dying in front of my eyes... and now she's gone and I don't know what to do."

He held me tighter, kissing the spot between my neck and my shoulder, leaving his lips there as his breath hitched. "It could've been you."

"It *should've* been me," I whispered. "He killed her because I made him think it was her you'd slept with. The knife may have been in his hand, but it was my words that took her life. Same as when he placed that whip in my hand and told me to strike. I'm just as much the monster he is… maybe even worse. It should be Anna sitting here. She could fix this… I'm worthless."

"You are not worthless and you are *nothing* like him, Red." He said it through his teeth, gripping my shoulders and turning my upper body so I could see the frustration in his eyes. "And I refuse to let you go down this same road of self destruction you went down with the last tragedy that touched you. You will not beat yourself up and slide into misery for this. You will not push yourself away from me or the rest of the people who love you. You will not let this man destroy us. *He* did this. Not you. You can mourn her death, but don't you dare make it yours."

"I wanna go home," I whispered, breaking into pieces at the word *'home'* because it didn't have the same meaning anymore.

Home should've been right where I was, in Jack's arms on the beach of our island with our babies, but it wasn't. Home was suddenly my mother's arms; the complete guiltless relief that would come from having the meltdown I so wanted to have while she held onto me. She wouldn't judge me or have any expectations of what I should and shouldn't feel. She'd let me be as weak and miserable as I needed to be, and she'd hold on to me until I was done, loving me all the same once the tears finally dried.

During the year and a half we'd been gone, I'd had brief moments of longing for my mother, but it all came to a head then. I missed her entirely as Jack pulled me against his shoulder in an attempt to comfort me and felt nothing like her. Why hadn't I spent more time in her arms? There were so many times, so many mistakes that could've been resolved if I'd just run to her and let her hold me until I was done crying. I'd been too proud and stubborn to show emotion to her as an adult, and I wondered how different my life would've been if I had gone to her when I needed to.

"We need to wash this blood off," Jack said softly, attempting to scrub my knuckles with his thumb. "Why don't we go up to the waterfall and clean up before it gets dark? There are still some old clothes in the cave you can change into. We can grab some guava on our way up. Get some vitamin C into both of us. Neither of us can be of any use to Cecelia if we get sick."

I looked back out toward the ship. "What if they come?"

"We'll take everyone with us. We'll spend the night in the cave. They won't find us there in the dark. It took us months to find it in broad daylight. I'll come down with Jim, Bruce, and Chris in the morning and we'll figure out how to handle them then."

Chapter Twenty

Chris

Chris sat at the nearly extinguished fire staring out at the massive roaring waterfall where Bruce was picking fruit as the sun began to rise.

They'd spent the night in the cave, and it had been a long one. No one spoke after all that had happened with Anna, and they'd all gradually fallen asleep with plans for the men to return to the beach the following morning to administer fruit and check the status of Juan Josef's location.

He hadn't been able to comprehend why the others were so sentimental about the island but, as he stood alone taking in the scenery around him, he was beginning to understand it. The place was beautiful in every way. Lush green trees grew abundant with pops of pink, white, lavender, and red, fruits and flowers spotting the landscape in abundance. It was quiet, with just a subtle pulse of the ocean's waves far beneath the sizzle of the leaves above him blowing with the breeze.

Everywhere he looked, there were remnants of the life they'd lived there. Inside the cave, there was bedding, baskets, candles, and markings all over the walls.

Outside, there was a cage they'd kept birds in, a wash bin, and a makeshift shower. The fire pit had a grill and seats carved out around it where he could just imagine them all sitting and sharing stories about their lives.

Of course, this place meant something. They became a family in this spot. Every inch of this island had been home to them for a year. Every part of it likely sparked some memory of them together.

He focused back on Bruce, noticing the way his left leg dragged a little as he moved from tree to tree, and he wondered how severe their injuries might have been after the crash. Becoming solely focused on finding a way through time and lying about their identities, he'd forgotten to ask the details of their own experiences after the crash. He'd known they lost the pilot - knew bits and pieces of their time on the raft and major events on the island, but he didn't know the details of how they'd endured here, and he felt guilty for it as he watched Bruce limp along the waterfall's edge.

There were two different fruits Bruce seemed interested in collecting. One was a small yellow-green color that grew nearer to the waterfall. The other was further out from the falls and was more oblong. It grew in smaller trees amid clusters of white flowers, and Bruce pulled down variations of red and green, tossing them in a separate basket.

He picked each piece of fruit with a lack of ambition, as though his entire existence was ripped away alongside Anna, and his body was just pressing on to do menial tasks without the mind to drive it. He seemed the most devastated by the loss of her; not in a verbal way - the man had barely spoken two words since it'd happened - but he carried his sorrow heavily in his sunken posture and distorted expression. Wherever his mind was, he was sure Anna was at the top of it.

Chris felt like he should help, but joining him in that moment felt like it might be an intrusion on the pain he was clearly down there trying to cope with.

"He ain't never gonna' be the same," Jim whispered, appearing at Chris's shoulder to look out in the same direction. "Poor summbitch never got up the nerve to tell her he was crazy 'bout her."

Chris touched his chest where Anna had once stitched a bullet hole that ripped through him. "I didn't know her like you did, but she seemed like an amazing person... I wouldn't be alive if it weren't for her."

"None of us would," Jim said, running a hand hard over his face. "She was the best of us. Only thing in this world that mattered to her was gettin' home to her boy, and it rips me apart knowin' she ain't never gonna' get there. That girl put every bit of her heart into healin' us while she waited to get back to him. Never complained about it neither. Just did what she had to... like keepin' us alive was gonna' get her there in the end. Don't make no sense why anyone would want to hurt a hair on her head."

Chris shook his head, keeping his eyes focused on Bruce. "Even if Juan Josef didn't know how good she was, she was the only person with medical knowledge and he's got a ship full of sick men... Why would he kill *her* of all people? Why not me or you or anyone else?"

Jim spat to one side. "Like I said, it don't make no sense. That poor woman wouldn't have hurt a fly... hell, she was down there with the sick tryin' her damndest to get 'em fixed up."

"He's obviously more unstable than we thought. And Jack's ready to swim out there and murder him the first chance he gets. What do we do now?"

Jim blew out and kicked a rock to one side, glancing back toward the cave. "Hoss ain't thinkin' right. Hell, who could after seein' their woman and baby covered in blood like 'at? I agree we gonna' have to kill the rotten summbitch, but we gonna' have to do it right... make it look like an accident." He shielded his eyes as he looked up toward the summit. "Plenty of places for a man to have an accident here."

Bruce was heading back toward them, the baskets weighing down both arms as he struggled to walk uphill. "Come on," Chris said, already starting down the path, "maybe he'll have an idea of how we can do it."

"Ay tiny," Jim hurried ahead of him, "let me get that for ye.'"

Bruce stopped in his tracks and turned a little to shield one of the two baskets behind his body. "I've got it," he said a little breathlessly. "Are you all ready to go?"

"You *ain't* got it," Jim scoffed. "Hell, ye' look about as wore out as a baptist church fan in the dead of summer. Let me take one of 'em."

"I said I've got it," Bruce insisted, scowling at both of them. "Where's Jack? We need to get going."

Jim stopped suddenly and crossed his arms over his chest, tilting his head to one side as he observed the basket Bruce was attempting to keep behind him. "What the hell ye' doin' with those?"

Chris looked between them, frowning as they both stared each other down. "What are they?"

"Sea mango," Jim said, as if Chris should understand why that was relevant. "Did you give that to 'em yesterday?"

Bruce nodded, his cheeks reddening slightly.

Jim looked behind them toward the cave and back. "Them men ain't got typhoid, do they?"

"No," Bruce said, looking down at his feet.

"And Anna knew that too?" Jim continued.

"Yes."

"And when was you gonna' tell the rest of us what y'all were up to?"

Bruce took a deep breath and looked up. "Once it was done."

Jim shook his head slowly. "Ye' know Alaina and Jack's both up there eat up with worry that their baby's gonna' die. You was just gonna' let them keep thinkin' 'at?"

"We couldn't risk anyone finding out before we had the chance to get to Juan Josef."

Chris crossed his arms over his chest. "Could one of you please explain what the hell's going on?"

"Sea mango is poisonous," Jim said. "Anyone that eats it'll be dead in days - if not hours."

Bruce nodded. "And it'll look like they died from typhoid."

Jim sighed. "But you didn't have no sea mango on the ship. How'd ye' get 'em sick in the first place? And how was you gonna' kill 'em if we didn't come here?"

Bruce's shoulders slumped in resignation. "Killing the men on the ship wasn't part of Anna's plan. We were just going to give them the illusion that there was typhoid onboard so they wouldn't suspect us of having a hand in it when we poisoned Juan Josef."

"But you didn't have no sea mango on the ship," Jim repeated, raising an eyebrow.

"No, but I had lye soap, and I put just enough in the food going below deck to cause the men down there to look sick. I didn't put a deadly amount in… that was reserved for Juan Josef and his sons."

Jim swept a hand over his hair, leaving it to stand on end as he stared at the baskets. "But you're killin' 'em all now, aint ye?"

Bruce nodded. "For Anna."

"We gonna' walk down to that beach and there's gonna' be a whole mess of dead or near-dead men down there… how we gonna' explain bein' the only ones left alive when Juan and his sons get to the shore?"

"Won't have to." Bruce adjusted the basket against his forearm. "We won't be outnumbered anymore. We'll take the sons and kill that bastard."

"Wait," Chris held up his palm. "Why would we take his sons? We could be done with them and go on with our original plan… leave them here."

Bruce straightened. "Two reasons. One, we need someone to sail that ship. None of us know anything about a boat that size. And two, *we're* going to kill Richard Albrecht's ancestor, and they're the only ones that know *which* Richard Albrecht we'll need to look for. If we can prevent them from ever passing through time, Anna will still be alive." He flashed Jim a look shrouded with warning. "And none of you is going to stop this. We've never done a single thing for Anna and she's done everything for us. We are doing this for her, and I don't care what you have to say about it. She's earned this."

Jim nodded slowly. "You're right. She's earned a hell of a lot more than that. But we don't know how many's left on that ship. And we ain't got nothin' but an old pistol here to fight 'em with."

Chris glanced back toward the path that led to the shore. "If the beach really is full of dead bodies, there'll be plenty of weapons down there."

"Assumin' Juan Josef and his sons ain't on the beach already. If they are, they'll be armed and we won't."

Bruce set the baskets at his feet and rubbed his arms where he'd been holding them. "If they are, then we continue with the typhoid plan. Wait until they fall asleep to arm ourselves. They'll be too preoccupied with the sick to be concerned about what we're doing."

Jim shook his head. "They just killed one of ours in cold blood. If I'd done it to them, I'd be sleepin' with one eye open and pointed in their direction. Sick be damned."

"You guys ready?" Jack called as he jogged toward them from camp. "I want to get back in case Cecelia gets worse."

Jim waited until Jack caught up to them, then nodded his head in the direction of the two baskets. "It ain't typhoid."

"What do you mean?" Jack asked, and Chris watched as Jack's eyes landed on the mango, then on Bruce, then on Jim as he put it all together.

"Your baby's got colic," Jim assured him. "*Not* typhoid. Nobody's got typhoid. They been poisoned... and we're 'bout to walk into a cemetery on that beach."

Chapter Twenty One

I paced in front of the cave. Every single hair stood on edge and every single leaf that blew in the trees had me searching down the trail for signs of Jack, Jim, Chris, or Bruce returning from the beach.

'God, please let it be them that returns.'

They'd filled us in on Anna and Bruce's scheme. When they'd told me there was no typhoid, I thought I might fall over from the sheer force of emotion that welled inside me. Relief came first. Knowing Cecelia wasn't sick with some deadly infection had made my eyes water. So had the anger, however temporarily it had surfaced.

For as much as I wanted to be angry at Anna and Bruce for concealing their plans and making me worry over the life of my daughter, my own concealed plans had done far worse. I should've trusted her. I should've trusted all of them. Had I not taken things into my own selfish hands; had I trusted that any one of them could've been just as capable of forming a plan to rid ourselves of Juan Josef as I was, Anna would still be alive to see her significantly better plan come to fruition.

I tried not to imagine the almost forty dead—*or near dead*—bodies laying on the beach. Would their death have been quick or painful? I remembered the day Anna had pulled a sea mango from its tree and Magna had insisted with vehemence she drop it immediately. She'd then explained that every part of the plant was poisonous if ingested. She hadn't clarified, however, what would happen if any one of us would've eaten it... I had no idea what those men on the beach might be going through; wasn't sure if I wanted to know either.

I wondered what Bruce might be feeling. He was down there to see it where I wasn't. Did he feel remorse? Should I? Surely, those men didn't deserve to pay for Juan Josef's crimes. I didn't know the crew. Did they know what their captain was doing? Did they know he killed her?

I considered Bruce's insistence that we move ahead with the Albrecht plan to bring Anna back. Could she still be alive if we were successful in eliminating Richard Albrecht's ancestor?

I had been opposed to the idea of killing anyone in order to change the events that had happened to us, but how could I contest the one thing that could prevent Anna from dying; that could prevent those men on the beach from dying? All my arguments against changing history, when stacked up against the death that surrounded us, felt moot. We needed to try. Didn't we?

"Lainey," Lilly cooed, placing a hand on my shoulder to snap me out of the daydream, "come sit down. Worrying won't bring them back any sooner."

I took a deep breath and turned to face her. She was holding Cecelia in one arm and brushing the hair from my face with her other, her big brown eyes attempting to smile at me.

"Lil," I said softly, "how the hell did we get here?"

She sighed and took my hand in hers, squeezing gently. "Just the cards we've been dealt, I guess."

I shook my head. "I hate these cards. I don't even recognize myself... Sometimes, the things I think of scare me to death... like I'm turning into the same kind of monster he is... plotting all the ways I'd like to kill him... feeling absolutely no remorse whatsoever for those men on the beach. And other times, I feel like I could crumble into the dirt and sob loudly... hoping I'll open my eyes and my mother will somehow appear to comfort me back to something more human."

"I feel the same, you know." She pulled me to sit beside her near the fire. "I don't even remember my mother and I've longed to have her hold me almost every day since we crashed. Especially now that Anna's gone. I'm so mad, Lainey. I'm mad about all of it. I want to be on that beach with Jimmy exchanging vows with you and Anna at my side... To be blissfully ignorant of time travel and still wondering when a plane is going to spot our distress signals while we go about our days as a family here... To have Jimmy to myself all day and all night, completely unoccupied by anything that's not me. The fact that I'm not makes me want to either lay down on the ground and pitch a screaming fit or strangle that man with my bare hands. I hate these stupid cards too. But they're what I've got... and doing either of those things isn't going to change them... it'll only change me. So the only thing I can do is pray we get a re-deal..."

"You really think it'll work? That we could change all this if we find the right Albrecht?"

She nodded, looking down at Cecelia and smiling. "I have to think it'll work. Otherwise, I'd be down in that dirt kicking my legs and screaming at the top of my lungs or killing people in their sleep."

I followed her gaze, noticing Cecelia was awake and wasn't screaming herself. Lilly seemed so naturally maternal just then, and a tingle of regret swept up into the pit of my stomach for having never asked about her mother before. We'd all experienced loss before arriving here. Many of us had lost parents or children or spouses and none of us spent much time explaining how. I cleared my throat. "How old were you when your mom died?"

"Two." She smoothed her palm over Cecelia's crown, tilting her upward to inhale her new baby scent. "It's weird that I long for her like I do, I know. I only know her face from pictures... but I have these feelings that are like a memory... like I know she was good at being a mom, not from what anyone told me, but just this knowledge somewhere deep inside... like I remember her being good at it. And I miss her. I have no memory of actually looking at her face, but I miss her face like I'd been looking at it my whole life. And anytime life gets even the least bit difficult, I miss her that much more... like somehow this woman I never knew could make it all better."

"How did she die?"

She laid her head on my shoulder and sighed. "Same as gramma. Cancer. God, I hate that word. Mom's cancer came out of nowhere. They said she was fine one day and then the next she was coughing up blood... they took her straight to the hospital, but it had spread too far too fast. She died less than a week after they took her in. Nobody was ready for it. It just... happened. My dad didn't cope very well. Pretty sure his version of a kicking screaming tantrum was to bury himself in work for the next twenty something years... I think about him a lot. Not knowing where I am or where his parents are... assuming we're all dead... This has to be especially hard on him. After mom died, we were all he had."

"I'm so sorry, Lil. The fact that you're not murderous or throwing a tantrum is a huge testament to your strength. I don't know how you're doing it."

She raised her head from my shoulder and repositioned Cecelia against the tops of her legs. "I have Jimmy. The whole world could be on fire and I could find a way to see past it with that man's arms around me. It's not quite the same as having a mother to embrace you, but it's... I don't know... Like a part of him is wrapped around me like armor... and the world can't quite touch me the way it could before him."

That made me smile for the first time since Anna died. "If you'd have said Jim Jackson would be your armor a year and a half ago, I'd never had believed you."

She echoed my grin. "Me neither. It's funny how life works, isn't it? I've had plenty of hard days; days like yesterday that I wished with all my heart could be erased... But then Jimmy came along, and I can't think of a single thing that wasn't worth going through to get to him."

Cecelia's lip curled upward as she looked between us. The rational side of me knew it was just her facial muscles developing, but the optimist in me was sure she was genuinely smiling at us.

Lilly laughed at it. "She's so beautiful, Lainey. How can anyone have a tantrum about life when they have someone so beautiful to look forward to? Just look at that smile…"

I leaned into her shoulder, both of us admiring my daughter's facial expressions with a collective audible sigh. "I overheard you and Jim the other night," I whispered. "I didn't mean to eavesdrop, but I think you're going to make an amazing mother someday."

She groaned. "If I *ever* become a mother. I mean, he's right, the timing is all wrong… especially now… but will it ever be the right time when we're in this century? Will life ever be still enough for us to plan a family?"

I draped my arm across her shoulders, pulling her against my side. "And if we don't stay in this century?"

She let out a long breath. "What about all the questions we'll raise when we get there separate from the ones that go through first? Didn't we agree that whoever stays behind stays? That it would be too hard to explain how it took so long for the rest of us to appear?"

I shrugged. "How many times can we explain that we were stuck on this island before they stop asking those questions? I don't care how long it takes. I want my mother and my sister and my uncle to be a part of my children's lives. I want Jack's mother and his sister to know them. I want your life to be still enough that my babies grow up with yours."

"And what about mine?" Kyle asked, creeping up behind us to look over Lilly's shoulder at Cecelia. "I can't leave Fetia, and I can't take her with me… My place is going to have to be here."

Lilly shook her head, patting the seat beside her. "We'll take her with us. There's only so many questions we can't answer, right?"

He looked out toward the waterfall where Fetia and Magna were bathing Zachary and Izzy. Fetia had wanted the practice, and I'd needed the help after Zachary spit up all over both himself and Izzy that morning. Kyle shrugged. "I don't know… what would she even do there? I feel like that world would be so overwhelming for someone like her… So much to take in at once. Her life was so simple before we showed up in it. I don't want to complicate it that much more by forcing her into a time that's so much different from the one she knows."

"We'll—

I froze mid-sentence as I caught sight of something down the trail headed in our direction. It was our men, and as they moved out of the cover of the trees, the fist in my stomach unclenched. Jim and Chris each held rifles aimed at their *three* new prisoners. Chris had a broadsword affixed to his hip once again, and Jack held a body I could only assume was Anna, wrapped tightly in white fabric and lifeless in his cradled arms. Bruce, despite his limp, was shoving Juan Josef ahead of him, nudging him with the butt of his own rifle and kicking him when he attempted to slow his pace. Juan Josef's arms were tied behind his back and his normally perfect attire was crinkled and stained with dirt.

I'd assumed, if our men took the upper hand, Juan Josef would've been killed on the beach. I'd hoped for just that, but seeing him disheveled and beaten was somehow more satisfying just then.

Juan Jr. and Dario were also tied. They didn't appear to be putting up a fight as they walked toward us on each side of their father, their clothing undisturbed by signs of resistance. They would've surrendered, but all three wore their defeat on their faces, unable to look directly at anyone as they moved up the trail.

Whatever response to seeing them my mind was conjuring up was interrupted by Maria as she bolted past us. I hadn't even realized she'd been nearby. In a cloud of sandy dirt, I watched as she sprinted at full speed, skirts held high over her knees until she reached them, reared her fist back, and punched Juan Josef in the nose with every bit of strength she could muster.

Lilly burst into laughter beside me as Juan Josef fell to his knees for Maria to pour Spanish obscenities over him.

I frowned. "I didn't realize she and Anna had been very close?"

Chris slid an arm around her waist and lifted her off her feet. Even from the distance we were from them, I could hear her spouting off every English and Spanish insult she could come up with as she tried to get out of his grip to land one more blow.

"They weren't," Lilly noted, watching the altercation with the same fascination I was while Maria kicked a leg in Juan Josef's direction. "Anna hated her. I wonder if she'd be down there throwing punches if she knew what Anna really thought?"

It was hard for me to picture Anna hating anyone. Even when she was most angry with me, she'd never once shown any bit of hatred. She was always kind, even when she was seething. "I imagine she would've come around... once she'd gotten to know Maria."

Lilly shook her head. "Doubt it." She handed me Cecelia and stood, brushing off her skirts. "Anna loved you, Lainey. She hated Maria for the way she spoke to and about you... She thought you deserved so much better than the insults that woman passive-aggressively pays you. And Anna was too loyal of a friend to let go of that grudge so easily." She sighed. "But maybe we'll erase it all, and I can be proved wrong soon enough."

I watched Lilly walk down toward them, guilt sitting even heavier in my chest with the knowledge that Anna had been so quick to become my defender.

I stared at her body in Jack's arms as they turned up the path leading to camp. How small she suddenly appeared. I'd never once seen her as a small woman... like all her knowledge and skill somehow made her larger than the rest of us. My eyes watered as the breeze caught a tendril of her hair and lifted it from the wrap to blow freely to the side of her lifeless body. I watched it, unblinking, seeing a piece of her left alive in that one strand of white blonde, waving at me as if to say *'I'm here and I am not done yet.'*

Of course she wasn't. She might've been timid on the outside, but she was more fierce than all of us put together on the inside. She would fight, even in death, to get to her son. And I was no longer willing to stand in her way. Whatever it took to erase her death, I would do, and I would fight alongside her.

They circled into camp, Bruce and Jim pulling the prisoners to a halt while Chris towed Maria to one side. She had been mid-insult and grew silent as Jack gently lowered Anna's body onto the grass at the side of where Kyle and I were seated.

"We'll bury her with Bertie," He said softly, kneeling over her body to tuck the small bit of hair back into the fabric.

"What are you going to do with him?" Kyle asked, standing and tilting his head in the direction of Juan Josef.

Bruce sneered; a cold, soundless laugh on his curved lips as he narrowed his eyes at Juan Josef. "He'll die the slow and painful death he deserves."

"No," Juan Jr. said firmly, standing taller against his restraints.

"No?" Jim eyed him, keeping his rifle aimed at his father. "You ain't exactly in a position to negotiate, *junior*. You saw what he did."

"I did, indeed." He drew in a long breath. "I understand that, through your eyes, he warrants no less than the death you wish to serve him, but through mine, he has done little else but defend himself—albeit in a rather cruel manner—in preservation of the mission I wish to see to fruition."

Bruce spat to one side, adjusting his rifle so it was pointed at the center of Juan Jr.'s chest. "And exactly what threat did that kind and gentle woman pose to him that could justify her death?"

Juan Jr. met Bruce's eyes, raising one brow. "My father is no fool. He knew it was no coincidence our men grew ill within weeks of you being allowed in the kitchens. Just as he knew the moment she spouted off her diagnosis that it would be by *her* hands he would fall." He looked at me. "My father knew, because he'd allowed himself to be distracted by your company, our men— men who did not deserve to suffer such painful deaths; who were only serving us as a means to provide for their families—would die from the poison you served them. He knew it was quite possible we too would die if we'd been served the same. He killed your friend, not only in defense of himself and his sons, but also to ensure our mission would live beyond our death if it was coming. If we are fated to die in the coming days, he knew that by killing her, you would continue to see our plan through, if only to prevent her death from happening."

Bruce shook his head. "Your excuse for his actions is not enough to save his life."

"Then let this be," Juan Jr. said, showing no signs of anxiety despite the rifle targeted at his heart. "I can only assume, as I've had no symptoms of illness, that you intend to keep me alive for the purpose of sailing the ship so you may return to the future and undo this. You'll need what little remains of my men to serve you as a crew and they'll not sail without my authority. If I am correct in these assumptions, you're going to need my compliance, and I'll not agree to it if you kill him."

I stood to face him. "Why should we believe you would comply? The men were already sick when you offered to help us escape. Why would you make the offer if you knew what we were doing?"

"Because I wished to stop you. I considered many of those men my friends and I'd hoped that by separating you all from my father, we could carry out our plans without anyone among us having to die."

I looked at Dario, whose head slumped on his shoulders to rest against his chest. "And you? You knew what he was going to do to her when you took her up there that night?"

Slowly, he looked up at me and shook his head. "I hoped I could save her from it... hoped if she saw me for something more than my father—if she saw we were willing to help you escape him, she might stop. I'm afraid I was too late."

Bruce aimed his rifle at Dario. "You deceived her into thinking you were interested in her."

"I liked her," Dario assured him, his tone earnest. "I didn't want this, I swear it."

"No one wanted *this*." Juan Jr. glanced around at all of us. "We've always been careful to only take the lives of Albrecht men. Even then, we knew we were risking our very own existence... we knew any death at our hands in this time would change the future we once knew... But, what you've done today is far worse than any damage my father may have inflicted upon you. You've altered time in a most egregious and careless manner; murdered generations of people who once existed only to save your own lives... It is not my father that is the monster among us anymore."

I looked at Juan Josef, whose blackened eyes were focused exclusively on mine, and bile burned the back of my throat when his bloodied lip curled ever so slightly upward, a hint of his teeth showing beneath his matted black beard. He didn't speak—didn't need to—his expression was a clear message that while he was the one beaten and tied, he'd still won. He'd driven us to commit a heinous crime, turned our souls as black as his, and he knew we would agree to keep him alive so we could attempt to undo it.

"We ain't lettin' him roam free. You know that, don't ye?" Jim lowered his rifle a few inches to make eye contact with Juan Jr. "He'll be locked up just like ye' did us."

Juan Jr. nodded. "I expect nothing less."

"And you'll sail the ship then?" I asked. "So long as we don't kill him?"

"I will. You have my word. I won't fight you or attempt to see him released." He looked at his father, a shadow of disgust sweeping over his features for a split second. "Our quarrel was never with any of you. It was only with destiny. I do not wish to see anymore unnecessary bloodshed, at his hands or yours. If you wish to take him prisoner, do so. I will command the remaining men and inform them that their captain has taken ill."

"How many men are left still alive?" Lilly asked, inching toward Jim's side. "And won't they have seen us take you prisoner... take the weapons...?"

Juan Jr.'s eyebrows raised high on his forehead as he met her gaze. "You've not seen the beach then? The result of your poison on those poor souls? They lie in pools of their own blood and filth, those left alive retching painfully, praying for an end to come. No one left still breathing had the strength to even turn their heads in our direction once we reached the shore. It may be that none of them are alive by now."

The bile rose further to sit in the back of my mouth, and I swallowed it hard as I imagined the copper beach where we'd once spent so many nights stargazing now stained with blood and death.

"Bruce, how many of 'em you think will live through the night?"

Bruce shrugged as he met Jim's eyes, guilt washing over his posture. "I don't know. I only knew the mangos were deadly from Magna's warning... I don't know how much is too much or if any of them even can survive... The ones that were sick from the lye will live... I didn't give them the mango yet... didn't want any of you to know what I was up to until it was done."

Juan Josef looked at me then, a flicker of hope in his eye. "You mean you weren't *all* a part of this plan?"

I shook my head, instinctively shielding Cecelia's head from his gaze with my palm as I rocked her against my shoulder. "No."

"But is that not why *you* created your little ruse about Jack's affair with another? To keep me distracted from what they were doing by seeming interested in me?"

"No," I shook my head, making sure I met his eyes as I added, "I intended to kill you in a much more... *intimate* way."

The little bit of hope that I might've been sincere in our moments together fizzled from his features, and I saw that my words cut him. Maybe Juan Jr. was right. Maybe his father wasn't the monster among us any longer.

"What will you do with the dead?" Lilly asked, turning to Jack, where he'd gradually made his way to stand protectively at my side during the exchange.

He sighed. "We'll have to go down there and bury them... do what we can to treat the ones that are sick. I'll take Magna to help heal and Chris to help dig the graves..."

"I'll help," Kyle said.

"As will my brother and I," Juan Jr. stated. "Those men were as much brothers to us as we are to each other. We should be there to bury them."

"And what are we gonna do with this summbitch while we're at it?" Jim asked, kicking dirt in the direction of Juan Josef.

Bruce adjusted his rifle to be targeted on him. "I'll watch him."

"And I'll watch *you*," Bud assured Bruce, emerging from the cave. "Take Jacob and Michael down to the beach. You'll need all the help you can get. I'll keep Phil up here with us."

"Red," Jack turned toward me. "I'd really prefer it if you and the women took Izzy and the twins to the other side of the island. It'll be late before we get back and I'd rather you weren't here with them. It'd just be for tonight. We'll figure out something more official to keep him detained in the morning."

I pressed my forehead against his side as he smoothed a palm down my hair, exhaling the breath I'd been holding and feeling his armor wash over me.

Chapter Twenty Two

"Alaina," Jack whispered, waking me from a light sleep. He rarely ever used my actual name and the fact that he'd done so late in the night with Juan Josef nearby made my pulse quicken.

I rubbed my eyes as I sat up suddenly, scanning our little camp to make sure Izzy and the twins were all where I'd left them.

We'd setup a small camp on the opposite side of the island, laying fabrics on the sand around a fire, not bothering with a canopy or shelter since the night was warm.

I squinted in the darkness to try to make out the shapes of their bodies.

I could just make out Jack's silhouette against the small bit of light coming off the smoldering ember of the almost dead fire as he knelt to run his hand over one of their sleeping heads beside me.

I frowned. "What's wrong? Is everything alright?"

"Come with me?"

I blinked heavily. "Where? What's going on?"

His hands reached out, and he took hold of my face just as his lips covered mine. I could taste his tears; could feel his complete devastation as his lips pried my mouth open and his breath hitched against it. He pressed his forehead against mine. "Come with me," he breathed heavily, "we won't be far."

"Oh," I managed, feeling my entire body come alive as he pulled me into his arms. "But the babies—

"I've got them," Lilly yawned from somewhere nearby, her voice groggy with sleep. "Go."

He didn't wait for my response, but slid his arm beneath my knees to scoop me into his chest as if I weighed nothing, and carried me down the beach.

Stopping far enough to be hidden by darkness, but close enough to hear Zachary and Cecelia if they woke, he lowered my feet into the cool, soft sand. I hadn't a second to think before his mouth was back upon mine, his thumb on my chin pulling my bottom lip down to invite his tongue to explore.

This wasn't a romantic kiss on the beach. It was Jack's grief… pouring into me with a pulse like the tide, each breath against my skin shaking with the wave of anguish behind it. This was three weeks in the grips of Juan Josef that he'd bottled and held deep down inside him until it could no longer be contained. It overflowed through his fingers where they wound tightly into my hair; through his lips where they pleaded against mine to allow him somehow deeper; through his body where it pulsed against mine, pleading for me to take the grief from him.

I took it, curling my fingers into the fabric of his shirt to bring him closer, letting everything I didn't recognize inside of me pour out through my lips; through my body where it fell into familiar rhythm against his; through my own shaking breaths as they spilled out and blended with his to drift out over the ocean.

With his forearm at my back he pulled me closer still, and I sobbed audibly, letting the tears stream down my cheeks as, somewhere between our joined mouths, I began to recognize little bits of myself returning… the monster I'd become fading into the blackness around us.

I let my hands glide over his shoulders, pushing his jacket down his arms. Not willing to release my mouth, he kissed me harder, as if doing so would prevent me from stumbling backward when his arms released me to let the jacket fall in a puddle at our feet.

They'd only been gone for a second, but when his arms returned to wind around me, I let out the longest sigh that had ever escaped my lips, feeling all the agony from the last three weeks leave with it in a quiver.

This was Jack's pain. His hands moved in frenzied motions over me. His fingers were in my hair, then sliding down my sides, then back on my face as his tongue reached deeper for reprieve. This was the noose around his neck, the image of Juan Josef's fingers against the nape of my neck, and the feel of Anna's lifeless body in his arms.

I took his pain, hurriedly working the buttons of his shirt until it hung open and my hands could slide inside, the warmth of his skin making me feel like my fingers might've been trapped in ice before that moment.

This wasn't a passionate embrace. This was *my* fear, seeping out of me with every pass of my hands down his spine, with every touch of my tongue against his. This was Juan Josef standing over my babies, his hand on mine at the table, the flash of movement in his arm as he took Anna from the world, and Jack's lips against mine took that fear from me.

In one quick motion, his hands at my back slid down to the hem of my shift and he separated our mouths and bodies long enough to pull it up over my head. I shivered at my instant nakedness, but only until his hurried palms returned to glide over my skin. "I just need to touch you," he breathed against my mouth, "need to feel you against me…" He pulled me off my feet to wind my legs around him and press my chest against his where his shirt fell open. He tugged gently on my hair to tilt my head and allow his mouth to explore my collarbone. "I don't need more…"

I whimpered as his breath and tongue against my skin ignited a pulse deep down inside me. Anna had told us we should wait four to six weeks, but I was only going to make it to three. He might not have needed more, but I did.

This was not my body against him, it was my emptiness without him needing to be filled. I coiled my fingers into his hair, pressing his mouth against my breast. My hips rocked in sync with his tongue while he took it softly. This was waking up without him. This was the nightmare that stung deep down in my soul when I'd thought I'd lost everything. This was the panic as I'd waited for him to return from the beach that morning.

He took my emptiness, making a sound deep in is throat when his mouth returned to mine, hot with traces of salt from my skin and milk from my breast. He lowered us down until the soft cool sand met my shoulder blades, a welcome contrast to the heat boiling over inside me.

He held my hips against him as he spread his jacket below me, then lowered me down and took my mouth again and again, each time with a stronger sense of urgency; a need to be rid of his pain and grief.

He rolled to one side, pulling my back against his bare chest as he coiled both arms tightly around me, one arm draped across my breasts so he could grip my shoulder while the palm of the other slid lower.

This was Jack's relief. His mouth was on my neck, on my shoulder, on my face, and on my lips, seemingly all at the same time. This was my uncut throat, Cecelia's health, and Juan Josef's arms tied behind his back. This was a war we'd won, and I was his prize. I took his relief on my sharp inhale as his hips moved against mine and his fingers found their destination.

We were both healing each other, and the life that Juan Josef had attempted to rip away from us was within reach. I needed to feel him in the depths of me, to cling to him and know that we too weren't wrapped in fabric waiting to be buried, but that we were alive and Juan Josef hadn't left a single scar on the lives we intended to keep on living.

I moved with him as his body pressed against mine in rhythm with his circling fingers. He needed it too. I could feel his own desire rising hard against me through the fabric of his breeches. "More," I breathed, grabbing hold of his hair to pull his lips back to mine, tasting him deep enough that he would understand how much more I needed.

His grip around my torso tightened, and he didn't wait for me to insist before he curled two fingers inside me.

I cried out at the suddenness of his estranged touch, tightening my fist in his hair as I moved against him again, pleading he'd never stop giving more.

"I don't want to hurt you," he said between breaths. "I just needed to feel you."

"I need to feel you," I begged, my breath hitching as he explored deeper. "We'll stop if it hurts."

His mouth covered my throat as his fingers left me, and I thought I might burst with anticipation and emptiness while his tongue and teeth and breath on my neck kept my body quivering.

"Are you sure?" He breathed.

"I'm sure."

And within seconds, he was erasing himself slowly inside me, his fingers still moving in a soft circle outside while every inch of me tightened around him.

He let out an audible exhale against my shoulder when the length of him had filled me, and I let out a similar sound in response, feeling my soul recognize itself in the burn of our bodies reacquainting.

He held there, waiting for me to unclench. Slowly, I did, and the burn gave way to euphoria, warm and bubbling from my toes to the top of my head. He was trembling with restraint as our hips worked slowly, growing bolder as we both remembered each other.

Unable to stop myself, I moaned, and his palm slid up to tighten around my mouth while he made a feast out of the length of my neck.

With his chest against my back and arms wrapped securely around me, he moved us both, his fingers matching the enthusiasm of our hips. He let go of his restraint and lost himself, growing harder as he thrust with more urgency. His mouth left my neck to cover my lips, his breath ragged against mine. He swallowed me in his kiss as the last bits of pain and grief surged through him to drive harder and faster into me.

He began to shake and I could feel the exhales of his sobs against my mouth where it panted against his, the final pieces of his torment leaving on the breeze.

He quivered and fought his release until, at long last, he collapsed around me and the pulsing sensation he left behind awakened my heart to set its new rhythm. As he dissolved inside me, his fingers continued, pushing me upward and upward, my breath washing over his cheeks as he studied my face. Everything in me shook as his breath washed over my exposed skin, and I let go in an audible gasp that forced my fist to tighten in his hair, pulling his mouth to mine once more until I, too, crumbled with the weightlessness of release.

I smiled as he laid small soft kisses against my lips, realizing just how much I'd needed this; how much I'd missed the feel of him inside me.

"Did I hurt you?" He gently pulled himself from me, moving my body to lie flat so he could smooth his palm over my stomach.

"You did the exact opposite of hurting me," I laughed as he curled himself over to kiss a trail along my arm and across my shoulder.

"I missed you," he breathed, rolling over to rest on his forearms above me. "God, I missed you." He was out of breath, his chest moving heavily against mine as he scanned my face. "You're sure I didn't hurt you? Cause..." He blew out an airy laugh, "I swear to God, I could do that six or seven more times before the night's over."

"I think I could too." I grinned up at him, smoothing my palms over the wide expanse of his shoulders, watching my fingers as they moved across his chest to outline the muscles that had been fine tuned by our time spent on the island. "You didn't hurt me... not at all."

His thumb caressed my cheek, then brushed over my lower lip. "Good. I'm not ready to be done with you yet." His smile faded as he looked over my face. "You heard what he said today. Nothing you did caused her death, and there was nothing any of us could've done to prevent it. He would've done it whether we'd schemed or not. You understand that, right?"

I swallowed the ridiculous little voice in the back of my throat that wanted to contradict him and nodded.

"I mean it." He combed the hair from my temple. "I know you, Red, and I can see your brain working, trying to find some way to beat yourself up over this. It's not your fault. Nor is it mine or hers or anyone's but Juan Josef's." He lowered his lips to brush them softly over the bridge of my nose, then over each of my eyelids, sending a wave of warmth from my crown to my toes.

When I opened my eyes again, he was smiling. "I could beat myself up with blame for leaving this island in search of help... but none of us could've known what was going to happen. We couldn't have known we would end up here." He lowered again, this time laying a whisper of a kiss on my lips. "But I will do everything I can to erase this for you... I will kill every Albrecht in this century just to see you smile again without the weight of him pulling it back down." He moved his nose over mine. "I mean it when I say I've missed you... I've missed the way you smile when you're not trying to claim ownership of all the world's problems; the sound of your laughter when you're completely at ease... Watching you take on the guilt of plotting that man's death was as difficult as when I'd watched you die in my arms. And I won't do that again. Your part in all this is over."

He smoothed his palm down my side, stopping just beneath my thigh to spread his fingers wide and slowly move it back upward. "I will take all of it from here. Taking care of you... of our children... that's what I *want* to do. Making sure you can smile at the end of the day, *that's* what's going to make me happy. So let it go however you need to. And let me take care of you."

I sighed, admiring the way the moonlight painted his face with bits of silver. I didn't deserve him. "I don't try to claim ownership of the world's problems, Jack. I just... My entire life, I've consistently hurt the people around me by either overthinking things or not thinking things through at all. Over and over, I've done this to everyone I love; everyone who's ever loved me. I've made colossal mistakes that would feel inhuman if I didn't carry the guilt of them. I said her name, Jack, as part of a vile lie. I said her name without thinking... Offered her up to a complete madman... and he called her a whore for it just before he killed her. God, I want to be able to let that go... to not blame myself for the look on her face when he said it... when he slit her throat moments later and that look was frozen in place, staring at me for an explanation as to why he'd referred to her that way... How can I ever let that go?"

He shook his head. "Do you remember that last night you and I spent alone together up on the summit? When I was going to propose to you and then you brought up Chris's family?"

I groaned. "I'll never let that go either. I'm sor—

"Hush. That's not where I was going with this." He traced the arch of my eyebrow with his thumb, a hint of a smile touching his lips. "I didn't think when I reacted the way I did that day... I let you cry alone in the cave and I listened to you all night. I can still hear that sound sometimes in my mind... and if something would've happened to you right then... something like that storm that nearly flushed us out of the cave the following night... I would've never stopped hearing it. I'd have spent the rest of my life blaming myself for letting you cry. We all make mistakes, Alaina. We all say and do things without thinking or after we've overthought something... But if she hadn't died just then, you'd have been able to explain why he called her that name; told her what you had planned, and she would've understood—just like you understood why I reacted harshly that night on the summit. She loved you and you loved her. She was lying to you too, but you're not mad at her for it, are you?"

I shook my head.

"I'd venture to guess that, wherever she is, she's not mad at you either." He kissed me again, this time deeper, before he raised up to linger a few inches from my lips. "Alaina, I don't love you because you are perfect. I love you because you are real and good and because I want parts of your authenticity to rub off on me; the depth with which you feel emotion—*good or bad*—is more genuine and honest than anyone I've ever met. You *feel* with passion. And I love that pieces of that passion *do* rub off on me and make me feel good about myself... the way I love you, our family, our friends... I love with passion because of you."

I saw the corners of his lips curl upward, his hips moving ever so gently against mine as the passion in him stirred. "And I'm gonna make love to you again now, and I hope part of me, the part that knows it's okay to be imperfect without guilt, will rub off on you, and you'll let go."

And so he did… and I let go.

I could still feel him on my skin when I woke, my breasts heavy and needing Zachary and Cecelia to relieve them.

We'd come back to camp in the night and had fallen asleep with the babies between us on a blanket in the sand. I'd never remembered sleeping quite as soundly as I had after the reprieve he'd given me.

Very gently, I pulled his arm from me and sat up in the soft grey of the early morning to smile down at his sleeping face. His lips were curled ever so slightly upward, forming the smallest hint of a dimple in his right cheek. His hand was curled in the fabric where I'd once been, and he looked just as peaceful as I felt.

I pulled Zachary into my arms, rocking him softly so he could wake just enough to be fed. Neither of them had woke in the night and I desperately needed him to take away the pressure.

My smile widened once he did. The sensation mixed with the memory of what Jack had given me the night before lulled me into a sort of euphoric trance. I was aroused in a new and unfamiliar way… It wasn't quite arousal, but similar in the areas that felt it. I should've felt guilty for it, since breastfeeding had never elicited this type of physical response from me, but it didn't feel unnatural. It felt like the deepest and most intimate connection I'd ever felt; like I was both a mother and a woman for the first time since I'd given birth, completely free and yet tethered entirely to my beautiful family.

Jack's eyes opened, and his gaze lingered on Zachary at my breast. I hadn't bothered with a blanket since everyone was asleep and all the other men were on the opposite side of the island. He didn't speak or move, just watched, and I wondered if he was feeling a similar bond to us. He certainly appeared that way. The curve in his mouth remained upward, and his eyes held a glint of mischief? Appreciation? Whatever it was, he was captivated by both of us.

My gaze moved from him to Zachary. And the strange feeling intensified as his tiny fingers curled and released against the movement of my breath, his eyelids, still heavy from sleep, opening to reveal blue eyes that were fighting not to roll backward.

Returning my focus to Jack, I watched him watching us, vowing to commit the image and the content I felt to memory before we set out on what was going to be a very difficult day. Today, we would bury Anna, and I wasn't ready to face that... Not yet. I would hold on to this silent moment with my family for as long as I could before facing that.

Jack's arm slid out so he could spread his fingers wide over my knee, his thumb moving gently over my skin. "You're beautiful," he whispered, so softly I wouldn't have been able to make out the words had I not been looking down at him. "Both of you."

I placed my hand over his, feeling a flutter in the pit of my stomach as he interlaced his fingers with mine and pulled our joined hands to his lips. "He looks like you, you know."

I didn't need to see the smile on his lips because I could see it in his eyes as they lit up. Pride swept over his features as he lowered our joined hands back to my knee. Sometimes I wondered if he forgot he too made our children... He always looked at them with the same sense of awe that he often had with me, and as he raised up on his elbow to get a better look, I realized he might be seeing himself in his son for the very first time.

I'd carried them, and I had always known them both as a part of me, but he was just discovering them, and watching him do so strengthened the sense of complete connection that had filled me.

I wondered, as I watched him, just how much was going on behind those blue eyes. With all that had happened since Chris had shown up on our shores, Jack and I hadn't had the same opportunity to share our thoughts as we once had. For as much as I'd missed his touch, I missed his mind; missed the pitch black cave where our souls once danced in the darkness, knowing every piece of the other after days and nights spent opening our hearts to one another.

Maybe we could return to that back cave just one more time before we left, and I could take whatever guilt he was still holding onto away from him as he'd taken mine from me.

Chapter Twenty Three

Jack carried Anna's body down to the beach. We couldn't go together with Juan Josef and his sons still at camp, so we left Chris, Kyle, Jacob, and Bud in charge to come say their goodbyes separately. Jim, Jack, and Bruce went straight to work digging a grave for her beside Bertie. Once she was laid inside, Bruce would stay to cover her with dirt after everyone had a chance to come and pay their respects.

Preparing to bury Anna didn't feel the same as burying Bertie. Maybe it was because we were so determined to see her revived, but it didn't seem like goodbye. It felt like we were writing a chapter we'd soon be ripping out of our story.

At least, that's how it felt for me... Bruce, on the other hand, was affected entirely differently. It was like a part of him had died with her; the part that was always chipper with some witty—albeit cheesy—one-liner to coax a smile out of us on a daily basis was gone. His lips had tightened hard across his features, aging him tremendously and making it appear as though he'd never again be able to smile or joke until she was returned.

We all had known Bruce had a crush on her. I was pretty sure Anna knew it too. It was hard to overlook the way he went out of his way to please her or smile at her or simply *be* next to her. We'd all alleged his draw to her had been circumstantial; that the rest of us had sort of paired off and he was naturally driven to the only other woman near enough his age to seek out for companionship.

Looking at his sullen expression; his vacant eyes as he dug into the earth with his bare hands, I realized it was much more. My heart ached for the words he never mustered up the courage to say to her, and I hoped we could give him the opportunity to speak them one day soon.

Lilly and I stood silently, each of us holding one of my babies, watching them while Magna and Izzy picked flowers nearby.

I wondered, as they lowered her down into the grave, if her spirit was nearby watching, feeling the same lack of finality in this ending I did.

I wondered if we would all remember what we'd prevented once it happened. Would she remember her death? Would she remember us standing here watching her body be laid into a grave that wouldn't eternally contain her? Was she there, standing beside us, curious as to what words we would have to say over her?

If this wasn't goodbye, what words *could* we say? There wasn't a single word that felt suitable, and if she was watching, I was mortified that anything we'd have to say would come up short.

We knew Anna as two things. She was a devoted mother and a fearless caretaker. But that wasn't all she was. She was a woman who'd been beaten by a man she'd once loved; a woman who'd had the courage to leave her aggressor, and yet, she kept that part of herself hidden. None of us knew the life she'd lived that made her a woman capable of that kind of strength. She didn't speak about her life or who she was outside of Liam. None of us knew the woman beneath the mother and caretaker; the things she dreamt of that were reserved exclusively for her; the subtle nuances in life that brought a smile to her face... it didn't seem fair that *we* were the ones standing there to speak on her behalf.

We all circled around the dirt she lay in, and Izzy tossed a bouquet she'd been meticulously constructing inside, the unwrapped flowers meeting the white fabric and spilling pink and white petals over Anna's body. My heart sat in my throat, not because she was down in that grave, but because she was outside with us, waiting for the words...

I wasn't sure how long we stood there silent. It might've been minutes or an hour before Jim spoke.

"Lordt," he started gruffly, "I ain't read the Bible much, and I know ye' seen me plenty of times daydreamin' through a church sermon or two, but I remember from somewhere the words, *'Though he brings grief, he will show compassion, so great is his unfailing love.'* Now I've asked ye' for a lot of stupid things I don't need in my life. And I don't care if you never answer a single prayer again. *Today*, I'm beggin' ye,' for compassion. Let it be your will that this be undone. I know ye' got her, and I know ye' ain't gonna' want to let go of one of your finest creations, but we're just loanin' her to ye. Let her heal the ones up 'er that need it, but then let her come back to the ones down here that need it more... I'll never ask ye' for another stupid thing again if ye' just give her back to her boy... Give her back to the ones that know her best; the ones that will stand over her grave when she's too old to go on and say the right things about the sort of woman she was. This world is too dark without her in it. Let her bring a bit of your light back for a while longer. Lordt, I ask ye' just this one thing, and I'll never expect ye' to answer me again. Give her back."

'Give her back,' I repeated in my mind.

And that was it. There was no goodbye. We didn't speak of her like she was gone; didn't share fond stories of all the ways she'd made our lives better. That was reserved for people you'd never see again, and we all felt her lingering... waiting to be resurrected.

Bruce carved a short inscription in the stone beside Bertie's epitaph that read: *'Anna Klein - We will meet again.'*

I took a very deep breath when we finally turned away from it, rattled by the lack of tears from both myself and everyone around me.

Returning to camp, I was absorbed in racing thoughts. We hadn't said goodbye, and that was unsettling. Everything was unsettling.

We were going to erase history...

How strange it felt to think of something so outlandish as being even remotely tangible. Having our airplane crash into the ocean was a strange enough reality, but to go from a plane crash to a fairy tale life with Jack to 1774 to a pirate ship to completely rewriting the events that we'd all just experienced seemed suddenly far too phantasmal to grasp onto...

Was I trapped in some very bizarre and lucid dream? Had I died in that crash and was my mind simply constructing the world around me in those final fleeting moments of brain activity; growing more fantastical as more of my core systems shut down?

"Red?" Jack nudged my elbow, pulling me from my stupor to realize I'd been frozen on the edge of camp, staring at Juan Josef where he was tied to the same tree where Phil had once been kept detained.

Jack was staring at the very same thing when I looked up at him.

"Now that we don't have to worry about our identities being exposed by doing so," he started, adjusting Zachary in the crook of his arm, "I think we need to do something about Phil. With Juan Josef to keep an eye on, it'll be harder to watch him like we did in Tahiti. I can't trust him to roam free."

Phil.

The memory of that night came rushing back to me as I stood, unable to move my feet, imagining him in the same spot Juan Josef now occupied.

I hadn't really processed what it'd meant to have Phil roaming freely among us. Between the high-risk pregnancy, Jack's return, Captain Cook, and now Juan Josef, somehow his attempted rape had become trivial... like a far-off and irrelevant memory... We'd been unable to detain Phil in the presence of Captain Cook for fear he might cause trouble by speaking up, but Jack and Jim had taken steps to keep him away from me, and as a result, I'd been able to avoid the memories his face may have conjured up...

But now, standing in a place so near to where it'd happened, I relived those emotions; that sense of helplessness and weakness as he'd pressed his body against mine... I relived the way he'd touched me... the way he'd put his mouth on me... the way I'd fought and kicked and screamed only to excite him more... and

that made my stomach turn. "What do you want to do about him?"
I asked.

His eyes met mine, and he offered a half smile. "I was hoping
you'd tell me. What do *you* want me to do with him?"

I shook my head. "I don't know… Didn't he help you escape
the Nikora?"

His expression hardened. "Why should that matter?"

"Well…" I pulled Cecelia up against my shoulder to relieve my
tingling arm. "I just… I don't know what's fair and what's just me
being angry. I never saw him as a bad guy before that day - *a
creep*, yes - but not an evil man… and he was very drunk… and
he's never done anything like that since he's been sober… and he
helped you escape… and I don't know whether punishing him
further after everything that happened on that island with you is
justice or vengeance."

Jack raised an eyebrow. "Alaina, he tried to rape you. He dug
his teeth into you… It doesn't matter if he helped me off that island
- he was only helping me to save himself. There's not a single day
that goes by where I don't picture your face when I came upon you
in those woods… your lip bleeding… the torn shirt and those
fucking bite marks on your skin… It's taken every amount of
willpower in me to prevent myself from finishing what I started
that day. Whatever you choose is more than fair, and would likely
be far less vengeful than a punishment of *my* choosing."

I bounced Cecelia softly, considering it. "What's the plan for
the one we have?"

He took a deep breath, and I knew by his expression that I
wasn't going to like what they'd come up with. "There's no way to
imprison him on the island. He's already loosened quite a bit of the
rope at his wrists. We think we should take him back to the ship
where a few of us can stand guard outside a locked door. We'll tell
the others he's quarantined in his room and we're preventing him
from infecting anyone else by keeping him locked inside."

"And *you're* planning to stand guard?"

He nodded. "We'll take shifts… just like their men did with
us."

"Could we lock Phil in with him?" I asked.

"That's what I was thinking you'd suggest. I can't see any reason not to. He won't come willingly though if he knows what we're planning and I'm far too exhausted to fight... I'll suggest he take the first shift with me - he's used to me telling him where he can and can't go - and then I'll throw him in with Juan Josef once we get there."

Chapter Twenty Four

"Ay, Sugar," Jim said as he entered the bedroom I'd chosen on the ship, "ye' can quit pacin' now. We got 'em squared away down there."

I spun around from where I'd been walking back and forth near the large bay window, my pulse slowing as I met his friendly gaze. "Phil too?"

He nodded, grinning wide with a playful laugh. "Ye' shoulda' seen his face. Hoss asked him to help us with Juan Josef's shackles... turned and placed a shackle on Phil's wrist just as soon as he was done with Juan's. He's madder than a puffed toad, I tell ye.' Don't know what he was expectin.' Ain't like we just forgot about what he done."

"Is Jack guarding them?" I glanced over his shoulder at the empty hallway behind him.

He winked. "Kyle, Michael, and Jacob's gonna' mind 'em for this first shift so we can all focus on gettin' our ducks in a row. We got lots to talk about before we sail out."

"Where are the others?" I asked.

He sighed, running a hand through his hair. "They're waitin' for us in the dining room. Juan Jr. and Dario thought it was the best place for it. They already cleaned it, so you know. If ye' don't want to go back in there so soon, it's fine... we can go up on the top deck."

"No," I said, feeling a shiver creep up my spine as I imagined the seat Anna had been seated in. "I'll need to go in there at some point and there's no point in putting that off."

I turned toward the fourposter bed, pulling the makeshift sling from the foot and wrapping it around both shoulders.

"Ay, while I got ye' alone," Jim leaned against one of the bedposts. "I wanted to ask ye' what your take is on all this. Killin' the ancestor, I mean…"

I shrugged. "When Juan Jr. first mentioned it, I was completely opposed to the idea. It doesn't seem right to kill an entire line of people just to change what's happened to us… But we have to now, don't we? We can't just leave things like this."

"Ye' mean we cain't just accept her death?"

I nodded. "And all the rest we killed."

"Why not?" He crossed his arms over his chest. "We accepted Bertie's… and Frank's… I don't want to sound like I ain't got a heart—I loved her too—but what we're plannin' to do… it feels a bit like we're playin' God. That prayer I said over her, it didn't sit right. If the good Lordt didn't intend for Anna to die, if it wasn't her time, or if he didn't intend for Juan Josef to come here and cross paths with us, then it wouldn't have happened, darlin.' At what point does *'thou shalt not kill'* become *'thou shalt not kill unless ye' benefit directly from it?'*"

"And what about all those men?" I asked. "That's a lot of people that would've went on to potentially father sons and daughters that might shape the world we know. If we do this, they don't die… and the generations that would spawn from them won't die, either. What's one death compared to all of them? Compared to Anna?"

He exhaled audibly. "I ain't sayin' what Bruce did was right neither… but what's done is done… and the more we creep down this dark path, justifyin' why we set out to kill, the less we'll resemble ourselves by the time we come out of it. And we might forget what we done here if we're successful, but I guarantee you, we shall be reminded." He looked up at the ceiling as if God himself were hovering just above him.

"Anyone else feel this way?"

He raised one shoulder. "I think Chris might. Rest of 'em are too eat up with grief to realize what they're agreein' to." He glanced down at the babies where they laid at the head of the bed. "This life ain't but a second in comparison to eternity. If we do this, can ye' live with this stain on your soul for eternity? I'm assumin' you still believe in the almighty?"

I knitted my brows. "Of course I do. That's why I want to change it... To bring those men and Anna back."

"Guilt and grief and anger can make ye' do all sorts of things you'll come to regret down the line. Talk to God if ye' believe in him; tell him what you're plannin' on doin,' and see if ye' still feel right about it afterwards."

I huffed. "What would you do if it were just up to you?"

He grinned. "I'd send that ugly summbitch through time with his passport taped to his forehead so they could arrest him for whatever crimes they was chasin' him for in the first place. And then I'd go find us a plot of land—here or there, don't matter none —and I'd live my life beside y'all, raisin' babies and bein' a good man; a man worthy of meetin' the ones I love in heaven one day. I would accept the path God put us on, and I'd mourn the ones we lost along the way. That's what I'd do."

I thought about our dream of Ireland, and how wonderful that life had sounded. I thought about what it might be like to see my children in my mother's arms; in Cece's arms if we went home instead... How far away plans for the future suddenly seemed when considering all we'd face in the months ahead if we moved forward. Was Jim right or was I? I hadn't thought about the consequences of what we were doing in terms of eternity. Maybe the blood wouldn't be on my hands, but would offering the name be the same as pulling the trigger? And where would that leave me in the eyes of God? Where would it leave me if I *didn't* try to save those men? Wasn't that worse?

I positioned Zachary in the sling, considering it. *'Your part in this is over.'* Acknowledging the strength Jack had given me, I looked back at Jim, where he was taking Cecelia in his arms. "Jim,

I'm giving this one to Jack because I trust him to make the right decision for his family. I'll go along with whatever he thinks is right, and if that decision is to kill the ancestor of Richard Albrecht, I'll pray God forgives us all for whatever part we play in it."

He held Cecelia against his shoulder, knitting his eyebrows together as he looked at me. "I ain't askin' you to make the call, Sugar, just askin' what ye' think." He rocked Cecelia softly. "A lot has happened since we come up on Juan Josef. It ain't all been bad..." He looked down at Cecelia to imply he'd meant the babies had been born after our first encounter. "And I ain't sayin' them good things would necessarily go any differently, but ye' gotta' consider that they could. If Juan Josef hadn't been on Eimeo asserting dominance over the people there, would the natives have been as willing to help us? Or would they have taken you prisoner for showin' up with the enemy? If ye' hadn't been worryin' about Juan Josef, would ye' still have gone into labor when ye' did? Or could ye' have gone to term? If it would've been days or weeks later, could it have gone as smoothly as it did with her breech? If it hadn't been Magna there with ye,' would Anna have known she was breech and done things different? And if ye' hadn't immediately been brought onto that ship and fed like ye' were, would the babies be as strong and healthy as they are now? We don't know them answers."

Instinct brought my palm to the top of Zachary's soft head, where he was nestled against my chest. I hadn't thought we'd be erasing the first several weeks I'd spent with them. Yes, those weeks had been brutal in many ways, but I'd gotten to know my children; bonded with them deeply, and I was suddenly sad at the idea any of that could change.

"Oh hell, I didn't mean to scare ye,'" he said, stepping around the bed to place a hand on my shoulder. "Don't give that no account. I'm just spoutin' off at the mouth is all cause I'm scared. I shouldn't have said none of that. Knowin' what will change in these last few weeks ain't no different from knowin' what kind of change tomorrow brings on any given day... I'm sure they'll be fine. Better than fine without that summbitch comin' into their lives."

I nodded, leaning against him as he pulled me to his side and turned us toward the door. I couldn't shake the feeling his words had implanted, though. As we made our way to the dining room, my heart stung at the idea that anything related to Zachary and Cecelia could go any differently. I wasn't ready to forget the bond I already had with them—even if there was a chance I could build it again under different circumstances.

I took a deep breath as we walked through the double doors, my eyes going straight to the head of the table to the seats Lilly and Jack now occupied where Anna and Juan Josef had been the last time I'd entered the room.

The blood was gone from the table and floor, and the room didn't hold the heavy weight of her death like I imagined. It felt like a room on a ship and nothing more.

Jim kept Cecelia against his shoulder as he made his way to the empty seat between Lilly and Izzy, and I couldn't help but reflect the smile that lit up Izzy's features when he tugged on one of her braids.

Everyone was there. Bud, Magna, Lilly, Izzy, and Jim lined the far side of the table, and Fetia and her father, Bruce, Chris, and Maria were seated opposite them. Jack sat in Juan Josef's seat, my normal spot beside it empty and reserved for me, while Juan Jr. and Dario stood leaning against the wall near the window.

I took my seat, adjusting Zachary to lie against the crook of my arm.

"Five of our men survived," Juan Jr. said, "along with a handful of service staff and the clergyman. That's thirty-eight dead who all served a purpose. We won't have nearly enough to man this ship, especially with the ones left alive in such a weakened state. We'll need help... to care for the livestock... to cook—*and not poison us*—and to help with the rigging and repairs... Once we're at sea, we'll need every man, woman, and child that's able to keep us on-course."

"We're all willing to do our part," Jack asserted firmly, both of his palms rested on the table. "We have a few weeks to learn what we need to know. But that's not what we're here to talk about... We've all spent too much of these last several weeks not talking to each other, and that stops now. Whatever we plan to do moving forward, we plan it together and agree on it *together*... Starting with whether or not we move forward with seeking out the ancestor of Richard Albrecht."

Both Dario and Juan Jr. pulled themselves from the wall to scan our faces, neither offering their input, but both seeming to hold their breath in anticipation of the response.

Bruce's brows furrowed. "We have to. For Anna."

Lilly nodded. "I agree. We have to try."

Jack scanned the room. "Is anyone opposed to it?"

Jim and I made eye contact, but neither of us spoke up. I wasn't sure I was opposed to it... Nor was I sure I agreed with it... I could see the same conflict in him, and the same relief I felt when Chris spoke up.

"I am," he said, avoiding Bruce's accompanying scowl. "We don't know what kind of damage we're doing. Every person we meet, every encounter or word we speak could change something. I think we should all wait until March and go home together where we can't do any more damage to the lives we once knew."

Juan Jr. coughed out an airy laugh. "Forgive me, sir, but the damage done on that beach likely changed far more of the lives you once knew than killing one man would do. You would return those thirty-eight men and all the generations they will parent... you would return every Albrecht we have killed along with their descendants... you would return Anna... and you would change the outcome of one line of people as opposed to more than forty."

Bud cleared his throat. "It can't hurt to do the research... Once we have the name, we could always decide not to do it."

Chris shook his head. "It's not as simple as a name, Bud. The locations throughout history of every single person that descended from that name need to be accounted for, along with the descendants of our own ancestors to ensure they can never ever cross paths. That's going to take a considerable amount of time."

Bud nodded. "I hired a company to map out my and Bertie's genealogy. They were thorough; lining out locations, occupations, and the history behind each member of our family trees. This dated all the way back to the 1400s. It took a year and a sizable investment, but we wouldn't need to go back that far. I have plenty of money to hire that same company and others like it to do the same for every single person on that flight log, along with Richard Albrecht. I would spend whatever it takes so they would work exclusively for us for a year. We could then rake over the details to make sure whoever we pick in this time cannot affect the lineage of any one of us."

"A year..." Maria whispered, looking up at Chris. "Who will go now that Anna can't?"

Jack took a deep breath. "We'll get to that in a moment. But first, we have to come to an agreement on this. It can't hurt to get the names... Whoever goes will come back with the information and *then* we can decide what to do with it. Can we agree on that?"

The sounds of agreement bounced off the walls around us as everyone expressed their version of it at once. Chris reluctantly nodded. "As long as we agree that we won't act on the name unless we all are willing."

"We won't," Jack assured him. "Now, assuming only three can go through, we need to decide who goes." He raised a hand as chatter began to pick up. "Before we do, Dario, it has never made sense to send you. You need an identity and you would be hung up in customs far too long to provide any value. You know we will come back. But you also have to know we can't send you."

Dario sighed and nodded. "I presumed as much after speaking with Alaina."

"Good," Jack turned toward Chris. "I think you should still go. Anna was adamant about getting your head checked out and even if there was no injury, I believe you are the right man for it. You're a natural leader and we need that kind of strength to stay on course."

There was a silent moment of appreciation that passed between them before Jack looked over to Bud. "And Bud, I think you should go with him. You could handle the genealogy while Chris is working out his medical affairs."

"I was hoping I'd get the opportunity to volunteer." Bud smiled warmly.

"And we'll need one more to work out personal matters," I said. "To find Liam and make sure he's safe and not a victim to his father... It's the only thing Anna cared about."

Maria raised her hand. "I can do this. I have no family to reunite with... nothing there to distract me. I can search for him and do whatever I must to make sure his father cannot take him... and I can be there to look over Chris if he needs it after treatment."

"And Izzy..." Lilly said, running a finger over Izzy's braid. "We'll need to figure out if she has a family out there looking for her... all of us should know what's happened to our families while we've been gone."

Maria smiled at Lilly. "If you give me names and locations, I will check on everyone."

"There was a tag on Izzy's suitcase with her full name and address." Lilly's eyes watered as she stared affectionately down at Izzy, struggling with the idea of giving her up at some point. "I saved it. I'll make a list for everyone."

Jack waited patiently, then peered around the table. "Then we all agree on sending these three?"

Again, the clatter of general agreement sounded throughout the table.

"Now for the hard part." Jack's brows furrowed, and he stared down at his hands where he smoothed them up and down over the wood surface of the table. "What if it only goes backward?"

Bud straightened, making eye contact with Lilly. "Then those of you that are left will need to agree on moving on with your lives here." He held up his palm as Lilly opened her mouth to object. "One year there will be six months here. I give you my word that if I make it to the future, I will be at that storm one year later. If you arrive there in March and we do not come through, then you will know with certainty it doesn't work the way we intended and you will build a life here just as we will build a life wherever we end up. Lilly, do not argue... not now. We will not be dead... and neither will you."

She closed her mouth and stared down at her lap.

"And if there is no storm?" I asked. "If we sail out there and it never comes, what then?"

Jim laid his hand over Lilly's, squeezing gently. "Then we'll build a life here and be done with all of it."

Jack nodded in agreement.

"And what would happen to us?" Juan Jr. asked. "If there is no storm, what would become of my father? Of me? Of my brother?"

Bruce's jaw tightened. "Your father couldn't be allowed to go free. You two would need to go back to your lives without him."

"Will you give your word that you will not kill him?" Juan Jr. asked. "I understand the need to see him punished for his crime, but if we're taking an eye for an eye, I believe we are more than even when it comes to murder. I have offered my service to you in exchange for his life. I will not fight you if you intend to see him imprisoned for the rest of it, so long as I know he will live."

"How can you beg for his life after you've seen the type of evil he is capable of?" Bruce asked.

"All men are capable of evil when their backs are against a wall. Whatever he is, he was made that way by circumstance. I owe him my life and I won't see his taken in exchange for it."

Jack's fingers curled into fists against the table. "And if he should rise up against us? If he should make any attempt to harm one of ours?"

"Then the agreement is null. I have asked him to submit, and he has promised to do just that. I cannot expect you not to react in the same manner he would if he should attempt to defy you."

"Then we will agree," Bruce snapped. "What now?"

Jack exhaled heavily, his fingers unfolding as his shoulders relaxed. "Now we figure out where the rest of us will go for six months while we wait."

"Can't we come back here?" Lilly asked, scanning the table for a reaction. "We won't have to hide our identities or impose on the Tahitians. There's plenty of food and shelter."

"And Uati?" Bud asked, looking at Jack. The air somehow felt chillier as whatever memory the name conjured up for the two of them crossed over the table. "He will always be a threat when we are this close to him."

Jack twisted his lips to one side. "He will be, but he doesn't have rifles or swords or cannons." He looked up at Juan Jr. "Do those cannons work?"

Juan Jr. nodded, smiling. "I assure you, they work quite well."

Jack considered it. "And we have the summit to watch out on all sides... we would see them coming and be able to send a signal down to prepare for them... I'd be far more wary of returning to Tahiti to run into Captain Cook than to stay here and fight the much more primitive Nikora... who are easily persuaded of just about anything."

I remembered their tales of Uati believing them to be *'gods'* and hid a smile. That smile was much more difficult to contain as I imagined spending time alone with my family on the summit where I'd fallen in love with Jack. "I like that idea," I said.

"Me too," Lilly agreed. "We could use a bit of peace while we wait."

"Anyone opposed?" Jack asked, glancing at Juan Jr. and Dario who both shook their heads. "Then we have a plan... Juan, Dario, why don't we spend the rest of the day going over what you'll need help with in order to get us there?"

Chapter Twenty Five

Chris

Chris kept the collar of his shirt balanced across his nose as he moved his shovel along the floor of the pigpen. He'd spent enough time down in the hull with the pigs on Cook's ship that he figured he would volunteer to care for the livestock to save the others from the stench. He'd overestimated his own tolerance to the smell.

Jim hadn't been phased whatsoever. Across from him, he did the same with no fabric over his nose to filter the odor, snickering every time Chris stopped to gag and spit to one side.

"I tell ye,' these summbitches reek enough to gag a maggot, but they sure as shit do taste good!"

Again, Chris gagged loudly, attempting to keep his shovel steady as he moved it to the barrel and dumped its still steaming contents.

Jim howled with laughter. "Aw come on now, beanstalk, it ain't that bad." He dug his shovel in again, wiping the moisture from his brow with the back of his hand. "I took a job once workin' for this old farmer back home. I's only maybe fourteen or so. Ooh, Lordy, I tell ye' shovelin' pig shit ain't nothin' in comparison to shovelin' manure. I like to never got that smell off me. Showered and scrubbed until my skin was raw and could still smell the stink." He looked up at Chris then, bobbing his bushy eyebrows. "Them summbitches taste good too, though." He proceeded, clueless of the nausea he incited. "I wonder who first looked at these stinkin' ass animals and thought, *'now that's good eatin?'*"

"I don't think I'll be able to eat for a week after this," Chris snarled.

"You'll get used to it." Jim set his shovel to one side, dusting his gloved palms off against each other before he reached for the bedding to re-cover the area. "We'll have to come down here every mornin' and clean this area. Ain't healthy for us or the pigs to breathe in these fumes. Gotta' keep 'em well fed... The goats too. Did ye' get some more milk from Wanda over there to take up to Alaina?" He tilted his head at a particularly noisy goat who'd been watching them through one of her black eyes.

"Not yet," Chris admitted. He was still working up the courage to get anywhere near the thing. He'd never been fearful of animals before, but there was something about *'Wanda'* that incited shivers down his spine, like she was peering into his soul. "Do you think the baby's okay? She hasn't been crying as much today... Will she need the goat's milk much longer?"

Jim shrugged dramatically, dropping the hay and straw in piles throughout the pen. "I don't know. If she was mine, the way she was carryin' on them two nights, I wouldn't risk givin' her anything else for quite a while."

Chris looked back at Wanda. "I've never milked a goat before..."

"Ye' say that like ye' milked something else... who you been out in the world milkin?"

Chris laughed loudly. "No one. I've never milked anything before."

Jim winked. "The way she's been eyeballin' you, I think she might just enjoy it!"

Chris shuddered. "I don't think I like goats... She's creeping me out."

"Here." Jim handed him a rake. "Go on ahead and spread the rest of this out. I'll milk her... Sissy."

Jim grabbed a bucket and fearlessly made his way into the goats' enclosure. "What ye' think it'll be like to go back now? You think the world will be different after what we done here?"

Chris focused on moving the straw and hay around evenly over the pen's surface. "How different could it possibly be?"

"Who knows what ye' might walk into?" Jim's voice was muffled beneath the sounds of liquid shooting against tin. "What if one of 'em boys on the ship was the great great grandaddy of someone like Winston Churchill? What if ye' go back and the outcome of World War II was different? Or… hell, I don't know… what if what would've been the wife of one of them pairs off with some other poor sap and spawns the son of satan and ye' go back to a nuclear wasteland? Ain't ye' scared?"

"Well, I am now, thank you very much." He moved the straw around with more force, pushing images of a scorched earth into the far recesses of his brain.

Jim cackled with laughter. "I'm just messin' with ye,' big man… Cain't help myself sometimes. Ay, can I ask you to do somethin' for me? Somethin' I don't want Lilly knowin' ye' done?"

Chris frowned, resting his hand against the handle of the rake and leaning into it as he looked into the goat pen. Beneath Wanda, he could only see Jim's knees in the bedding and his hands working her teats over the tin bucket. "What's that?"

"They's a woman named June McLendon. I don't know where she is now, but she lived in Boise City, Oklahoma with her momma' for a time… Born in Texarkana. First thing I done when I won that money was put it in a safe-deposit-box." He grunted as he rose with the bucket and moved around to the front of the enclosure, scratching Wanda behind one ear. "Didn't want to put it in a bank with all the chaos goin' on in the world. I got the key sewed into my boot. If ye'd be willing to look for her, I want to give her the key… make sure she gets that money. And…" He pursed his lips, frowning as he stared down at his feet. "Well, she was pregnant last I seen her. I's wonderin' if ye'd find out for me whether she had a little girl or a little boy… and… what she named it."

Chris nodded, curious, but unwilling to pry. "I can do that. Boise City, you said?"

"Yeah," Jim sighed. "I'll write down everything you need to know. I don't mean to add another burden—"

"It's no burden at all." He wanted to ask more; to confirm the suspicion Jim had a child out in the world and ask why he didn't know whether it was a boy or a girl, but that wasn't his place just then.

Jim nodded, still unable to look him in the eye. "Thank ye.' It'd mean the world to me to know she got that money."

"I'll make sure of it."

"All right beanstalk," Jim shifted his tone, meeting his eyes then with a grin. "Let's go dump this shit over the side and see what's for dinner. Eh?"

Chris laughed at that. "I don't have the luxury of a shower to scrub this stench off."

"You stunk long before you started shovelin' shit," Jim teased, grabbing one side of the barrel's handles and waiting for Chris to take the other. "We all do. We just got used to our stink. Lordt help whoever finds ye' first out in the future. It'll be them with their shirt up over their noses."

Chris snuck a sniff in his armpit as they worked their way out of the hull with the barrel. All he could smell was the pigs' filth. "You really think we smell that bad?"

Jim laughed. "We smell like men, beanstalk... Like sweat and muscle and testosterone and toughness... Although..." He sniffed his own armpit and winced. "...it wouldn't hurt to go for a swim before dinner. That firecracker of yorn will certainly appreciate it if ye' don't smell like pig when ye' crawl in bed beside her."

A quick swim later, they dined in the dining hall, Bruce using the process of perfecting a pork roast dinner to bury his grief. Over the meal, they discussed further details of the trip ahead; how they'd handle potential settlements with the airline, the story they'd tell in customs, how they'd search for Liam and check in with other families, and the final meeting in Los Angeles where they would sail back to the coordinates on Bud's yacht.

Every muscle in his body ached after a long day tending to the livestock and working on the ship's repairs. He sat heavily on the edge of the bed, his eyelids betraying him before he could even begin to unbutton his shirt.

"Hey superman," Maria whispered, climbing into the bed behind him to slide her hands over his shoulders, gently working her thumbs into the muscles at his neck. "You look like you are asleep already."

He tilted his head back against her stomach as she raised on her knees to work her thumbs deeper.

"I have to ask you something." She moved her thumbs in small, tantalizing circles. "About the trip…"

"Hmm?" He hummed, nearly hypnotized by her touch.

"I thought of something when we were at dinner and I was too afraid to speak up. I want to go with you, but if it has really been three years, my visa will be expired. They could send me back to Cuba… and I will be of no use to any of you."

He reached up to place his hand over her fingers where they rested between his shoulder and throat. "I'm sure, given all that's happened to us, they will renew your visa, Maria."

"What if they don't, Kreese? There are enough risks in all of this. I don't want to be one more. Maybe we should send someone else?"

"No," he whispered, squeezing her hand. "I never wanted to go without you… I won't go without you now. I'll apply for a marriage visa the minute we get to customs, just in case."

She stopped massaging. "Just in case?" She huffed, pulling his hair so he was forced to open his eyes and look up at her face. "What do you mean, just in case? I don't want you to marry me *just in case*."

He laughed at the scowl on her features. "Fine, then I'll marry you *just because*. That better?"

She pushed him away from her and sat, crossing her arms over her chest. "I didn't bring this up to squeeze a marriage proposal out of you estúpido. I'm being serious and you're being... an asshole. I don't want my citizenship status to stand in the way of everything we promised them we would do."

He turned toward her, running his palm down her arm. "You're right, I'm sorry. I wasn't thinking about how unromantic that came out... I just... don't plan on marrying anyone but you... I don't want to go with anyone else. If it doesn't work the way we hope it will, if it only goes backward, I can't go without you. I won't. So... if I have to have this unromantic marriage proposal to make sure I can take you home with me, so be it."

"You really want to marry me? I am such a pain in the ass. You tell me this every day."

He laughed, running a hand over her dark hair. "Of course I do. You're *my* pain in the ass, and I love you."

She rolled her eyes. "You are so cheesy. And what do you mean home? Where will *we* go?"

"Well, I'm not sure yet. We could stay with Bud or we could go back to Chicago. I had a house there... I don't know if it's been sold, but we could stay with my parents or get a hotel in the city if it has... if I have any money. We'll figure that out."

"You think they'll hate me? Your parents? Because I am not Alaina?"

He reached for her then, pulling her against his chest. "No, baby. They will love you because I love you."

She sighed. "But Alaina's family will hate me. I'm sure they will want to see you."

He brushed his fingers through her hair, kissing the crown of her head. "They'll have to get over it if they wish to *continue* to see me."

"Are you going to tell them she is alive?"

He shook his head. "No. They won't understand. No one will... and we can't take a chance, with my already damaged brain, that any of us might be locked up for seeming delusional."

She laid still against his chest for a moment and he nearly fell asleep again, but she sat up and frowned at him. "Did you just call me *'baby?'*"

He laughed. "Did I?"

"Sí."

He continued to chuckle. "I'm... sorry?"

She pursed her lips. "I don't know if I liked it... call me that again."

"Baby."

"I hate it," she punched his arm. "Don't ever call me that again."

He fell onto his back, crossing his arms behind his head as he smiled at her. "Never again."

She crawled over him, straddling his midsection. "But I like that you want to call me something sweet... No one ever called me that kind of thing before... try something else."

Tired as he was, he was unable to take his eyes off her from such a perfect angle. His hands roamed on their own up her thighs. "Darling?"

She snarled her nose. "No."

"Dearest?"

"I'm not an old lady."

He snorted. "Honey? Gorgeous? Goddess?"

"No... No... *Maybe.*" She slowly lowered over him, a mischievous smirk on her expression as her hair tumbled down around their faces like thick velvet curtains. "What else?"

"Mrs. Grace." He raised an eyebrow, unsure if he should expect a punch to the ribs or something sweet.

She twisted her lips to one side. "That's twice now you've brought up marrying me in a most unromantic and non-cheesy way. Who are you and what did you do with my beloved Kreese?"

"I'm serious. We know we love each other. We know all the best and worst sides of each other after all this time spent together. I want to marry you. Why wait? Don't you want to marry me?"

She shook her head, but her playful smile remained. "No."

"No?" He laughed in mock offense, sliding his palms over her spine to pull her closer. "Why not?"

"Because one, that is not how you propose to your wife, and two, I am not that easy to settle down." She swept her lips tauntingly over his. "…but call me that again…"

He grinned. "Mrs. Grace."

She smiled. "We'll see."

Chapter Twenty Six

I had the machete in one hand, a large breadfruit that was refusing to let go of its branch in the other as I hacked at the stem, blinking the sweat from my eyes from a day spent in the scorching sun.

We'd spent the week gathering food and water in preparation for our trip. We were a week and a half away from departure and I wanted to make sure Chris, Bud, and Maria were prepared for weeks on the water.

"That's not poison, is it?" Juan Jr. asked from below, causing me to jump nearly out of the tree.

Recovering my balance, I peered down at him. "No, but if you sneak up on me like that again, it could serve as a pretty good weapon." I hacked at the stem again and it came loose, allowing me to shimmy out of the tree to drop it into our basket. "It's breadfruit," I managed, wiping the sweat from my brow. "What are you doing out here?"

"I don't know," he admitted, frowning. "I've been following you for a while, watching... but I'm not entirely sure why."

"That doesn't sound creepy at all." I plucked up my bottle of water and took a massive swig. I offered him a drink and he raised a hand in dismissal.

"Where are your children?" He asked, picking up my basket for me.

"Magna and Fetia offered to watch them so I could help gather food. Why?"

He shrugged. "Curious is all."

I stopped, feeling a little put off by the son of my enemy's sudden curiosity in me and my children. "What do you want, Juan?"

He put the basket down and ran a hand over his thick, dark hair. "I'm just curious I guess... You seem to have this effect on everyone... My father and brother are both mesmerized by you, you've a husband and a fiancé among your party... And I've spent the least amount of time with the one woman everyone is most fascinated by. I was hoping to learn what it is about you that draws them."

My shoulders eased a little, and I let out a very unladylike snort. "Honey, if you figure that out, you let me know. I'm the least fascinating person here. I overthink everything, complain even on a good day, and thanks to lingering pregnancy hormones and your father, I tend to have outbursts of either rage or tears. There is nothing about me that should draw anyone, and I assure you, I am just as confused by it as you are."

He grinned, a rare thing in the world of Juan Jr. It was almost out of place against his pointed and dark features. "So excessive vanity is not how you lure them, I take it?"

I rolled my eyes, pointing toward another breadfruit tree. He picked up the basket and followed me to it.

"Perhaps it is your uncanny ability to walk up small trees?" He teased as I clambered up the trunk.

I giggled, hacking the stems of two breadfruits and letting them fall to the ground. "A trait most men search for in a wife, I'm sure."

"Have you always been so... boy-ish?"

At this, I bent over with laughter once I'd landed on my feet. "I see that you are not the same hopeless romantic your brother is. And no... I was never wildly outdoorsy back home. My time here has changed that. You have to be a little *boy-ish* if you want to eat on a deserted island." I squinted up at him, shielding my eyes from the sun. "I've been meaning to ask you, where do your men think we're going? How much do they know?"

Juan Jr. offered a wry smile, rubbing the back of his neck. "They know we're in search of a bizarre storm on the ocean. They don't know *why* exactly we're in search of it, but they don't ask a lot of questions so long as they're paid for their time. Sailors are quite superstitious, and I've overheard plenty of fascinating theories as to what they think we might find."

I raised an eyebrow. "Such as?"

"Sirens, sea creatures, gold rain, and even God himself."

"What will they do if they see our people disappear into thin air?"

He shrugged. "I would venture to guess they'd write songs about it after they were finished hiding below deck."

I laughed at that, but he didn't, and was studying me so intently, I was forced to look away. "Why are you looking at me like that?"

"My father calls you Gloria sometimes when you're not around." He scanned my face as if he were trying to recall a memory of the woman. "But you're not her. I remember her face. I remember the way she looked when she laughed. Your nose is different, and your eyes aren't as slanted as hers were..."

I raised an eyebrow before turning to the tree beside the one I'd slid down. "I'm glad one of you can see that. It's very odd the way they look at me sometimes. Like they are waiting for me to do something that would expose me as her."

"You had another child?" He asked, forcing the hand I'd placed on the trunk to release its grip.

I took a deep breath and turned toward him. The smile was gone from him and I recognized the heartache that pulled his features downward as he thought of his own lost children. "I did... several years ago. A daughter. She only lived for a week."

"That necklace... where did you get it?"

I frowned, wrapping my fingers around the small pendant as if he might pull it from my neck, feeling the subject matter of Evelyn and her necklace a bit too intimate for the two of us. "Chris gave it to me as a gift one year for my birthday. Why?"

"Where did he get it?" His eyes remained fixed on my fingers where they shielded it from his view.

My pulse was quickening, and I wasn't sure why. "He had it made for me. And I'm sorry, that's all I'm willing to say until you tell me why you're interested in it."

"Do you know why my brother thinks you are somehow our mother? Why my father looks at you the way he does?"

I swallowed, shaking my head.

"Because she wore the exact same necklace."

My knees felt weak and suddenly all the exertion from the day caught up so I was forced to sit down on my butt in the dirt. He followed alongside me, kneeling.

"I'm sorry," he said, "I know how strange that must be to hear, but I couldn't contain it any longer. I have to know where that necklace came from... I have to know why my mother wore it and how it's possible she looked so much like you. Maybe time doesn't work the way we think... And if that's so, then what part do you play in my own history? I thought maybe I was wrong about your features... Maybe you could somehow end up in the 70s... but you're not her. My father won't answer questions about my mother, but you have her necklace. How?"

I blinked. None of what he was saying made any sense. I didn't plan on going anywhere near that storm. I wouldn't go to the 21st century, let alone the 1970s.

Sighing, I raised the little globe against the light. "Do you see this pattern? How it looks like marble from a distance? Look closer. It's hair... my daughter's hair."

He leaned in to inspect it, his eyes widening as he made out the tiny golden red fibers.

"Chris had this made for me so I could carry a part of her with me after she died. There's no way it could be the same as your mother's. Maybe she had something similar, but it couldn't be the same."

He sat back on his butt, folding his arms over his knees while he blew shakily out. "I used to sit in my mother's lap when I was a boy and play with it while she sang to me. I remember turning it in my fingers and thinking those exact same strands of hair were some sort of magic inside the pendant. I'm sorry, but it *is* the same."

I held the pendant out, observing the way the hair shimmered in the sunlight. "Maybe she had one made. I don't know when they started making these, but maybe she lost someone too."

"So I'm to think that a woman who looks almost identical to you had it in her mind to have an identical necklace made and not think that too much of a coincidence?"

I let the globe fall against my collar. "Juan, I have no intention of ever going anywhere near that storm. There would be no way for me to end up in the 1970s. It *has* to be a coincidence."

"Maybe you're right." His eyes finally left the pendant to meet mine. "And if you're wrong, I suppose we'll all find out soon enough."

After this exchange, I wasn't sure I was willing to accompany the others anywhere near the coordinates. I wasn't Gloria, I knew, but... what would happen if I got too close? My necklace being a part of their history seemed far too coincidental.

He pulled something from his pocket, a small dark leather wrapped in twine. "I kept something from mine, too."

I watched him as he ran a thumb over the knot, memories of his family playing out beneath his lowered lashes.

"This is her hair... My Elizabeth... I created this by braiding and knotting it... and inside..." He let out a breath of a laugh. "A tooth for each son I lost... I'd considered their hair, hoping to make a braid out of the three, but we'd kept their locks short after they got the fever... to keep them cooler... And so I pulled a tooth from them myself... to remind me of why I'm fighting this hard to undo it."

"Your father said it's the only reason you still live?" I asked, laying a hand over his.

He looked up at me then, scanning my face once more for indication of his mother. "It is... Saving her from me... knowing my Elizabeth will live and grow old with another and never know the pain of watching her sons die first... of then suffering through her own death... it's the only thing that matters to me."

"What if it doesn't work?" I asked. "If we don't find the storm or we kill the ancestor and nothing changes... what will you do then?"

His dark lashes lowered as he looked down at my hand over his. "I wanted to die so I could be with them... but I'm afraid I've grown accustomed to living again... How could I want to go on after all that? And what would I do with the rest of my life when all my happiness has been stripped away?"

I squeezed his hand. "You know, I thought I'd never smile again after I lost my daughter. I know it's not the same, I barely knew her in comparison, but I know what it's like to crave death... to feel guilty for wanting to live past it... I know how it feels for every smile and laugh to seem like a betrayal because they're not there to share in it..." I closed my eyes, remembering all those same feelings boiling over on that very beach. "Someone once told me that letting yourself love and be loved now doesn't mean you stopped loving the ones waiting for you. It doesn't mean you won't see them again and love them still. He said being happy now doesn't take away from the happiness you had then... You can be happy, Juan. I'm a testament to that, if nothing else. It might take time to get there, but it's possible."

"Maybe that's what lures them to you..." He noted, smiling once again against his dark features. "Hope."

An arm slithered around my waist and pulled me behind a familiar cluster of boulders on my way back toward the beach. I laughed like a child as I dropped my basket and let Jack's hands roam over my sides once my back hit the cool, damp rock.

"I almost forgot what you looked like in a pair of shorts and a tank top," he breathed against my mouth, his hips pinning mine securely to the stone. "I don't care where we end up, so long as you never have to cover up these legs again."

Giddy with the excitement of being felt up, my giggle turned airy as his fingers swept over my exposed legs and his mouth covered the crook of my neck.

"Jack," I sank my fingers into his hair, "I've... been... gone too long..." I managed between gasps for air while he tasted the length of my neck. "The babies..."

"Just a sec," he whispered, nibbling on my ear and liquifying every bone in my body. "This won't take long... especially if you keep making those sounds."

"Jack, seriously," I attempted to protest, not very convincingly, as I pulled him closer. "They'll be hungry soon."

"*I'm* hungry," he answered from somewhere deep in his throat. "And we can hear them from here."

"But..." I tilted my head to give him more room to consume, "it's broad daylight... someone could see us."

His hand slipped up my thigh, beneath my shorts, to grip my bottom, his fingers working inward until they found the source of my liquified bones. He groaned as he pressed against me, finding my ear once more. "If someone's looking for us here, they know exactly what they'll find... That's on them for being perverts, not us."

"Jack..." I tried to come up with something—*any* kind of excuse for why we shouldn't be doing exactly what we were doing, but could only say his name... over and over as his fingers began a steady rhythm against me and his mouth grew more and more heated against my neck.

"Do you remember when I told you I wasn't a jealous man?" he whispered against the moistened skin, unlatching the button on my shorts to slide his hand around to the front.

"Uh huh..." I managed on a gasp, my hips surrendering to the magic he was doing, rolling in sync with his fingers.

"I lied." He slid a finger inside, and I gripped his hair, every part of my body quivering as he worked his tongue and fingers in euphoric synchrony.

I couldn't see or hear or think. There was no island, no ship, no time travel or necklace, no Anna or me or anyone else... If someone had asked me my name, I'd have no answer. All I could do was feel. My entire body was merely a series of nerve endings, all pulled taut as they reached for him, begging for more.

He gave more. His thumb circled, his teeth scraped, his body moved against mine as what he was doing seemed to excite him just as much as it was exciting me. He was an animal... and so was I; my legs tensing, hips flinching as I neared the release my entire being was reacting for.

"I am a very, *very* jealous man." He purred against my ear.

My body writhed against him as his rhythm matched the fervor of his words, my vision filling with bright white stars as I reached the height of my ecstasy.

Not stopping his pace, he slid the shorts down my legs with his free hand, hurriedly unlacing his breeches between us.

I spasmed and cried out, every taut nerve ending dissolving in relief.

"Not done with you yet," he managed, lifting my legs to wrap them around his waist and surge his entire length inside me.

His mouth covered my lips when I screamed out and he pushed deep into me, each thrust feeling like it reached further inside me than he'd ever been. Once again, my vision tunneled and I couldn't hear or see or feel anything but him.

My spine pressed securely against the forearm shielding it from the cold stone, he knitted his fingers into my hair, moving back to my neck to entice noises I wasn't aware I could make while he moved unapologetically, claiming ownership over every inch of my flesh.

He shook and tensed, his breathing more erratic than I'd ever felt as he surged into me one final time. I felt his release all the way down to my toes, and was sure I'd melted somewhere in the process, unable to feel the bones in my legs in order to lower them.

He panted against my shoulder. "Told you it wasn't going to take long with those noises."

"I'm not complaining," I chuckled, scratching the back of his head softly, "but what the hell has gotten into you?"

He breathed out a laugh, slowly lowering my legs for me and assisting while I stepped back into my shorts. "I have no idea... I saw you earlier with Juan Jr. and... I don't know... I just... couldn't stop myself."

I tipped my head back in laughter. "Maybe I'll ask Juan Jr. to walk with me more often, then. That was *surprising*."

"Good surprising or...?"

"Very good." I grinned.

He laid gentle kisses over my forehead then in contrast. "What were you talking about with him for so long?"

I rested my palms on his chest. "Oh, you know... just plotting ways to kill you so we can run away together."

His lips curled upward, but then dropped. "Seriously. Whatever you two were discussing seemed like it bothered you. Is everything all right?"

I nodded. "I think so..." I touched the pendant on my necklace. "Their mother... the one who looks enough like me that Dario reverts to some boy-like state and Juan Josef calls me by her name? She had the exact same necklace as me. That can't just be a coincidence, can it?"

He frowned. "Well, now I'm even more disturbed than I was when I pulled you in here... what does that mean?"

"I think it means I need to stay far, far away from that portal."

He nodded. "I agree."

"Do you think you and I should stay here with the babies while they go to the coordinates? Juan Jr. was convinced that the necklace was identical and I'm a little shaken by it. How could my necklace end up in the 1970s if I don't? And how the hell does that portal work?"

He looked around us, running a hand hard over his face. "It'll be unsafe to stay without the protection of the ship and Uati close by... but... I don't want you anywhere near the storm. Maybe we could go up to the summit until they come back… take a few rifles just to be safe. If the coordinates are off in any way… you wouldn't be safe on that ship."

"So we're staying?"

He smiled down at me; the anxiety melting away as the same realization I was having washed over him… We would be alone on our summit with our children.

"Yes, Red. We're staying."

"Good," I reached up to kiss him one last time, "but before they sail off, there's something I need your help with… And you're not going to like it."

Chapter Twenty Seven

My hands were shaking beneath the table. After my conversation with Juan Jr. and then Jack, I was unnerved by Gloria's connection to me. I needed answers, and there was only one person who could give them. Juan Josef.

I could've easily gone to his room and asked, but I wanted a little piece of myself back, and it seemed more fitting to have him brought to me.

I heard their footsteps coming down the hall, warnings from both Jim and Jack as to what they'd do if he tried anything, and I straightened my back, attempting to look as intimidating as he once had when he sat in the very same seat.

"Are you alright?" Juan Jr. whispered from his seat beside me.

I nodded as his father was ushered into the dining room.

The time he'd been a prisoner had not been pleasant by the looks of him. I was no longer worried about the men seeing him and assuming he was in good health. As a precaution, we'd previously sent them to the top deck to assist Dario in preparing the sails.

His hair and beard were matted, and he was stripped down to a white shirt and black breeches. The white on his collar was showing signs of extended wear and hung loose where he'd evidently lost weight.

"Try anything," Jack growled as he pushed him into the chair, "and I'll kill you."

Jack looked at me, raising both eyebrows in a final plea to let him stay close, but I shook my head and smiled. I was safe.

I waited for Jack and Jim to take their positions outside the door to pick up my silverware and begin slicing my pork. "Eat," I instructed Juan Josef, unable to hide the smile that the order provoked.

Whatever notion of leverage I thought I had over him in that moment dissipated when he slowly pulled his head from his chest and met my eyes. The man looked half-starved and ragged, and yet his eyes pierced into me and made me feel minuscule.

He took the fork and knife in his hands, not lifting his gaze from mine as he sliced through the meat and brought the fork near his lips. "What is it you've summoned me for, my dear?" He casually slid the pork into his mouth and stared as he chewed.

"Why do you call me Gloria when I'm not around to hear it?" I asked, cursing my voice for sounding as feeble as I felt.

He lowered his silverware to pick up his wineglass, swirling the liquid just beneath his face until he'd finished chewing. "I've called you *far* worse names when you are not around to hear it." He sipped his wine as if he were the one sitting in my seat, lowering it slowly to the table on his exhale. "Why should it be any of your concern I call you that one?"

I cleared my throat. "Juan Jr. said she wore the same necklace. I need to know what you're not telling me."

The corner of his mouth drew upward as he glanced at Juan Jr., clicking his tongue. "And here I thought it'd be your brother that'd be the one who would tell her. My my, you surprise me, Juan."

"What are you not telling me?" I asked again. "What do you know about this necklace?"

His piercing green gaze found me again, and his nose twitched. "I know that it doesn't belong on your neck."

"Where did you meet Gloria?" I demanded, my voice showing the frustration that was welling inside me.

He raised an eyebrow, digging back into his food and speaking lackadaisically. "Maybe I met her through a friend..." He narrowed his eyes in simulated thought, biting a piece of pork. "Or maybe I ran into her at a party..." He cut into his meat, waving his fork around as he added, "...or maybe she washed up on my shore..."

"She's not mom," Juan Jr. insisted. "It's not the same face... don't play games, father. Not now. Where did mom get the necklace?"

Juan Josef took a deep breath, rolling his eyes. "I could've drawn that out long enough to finish my dinner." He sighed, hurriedly biting another piece of pork, evidence of his hunger now showing in the way he chewed quickly. "She only ever said it was a gift... nothing more. I don't know how you have it in your possession now, but I had intended to find out before all this..."

"A gift from who?" I asked.

"From *whom*..." He corrected, smiling and straightening his posture. "She never said."

"And it was exactly the same?"

He leaned closer to observe it, the hairs on my arms standing up as his breath landed upon my collar.

"Yes." He lingered there, meeting my eyes with a very ominous grin that told me he knew exactly how uncomfortable his nearness made me. "I've been close enough to have seen every detail of this globe on several occasions and from *many* different angles." He leaned back in his seat. "It is the same."

I shook my head of the implication. "How is that possible?"

He picked up his utensils. "Only time will tell, my dear. I'm sorry, I do not possess the answers you are hoping for."

I drew in a breath, trying to keep my composure. "Well, you know more than either of us. Was Gloria from Columbia?"

"Ah," he chuckled with a mouthful of food, "finally an intelligent question. No, she was not. She was an American."

"How did you meet her, then?" I insisted. "Please... I need to know what my necklace was doing in the 1970s."

He plucked up his wineglass again, closing his eyes as he breathed in its aroma. "She was a photographer. She had been in Columbia to take photos of the Valle del Cocora." He opened his eyes and tilted his glass toward me. "It's very beautiful. I suggest you take a trip there yourself…"

He sipped the wine and sat back in the chair, sliding down to rest his head against the back of it while he held the wine between the fingers of both hands, conjuring up the memory as he stared at the liquid inside. "She'd been hiking in the valley all day with her little camera. She took the most beautiful pictures. That day, she managed to catch the mist rolling off the peaks of the valley. When she was done, she and her companions went down to this small cafe afterward for dinner. I was preparing to leave when she walked in."

He shook his head. "Oh, but I couldn't leave once I saw what was behind those big hazel eyes of hers." He grinned and looked over at me. "She had that same spark you have… I knew, the minute she looked at me, she wasn't in Columbia just to take pictures… she was looking for adventure. She was looking for something far more exciting than the valley. So I stayed… I waited for her companions to leave one by one by one… I watched her watching me wait… and then I gave her her adventure that night." He sipped the wine then, clearing his throat after he'd swallowed it. "And yes, she was wearing your necklace then."

I frowned, taking a hefty sip of my own wine. "Where was she from in America?"

He combed his beard. "Let's see… She grew up in Virginia. Went to college at Rutgers University in New Hampshire… We met the summer after she graduated… And she never left Columbia after that night in the cafe. That night was the one and only time I ever asked about the necklace… she said it was a gift and…" He winked at me. "…we didn't do much talking after that."

I shuddered at the image. "That's all you know?"

He chugged the remaining wine, then sat up in his seat, placing the empty glass onto the table. "That is all I know."

"Jack?" I called out, feeling all my muscles ease when he and Jim appeared inside the door. "We're finished here."

Juan Josef rose from his seat, keeping his eyes on me as he willingly crossed his arms behind his back. "I must warn you before I go, my patience with the lawyer has run out and if you wish to see him survive the night, I advise he be moved to another cabin. I've given my word that I will submit, but I cannot take a moment more of his incessant chatter."

Jack pulled him away from me, pushing him toward the door. "Nobody gives a shit what you can and cannot take… nor does anyone give a shit about the lawyer."

"Ye' alright, Sugar?" Jim asked, looking between me and the corridor Jack and Juan Josef had disappeared into. "Jack's got him handled. I can stay if ye' want…"

"I'm fine," I assured him, slinking down in my seat with my wineglass. "I just… hoped there'd be some kind of explanation." I sighed audibly. "You go ahead. Tell Jack I'm gonna head to our room. The babies will be hungry soon."

"I'm sorry he didn't have more answers for ye.' Goodnight baby girl."

"Night."

I blew out, sitting up to finish off my wine.

Juan Jr. was doing the same. "So what now?"

I stood. "I can never go home… If I get anywhere near that portal, who knows what happens to me? I'm not going with to search for the storm. I'll have to wait here."

"And after we kill the Albrecht? When you forget every connection that necklace has to my family? What then?"

I shrugged. "We haven't agreed on that yet. I've added your genealogy to our list. We need to know who your mother was before we can change anything."

Once I'd gotten the babies fed, bathed, and asleep in the cradle, I slid out of my clothes and into a clean shift. I'd been able to use some of their warm water to wash off, and the exhaustion set in as I sat heavily at the vanity to brush the tangles out of my curls.

My reflection in the mirror, lit by the surrounding oil lamps, looked as tired as I felt. My eyes were red and slight bags had formed beneath them. My shoulders couldn't hold themselves up and…

I blinked heavily, rubbing at my neck. "Are you kidding me?" I growled into the mirror, careful not to wake the babies as I tried to scrub the mark off.

"What?" Jack whispered from where he'd snuck into the room and was leaning against our cabin door watching me.

I stood, whirling around at him as I pointed at my throat. "This is *what*," I hissed, keeping my voice down. "I was sitting at that table pointing at my necklace, calling attention to this very spot, and then I come in here to find that I, a thirty-three-year-old woman, have a goddamn hickey on my neck!"

"*I* did that?" He legitimately looked surprised… and amused… which aggravated me more.

I huffed. "I don't know anybody else that's been sucking on my neck lately. Of course you did this!"

He smoothed over it with his palm, shaking his head. "I'm so sorry. I didn't realize."

"You didn't see it there when I was sitting in the dining room like a damn fool trying to act all intimidating?!"

He chuckled, the laughter reaching his eyes. "Red, I swear to you, I didn't do it on purpose, and I had no idea it was there. I guess I got a little carried away."

"Oh, you think?" I turned away from him, hurrying back to the mirror to rub at the dark purple blemish. "I've never had a hickey in my whole life… A grown-ass woman with a friggin' hickey! God, I feel like an idiot that I kept calling attention to it! How could you not notice this?! How didn't I?!"

He came up behind me, looking at my neck in the mirror as I continued my feeble attempt to wipe the mark off. "Red," he was containing his laughter. I could see his shoulders shaking with the effort of keeping it in. "I'm really sorry… You were up in those trees all day… maybe they thought you—

"Thought I what?" I spun around in the vanity seat, glaring up at him. "Ran into a vacuum on my way down one?!"

He knelt in front of me, sliding his palms along the sides of my hips. "Who cares what they think? To me, it looks like you wore shorts today and the man who loves you very much *and is very sorry* couldn't control himself at the sight of these glorious legs." He grinned, continuing to work his fingers down the side of said legs. "How can I make it up to you? You want to give me one?" He tilted his head to one side in offering. "Go ahead, I'll wear it proudly."

I rolled my eyes, sighing. "No, I don't want to *give you one*."

Mischief sparked in his expression as his neck straightened. "You want me to give you another one? Someplace more... discreet?"

"No!" I laughed at that, attempting to push him away but only ending up closer as he made his way between my legs to coil both arms around my lower back.

"You sure?" He laid a kiss against the mark in question, letting one hand loose to roam back down the side of my thigh. "Cause... these legs are out again and I've got a few ideas..."

I laid my forehead against his shoulder, breathing him in as I let the anger distinguish and my body relax. "I think we're both too tired for that."

"Mmm," he pulled me to the edge of the seat as he tightened the forearm wrapped around my back. "I'm never too tired for *that*."

I breathed out a laugh, adjusting my head to rest my cheek against his shoulder. "Then you have far more energy than I do after today."

"You won't have to do a thing," he whispered. "I'll do all the work."

"Seriously, what's gotten into you lately?"

He shook with a chuckle. "I don't know... But something has definitely changed." He pulled me even closer, petting my hair. "It's like I just realized there's this... I don't know... this deeper connection between us... like I can just be me; say whatever I want, do whatever I want, feel however I want with you, and there's no shame in it. You carried a part of me inside you... you brought life to our children, and I just... I know you more than I've ever known anyone. I feel you all over me. And now all the impulses I would normally contain feel like they're free... It feels like hiding things I want to do or say would be like hiding them from myself."

I hummed happily. "I know exactly what you're saying." I buried my smile in his shoulder, a blush forming on my cheeks as I realized I wouldn't be sleeping any time soon. "What kind of impulses *exactly* are you having right this moment?"

"Mmm," his hands began exploring again, gliding down my back to my thighs to slide all the way down to my calves and back up. "I want to wrap these legs around my shoulders... pull you down into this floor, and bury my face between them until you forgive me for leaving that mark on your neck."

Just the thought of it made all the parts he'd just referenced tingle. He'd never spoken to me like that, and it excited me.

"And then I want to leave more marks... all over your body to pull those same noises out of you that you were making earlier... Marks that'll get you just as angry at me as you are now so I can earn your forgiveness over and over again."

My cheeks burned, and butterflies like I hadn't felt since our first kiss fluttered madly against my stomach on each inhale. "Where would you leave them?"

He pulled my head from him and offered a wicked grin, lowering onto his bottom to pull one of my legs over his shoulder. He pushed the fabric of my shift up, drawing a circle with his thumb on my inner thigh. "I'd start here..."

I leaned back against the vanity, my pulse thrumming as his face grew near enough to the spot for his breath to warm it.

"Then I'd leave one here..." He moved his thumb inward a little more.

"And then..." His thumb made one fleeting pass over the sensitive flesh at my center and sent a chill through me. "I'd finish here."

"Do it then," I breathed.

He looked up at me and raised an eyebrow.

The wildness I felt in that second he stared up at me was freeing. I realized I too could do and say and feel whatever I wanted and there was no shame in any of it. I wanted to give in to whatever impulses we had together... So I grinned at him. "Make your marks."

And then we were both lost. I was gone in the feel of tongue and teeth and breath against my inner leg. I held onto the vanity as his face moved inward and felt every noise he'd warned I'd make escape me when he pulled me onto the floor and made me forgive him... over and over.

Chapter Twenty Eight

The following nine days had gone by quickly. With no further explanation about the necklace, Jack and I had accepted that neither us nor our children should go near enough to that storm to risk going through. The whole thing had put everyone on edge. Unsure what century they'd be going to, Chris, Maria, and Bud treated our time together like a final goodbye, spending every minute they could with the group to soak up our final moments together.

It was their last day on the island when Chris joined me on the beach. I'd been sitting on the sand, happy to have a cloudy and comfortable day, the babies wiggling in front of me on a blanket when he sat down beside me.

"You look happy, Ally." I could hear the smile in his voice. "Like... truly happy."

I grinned. "I think I am... *truly.*" I looked over at him, memorizing those massive green eyes and long nose, praying this wouldn't be the last time I'd ever see my first love in the daylight.

"I'm happy too." I knew he was, and that made my heart warmer.

"Are you scared? About going?"

He nodded. "Yes. And that's why I wanted to talk to you. If we do somehow make it to our own time, I need to know what you want me to say to your family. I know them as well as I know my own and they're going to be on the first flight to wherever I end up to ask questions about you."

I took a deep breath. I couldn't commit to a chance I'd go back. Not with so many unanswered questions about the necklace... It was far more likely I would have to make a life in this time, and giving my family any hope they might see me again wouldn't be fair to them. They'd had three years to mourn my death. They'd be over the worst of it when he showed up. To tell them the truth would be cruel. It would break my mother... if she could even believe it.

"Tell them the same story you tell customs," I said. "You saw me get on the raft and you never saw me again. I can't go back, and telling them anything else... well, it wouldn't be right."

"Are you sure? You could write a letter to prove it... they'd at least know you were happy."

I shook my head. "They'd never believe it, love. A letter from me about being stuck in the 18th century would only serve to incriminate you in their eyes. We can't be sure they'll ever see me again so let them have the peace that comes with the acceptance of death... Let them think they're talking to me from time to time and go on with their lives. I'll tell them the whole story one day when we're all dead and gone."

He let out a long airy breath, placing his hand on the center of my back and scratching softly. "I'm sorry. That has to be just as hard for you to come to terms with."

I watched as Zachary smacked his lips in a dream. "I accepted it a while ago. I know they're okay."

"So you're really going to stay here forever?"

I brushed a few stray beads of sand off the edge of the blanket. "I think so... it's kind of exciting. The freedom to go anywhere... do anything. Be anyone."

He laughed. "It's definitely going to be strange to get used to life there for a year... all the noise..."

"You think, after all is said and done, you'll go back to stay?"

He shrugged. "I don't know yet. I'll use this year to decide, I suppose... hopefully I can still remember my decision if we go through with Juan Jr.'s plan."

I stretched my legs out in front of me, placing them on each side of the babies' blanket to dig my heels in the sand. "What a life we've lived so far, huh? Traveling time and toying with history..."

"It certainly hasn't been boring." He looked out over the ocean. "Speaking of the life we've lived... I wanted to ask for your blessing. I'd like to marry Maria when we go home... and since you and I can't really give each other a divorce, I hoped an approval might suffice."

My entire face felt like it smiled. "Of course you have my blessing." I couldn't help but reach for him, pulling him into a light hug. "Of course! I'm happy to give it!"

He laughed as he pulled out of the hug, remaining leaned in toward me. "You mean it? It's not too soon?"

I shook my head. "What is time after all this?" I waved my arm out to illustrate our surroundings. "I want you to be as happy as I feel, and if marrying her would give you that, then do it."

He raised both eyebrows. "Your sister is going to be difficult about it."

I giggled at that, imagining Cecelia's face when she laid eyes on Maria. "Oh, she's going to be a *nightmare*. You may want to steer clear of her for a while." The smile remained fixed on my lips. "Oh, but your dad's going to love her... he'll hear that accent for the first time and she'll have him wrapped around her finger. Do you remember when we went to that Mexican restaurant downtown, and he forgot how to form words when the waitress came to ask for his order?"

He burst into laughter, moisture forming in his eyes. "And he asked her to bring him whatever her favorite was, and it was the spiciest thing on the menu?!"

I bent over, unable to catch my breath from the memory. "Oh, and he kept eating it and asking her to bring him more milk! His nose and eyes running like crazy! I don't think I've ever seen your mother laugh so hard!"

"All because of her accent! She wasn't even that pretty!" He wiped his eyes, still lit up with joy.

I snorted. "I hope Maria doesn't like cooking spicy food. She'll kill the poor man. We both know he'll eat every bite!"

He sighed deeply. "God, I didn't realize how much I'm looking forward to seeing them again."

"Probably not nearly as much as they're looking forward to seeing you. I'm happy for you, Chris. Really."

He smoothed a hand over my hair. "And I'm happy for you, Al. You didn't ask for it, but you have my blessing, too. I know he proposed to you. And I'm not sure if you needed it, but in the event you did, you have my entire support."

I leaned into his shoulder, unable to stop grinning because I realized I might've been waiting for just that. "Thank you... Please be careful out there and... try to come back."

"I will." He laid his cheek over the top of my head. "You be careful here too. Take care of yourself and these babies. I can't wait to see how much they've grown by the time I get back."

"If you make it there, will you bring back some photos I can keep with me? Of my mom and Bill and Cece... and Owen and Maddy? ...And your mom and dad? And gramma? I don't want to ever forget their faces."

"Of course I will."

"And I want photos of your wedding... of you and Maria... of everything I'm going to miss."

"Ally, I'll fill Bud's yacht with photos just for you."

That night, Jim, Lilly, Maria, Bud, and Chris all insisted on staying with us on the island before they set sail the following morning.

We laid out several blankets on the sand and lit a small fire. Passing around three bottles of port wine, we cozied up together in what very well could've been our last night together.

I was snuggled against Jack's chest where he sat behind me, the babies both asleep on my folded legs. Across from us, Maria was wrapped similarly in Chris's arms, and Lilly laid with her head rested in Jim's lap, staring up at the stars. Bud watched them fondly from his seat beside Jack.

We were all surprisingly silent as the bottles made their way around the circle, absorbing the comfort of being in each other's company as the fire crackled and popped between us. Everyone felt the potential finality of the moment, and time seemed to stop the longer we all went without speaking.

"Ay, Hoss..." Jim whispered, breaking the silence and scratching Lilly's head softly.

"Yeah?"

"What do ye' call a fish with no eyes?"

I laughed to myself, relieved at the familiarness of Jim's bad jokes around a campfire.

"What?" Jack asked.

"A Fsh." Jim cackled for a second and sighed.

"That was dumb," Lilly added, looking up at him with a lack of amusement.

"Alright then," he grinned down at her, "Two muffins are sittin' in an oven. First muffin says to the other, *'holy shit, it's hot in here,'* and the second muffin says, *'holy shit, a talking muffin!'*"

Lilly covered her face with the crook of her arm. "Oh my God. Just stop."

"I got one," Bud smiled, taking a sip of the wine and handing the bottle to Jack. We all watched him as he straightened and placed his hands out in front of him to illustrate for effect as he always did when he told a story. "So there's this penguin... he's out driving around one day and his car starts making a funny noise, so he pulls into this little mechanic shop. The mechanic says to him, *'it's gonna' take me about an hour to check it out.'*"

I laughed as Bud adjusted his voice for the mechanic.

"So the penguin nods and decides to take a walk. The penguin makes it a few doors down and he's burning up... you know, penguins aren't meant for warm weather... so he ducks into this little ice cream shop and orders a big ice cream sundae. Now," he lowered his hands to peer around the group, "I don't know if you've ever seen a penguin eat ice cream, but with no opposable thumbs, it gets messy quick. The penguin doesn't care. It's the best sundae he's ever tasted, and he devours it. By the time he's done, there's ice cream and chocolate dripping all down the front of him."

He smiled, raising his hands back up to continue. "Anyway, the penguin looks up at the clock on the wall and realizes it's been an hour, so he hops off his little bar stool, waddles out the door and back down to the shop to check on his car. The old crotchety mechanic comes out from under the hood and says to him, *'it looks like you blew a seal.'* And the penguin says, *'no... it's just ice cream.'*"

There was a pause for a moment before Jim absolutely howled with laughter, prompting the rest of us to join alongside him.

The excitement woke Zachary, and I brought him up against my shoulder before he could begin screaming.

"Grandpa! That's dirty!" Lilly snorted while Jack took Cecelia into his arms to rock her softly.

"You know who told me that joke?" Bud asked, wiping his eyes as the group settled down.

"Who?" Lilly asked.

"Your gramma."

Lilly gasped with fake outrage, lifting her head off Jim's lap. "My grandmother was a saint and would never!"

Bud smiled fondly, some whisper of a memory dancing behind his eyes to cause the smile to grow warmer. "Your grandmother was so much more than a saint. She was... everything a man could ever ask for all wound up in a single beautiful person. Smart, kind, funny, and the most insightful human being I ever met." He let out a long exhale and his tone turned more solemn. "And you're just like her. Now, I know none of us wants to acknowledge that this might be the last time we all are together, but I need to say this much. She was proud of you and so am I. I don't know where we'll end up after we run into that storm. I pray we'll make it back, but if we don't, I know you'll be all right. Jim, don't you ever stop taking care of her the way you do now."

"I won't."

"And you keep both of our rings and use them to get married. It's what we both wanted... don't wait too long to use them." He playfully narrowed his eyes at Jim for dragging his feet. "I mean it. Bertie and I had fifty wonderful years of marriage with those rings. Jim, you're not getting any younger. If you want to get fifty years out of it too, you better start letting go of those notions of grandeur you think she wants." He turned toward Jack and I. "That goes for you two as well. Marriage isn't about flowers and dresses and fancy food or music... it's bigger than all of that. It's a bond between the two of you and God; a promise to love each other in his light and be that light when the other is in darkness. Life is shorter than you realize... and once you make that promise, it makes better every single thing about what's left of it."

I glanced across the fire at Chris. We'd made that promise to each other a long time ago, and now both of us were preparing to make it to someone new. I was sad our marriage hadn't been the life altering eternal picture Bud was painting, but I was happy it had been life altering for the ten years it was. We were still each others' light in a way, but we wouldn't be the brightest to each other anymore. I was glad he found something brighter.

He must've been feeling similar because his eyes met mine and he offered a knowing smile, glancing at Zachary where he was gradually falling back asleep against my shoulder.

"What I'm saying is," Bud continued, "take care of each other. Stick together. Don't you worry about us if we don't make it back. I'll take care of these two and we'll be thinking fondly about all of you."

There was an even longer silence then. All of us looked at each other, studying faces like it'd be the last time we'd see them. The wine bottles continued to be rotated around the group until they ran empty.

At long last, and much to my surprise, Jack spoke. "There's this image I always had about what a father should be like... The type of man he should be, the way he should make you feel... the kind of wisdom he would bestow... My father was never that. But you are. And the example you have set as a man will serve as my inspiration for the way I raise my children. I want to say thank you. For everything you've taught us... for everything you did for us... For everything, period."

"I second that," Jim added. "Ye' been the voice of reason in a place where reason is hard to come by. Hell, just sittin' next to ye' makes a man feel like he's got some kind of handle on things... Like ye' been guidin' us this whole time. And you," he grinned at Maria. "You been a spark of lightnin' since ye' got here..." He laughed. "Hell, I gotta' hide behind Bud on the days ye' get worked up about a thing; scare the shit out of a man just by lookin' at him. Ye' keep us all on our toes with that firecracker of a personality ye' got, and I'm gonna miss ye.' You too beanstalk. You're a good man, and I'm proud to call you my friend. Ain't nothin' gonna' be quite the same until y'all get back."

Lilly laid back against Jim and let out a long sigh. "And you're all coming back. This isn't goodbye yet."

"I agree," Maria said. "If God has really led us all here, then he wouldn't prevent us from coming back to finish what he set us out to do. We will be back."

Jim grinned. "See? Even that sounds kinda' like a warning coming from you! But you are absolutely right, Sugar. The good Lordt didn't send ye' all this way just to leave things unfinished."

"I hope you're right," Bud said, taking a minute to lift himself up off the sand with a grunt. "We've got a long couple days ahead so I'm gonna' get some sleep. You two give me a hug before I go." He looked down at me and Jack. "I don't plan on saying another goodbye in the morning, and I want both of you heading up to that summit before the ship sails off."

"Here," Lilly sat up and reached her arms out, flexing her fingers. "Give us those babies. I want to get some snuggling in with them if I'm gonna go a week or two without it."

Careful not to wake them, Jack and I handed both babies off to Jim and Lilly as we rose off the sand.

Bud embraced Jack first in a very tight hug. Close enough that I could hear, he whispered in his ear. "You remember what I said to you now. You did what you had to do and you're here now. Being here is all that matters. You let it go and take care of the ones you worked so hard to get back to. Let it go now."

His words tugged at my heart. I knew Jack killed a man during the time he and Bud were imprisoned, but he never spoke about it, and I wondered just how much he thought about it. He'd encouraged me to let go of all the guilt I'd been holding onto... I should've been doing the same for him.

Bud stepped back, shaking Jack's hand before he moved onto me.

"And you," he pulled me into his arms. I'd never been hugged by Bud before and I suddenly regretted that because the sensation felt like a warm blanket in the coldest of winters. "You take care of all of them. Especially those two babies. I know you will. I love you like one of my own... and I hope to see you soon."

I held on tightly, soaking up the comfort of the father figure he'd become to us all. "I will. Thank you for bringing him back to me."

He moved closer to my ear. "It's you that brought him back, sweetheart, not me. And it'll be you that'll need to keep bringing him back when his mind returns to it."

"I will."

He let go and looked down at the group. "I'll see the rest of you on the ship tomorrow. Goodnight."

"We should go too," Chris said, pulling Maria up with him. "It's late."

If I hadn't been ready to say goodbye to Bud, I certainly wasn't ready to say goodbye to Chris. I was frozen in place as they moved around the fire, and a lump formed in my throat that made breathing difficult as Maria coiled her arms around my neck.

I squeezed her while Chris and Jack spoke in hushed voices beside us, tears pouring out of me beyond my control. "Take care of him," I told her.

"I will, and I'm sorry for every stupid thing I ever said to you. I am so happy to know you and I cannot wait to come back and know you more."

"Don't give up on him," I begged. "Ever."

"There is nothing in this world that would make me give up on him. I will be with him until my last breath, I promise."

We slowly unwound our arms, and I took a deep breath just before I fell into Chris's chest.

There were no words.

We held onto each other tightly, probably for far too long, and the words didn't need to be there. I closed my eyes and committed the feel of him to memory, promising myself I'd never forget the way he smelled; the way his arms felt against my back; the way he'd held me all our lives. And I sobbed.

"It's not goodbye," he finally whispered, resting his cheek against the top of my head and waiting until the tears had stopped to let go. He ran his hand down my hair and held the side of my face. "Even if I can't come back, it's not goodbye. You'll always be with me and I'll always be with you."

I nodded, sniffling. "Be careful… And be happy."

He smiled. "I will and I am. You do the same."

He lingered there for a moment more, scanning my face before he straightened and looked back at the rest of the group. "That's about all the goodbyes I can handle tonight. I'll see you two on the ship. Goodnight." He turned quickly away from me, taking Maria's hand in his and disappearing into the shadows as they made their way up the beach.

Chapter Twenty Nine

"Wake up, Red." Jack whispered sweetly, laying a soft kiss on my temple. "We should head up before they sail out."

I sat up, blinking my eyes against the rising sun. "Did they leave already? Did I miss them?"

He ran his palm over my hair. "They went out to the ship about an hour ago. Chris didn't want to wake you for another goodbye. He said the one last night just about killed him."

My nose burned, and tears wanted to come, but I blinked them away and nodded.

"You alright?" Jack asked.

I smiled up at him, touching his face where he'd shaved his beard at some point while I was sleeping. "I will be. Thank you for being so... *you* about all this."

He grinned, turning his face in my hand to kiss my palm. "So does that mean you still like me, then?"

I laughed. "I suppose I do. But you know what I mean. It was hard to let him go last night and I'm sure that must've been... a little awkward."

He shook his head. "I'm not so greedy that I expect every ounce of love you have to be reserved exclusively for me. I know you loved him and I know it was hard to say goodbye. You're allowed to feel that." His eyes lit up with mischief. "And besides, I have an entire island alone with you for an indefinite amount of time to work out whatever jealousy I might feel because of it."

I raised an eyebrow. "Oh? The same kind of jealousy walking with Juan Jr. provoked? If so, I'm going to need to eat something first."

He leaned in. "Honey, you didn't give Juan Jr. a very long, drawn-out hug. You'll want to make sure you're well-fed all week."

Before I could respond, Zachary began to whimper. I sighed, leaning in to kiss his lips. "Your jealousy is going to have to wait. I need to feed him, and…" I bit my lower lip, placing my thumb at the center of his slightly dimpled chin, *"you're* gonna' need to milk Wanda."

He glanced over his shoulder where the devilish black and brown goat was tied beneath the canopy, chewing grass on one side of her mouth as she stared at us with her creepy black eyes. He shuddered. "I swear to God that goat's plotting to kill us."

I pulled Zachary into my arms as he worked himself up into a full fit, glancing toward the ship still anchored off our coast and back. "I think you can handle the goat, dear. You're gonna' want to hurry. Cecelia's patient, but she's not *that* patient. We'll head up once they're both changed and fed. I want to be able to watch them sail out from up there."

He watched as I loosened my tank top strap and positioned Zachary at my breast, then groaned and stood. "Stupid ugly goat," he said to Wanda, marching toward her with the bucket. "Don't look at me like that… neither of us wants this to happen."

I laughed, pulling linens from one of our cases and wondering if I was talented enough to change Zachary's soiled diaper and feed him at the same time. I wasn't, and I gave up almost the second I started, deciding I'd need to wash him thoroughly before I changed him, anyway. "They both need baths, too."

"You know…" Jack called, his voice a little forced as he worked Wanda's teat. "We could just let them be naked… they're babies. Babies are allowed to be naked. It'd save us from constantly having to wash both the linens *and* the children several times a day."

I rolled my eyes. "I'm not leaving my babies naked for spiders and bugs and God knows what else to eat up their little crevices."

"We've seen like two spiders and a handful of ants since we got here. I'm sure their *crevices* will be fine. I know mine will." He chuckled. "The minute we get up there, my clothes are coming off and they're staying off until that ship comes back."

"Is that so?" I smiled, combing the little bits of fluffy blonde hair on Zachary's head.

"You're taking yours off too, you know. We're gonna' do four things this week. Eat, sleep, bond with our babies, and *bond* with each other... None of those things require either of us to keep our clothes on."

"I'm not walking around naked in broad daylight, Jack."

He stood with the bucket, circling back into camp to stick out his lower lip. The pout on such a large man was ridiculously out of place. "Oh, come on Red, live out my island fantasy with me."

I shook my head. "Darling, you might be comfortable walking around in that glorious body of yours, but you didn't just host two small humans inside it to stretch you out in awkward places. I'd prefer to keep my clothing on when the sun is up, thank you."

He knelt to tip the contents of the bucket through a canvas filter and into the little porcelain bottle. "Red, I've seen your body before you were pregnant, during, and after, and I think it's been *glorious* in every single form. If I haven't made it clear that I worship every inch of you, then I've got my work cut out for me this week." He looked down at Cecelia and his eyebrows shot up high on his forehead.

"She smiled at me!" His wide eyes met mine and then went back to her. "She's smiling at me!" He leaned over her, his entire face lit up in a laugh. "Oh, there it is again! I see you smiling, baby girl. You agree with your daddy, huh? Tell your mommy you just want to be naked and free with your parents. We don't need all these stinking clothes, do we?"

He maintained his baby talk as he pulled her up into his cradled arm. Her lips curled up again, and she made a soft and happy sound. "That's right!" He beamed. "No, we don't. We want to be naked and free and oh my God, if you keep smiling at me like that, I'm not going to be able to do anything else all day but look at you." He held the bottle in one hand, grinning at her. "How am I supposed to feed you when you're smiling like that?"

"Well, that didn't take long." I raised an eyebrow.

He didn't look away from her and continued to watch her in wonderment. "What didn't?

"For her to wrap you around her little finger."

He pulled her closer, reflecting every expression she made back to her. "No, it didn't. That's cause she's a daddy's girl, aren't you? Yes, you are. God help any boy that looks at you twice. He'll be dead in his tracks, yes he will. We don't want no stinking boys around here... just like we don't want these stinking clothes, right, baby girl? Look at that smile!"

I'd never seen Jack so entirely at ease, and I loved every second of watching them together. For as much as I would miss everyone that was now on the ship, I was going to enjoy watching Jack interact with his children without the veil of masculinity he kept behind when others were present. I instantly loved him that much more just for the way he spoke to our daughter, and I wondered if I would forget this moment when the time came to change history.

"You're adorable with her," I noted once he finally tipped the bottle to her lips.

His eyes met mine, and his playful expression melted away to something much more wicked. "Don't let that fool you, Red. I'm still quite deadly."

I grinned, shifting into my own baby talk as I responded with, "yes you are, aren't you?"

Trekking up the side of the volcano had been challenging enough when it had only been the two of us. Making the trip with two babies, weapons, ammo, food, linens, and a goat in tow was almost impossible.

We'd each made a sling to carry a baby against our chests. Jack was unwilling to let go of Cecelia, so he carried her along with most of the supplies while I carried Zachary and towed Wanda by her rope. She wasn't too difficult; she followed willingly for the most part, but made frequent stops any time a blade of grass or leaf looked the least bit appetizing.

My sides were on fire by the time we reached the oasis and the bottom cave, but I was relieved to be free of Wanda. We tethered her to a tall palm tree with enough rope that she could easily access the water and as much grass as she could fill up on.

I sat down on a boulder at the edge of the small creek, giving my burning calves a moment to settle. With the pregnancy, I'd been limited to minimal movement, and climbing uphill for hours after months of relatively no exercise felt like it should come with a medal.

"You want to set up a small camp here for the night?" Jack asked, looking back at the cave. "I can go up every hour or so and look out. You're exhausted."

"No, I just need a minute," I assured him. "My legs feel like jello... *burning* jello."

"Tell you what," he unwrapped Cecelia and laid her on the fabric beside me, quickly taking my calf in his hands and kneading the muscles with his thumbs. "I'll run up and take a look, set up their baskets and our bedding, and then I'll come down for you... Give your legs a bit to rest."

I hummed with ecstasy as his thumbs worked in circles, closing my eyes. "Okay."

"Here..." he let go of my leg to pull off one of the rifles strapped to his chest and leaned it against the rock beside me. "It's already loaded. You know how to shoot it?"

I nodded. Jim had shown me a few days prior when we were out searching for boar. "I doubt Uati is going to show up in the half-hour it'll take you to set up our beds and come back."

He smiled sweetly. "I know, but I've left you without a weapon too many times, Red, only to come back and find you close to dead or taken prisoner. I won't ever make that mistake again." He pulled a dagger from a sheath strapped to his thigh. "Take this. You want the sword, too?"

I took the dagger, laying it on the rock beside the rifle. "No. We'll be alright. We're safe up here."

He looked around us, his lips curling upward once his gaze met mine. "I've spent so many nights dreaming of having you up here again... I'd almost forgotten the way the sunlight hits your face and lights your hair on fire up here... my God, you're beautiful."

I snorted. "Jack, I'm sweating from parts of me I didn't know could sweat. You can call me beautiful all you want after I've bathed, but at the moment, I am very much aware of what I must look like."

He shook his head, gripping my chin lightly as he looked over my face. "Even sweating out of mysterious parts I want to know about later, you are beautiful... I'll be right back. Please don't get captured or maimed while I'm gone."

"Unless there's a pirate or a boar in that water, I won't." I grinned. "Leave the soap."

Soap was a coveted commodity, and the moment we took control of the ship, we raided its soap supplies. I was beyond excited to fully submerge in the much warmer water of the oasis pond with a fresh bar of lavender scented soap.

He fished it out of our duffle bag and placed a kiss on my forehead before he stood and headed for the cave, looking over his shoulder at us every few steps.

I glanced back in the direction we'd come for signs of the Nikora I knew weren't there. Jim and Chris had paced the beaches on all sides in search of canoes or footprints and had found none. There was nothing up here to be afraid of. Even the boar didn't venture up this far.

I laid both babies on a blanket on top of a flat boulder I could both reach and see from inside the pond. Looking back at Wanda, who was also exhausted from the hike and had curled her legs beneath her to rest in the shade, I began unlacing my boots.

I slid out of my top and shorts and stepped into the warm water, sighing with relief as the wear of the hike melted away. I spun the lavender soap between my hands until I'd made suds and I scrubbed every corner and crevice of my body. I washed my hair twice and felt cleaner than I'd been since the plane crash by the time I was done.

Cecelia whimpered, and I pulled myself up on my forearms on the boulder to look over her. Of course, she'd soiled the diaper I'd put on her less than a mile from reaching the oasis.

"We're not leaving you naked." I whispered, gently pulling the dress and diaper off her. "I don't care what your daddy says. It's not civilized… so don't sass me." I pulled her against my shoulder and walked her to the more shallow water. There, I rested her on my forearm to submerge all but her head, working the lavender soap over her tiny body and into her fuzzy amber hair. She watched me and smiled as I cupped water in my hand and poured it over her head.

"Oh, you *are* smiling!" I cooed. "Look at you… my beautiful girl… You like that?" I poured the water over her head again and she stiffly wiggled her arms and legs, her eyes widening as she made a happy sound. "You do like that, huh? My little fish."

Again, the corners of her mouth rose upward while her blue-grey eyes moved between each of mine. "Look, you can be a daddy's girl all you want when he's around, but… we both know who your favorite is, huh?"

She yawned as I turned back toward the boulder. "I suppose we should bathe your brother while we're at it… He's gonna' be cranky when I wake him up…" I pulled her up against my shoulder, inhaling the mix of new baby scent blended with fresh lavender. "I love you, my little fish." Wrapping her up in a linen, I cuddled her for a moment more, then laid her beside Zachary.

I tugged gently on Zachary's toes. Waking him up with water was not going to bode well for any of us. "Wake up, little man," I whispered, running my palm over his chest. "And please be pleasant."

His eyes opened, and he looked at me, his little brows furrowing as he stretched and yawned. He really was starting to look like Jack. Where Cecelia's eyes were still a darker muted blue, his had lightened and were almost the same translucent color as his father's. His head had the same shape as Jack's, and his brow and cheekbones were angled similarly.

I pulled off his dress - it was too difficult to sew baby pants that he'd grow out of in weeks - and unwrapped his diaper, then pulled him against me.

He made a few cackling noises that indicated he was less than thrilled to have been woken without food, but his annoyance disappeared the instant I dipped him into the water. His eyes widened, and he made several airy gurgling noises that generally meant he was surprised.

I hadn't had a chance to submerge either of them before. I'd heated water and washed them with a rag, so this sensation was new for both of them, and where Cecelia was in her element, Zachary was anxious.

"Momma's got you," I sang, working soap over all his little folds before I dipped his lower body back in. "You're safe baby. Calm down."

His eyes darted from me to my hands, to the trees overhead, to the reflections on the water and back. He scrunched his face and made sounds, but he didn't cry, so I assumed he wasn't all that annoyed with me.

I massaged the suds into his scalp, scratching gently at the flaky skin on top, then cupped the water and poured it over him, laughing as his eyes rolled back in his head. "Oh, you like that too, eh?"

I rinsed his hair a few more times than I needed to just to watch his reaction, then walked us both out of the pond and back to the boulder. Since Cecelia seemed content wrapped tightly in her blanket, I wrapped him similarly and fed him first, not bothering with my clothing since the sun had warmed the boulder I sat on.

A few minutes into feeding him, a small shimmer of light caught my eye, and I looked out to find Jack leaning against the side of the cave watching us, the sunlight bouncing off the sword at his hip. Or maybe that light was the way he made me feel reflecting back at me. The way his eyes scanned us, the slight upward curve on one side of his lips, he beamed devotion, love, and pride in my direction.

Jesus, I loved that man. My pulse thickened and my throat tightened just looking at him. I realized, as he pushed off the wall, smiling at me as he made short work of the distance between us, that I would never love anyone like I loved him and his children ever again. They were everything, and I knew, even as our ship was sailing away in pursuit of it, I wasn't willing to let anyone take even a second of our memories away from us. In the last few weeks, we'd become a family, getting to know each other on a much deeper level than we ever had, and I didn't want to forget those little moments... the way he'd spoken to Cecelia... the way he'd looked at me and Zachary... the bond we'd formed since I'd given birth... How could I give that up?

I grinned as he sat down beside me, his eyes roaming over my face, exposed skin, and breast where Zachary fed. "Is this what you had in mind for your naked island fantasy?" I asked.

He shook his head, combing his fingers lightly over Zachary's crown. "No..." He let out the breath of a laugh. "No, this is so much better."

Chapter Thirty

Chris

Chris sat in the cutter looking out at water that was a pristine and still reflection of the cloudless moonlit sky over his head. The ship had stopped just short of the coordinates written in Zachary's journal, lowering him, Bud, and Maria down in a well-stocked cutter before sailing a safe distance to the east to wait. It hadn't taken long at all to get there from the island on Juan Josef's ship. Two days of perfect winds and mild weather made the trip an easy one.

They'd spent those two days speaking at length about all the tasks they'd need to manage over the course of the next year should they make it to the future. Outside of locating the right ancestor, charting their genealogy and connecting with families, they needed to find anything they could, be it folklore or hard evidence, that could clarify how the portal worked and look for any indication of anyone ever crossing continuously through it to alter historical events. History as it pertained to Captain Cook's return to Tahiti and the thirty-eight men they murdered needed to be looked into as well, and any strange changes needed to be documented.

Chris also had tasks of his own. Whatever was going on with his head needed to be dealt with right away. The headaches were becoming more frequent. Worse still, his dreams had become increasingly lucid since they'd reached the island.

Nearly every night, he was wide awake inside an old memory with Alaina, only the memories played out differently. In his dreams, she hadn't left, and the problems that had broken them were mended. She felt different—*he* felt different. The dreams had become so real that it took him longer and longer upon waking to differentiate reality from dream, and he felt himself slipping further away from Maria as the nights dragged on.

This made the need for a neurologist more urgent than ever. He loved Maria and had every intention of marrying her. Waking up with her in his arms, thinking she was Alaina, was not going to work out for anyone. It wasn't what he wanted for her—for either of them.

He tightened his arms around Maria, his shoulders tense as he caught sight of the ship—now a small yellow dot in the corner of his vision where the lanterns onboard were lit.

He, Maria, and Bud had said their goodbyes the instant they were close to the coordinates, wasting no time getting on the cutter. Unsure whether the storm would hit on or around September 3rd, they didn't want to take any chances that they might miss the only opportunity they'd have for six months to go back. They'd sat still in their lifejackets on the water for two days and nights, raising their makeshift canopy when the sun was at its highest. The others watched at a safe distance through the spyglass and would remain there until the storm cleared. If he didn't make it through time, he would light the oil lantern to signal them back. If he did...

Uncertainty had been stuck to the back of his throat almost since they'd set sail. *If* the storm came... *If* they survived it... what would they find on the other side? *If* they somehow made it back to the world he once knew, would it still look the same after all they'd done?

He tapped his jeans to ensure both his driver's license and his grandmother's ring were still safely tucked inside his front pocket —well, Jack's front pocket. Since his own 21st century attire had been lost more than a year ago, Jack had loaned him his own jeans and a navy button-up shirt. He was surprised to find both fit him well. Lilly had done the same for Maria, loaning her a paisley blue and white tank and tan shorts.

He shoved the tips of his fingers into the pocket, his pinky hooking around the ring to settle his mind. Since he was the only descendant left of his grandmother's bloodline, and because she'd wanted it to stay in the family, there was no one else he could hand the ring over to. It didn't feel right to offer it to Maria after it'd been on Alaina's finger for ten years. Any woman would feel strange about sharing a wedding ring with an ex-wife, Maria... well, she'd lose her mind if she even knew he'd considered it. He'd buy her a new one, and someday, if they had children, they could pass his grandmother's ring down to them.

He stared at the unmoving water around them. There wasn't even a hint of a breeze. Was this how it'd been in the moments before they'd flown through the storm? He closed his eyes, remembering the sensation of falling out of the sky; the shock, the panic, the... weightlessness... Would it be the same going through from this side of time? And if they made it, how long would it take to find rescue on the Pacific Ocean?

"Mi amore," Maria whispered, leaning into his chest, "are you having second thoughts? You are fidgeting. If you are scared... we could send someone else... we don't have to go."

He grinned, laying a kiss on the top of her head. "For the thousandth time, Maria, I'm not scared." And that was a lie each time he'd said it—a lie he was praying he'd start to believe.

"It's okay to be scared, Kreese. I'm not going to judge you."

He draped both arms around her waist as they looked out over the ocean. "What about you? Are you afraid?"

She rested her head against his chest, letting out a very long breath. "Not yet." She ran her fingertips over his forearms. "I've never seen the ocean so calm."

He tucked his chin into the crook of her neck, inhaling the sweet smell of roses that drifted off her hair where it hung loose between them. "I don't think it'll be this calm for long."

"Will you hold me like this when the storm comes?" She breathed, lacing the fingers of both her hands into each of his and squeezing.

He tightened their joined arms around her, feeling the small tremors working their way through her body to contradict the brave face she was trying to put on. "There's not a chance in hell I'm letting go of you."

She shivered despite the warm temperatures. "I love you, you know… I don't say that to you enough."

He breathed out a laugh. "You don't need to say it. I feel it. And saying it right now feels like you're scared we won't make it."

She twisted her head to look up at him, the whites of her eyes illuminated by the silver moonlight. "I *am* scared. I'm scared of so many things, but more than anything, I am scared I will lose you. I keep dreaming of the first storm, when the ocean swallowed you and I was alone in the water reaching for you… but in my dreams, I cannot find you."

He slid his palm down her dark hair to rest it against her cheek. "You won't lose me because I will not let go of you. Not ever."

Bud cleared his throat, calling their attention to the opposite side of the cutter as he shifted his gaze from the horizon to them. "Have you given any more thought to where you'll stay if we end up in the right time? I know you'll want to see your family and spend time with them, but it may become difficult to slip away to return for the others the longer your family grows accustomed to having you there."

"We have," Chris said, thinking it odd they all felt the need to talk softly when the sun went down. "We'll go to Chicago first so I can see a neurologist at Rush while spending a few months with my family. Once I have answers, we'd like to go to L.A. so we can check in on Liam. I think we can use social media to locate the rest. I'll let my family know I'm leaving to search for signs of the raft."

Bud nodded. "I can meet you in Los Angeles. I need to go to New York first and settle affairs, spend some time with my son, and meet with the genealogists, but then I think it'd be good to remain together... assist each other in locating the families and researching any changes in history."

"I agree—

A bright flash of lightning lit up the sky, silent as it struck the water ahead of them.

"Bud... take my hand..." was all Chris could say before the entire sky turned white and all sound around them went completely dead.

White light enveloped them, and whatever was in the lightning seemed to seep into Chris's brain, tendrils of electricity stretching from the base of his skull to reach for his eyes, ears, and every facet of his mind, unraveling whatever was left of it.

The light dissipated, trickling down into the ocean to leave a pulsing glow around the edges of the boat. Chris blinked, attempting to get his eyes to adjust to the dark after being blinded.

With his head pounding and ears feeling like they'd sunk deep beneath a body of water, he couldn't focus on any one thing. His entire body felt like it was being ripped apart. Memories and dreams oozed into each other as remnants of the lightning continued to fire on all sides of his brain, scenes from his entire life playing simultaneously; some familiar, some new in the seconds before the next strike.

The second flash of lightning stayed over them for far too long, soundless as it raised the water almost in slow motion against the sides of the cutter. Once again, the light crept in through his skull, sprawling out across his body where he felt like it was being lifted.

Weightless and absorbed in the light, he saw Alaina in the hospital, holding Evelyn. In another accompanying bolt, he saw her singing on stage before a crowd. In another, he watched her climbing over the kitchen island to cover his lips with her own, both of them desperately pulling at the other's clothing.

Was he dying? He hadn't felt the lightning strike him, but he was sure it'd hit him over and over. His skin was crawling with its charge.

The dreams that had been plaguing him nightly seemed to take over, blending into sync with the storm, playing out in full through the millisecond blasts of light. Where Maria buried her face in his chest and Bud shielded his head with both arms, Chris stared ahead, unable to look away. The ocean came alive around them as if they were caught in the center of a waterspout with his dreams plastered on every curve of its twisting surface.

The boat dipped forward and back; the waves swelling in all directions, and even as the light over them disintegrated and rain plastered the hair to their heads, no inkling of sound made its way through whatever barrier sat at the edges of his ears.

Another bright white streak of lightning pierced the water all around them, stabbing into the dark surface sharply and sending iridescent ripples along the sides of the boat. For a moment, everything froze. His breath stopped, and even though he couldn't hear his pulse, he knew his heart ceased its beating.

Suddenly, he was standing on his front porch—the world completely silent around him. Alaina's lips moved without sound, but he knew the words even through muted ears.

"Show me how a husband kisses his wife," she said, her eyes and face swollen from tears she'd cried for weeks on end. "And take this pain away for good."

He'd dreamt this before. In the dream, she'd said this instead of asking that he take her to Minnesota. It was a moment that could've changed everything… but it didn't happen. On that same porch, on that same day, she'd said she needed to get away, and she suggested Cecelia's campground. In *this* moment—one he was having a hard time figuring out how he'd gotten to, she didn't. She waited for that kiss. A kiss he somehow knew could change all of it.

'But Maria…'

Maria was on the boat… he wasn't. He could feel the wood boards of the porch beneath his boots… not the shoes he was wearing on the boat, but *his* work boots. He could smell the last blooming hydrangeas on the warm August breeze. He could see Alaina's face, could feel her breath on his lips as she stood inches from him.

Had he been pulled through time to land in this moment before any of it could happen? If he kissed Alaina now, would he erase everything that had happened—both good and bad over the last several years? Is that something he wanted? Is that something *she* wanted?

Before he could move a muscle, a roar of thunder blasted through his lost hearing to force his eyes open. He was back on the cutter, staring out at the amazingly calm ocean; an unmoving reflection of the sky overhead.

Had he dozed off? Was this yet another cruel trick of his mind? Or did the storm hit and take what little was left of his mind with it?

He frowned, sitting up to search for storm clouds, oncoming waves, or remnants of the porch he'd just been standing on. There was nothing but the soft sound of the water sliding gently against the wood frame, the static of their collective breathing, and the pulse of his heart still racing in his ears.

He swallowed, tightening his grip around Maria as he watched Bud slowly uncover his head.

"You…" Bud frowned, shuddering. "You both felt that, right? I didn't dream that?"

"Sí." Maria sat up, her head moving rapidly as she searched the horizon around them. "Did it work? Where are the waves? Where's the rest of the storm?"

"On the other side?" Bud suggested, sitting up to scan their surroundings. "This one felt much different… like… it swallowed us and spit us out."

"But where did it spit us out at?" Maria asked, squinting as she stared over the boat's edge.

Chris followed her gaze to a speck of white on the horizon, a green and red light sitting on each side of it. "Light the lantern and get the flare ready. Bud… grab that other paddle… that's a barge."

Chapter Thirty One

Jack's naked island fantasy was just that: a fantasy. We'd made it back to our summit; the source of our whirlwind romance; the place I'd dreamt of night after night, and neither Cecelia nor Zachary wanted any part in its sentiment.

I'd thought we'd gotten lucky to have two babies that slept frequently and didn't fuss. Yes, they cried, but it had been minimal until the first night we'd all settled down on the landing.

Under a sky full of stars, the hysteria broke loose and hadn't stopped for seven straight days and nights. The entire week was spent consoling one or both of them. They were either hot or cold or bored or wet or hungry or gassy or lonely almost round the clock. Their sleep schedules fell out of sync so that one would wake almost the instant the other fell asleep... which meant neither Jack nor I got more than an hour or two of sleep a night, and that one or two hours was plagued with strange dreams.

Cecelia didn't want to be put down... *ever.* She smiled frequently and was starting to make the most adorable little noises so neither of us really minded holding her, but the moment either of us laid her down, even once she'd fallen asleep, she screamed..

Zachary hadn't quite developed the same social skills she had, but he was cranky and sweaty, and every little thing set him off. If Cecelia cried, he cried. If one of us picked him up, he cried. If we laid him down, he cried. If I stopped feeding him, he cried. Not once, not twice, but three times, he'd filled his diaper so it crept up his back and down both arms. I'd had to take him down to the pond each time to bathe him, since Cecelia would not be transferred from her father's arms to give him a turn at cleaning the mess.

Even when they weren't crying, my ears throbbed with the resounding echo, and my eyes felt like they were constantly fighting against lead weight just to stay open. For seven days, we'd each paced the landing, bouncing, rocking, or feeding them. Up and down we'd gone to the oasis to bathe them or milk Wanda or collect firewood, and each return back up took more and more effort.

My whole body was heavy that final night as I leaned back against the big tree. Cecelia had fallen asleep in my arms and I dared not move her. Zachary was asleep in his basket beside me. I would not make the mistake of carrying them down to the cave. I would sleep against the tree for however many minutes they both remained quiet.

Jack, too, walked as if he was acutely aware of the weight of his bones, his feet dragging as he crossed the landing to collapse onto his butt at my side.

"I've never been so tired in my life," he whispered. "Our kids are assholes."

I snickered, careful not to move Cecelia. "They really are. They're so cute when they sleep, though."

"Yeah." He let out a wide and dramatic yawn, stretching both arms high over his head. "I suppose we'll have to keep them."

"I suppose." I leaned into him as his arm fell gently over my shoulders, his yawn becoming contagious as I was unable to prevent one from escaping my own lips. "God, I miss sleeping."

"Me too. This is a week I would *definitely* erase," he teased.

I laughed. "Oh? So we could live it all over again in a different setting? They'd still go through this crying phase, and we still wouldn't sleep... and we'd miss all those little moments that were good in between." I sighed. "I want to save Anna and all those men buried on the beach, but the idea of losing any of these memories with you and them, it just doesn't seem fair."

"So you've been thinking about that too?" He ran his warm palm over my thigh, the broken calluses on its surface scratching the sensitive skin.

I nodded. "Is that a terrible way to think?"

"No... maybe..." He pursed his lips. "If it is, I suppose I'm terrible, too. Since she died, I find myself cursing every moment we make another memory that could get erased. Hell, just looking at you sometimes, the way I feel about you in those small moments... I don't want to lose even that. I try to warn myself not to do anything memorable... not to think a certain way... but I can't avoid it. We have to try to save those men... to save Anna. I have to think my memories with you and our children aren't worth more than the lives of them. Right?"

I leaned to the side to look up at him. "I suppose we'd make new memories; find ways to feel those same things. It's just hard to knowingly let go of the ones we're making. What if I piss you off royally in another version of the last several weeks?"

He grinned, the moonlight overhead illuminating his amusement in a brilliant glowing blue. "Red, there's nothing you could do to piss me off *royally*."

"Oh, I'm sure I could. Give it time. I'll find a way."

He smiled, running a hand through his hair as his lips turned back down. "Do you think they made it through? It's got to be... what? September 6th, now?"

I nodded. I couldn't say how, but I knew they had made it. I dreamt it, and those dreams felt very real. I had no doubt in my mind that Chris was in our time, just as I had no doubt they would return in six months with the answers we all needed; answers about the necklace, about the ancestor, about the portal, and about our families...

"Do you miss your family?" I asked.

He bent toward me, hovering over my lips as his hand swept over my hair. "My family is right here beside me."

I ran my nose over his, inhaling the scent of him; a sweet mix of the island flowers, fish, coconut, the babies, and sun kissed skin.

"I mean Macy and your mom... don't you miss them? When was the last time you saw them both?"

He shrugged, kissing my forehead before leaning back against the tree and letting out a long breath. "It'd been a while since we were all three together in the same place. Things were... *strained* between my mother and me after the accident with Macy. We tried for a time... holidays and birthdays, but it was hard for her to pretend there wasn't deep resentment there on her part. I knew she didn't mean to, but she'd look at me a certain way when Macy would limp... like I could've possibly forgotten for a second that it was because of me she did. She'd stare at the scars on her face, then look at me as if I wasn't fully aware who'd given them to her. I'd taken Macy's beauty and her disappointment in me couldn't be contained whenever we all got together. I came around less and less over the years. I didn't want to be angry at my mother when her anger for what I'd done was perfectly justified... The wedding would've been the first time we would all be together in... God... maybe four years? I miss them, but it isn't exactly abnormal for me to have gone so long without seeing them."

I laid my free hand over his. "I'm sorry."

"I'm not. I know what I did, and I'm not allowed to feel sorry for myself for the way that affected them."

I frowned. "Do you think about it often? The wreck?"

"I do... I try to remember more... I ask myself if I were sober, would I have had the clarity of mind to react differently? If I hadn't pulled the wheel so hard, could we have avoided the flip? Could I have seen the truck sooner? Every time I think of it, I see myself doing a million things differently in order to prevent Macy from getting hurt. Even just stopping at a gas station to get a damn Gatorade... I wasn't even thirsty. Why did I stop? I could've bought something to drink when we got to the dress store... if I hadn't stopped right then, if I hadn't spent those extra precious seconds scanning the different flavors as if I didn't always reach for the same one, if I hadn't signed an autograph just outside the door, or if I hadn't fumbled with the radio for those seconds before we got back on the road... the truck wouldn't have passed at the moment it did. And Macy wouldn't have a scar on her face or a leg that dragged the floor."

I shook my head, looking up at him. "But if you hadn't done any one of those things and you'd avoided the crash, she might never have met Robert... you might never have ended up here with these two perfect little asshole children of ours. It was a mistake—an ugly, tragic mistake, but one I think was meant to happen."

"Maybe..." His nose twitched as he bent one leg to balance his forearm over it. "But if I could erase those scars and know everything would still work out for the best, God, I'd do it in an instant."

I knew that feeling. I'd been having dreams of my life with Chris, alternate and happier versions of our marriage—ones where I never left him or pushed him away. If I could erase the scars I'd given him and replace them with the dreams I'd been having instead, knowing I could still end up here, I too would do it in a heartbeat.

I ran my finger over his jaw. "I wish I could erase it for you... all of the things that hurt you... if I could take your pain the way you've taken mine from me... I'd love to give you that."

"You *do* give me that." He turned his face into my palm, closing his eyes as I dragged my thumb over his lips. "You give me that every single time you touch me... or look at me... or laugh when I'm near enough to hear it... The things that hurt me can only hurt until I am near you, and then they fade far into the background so there is only you and me."

My eyes watered, and my lips curled upward on their own. "You have the same effect on me. Even before we came up here for the first time, your nearness made void every painful memory so there was only you and me in whatever moment we were in."

He smiled as I moved my fingers over the scar on his eyebrow. "You should really stop saying important things I'll forget, Red."

I bit my lip, letting my thumb trace the bridge of his nose. "I'll tell you again, I'm sure... There was a night on the raft, you put your arm around me, and I felt guilty for it later, but... that night...

I forgot the whole world, and I was perfectly at peace for the first time in years just being held by you."

He breathed out a soft laugh, placing a kiss on my palm before he rested his cheek inside it. "On the plane. You sat down beside me and I had to close my eyes to keep from staring at you. I wanted you the second I saw you, but I saw that ring and knew better. I'd never been so jealous of a man I'd never met until I looked at that ring. I'm pretty sure my heart melted when you grabbed my hand during takeoff." He reached out and spun a strand of my hair around his finger. "I watched you sleeping that night, you know... wondering what you'd be like to kiss... to touch... and I swear, when your eyes opened and met mine, I forgot we were crashing."

"I watched you in the terminal." I hid my smile, blushing slightly as he rested his head back against the tree and closed his eyes. "I wondered what you were like underneath all that attitude... what it'd be like to have your affection exclusively."

"Stalker." He grinned with his eyes closed. "I saw you watching. And I enjoyed it." He opened one eye to peek down at me. "Am I what you thought I'd be?"

"No." I kissed his shoulder. "You're so much more."

"Mmm." He closed his eyes again. "If every muscle in my body didn't feel like it weighed a hundred pounds, I might be tempted to peel these clothes off you and make another memory we won't want to forget."

I grinned, feeling the weight of my own muscles pulling me toward sleep. "We should sleep... one of them is bound to wake up any minute."

He nodded, not opening his eyes. "You know, I've fought grown men and trained for days on end, battled massive waves on the ocean, built a boat with my bare hands, even killed a man after being starved for months... and I've never been as worn out as these two babies have managed to make me."

I yawned, closing my own eyes. "I heard what Bud said to you before they left. You don't talk about what happened on that island... But—

"I don't need to, Red." He pulled me against him, kissing the top of my head. "It's all faded far in the background."

"If you ever *do* need to," I laid my head on his shoulder, "I'm here."

I might've slept for an hour before Zachary woke up agitated. I'd ended up on my side in the moss, Cecelia curled up in my arms and pressed against my chest. Jack was no longer beside us.

I groaned as I pulled myself up off the ground to rub the sleep from my eyes.

"I'll get him," Jack assured me, appearing from the edge of the landing to kneel down next to the basket. I could smell what ailed Zachary and was grateful not to be the one to clean this particular mess. "Looks like the ship on the horizon," he said, smiling. "I can see lantern light."

I yawned, glancing in the direction he'd come from, excitement welling in my stomach at the promise of additional help. "You think we should head down since we're up?"

He shook his head. "Neither of us is capable of heading *anywhere* any time soon. We're both running on empty." He pulled Zachary from the basket, holding him out at a distance as he caught a whiff of his diaper. "Jesus…it's everywhere again! How does he keep doing this? Nobody has that much shit inside them!"

I laughed out loud at that. "Your son does, apparently."

He gagged to one side. "I'm gonna need to take him down again to clean this up in the pond. We used the last of the water on the last one. You think something's wrong with him? This can't be natural… can it?"

I shrugged. "I don't know what's normal. He doesn't seem sick. He doesn't have a temperature or anything. I think it's just diarrhea."

"Well, he's blown through every clean linen we had with these explosive—*Oh my God*, is he seriously going again?"

A rumbling sound from Zachary's bottom clarified that he indeed had more to give, and once again Jack gagged loudly, keeping Zachary at arm's length while he stood.

"Jack, honey," I pulled Cecelia into my shoulder as I moved to stand, "I can take him."

"No, no, I can do it," he assured me through queasy vocal cords. "You've cleaned him every other time. It's... my turn."

I stood anyway, unable to hide my amusement at the sight of Jack holding our child as if he were a ticking bomb about to explode. "I'll come down with you, anyway. Cecelia spit up in my hair earlier and I didn't have the energy to do anything about it."

"Oh, you knew?" The corner of his lips curled teasingly upward. "I didn't want to say anything earlier..."

I rolled my eyes. "I hate to be the one to tell you this, Jack, but you're in no better condition. That shirt you've got on has at least five new stains on it and I can't be sure how many of them are spit up and how many might be... other."

He stifled a gag, his eyes widening as Zachary's bottom bubbled again. "I told you to let us all be naked. You didn't listen. Now every bit of fabric we have is soiled."

I giggled. "It's really been the most romantic week, hasn't it?" I looked over his shoulder at Zachary's puckered face. "Darling, you can't hold him like that the whole way down."

"You wanna bet?"

I shook my head, juggling Cecelia as I removed my top. "Here. Trade me. I'll bathe with him."

He sighed, allowing me to swap them and pull Zachary against my skin. "So very, very romantic."

I cringed at the feel of his slick skin against mine, avoiding looking down. "The sun will be up soon. We'll wash them and our clothing and the linens. While everything's drying, we'll squeeze in a nap down there, then we can start heading down. I want to know what happened and get Magna's opinion on whatever might be causing his diarrhea. Plus, honestly, we could both really use a couple extra sets of arms for an hour or two."

Chapter Thirty Two

The sun was high overhead when we made it down to the beach to greet the others. Lilly was reaching for Zachary before I was even off the trail, and I was beyond happy to hand him over.

"Keep him," I managed, collapsing onto the sand by her feet once she'd cradled him against her chest. "I haven't slept in days."

She giggled. "You heard your momma," she cooed, snuggling him against her cheek, "You're mine now. She can't take it back."

I covered my eyes with the crook of my arm as I laid back against the warm sand. "Oh, you'll change your mind the minute he fills his diaper again. How'd it go?"

She sat down beside me, pulling Zachary against her shoulder and cautiously checking his diaper. "It went well, I think. It was... crazy, really. They disappeared into thin air. The storm came out of nowhere, and we all knew what it was. Everyone on the ship lost their hearing, and we were scared we might get sucked up with them... but then they went through, and the waves came after... they were worse than I remembered. It was all we could do to get the ship out of there without capsizing. I've never been so scared in my life. Jimmy puked!"

"Did not!" Jim sat down beside Lilly, Cecelia curled inside one arm as he grinned down at me. "By the looks of things, ye'd think yuns was the ones out there battlin' the ocean. Sugar, ye' look like ten miles of bad road. What the hell happened to ye?"

I groaned, sitting up to glare at my two children who were behaving like perfect angels in their arms. "Those two happened."

He chuckled. "These two little bundles of joy? I don't believe that for a second."

I waved him off, running a hand over my face. "Tell me more... you're sure it worked? Did you go back to look for them?"

Jim nodded. "Yeah, we circled back once the storm died down. Went straight to the coordinates and waited til mornin' and there wasn't no sign of them whatsoever. We sailed all around the area for a full day before we come back."

I exhaled heavily. "I dreamt that they made it through... it felt real... I've been dreaming all kinds of things that feel real lately since these two barely leave me any time to sleep. I hope they're alright."

"Time will tell, darlin.'" He shielded his eyes as he looked up at the source of the large shadow that suddenly cast over us. "Ay, Hoss. Ye' ain't gonna' believe the week we had out there. Did ye' get a look at Phil?"

"No," Jack yawned, sitting down beside me. "Why?"

Jim rolled his eyes and shook his head. "Well, the minute we sailed off, we had to separate Phil and ole' Juan Josef. That summbitch stabbed Phil right through the cheek with a dang paperknife. I don't even know how he got a paperknife, but I'll be damned if it didn't go all the way through! Pretty sure it's infected. It don't smell right and his face is so puffed up and bruised it'd scare a buzzard off a gut pile. I almost feel sorry for the ugly bastard. *Almost.* We gonna' have to figure out somethin' to do with him. I got no love for the man, but it ain't in me to let anyone suffer like 'at."

He scratched at the growth of beard forming along his jaw. "And then, if that wasn't enough, one of them men figured out Juan Josef wasn't sick. He musta' overheard us talkin' one night cause he turned a dang pistol on me and Kyle when we was down there keepin' an eye out. He demanded we let him see the captain... and well... I wasn't too keen on havin' a gun pointed at me just then. So... long story short, we got us a third prisoner now."

"Jesus," Jack muttered. "Which one?"

"That scrappy lookin' one that's missin' a tooth right here," he pointed at his left canine. "Eli... I tell ye,' them sailors sure can put up one hell of a fight. Was all I could do to get the scrawny lil' summbitch wrangled and in them shackles. *Then*..."

"There's more?" I asked.

"Lots more, darlin. Try to keep up.'" He winked. "One of the pigs died... ain't no tellin' what was wrong with it, but it up and died without reason. Wasn't old enough to die of old age... and 'em pigs been eatin' better than the lot of us. Pen was kept up too. If it had some kind of disease, the rest of 'em pigs got it too. So we ain't eatin' none of 'em till we can figure what's wrong. Don't want none of yuns goin' near 'em neither. Gonna' have to wrangle up the local boar if we want pork for supper till I can figure out what happened. Otherwise, we gonna' be on a strict fish diet for a while."

Jack ran a hand over his beard. "That's not ideal, but we can replace them. Not the worst news."

"Ain't done yet." Jim looked back toward the ship where it was anchored on the water. "We took some damage in that storm. The men are all in there workin' on it with Michael and Kyle... and while Kyle's gone, there's one more thing..."

I frowned as both his and Lilly's expression turned solemn. "What?"

"Fetia's bleeding," Lilly said. "It started a few days after the storm... spotting mostly, but Magna's in with her. We don't know if it means anything yet, but we thought we should warn you just in case... Kyle doesn't know. Maybe we could send him up to the summit with Michael for the first watch until we know what's going on. The way he worries about her might make things worse."

"Oh no," I looked back toward the ship. "I hope it's nothing... that poor girl. Whatever I can do to help, I will."

"Well," Jim grinned, "ye' can start by gettin' some sleep. Ye' ain't gonna' be able to help no one like ye' are. Hell, you look like you're about to fall over."

I sighed. "Zachary's had diarrhea almost since the moment you left, and Cecelia's just been crying constantly…"

He looked down at Cecelia, who was as docile as she could be, staring happily up at him. He closed one eye and looked back at me. "What ye' been eatin' all week?"

I pursed my lips as I tried to remember. "Mostly the fish from the pond up there. We took some guava and F'ei and a bit of bread, but it didn't last."

He smiled and shook his head. "Well, that's why, sweetheart. That pond up there's got crystal clear water. 'At means 'em fish are probably loaded up with mercury. Hoss, ye' shoulda' knowed that. Everyone knows mothers ain't supposed to eat nothin' with mercury cause it'll upset the baby's stomach. Stay away from the fish in that pond and the ones at the fall. Eat plenty of bananas and bread and I bet money he'll be right as rain by tonight." He touched Cecelia's nose. "And so will she. She's probably just pickin' up on his bad moods. Twins been known to do that, ye' know."

I smacked my palm to my forehead. Of course, that was it. He'd gotten diarrhea the first night we were up there and had it the entire time. I hadn't even considered it would have anything to do with my diet. "Well, now I feel like an idiot. I should've thought of that…" My eyes began to water as I looked at Zachary's tiny body against Lilly's shoulder. "My poor baby…"

"Don't you dare start squallin' now," Jim reached over and put his palm over my hand. "He ain't hurt. Now, you're wore out, both of yuns, and wore out folks ain't exactly of sound mind. Go on and lay down for a little while. Let uncle Jimmy handle it."

Chapter Thirty Three

Chris

Chris held onto the armrests of his seat tightly as their plane moved toward the runway. He hadn't considered, in all their endless preparations, just how difficult flying would be after they'd survived a commercial plane crash.

They'd made it onto a barge headed into Los Angeles. During their time onboard, he'd learned from the ship's captain, Dennis Mitchell, that they'd come through the storm and into the year 2020. Dennis was a friendly and laid back man, one who was quick to fill them in on *all they'd missed* as it pertained to the global Covid-19 pandemic. Chris couldn't help but wonder if their time in the past had somehow contributed to it, far-fetched as it may have been that any man onboard Juan Josef's ship might've been an ancestor to someone who could've prevented it. Dennis had also informed them that the search for flight 89 was a bit of a worldwide sensation for quite a bit of time. Nothing from the plane had ever been recovered, which gave Chris a chill since he assumed only the front part of the plane had actually gone through time. Where had the rest ended up?

At customs, the airline had made a show out of welcoming them back, showering them with food and drinks before they were taken to be questioned over and over as to what they remembered of the crash and where they'd been. All three had been kept separated for days as they answered the way they'd rehearsed: they hit a storm, the plane went down, there were others on a raft, they ended up on an island, after years of waiting, they ventured out on a small boat they found in a cave there.

Mid-questioning, he'd insisted on contacting his parents and had sobbed when he heard their voices over the phone. Both his mother and father had known he was alive before he had the chance to call. With Covid travel restrictions, they were unable to fly out to greet him, but would be waiting for him at O'Hare when he got there. His mother informed him they would likely not be the only ones there to receive them.

He, Maria, and Bud had apparently gained celebrity status before ever even making it to the border. Within hours of Dennis contacting his superiors with news of their rescue, their faces had been plastered all over every major news media outlet. Due to its previous global coverage, family, reporters, lawyers, doctors, and even long-forgotten friends were lining up to vie for their time.

Due to the extreme circumstances, Maria's visa had been renewed for six months to allow them time to apply for a fiancé visa. She'd been uncharacteristically quiet about the whole matter; nervous and docile from the moment they'd been brought onboard the barge.

Even as she sat in the seat beside him on the plane, she chewed her lower lip and stared forward.

"It's going to be okay," he whispered, releasing his grip on the armrest to take her hand in his. "We'll be back on the ground in no time."

She frowned up at him. "I am not afraid to fly, superman. I am afraid of being back on the ground. Everything is different now."

He sighed, pulling his newly secured phone from his pocket to pull up an article he'd been reading on Covid. "I don't think this pandemic has anything to do with what we did. Here... read this. It sounds like it would've happened either way."

She shook her head. "I don't mean that. I mean you. *You're* different. You can't even look at me. What happened in that storm?"

His cheeks flushed, and the hairs on the back of his head stood on edge. "I'm looking at you now."

She narrowed her eyes. "You are looking at me differently. Something happened to you in that storm. On the ship… at the hotel… you can't touch me, and you don't see me the same. You haven't kissed me once since we came through. What happened to you? Tell me the truth."

"It's nothing, Maria." He shifted uncomfortably in the seat. "It's just my head. I've been having weird dreams and headaches and I'm sorry. I didn't realize it was affecting you."

"Dreams about what? Or should I be asking *who*?"

The plane beneath them vibrated as it readied for takeoff. He laid his head back against the headrest and squeezed his eyes closed, visions of the last time he was on an airplane racing through his mind. "It's nothing, I swear. There's just a lot on my mind. I'm sorry."

"You are afraid of this plane?" She taunted as it sped forward. "You should be more afraid of this conversation. Tell me what you are dreaming of that prevents you from seeing me."

He couldn't tell her he was living out alternate versions of reality almost on a constant loop in his brain, regardless of whether he was awake or asleep. Nor could he tell her those versions felt as real as the ones he remembered. He couldn't tell her he felt a guilt when it came to her presence beside him because of a newly regained closeness to Alaina as a result of dreams where she still loved him. None of it would matter once he got to the neurologist and could prevent the dreams from happening altogether. "It doesn't matter, Maria. We're going to get it fixed soon enough."

"Are you dreaming of *her*? You said her name twice last night in your sleep. Tell me what is happening with you. You are the man I love, and I don't want to be kept in the dark while you are struggling, even if what you are dreaming is not something I want to hear. Tell me why you can't look at me."

He opened his eyes, forcing his gaze upon her as the plane shook around them. "Yes, I'm dreaming of her… and I can't stop it. It doesn't mean anything. Whatever was in that storm unraveled my already deteriorating mind and now it's a little... scattered. We'll get it cleared up. Okay? It's nothing."

"What kinds of dreams?" She asked as the wheels lifted off the ground and his stomach danced.

"Maria," he took a deep breath, clinging to the armrests, "I have no control of them... They just... keep happening. They don't mean anything. We have bigger things to worry about right now."

Her eyes watered. "Mi amore, there is nothing bigger for me to worry about than you. I am not angry about dreams you cannot control. I am angry you will not tell me about them. All I want is to be beside you; to help you. I came with you so I could do that. I have no one here... no place to go but where you are. If you cannot look at me, I need to know why. I need to know what I can do to help you through it."

She was right. Keeping her in the dark was unfair... being unable to look at her the same was even more unfair. "I keep seeing this version of our lives where she didn't leave... where I never cheated... where we fixed it and were happy; as happy as we were when we started dating... and they keep coming; one after another after another as my mind slips further out of my control. I don't want to think of these things, don't want to feel the way I do when they come in, and the sooner I can get to a doctor and get it taken care of, the better. I love *you*, Maria."

She nodded, resting her head against her headrest as she let out a long exhale. "I know you do. And I didn't come through time to judge you for thoughts you can't control." She laid her hand over his. "Even if you can't look at me, I'm here. And I want to know every time this happens. Don't hide from me, Kreese."

"It's happening now," he admitted.

"Right now? You are thinking of her right now?"

He nodded, closing his eyes. "We're on the first flight and she's playing with my hair, telling me about this snorkeling spot she read about that she can't wait to see. One of her hands is holding onto mine... she's been talking the whole flight about all the things she wants us to do when we get to Bora Bora... She's smiling... but that's not how it happened. We barely said two words to each other. She had her nose in a book through half of the first flight, then passed out for the rest. I don't think she even looked at me for the duration of the trip... but this... it feels just as real."

He opened his eyes and watched as Maria attempted to cover her frown with some semblance of compassion. "What do you think it means that this is what you are thinking of?"

He shrugged. "Maybe it's some weird reaction to leaving her behind... Like maybe my mind is trying to mend the relationship we both ruined before I come face to face with her family?"

"You think they will be at the airport?" Her eyes widened.

He pulled her hand into his lap, surrounding it with both of his. "They will be. My parents mentioned they were coming. It's okay."

"Is it?" She turned toward him in her seat, panic settling over her features. "Do they know about me?"

"Yes."

She sucked in sharply. "Ay Dios mío, I'm not ready for that. I could've pretended to be someone else... You're not ready for that... What the hell am I going to say to them? They're going to hate me."

He shook his head. "If they're going to hate anyone, it'll be me, and they'll get over it. Don't worry. You're safe."

Her breathing grew ragged. "I don't know if I can do this... maybe you go without me... I'll meet you somewhere after you are done with them... I'm too afraid."

"*You're* afraid?" He laughed softly. "Maria, you've faced far worse than the McCreary's and didn't show the slightest bit of fear. You'll be fine. I promise. No one is going to hate you."

She let out an audible sigh as she pulled her hand away. "You should've told me. Now I only have a few hours to figure out what to say to them."

"Maria—

"¡Cállate! I have to think now. I don't have time for your nonsense. There's too much to plan."

He snickered, laying his head back against his seat and closing his eyes as the plane leveled out. What *would* he say to Alaina's family once he saw them?

The wheels of the plane touching down on the runway woke him from a deep sleep; one where Alaina had been lying in his arms on their bedroom balcony. He was looking up at the stars while she was looking up at him. They'd been talking about pie… playfully arguing in support of either chocolate or cherry being the better option, and she would kiss him each time he moved to make his case for chocolate. He shuddered, attempting to shake the intimacy of the dream from his skin; to remove the feel of her lips from where they'd been making their way down his jaw.

He looked to his right. Maria's head was rested against the window. Her eyes were open, but she was lost in some kind of dream as she stared out at the moving runway.

Probably a dream of him… what was he going to do until he got help? He couldn't keep pushing her away. He had to find a balance. Maybe there was some kind of pill he could take… something natural to help ease the illusions.

"How are you two doing?" The tall blonde flight attendant asked, leaning against the seat in front of them.

They were two of only six people total on the flight, and the attendant had recognized them from the news, taking extra steps to check in on them after take off and now that they'd landed.

"We're fine, thanks," Chris told her. "Ready to be home."

"I can imagine." She winked, then proceeded down the aisle toward the other four passengers.

"Home," Maria said softly, fogging the window with her breath and drawing a heart in it with her pinky as the plane turned into the gate. "I have no way of being prepared for what's about to happen."

"It'll be over before you know it, and we'll be alone soon enough."

She sighed, unlocking her seatbelt as she straightened and turned toward him. "Can I kiss you, or is it weird?"

He smoothed a hand over her hair and smiled. "You can always kiss me. It's not weird." He leaned in, pressing his lips gently to hers.

"It *is* weird," she whispered after she pulled away. "When will you see the doctor?"

He swallowed the lump in his throat. "Three days."

She took a deep breath. "Okay. Then I will spend three days avoiding you to look for Izzy and Liam's family online."

He remained inches from her lips. "I'm sorry."

"It's not your fault." She patted his cheek, shifting her tone back to cool and suppressing whatever emotion had started to surface. "I have gone much longer than three days without kissing you before. I will be fine now. Come on… let's go see this family that isn't going to hate me, eh?"

She stood and waited for him to unlatch his belt and lead the way. They had no luggage to reach for, and that in itself was a strange thing. He took her hand, and they walked silently through the jet bridge and into the gate. He kept her hand in his as they made their way through to the arrivals area.

He could see his mother pacing in front of where the others were seated, and that image made his knees tremble.

He'd been unable to conjure her face, but now she was there, the worried lines creasing in the corners of her eyes and brow. Her salt and pepper hair fell in layers over her baby blue peacoat. She turned, and the moment her green eyes met his, his heart stopped. "Mom," he managed, squeezing Maria's hand as he was unable to move his legs to take another step.

Maria stared at him, then at his mother as she raced toward them. She let go the moment his mother was within reach, and he collapsed around her small figure, clinging to her as he pulled her tightly against him.

"I knew you were alive, my angel." She kissed his temple, weeping as her arms tightened around him. "I knew it all along! I told everyone you'd be back. They all said I was crazy."

"I'm here," he cried against her, his cheeks burning from the smile he couldn't contain. "I'm here, mom."

"Son," his father said from somewhere nearby, and suddenly another set of arms were around both him and his mother. "I missed you so much."

They held onto each other until their tears dried. Unwinding slowly from the embrace, Chris looked past them to find Alaina's mother, Sophia, her uncle Bill, and her sister Cecelia waiting patiently for their opportunity to receive him.

Taking a very deep breath, he stepped toward them, unsure what would come next.

Sophia was trying very hard to keep her tears at bay. Her entire body was trembling with the effort. It was amazing how much she looked like Alaina when she was fighting tears.

She forced a smile as she met his eyes. "Well, come and give me a hug already."

He did so, happily, and he felt her breathing hitch as a few of those tears escaped her while she held onto him. When she pulled back, she straightened, running a hand over her pristine red hair as she inhaled deeply. "Your mother said you saw her get on a raft," the word *'her'* trembled, nearly exposing the breakdown she was holding in, but she recovered quickly. "So she lived through the crash?"

He nodded. "The raft disappeared in the storm. That's all I know."

She sniffled. "Well, that's enough for me to hold on to."

Cecelia was standing next to her and hadn't taken her eyes off him for even a second. "And you were stuck on an island all this time?" She asked, her tone incriminatory.

He cleared his throat. "Yes."

"And… you never thought maybe, since you saw her float away on a raft, she could've been rescued?"

"I hoped she had been… prayed for it almost every night I was on that island." And that was true.

"But you still…" her eyes drifted to Maria, who was standing uncomfortably to one side, her arms hugging her chest while she stared at her feet. "Are you even going to introduce her, or are you going to leave her standing there like that?"

He curled an arm around Maria's waist and pulled her against him. "I have spent countless hours trying to figure out how I could possibly introduce her to any of you after all this… And there's only one way. This is Maria, my fiancé." Maria's eyes went wide as she jerked her head to stare up at him. He smiled down at her. "I fell in love with her. And I didn't do that with the intention of hurting anyone. It just happened, and there was nothing either of us could do to prevent it." He refocused on Cecelia. "That doesn't mean I ever stopped loving your sister. I cannot begin to explain to you what we've been through together, but I will say that if you intend to have a relationship with me, you will also have a relationship with her. That's not negotiable."

His mother extended both arms to Maria. "It's so good to meet you, dear. I'm Evelyn, everyone calls me Eve."

Maria awkwardly moved into her embrace.

"And I'm Mike," his dad beamed, pulling her into a tight hug. "Welcome to the family."

Chris watched as Sophia and Cecelia struggled with the scene playing out before them. He knew it had to be difficult, and his heart ached for them… it ached for Alaina as well.

Bill extended his hand to Chris. "Well, I'm happy for you. I never thought I'd see you again. Welcome home." He looked over at Maria, who was recovering from the bear hug his father had forced upon her. "Both of you."

Sophia snapped out of whatever daze she was in, blinking as she made eye contact with Maria. "I'm Sophia. I brought you some clothes… I thought you might need them… and…" she glanced between Cecelia and Chris. "We kept the house… in case you ever showed up. Cecelia's been taking care of the place while you were gone. All your things are still there."

Cecelia nodded. "I'll need a few weeks to pack my things and find a new place to stay. I hope you don't mind?"

Chris frowned. "What about Owen? And Maddy?"

Cece looked at her mother, then back up at Chris, both of them with matching puzzled expressions. "Who are Owen and Maddy?"

Chapter Thirty Four

"I think we changed something big," I said, glancing over my shoulder toward camp before looking back at Lilly as she dramatically lowered her upper body into the water.

Jack and Jim had taken the babies to allow us both time to slip away for a much needed bath before we all headed back to the ship for the night. "What do you mean, *changed something big?*"

I ran the soap along my forearm. "I mean... I've been having these dreams... but they're not dreams... they're *memories.* I thought, at first, it was just from a lack of sleep with the babies being up all night... but no. Lilly, I have new *and* old memories of my life."

She tilted her head to one side. "Such as?"

I spun the soap between my palms. "Well, I've realized after running through them over and over in my mind, there's one core change that set the rest in motion. My sister never married Owen."

She frowned. "How could what we did here affect your sister's marriage?"

"He had to be a descendant of one of those men buried on the beach. That's the only thing I can think of... There's no other way we could've changed that. But if Owen doesn't exist, then Maddy doesn't exist, and those two were my sister's whole world."

She stole the soap from me to create a lather between her fingers and work it through her hair. "How can you know for sure these aren't just weird dreams?"

I shook my head. "Her not marrying him changed *everything* about my life before the crash, Lill. And all those changes are alive in my mind; just as real as the originals. I can feel them. I didn't leave. Chris didn't cheat. We fixed it. We were happy. Like... *really* happy. Perfect even. I didn't suggest the trip to Bora Bora. He surprised me with it." I dipped my arms under the water, my mind racing as I tried to organize the stacks and stacks of memories that were playing behind my eyes. "I still ended up here though, even with the change..."

"Stop," she held up her palm, squinting one eye as soap crept down her forehead. "You're going too fast. Start with the very first thing you can remember that's changed. Walk me through everything different that led up to the crash."

I waited until she'd rinsed her hair, measuring my new inventory of life against the old for differences.

"The first thing would be our second official date... it used to be Cece's wedding, but that changed. Instead, he took me out to this absolutely gorgeous rooftop restaurant in the city. Then afterwards, we walked to this little bar that had an open mic night. He pushed me to sing for him... and after several drinks, I did... I was so nervous when I got on that stage... so many more people were there than I remembered and my hands shook over the keys of the piano, but I did it. I sang one of my songs and I remember feeling so good because all those people cheered for me afterward... I can't even tell you how many people came up to shake my hand when I came offstage... and Oh!" I covered my mouth as the memory flooded my mind. "We had sex for the first time that night... at his apartment."

"So the new you is more slutty than the old one?" She teased, bouncing her eyebrows.

I shook my head. "But... wait..." I frowned. "The first time we were supposed to have sex was after he told me he loved me at the waterfall... but... we never went to the waterfall in the new version. And..." I squinted my eyes. "The first time he said he loved me was the morning after that second date... over breakfast in his apartment."

"Well, you still fell in love then."

I nodded. "Yes... and we still lost Evelyn... and he still made me the necklace... but the day on the porch when I originally asked him to take me to Cece's because I couldn't take it anymore, I asked him to kiss me instead... and we both let it go." I huffed. "And that was because of Cece. She was with me through the worst of the grief. She stayed with me and held onto me when I got back from the hospital... she's the one that pushed me to let it go... to focus on my relationship with Chris instead of Evelyn's death... and I did."

"Does Cece seem happy in the new memories?"

"Cece always seems happy," I smiled. "No one would ever know if she wasn't. But... Maddy... Maddy and Owen made her happy on another level. I have to give that back to her."

"Then we will. I mean... That's the plan, isn't it? To prevent Juan Josef from coming through. That's what we're working toward, right?"

I sighed, nodding. "I suppose it is. I just... saving Anna and those men is important, and I don't want to seem shallow, but it's scary to think that some of the things that have happened since we met Juan Josef could go differently... or certain memories we've all made since then might change."

She raised an eyebrow as she handed the soap back to me. "But this means we can change things and still remember everything that happened before we changed them, right? If you have new and old memories, then shouldn't we all if we go through with this plan?"

I shrugged. "Maybe?"

She held a piece of her hair near her eyes, staring at it as if it might come to life. "I think it does. It doesn't make sense that you can remember both, but you do. So if that's how it works, then whatever happens while we wait won't be erased in our minds, even if we erase it from existence. All these memories we've all been making should be fine, right? Even if we gain new ones?"

"In theory..."

She dropped the strand of hair and looked at me. "Do you think Anna will remember dying? And whatever happened to her after she died?"

That thought sent a chill up my spine. "I hope not."

She shot me a sideways look. "Why do you say you hope not? Don't you want to know what happens to us when we die?"

I scrubbed my arms, considering it. "I do, but I'm thinking about Anna, specifically. If she remembered everything about her death and what came after, what would it be like to suddenly be sucked back into this world?"

"Anna cared about one thing above all else, Liam," she reminded me. "She'd be grateful for the chance to see him again. Even if she got to spend six months in heaven, nothing would be more important to her than seeing him again."

I knitted my brows. "That's another thing. What are we going to do for six months? With several prisoners and a spooked crew? The men are going to get restless on the island and start asking questions about what they saw and what we're waiting for. What will we tell them happened? How do we keep them under control for six whole months? They're not going to believe Juan Josef is sick for much longer."

She grinned. "Oh, I didn't tell you about Abraham! He's the ship's clergyman. The entire crew has turned to him for answers after watching the others disappear. He's got theories of his own about what he saw. Something about God's chosen *'rising in the clouds to meet the Lord in the air.'*" She chuckled. "I think their prayers and sermons will keep them docile for a bit as they await their chance to be offered up in the same way. I'm pretty sure they're all on the beach now, listening to Abraham read scripture and repenting for their sins. Not one of them has even asked about the captain's wellbeing since the storm."

"Oh..." I gave her the soap, imagining the very rugged and foul-mouthed crewmen down on their knees in the sand praying. "Well... I guess that solves one issue. I don't think I've met Abraham. I remember Juan Jr. mentioning a clergyman, but I don't recall seeing him."

"Well," she smiled, "he doesn't look like what you'd imagine when you think of a typical minister. He's the short guy with the baby face that's always got his nose buried in a book on the bow."

"Oh, I've seen him! I thought he was kitchen staff. He's so young!"

"He is, but he's very committed to his title." She mindlessly dragged the soap over the surface of the water. "And I've been thinking a lot about what grandpa said before they left... about getting married and not waiting too long. I talked to Abraham before the storm. He could perform the ceremony. And if we can make memories without forgetting... Maybe I could marry Jimmy while we're waiting? Here... on our island... where we fell in love with each other. What do you think? It'd give us something to focus on so we're not obsessing over whether or not killing the Albrecht is the right thing to do."

I smiled, working my soapy fingers through my matted hair. "I think that's a beautiful idea, Lill."

"Good. I'm going to need your help."

"Help with what?" Jim asked from the water's edge, kicking off his boots.

"What are you doing?" I asked, self-consciously lowering myself so only my head was above water. "We're naked..."

"Sweetheart, believe me I *know* you're naked," he snickered, "but I've got throw up all down my hair and back and I'm sorry, but I'm gettin' in. That child of yours..." He tugged off his shirt. "I swear to God, she waits 'till I got her pulled up against my neck to throw up every single time! It's like she's aiming! Now," he pulled off his breeches, revealing a completely naked—

"Oh my God, Jim!" I squeezed my eyes closed and held both hands up to block any potential view should my eyes be pried back open.

"What? Aw hell, it ain't like ye' never seen one before." He chuckled as he splashed into the water. "Ain't Hoss's fault the good Lordt blessed some of us more than others! Oh quit. I'm covered now."

I heard Lilly smack his arm. "Not everyone wants to see that much of you!" She smacked him again.

"Ah ah ah! Whatcha' smackin' me for woman?!"

"You're disgusting! I'm so sorry Lainey." She splashed water at his face. "I changed my mind about what I said earlier."

I laughed. "It's fine. I didn't see anything. *Really.*"

"What'd ye' say earlier?" He tugged on her hair, bouncing his eyebrows. "Yuns come down here just to talk about me?"

She swatted his hand away from her. "No. We came down here to bathe in peace without having to listen to you jabber on and on just to hear yourself talk."

He gasped in fake outrage, holding his palm to his chest. "But ye' said you like the way I talk." He lowered down into the water so only his head was above it as he moved closer to her. "Specially last night… you 'member when I was—

She placed both hands on his head and pushed him beneath the water, laughing playfully when he came up spitting water in her direction. "You're such an idiot."

I couldn't help but smile at them as they tried to avoid touching each other too intimately while they continued to play fight.

"How's Fetia?" I asked.

"Doin' good." Jim combed Lilly's wet hair with his fingers, a peace offering she always accepted. "Magna says she ain't bled at all in two days, so that's a good sign…"

"Good," I sighed in relief. "I went to check in on her earlier, but she was asleep."

"I think she'll be alright. She's a good girl, ye' know. Smart and sweet." He let Lilly work the soap over his neck, closing his eyes as she circled around the back of him to work her nails over the top of his head. "Her English is gettin' better than mine."

I laughed at that. "It really is. She's picking it up fast."

The corner of his lip curled up. "Well, there ain't much else for her to do with Kyle up on the summit. Lordt knows the minute he comes back down they'll be laid up together somewheres playin' hide the sausage for days on end."

I shuddered. "Please, don't remind me... it's bad enough I know they did it *once*."

He cackled with laughter. "Oh, come on, freckles. Don't act like you and Hoss ain't goin' at it in every shadowy corner ye' can find. Every man, woman, and beast on this island's had to have seen yuns doin' the deed at least once or twice."

I sucked in the air, my entire face burning suddenly. "No..."

Lilly hid a smile behind his shoulder. "Or at least heard you..."

I covered my face with my hands. "Oh my God, stop it. You're messing with me... please tell me you've never seen us."

"Hate to be the one to tell ye,' but ye' ain't exactly discreet once y'all get goin.'" He giggled as my entire face turned beet red. "Ain't nothin' to be ashamed of, sometimes when the urge hits ye'—

I held up my hands. "Alright, I've heard enough... I'm gonna go and hide and never speak to any of you again for the next... twenty years."

Lilly dunked his head to rinse the soap, and he came up with one eye open. "Oh, quit bein' so coy when we all know you ain't. We're all doin' two person push-ups every chance we get... Like I said, there ain't much else to do."

Lilly howled with laughter. "Hiding the sausage? Two person push-ups?"

He grinned, grabbing her beneath the water. "Well, if you insist... might get a little awkward with that one over there watching, but I'm willin' to give it a go..."

This prompted a shrieking giggle from Lilly as she wiggled away from his grip. "Alright, quit... Quit!" She pushed him back into the water as she moved to my side, a perfect smile lighting up her entire face. "Do you want me to get rid of him? He's clean now and is just hanging around to annoy us."

I shook my head. "No, you two are adorable. I should go."

"Wait." She grabbed my arm. "You said you were happy..." She looked back at Jim who had caught sight of a fish and was entirely distracted in his futile attempt to catch it with his hands.

"Are the memories of being happy with Chris affecting the way you feel about Jack? Have you talked to him about it?"

I blew out. "Not yet, and they're not affecting how I feel about him, but they *are* affecting the way I feel about how he and I got here. I wouldn't have ever let go of what I had with Chris in this new version of my life. I wouldn't have moved on so quickly had I not felt like our marriage had been over for years prior... In the new memories, we were perfect... and yet, I'm still here. With Jack. Our marriage hadn't failed, and I was beyond happy. Shouldn't that have changed everything about me and Jack the minute Owen's ancestor died? I don't have new memories with Jack. Everything is just as it happened. But it shouldn't be. And that makes me wonder... will killing this ancestor do anything or will it just be one more death we've caused in this place?"

She frowned. "Nothing's different at all in your memories since the crash?"

I shook my head. "Nothing. What if we can only make changes in the future and not here? What if we can't save Anna?"

She ran her palms over the water. "But... killing the Albrecht... that technically changes the future, doesn't it? If we kill the Albrecht, Juan Josef won't have a reason to come here. I don't understand how it *wouldn't* change things here."

I met her gaze. "That's the other thing. Chris and I were in a good place and we still ended up here. I came up with the trip to prevent the divorce the first time around. He came up with the trip as a surprise on the second. What if something similar applies to Juan Josef? Killing the Albrecht might prevent *Richard Albrecht* from driving Juan Josef to that spot, but it might not prevent him from getting there another way. I asked your grandpa to pull Juan Josef's lineage too... When they get back... Maybe we should consider looking into hunting a different ancestor."

Chapter Thirty Five

Chris

Chris stood in his kitchen staring at the coffeepot, watching as the dark liquid dripped slowly into the carafe. Maria was still asleep on the living room sofa where the two of them had decided to take up residence for the two weeks they'd been there. All other rooms in the house seemed off limits to their relationship. Cecelia was asleep upstairs in the master bedroom that he'd insisted she keep.

He hadn't even stepped foot in his old room for fear of the memories he might relive once he did.

It'd taken time for him to work out, but he realized they'd changed their history, preventing Owen and Cecelia from meeting somehow, and the result had altered all his memories with Alaina. They hadn't fallen apart, but were stronger than they'd ever been when they crossed through that storm. He wondered if she was experiencing the same memories on the other side of time.

He wanted to search for Owen; to see if he'd been a descendant of one of the men they killed or if they'd merely adjusted critical moments in time that prevented Cecelia from ever crossing paths with him. If they couldn't reverse what was done, and if Owen was still alive out there somewhere, he could at least introduce them to each other before he left again. Cece had been much happier with him and their child than without, and he felt guilty he'd contributed to the loss of both of them from her memory.

The new Cecelia was different; colder and untrusting. She held back on expressing her suspicion of him and Maria and their story, but he felt her eyes on him with every move he made. It was like she was waiting... searching for something that could expose him in a lie.

The only time he could really speak openly was during the hours she was tied up running errands, but those hours had been mostly spent in the hospital getting CT Scans, MRIs, and bloodwork.

After two weeks of testing, his neurologist had been able to determine that Chris had an intracranial hematoma, which, translated into terms Chris could understand, meant he had slow internal bleeding that was causing pressure on his brain. The doctors were sure he had to have continuously reinjured it in order for the damage to be as significant as it was. Chris knew he had hit it several times during the storm while taken prisoner by Captain Furneaux and had taken quite a few blows to the head when Juan Josef's men took him captive. He wondered just how long he could've gone without treatment if he'd never left.

The injury warranted surgery. He was scheduled for one in two weeks where they would cut open a part of the skull to drain and remove the hematoma.

It was a risky procedure. With a fiancé visa now in his possession, he intended to marry Maria before surgery to ensure she would secure her citizenship and be able to see their mission through should he not make it. He'd also filled her in on his promise to Jim so she could search for June if he was unable to.

The coffee hissed and bubbled as the final drops spilled out, snapping him out of his daze and back into the early morning reality. He quietly pulled a coffee mug from the cupboard over the island, feeling unnerved by the fact that Cecelia had left nearly everything in the house exactly as it was. He poured himself a cup and stood at the island, staring over it at Maria where she slept deeply on the couch, one arm draped across her face.

Things had been tense between them since they arrived in the 21st century. He knew he wanted her—loved her—but the new memories of his old marriage pulled at the strings of his heart, so much so that he couldn't quite get himself back to the man he'd been to her before the memories had come. She didn't deserve to feel the way he was sure his confusion was making her feel, especially when they were planning to be married within the next two weeks.

"Can we talk?" Cecelia whispered, forcing him to jump as he spun around to face her. Her bright blonde hair was knotted on the top of her head and her expression was tormented, battling between tears, anger, and guilt as she hugged her arms over her chest. She glanced across the island at Maria, then back up to him. "Outside, perhaps?"

He nodded and followed her as she made her way through the dining room to slip out the patio doors, barefoot and still wearing her pink plaid pajamas.

They'd gone through the storm in September of 1774, but had come out in March of 2020. The early morning air was icy on his cheeks as he stepped out behind her.

She whirled around the moment he slid the door shut behind him, her eyes full of tears. "Chris, you can't marry her."

He held up one hand, standing straighter in defense. "Cecelia, this is not up for—

"Let me finish," she sniffled, running both palms over her cheeks in frustration. "I saw your search history on the computer. I know you were looking up the crash coordinates, and I know you're secretly hoping my sister is alive. If this is about a green card, I can find—

"It's not about that."

She growled. "Right, it's because you *fell in love* with her. Your father told me what the doctor said. You're obviously not thinking clearly." She pointed toward the house. "That woman might be beautiful, but she'll never be A.J., and you know it. Even if A.J. is dead, which neither of us truly believes, I can't let you do it. I'm not saying that to be mean, I'm saying it because I love you and I care about your happiness. You're like my own brother, Chris, and I'm telling you she's not right for you. I saw how happy you were with my sister... this woman will never give you that."

He shook his head. "You don't know her."

"I know enough." She glared at the patio doors as if she could see Maria through them. "I know she's got her nails in you somehow and you're hanging onto every word she says, but I can see it in you that you can't let go of my sister. What will you do if A.J. walks through that door in a few months or in a year? You gonna' stay married to this woman who clearly has found a meal ticket in you?"

"You're crossing the line, Cece. You don't know anything about her or what's happened between us."

She crossed her arms over her chest. "Then enlighten me, Chris, because the man I know would've seen my sister float away on a raft *alive* and then he'd devote every second of his life trying to find her. He wouldn't just move on to the next one as if she'd never existed!"

He ran a hand through his hair, wishing he could tell some version of the truth so she could understand. "I don't owe you an explanation. I loved your sister, but she's gone. If the raft had made it out of the storm, she'd be here."

She shook her head. "You don't believe that. If you did, you wouldn't be looking up those coordinates online. What's the plan, Chris? Marry this woman, then take her out with you while you search for A.J.? And what happens if you find her?"

He took a sip of his coffee to wash down the ice in his throat. As he swallowed, he set his jaw. "I'm done with this conversation, Cece. What I do with her, what I search for online, or what I decide to do with my life is not anyone's business but my own."

Her nose twitched in the same way Alaina's did when she was suppressing an outburst. He'd never noticed just how much the two looked alike until that moment. Cecelia had the same freckles, the same upward curve in her lips, and her eyes were the same almond shape. The way she stood and the expressions she made made it difficult for his heart not to swell with new memories of his relationship with Alaina; ones where she really did make him the happiest man alive. Cecelia had a point. He was having a hard time letting go, and he *wouldn't* have moved so easily on to Maria with the life he was now learning he'd lived as a result of killing those men.

She blew out the breath she was holding. "For three years, all I have done is search for signs of her. The airline paid out a settlement to the families. I'm sure your father has told you. We took every penny mom got and bought a boat. I quit my job and spent a year with mom and uncle Bill on that ocean looking for her —for *you*. We intended to go back this summer to keep searching. When we're not out there, all three of us have lived on the computer or on the phone trying to find ways to find you. I have called the airline, border control, the coastguard, and endless commercial fishing charters begging them to keep searching. What you do with that woman in there—

"Her *name* is Maria."

Again, she took a deep breath. "What you do with *Maria* may be none of my business, but if you intend to go out and search for my sister—for my *best friend in this world*, that *is* my business. *She* is my business. I will spend my entire life searching if I have to, and if your intention is to search for her too, I'm coming with you."

"My intention, Cecelia," he said through his teeth as the familiar sting of a migraine swelled behind his eyes, "is to make it through this brain surgery… to make sure Maria is taken care of should I not come out alive. Planning anything beyond the next two weeks is not something I have the luxury of doing."

Her expression softened. "So you're having the surgery then? Your dad made it sound like you hadn't agreed to it. I mean… you made it three years without treatment… Will you die without the surgery?"

He shrugged. "The doctor says it could worsen over time. I could fall into a coma or a vegetative state. Will I be able to *really live* if I don't have it? I'm not willing to lose my mind."

A tear rolled down her cheek, and she quickly swatted it away. "Is that why you're marrying her so soon? So she'll have the house and her citizenship if something happens to you?"

He sighed. "Is it really so hard to believe I care about her?"

She sniffled. "It is... but only because I've seen the way you cared about my sister and it didn't look like that. I'm sorry if I've been cold. I just..." She pressed her palms to her eyes to catch the tears that were threatening to spill out. "I'm making things uncomfortable for you here, and it's your home. I can go stay at a hotel. Give you both some space."

"You don't have to do that." He offered her his coffee, and she accepted it, wrapping both hands around the mug for warmth. "This is your home now too and Alaina would want you to stay here—*I* want you to stay. I know it's hard to see Maria as anything but a betrayal. I struggle with it myself sometimes, but I really do love her, and I'd like it if you got to see why... the person she is that isn't the betrayal... It'd mean a lot if you tried to get to know her."

She sipped the coffee, gathering her composure as she did so. "I will try... for you."

He smiled, taking the mug back when she offered it to him. "Thank you. Come on, you're freezing. Let's go back in."

"Wait." She chewed on her lower lip the same way Alaina always did. "There's something else I wanted to ask you... You mentioned a man named Owen at the airport and for some reason, that name felt like it meant something; seemed familiar. Who is he?"

He frowned. He couldn't tell her the truth; couldn't tell her that Owen was once her husband and that they'd had the sort of marriage he'd been envious of. "Just... an old friend of mine from school. The injury sometimes causes confusion, overlaps old memories with new ones... And I had him confused as someone associated with you."

"Oh," she pursed her lips, a hopeful expression washing over her features. "Did I meet him once? Maybe at your birthday party a few years ago?"

"You might've." He rubbed the back of his neck where the guilt was sitting heavily.

She hugged her shoulders and sighed, looking up at him and tilting her head. "Are you afraid of the surgery?"

He wanted to tell her he wasn't. How could he be afraid of the surgery after everything he'd been through? He'd been on the edge of death so many times. What was once more? But he *was* afraid. He wasn't ready to die and the possibility that he could terrified him. There were too many things he'd leave unfinished and unanswered if he went now.

"Can I drive you to the hospital when you go?" She asked, not needing a response to the question as she apparently read his thoughts. "I could wait with you until you're recovered, and—

The phone in his pocket rang loudly, cutting her off until he could reach inside and tap the side button. He hadn't realized how intrusive technology had been in his life until he'd been ripped away from it. "Sorry." He glanced down to see Bud's name on the screen. "I'd love it if you were there with me."

She forced a smile. "I'm guessing anyone that's calling *that* number is probably someone you need to talk to… I'll go fix us some breakfast… see if I can dig up some more clothes for Maria."

"Thank you, Cece," he said, sliding the answer toggle on the screen and holding the phone to his chest. "And I'm sorry it's not Ally here in my place. If she's out there… and if I make it through this surgery, I'll do my best to find her."

"I know you will," she said, sliding the door open and slipping back inside. "Because you still love her."

He watched through the doors, waiting until she was back in the kitchen before he pressed the phone to his ear. "Hello?"

"Chris," Bud's voice sounded tired. "I found something."

Chris glanced back into the house before stepping out into the yard, pacing outside of earshot to the large oak tree. "What?"

"Well… I was doing a bit of my own research while waiting on the genealogy reports and I decided to do a search for our people to see if there's any indication of their continued lives in the 18th century."

"And?" Chris asked. "Did you find any of them?"

"I did," he said, clearing his throat. "But... I can't be sure of the legitimacy of this. I've contacted my genealogist and asked him to push this to the top of the list to confirm the date. You can't always trust something found on the internet, so don't panic..."

Chris swallowed. "Panic over what?"

Bud blew out heavily. "It's Jack... I found his name on a registry... a registry of *deaths at sea* reported in 1775. There's only the year, no month or cause of death or even a label for which ship reported it... I'd hoped this was the wrong Jack Volmer or the date reported in the article is wrong, but, I traced it to an ancestry page and... How many Jack Volmers could there be at sea in 1775 that would also be married to an Alaina J. M. Volmer?"

He could feel his pulse in his throat. "We left in 1774... where did you find that registry?"

"Someone uploaded it to an ancestry site. It's just a small section of a page with a list of names on it. I've reached out to the person who uploaded the photo to see if they have the original registry or know where to find it. It looks like she hasn't been on the site in a while, though. I'll have to rely on the genealogists to come up with answers if she doesn't respond. If the date is outside of March 1775, and if we can find out the cause of death, we can prevent it."

Chris leaned back against the tree. "Send me the link. I want to help while I'm able. You said it was on an ancestry website? Does the woman who uploaded it have her name and ancestry visible? I know when Alaina played with hers, you could look at other similar ones and see their trees. Her full name should be on there somewhere."

"Not sure... I'm emailing it to you now." He could hear Bud typing slowly. "This is the first time I've really used one of... Oh... hang on... yes, her name's on here... It's oh... You're not going to believe this. Her name is...Dahlia... Hernandez."

Chapter Thirty Six

"How are you feeling?" I asked, inching into Fetia and Kyle's cabin, delighted to find them both standing at the floor-length mirror. Kyle was smiling at her reflection as she turned to each side with her hands over her midsection.

"I good." She said, beaming when she caught sight of both babies in the sling affixed to my chest. "Baby good too."

Jacob and Fetia's father had relieved Kyle and Michael on the summit the day before. They'd arrived after I'd gone to bed, and I was anxious to see him after so long apart. "And you?" I asked, messing his too-long hair where it was beginning to curl. "How was your week away from us?"

"Miserable, mostly," he groaned, combing back the hair I'd ruffled. "Michael still acts like he's twelve. I had to do *everything* up there while he played around. How are things here? My dad... is he..." He waved it off, attempting to appear as though he wasn't concerned about the stab wound in Phil's cheek.

I knew Kyle had been struggling with his relationship with Phil from the moment he'd pulled that trigger and the gun hadn't fired. For as much as he wanted to appear as though he loathed him the way the rest of us did, Phil was still his father, and I knew, from experience, giving up on a parent, however awful their actions might be, was no easy task.

"He's healing nicely," I assured him. "We gave him what was left of our antibiotics and have been keeping it washed. Magna's been checking the stitches daily. She really did a good job on them. You're welcome to go see for yourself. No one will think less of you if you wanted to see him, you know."

He shook his head. "*I* would think less of me. It's a waste of our antibiotics, if you ask me," he lied. "Let's not dwell on it today. Today, I just want to take in this glorious new bump that's formed while I've been away" He took Fetia's hand in his and turned her to face me. "Look!"

She grinned down at their joined hands where he'd laid them over the swell in her stomach. "It girl."

"Good morning!" Lilly beamed from the doorway, a bundle of white fabric in her arms as she and Izzy joined us.

"Morning, Lill." I sat down on the bed, pulling Zachary and Cecelia out of the sling one at a time to lay them on their stomachs over the soft mattress. "What's all that?"

She bounced her eyebrows. "My wedding dress. It's going to be ridiculously excessive and marvelous. This... this is just the bodice." She winked. "What'd I miss?"

I laughed. "Apparently, Kyle and Fetia are having a girl."

Lilly sank down into the armchair near the window to unwrap the already cut fabrics. "How do you know it's a girl?"

Fetia gently patted the bump with her free hand. "My father say... Here, girl." She then motioned a little lower on her stomach. "Here, boy. It girl. I know."

I shook my head and laughed. "Could be both." I presented mine, both of which had begun raising their heads and looked like two little aliens with their tottering faces pointed up in my direction.

Kyle chuckled, releasing Fetia to kneel down in front of the bed and make a face at each of them. "Her English is getting good, isn't it?" I nodded as he slid his pointer finger toward Cecelia, who immediately clenched it inside her tiny fist and attempted to pull it to her wide mouth. "She still only drinking Wanda's milk?"

"Mostly," I yawned. "I've been reintroducing her to mine slowly at night since she's been more demanding lately and nobody likes milking Wanda. So far, we haven't had any issues."

Lilly pulled out a needle and thread and smirked. "If you call waking up the whole ship every night *'no issues.'* That girl's got pipes on her."

Fetia knelt down beside Kyle, one hand on his shoulder as the other combed over Zachary's blonde hair. "Twin. That right word?"

I smiled at her, surprised by how many words she'd already learned. "Yes. Twins."

"It hurt? *Twins*?" Her flawless skin didn't create a single line on her face when she frowned at them.

I laughed. "Yes, but it was a good hurt. Worth it."

"Kyle scared," she mused, the fingers of the hand at his shoulder raising to caress the side of his throat; an act so affectionate it had me torn between acceptance and defense. They were both so young, and yet, what they were doing at their age wasn't uncommon in the century we were stuck in. I wanted them to be happy—which they both appeared to be—but I also wanted them to be responsible.

"It's okay to be scared." I brushed a lock of her silk black hair away from her face so I could admire its perfection. She truly was one of the most beautiful women I'd ever laid eyes on, and it was difficult not to stare. "You're both young. Having a baby at your age is scary."

"I'm not scared." Kyle asserted, playing a game of tug of war for his finger with Cecelia and losing that battle as she pressed her mouth over his knuckle. "I just... How am I gonna take care of a baby in this time? How will I support it with one arm and no real skills to fit this century?"

"We'll support each other," Lilly said. "You have plenty of skills. I've seen them. After grandpa gets back, and after we do whatever we can to save Anna, we'll find a place to settle down. Together. We don't know if we're staying in this century, anyway. It all will depend on what they come back with."

He pursed his lips, gently pulling his hand away from Cecelia and wiping the knuckle on his pants. "Do you think we'll go back to Tahiti to get Noona?" He asked, his grey-blue eyes meeting mine as he knitted his eyebrows. "We promised to take him with us, and I'm worried about him."

After all that had transpired since we'd been taken against our will, I'd almost forgotten about Noona. His grandfather had healed Chris in Eimeo and asked only that we take his young grandson with us to England so he would have more opportunities. Kyle had taken the boy under his wing during our time in Tahiti and had grown attached.

I offered him a smile. "I'll talk to the others. We haven't really discussed where we'll go once Chris gets back, but Tahiti isn't too far. Maybe we can go check on him and take Fetia's father back before we set out to do... whatever it is we decide to do. And if whatever that is works, we may not ever have to make that promise. It was made in exchange for their help escaping Juan Josef. We can't very well take him with us on a mission to kill someone. He'd be safer in Tahiti." I noted the disappointment in Kyle's features. "If it doesn't work, we'll hold true to our promise."

Kyle stood and ran his hand over his hair. "You really think killing Richard Albrecht's ancestor—murdering a whole lineage of people we've never met, who have never wronged us—will change everything?"

Lilly smirked at the fabric in her hands. "No, but killing Juan Josef's ancestor will."

My gaze immediately darted to the open cabin door. "Lilly," I hissed. "Keep your voice down when you say things like that."

"Dario and Juan Jr. are on the island," she assured me, weaving the needle meticulously through the fabrics. "I watched them paddle to shore before I came here. We should take any opportunity they're away to discuss our plans."

"You want to destroy Juan Josef's lineage?" Kyle probed, rubbing his jaw as he considered it. "Juan Jr. and Dario... we'd be killing them, too."

Lilly raised one unconcerned shoulder, not lifting her eyes from her work. "So? They both know what their father is, and neither of them did anything to stop him when he took us against our will. Dario practically served Anna up to him on a platter to be slaughtered. We owe them nothing."

"Juan Jr. has helped us," he argued, "he stopped the whipping and the hanging... he plotted to abandon his father with us... he's not a bad man. Alaina, you know this. I've seen you talking to him. You can't seriously be considering killing them?"

I liked Juan Jr., but if saving Anna and Owen was our initiative, then I couldn't allow myself to care for any of them. They were still our captors, after all. "My memories have changed," I told him. "When we killed those men on the beach, it altered my history. I shouldn't be here with the altered past, and yet, here I am. I still ended up getting on that plane. If we want Anna back; if we want to save those men from dying, the *only* way is to eliminate Juan Josef altogether. We can't risk him crossing through time by some other means."

"And Jack agrees with this? And Jim?" He looked between me and Lilly, his expression full of disbelief.

I nodded. "If we eliminate Juan Josef, we can go home. *All of us*. Anna too."

"And just how are you planning to slip that by them?" Kyle asked, ignoring Izzy as she spun in circles around him and Fetia. "If they're sailing the ship, they'll be with us all the way."

"They're looking for a name," Lilly said, looking up from her dress to raise one perfectly arched eyebrow. "So we will give them one. They won't know it's *their* ancestor, will they?"

He shook his head. "This doesn't feel right... None of it. It feels like cheating."

Fetia made a tsk noise, smiling down at Izzy where she'd taken her hands to dance in a circle with her. "Is no cheating. Is life."

"She understood all that?" Lilly asked, lowering the fabric to gawk at Fetia. "Does she know everything, then?"

Scratching at the back of his neck, he sighed. "Yes. And while she doesn't seem concerned with changing our history, I am. There are so many things..." he motioned toward the small swell in her stomach, "...that could go differently."

The door to the cabin creaked as it was pushed open, and I smiled to find Jack in the doorway. The smile promptly disappeared as I took in the fresh blood stains covering his white shirt. "Jesus," I jumped up from the bed. "What happened?"

He took my hands in his before I could place them on him, squeezing gently. "It's not my blood. It's Eli's."

"Who's Eli?" Lilly and I both asked in unison. She'd dropped her fabrics and rushed to stand beside me, peering past his shoulder to the hallway in search of Jim.

"The sailor we locked in with Juan Josef," he said, rolling his head to one side and then the other. "Jim's fine. He's with him now. Juan Josef stabbed the man in the stomach with a kitchen knife. I was hoping to find Magna… to see if she could help us try to stitch him up. It's not looking good."

Fetia stopped spinning. "Magna go collect food. I help."

"No," Kyle put his arm out to stop her. "You need to be taking it easy.   Bruce is on the top deck with the preacher. They can handle it."

She swatted his hand away. "I help." Pointing at Lilly's discarded needle and thread, she stomped her foot. "I do this."

Their eyes met, and I watched as he silently pleaded and she silently insisted, placing both hands on her hips in defiance. His shoulders slumped in surrender. "I'm coming with then, and if he so much as looks at you funny, we're out of there."

I frowned at Jack as the two of them made their way out into the hall. "Why would Juan Josef want to kill one of his own men? And how did he get a kitchen knife?"

Jack shook his head. "Beats the hell out of me. I intend to find out soon enough. Me and Jim searched that cabin for any weapons after the incident with Phil, and there was nothing. Someone *had* to give it to him." He quickly kissed my forehead and turned to follow them. "We'll need to take inventory. Forks, knives, daggers… anything that could be used to inflict damage. Jim and I will do the same in the armory. If someone's giving him weapons, I want to know about it."

"I can go down to the kitchens now," I offered. "Bruce and I can start marking the forks and knives with numbers. Start a system to keep track of who has which ones."

Lilly nodded. "I'll come with."

"Good. I'll have Kyle and Michael take over guard when we're done with Eli." He hurried out of the room, adding over his shoulder, "Jim and I will meet you in the kitchens after."

I chewed on my bottom lip as I reattached the sling to my shoulders. I knew Juan Josef was a calculated man. He didn't do anything without purpose. Killing one of his men made no sense when his plan to eliminate Richard Albrecht was better served by him remaining a docile prisoner. There had to be some reason for it, and a shiver ran down my spine as I realized that, even though he was the one imprisoned, we were still his captives.

Chapter Thirty Seven

Chris

Chris stared at the computer screen, glancing over his shoulder from the desk in the kitchen for signs of Cecelia's return. She'd left to pick up groceries that morning and, since he was ten days away from surgery and three days away from getting married, he took any opportunity of solitude to use the computer for research. Given her prior admissions, he made a habit out of clearing his history after he was done.

He followed the genealogy chart Dahlia had put together over and over again as if he could find some mistake by the fifth or sixth sweep from top to bottom. She'd put quite a bit of time into tracing her ancestry. When he zoomed out, the screen was an intricate web of crawling lines and names.

There were two distinct sections with highlights along each branch of the tree where the two people at the top on each side connected to her name. On the right path, those two names read:

Jack M. Volmer, Birth Unknown - 1775

Alaina J. M. Volmer, Birth Unknown - 1827

Beneath their boxes was a line connecting their names to two more:

Cecelia B. Volmer, 1774 - 1831

Zachary W. Volmer, 1774 - 1779

"So, they don't ever come back," he mumbled, frowning at the death dates listed for both Zachary and his father. If there was nothing he could do to change this chart, Alaina would lose both Jack and Zachary within the next five years. Losing another child, particularly so soon after losing Jack, would absolutely destroy her. He couldn't let her go through that.

His pull toward the new memories of her had intensified with each passing day inside their old home. Photos left untouched hung from nearly every surface of the house to serve as a reminder of the happy and non-broken relationship they'd had before leaving.

It was strange to hold two sets of memories of their lives. The more time he spent in the house, the foggier the original versions became, and his guilt for the fact that he and Maria had still somehow come out of it as a couple put strain between them. He hadn't been intimate with her since they'd arrived—hadn't been capable of it—and he knew it was eating away at her.

He looked toward the staircase, as if he could see Maria somehow in the upstairs shower. The sound of running water over his head indicated she was still inside. She'd taken every opportunity to shower since their return; often remaining until the water ran cold, claiming she could still smell the "stink on her skin."

Forcing the memories of Alaina far back, he let the ones of Maria play out to remind himself of the relationship they'd built over the past year and a half. Harping on an alternative version of reality would do nothing but sabotage the life he'd been looking forward to building with her.

The storm had done something; jumbled his thoughts so he couldn't organize them; couldn't prioritize or clear them out. His endless and erratic thinking had become a handicap, and scared as he was to go into that hospital in ten days, he couldn't wait for the potential reprieve the surgery might offer.

He returned his attention to the computer screen.

'Focus.'

Zachary's path was not the highlighted of the two, so he tucked thoughts of his death away temporarily and continued down

Cecelia's. At 21, she married a man named George Davis and had four children of her own.

He smiled at that; that Alaina's daughter might find a happy life, might fall in love...

He traced the highlighted branches as the Davis name carried them through most of the 19th century before becoming Anderson in 1895.

The descendant of those first two Andersons was named Sarah, and Sarah Anderson had a photo. His heartbeat quickened when he realized he could click on it. Suddenly filling the screen was a dull Sepia-toned portrait which had been scanned and uploaded. Even though it was faded, he could tell Sarah had the same eyes and nose as Alaina, her jaw was shaped the same, and around her neck, she wore a necklace that looked—no, *was* the exact same necklace he'd gifted Alaina after Evelyn had died.

He could make out the delicate silver swirl that housed the pendant. Although the globe appeared marble through the worn image, he knew it was clear with fibers of golden red hair.

"It must've gotten handed down," he said to himself, "generation after generation..."

He stared at the portrait, her likeness conjuring up new images of nights spent laughing, kissing, and making love in this very kitchen days before they'd flown out... images of that very same necklace around her neck while she lay naked before him—

He blinked those thoughts away, closing the image window to venture to her highlighted child.

Sarah Anderson had a daughter who also had a photo: Gloria Collins, born in 1950. Because of the direct link to Dahlia branching off her icon, this had to be *the* Gloria.

His heartbeat quickened. He knew, had known after viewing the image of Sarah, that the necklace's involvement in the 1970s had been a result of it becoming a family heirloom and not that of Alaina getting too close to the storm. She and Jack could come home.

He clicked on the photo icon for Gloria and was delighted to find an entire album attached. Each russet-tinged photograph had been taken in the 70s, and every single one looked like it was a photo taken of Alaina. Every expression, feature, and pose was identical to the ones she so often made. Gloria had the same hair, the same mouth, the same eyes... it was as if Alaina herself had stepped into the 1970s and, from the look on her face in every single image, had an absolute blast.

There were photos taken from all over the world. Some of them were hard to make out - dense forestation or mountains photographed at an angle that was hard to identify. Others, she stood in front of iconic locations: The Eiffel Tower, the Empire State Building, the Great Wall of China, the Alps... In each one she was smiling from ear to ear, a black and silver camera hanging from her neck, usually with friends draping their arms over each of her shoulders...

He clicked through a rolling slideshow, unable to contain the contagious response to smile after smile of hers on his own lips... Until... a wedding photo.

In this photo she looked happier than every other image he'd seen, but the upward curve of his lips vanished as he noted both arms wrapped around a tuxedoed young Juan Josef.

She wore a timeless satin and lace white gown, well-fitted to her curves, a long veil reaching the floor, and a distinct glass globe necklace around her neck.

He flipped to the next photo, a closeup of Gloria's face that had to have been contained in the same wedding album. She wore the veil, and the photo was taken from above as she smiled up at the camera with one hand propping up her chin. While this woman could've been Alaina's identical twin, he could see the distinction in her features. The freckles were more spread out, the eyes ever so slightly more slanted, and there was a hint of difference in the jaw when she smiled. In the other photos, those slight differences were harder to decipher due to the lower resolution, but this... this was taken by a professional and he could make out every subtle variation from the shapes and features he'd memorized on his wife's face.

His wife... Again, he looked toward the stairs as Cecelia's words ripped through him. *'The man I know would've seen my sister float away on a raft alive and then he'd devote every second of his life trying to find her. He wouldn't just move on to the next one as if she'd never existed.'*

That was true. While each old memory filled with fog, the new ones felt like they were illuminated in sunshine. He wouldn't have moved on... not *ever.* Not from that. But nothing past the plane crash had changed... Every memory from the moment he woke up in that bathroom remained intact. And it clawed at him. If their marriage had been happy, he'd have swam that ocean to get to the raft instead of giving up and going to that island... he'd have leapt out of that doorway to get to her, ignoring any cries for help on the plane...he'd have waited to catch a flight where they could've been seated together... He would've done *everything* differently... And yet—

He heard the upstairs shower squeal as Maria turned off the faucet. He looked back at the photo, the likeness so close to the woman he would've spent the rest of his life with.

He wasn't being fair.

'We're going to put it back,' he reminded himself. *'These memories aren't the real ones. They're temporary.'*

What if Alaina was being flooded with the same memories? Was it building similar obstacles between her and Jack?

Closing his eyes, he sifted through every crevice of his mind, new versions and old, for an image, one *single* image where she'd looked at him in the way he'd seen her look at Jack... With eyes that told the world it didn't exist; that the *only* thing that existed was the man she gazed upon.

Even in the happiest of their times together, she'd never regarded him in such a way. There was love, sure—love that would've been infinitely enough for him, but he realized now, it never would've been enough for her. He'd never be able to give her the kind of happiness Jack did.

Giving Alaina happiness would be to give her Jack; to prevent the 18th century from robbing her of him. He could do that, and perhaps, in doing so, he could unscramble his thinking enough to focus on the life he'd been so looking forward to alongside the woman he could hear making her way across the foyer.

"Good morning, superman."

He turned to where she grinned from across the kitchen island, her wet hair dripping down her bare shoulders where she stood wrapped in a towel.

He smiled as he recognized the look; the look that told the world that no one existed to her but him. He'd been so caught up in trying to find that very expression in his memories of Alaina that he'd forgotten he had it right beside him on this beautiful face.

'There is only you, Maria,' he'd once told her. And it had been so utterly true when he'd said it. With the muddying of his memories, it felt increasingly like deception... Deception that added another heavy layer of guilt on his already weighted shoulders.

She peered past him at the ancestry chart, squinting her eyes as she took in the screen. "Who the hell is Juliana Martinez?"

He spun back around in his chair, gazing at the unhighlighted line connecting Juan Josef Perez Hernandez to another box: Juliana Martinez... and beneath the two of them, a familiar name: Juan Josef Perez Hernandez Jr.

Gloria was not his mother... And it made sense. He and Dario didn't share the more feminine features Dario had inherited from Gloria: the red tint in his hair, the lighter eyes, the more delicate cheekbones.

"Juan Jr.'s mother," he said, clicking on her icon to reveal a photo. She looked like Juan Jr. Her features were sharp, her lips tight, and she didn't have that glow of happiness that radiated from Gloria's photos. She seemed taut and serious, like she'd been groomed to play the dutiful role of wife and mother. Juan Jr. held that same serious air about him.

He wondered what happened between Juliana and Juan Josef. She had no death date, and might possibly be alive somewhere to offer answers. Had she abandoned Juan Josef and her child or had he left her for Gloria after that day in Valle del Cocora? Did Juan

Jr. know this was his real mother, or had he been raised to assume Gloria was? He'd only ever heard him refer to Gloria as *'mom.'* Was this information relevant somehow?

"I am very good at finding people, you know," Maria informed him, turning his focus back upon her as she toyed with an apple in a basket on the counter between them. "Maybe I could find her. While you've been avoiding me, I found Anna's family."

His heart sank. "I'm not avoiding you."

She ran a finger along a line in the marble countertop, evading his gaze and the statement. "Her parents are very private people online, so I couldn't find very many photos or information, but I was able to find an Instagram account for Anna's sister, Melissa. She has lots of photos and there is a little boy in some of them. She bought a house last year in Irvine, California, and posted pictures while she renovated. I looked through realty websites until I found the old listing that matched her photos. Now I have her address, and I'm guessing Liam lives nearby. From stalking her Instagram, I know she does yoga and with the address, I assume it is at a place just two minutes from there. When we go to stay with Bud, I could go to Irvine for yoga, make friends with Melissa and find out where Liam is." She frowned, pursing her lips as she stared at her finger tracing the lines in the marble. "I enjoy this, you know... the investigating and planning. I could do the same for Juliana. See if she knows anything about Richard Albrecht or Juan Josef that could be of use to us. I need something to... keep myself occupied."

He shook his head, standing to lean over the counter and take her hand. "I'm not avoiding you, Maria."

Her brown eyes met his then, and she forced an unconvincing smile. "You have not even noticed that we are alone in this house and I stand before you in only a towel. You *are* avoiding me, but I cannot pretend I don't understand why."

He moved to defend his actions but she held up her hand. "You forget I know you, Kreese. I know this is hard for you; the new memories of her, being in the house you shared with her... and I see your guilt. We are rushing into this and you are not ready. *I* am not ready to be married to a man who cannot look at me. That doesn't mean I don't love you or I don't wish to marry you some day, but... not yet. Not when you are torn between us. We have ninety days. The wedding can wait until your heart is wholly mine once again. And if it is not..." She trailed off, shrugging. "I will not start *our* marriage off where yours ended. *I* will not be the woman you can't see as someone you need to touch. Understand?"

"You're calling off the wedding?" He asked, swallowing.

"Standing before a judge in a courthouse is not a wedding, mi amore." She met his eyes then. "And I am calling off whatever that is... for now."

"But the surgery," he argued, "if I don't come out of it, they could send you to Cuba. We don't have time to postpone."

"If you don't come out of it," she said evenly, "I do not care where they send me."

Chapter Thirty Eight

Eli died. Slowly. I'd never even seen the man's face, but I had spent the following several days with an ache in my heart for him. Jack had told me that the man screamed until he'd lost his voice, then his eyes continued screaming until they finally closed for good.

Jim, Jack, and even Juan Jr. and Dario had interrogated Juan Josef about his motives for the attack. He'd simply informed them that he'd grown "tired of his company."

We all knew there was more to it—*had* to be more. Eli had been the only man aboard the ship that had come to Juan Josef's aid, discovering during their trip to the coordinates that the captain wasn't in fact sick, and threatening to expose us for locking him up. That's why he'd been imprisoned. For Juan Josef to then kill him made no sense... unless it was a calculated move. But what exactly was he calculating?

Dinner plates clanged around me as Lilly, Jim, and Izzy set out place settings around the dining room table while Bruce placed the steaming plates of dinner at the center. The aroma was heavenly.

Jim and Juan Jr. had killed another boar. We still had no explanation for the death of one of the pigs, and even though no more had died, none of us were ready to eat any of them for fear they might be diseased. Instead, we hunted the ones on the island and, more often than not, ate fish.

For whatever reason, we'd all made it a point to clean up for dinner—ham seeming like a proper occasion to abandon our plotting for an evening of normalcy. My mouth watered as I waited for everyone to take their seats around the table, staring at the glazed ham, buttered boiled potatoes, bread, cheese, spaghetti algae, and boiled F'ei that covered its center.

I felt Jack's calloused palm slide over my knee as his breath reached my ear. "You had to wear *this* dress…"

I hid a smile as my entire body heated at the touch. I'd lost much of the pregnancy weight and finally felt confident enough to slip on the blue dress Lilly had made me for her grandparents' anniversary. If we were having a night off from our problems, I wanted it to last well past dinner. Neither of us had been sleeping much between feeding the babies, checking inventory, and guarding the prisoners, and what little opportunity we might've had for intimacy over the past week had instead been used to squeeze in a nap. "Would you prefer I'd worn something else?" I whispered back.

His palm slid a little higher. "I'd prefer if there were no one else in this dining room so I could have you right here on this table while you wear it."

I hurriedly took a sip of my wine, praying it would cool the flush of heat that'd washed over me at the image. Clearing my throat while his thumb dared to climb higher up my inner thigh beneath the cover of the tablecloth, I looked toward Lilly. "How's the dress coming along?"

She piled a healthy serving of boiled potatoes onto the plate in her hand, smiling. "The bottom layer is done." She added a chunk of ham and a generous amount of spaghetti algae before placing the plate in front of Jim and picking up her own. "Fetia's going to help me pin the second layer tomorrow."

Jim snarled at the spaghetti algae, moving it to one side with his fork so it wasn't touching his potatoes.

"I was thinking," she continued, setting the second plate she filled down in front of Izzy in exchange for her empty one, "once the dress is finished, maybe we could spend a few nights on the island to set up the decor for the wedding. Just us girls.. Have something like a bachelorette party… What do you think, Lainey?"

Jack's palm slid higher, and I had to work to keep my voice even. "I'd be happy to." I kicked his shin and his fingers retreated a few inches.

He chuckled to himself, using his free hand to fill the plate in front of me with bits of everything. My heart warmed as I watched him do it. "Thank you," I whispered between us.

Juan Jr. frowned at Lilly from the head of the table, swirling the wine in his glass as he waited patiently for the opportunity to serve himself. "If we are to change our history, would not a wedding be bereft in the aftermath?"

Lilly shrugged. "If it is, then we'll do it all over again in another place and time. Either way, I'll have married the man I love," she looked to her right at Jim who had shoveled ham and potatoes into his mouth until his cheeks bulged, "and what woman wouldn't jump at an opportunity to relive their wedding day again?" She pointed at the untouched spaghetti algae on Jim's plate with her fork, raising an eyebrow. "You want to get scurvy? Eat it."

He rolled his eyes, sitting back to finish chewing.

Dario laughed at their banter. "I think a wedding will make a perfect diversion while we wait. If there is any assistance I might offer, I'd be honored to be of service."

"That's mighty kind of ye,' Dario," Jim mused, swirling his fork into the green ball of algae as if he might actually eat it. "Ye'll be sorry when she's got ye' runnin' around that island busier than a one-armed monkey with two bananas. I'm tellin' ye' now, she's got a picture in her head of how this whole thing's gonna' go…" He unwound the fork and pierced a potato instead. "…and not a one of us will get any rest until she sees that picture brought to life. Ain't that right, Princess?"

Lilly flipped her hair over one shoulder. "For your information, I was *planning* to keep it simple."

He launched the potato into his mouth, moving it to one side as he raised one bushy eyebrow in amusement. "Simple? Woman, ain't nothin' been simple about you and me from the start. I don't believe you even know what that word means. Ye' gonna have that whole island decorated with flowers and frill 'for this is over."

She bit her lower lip to hide the knowing smile that would verify the truth to the words he'd spoken. She'd told me her plans for the ceremony, and absolutely none of it was *'simple.'* She wanted an arbor covered in island flowers, chairs erected, fabric strung and dyed, candles everywhere, and petals covering everything. Lilly, indeed, had no concept of the term *simple*.

Juan Jr. fixed his gaze upon Jim, contemplating, I imagined, what it was Lilly saw in him that made her so anxious to get married, particularly as Jim's cheeks once again bulged after a too-large bite of ham and potatoes. Deciding better than to express whatever might've been at the top of his mind, he instead raised his wineglass, the corner of his lip curving upward. "Congratulations to you both, then. I would also be happy to offer my assistance in any way I can. Flowers and... frill included."

Jim grinned. "Oh, yuns don't know how sorry you're fixin' to be. She's probably dreamin' up a chapel right now just to keep ye' both honest."

I laughed heartily at that, and Jack squeezed my leg, pulling my gaze up to him. The mischief that had been in his eyes moments prior was gone, and in its place was a tenderness I hadn't been expecting. It was as if there was a tether running between us, and down it, he sent the words *'I love you.'* I returned the unspoken words back along that invisible cord, and he gently squeezed my leg again in acknowledgment before turning his attention back to the table—to the two men seated at each end of it.

He'd been wary of Dario and Juan Jr. after the incident with Eli, and even on our night off, even while his fingers gently traced circles against my thigh, he was watching their every move. He'd placed marked knives at each of their place settings, and I knew he was testing them.

"A chapel *would* be more proper," Dario noted, using his marked knife to slice into his ham.

Lilly shook her head. "Maybe for you, but not for me and Jimmy. We want to be married surrounded by the same landscape we fell in love against... the sun setting at our backs... the smell of the flowers all around us... a warm breeze touching our faces as we exchange vows." She lovingly exchanged a glance with Jim. "We don't need a man to build us a chapel when God built us a paradise."

"That's right, Sugar," he beamed at her, wrapping a small bit of spaghetti algae on his fork alongside the ham already skewered there and filling his mouth again. He winced only a little at the flavor before taking a hefty swig of ale to wash it down.

Again, there was a small squeeze against my leg, and I imagined Jack was feeling similar sentiments to mine. The image she'd painted of their wedding had been serene. It also was something I wanted for myself... to say the words to him in the place we fell in love. We hadn't spoken of our own marriage plans with all that had come after the engagement, but I was fairly certain he was thinking of them just as I was.

Throughout the dinner, the small squeezes and wordless glances continued any time there was mention of the wedding. By the time we'd said our goodnights and made it to our cabin with two full and sleeping babies, I was pretty sure we'd silently agreed to carving out our own bit of time to get married on the island before we left.

I laid Zachary in the cradle as Jack carefully lowered Cecelia in beside him. Turning toward me, he tucked a stray curl behind my ear. "So... we're getting married here, then?"

I laughed. "It appears that way, yes."

"Would you like me to build you a chapel? Fill the island with flowers and frill?"

I shook my head. "No. I only want you."

He held my face, running a thumb over my lips. "You're sure?"

"That I don't want a chapel and flowers and fabric littering our perfect island? I'm sure, Jack."

"No," he coiled his other arm around my waist. "I mean, are you sure you only want me? With the memories..."

"Do you know what it's like to have these new memories?" I asked, smoothing my palms over his chest. "It's like... this book you've read a thousand times gets made into a series and you're excited to check it out... only they've changed all the key events... It might play out differently, but you know, even as you watch, what really happened. The new memories change nothing, Jack. I want *you*."

"Why?" His fingers traced my spine, and he smiled despite the heaviness of the question. "What is it about me that made you choose this life over that one?"

I slowly shook my head and grinned. "Everything, Jack. Everything you and I have become... From the beginning, it was going to be you. That first time you put your arms around me, I felt all my pain melt away. And as it did, I started to see myself through your eyes, and it made me feel like I was capable, strong —not because I was beside you, but just because that's who I was deep down. I didn't need a crutch to hold on to to get food or fire or face a storm. Through the mirror of your eyes, I saw someone strong enough to do all that for myself. And as I became the person in the reflection—a person I'd always wanted to be, I *saw* you. Not the actor or the big man who bossed everyone around and built things... but the *real* you. The one that cared about all of us; the one that stayed up to make sure I was alright, the one that sat with Izzy until she'd stopped crying and fallen asleep, the one that jumped in the ocean to save a stranger from drowning, the one that held me up when I crumbled... and for the first time in my life, I stopped thinking about my happiness, and I craved yours. I watched you smile—*really smile*—up on that summit, and I wanted that smile to stay; realized I'd do just about anything to give you that smile over and over again. And that desire gets stronger every day I look at your face. Making you happy... watching you with the children we've created... feeling your hands on me now... it's like I stepped off that raft and into the life I was made for. I might've had glimpses of happiness in my old life, but once I recognized the real thing, there was never any turning back. I choose you because I was made to be with you."

That smile appeared, lighting up every feature on his face as he drank in mine. "You know," his thumb danced softly down the side of my jaw, "I thought I loved you that first night on the beach. I remember you said you loved me and every piece of my heart shattered and healed in the same instance. But then..." his hand at my back tightened around the fabric of the dress, "when Jim got trapped and I saw you heaving boulders off the wall, I realized I couldn't have loved you on that beach because it was nothing compared to the way I felt seeing you there... this fierce little creature that was giving everything she had to save her friend and then stood over me to wash the dust from my hair... In that moment, I thought *that* was all the love a man could possibly feel..." his hand at my back slid along the silk to my stomach. "But then I watched you carry our children, held you and them in my arms, and then I was *positive* I couldn't have loved you up on that summit because what I felt in that moment was... everything."

He grinned, cupping my face with both hands. "And then I walked in that dining room tonight and I saw my future wife in this dress, and I just about dropped to my knees at your feet. Couldn't keep my legs under me at the sight of you. I don't think I'll ever stop loving you more than I did the day before... and I can't wait for every one of those days."

I turned my face into his hand, humming happily. "Me neither."

He scanned my face, his fingertips following every place his eyes landed upon, tracing my eyebrows, the bridge of my nose, the curve of my lips as I smiled.

"When?" He breathed, leaning in so his lips hovered just over mine.

"Tonight?" I bit my lip. "Tomorrow? Doesn't matter. I don't need anything but you, a preacher, and our family around us..."

He slid a hand down to my waist and rocked us slowly. "Should I go wake them all up? Jim had quite a few drinks at dinner... but I'll drag him to shore if you'd like."

"Tomorrow," I laughed. "I've got other plans for tonight."

"Is that so?" He spun us slowly in our silent dance. "Isn't it bad luck to spend the night before your wedding with—

Unable to go a moment longer without doing so, I pressed my lips to his. "We make our own luck," I breathed against his mouth. "And I didn't put this dress on so you could sleep somewhere else tonight."

He made an approving noise deep in his throat as his lips met mine again. "What exactly did you have in mind, then?"

I pulled away enough for him to see the fire I was sure was blazing in my eyes. "Oh, I intend to make you smile…" I loosened the laces of his breeches as I slowly lowered myself down to my knees. "Over and over…"

Chapter Thirty Nine

Chris

Chris stared up at the fluorescent lights over his head. His entire body was trembling both from the cold of the hospital room and from the nerves that had overtaken him as the clock over the bed grew nearer to 8:30AM... the scheduled time for his surgery.

With Covid, neither Cecelia nor Maria or even his own parents had been allowed to come in with him. They'd all protested unsuccessfully, and he knew they were all sitting in Cece's Jeep in the parking lot waiting for confirmation that the surgery went well. There was some comfort in knowing they were nearby, but still...

He looked at the clock. 8:20. His breathing was erratic, his heart racing. There were so many things that could go wrong... He wasn't ready to die. Not with so much left unsettled.

He needed to live; needed to get back to the storm to tell Alaina about her descendants... to tell her they didn't need to kill Richard Albrecht's ancestor. She simply needed to come back to the 21st century. If she came home and stayed there, Gloria would not be born to marry and expose Juan Josef to Richard Albrecht. He would then have no reason to go out on the ocean the day he did. They would erase all of it the moment she stepped through time.

He and Bud had discussed the new option. Bud's genealogists were reviewing Dahlia's charts, although he didn't need any confirmation after seeing the photos. He knew all he needed to know. If he could've gone back that day, he would've.

Still, Bud had insisted on seeing the research through. They'd promised to come back with information and make a decision as to what would happen next as a group. Bud said it was their obligation to deliver as much detail as they could.

8:22. He shivered, contemplating how long a person could survive with a growing hematoma. He'd gone this long... what was another few years? Was it too late to run?

He stared down at the needle digging into the vein of his right hand where the I.V. slowly was dripping what felt like ice into his body. Technically, he was fully capable of ripping it out and bolting for the car that was somewhere in the adjacent parking garage. But what good would he be to anyone if he eventually went brain dead?

8:26. He couldn't remember ever having felt so terrified. Not even when that plane was crashing... in that moment, he'd only felt... regret. He'd been calling out for Alaina... not because he was afraid to die, but because he was afraid they'd die before they'd had a chance to fix things... and now? Now he was afraid of the same things, but with a new woman he'd managed to screw things up with.

"How are we feeling, Mr. Grace?" A woman in scrubs asked from the foot of the bed. Her eyes were bright beneath the plastic shield she wore. She was O.R. staff, he could tell by the scrub colors and the blue hair cap. His anxiety shot through the roof.

"I'm second-guessing my decision to go through with this, to be perfectly honest."

He couldn't see her lips beneath the mask she wore, but her eyes crinkled in the corners enough to indicate she was smiling. "Dr. Shah is one of the best neurosurgeons in the country." Her eyes darted to the machine beside him, its incessant beeping his constant companion for the past hour. "You're safe. Take a deep breath, honey."

He did so, listening for the beeping to slow.

"You are one of the three most famous people in the world right now, Mr. Grace," she said, moving to the side of the bed and working a blood pressure cuff up his left arm. "Dr. Shah would not risk his reputation if he didn't think you'd survive this surgery. I promise, you're safe. Breathe."

Much to his surprise, she took his hand and squeezed. It was oddly comforting, and he heard the machine beeps spread out a little more as a result.

"What's your name?" He asked.

"Tiffany," she said sweetly, patting his hand once before she released him to inflate the cuff. "I've been working with Dr. Shah for the past ten years. He's the best of the best. He truly cares about his patients. I know this is hard—especially without being able to have family here with you, but I promise you, you're in good hands. We've got you."

"Has he ever... lost anyone?"

Again, the corners of her eyes crinkled in a smile. "Not a single one that came in for this procedure. And I couldn't even tell you how many of these we've done over the years. It's a lot."

He felt those words ease the tension that had been sitting in his shoulders... in his whole body, and he sank somehow deeper into the hospital bed.

"Are you ready?"

Too nervous to say the words, he nodded once.

"We're going to take you to the O.R. now. Once we get in there, they're going to ask you your name and what procedure you're having done. Then we'll insert a spicy little liquid into the I.V. and you'll be asleep within seconds. I'll be there the whole time to make sure you're safe. Then I'll be right here beside you when you wake up. There'll be no pain. Okay?"

Again, he nodded, and as she released the brakes on the bed and the lights above his head began to pass by, he focused on keeping his breaths even.

"Good morning, Mr. Grace," Dr. Shah said beneath his mask as he placed a hand on the bed's railing and walked alongside them through the corridor. "Are you ready to get rid of these headaches once and for all?"

He hated the way they talked to him like a child, but he knew it was a means to keep him calm... and to their credit, it was working.

"Afterward," he said, "will my family be allowed to come up?"

Dr. Shah shook his head. "Unfortunately, no visitors this week. We've had a spike in Covid cases, but Tiffany has an iPad she brought in for patients to use to video chat with their families while here. Since you're our V.I.P., I imagine she'll let you hog it for as long as you'd like."

His heartbeat quickened as a set of double doors opened and the bright circular O.R. lights shone over his head.

"Breathe," Tiffany whispered near his head. "You're safe."

"Mr. Grace," the tall dark-skinned anesthesiologist he'd met earlier greeted him. "You're looking like you're ready to get this over with. Don't worry, I'm here to make sure you don't feel a thing."

"Alright, honey," Tiffany said sweetly, lowering the railing on one side of the bed. "These boys are gonna move you onto the table here. I want your right hand here. You just keep breathing. We'll do everything. You alright?"

He nodded, closing his eyes as he was transferred seamlessly from one bed to the other.

Dr. Shah stood over him with a chart. "Okay, tell me your name and the procedure you are having."

"Chris Grace, craniotomy."

"Very good." Dr. Shah said, moving out of his field of vision.

He was freezing now. Despite his best attempts to hide it, his entire body was shivering.

"I got you, handsome. Put your right hand here." Tiffany tapped on a block to one side of the table he laid on, then wrapped him in a warm blanket, tucking the edges around his legs and torso. "Better?"

"Better."

"We're going to put this oxygen on you now," Tiffany informed him, placing a mask over his nose and mouth. "I know it's cold, but just breathe. We're gonna add the spice to warm you up now. You ready?"

He nodded, staring at Tiffany's eyes as he felt a warmth in his right hand.

'Better,' he thought. That might've been the last word he ever said... *'better?'* His mind echoed as his eyelids grew heavy. *'Fucking better? That's your last word? A response to a warm hospital blanket??!'*

And then there was nothing.

PART III

All that I am I give to you.

Chapter Forty

"Today?" Lilly asked, holding a piece of bread in front of her as her mouth fell open. "As in… a few hours from now?"

I laughed at her from across the table, adjusting the blanket over my breast where Zachary was feeding, the morning sunlight streaming through the window to warm the soft fabric. "Yes, Lilly. We don't want anything fancy. We just want to exchange vows and be married. Jack's up on the deck talking to Abraham now."

"But… it's you and Jack. You deserve to have something fancy!"

"The island is fancy enough. And having you all there to witness it, that's all we care about."

She shook her head. "Can you at least give me until this evening?"

"For what?" I asked, amused by how perturbed she was by my wedding plans.

"To finish the dress I was sewing you before we left, put together a few bouquets, and arrange for some food and music afterward. This is a lot of pressure you're putting on me, you know!"

"Lilly, putting pressure on anyone is the last thing I want today."

"As your maid of honor, it's my responsibility to take on that pressure and to make sure your wedding day is perfect. I've been so preoccupied with my own wedding plans, I failed you as a friend by not asking about yours! Consider this my gift to you. Please, let me do this. Give me until this evening? *Please*?"

"Fine. But only if you promise not to go crazy and tire everyone out before the evening even gets here."

She gasped. "As if I have ever done anything of the sort!" She stood, her seat scraping against the floorboards as she hastily spread jam on her bread to take with her. "Go wash your hair and relax. I'll come back to the ship in a few hours to get you ready. I gotta go find Fetia and Magna... and Jimmy... and Bruce... and maybe Dario..." she smirked. "So I can *not* tire them out..."

"Seriously, Lilly. I don't want anything crazy."

"Wouldn't dream of it, doll." She winked and hurried out, leaving me alone with Zachary and Cecelia and a grin still smeared across my face.

Adjusting Zachary's position against my breast, I reached out for a piece of bacon, leaning back in my seat to chew it as I considered what it might be like to stand on that beach at sunset and promise myself to Jack.

I was giddy with excitement, every nerve in my body feeling like it was dancing with anticipation. The evening couldn't come soon enough. I couldn't wait for him to call me *'Mrs. Volmer.'*

I hadn't felt this way when I'd married Chris. I'd been excited, yes, but I was scared that morning when I slipped into the little white dress I'd bought at a thrift store the day before.

We'd been so young and so hasty in our decision to get married. I remembered staring at my reflection and wondering if I was too young to be getting married; asking myself if we really knew each other well enough in the six months we'd been dating to make such a huge commitment. I remembered pacing from one side of my bedroom to the other, weighing the options of getting married against calling it off. I'd been so terrified that if I called it off, he might think I didn't love him, so I decided to go through with it. And that was not a good enough reason to marry someone; even if I loved him. I hoped it was different for him now.

I wondered if he was off in the 21st century somewhere getting married to a woman who wouldn't be asking herself those questions. Was Maria sitting in a room with her skin tingling as I was now, waiting for the moment she'd say *'I do?'* Were they married already? For as much as I couldn't wait to say my own vows, I also couldn't wait to hear every detail about theirs.

Zachary had finished feeding, pulling me from my thoughts to burp him and exchange him for Cecelia and the porcelain bottle of Wanda's milk. Holding her and the bottle with one arm, I finished my breakfast while she finished hers.

Just as I laid her back in the basket and began to rewrap the sling so I could take them both back to our room, Jack appeared in the doorway, a wicked grin on his face. He gripped the doorframe over his head and leaned slightly into the dining room. "I ran into Lilly on the deck."

"Sorry," I chuckled. "I couldn't tell her no."

"I've been told to keep you occupied for the rest of the morning..." There was mischief in his eyes. "...I had some ideas for a few things I wouldn't dare do with my wife."

My heart fluttered at the word *'wife.'*

"Is that right?" I crossed my arms over my chest. "We've only got a few hours... what'd you have in mind?"

"Nothing I'd want my children present to witness," he said in a dark, throaty voice, his arms flexing slightly where they gripped the frame. "If you're done feeding them, Magna offered to take them off our hands for a bit."

"They're fed..." I answered in the same sultry tone. "Shall I take them to her?"

He slowly shook his head, undressing me with his eyes as he lowered his arms. "I'll take them. I want you right where you are when I get back."

"In the dining room?" I balked, leaning against the edge of the table. "Where anyone could just walk in and find us?"

He bit his lower lip. "And a few other places, too."

Hours later, we both laid naked in a tangle of sheets and blankets in our room. I ran a finger over the curves of his abdomen where my head was rested. "I'm not sure that's how you're supposed to spend the morning of your wedding day."

His stomach vibrated with a laugh, moving my head with it. "I can't imagine there's any better way to spend the morning of your wedding day… wait until you see what I have in store for tonight."

"I thought those were all things you *wouldn't dare do with your wife*?"

"To be sure," he teased. "Once you're my wife, it gets far less delicate."

I snorted, turning my face toward him against his flushed skin. "*That* was delicate?"

He bounced his eyebrows, tracing a line down my jaw. "You'll find out soon enough."

I sighed, hugging my knees to my chest. "You don't have cold feet?"

"Not at all," he said, brushing the hair away from my face as he folded his other arm casually behind his head. "You?"

"Not even a little. You spoke to Abraham?"

"I did. That's what took me so long." He tugged my arm, pulling me up to lie curled into his side. "He made me go through scripture and pick out a verse for the *'reading.'*"

"The reading?" I asked, searching his eyes for any bit of distaste. "Are you comfortable with that? We can keep it short and sweet if you'd prefer."

He laid a kiss on my brow. "No. I want this day to last as long as possible. Besides, I like the piece I picked out. It felt like it fit us."

"Which one did you pick?"

"You'll see." He winked, pinching my bare bottom. "We should probably get you washed up before Lilly gets here… She'll have my ass if your hair isn't clean and you smell like me."

"Mmm. I don't mind smelling like you," I buried my face in his shoulder. "She'll get over it."

"Will she?" He sniffed my hair.

"No," I groaned, peeling myself off him.

He grabbed my hand, preventing me from completely leaving the bed. "I have a surprise for you." He glanced at the grandfather clock in the corner. "It should be ready now."

"What should?"

His lips curled upward. "Put your dressing robe on. It's down the hall. I'll show you."

Hastily, and giddy with anticipation, I slid the nearly sheer dressing robe over my shoulders, tying it at the waist and bouncing from toe to toe while he lazily pulled on a pair of breeches.

"So impatient," he mused, sauntering to the door and taking my hand to lead me down the corridor.

It was only once we were working our way down the hall that I became aware of how scandalous we might look. He, in only a pair of pants that hung low enough on his hips to expose the edges of the angled V that led down beneath them. I, with hair that was likely a dead giveaway to the *'delicate'* things he'd done for the past several hours, plenty of which involved his fingers being tangled in my curls. I prayed none of the men would pass us by.

Luckily, my prayer was answered, and we arrived uninterrupted at a door on the opposite end of the hall. He opened it, revealing a small candlelit room, a copper soaking tub filled with steaming water sitting in its center. "A bath?" I drooled. "A *real* bath?"

He nodded. "I had Georgie from the kitchen crew heat and fill it while we were… occupied. Get in while it's still hot."

"Oh my God." I practically ripped the robe off and skipped to the edge. "This is the greatest wedding day anyone could ask for!"

"I agree," he said, scanning my naked body as though we hadn't spent the past several hours doing precisely what I could see him contemplating beneath those fiery eyes. "Get in," he instructed. "Lilly gave me some of her dwindling stash for you. She ordered me to wash *and* condition your hair."

I lowered a leg into the gloriously warm water. "Oh…" I moaned, stepping over the edge and slowly sinking down onto my bottom, every muscle in my body instantly turning into liquid. "This is heaven. You're going to have to drag me out of here."

"Oh, I most certainly will if I must. I want a little bit of that hot water for me." He knelt to one side, presenting a pitcher, a bar of lavender soap, and Lilly's coveted shampoo and conditioner bottles.

"You're not getting in with me?" I asked, pouting.

"This tub's not big enough for the both of us," he kissed my forehead, dipping the pitcher into the water as he guided my back away from the edge to tilt my head back. "Besides," he poured the water over my hair and every part of me went slack with relaxation. "If I get in there with you… neither of us is getting clean… And I'd like to marry you at some point today."

"Mmm," I hummed as he scratched my scalp. "Marry me in this tub."

"I'd be glad to, but I don't think Abraham could make it through the sermon with *this* view."

I smiled, unable to prevent the ecstatic sounds from escaping my throat as he worked Lilly's shampoo into my scalp, his nails awakening every follicle on my head while the room filled with the sweet, fruity scent of cherry blossoms.

"If you don't quit making those noises," he whispered close to my ear, "we're never going to leave this room."

Tilting my head back, he poured the water over my head again and again, repeating the entire blissful process once more with the conditioner.

"You're not done yet?!" Lilly hissed from the doorway, promptly putting an end to our romantic morning. "It's almost one o'clock! She was supposed to be in the room with *dry* hair by now!"

"One o'clock?" I sat up suddenly. "I need to feed the babies."

Jack calmly shook his head. "I milked Wanda this morning. There's enough for both of them. Magna and Fetia have it covered."

I felt my breasts grow heavy in response and placed my hand over them. "No Jack, I *have* to feed them…"

He looked down to where my palm was rested. "Right, sorry. Lilly, can you go get them and meet us in the cabin?"

"On it," she said, closing the door behind her.

"I guess that's the end of that." He teased as I quickly ran the bar of soap over my body. He offered me his hand and assisted me out of the tub to wrap me tightly in a towel. "I'll see you at our wedding."

"You're not coming back to the cabin?"

He laid a kiss on my lips. "No boys allowed. Lilly's orders. Besides, Jim has something planned at the cave."

"Oh God, I'm sure it's something scandalous."

He kissed me once more, grinning. "The next time I kiss you, you'll be my wife…"

I ran my thumb over his lower lip. "I can't wait."

I turned to one side, then the other, gaping at the reflection staring back at me. "Lilly, how did you get this done in a few hours? This is exquisite!"

The dress was more than I could've ever imagined. It was elegant and simple, a sleeveless and fitted top, fabric bunched in the corners to create a pattern that swirled down into a full floor-length A-frame.

"Well," she said, admiring my reflection from where she stood behind me in her favorite green dress. "I didn't have time to finish the bottom layers, so I sewed mine into it. It can be your *'something new'* and your *'something borrowed.'*"

"It's perfect!" I spun to face her, wrapping my arms tightly around her. "Thank you!"

"Stop." She pried my arms away from her. "I've spent way too much time on our hair and makeup to have it get messed up before we even get to the shore. Cry later."

I looked back at my reflection, my hair braided and draped down one side, white and pink flowers sprinkling the braid where it nearly reached my waist after going so long untrimmed. She'd added rouge to my cheeks, a little bit of eyeliner, and used the softer pink rouge on my lips as well. I'd never thought of myself as an unattractive woman, but I'd never considered myself beautiful. Until that moment.

"Lilly, you've outdone yourself."

"That's nothing." She winked, handing me a bouquet of pink and white flowers. "Wait until you see the rest. You ready?"

"I've never been more ready for anything in my life."

"Jimmy!" she called out, nearly deafening me in one ear. "We're ready!"

He appeared in the doorway as if he'd been standing just outside it the whole time, clad in the grey suit jacket he'd worn for Bud and Bertie's anniversary with a white flower tucked into his breast pocket. I knew he was miserable in that jacket, noted the beads of sweat forming on his brow, but he didn't complain one bit. He flashed his teeth in a wide smile as he scanned my reflection, letting out a dramatic whistle. "Honey, you're just about the prettiest bride I ever laid eyes on. If the sight of you don't bring that man to his knees, he ain't right in the head."

"Is everything ready on the beach?" Lilly asked.

"Just waitin' on us. Come on with yas, before I keel over with heat stroke."

He led us up to the top deck, where Juan Jr. was waiting at the side of a sloop. He bowed his head. "Alaina, you look stunning."

"Thank you." He and Jim assisted both me and Lilly into the sloop before they joined us inside. Juan Jr. stood and lowered us down.

On the shore, after what felt like ages of paddling to get there, Jim lifted me up into his arms to carry me onto the dry sand, returning to do the same for Lilly.

I heard him mumble to her as they approached. "The second she says *'I do,'* I'm tearin' this thing off and chuckin' it in the ocean."

I laughed, but then I caught sight of what was awaiting us down the beach.

Lilly was truly a magician. With the ocean sunset as a backdrop, she'd created an aisle leading toward it, a long strip of white fabric rolled out on the sand, littered with pink and white petals. To each side of it, she'd had someone bring in chairs from the ship, all of them filled with our family. Bruce sat at the back with his violin at the ready. Magna and Izzy were on the opposite side.

Juan Jr. hurried ahead to take a seat beside Dario. Kyle and Fetia sat in the front, each holding a baby. And waiting at the center, Jack stood tall, Abraham dressed in his ceremonial black beside him.

There was not a hint of hesitation in my steps as I followed Jim and Lilly to the edge of the aisle and waited.

Bruce pulled the violin to his shoulder and began to play the moment they took their first step onto the fabric.

I stared exclusively at Jack, and he stared exclusively at me the moment I stepped onto the fabric.

Chapter Forty One

Abraham, with his young full cheeks and stoic posture, stood proudly before us in his dark black robe and white collar, holding a very-worn leather-bound bible in both hands. His dark hair was covered by a white powdered wig that sat a little too far back against his forehead, revealing the true darkness of his hairline. He cleared his throat, smiling between the two of us before he addressed the ones seated behind us. "The grace of our Lord Jesus Christ, the love of God, and the fellowship of the Holy Spirit be with you."

He paused.

"And also with you," a few of them that were familiar with the custom said back. Jim giggled on the opposite side of Jack, prompting a very sinister-looking scowl from both Abraham and Lilly. He quickly straightened.

Jack's smile grew broader in the corner of my eye as his knuckles softly grazed mine.

"God is love, and those who live in love live in God, and God lives in them," Abraham recited. "Let us pray."

As everyone bowed their heads and Abraham began the prayer, I felt Jack run his finger over my wrist, inciting goosebumps upon every inch of my skin. Even the roots of the hair on my head felt like they pulled upward at the touch.

"You look beautiful," he whispered.

So entranced was I, that I didn't hear a single word of Abraham's prayer. The only thing I was aware of was the man standing beside me, finding every excuse to sneak a touch where our arms hung close together.

"Amen," Abraham said loudly. When I opened my eyes, he was looking past me at the rest of our group. "We have come together in the presence of God to witness the marriage of Jack Michael Volmer and Alaina Jane McCreary Grace, to pray for God's blessing on them, to share their joy, and to celebrate their love."

I tucked my lips in to hide the smile. Jack had given Abraham our full names, and I was grateful he'd left *'Grace'* as a part of it. It was a part of me, and leaving the name felt like an acknowledgment of it.

As Abraham continued to address the others, I stole an opportunity to look up at my groom. He'd apparently had the same idea, his gaze turning to greet mine at the precise same moment. There was not a hint of doubt in those clear blue eyes. There was nothing but confidence, pride, and unrestrained love... and a perfectly shaved face.

I drank in the sharp lines of his jaw, the upward curve in his full lips... He wore a white shirt; one suited for the 18th century, with plenty of frill at the collar where it sat over his black jacket and breeches. He was a blend of 18th and 21st century attire with his stockinged calves and shoes, but it was absolutely perfect.

Bertie had been right. This... the way he looked at me right then... this is the image I would remember forever.

"You look beautiful too," I whispered between us, prompting the corners of his lips to curl upward.

"...Jack and Alaina are now to enter this way of life," Abraham said a little loudly, an attempt, I assumed by the stern expression on his face when I met his gaze, to get us both to pay attention. "They will each give their consent to the other and make solemn vows, and in token of this, they will each give and receive a ring. We pray with them that the Holy Spirit will guide and strengthen them, that they may fulfill God's purposes for the whole of their earthly life together."

He glanced between the two of us. "The vows you are about to take are to be made in the presence of God, who is judge of all and knows all the secrets of our hearts; therefore, if either of you knows a reason why you may not lawfully marry, you must declare it now."

We both remained silent.

Abraham broke character for a moment, grinning playfully. "*Now,* you may face each other."

We both turned, my cheeks on fire from the smile that felt like it might never fade.

"Jack, will you take this woman to be your wife? Will you love her, comfort her, honor and protect her, and, forsaking all others, be faithful to her as long as you both shall live?"

"I will," he said, a slight tremble in his voice that made my throat burn.

"And Alaina," my heart danced, "Will you take this man to be your husband? Will you love him, comfort him, honor and protect him, and, forsaking all others, be faithful to him as long as you both shall live?"

"I will," I managed, every bit of restraint caving at the spoken words and forcing tears to run down both my cheeks.

Behind me, I heard Lilly echo my own sniffle.

"And will you, the families and friends of Jack and Alaina, support and uphold them in their marriage now and in the years to come?"

"We will," the group around us answered, only heightening my emotional collapse. In every way, I felt like I was exactly where I was supposed to be, with the people around me that were meant to be there. The joy I felt as a result was overwhelming to every one of my senses.

"Let us pray," Abraham said again, and I relished in the opportunity to compose myself, wiping my eyes and nose quickly while the heads around us bowed and he recited:

"God our Father, from the beginning, you have blessed creation with abundant life. Pour out your blessings upon Jack and Alaina, that they may be joined in mutual love and companionship, in holiness and commitment to each other. We ask this through our Lord Jesus Christ your Son, who is alive and reigns with you, in the unity of the Holy Spirit, one God, now and forever. Amen."

Much more together now, and committed to making it through the remainder of the ceremony without another breakdown, I took a deep breath and opened my eyes. Jim winked at me from his place behind Jack.

Abraham opened his bible and balanced a pair of circular glasses on his nose. "A reading from First Corinthians..."

Then he read, loud and clear, the piece of scripture Jack had selected.

"Love is patient, love is kind. It does not envy, it does not boast, it is not proud. It does not dishonor others, it is not self-seeking, it is not easily angered, it keeps no record of wrongs. Love does not delight in evil but rejoices with the truth. It always protects, always trusts, always hopes, always perseveres. Love never fails. But where there are prophecies, they will cease; where there are tongues, they will be stilled; where there is knowledge, it will pass away."

"Jack and Alaina," I broke free of my daze; my absolute appreciation for the words Jack had selected. "I now invite you to join hands and make your vows, in the presence of God and his people."

I placed my hands in Jack's without hesitation and he gave them both a reassuring squeeze. I was home. I was safe. I was *his*.

"Jack, repeat after me..."

The emotional grip I thought I had broke into a thousand pieces as Jack echoed the words Abraham provided.

"I, Jack Michael Volmer, take you, Alaina Jane McCreary Grace, to be my wife." A broad smile, one I could only imagine was the mirror image of the one on my face, washed over his as he continued.

"...to have and to hold from this day forward; for better, for worse, for richer, for poorer, in sickness and in health, to love and to cherish, till death us do part."

He'd spoken the words without looking away for even a second, his eyes remaining fixed upon mine, his fingers tightening around my own. I was a sobbing, trembling wreck by the time he'd finished and Abraham turned to me.

"Alaina, repeat after me…"

I did my best to recite the same words back with the level of unwavering sincerity Jack had. I meant every word as I echoed it, despite the sob that prevented each word from being discernible from the next—most of it coming out as one long, high and low-pitched sound.

Jack chuckled as I made my way through it, releasing one hand to pull a handkerchief from his jacket and dab my eyes.

Even Abraham suppressed a laugh when I'd finished. Straightening his back, he looked toward Jim. "Who has the rings?"

Jim stared forward at the people sitting on the beach, attempting poorly to conceal his own battle with emotions.

Abraham cleared his throat. "Who has the rings?" He said again, snapping Jim out of his stupor.

"Oh shit, I got 'em." He closed one eye as he shoved a hand into his pocket, fishing around long enough to warrant a small groan from Lilly behind me. He handed them both to Abraham, mouthing a *'sorry'* in the direction of Lilly after he'd returned to his place.

Abraham handed one to each of us and I grinned at the gold band in my fingers… Bruce's old wedding ring. I looked out at the small group of spectators and found him smiling from ear to ear.

I noticed something on the inside of the ring—an engraving. It wasn't the perfect engraving of a machine, but rather, one hammered by hand… I turned the ring in the light to read: *'I go where you go.'*

"Heavenly Father, by your blessing let these rings be to Jack and Alaina a symbol of unending love and faithfulness, to remind them of the vow and covenant which they have made this day through Jesus Christ our Lord. Jack, place the ring on the fourth finger of Alaina's left hand and repeat after me…"

He did as instructed, reciting the words: "Alaina, I give you this ring as a sign of our marriage. With my body I honor you, all that I am I give to you, and all that I have I share with you, from this day to the last of my days."

I did the same, reciting the words this time with perfect clarity.

I held his hands, smiling at the gold band on his finger that would bind him to me forever, my heart dancing at the sight. He was mine...

"In the presence of God, and before this congregation, Jack and Alaina have given their consent and made their marriage vows to each other. They have declared their marriage by the joining of hands and by the giving and receiving of rings. I therefore proclaim that they are husband and wife."

At these words, my knees trembled. Jack squeezed our joined hands a little tighter, his eyes watering ever so slightly.

"Those whom God has joined together let no one put asunder." Abraham's shoulders eased, and he removed his glasses to add, "Jack, you may now kiss your wife."

He barely waited for Abraham to finish the words before his hands were on my face, his lips covering mine to add exclamation to the vows we'd both spoken.

Around us, there were cheers and the sounds of Bruce's violin. I coiled my fingers in the lapels of his jacket, parting my lips for him as I pulled him closer for just a moment more, not quite ready to be done.

He pressed his forehead to mine when he finally released my mouth, whispering, "I love you more today than all the days so far, Mrs. Volmer."

"And I love you." I smiled up at him. "Who engraved your ring?"

"I did," he said proudly. "Bruce gave it to me months ago. I've been slowly adding the words to it during my shifts standing guard over Juan Josef."

"Yuns gonna' stand there like 'at the rest of the night?" Jim teased, his jacket already discarded in the sand at his feet. "Bruce's been cookin' up a storm and I'm so hungry, I could eat the north end of a south-bound goat."

I giggled as Lilly shushed him, curling my arms around Jack's waist to let him lead me back down the little aisle to allow the others waiting to disperse.

Once my toes were back in the sand, the ceremony felt officially over, and everyone began to talk at once. Lilly pulled me to one side. "I wanted to do dinner and dancing in the cave, but it was too short of notice to pull it off. I had the kitchen staff setup the top deck instead. Is that okay?"

I pulled her into a hug. "Lilly, everything about today is perfect. Thank you."

Chapter Forty Two

Chris

There was a steady beeping as Chris's eyes opened to find Tiffany standing at one side of the bed jotting down numbers on a chart.

When he opened his eyes again, the lights were off and she was gone. There was no pain, but everything felt foggy.

The third time he opened his eyes, Dr. Shah was in the room with Tiffany, both of their masked faces hiding smiles as their gazes fell upon him. "The surgery went well, Chris," the doctor informed him in the soothing tone he always used. "We've contacted your parents to let them know. When you're feeling up to it, the iPad is ready for you."

Before he could respond, his eyes were closed again.

This happened several times, and just how much time had passed between each round of consciousness, he wasn't sure. The only thing that told him he was alive was the steady beeping of the heart monitor behind him.

The next time he opened his eyes, he was staring up at the lights over his head. This time, he felt significantly less groggy.

"Mr. Grace," a thick, deep voice said from near the foot of his bed.

He blinked, adjusting his eyes to the light to focus on the tall man leaning against the opposite wall. He wore a grey suit, well-tailored to his large build, and the lights over his head reflected off his smooth bald head.

Beside him, seated in the lone chair in the corner of the room, was a woman. In comparison to the nearly onyx complexion of the man beside her, her skin was pale under brown hair that had been pulled back at the base of her neck.

"Mr. Grace," the man repeated, his rich baritone feeling like it shook the blankets laying over his chest. "My name is Detective Haywood. This is my partner, Detective Morris. We have some additional questions regarding your recent experience on flight 89. Dr. Shah has lowered your meds to allow for clarity in our conversation. Are you in any pain?"

"No," he managed, his throat feeling as if he'd swallowed gravel. "Water?"

Detective Morris stood from her seat to collect a pink cup from the table beside him, positioning the straw at his lips.

He took several hefty gulps, staring up into her light brown eyes over her mask before he let her place the cup back on the table and return to her seat.

Sitting up a little straighter in the bed, Chris winced at the ache in his bones—not his head, he noted, just his body. "How long have I been out?"

"You'll have to save those questions for your doctor," Detective Haywood informed him. "Are you feeling well enough to answer a few questions?"

"I think so," he said softly, "although I told the men who questioned me in customs everything I could remember several times over."

Detective Haywood removed his face mask and smiled, exposing bright white straight teeth in a wide set mouth. It was the first person whose full face he'd seen since he'd entered the hospital and he was appreciative of the gesture. "I'm sure you're quite tired of answering questions. I apologize for the inconvenience. We'll try to be quick so you can rest."

He noticed Detective Morris had pulled out a small voice recorder and a notepad. She clicked her pen once in preparation to document everything that would follow. It was strange that, amid a pandemic, the two of them would venture into this hospital to ask him all the same questions he'd already answered... Very strange. Suddenly, he was uncomfortable.

Detective Haywood cleared his throat, pushing himself off the wall to stroll to the edge of the bed. "Some of these questions might seem a little out of place, but this is a very large investigation and there's no detail too big or too small."

"Okay..."

Again, Detective Haywood offered him a warm smile. "There's no need to feel uneasy, Mr. Grace. This is simply a formality. We'll be on our way in no time."

Chris relaxed a little.

Detective Haywood ran his palm over his jaw. "I've interviewed your wife's family several times over the course of the last three years. I know you all were together the night before you and Mrs. Grace left for your vacation, and I know they exited your home around seven thirty. I'd like to start there, if you don't mind. Walk me through the events that took place between their departure and yours."

"Between me and my wife?" Chris asked, frowning.

Detective Haywood breathed out a laugh. "Like I said, some questions might seem out of place, but the details, even if they seem obsolete, might expose some missing piece we're not seeing. I've been investigating flight 89 for three years, and there is no leaf I am willing to leave unturned in my search for answers. I've asked similar of the other two survivors."

"Maria? She's—"

"She's fine, Mr. Grace. She's with your parents, anxiously awaiting a video call from you."

He let out a long, relieved exhale.

"What happened after Alaina's mother and sister left?"

Chris sifted through his memories. There were two answers to that question, but he decided to go with the newer account of events. "We went upstairs to finish packing." He recalled that they'd managed to get a few essentials into the larger suitcase before tearing at each other's clothing and spending the following hour making love on top of the scattered items on the bed. Was that a detail he should share? Deciding that wouldn't be relevant information in any way, he skipped over it.

"It was late by the time we'd finished loading up the cases. We decided not to sleep since there was snow in the forecast and she wanted to leave earlier to get to the airport in case the roads were bad. We left around 3—"

"Stop there," Detective Haywood placed a large palm up in the air. "I need to know the details, Mr. Grace. From 7:30pm to 3:30am, what did you and your wife do other than pack?"

"I really don't see how any of that is relevant." This seemed too personal.

"It's likely not, but I have to ask."

"Why?"

Detective Morris lowered her notepad, looking at him over the rim of her glasses. "Because you and the other two survivors are the only bit of evidence we have regarding flight 89. We have to ask these questions. Please, try to answer."

He toyed with the edge of the thin blanket draped over him, resolving to give them what they wanted so he could check in with Maria. "We packed, we made love for an hour, then we packed some more. We brought the cases downstairs, and she turned on the t.v. to check the weather. We debated about what time we should leave and whether or not it would be smart to try to sleep a few hours before doing so… she won that debate and we stayed awake. She put on reruns of Friends. We made love again on the sofa, then we ate cereal while we watched two more episodes, then we left."

Detective Haywood paced the few steps to one side of the small room and turned back to do the same in the opposite direction. "And then you drove to O'hare. Tell me about the drive. What'd you talk about?"

"We didn't really talk during the drive. The snow was thick, and the roads were awful. We were both just focused on the road. You couldn't see ten feet in front of you, and I was barely able to drive faster than 30mph without sliding. We passed a nasty accident on the way up and that only intensified our silence. I don't think we spoke a single word until we pulled into the parking lot."

Another pace to the wall and back. "Tell me about O'hare. You were delayed there. What happened at the airport?"

He squeezed his eyes closed, attempting to decipher between the two different memories of that morning. "There weren't many people there so early. We got through security in no time. We went to a Starbucks and got coffees, then we sat down in our terminal. She pulled up the resort on her phone and we started planning where we'd have dinner on our first night there... then we looked at the various attractions to start planning what we'd do first the next morning. We decided on snorkeling and a massage. Then we got the announcement we were delayed."

"And what was her reaction to the news?"

"Her reaction?"

"Was she angry?"

Chris huffed. "Of course. We both were. Well... frustrated anyway, and worried we might miss our connecting flight... which we inevitably did."

"So you're delayed and stuck at O'hare, both of you are angry... what happens during the wait?"

Again, these questions felt far too personal. Chris couldn't understand how anything that had happened between himself and Alaina could assist in their investigation. He answered, though, anxious to be rid of the detectives. "I napped while she read. I woke up when they were boarding the flight, then both of us fell asleep during the flight. She was out before she could even get nervous about takeoff."

"She was a nervous flyer?" Haywood asked, one thick eyebrow raised.

"Very nervous."

"Did she take anything for the nerves? A drink or any anti-anxiety medications?"

Chris frowned. "No. Alaina wouldn't even take an aspirin if she needed one."

"So you both slept through the entire first flight?"

Shit... They did in one of his sets of memories... In the other, they'd talked through the whole first flight. The two timelines were starting to scramble. Did it matter that he'd given the former account of events? He didn't see how.

"Yes."

He was really getting tired of this interrogation—that's what it felt like, an interrogation... like they were waiting for him to say something to expose himself as some great mastermind who'd stolen the flight and hid it... Was that what they thought happened? That the flight might've been hijacked? Did they think he might be involved? Is that why they were asking such personal questions?

"So you arrive in Los Angeles. What happens there?"

"We were late. We sprinted to the shuttle and then once we got to Tom Bradley, we again ran as fast as we could to the gate, only to find out we'd missed the flight."

This is where the new memories had stopped entirely. Everything from that moment on was identical in both versions of his past. He ran them through their experience at the airport, the separated seats, seeing her next to Jack Volmer on the plane, and the crash. He left out no detail, big or small, and was sure there was nothing left he could offer.

"So, you saw the raft disappear," Haywood said, running a palm over his smooth head. "And you never saw the raft again after that?"

"Correct."

"The raft never made it to your island?"

Chris took a steady, deep breath. "No."

"And you said a single piece of luggage washed up on the shore, but it did not belong to either you or your wife?"

He shook his head. "No."

"And at no point between the moment your wife's family left your home and the moment you took your seat on flight 89, did you and your wife have any sort of argument, correct?"

Taken aback, Chris's response was significantly shorter as his temper welled in his chest. "No, my wife and I did not have any sort of argument."

At this, Detective Haywood pulled out the rolling stool from the counter, sliding it to the bedside to straddle it. "So then, at what point did she remove her wedding ring?"

"What?" The word fell out of his mouth before he could even process what the detective had asked. He felt the same as he had when the search party had caught him with Sergeant Harris's body at the waterfall in Oparre. He couldn't afford to make the same mistakes as he had then; couldn't afford to look guilty in any way. How careless he'd been forgetting that the ring was among his belongings. With Cecelia sniffing around every corner he'd been in, of course, she'd found it. He needed to think clearly before he answered.

"When did your wife remove her wedding ring, Mr. Grace?" Haywood asked again, his tone shifting from the warm and friendly one he'd used throughout to one laden with accusation.

He and Alaina were happy in the new version of his memories. She'd never willingly take off that ring, he knew. And he knew Cecelia wouldn't believe she'd taken it off for comfort. Even when her fingers were swollen during pregnancy and the ring threatened to cut off her circulation, she refused to remove it. He ran through various situations and then landed upon a story he prayed would cover his mistake.

"She took it off just before she boarded the second plane, when I asked for it," he said in a casual tone, working hard to make himself appear as though he found the question comical. "She was very confused by it, but I promised to give it back once we were in Bora Bora. You see, we got married in a courthouse... Both of us too excited to get married to plan a proper ceremony. I knew there was a part of her that regretted being so hasty. We didn't write vows and there was nothing romantic about it. I wanted to surprise her by offering her vows and the ring on the beach. Give her a ceremony she could look back on."

"Why didn't you mention that when you recounted the events at the airport?"

Chris shrugged one shoulder, smiling as if he was reliving the moment. "Forgot about that part of it."

Detective Haywood narrowed his eyes. "Did you tell your new fiancé about the ring? About what you had planned for your wife?"

Maria. If they'd gone to her first to enquire about the ring, she, no doubt, would've said something to unknowingly incriminate them both in her defense of him. God, he wished he'd been awake enough earlier to call her before they'd arrived. What might she have told them? What was it they thought he might be guilty of? Murdering his wife? Hijacking the plane? All because they found a wedding ring?

He shook his head, treading carefully as he simply responded with, "no."

"Interesting," the detective responded, combing his fingers down his chin. "Is there a reason she claims the ring was purchased specifically for her, then?"

Chris forced a chuckle, despite all the warning alarms firing in his brain. "We're engaged. She *would* assume that."

Nothing about Detective Haywood's expression indicated whether or not he believed a word Chris had just said, and he made no move to rise up from the stool, but instead sat inspecting him.

Detective Morris stood. "Mr. Grace, did you know Bud Renaud prior to boarding that plane?"

"No."

Suddenly, the room felt too small as she stood on the opposite side of his bed, sharing the same accusatory expression as Detective Haywood. "But you knew of him? Did you know he was going to be on that flight?"

"I knew of the Renaud family, of course, but I didn't *know* he would be on the flight." He straightened, fed up with the situation and the possible accusations he was backing himself into. "I'm sorry, what are you implying? Are you planning to arrest me for something?"

"No," Detective Haywood said evenly.

Common sense washing over him, he lifted his chin. "Well then, I've answered all the questions I'm willing to answer without an attorney present. Had I known this would be an interrogation— *one I'm not sure is legal given that I am recovering from brain surgery*—I'd have insisted my lawyer be brought in before answering anything. I'm asking you to leave now and to send my nurse in so I can call my fiancé."

Detective Haywood grinned as he placed his mask back over his nose and mouth and stood. "Thank you for your time, Mr. Grace. We'll be in touch again. Soon."

Chapter Forty Three

I held Jack's left hand in my lap, tracing the gold band on his ring finger where we sat at a long table on the ship's deck surrounded by stars, candlelight, steaming food, and our island family. At the far end of the table, Juan Jr. had set up the gramophone, and John Coltrane's *'Blue Train'* album provided the perfect soundtrack for our wedding reception dinner.

With Bruce and Michael taking turns guarding our prisoners, Jack was more relaxed than I'd seen him in months. He drank wine and laughed alongside me as toasts were made in our honor and stories were told as the moon grew higher in the sky.

Once we moved past the embarrassing tales of where and when each of them had caught Jack and I in questionable positions—accounts ranging from the early days in the cave to the big house in Tahiti to this morning in the dining room—people began sharing their own marriage stories.

Lilly recounted the details of Bertie and Bud's wedding; the ones she'd laid out for us the day she died, and my eyes watered as I heard it retold. Magna told us about her beach wedding, a traditional Polynesian handfasting, followed by the exchange of flowered crowns and leis. I could see the gears in Lilly's head turning as she described the traditions. Kyle and Fetia shared their similar experience, and even Bruce shared happy memories of his marriage before it fell apart.

Juan Jr. and Dario dined with us, and although neither opted to share any personal details, they were alight with smiles and laughter as they listened.

"Y'all wanna hear a funny wedding story?" Jim asked, chewing to one side and raising his wineglass in our direction. "It ain't mine, but I was there."

Too full to eat another bite of my steamed crab, I plucked up my wineglass and leaned in, still clutching Jack's hand in my lap. "Yes!" Jim-stories were always my favorite.

"Wait," Lilly said, narrowing her eyes at him. "This isn't the one with the mechanic's daughter, is it? Because if it is, that's not appropriate dinner conversation."

He shook his head, winking at me. "Nah, I'll save that one for later. This one's about Timmy and Betty Rea Downing."

I watched him get comfortable in his chair, his eyes fixed on the glass of wine in his hand as he was transported to the memory.

"See, before my momma moved us to Oklahoma, I spent about eight years growin' up in Little River County, Arkansas alongside Timmy and his sister Betty. They was the closest thing I ever had to siblings. We grew up runnin' from one side of the county to the other, swimming, fishing, and finding trouble just about everywhere we went."

He crossed his ankle over his knee, swirling the liquid in his glass. "Now, me and Timmy and Betty was family, no matter who we were born to. So even when I moved away, we stayed in touch. When Betty Rea decided to get married about fifteen years ago, you can bet your ass me and Timmy was standin' in that wedding."

He grinned. "But a regular ole' Arkansas wedding would not do for little miss Betty Rea. No, she wanted a fancy beach wedding down in the Keys. So… we loaded up Timmy's dilapidated van and the two of us drove down to Key Largo."

He smiled to himself. "Now, unlike the rest of us, Betty Rea was movin' up in the world. She snagged herself the son of a pretty well-to-do lawyer while she was in college. Needless to say, rednecks that we were, me and Timmy didn't exactly fit in at their hoity-toity rehearsal dinner. We was about as stiff as a badger's ass walkin' into that resort."

He laughed, "I tell ye,' between the two of us and an open bar, we must've drank two whole bottles of Jack Daniels by ourselves... and Timmy... well, all night he was ramblin' on about how he'd never been to Key West—never really been anywhere outside Arkansas. I hadn't either, save Oklahoma, which to me, wasn't much different from Little River County. And our dumb, drunk asses decided, somewhere around three in the mornin' that it'd be a good idea to go check it out. See what all the fuss was about."

He squinted one eye at me. "I don't know if ye' ever been down to the Keys, but Key West is about a two-hour drive from Key Largo. Neither one of us knew that little detail when we got in the van and headed in what we *thought* was south. We was too dumb and drunk to notice we was actually goin' north. I think we made it about thirty minutes down the road before we saw blue and red lights in the rear-view mirror."

Jack's thumb ran over my knuckles, and I laid my head against his arm.

"Now," Jim continued, placing his drink on the table and holding his hands out to add to the theatrics. "If ye' ever been north from Key Largo, you'd know that about thirty minutes into that trip, we had swampy Everglades on each side of us. And would you believe, Timmy, my best friend in the world, pulled his van over, looked me dead in the eye, and said *'I ain't goin' down like this,'* before he jumped out of the vehicle and bolted into that swamp?!"

"Into the Everglades?!" Jack howled. "What'd the cops do?"

"Not a damn thing," Jim snickered. "Timmy climbed up the fence faster than a haint and plum disappeared. Left my happy ass sittin' in the passenger seat with my face hangin' out."

He rolled his eyes. "Them cops wasn't goin' nowhere near that side of the fence. They shined their flashlights out there and hollered for him, but he was gone. And the police officer looked at me and said, *'where was yuns goin'?'* And so I told him—*as if he oughta know*—we was goin' to Key West!" He cackled. "As ye' can imagine, he just about fell over laughing. Here was these two young kids, drivin' north to get to the keys and one of 'em decidin' it was a better idea to run into the swamp with crocodiles and snakes and God knows what else in the dead of night than to get a D.U.I. and miss his little sister's wedding."

The whole table roared with laughter.

"Did he come back?" Jack asked, squeezing my hand.

Jim shook his head, the smile widening. "Me and 'em two cops stayed on the side of the road waitin' all Got damn night for the summbitch to climb back over. Would you believe he *fell asleep* in there? Curled up in the Everglades like it was nothin.' Came hobbling out about two hours before Betty Rea was supposed to walk down the aisle covered in filth. Them cops took one look at his torn clothes and mud-soaked hands and feet and figured he'd served his sentence. Let us go with a warning. Oooh, Lordt, but he stunk to high heaven, and I spent thirty minutes cooped up in the van—*with windows that didn't roll down, mind you*—drivin' him back to the resort. Even after he'd showered, he still stunk like swamp through the whole damn ceremony." He glanced at Lilly. "And so I want you to remember that story the next time you roll your eyes at me for doin' somethin' dumb and know it was *me* that had the sense to stay in the damn car. I might be a redneck, but there's much worse than me out there."

"I don't roll my eyes at you," she said, taking a considerable amount of effort not to roll her eyes as she said it.

"Woman, you've rolled your eyes at me at least ten times since we set down at this table." He held up a hand to silence her retort, "and you're fixin' to roll 'em now cause what in the Sam Hill kind of music are we listenin' to? I cain't hardly stand it no more. Y'all ain't got nothin' that's got a melody to it?"

"It's John Coltrane," I informed him. "You don't like it?"

He snarled his nose. "Lordt, no. It's too much goin' on. Scramblin' my brain."

"I never cared for it either," Dario admitted. "Couldn't understand why my father always listened to it."

"See?" He stuck his tongue out at Lilly. "Go find somethin' we can dance to. Ye' cain't dance to this noise."

"Lainey, why don't you help me pick something?" She said sweetly. "It's your wedding day, you should pick your first dance."

"That's a perfectly terrible idea," Jack teased, kissing the top of my head. "You give her a box of records to choose from, and we'll be here all night waiting for her to make a decision."

I laughed, raising my head off his shoulder. "Alright smartass, help me pick one, then."

He pulled me off my feet.

Juan Jr. rose from his seat to escort us. "I wasn't sure which ones were which, so I brought all three crates up," he said, motioning to three crates on the deck at the side of the table the gramophone sat on.

Jack nudged me toward the one closest. "I'll take the far one."

I knelt, deciding to give the case a once-over before scanning each record's contents.

Juan Josef and Gloria had amazing taste in music. It was organized by genre. I flipped through classics from Miles Davis, Duke Elllington, John Coltrane, Art Blakey, and more before reaching albums from Smokey Robinson, Gladys Knight & the Pips, Jackie Wilson, Ben E. King, and Solomon Burke. Jack was right. I could be there all night attempting to find the right song. I made a mental note to ask Juan Jr. if we could set up the gramophone in a shared space to allow me to listen to each in its entirety.

"Got one," Jack said, holding a record over his head.

"There's no way you could pick something that fast." I stood, and he promptly hid the record behind his back.

"Don't trust me to pick something good?" He teased, spinning as I attempted to get a look at what he held.

I giggled, still trying to get a look around him. "I honestly have no idea what your taste in music even is!"

He winked. "Polka… mostly…" Biting his lip, he turned faster than I could move around him. "You really don't trust me to pick a song?"

"You picked a song in less than a minute. Don't you want to at least look through all our options before deciding on what will be *our* song for the rest of our lives?"

His lips remained curled upward, a sparkle of amusement in his eye as we continued to dance in circles. "Nope."

Spinning again, I laughed heartily. "That confident in your decision?"

He nodded proudly. "You gonna let me have this or not?"

Giving up my futile attempt to move faster than him, I crossed my arms over my chest. "On one condition."

"An ultimatum already, Mrs. Volmer?"

I raised an eyebrow. "Yes. I'll let you pick our song, as long as while we dance it… we do the move."

A thick rumble of amusement rolled through him. "You sure you're up for it in that dress?"

"Woah woah woah," Lilly leaned forward from where she'd been snooping from her seat at the table. "You guys have *moves*?"

I grinned, "Oh, Jack has *lots* of moves… You know, he used to be quite the—

"Alright," he said quickly, flashing his teeth in warning before I could finish the sentence. "We'll do it… but you better not mess it up, Red," he joked, turning his back to place the record on the player, "can't have you making all my years of practice look like child's play, ya know."

"Wouldn't dream of it, darling." I took my place in the open area of the deck they'd cleared for dancing, and I smiled when a gentle flute and trumpet intro poured from the gramophone's horn. The song was familiar, but I couldn't quite place it.

He joined me quickly, taking my right hand in his left, that glorious gold band catching the candlelight surrounding us as his other slid around my waist.

He led us effortlessly into dance the moment Ray Charles' voice began. I recognized the song instantly as *'Come Rain or Come Shine,'* and I couldn't have picked a more perfect song if I'd spent the whole night trying.

He held me close, moving us gracefully around the expanse of the dance floor in smooth, weightless circles. "It took me more than a minute to pick, you know," he breathed against my ear. "I went through the records while you were getting ready. I knew which song I wanted before I even stood up."

"It's my new favorite song," I assured him, unable to stop smiling.

Eyes ablaze, he spun me out of his arms and back in one fluid motion, grinning scandalously when my focus returned to his.

That was the thing I loved about dancing with Jack. He moved in such a way—led with such surety—that he made me look like I had some inkling of what I was doing. I certainly didn't, but I enjoyed every second of it all the same.

"I can't believe you're my husband," I said a little shyly. "*Jack Volmer* is *my* husband."

He chuckled, turning us slowly. "I most certainly am. You'll never get rid of me now."

"I can't stop looking at that wedding band on your finger," I confessed, my eyes darting to it and back. "I love the way it looks on you."

He brought our joined hands closer to admire it. "It's you, you know... this ring. It's a piece of you against my skin, a reminder of who I belong to, who I look forward to... I'll never take it off."

I gently combed the hair at the nape of his neck. "When all this is done, what do you want for the rest of our lives?"

"Just you, Red. You and Zachary and Cecelia. As long as you three are in the foreground of my life, the background scenery doesn't matter to me. What about you? What do you want?"

"The same," I raised on my toes to steal a kiss, the hand at the small of my back pressing me into his body as he instantly deepened it.

"You know what I really want?" He breathed, resting his forehead against mine while our bodies continued to sway with the rhythm. "I want us to live a life where we never have to plot or scheme again. Where we're just us... no wild adventures... no lies... just plain old us living plain old lives... Worrying about normal things like… what color curtains we should hang in our living room."

I laughed as he spun me out of his arms and back, this time ensuring my back met his chest while he coiled our still joined hands around my waist. I laid my head against him and sighed. "How wonderfully bland and perfect that life sounds."

His teeth grazed my ear. "Oh, we'd find other ways to keep it from being bland, I promise."

My entire body warmed, and glancing down at his ring finger against my abdomen, I no longer cared about the reception. I wanted to watch that hand move over my bare skin; wanted to make love while he called me Mrs. Volmer; wanted to lay tangled up in each other until the sun came up…

Releasing my hand, he laid a breathy kiss on my temple. "Arms up." He skillfully raised them for me, his fingertips slowly skating down the sensitive flesh of my inner arms, calling every hair on my body to attention.

I felt his fingers wrap around my waist on one side as the palm of his other hand found the small of my back. "Are you ready?"

Before I could say yes, he lifted me high over his head. I arched, sliding one foot back as he'd taught me before, and felt, maybe for the first time in my life, graceful doing so.

The hand at my waist released and the single palm supporting me at the small of my back raised me higher into the air. Even over Ray Charles, I heard Lilly's gasp.

I waited a bit for the song's climax before I bent my knee and he spun me around and down so his face was hovering inches over my own. I wasted no time pressing my lips to his just as I'd wanted to the first time he'd done the move, and he slowly straightened us, his fingers coiling into my hair to deepen the kiss as the final note rang out.

Somewhere behind us, the table erupted with applause, but I was too entranced in his kiss to let go. It was soft, slow, and attentive. He explored my mouth as if he'd been kissing me for the first time, and I did the same. The smooth metal of his ring slid over my cheek as he cupped my face and I melted against him.

"Why don't we have moves like that?" Lilly teased, pulling my and Jack's attention toward them at the table.

Jim snorted. "Hell, all he did was lift her up over his head. I could do that."

"No, you can't," she smiled at me. "That was beautiful, you guys. I've never seen two people dance like that. You looked like you were both floating. Jack, maybe you could give Jim some lessons."

"I don't need lessons, woman." He dragged her off her feet and hauled her to the dance floor, standing there patiently while Juan Jr. flipped the record over and rewound its handle.

'*Let the Good Times Roll*' erupted and Jim led Lilly into a ridiculous and overdramatic interpretation of the moves Jack and I had run through before the lift, spinning her awkwardly every few seconds.

Chuckling, Jack brought us back into a steady sway as the rest of the table stood, pairing up to join us on the floor.

Kyle rocked beside us with Cecelia held in his arm while Fetia did the same with Zachary. Dario escorted Magna to the dance floor and her resulting smile was bright white against her dark features. Juan Jr. even joined the dance, sweeping Izzy off her feet to spin, much to her enjoyment.

Bruce, with no partner, hilariously created an invisible one, stealing kisses from his imaginary mate as he turned her across the deck. It was good to see him smiling and joking again. He hadn't since we'd buried Anna, and it warmed my heart to see the color returning to his large cheeks.

Gliding through them nimbly in our own dance, I coiled my arms around Jack's neck. "So... what'd Jim have in store for you at the cave? Was it the scandalous bachelor party I have in my mind?"

He shook his head, peering past me where Jim continued to whip Lilly around in dizzying circles. "Given the shortage of strip joints on the island—which he made sure to express his disappointment in, it lacked the scandal Jim surely would've dreamed up had we been in our own time. Instead, we shared a bit of whiskey and he gave me some advice. Then we joked about the single life before we helped each other get ready."

"Advice?" I snickered, looking over my shoulder where Lilly squealed as Jim attempted—and *failed*—to raise her over his head. "What kind of advice?"

He hid a smile, clearing his throat. "Apparently, he thought I could use some sex advice."

I collapsed against him with laughter. "Learn some new tricks, did ya?"

He pulled me closer. "Nothing that'd be considered appropriate. Although… I might be inclined to try them, anyway. And soon."

"Mmm," I nestled against him as the song transitioned into *'It had to be you.'* Sighing, I ran my palm over his chest. "How long do you think before it's acceptable for us to slip away?"

He toyed with a strand of hair that had come loose from my braid. "Hopefully not much longer. As much as I love seeing you in this dress, I can't wait to get you out of it."

"I need to feed the babies first," I reminded him, looking out at Fetia and Kyle, both babies content for the moment being rocked between them. "But I've had too much wine… I'll need at least another hour before I can feed them. Jim and Lilly offered to keep them for the night."

He followed my gaze. "I imagine they'll regret that sometime around 2AM when Cecelia decides she's still hungry."

I rested my chin on his chest and smiled up at him. "That's precisely why I agreed we'd stay in the big room tonight. Since it shares a wall with theirs, I figured we'd be able to hear her if she starts crying."

"Hmm." He twirled me out and back. "They'll regret that shared wall even more with all these new tricks I'm planning to try out."

My smile remained affixed as we danced through another song and he showed off a few additional skills, lifting me off my feet on more than one occasion.

The party officially kicked off, everyone took turns at the gramophone. I danced with Bruce during Solomon Burke's *'Cry to Me,'* then Jim for Jackie Wilson's *'Higher and Higher,'* regretting the faster tempo and feeling like I'd suffered whiplash by the end of it. Kyle chose Ben King's *'Stand by Me'* for our dance, and I ended my exploits on the dance floor with Juan Jr., his choice of Jimmy Durante's *'Make Someone Happy'*, a stark contrast to his stiff and regal demeanor.

No longer feeling like my head was swimming from the wine, I supposed it was safe to nurse just in time for Zachary to inform the entire celebration he was starving.

Jack and I ventured back to the table while the others remained on the dance floor. He used the porcelain bottle to feed Cecelia Wanda's milk while I nursed Zachary beneath a blanket.

"You're not afraid you will lose this memory?" Juan Jr. asked, watching the dance floor as he leaned against the table beside us.

"No," I smiled, and forgetting myself, added, "I didn't lose—

I sucked in my lip, realizing what I'd just been about to say. Jack's eyes widened as well.

'Stupid stupid woman!' I thought, my heart suddenly racing. *'What the hell did you just do?'*

Juan Jr. was only looking to change the past because he thought he might erase his pain and come out a different person. What had I just exposed? And what would he do with that information?

Juan Jr. crossed his arms over his chest as he frowned down at me. "Didn't lose what?"

"Nothing," I corrected, trying to form a natural smile.

But Juan Jr. would not be dismissed. He raised an eyebrow. "We changed something about your past?"

"It's nothing," Jack assured him, sounding far more collected than I had. "A small detail she's not even sure about."

Juan Jr. picked up his wineglass. "You're afraid of what I might think if you tell the truth. You remember something we changed, and if *I* can remember what's happened here, you're afraid erasing all of this will be for not. Correct?"

I chewed on my lower lip, wishing I could somehow erase the last thirty seconds.

He smiled warmly, his eyes moving between the two of us. "If one of you lost the other... if you lost your children... you'd want to do anything within your power to change that... even if that meant losing all the good memories of each other." He swirled the wine in his glass. "But I *want* to remember them... to remember who I was, even if I am to become someone new. I want to remember my wedding day, to be able to recall my beautiful wife and know that she still lives, untainted by my involvement in this time. Tell me that is possible?"

I looked at Jack, unsure of what to say.

"We think it's possible," he said slowly. "She started gaining new memories after we killed those men, but the old ones remain."

At that, a deep rich laugh escaped Juan Jr., and his entire face lightened. "You have no idea how happy that makes me. I've spent so long asking myself if I could bear to forget her. Thank you. Thank you."

"For now," I said softly, "can we keep this just between us? If your father—"

"You've my word, madam." He pushed off the table. "I shall tell no one, especially him. Let him learn the hard way that his sins in this place shall follow him there." He bowed gracefully. "Thank you again. And congratulations to you both."

I looked at Jack after Juan Jr. rejoined the festivities. "I'm an idiot. I'm so sorry. It just slipped."

"You're not an idiot," he assured me, his focus remaining on Juan Jr. "Christ... To be willing to sacrifice his own memories of his wife just to save her... To go through with this and know he'd give her up forever... That'd be eating me alive if I were him... I still don't trust him, but I don't think for a second telling him was a mistake. You gave him peace—we both witnessed it—and I think he's just grateful enough to keep his word and not tell anyone."

"I'd do it for you, you know," I said, pulling his gaze to mine. "If I were faced with the same decision, I would give you up to save your life."

"I told you, you'll never be rid of me now." His playful grin slipped away though, and he furrowed his brow. "You meant the plane..."

I nodded. "Like Anna mentioned before. I could trace Frank's lineage... disrupt it somehow to make sure someone else was flying that day."

"No," he said flatly, setting the bottle on the table and hoisting Cecelia to his shoulder to rub his palm over her back. "Not that. If I die your husband, whether that's tomorrow or forty years from now, you leave me be and know I died a happy man. We don't know what happens when the ones that die come back, and I don't ever want a life where I can't remember you."

"But if *I* could remember it all, I could find you again... we could start it all over."

"No," he said simply. "Would you want to wake up in bed with Chris someday and never know this life had happened to us?"

"No..."

"Then I promise to never do that to you, even if I would only be doing it to save your life. I want you to promise me the same."

I swallowed, acknowledging the weight of the agreement. Even though we had it within our power to alter events that could lead to our deaths, we could never alter the one that led us here. "I promise."

"Good." He grinned. "Because I've got a handful more memories I'd like to make before our wedding day is over. I think I've shared you long enough." He eyed the wriggling lump I held beneath the blanket. "Is he finished?"

"Mm hmm." I adjusted the dress and moved Zachary up over my shoulder atop the blanket. "Shall we go hand them off to their babysitters, then?"

"Probably a good idea. I don't think I can keep my hands off you much longer."

Chapter Forty Four

He'd been right. The moment we exited the stairwell, his hands were on me, gliding over my bare arms and down the sides of my dress as I led him toward the double doors at the end of the hall.

"So impatient," I teased.

"I've never made love to my wife," he said, wrapping his arm around my waist. "Forgive me if I'm a little excited about it."

He left a trail of wet kisses down my neck as we inched slowly down the corridor. "Mm, you taste different as a Volmer."

"Saltier, perhaps?" I snickered.

"Sweeter." He scooped me up off my feet and into his cradled arms, carrying me the rest of the distance to push through the double doors.

The big room—the one we'd all been locked in prior to taking control of the ship—had been sprinkled with petals, and the candles around the bed were already lit, covering one side of the large space in a warm orange glow.

He gently placed me on my feet and closed the doors behind us. When he turned back toward me, he was no longer Jack Volmer, but a predator taking one last look at his prey before he devoured it. I took a cautious step backward before he could pounce, holding up the wine bottle I'd snagged before our departure as a peace offering.

"Here," I said, "pour us a glass while I take the pins out of this dress. It's half Lilly's and if we mess it up, she'll kill us both."

He took the bottle, making no move to abandon his pursuit as he took a step forward for each of my steps back. "She should've thought of that before she loaned it to you…"

I giggled as he continued stalking me all the way to the mirror. "Seriously, Jack, she worked really hard… I'll have it off in no time."

He discarded the wine bottle on a side table, one corner of his lip curving upward. "Oh, but I'll have it off quicker."

I turned to face the mirror, admiring my reflection in the dress once more. Behind me, he lingered, watching me as I smoothed my hands over the bodice in search of the small pins Lilly had used to attach the dress to my stays.

"You know," I smiled at his reflection as I pulled out the first, "now that I've bagged you and you can't be rid of me, I have a confession to make."

"Oh?" He kept his eyes on mine as he lowered his lips to my neck and laid a fleeting kiss there that sent my whole body afloat. "What kind of confession?"

His hands slid down the sides of the bodice and he plucked out a pin from the waist.

I leaned back into his warmth as I tugged out another. "When I was a teenager," I sighed audibly as his lips found a path from my neck to my shoulder, "I had a poster of you in my bedroom…"

"Stalker," he chortled, grazing the skin of my shoulder with his teeth while he removed another pin near my ribs.

"I used to kiss it goodnight," I continued, "every night."

He buried his face against my braid, laughing softly while he pulled me back against him, that glorious gold band shimmering with the candlelight in the mirror against my stomach. "I have a confession, too."

I watched him while I extracted two more pins and the dress began to give way.

"When we were on the plane," he whispered, removing the final two pins to allow the dress to fall to the floor, "I watched you sleeping… and I…" he ran a fingertip down my spine until he'd reached the laces of my stays, then began to pull them loose. "…I didn't know why, but I had this uncontrollable desire to touch you in some way. I felt like a creep for it, but I…" He met my gaze in the mirror, "I took a piece of your hair around my finger, and I smelled it."

I gasped in mock outrage. "You creep!"

"That's not even the creepy part," he bounced his eyebrows in the mirror, loosening the stays enough that I could finally breathe deeply without their sting against my ribcage. "The minute I did that, I was more aroused than I've ever been in my entire life. And I was mortified you'd wake up and see it."

He tugged the stays off, tossing them to one side. "So I fumbled with the display and found some movie, popped my earbuds in, and prayed it would go away… taking deep breaths over and over and attempting to focus on the movie instead of what you'd look like naked in that airplane bathroom."

"What movie?" I asked breathlessly, his teeth tugging on my earlobe.

"No clue," he growled as he took in my naked reflection. "It was an unsuccessful distraction."

I laughed. "How'd you know I wasn't pretending to be asleep just to avoid talking to you?"

A mischievous grin responded in the mirror. "If you were pretending, you were doing an amazing job of it. Your mouth was open, and you were snoring."

My cheeks burned with my own mortification. "I snored?! On an airplane?! And you sniffed my hair while I did and got a hard on?!"

He roared with laughter, both hands now exploring my upper body. "Mmmhmm."

"Do I still snore when we sleep together now?" I asked, feeling weirdly self-conscious about my sleep behavior.

He nodded, holding me tighter against him so I could feel his arousal against my back. "And I still sniff your hair and get turned on while you do."

"There's something very wrong with you," I chuckled, attempting to turn to face him. He held me tighter, though, his eyes on fire in the mirror.

"Not yet, Mrs. Volmer," he smiled, resting his chin against my shoulder while he smoothed his left hand over my abdomen. "I like this view."

I reached up to run my palm down his cheek. "I'd like this view a lot better if you didn't have all those clothes on behind me, *Mr. Volmer*."

"Who's impatient now?" His fingers circled lower, and he watched the skin of my reflection flush. "My God, I could stare at this all night... Look at my beautiful *wife*."

My hips moved against him as his words heated my core. *Wife.* I was Jack Volmer's wife now... I stared at the gold band on his finger, still reeling at the sight of it—of *me* on him.

He pressed his nose against my braid, inhaling deeply while his hand slid lower. "You like it when I call you my wife?"

"Yes," I managed, desire burning my veins as I watched his ringed finger make one long, slow pass over my center.

"Look how *my wife* glows when I touch her here," he breathed, his other hand moving over my breast as his finger made another pass. "Look how she moves with me..."

I was indeed moving, my body begging him to soothe the ache he'd created inside it. I watched myself react as he touched me again, moving his finger in slow tantalizing swoops, my breathing quickening rapidly. I was teetering as close to the edge as if he were touching me for the very first time.

I watched him watch me beneath his lashes while he lowered his mouth to my throat, hot and wet as every part of me felt in that moment.

"Sweeter," he rasped, his breath chilling the warmth he'd left there. "I wonder if the rest of you is sweeter too..." He turned his face against my palm and kissed the inside of it before lowering himself to his knees behind me. "Don't move, Mrs. Volmer... I want you to watch..."

Obediently, I did, as he carefully moved the dress onto the chair at his side, then adjusted my stance so he could slide between my legs on his knees. He turned his head to look at us in the mirror, gripping each of my hips. "I want you to watch how *my wife* commands me; how I worship her... how I will worship her every single day for the rest of our lives."

And then there was nothing but pure molten fire as he turned and tasted in one long slow sweep of tongue against the sensitive flesh. Knees trembling, I observed as my reflection curled her fingers into his hair and urged him to do it again.

"Definitely sweeter," he hummed against my skin, returning quickly for another sample.

The shadows behind me felt darker, as if all the light in the room shone solely upon the two of us; as if all the world was void of life and there was only the life inside me, beating bright with the feel of his mouth against me, tasting... and tasting... and tasting. My entire body thrumming in tune with my racing heartbeat.

Perhaps it's because I was watching myself, but as he took me to the edge, the hair at the back of my neck stood on end and the feeling of being watched overwhelmed me. I found myself staring into the shadows beyond my reflection as I clutched his hair in my fists, unable to stop my knees from collapsing as I curled over him and crumbled the instant he slid a finger inside me.

I sank into his lap on the floor, boneless and throbbing.

He laughed, brushing my braid back over my shoulder. "I hope you're not planning on napping yet... I'm just getting started."

An hour later, entangled in each other's warmth, we'd both fallen asleep. In a dream, the feel of someone watching me had lingered, and I found myself inching toward the shadows where they reached for me, searching for the set of eyes I felt upon my naked skin.

Someone was there... a slight flicker of movement in the blackness... I crept closer... closer... I could hear whoever it was breathing... closer... until I was surrounded in the nothingness, my arms outstretched, feeling for whatever lurked there. Then it screamed.

I woke with a jump, the sound of Zachary crying on the opposite side of the wall forcing me to instinctively turn toward a cradle that was not at the side of this bed.

Jack placed a heavy hand over my thigh as I blinked at the darkness, searching for the same movement that had called to me in my dream. "I'll get them," he said into his pillow, yawning as he rose up to kiss my shoulder. "You stay just like this."

He squeezed my bottom, then rolled away while I attempted to settle my racing pulse. I rubbed my eyes and pushed myself up into a seated position, leaning my bare back against the cool wood of the headboard.

The lantern light slowly sprouted into a glow as Jack stood and stepped into his breeches, not bothering to tie them. He paused mid-step. "Are you alright?"

I smiled. "I'm fine."

"Fine?"

I nodded, stretching my arms over my head. "I just had a weird dream is all. I'm perfect, I promise."

"You're sure?" He made no move for the door despite Cecelia's cries now joining her brother's.

"Go, I'm fine. It was just a dream."

He inspected me warily, but nodded. "I'll be right back."

He hurried out the door, and I listened as he exchanged words with a groggy Jim and Lilly on the other side of the wall.

I wasn't fine. The feeling of being watched from something on the far side of the room still sat on my skin. Maybe it was just the room itself. When we'd been locked in it previously, we'd all had the constant feeling of being spied upon by Juan Josef. Even though it was immaculately decorated, there was something creepy about the way the light didn't quite make its way to all the corners. I couldn't wait to return to our smaller cabin.

Jack was just on the other side of the wall, I reminded myself, staring at the shadows, unable to settle my pulse. I was legitimately scared; scared like I hadn't been of the dark since I was a child... Paralyzed by fear as I pressed my back even harder into the headboard.

'You're being ridiculous,' I told myself. *'It was just a dream. You're thirty-three damn years old. Too damn old to be frozen with fear over the dark.'*

Frustrated with my own ridiculousness, I forced my legs to move, crawling across the bed to grab the lantern. I held it out as I stood, crossing the room with my spine stiff to shine its light in all the shadowy corners that had taunted me. Nothing... There was nothing there.

"Now that's one hell of a sight to take in." Jack smirked from the doorway, both babies held against his shoulder. "What on earth are you looking for?"

"Nothing," I groaned, feeling a bit sheepish as I joined him at the edge of the bed and put the lantern back on the side table. "I'm just being ridiculous."

I took Zachary from him first and climbed back into bed, positioning him at my breast before he could wail. "Help me get her on the other one? I'm too tired to feed them separately."

He kissed the top of Cecelia's head. "Your mommy thinks she can use you as an excuse to change the subject, baby girl."

I laughed as he crawled into bed beside me, continuing his adorable conversation with our daughter.

"But we're not going to let this one go, are we? We want to know why your mommy was lurking around the room naked. Don't we?"

I stretched out my free arm and he placed her in it so I could bring her to my breast. Both of them latched on and quickly working my nipples raw, I laid my head back against the headboard and closed my eyes. "I had a dream someone was in the shadows over there watching us. I couldn't shake it so I went over there to make sure."

He chuckled, adjusting the pillows to help support my arms. "And what exactly would you have done if you'd found someone? Naked with no weapon?"

I opened one eye in his direction, finding him leaning on one arm over my outstretched legs. "I hadn't really thought that far ahead. I just meant to silence the fear in my head by proving to myself there was nothing there."

He bit his bottom lip, glancing over his shoulder to where I'd been and back. "You should've told me before I left. It's my job now to check for monsters whenever any of you are scared."

I rolled my eyes, nudging his chest with my knee. "And what would you have done if you found one? *Half* naked with no weapon?"

He caught my knee before I could lower it, raking his teeth over the cap to incite a squeal from me. "I'm quite deadly, you know... even half naked. Especially when it comes to you three. A monster'd be no match for my protective instincts."

"Mmmhmm," I slid my leg back down beneath him. "Can you take your protective instincts over to the pitcher and grab your wife a glass of water?"

He laid a kiss on my leg and rolled off the bed. "Anything else I can do for my wife?" He asked as he poured a glass and returned with it and the pitcher.

"Don't tempt me, my love," I teased, taking a sip when he brought the glass to my lips. "I could come up with all kinds of ways for you to please me. It won't bode well for you long-term to set that kind of precedent so early on in our marriage."

Laughing heartily, he continued to bring the glass to my lips until I had finished it. "I wouldn't mind." He placed the glass on the table and leaned back on his palms. "As long as—

He turned toward his hands. "What the hell is this for?"

"What?"

When he swiveled back to face me, my heart stopped. He held a kitchen knife in his hands, and as he turned it between them, I noticed there was no inventory mark on its handle.

"Someone's been in here," he growled, leaping up from the bed.

Chapter Forty Five

Chris

Chris carefully pulled his shirt on over his bandaged head, watching the door for signs of Tiffany's return.

Detectives Haywood and Morris hadn't returned, but the encounter, as well as all that had led to it while he'd been in the hospital, shook him.

He'd been able to connect with Maria via video call where she'd informed him through tears that Cecelia had found the ring, questioned her on it, then accused her of murdering Alaina and thrown her out of the house.

Luckily, he'd bought her a phone and put his parents' numbers in it before he'd gone into the hospital. She'd been able to call them and they'd taken her in.

He'd tried to connect with Cecelia to smooth things over. Neither she nor Sophia would answer his calls.

Bill, however, had answered, and Chris did his best to give the same story he'd given Detective Haywood, explaining that it'd all been a misunderstanding. While Bill had been kind, Chris could feel his disbelief and disappointment.

He didn't answer a second time.

Bud, unlike both him and Maria, had immediately insisted a lawyer be present when the detectives showed up at his door. He'd simply said that he'd already told the authorities everything he knew about the crash and if they wanted to question him further, they'd need to contact his attorney first. Chris wished he'd had the foresight to have done the same.

He knew what it was to incriminate himself. He'd already done it once in Oparre and had paid heavily for it. He'd spent the past five days in the hospital replaying his conversation with the detectives over and over. They knew something wasn't right about their story—of course it wasn't... and the more time they spent in this century lying about what happened, the more they would paint themselves as guilty of whatever crime the FBI assumed they'd committed. They couldn't afford to stay a year. Hell, they couldn't afford to stay six months... particularly if they were going to be watched the whole time.

"Mask on, Mr. Grace," Tiffany reminded him as she propped the door open and pulled a wheelchair in. "You can take it off once you get to the car, but you gotta have it on in here."

"I'm not going down in a wheelchair," he insisted, snagging the mask from his bed and fastening its loops behind his ears. "I can walk."

"I know you can, handsome." She winked. "But rules are rules, and I gotta take you in this. Come on, you don't want to keep that pretty little Latina that's at the front doors waiting, do you?"

"Why can't I walk?"

She rolled her eyes. "Because you've had brain surgery and you're on pain meds. If you fall between here and the front door, we're liable for whatever injury you might suffer as a result. Just get in the chair. You can do whatever you like once I roll you out those doors."

Huffing, he sat down in the chair, ready to be out of the hospital and anxious to see Maria after all she'd been through with Alaina's family. He was livid with Cecelia for throwing her out and had every intention of paying her a visit as soon as he was able to drive.

"Now," Tiffany started, rolling him out of the room and strolling casually down the fluorescent hallway. "Remember, no strenuous activity for at least four weeks. No work, no lifting anything heavier than ten pounds, and no exercise." She parked him at the elevator and pushed the down button. "Doctor wants to see you next Monday at 10AM to check on the sutures and run another scan."

"I know," he shifted in the chair. "He said I could walk, though."

"The minute you're out the doors, handsome." She sighed as the elevator doors opened and she wheeled him inside. "You know, I'm really gonna miss you and your snarky little attitude."

He managed a laugh even though his mind was racing—racing, but clear, thank God. He had so much to do—had to search for June and give her the key to the safe-deposit-box. He'd memorized the numbers and had put the key safely in his boot, just as Jim had. Maria was going to check on Liam. Bud had looked into Isobel's living relatives and found only a grandmother in Oregon, and he needed to learn more about her condition and living arrangements. With the detectives nosing around, he hoped he could convince Bud to speed up his remaining research so they could leave in September instead of waiting until next March. The way he tended to put his foot in his mouth, he didn't think they'd make it to March without being tried for stealing and hiding the plane and its passengers.

He had a wedding to plan, a boat to secure, medicine to stock up on, and money to acquire in a form that could get them by in the 18th century if they needed it.

All that aside, he really needed to find some way to smooth things over with Alaina's family. He couldn't leave with them thinking she'd been murdered... Especially if Alaina and Jack decided not to come back... And the detectives... How could they ever come back if the FBI assumed the plane was hijacked? Wouldn't those returning risk becoming a part of the investigation?

Wouldn't it be easier to tell Detective Haywood and Cecelia the truth? Hell, he could even prove it in September if he had to... no... not if only three could pass through... if that was even the way it worked...

The elevator doors opened and Tiffany wheeled him through the much more aesthetically pleasing first floor. Rich wood and glass windows replaced the stifling dull colors of the upper floors he'd grown accustomed to. It was almost deceitful, he thought, as they grew nearer the front entry.

All other thoughts escaped him as he caught sight of Maria pacing from one window to the next in front of the building.

Her hair and floral dress forced violently to one side as the heavy wind threatened to blow her away, she battled to stay upright, peeking through the windows she paced between.

He laughed when she spotted him and shrieked, her voice reaching him even through the thick glass as she shouted "Kreese!" Waving her arms, she skipped from window to window alongside him until Tiffany led him through the two sets of double doors and he hastily stood.

"Mi amore!" She wound her arms tightly around his neck, a barrage of Spanish prayers spilling out under her breath before she added, "thank you, thank you, thank you God." She pulled his lips to hers, kissing him over and over as if she'd thought she'd never do it again.

"Careful with him," Tiffany warned. "He needs to take it easy for the next several weeks."

Chris hid a smile as she slowly pulled away. Tiffany and Maria had interacted for an entire thirty seconds via the various video chats Tiffany had facilitated between them. They did not like each other one bit, although *one of them* did a much better job of hiding it than the one in his arms now scowling at her.

"Oye, I'm not stupid." She attempted to look mean despite the wind whipping her hair over her face. "I know how to take care of him. I'm not going to jump up into his arms like a crazy person. Gracias for bringing him to me. I have him now. You can go." She flicked her wrist once in dismissal before returning her attention to his. "I have made such a mess, superman... the ring... I didn't know... I am such an idiot for saying it was for me... I just assumed. I'm so sorry you had to wake up to this headache I created."

"I should've told you," he wound his arms around her, pressing his bandaged forehead against hers. "It's me that's sorry. I should've told you right away she'd given it back to me. It was thoughtless for me to leave it."

"Come." She grabbed his hand and tugged him toward his father's white truck where it was idling down the street. "This wind is gonna' blow us both away. We'll talk about it when we get home."

He set his feet, though, and she bounced back to face him.

He cupped her face in both hands. "That ring was my grandmother's ring, handed down for generations. She gave it back so *you* could have it. For as much as I wanted you to wear it, I didn't think you'd respond well to my giving you a ring that had been on her finger for so long. It wouldn't have been fair to you. I would've never given her that ring if I'd met you first. And I need you to know that the memories… they mean nothing. What I put you through before I came here—what her family put you through while I was in here… Maria, you didn't deserve any of it. I'll never be able to tell you how sorry I am for all of it."

She raised her palm to his cheek. "There is nothing to forgive, mi amore. You are here—*alive*—in front of me. I have spent the last five days praying for only that… I do not care that you loved someone else before me. I do not care that sleeping in the house you shared with her made it difficult for you to touch me. And I do not care what ring I wear so long as it is one you give me. Okay?"

He bent, brushing his lips over hers. "I love you."

She grinned. "You're going to love me more when I tell you what I found yesterday."

"What'd you find?" He hovered over her lips.

"Juniper McClendon," she said as if it were no big deal. "She's in Albuquerque. She works at a bank called Dawn Financial downtown."

He smiled widely, running a hand over her windblown hair. "Are you serious? How?"

"I told you, superman, I'm very good at finding people."

"But I've been searching for her since we got here and couldn't find anything."

She turned her face in his hand and kissed his palm. "That's because you're not as good as I am. Now, come, let's get out of this wind before we both blow away. I'll show you everything when we get to the house."

Inside his old bedroom at his parents' house, he sat on his bed, staring at the relics of his childhood that surrounded him. Other than a few dusty boxes stacked in a corner, his parents hadn't changed a thing since he'd moved out nearly fifteen years ago.

On the wall directly across from him, black and white posters he'd spent years admiring hung on each side of the plaid curtained window; to the right, Jimi Hendrix, to the left, Pamela Anderson.

Directly beneath the window sat his desk, its surface littered with sentiment. A line of baseball and track trophies framed its upper counter, and beneath, a Rubik's Cube he'd spent countless hours trying to master, a cup of mechanical pencils, a random green model Nova SS, and a magic eight ball. He laughed to himself, remembering the many nights he'd spent asking that ball if tomorrow would be the day Ashley Lambert would talk to him.

The closet door to one side of his bed was littered with photos. He scanned them, reliving nights in his best friend Mike's basement with their inseparable group of friends, sneaking beers and cigarettes and weed... He hadn't seen them in years. He wondered where they were now.

Maria stood in the doorway, leaning against its frame with her arms crossed. "I've been sleeping in here all week. What are those weird toys over the bed and why are they all in boxes?"

He looked up at the shelves over his head, chuckling as he recalled his horror movie phase. "They're action figures, not toys.

One for each of my favorite horror movie villains. They're collectables."

"They're creepy."

He nodded, patting the bed beside him in invitation. "I know."

She closed the door and sat beside him on the blue and green plaid comforter that matched the curtains over his desk. "Did you actually bring girls to this room?"

He laughed at that. "A few."

She nodded at the Pamela Anderson poster. "And they stayed?"

"Not usually."

She grinned, looking over at the closet. "Who's the blond girl in all the pictures with you?"

"Sam," he said affectionately. "My first girlfriend. She was our friend Ethan's younger sister."

"You look like you were madly in love with her."

"Oh, I *most definitely* was," he snickered, scanning the photos that had her in them. "Obsessed, really. She wore cool band t-shirts and smoked Marlboro Reds. She could hang out with the boys and keep up with conversation, and she always had something funny to say. She was so much cooler than I was. And about halfway through our junior year, she realized how much cooler she was. Started dating a college guy that played guitar in a cover band. I was no match for that kind of cool."

"Maybe I should buy some band t-shirts, no?"

He bit his lower lip at the thought of Maria wearing nothing but an oversized Pearl Jam t-shirt. "She might've been cool, but she's got nothing on you and that accent."

Her smile remained as she touched the bandage on his head with her fingertips. "Does it hurt?"

"No, but it might if I stop taking the pain meds."

"Does it feel... different? Better?"

He reached up and curled his fingers around hers, bringing them to his lips to kiss her knuckles. "Much. I feel like I can focus... like there was a haze over everything before and it's clear now."

"Good. We need to talk about the FBI agents and what we're going to say when they come back. I didn't want to say too much on the video call."

"I know. Tell me everything they asked you."

"They asked about the ring... You know how that went. Then they kept asking about Bud... if I knew he would be on the plane with his granddaughter, and if we were in trouble and afraid to talk to them. They asked if I had the code to open the cockpit. I said I did—of course I did, and they kept asking if I opened the door. I told them I didn't."

He blew out. "I knew there'd be questions around our reappearance, but I never thought they'd accuse us of hijacking the plane and taking prisoners."

"That's what they think?" She raised an eyebrow, her brown eyes going wide.

"I believe so. Bud Renaud is one of the wealthiest men in the world. That plane disappeared and not a single trace of it was left behind. No parts, no bodies... so why wouldn't they assume someone stole it? Took the passengers hostage in an attempt to get their hands on Bud's fortune?"

She pursed her lips. "Where did the other half go? We all assumed it stayed here while we went to the future... wouldn't they have found something if it did?"

He shrugged. "I don't know. There's so little we know about how the portal works, particularly for the ones that don't make it through."

Maria leaned back. "What about Dahlia? She made that chart. She is alive somewhere. We know she was on the boat with Juan Josef. I could find her and try to talk to her. See if she can remember anything. We have time."

"Might be a good idea, but time..." He shook his head. "I don't know if it's a good idea to stay for a year. If they start throwing around words like *'terrorism,'* they could take us into custody with very little evidence. I think we need to go sooner. Juan Josef and the guy in those journals went through in September from this side. We know it's possible."

"But the ship won't be there to meet us."

"We'd need to stock up on fuel. Enough to get us to the portal and then to the island…"

She chewed on her lower lip. "But what about your treatment? If you need another surgery or medication?"

"I'll live," he assured her. "But Jack might not if we wait. Going back in September would ensure we could arrive *before* his death year. If we can convince him and Alaina to bring Cecelia back, we erase everything. We save Anna, those men, Owen, and Maddy. No one else would need to die."

She toyed with a loose thread in the comforter. "It is a good idea. But that's only if they are still in control when we go back. If Juan Josef and his sons have taken them captive again, we'll need to have the lineage. And he can never know that her return would remove Gloria and Dario from his history."

"I'll call Bud to see if he can expedite the research. We'll drive down to Albuquerque after my check-up, then we'll head to L.A. You can check in on Liam while I see if I can get in touch with Dahlia… we'll keep a low profile until we can take off… and the three of us can go over all this, come up with a plan A, B, C, and D for every possible scenario."

She tugged at the thread of the comforter. "Las Vegas is between Albuquerque and L.A., yes?"

He tilted his head to one side. "It is…"

She met his eyes then, a small smile tugging at the corners of her lips. "Maybe we make a stop there on the way? If you still want to marry me after I called off the last one…"

He tucked a lock of hair behind her ear, leaning into her. "Of course I do."

Chapter Forty Six

Everything changed after Jack found that knife in our bed. Someone wanted us to know they'd been there... to show us how easily they could've killed us... That seemed like a move Juan Josef would make, but when Jack had gone straight to the room that held him, he found Juan Josef securely locked inside, fast asleep in his bed.

Not trusting anyone outside our family on the ship, Jack and Jim suggested we lock the others in rooms on the floor we kept Juan Josef on so they could be guarded, but Lilly and I argued against it.

We needed the crew in order to get back. None of them had shown us anything but kindness. Most of them referred to us as *'God's chosen people'* and wouldn't dare do anything to put them out of God's favor. It wouldn't be fair to lock them all up for the actions of one. We had to do what we could to identify the culprit without losing the goodwill of the rest of the crew.

Not feeling anyone was safe to be left alone, we'd all returned to the big room at night, pulling mattresses from nearby cabins to accommodate comfortable sleeping arrangements. Someone always stood watch outside the locked doors while we slept, be it Jack, Jim, Bruce, Michael, or Kyle, and no one ventured out through the day without a weapon or an extra set of eyes alongside them.

It'd been two weeks since the incident, and we still hadn't narrowed it down to any specific suspects. It was taxing on us all and the summit was the only real reprieve. Returning to a normal rotation, Kyle and Fetia had gone up to relieve her father and Jacob, and the following week, Magna and Bruce went up to replace them. There was debate about who would go next. Jack and Jim didn't want to leave the ship without a suspect, but Lilly and I both wanted nothing more than to give them a much needed week away.

Lilly laid in the bed facing me, the babies wobbling their raised heads between us as the mid-afternoon sunlight seeped in through the window. They'd both been sleeping better through the night over the last week, and we were working hard to limit their daytime naps to keep it that way.

She lazily combed her fingers through my hair. "Do you think it's ridiculous that I want to keep planning my wedding with all this going on?"

"No," I said softly. "We can't very well stop living because someone left a knife in my bed."

She pursed her lips. "That's what Jimmy said too. Jack saw me working on my dress yesterday. I think he thinks I'm ridiculous."

I groaned. "Jack thinks anyone that's not interrogating or spying on the entire crew round the clock is ridiculous. He's obsessed; barely sleeping or eating. I've hardly seen him since it happened."

"Can you blame him? Someone snuck into your room while you both were in there and threatened his whole family. Every day he goes without catching the person who did it, he feels like he's failing you."

"I don't blame him at all," I said, sighing. "I just... I felt like we were *this* close to something resembling normal before that happened. I thought, naively so, we might have at least a few months of peace while we wait. I'm so sick of this ship and these men... of all this."

She raised up on her elbow. "We *could* just kill Juan Josef now and be done with it. Whoever left that knife was doing it under his orders, right? We kill him, whoever's helping him will either reveal themselves and come after us or they'll abandon whatever orders he's given them. If they come after us, we'll take them out too. If they don't, game over either way."

Wiping a bead of drool from Zachary's mouth before it could reach the comforter, I chuckled. "You're so violent."

She inspected her nails. "Oh, don't act like you're not thinking about it. We all are. And before you make an excuse about the deal we struck with Juan Jr., I should remind you, the deal we made was that we'd keep him alive as long as he submitted. He's not exactly playing the obedient little prisoner he agreed to be, is he? He killed Eli and *tried* to kill Phil—although no one would really blame him for Phil—and now he's sending his minions in to leave threats on his behalf? How is that submitting? We should've killed him the minute he put that knife to Anna's throat and you know it."

"Red, Lilly..." Jack peeked around one of the doors, his eyes tired when they met mine. "Kyle wants us all in the dining room; says there's something we need to hear while Dario and Juan Jr. are on the beach."

Lilly and I sat up abruptly. Pulling Zachary against her shoulder, she furrowed her brow at Jack. "Did he find out who left the knife? Can we go back to normal now?"

He shrugged, running a hand over the half-inch of blond and brown stubble covering the lower portion of his face. "He didn't say. He just said the four of us needed to meet him in the dining room right away. Jim's already up there waiting for us."

Lilly squealed, "Oh, what if it's the news we've been waiting for? I can't live like this much longer!" Not bothering with shoes, she padded out of the room with Zachary in her arms. "Come on!"

Following suit, I tugged Cecelia up into the crook of my arm, leaning against Jack as we made our way toward the stairwell she'd already scaled.

"You need to sleep, you know," I said between us, gently massaging the small of his back. "You look awful."

Scratching the top of my head, he forced a smile. "I'll sleep soon enough. I promise."

"Maybe we should go up to the summit for a few days. Take a break from all this."

He slowly shook his head, remaining at my side as we ascended the steps. "I can't. Not until we figure out who got in there and why they did it. Maybe you and the babies could go up with Kyle and Fetia tomorrow? It'd be safer there than on this ship."

"We're not going anywhere without you. The safest place for us is wherever you are."

"Is it?" He asked defeatedly. "Whoever was in our room that night got in while I was lying right beside you... You felt it. And I left you sitting there."

"What happened that night is no more your fault than it is mine," I said as we stepped into the hallway that led to the dining room. "They caught us *both* off-guard, and that's neither of our faults. They won't be able to do it again. You're my husband and it's just as much my job to look out for you as you think it's yours to look out for me. I can't do that from the summit, so don't ask that of me."

Thankfully, he didn't push the subject, but instead kept his eyes on his feet and said nothing further.

We filed silently into the dining room to take our seats alongside Jim and Lilly, facing the doors, and I slid my hand into his beneath the table, needing him to know we were both in this together. He squeezed it ever so gently in return, and I relaxed against my seat.

"Ye look like shit, Hoss," Jim observed, not looking much better himself. His eyes were just as bloodshot, and he had a considerable amount of patchy stubble along his jaw as well.

"Thanks, *dick*," Jack muttered.

"You both look awful," Lilly cut in before Jim could deliver the insult he'd been preparing to return. "When was the last time either of you slept?"

Jim scrunched his nose. "I got a good hour or two in this mornin.'"

"That's not enough," she said matter-of-factly. "You two are worse than toddlers when you're tired. You're both cranky and awful and you're too damn stubborn to listen to anyone who cares about you. If you don't sleep, you won't need to worry about one of Juan Josef's men killing you because *I* will."

Jim huffed. "With two of us up on 'at summit at all times, we're outnumbered down here. We cain't afford to be sleepin' in when we don't know who we can trust."

"You can't afford not to," I noted. "They caught us off guard once. One look at your bloodshot eyes, and whoever's responsible for this will take advantage of your fatigue to try again. You can trust *us* to guard the door once in a while... at least through the day when everyone's up and moving around—*for more* than an hour or two. Lilly and I are just as capable of shooting or stabbing someone as you two."

"Ye' know, I don't think it's *us* that's the crab-asses at this table," Jim said, crossing his arms over his chest and leaning back in his chair. "You two's the ones all hot and bothered. Me and Jack's just sittin' here."

"*Hot and bothered?*" Lilly narrowed her eyes at him. "You haven't even seen—

The doors cracked open, and Kyle stuck his head through the gap. "Alright, now... don't freak out. Okay?"

Everyone sat up straighter in their seats, and when he opened the doors the rest of the way, he revealed Phil waiting in the corridor behind him. His hands were tied in front of him, and he kept his head down.

"My dad's got something he wants to say," Kyle said, beckoning Phil to enter. "And I think we should listen to him." Kyle pulled out a seat across from the four of us, motioning for his father to sit.

"We ain't got time for whatever horseshit he's about to spew at us," Jim began to raise up from his chair, but Jack placed a hand on his shoulder to push him back down.

"Sit down, Jackson," was all he said. He was indeed cranky.

Jim froze, eyeing Jack incredulously. "Ye' really intend to sit here and listen to him piss and moan about why we oughta' turn him loose when we got bigger problems to worry about right now —particularly one that includes a lunatic walkin' around leavin' knives in our dang beds?"

Ignoring Jim, Jack folded his hands on the table. "What's this about?"

Phil sat down in the offered chair while Kyle leaned against it. Slowly raising his head, I caught sight of the large gash on his cheek. It'd healed, but a dark red line ran from his cheekbone nearly to his jawline. His muscles and fat had dwindled away, and his clothing hung loose. Whatever he was once, he wasn't anymore. This pitiful thing was not the man that had pinned me down and tried to rape me. He resembled a cornered and desperate animal... One that had been beaten and tortured until there was nothing left of the beast he'd once been.

His eyes met mine, and I refused to look away.

"Telling you I'm sorry won't change what I did to you." His voice fought against the swelling in his cheek, unable to close his mouth enough to enunciate the words properly. "I am sorry, though. And I know it's no excuse, but I haven't touched a drink since."

"Didn't I tell ye? He's fixin' to ask us to—

"I want you to lock me back in with Juan Josef," Phil said, keeping his gaze on me alone. "Kyle told me what happened, and I wanna' help. If I'm in there with him, I could find out who's working with him."

"Why?" Jack asked, leaning forward on his elbows. "Why on earth would I believe you actually want to help us?"

Phil frowned. "I helped you on that island, didn't I?"

Jack tilted his head to one side, his chin grazing his hands where they were held folded in front of it. "You helped *yourself* on that island. Didn't change what you did that got you there."

Phil nodded. "No, it didn't. Nothing will. But I'm stuck here just the same as you are... in this time... with these people. My son and my unborn grandchild are just as much at risk by whoever's helping him as any of you. Lock me in there. Let me find out who it is."

Jim narrowed his eyes, pointing at the scar on Phil's cheek. "What makes ye' think he won't just go ahead and finish what he started?"

Phil shrugged. "He'd need to obtain a weapon first. Check his cabin beforehand. Keep eyes on every man onboard. If one of those men gets close to that room and afterward, he makes another attempt at my life, you'll not only have your culprit, but you'll potentially be rid of me."

Cecelia squawked, and I hoisted her up against my shoulder to rock her. "Juan Josef is too smart. He would suspect you of working with us. He wouldn't expose whoever's helping him with you in the room."

"Yes, he would," he assured me, looking back down at his lap. "As far as he knows, I want you all dead... I spoke of little else when you locked me in with him the first time."

Lilly pursed her lips. "What reason would we have to put you back in there after we've kept you separated for so long?"

Kyle piped up. "We're shorthanded. We've got a bunch of men to spy on and our own door to guard at night. Moving our two prisoners into *one room* on the same floor as ours makes more sense. We wouldn't be so spread out. He's smart enough to see the sense in that... and if dad's in there, he can help us narrow down our suspects."

Jim scratched his jaw, looking at Jack and back. "It would be easier to keep 'em on the same floor... Would only need one guard instead of two at night... Whatcha' thinkin, Hoss?"

"I'm thinking that if we're considering it, we'll want to secure the windows in whatever room we put them in... check it thoroughly for anything that could be used as a weapon... I'm also thinking this sounds like a big risk for you to take, Phil. What's in this for you? You looking for us to forgive you? Let you go free if you help?"

"No," Phil looked between us. "Whatever I am guilty of, I'm still a father, and I still care about Kyle's safety. I'm not giving an ultimatum here. I'm simply offering to keep my child and his family safe."

Jack sat observing him for a long moment. Not looking away, he spoke to Jim. "How long would it take to clear out your room?"

"Half hour at most."

Jack massaged his jaw, considering it. "And you believe him, Kyle?"

Kyle glanced down at his father before slowly nodding. "I do."

"Alright then," he pushed back from the table. "You and Jim take him to their old room. Clear it out and make sure there's nothing that could be used as a weapon. Haul a second mattress inside. I'll go out and secure the window so he can't get out of it... Jim and I will bring Juan Josef up before dinner."

"What can we do to help?" I asked, standing beside him.

"Set the narrative," he said simply. "You and Lilly go up on the deck for tea and make sure every man onboard hears you when you talk about how we're moving them so we can guard both rooms."

"What about the summit?" Lilly asked, standing with Zachary. "We still haven't decided who's going and we need to relieve Magna and Bruce tomorrow."

Kyle rubbed his neck. "Jacob said he'd be willing to go again. Michael offered to go with him."

"Perfect," Jack said, moving around the table toward the doors. He stopped just before he reached them and turned back to Phil. "Don't make me regret this."

Chapter Forty Seven

"Come to bed," I urged Jack, balancing on my knees on the mattress as I reached my arms out to him. "Jim and Kyle have us covered."

With the prisoners relocated, there was considerable debate over who would stand guard first. Michael and Jacob needed rest before their hike, and Fetia's father could barely stay awake a full twelve hours on a good day, which narrowed it down to Jack, Jim, and Kyle—because Bruce was on the summit and *God forbid a woman stand guard*. They'd drawn straws—or, rather, sticks—and Jack, much to his frustration, had not drawn one of the two shorter ones.

He hovered between the bed and the door, listening for any sounds in the hall or on the other side of the wall separating us from our prisoners.

Lilly yawned from her mattress in the center of the room, having similar difficulties getting Izzy to lie down. She stood defiant in her little nightgown between my bed and theirs, signing. "Not tired, want dog."

"We're not sleeping with the dog," Lilly said, matching her spoken words with hand movements. "You can play with Luna tomorrow."

"No." Izzy said out loud, stomping her foot, then returned to her sign language to add, "Not tired."

"Izzy, Luna is Dario's dog. Dario needs her so *he* can sleep. You can see her tomorrow, I promise."

Izzy shifted her gaze to Jack and raised both eyebrows, creeping a little closer to our side of the room. "Yag nah sleeping…"

We'd been teaching her to practice sounds with her sign language, unsure where we'd end up and worried she wouldn't adjust to the correct signs if she returned to the 21st century. We'd worked with her to show the correct mouth movement to make each sound. The muscle memory was there since she'd spoken prior to losing her hearing, so she picked it up quickly and had even begun to read our lips on occasion. J's proved difficult for her to differentiate between Y's and the best she could do for Jack was *'Yag.'* We all thought it was adorable and didn't press the correct pronunciation.

"*Yag* is going to sleep now," I assured her, grinning while I translated with my hands, "otherwise he's going to be in *big* trouble."

She frowned at me, signing, "Jack not scared of you." She inched closer to where he stood near the wall listening and raised both arms toward him, encouraging him to pick her up.

He softened, his shoulders relaxing a bit as he kneeled down in front of her. "You're wrong. I'm *very* scared of her. Why don't you want to go to sleep?"

She pouted, moving her signs now in a pitiful motion as if he might cave to her wishes if she looked sad enough. "Want dog. Scared."

"What are you scared of?" He asked, both out loud and with his hands. He used a gentle tone despite her inability to hear it, and it warmed my heart to watch him. "I'm here. And I won't let anyone hurt you."

She looked toward the locked doors and back. "Man who took me come back. Dog will bite him."

Jack swept the fine golden hairs away from her face and shook his head. "He will never take you again. I bite too."

She giggled at that. "I sleep with you?"

Jack glanced at me briefly, and I gave him a nod. I didn't care if the whole ship made their way into our bed, so long as it meant he'd lay down for a while.

"Okay," he said, pulling her against his shoulder and rising with her to run his palm soothingly over her back. "I didn't realize she was so scared."

Lilly huffed, lying down on her mattress and turning in our direction. "This is the first time she's ever mentioned him. I'm not entirely sure it isn't a ploy to get Luna in here. She's not as sweet and innocent as she looks, you know. She's conniving when she wants something."

Sitting on the edge of the bed to toe his boots off, he held her tightly, and I inspected her face where it was smashed against his shoulder for any signs of deceit. "She doesn't look like she's faking it, Lill. This whole experience has been traumatic for all of us, and we're adults. I can only imagine what she might be going through in that brain of hers."

Jack slid back in the bed to rest his back against my chest as she sat up in his lap, her big eyes scanning his face. Tilting her head to one side, she took two thumbs and pressed them to the corners of his lips, pushing them upward.

He laughed at that. "Are you implying I'm cranky, too?" He didn't sign the words, but squeezed my thigh.

She nodded, evidently understanding the general concept, and pointed to her own face as she scowled.

"That's what I look like?" He asked, echoing the words with his hands.

"Yes," she said out loud. "Yag mad."

I combed my fingers through his hair, scratching gently at his scalp as I watched their interaction.

"Not mad at you," he signed and spoke. "Mad at the man who took you. *Want* to bite him."

She giggled, returning her thumbs to his face to peel back his upper lip and inspect his teeth. He growled in return, prompting a delighted squeal to escape her.

"Both of you need to go to sleep now," I informed them, adjusting the pillows to support Jack's head where it was rested against my overly tender breasts. "*Especially* if you want to see Luna tomorrow."

Izzy sighed and laid her head back down against his chest, curling her legs up into a fetal position in his lap.

He pulled the blankets over them both as I worked my thumbs into the too-taut muscles around his neck. He groaned. "If this is my punishment for not going to sleep, I might stay awake all night."

"Five bucks says you're asleep in minutes, Volmer."

"Mmm," he muttered, his heavy upper body melting into mine. "You want me to move?"

"No," I whispered, kneading outward to work the muscles over his shoulders. "It's my turn to watch over you. I'll listen for a while until I get tired... We both know I bite harder than you do, anyway."

He combed his fingers over Izzy's hair, chuckling softly. "Will you promise to wake me up if you hear anything?"

Laying a kiss on the top of his head, I smiled. "If someone so much as sneezes on that side of the wall, you'll be the first to know about it, *Yag*."

He stifled a laugh. "I'm sorry if I've been cranky. This isn't how I wanted our marriage to start out."

"Oh, I remember how it started out just fine," I teased, softening my touch to run my fingertips down his upper arms. "And I have every intention of taking that mirror with us wherever we go."

I felt his smile just before his body sank deeper into me and his breathing grew deeper. How adorable he looked with Izzy snuggled up in his massive arms.

From the angle we were positioned, I could just see his thick dusty lashes where they were closed for the night, Izzy's little fist tucked up against her face at his shoulder. I couldn't imagine ever loving anything more than I did watching the two of them sleep.

Movement at the foot of the bed caught my attention, and I grinned to find Lilly standing there in the dim lantern light with her pillow clutched to her chest. She glanced at Izzy and Jack, then back at me. "Would it be weird if I stayed up with you for a while? I can't sleep without her."

I patted the bed beside me. "Not at all, you big chicken. Should we invite Fetia too?"

She rolled her eyes, sliding gingerly onto the bed and positioning her pillow as a barrier between her body and Jack's. "She passed out almost instantly. I swear, nothing phases that girl."

"She's also, what? Nearly four months pregnant now?" I noted, speaking quietly so as not to disturb Izzy or Jack. "When I was at that point, sleep was all I thought about."

She smirked. "You think I'll look that perfect at four months pregnant?"

"*No one* looks that perfect at four months pregnant," I joked, mindlessly running my fingers through Jack's hair. "I'm not entirely convinced she's human."

Curling her legs up and facing me, Lilly let out a long breath. "You think Grandpa and Chris and... *Maria* are okay?"

I noted the disdain in her voice when she'd said Maria's name, like she didn't really want to include her, but felt obligated. "I'm sure they're all fine. Probably diligently working to get answers so we can get out of this mess."

"You think Chris got his brain injury figured out by now?"

I frowned, my fingers pausing against Jack's scalp. "I hope so."

One side of her lip curled menacingly upward. "Maybe they'll come back minus one with his thinking more clear."

"Oh stop." I shook my head. "She's really not that bad. And he's happy with her. I want him to be happy."

She laid her head back against the headboard. "Is he? She spent the last year and a half demonizing you so she could steal him away. Granted, you had Jack, but what if you didn't? It's obvious she'd been working him the whole time, trying to get a married man to warm her bed... it worked, but maybe that's only because he wasn't thinking clearly. I'd throw a party in his honor if he came back without her."

"Lill, I love you, but you're bigger than this type of gossip."

"It's not gossip," she said, pulling a lock of hair in front of her eyes to inspect the ends. "I said as much to her on a few occasions. She didn't deny it. You know what I think?"

"I'm sure you're going to tell me."

"I think she clings to him for her own sense of security. She thinks that's love. She needed him to get by in this time... to feel safe and cared for. But when she's comfortable and something she deems better for her security comes along, she'll toss him aside. You watch. I've lived my whole life around the narcissistic women of New York's upper class. I recognize an egomaniac when I see one."

Resuming the gentle sweeps of my fingers over Jack's hair, I considered it. "You want to know what I think?"

Still inspecting the ends of her hair, she lifted a mocking eyebrow. "I'm sure you're going to tell me."

Suppressing a laugh, I turned my face toward her. "I think she's just different. Different for us means we immediately assume the worst. She's boisterous and demanding and she fibs more often than she should, but it's not narcissism that makes her that way. It's insecurity. I imagine most women—and men—react to her the way you do, and I can tell she craves our friendship even despite the judgment. She loves differently... and we see that as deceit instead of truth because it is unlike what our definition of love might be... But maybe her way is better... Who knows? I've seen her with Chris, and I think she'd take a bullet before she ever tossed him aside. Sure, she demonized me, but she wasn't wrong. I wasn't good to him during our relationship, and then I fell in love with another man while he spent a year searching for me. I can't say I wouldn't have demonized a woman I never met if Jack had come to me with similar stories of a broken marriage."

She pulled her lips in, closing her eyes. "No, you wouldn't. You're better than that." Sighing, she let the lock of hair fall back to her shoulder. "I'm not though. You know, Jimmy told me about

June... About what she did to him, taking off pregnant... I've called her just about every name in the book. You know he asked Chris to find her? To give her *all* of his lottery winnings?"

"He did?" I asked a little too loudly, causing Jack to roll onto his side, Izzy still cradled in his arms.

She nodded, lowering her voice as I eased myself out from behind him to allow them to sleep in peace. "And I asked him, what if there was no baby? What if she lost it or aborted it or faked it in the first place? You know what he said?"

"What?" I whispered.

"He said it didn't matter. He said he wanted her to have it either way. Lainey, it boils my blood that a woman like that—a woman that absolutely tormented him for years; that still torments him—is just gonna have this handed to her... like it's nothing that she destroyed his life."

I laid my hand over hers on the blanket. "He's a good man, Lill. And he's not doing it for her. He's doing it for him... because in his mind, giving her that money is the right thing to do, and Jim will always be the sort of man that does the right thing."

She smiled, looking toward the door and back. "He really is. I hope to God I never cross paths with that woman... because the right thing *for me* would be to rip her cold heart right out of her chest."

Chapter Forty Eight

Chris

Chris leaned against his father's truck, watching the numbers on the gas pump climb rapidly as the New Mexico heat beat down on him.

Finally cleared to drive, his father had given him his truck and no small amount of cash from their settlement with the airline. He'd told his parents he and Maria needed to get away from the spotlight while his head continued to heal.

And that wasn't entirely untrue. The detectives had returned to ask all the same questions several nights ago the moment they'd all sat down to a family dinner. While he'd attempted to take the same stance Bud had, insisting they speak with his attorney, his mother had been overly accommodating, inviting them to join them for supper.

By the time they'd left, his head was pounding. He was anxious to get away from them, and fulfilling his promise to Jim seemed like the perfect opportunity.

He'd assured his mother and father he'd remain in touch, hugging them both for far too long before they'd taken off, unsure whether or not he'd see them again for quite some time.

He didn't intend to return to Chicago. While Bud wouldn't agree to the shortened timeline before checking with his genealogists, he had approved their early arrival at his vacation home in Santa Monica and was having it prepared for them. They planned to go straight there after their stops in New Mexico and Las Vegas.

They'd driven ten hours to Tulsa before stopping for the night. Ten hours in a truck with Maria, the wind blowing through the open windows, had reminded him of their time together on the island. They joked and told stories about their lives, bickering on more than one occasion about nothing.

Fully rested after collapsing in the hotel bed, they'd departed just after sunrise, and eight hours later, they were an hour outside Albuquerque, the key and instructions tucked in an envelope and labelled '*June.*' What they'd do from there, he wasn't sure.

Returning the handle to its pump, he climbed back into the truck and staunched a laugh when he caught sight of Maria in the passenger seat.

Sporting a Nirvana t-shirt and ripped jean shorts, she sat with her bare feet propped on the dashboard, a piece of red licorice hanging from her lips, and a newly purchased straw cowboy hat sitting atop her head. "You like my new hat?" She grinned, twirling the licorice to one side of her mouth.

"I absolutely love it," he chuckled.

"I got you one too." She tossed a white plastic bag into his lap when he closed the door. "It's black." She noisily dug around inside a second bag in her lap. "I didn't know what kind of sunglasses you'd like, but these seemed like they'd look good on you." She handed him a pair of reflective aviators along with a bottle of water.

He smiled at the gesture, fishing the hat out of the bag to examine it. "You know, I've never worn a cowboy hat in my life."

She tugged the licorice, biting off a piece as she inspected him. "Well, put it on already! I'm dying to see what you look like in it! I have always wanted to kiss a cowboy."

Unable to stop smiling, he carefully positioned it over his head, mindful of the healing bone at the back of his skull, then slid the aviators on and looked over at her. "Well? What do you think?"

Her eyes went wide. "Oh my God. You will never take that hat off again."

Shaking his head, he pulled down the visor to get a look at himself in the mirror. Bursting into laughter at his ridiculous reflection, he turned on the ignition, dialing the air conditioning up high. "I look like a cartoon character trying to conceal his identity."

"No, mi amore," she leaned toward him, pressing a kiss to his lips, "you look sexier than I have ever seen you. You leave that hat on tonight when we get to the hotel."

"I don't know if we should be staking out a bank in sunglasses and weird cowboy hats. We might look just a tad bit suspicious. We wouldn't want to draw any more heat than we already have on us."

"Take it off when we get there, then," she said in a sultry voice, her eyes all but undressing him where he sat.

"What *are* we going to do when we get there?" He asked. "We can't exactly walk in and hand her the key, no questions asked."

She held up a pointer finger, leaning to the side to pull her phone out of her back pocket. Masterfully, she pulled up a search, clicked a button, and a phone rang as she put it on speaker.

"Dawn Financial, this is Carissa. How may I direct your call?"

Maria winked at him. "Hi," she said in the whitest voice he'd ever heard from her. "Is June McClendon working today?"

"Yes, ma'am, but she's with a customer. Can I take a message?"

"Oh, you know, I can just call her cell phone later so I'm not interrupting her at work," Maria drawled. "Do you know what time she gets off?"

"Five o'clock."

"Thanks so much." She hung up the phone, returning the licorice to her mouth and grinning proudly. "We wait for a little blond woman to leave the bank at five o'clock. Then we meet her by her car."

Chris narrowed his eyes playfully behind the sunglasses. "Done this before?"

She pulled a water bottle out of her bag, twisting the cap off to hold it near her lips. "I might've hunted somebody down once."

"Who?" He asked in disbelief.

"A woman who thought she could send dirty photos to the man I was dating and get away with it."

He snorted, putting the truck into gear and navigating them back toward the highway. "What'd you do after you hunted her down?"

She chewed on the licorice for a moment, staring out her window. "I showed her the pictures on my phone and threatened to share them publicly if she didn't find another man... I also threatened to do... a couple other things."

"Did it work?"

She shrugged. "How should I know? I wasn't going to stay dating a man that kept naked pictures on his phone of other women!"

He howled at that. "Then why'd you bother hunting her down?"

"It made me feel better." She sighed. "Are you going to ask June why she ran away from Jim?"

He shook his head. "I wasn't planning to ask her anything... I was hoping I could just give her the envelope and walk away."

"No, that'll creep her out," she noted. "A strange man hands me an envelope while I'm walking to my car, I'm going to drop it and run. I might even mace him if I have it on me."

"Well, I can't very well explain how I have it... especially with our faces being all over the news and Detective Haywood snooping around."

She frowned, sipping her water slowly as she wiggled her toes on the dash. "What if we watch to see what car she gets in today, then we come back tomorrow and leave the envelope on it?"

"The letter inside says there's five million dollars in a safe-deposit-box with a key and an address of where to find it. If someone were to take it off her car..."

"No, you're right. We can't do that." She huffed. "She will know our faces from the news. And she has to know by now that

Jim was on that plane with us. I could tell her, as a flight attendant, he gave it to me with the instructions to give it to her while the plane was going down."

"That implies he's dead," he reminded her. "If they decided to come back, that would only serve to confuse things."

"Aye, you come up with something then!"

He pursed his lips, checking his blindspot as he merged onto the highway. "Hell, I don't know. We've got an hour and a half to think of something."

That hour and a half yielded very little in the way of ideas, and before he knew it, they were sitting in the small parking lot for Dawn Financial, his palms sweating against the steering wheel.

"That's got to be her," Maria said, pointing at a small blond woman in grey dress pants and a white shirt exiting the bank. She slid a pair of dark sunglasses over her eyes and walked hurriedly toward the parking lot.

Chris plucked the envelope from the dash and leapt out of the truck before he could think of the words to say, speed walking to catch up as she passed their truck.

"June McClendon?" He called out, surprised by how fast her short legs moved her.

She waved one hand in dismissal, not bothering to turn around or slow her pace. "I done told them other two shitbag detectives I don't know nothin,' so ye' can go back to whatever cuntpuddle you climbed out of and tell whoever sent ye' to leave me the fuck alone."

Taken slightly aback by her choice in vulgarity, he had to quicken his steps to catch back up. "I'm not a detective."

She didn't turn toward him, but kept her eyes straight ahead, likely calculating the distance remaining between herself and her vehicle. "Whatever the hell ye' are, I ain't got no answers for ye.'"

"I'm not here to ask you anything, either. I just want to give you this." He offered her the envelope. "It's from Jim."

She stopped then, slowly turning to face him as she crossed her arms over her chest. "Jimmy Lee's been dead for three years and I ain't seen the sorry sack-a-shit in close to ten. Whatever the hell is in that envelope is gonna' stay there. I don't want nothin' from nobody. I already told the last group of yas that came down here I ain't gettin' involved. Now, I got another job to get to. I ain't got time to be standin' here jackin' jaws with ye.'"

He removed his sunglasses, keeping the envelope held out. "You know who I am?"

She removed her own sunglasses, shielding her eyes as she squinted up at him. "Got dammit!" She spun on her heel and rushed to a little red car, hurrying to insert the key into the rusty door. "You stay the fuck away from me. Them FBI agents ain't left me alone since y'all showed back up. They'll be bustin' down my door if they find out ye' came here. I don't wanna know why the hell ye' came lookin' for me and I don't want ye' to give me jack shit."

"He wanted you to have it," Chris insisted, leaning against the passenger side roof. "Please," he extended the envelope over the car. "I'll leave and you'll never see me again if you just take it."

She scowled at him from the driver's side. "After all this time, *why* am I still caught up in this?"

Given her general mood toward speaking to anyone, let alone the detectives, Chris abandoned all caution, not caring if it incriminated him to speak some bit of truth. "You were pregnant the last time he saw you. This is a key to a safe-deposit-box with all the money he won in the lottery. He wanted you to have it to take care of his child."

"*His* child?" She cackled with laughter. "That piece of fucktard don't deserve to call nobody *his* child."

"Look," Chris huffed, "it's none of my business. I'm just here to do what's right. There's five million dollars in that box for you."

She narrowed her blue eyes at him. "This some kind of trap? Ye' tryin' to trick me into acceptin' this envelope so I'll talk or *not talk* to whoever comes next? Tellin' me it's from Jimmy Lee so I'll think it means something? What do I look like? Some kind of fuckin' moron?"

He shook his head. "No ma'am. You can do whatever you want with it. You can throw that envelope in the garbage for all I care. I just need you to take it so I can sleep well knowing I did what I said I would."

"I don't know nothin' about that plane, so if you're bribing me…"

"I'm not bribing you," he said, taking a deep breath. "There's nothing to know about that plane. It crashed. That's all. He wanted you to have this, so I'm giving it to you. That's it."

"That's it?" She eyed the envelope where he still held it over the roof of the car. "You knew him?"

"Does it matter?" He countered.

"No," she looked suspiciously around the parking lot. "You know they think you're either hidin' that plane or you're a hostage to someone that is?"

"I know."

"And ye' still came down here to give me this?" She shook her head. "You must be the worst kind of stupid. They're gonna' be watchin' every move you make. Probably got a GPS on ye.' What am I supposed to tell 'em when they come askin' me why you showed up at my work and why I suddenly come up with five million dollars when I didn't have a fuckin' pot to piss in the day before?"

"You tell them whatever you want, June. I didn't steal the plane and I'm not a hostage. I'm just giving you what he wanted you to have."

She placed a finger on the edge of the envelope. "He gave this to you? Told you to give it to me?"

Chris nodded. "He gave me the key. I memorized the number and the address… wrote it down as soon as I could."

She chewed her lower lip, taking a deep breath. "And if I take this envelope, you'll leave here and ye' won't never come back?"

"Correct."

She took the envelope, and Chris began to turn away. Remembering Jim's wishes, he turned back. "Will you tell me one thing... just for my own peace of mind? See, I've been holding onto that for three years and... I need to know for myself. Did you end up having the baby?"

She raised her chin. "I ain't no baby killer. 'Course I had it."

"And was it a boy or a girl?"

She inspected him for a long moment before letting out the breath she'd been holding. "A boy. Beau." She scratched her nose, squinting across the car at him. "Beau Lee Jackson."

Chapter Forty Nine

Both babies content with Magna, Fetia, and Lilly during a rare break in wedding plans, I ventured up to the top deck of the ship alone. I'd been cooped up too long and needed to stretch my legs.

Since Lilly had been having me sew my own bridesmaid's dress, I'd lost track of the weeks that passed after we'd relocated Juan Josef and Phil. I knew it had been at least three, maybe more. In that time, there'd been no additional threats, and Juan Josef hadn't made any attempt to murder Phil while they'd been locked together—he also hadn't exposed who'd been helping him. I was starting to wonder if the dog hadn't brought the knife into our room that night and we'd all been overreacting.

On the top deck, Kyle was standing among two of the younger shipmen and Abraham, engrossed in a story one of them was telling. He'd started growing a short beard, hoping the other men would see him as more of an adult, and, with a thick inch of dusty blond now covering his lower face, it was working. He did seem older. The shipmen who normally paid him no mind were more accepting of him as part of their conversation.

At the small bistro table on the opposite side of the deck, Jim sat with his feet propped up on the empty seat across from him, Abraham's reading glasses balanced on his nose where it was buried in a book. His gaze would lift from its pages on occasion to check on Izzy where she and Dario played fetch with Luna in the center of the deck.

"Ay Sugar." He smiled at me, lowering the book to massage the bridge of his nose. "I see you've managed to escape the drill sergeant. You want some tea?"

"Nah." I stretched my arms over my head, basking in the warm sunlight. "Just needed to walk around for a bit before she finds something else for me to do."

He snickered, setting the book and glasses on the table to stand and stretch his own arms. "She's gonna run us all ragged by the time any of us can walk down that aisle."

"She's certainly not running out of ideas to keep us all busy." I motioned to the table. "What are you reading?"

He glanced at the book on the table, tilting his head to read the spine. "*One Hundred Years of Solitude*. It was in Juan Josef's office. Ain't half bad if ye' wanna read it after me." He looked beyond me toward the island. "Ye' wanna go to shore for a while? I could do for a walk myself."

"I don't know…" I gazed back toward the stairwell, pondering whether or not it was too presumptuous to assume the women would be alright keeping the babies for an extended amount of time.

Reading my thoughts, he looped his arm through mine, tugging me toward the sloops. "It's good for 'em to keep the babies for a while. Fetia needs the practice and Princess needs the dose of reality so she ain't pesterin' me about havin' one every chance she gets. Besides, you and me ain't spent nearly enough time together since we been back here."

"Alright," I leaned into his side, excited to take a casual stroll on our beach. There was so little we did anymore just for enjoyment. Between Lilly's wedding plans, guarding the prisoners, taking care of the babies, and the everyday tasks required to keep food and water on the ship as well as maintain it, our days were almost always chalked full. "But only for a little while."

"Deal. Kyle, will ye' keep an eye on Izzy for a bit?"

Kyle nodded. "Will do. I'll take her down to Lilly before my guard shift if you're not back."

"Thank ye. Ay precious," Jim called out to Dario, a nickname that made him cringe every single time. "Come lower us down, will ye?"

"Where are you headed?" Dario enquired, abandoning his game of fetch to join us at the ship's rail.

"Just takin' a walk with a beautiful woman." Jim winked, assisting me over the rail and into the small boat. "Might see if I can talk her into runnin' away with me. Ye' never know."

Dario, the epitome of chivalry, straightened and looked in my direction for confirmation of my consent.

"I'm fine," I assured him. "And don't worry, there aren't too many places on that island we can run away to."

Jim blew him a kiss, hopping into the sloop and waiting until he'd started lowering us down to ask, "how bad ye' think he wants to punch me in the mouth?"

I laughed, looking up to where Dario was keeping his facial expression neutral as he worked the pulley. "Oh, I imagine he dreams of little else. Why do you poke at him the way you do?"

He leaned back, resting both arms against the sides of the sloop. "Somethin' to do, I reckon. Plus, if I had to put money on it, I'd say he's the one that put that knife in your bed, just to please his daddy."

I shook my head. "I don't think so. I saw the way he and Juan Jr. reacted when Juan Josef slit Anna's throat. It shook them both. They don't want the violence or the head games. They just want to try to erase the damage that's been done."

"And you?" He raised an eyebrow. "You still want to go forward with it? Did ye' pray on it like I told ye' to?"

"I did. I went back and forth with it for a while, but then the new memories came." I smoothed the edges of my shorts as we hit the water, the boat rocking when Jim rose to release the ropes. I waited for him to take his seat and the oars before continuing. "Killing those men stole a good husband and a child from my sister. Even if I disagreed with the morality of what we're talking about doing; even if I decided bringing Anna or those men back wouldn't be worth the risk, I'd take the eternal punishment to see my sister's happiness restored. She was my best friend in the world and I'd never be able to forgive myself if I didn't try to give her life back to her."

He rowed us steadily, nodding in understanding. "I been thinkin' on it a lot lately. 'Specially with the wedding comin' up and us talkin' about buildin' a family and a life together. Lilly's got her heart set on savin' Anna. And I cain't think the good Lordt would sentence someone like her to eternal damnation just for doin' what she thinks is right. Or you for wantin' to give a life back to your sister. If he does, well, I'll be burnin' in hell right there beside yuns. God knows I cain't bear the thought of her goin' nowhere without me. So, ye' got my vote when it comes the time to make that decision. I cain't vote against neither of yuns, even to save my soul."

We sat silently for a moment, considering it as we moved away from the ship. "You excited? About the wedding?"

He grinned. "Sugar, excited ain't the right word for it. A woman like that don't end up with a man like me in the real world. I ain't never felt no kind of love like what she gives. Don't seem right to have so much of it all directed at me. I keep wonderin' when I'm gonna' wake up."

"Me too," I admitted. "You deserve every bit of that love, you know. You're a good man, and you don't give yourself nearly enough credit for it."

He chortled. "Said the queen of self-loathing. If that ain't the pot callin' the kettle black, I don't know what is."

"Not lately," I admitted defensively. "I've been working on ways to love myself. You should too. Lilly told me about what you're doing for June. That's no small act of kindness, giving away all your money."

He winked, raising his left boot. "I might of kept a little bit in a separate box for myself, just in case. Couldn't fit it all in one anyways. It's pennies compared to the kind of money Lilly's got comin' to her, but I ain't no kind of man if I marry her with my hand out."

"See?" I smiled as we pulled into the shallows. "You're good, Jim, and you deserve every bit of the love she offers you... and then some."

Hopping out of the boat into the shallow water, he dragged us onto the sand and assisted me out of the sloop. "Thanks Doctor *Volmer.* Still gettin' used to yuns sharin' that last name. Is it different now that you're married?"

"Different in a good way," I said, curling my arm back into his as we strolled down the familiar beach. "Like there's some deeper bond between us now that we can call each other husband and wife. There's nothing to be afraid of from the person who agrees to spend their life beside you... You know?"

"You were afraid of him before?"

I shrugged. "I was afraid he might wake up one day and see me differently. I'm not anymore."

"Shoot, I could be married to Lilly for twenty years and still be scared shitless she'll wake up and regret marrying down."

I playfully punched his shoulder. "You don't give her enough credit either. She would never regret marrying you. Have you seen her lately? She's got the whole ship sewing frill and testing out various centerpieces."

Chuckling, he patted my hand between us, leading me around a cluster of rocks in the sand. "Wanna' ask ye' somethin.'" He stared ahead, squinting his eyes against the blaring sun. "Let's say they come back and we find out that necklace don't mean nothin' and they got proof we could all pass through safely—even them babies. Would ye' go back?"

"In a heartbeat." The quickness with which I said the words surprised me. I hadn't realized how much I wanted to go back until then.

"That's what I figured." He unlocked our arms to drape his over my shoulder. "Where would ye' go once ye' got there?"

"Haven't allowed myself to even think about that," I admitted. "It feels wrong to hope for a future that isn't going to be possible; like I might be setting us up to be disappointed in the lives we end up with, and I don't want that for myself or Jack."

"What is it about the future that makes ye' want to get back to it *in a heartbeat*?"

"My family," I said, leaning into his side. "My mom and sister and uncle... If they weren't there, I wouldn't care where we ended up. I don't particularly miss anything else about our time—except maybe ice and hot showers—but I miss them, and I hate that Zachary and Cecelia will never know them the way I do. What about you? Are you anxious to go back?"

"Nah, I never fit in there as it was. I'd be perfectly content parkin' my happy ass right here on this island and never meetin' another soul but yuns for the rest of my life. But Lilly wouldn't. She dreams bigger than what this century has to offer."

I grinned. "Lilly dreams bigger than what our *own* century has to offer. She's larger than any life she ends up in."

"That's true." He stopped and plucked a white seashell from the sand, tucking it into his pocket. "She wants the white ones for somethin,' and I figured if I asked what, she'd put me to work on it." Snickering, he draped his arm back over my shoulders, and we continued along the shore. "Anyway, she ain't leavin' yuns, and I ain't either. But it cain't hurt none of us to start thinkin' about our options when all this is through. If, by the grace of God, it's possible to go home, we could at least talk about where we all might settle down... In addition to plannin' for where we might go if it's not."

I nodded. "The war's already begun by now in America. We can't go there. And we can't risk going to Britain and getting caught up in it. Jack and I talked about Ireland. Maybe we could build a life there or at least wait it out until the war's over and migrate. There'd be lots of opportunity in America after the war to settle on a piece of land."

"If we had money to buy any of it, sure," Jim noted. "As it stands, we're piss poor. But we ain't gotta' stay that way..." He unraveled his arm from my shoulders and turned to face me, a wicked smile slowly spreading across his lips. "See, I been talkin' to Juan Josef's men. There's an older man named Walter that's been sailin' with him for years. He claims Juan Josef keeps a stash of gold hidden on that ship right beneath our noses. He stole it from an English captain. Says the whole crew made a game out of searchin' for it. Since we ain't doin' nothin' but sittin' around waitin, I say we have us a little fun. I ain't got no beef stealin' stolen gold from a pirate. What about you?"

"I always dreamed about searching for a hidden treasure... Could be fun..."

"Fancy a wager?" He bounced his brows.

"Oh, you think you can beat me to it? I've got a lot more free time to search than you do since you chauvinists won't let us *lowly women* do a damn thing to help. What's the wager?"

"If I find it first, I want a good ole' fashioned southern breakfast made by *your* hands. I'm talkin' biscuits and gravy, grits, eggs, sausage, bacon... no skimpin.'"

"Even your wager is chauvinistic," I laughed. "Deal. And if I find it first, you let me and Lilly take a shift guarding the door."

"Deal." He stuck his palm out and I shook it, excited to get back to the ship and turn it upside down, not so much for the promise of money, but more for the opportunity to be given equal responsibility. I was tired of being treated like something to be coddled while the men wore themselves ragged attempting to shoulder everything.

Chapter Fifty

Chris

Chris stood at the window of their hotel room, the phone pressed to his ear as he stared down at the Las Vegas strip thirty floors below. Clusters of people moved along the main road, likely preparing to transition from dinner-mode to party-mode as the sun lowered in the sky and cast a warm hue over the city.

"I pulled Bruce, Frank, and Anna," Bud said on the other end of the phone, "and sent their info to another genealogy firm since the two we're using are at capacity as-is. They said they can have their reports done by mid-August. My original firm wasn't too excited about the new deadline, but they're going to make it work."

Chris paced along the floor-to-ceiling windows that lined one wall of his room. "So you agree we should leave in September?"

"Honestly, if we could leave sooner and lay low until September, that'd be even better." Bud sighed. "Detective Haywood was here again yesterday. My attorney is getting anxious. The fact that it's the FBI investigating us as opposed to the FAA or the NTSB is cause for concern. They're likely looking at us for evidence of terrorism, and they don't need much to take a suspected terrorist into custody."

"I was thinking the same." Rubbing his temples, he balanced the cell phone against his shoulder as he poured out his evening dosage from the inventory of pill bottles on the bedside table. "Do we have somewhere we could lay low with access to the internet?"

"I'm working on that," Bud assured him. "When will you get to the vacation house?"

"Tomorrow afternoon," Chris said, popping the rainbow of pills into his mouth and washing them down with the beer he'd opened when they returned from dinner. "Had to make a quick stop on the way."

"Everything went smoothly in Albuquerque?"

Chris laughed. "I wouldn't call anything about our encounter with June McClendon smooth, but we got it done. We'll have to have a much better plan for when we approach Anna's family. With our faces all over the news and the FBI sniffing around, Maria's idea of walking in to the yoga studio isn't exactly going to work."

"I have a few friends out there I might be able to employ to help. Where's Maria now?"

Feeling a little lightheaded, Chris turned back toward the room and sat down heavily on the bed. "Downstairs. Picking out a wedding dress. I'm meeting her in an hour in the lobby bar."

"You don't sound excited. Everything okay with you two?"

Blinking a little heavily, he looked over at the pill bottles covering the side table. "Everything's fine. Just took my meds and I'm feeling a little dizzy is all. The antiseizure medicine has that affect... so does the tramadol."

"Tramadol?" Bud balked. "I thought they took you off that? You're definitely not supposed to be driving on that."

Chris sighed. "I only take a half of one in the evenings, and only if the pain flares up. I don't drive until I'm certain it's out of my system."

"I really think you should go see my neurologist in L.A. when you get there. It's too soon for you to be doing so much and you should've stayed in Chicago and kept up with your appointments. I could've handled this."

The room starting to spin around him, he forced himself up, crossing to the floor-length mirror to focus on his reflection. He'd bought a dark grey suit for the occasion and had left the bowtie to hang loose beneath his white collar. Too dizzy to attempt a knot, he leaned against the mirror and tried to get his bearings. "I'll make an appointment when I get there. Maybe he can change out some of these meds."

"That bad?"

Chris took a deep breath. "Almost unbearable. Honestly, I'd rather hear voices."

"Maybe getting married today isn't the most important thing," Bud said, switching into his fatherly tone. "Does she know you're feeling this bad?"

"I'm fine," he lied, plucking his key card from the dresser to tuck it into his jacket pocket. "I'm only dizzy for a little while right after I take them. By the time we get to the chapel, the worst of it will be gone."

Bud made a disapproving sound. "You gotta be honest with her, kiddo. Don't hide it if you're feeling sick just to please her. She wouldn't want that, you know."

Chris knew that, and he had every intention of filling her in on the unpleasant side effects of his medication at some point. But he'd already screwed up enough, and to turn away from their wedding just because he was dizzy didn't feel right. "I will."

"Alright," Bud said, giving up his attempt to parent him. "Let me know when you get to the house. I'll text you the number for Dr. Evans, and I'll let you know about my contact regarding the Liam situation. I want you to relax when you get to the house. No more driving and no more stress. Okay?"

Chris smiled. "Yes, boss."

Bud chuckled. "Good luck tonight. I'll see you soon."

"Thank you, Bud, for everything. Talk to you tomorrow."

Hanging up the phone, Chris squinted at the mirror, taking several deep breaths while his reflection blurred, took shape, and blurred again. This wasn't the normal effects he had grown accustomed to. He was significantly less functional than usual. Closing his eyes, he tried to remember if he'd taken his pills already when they'd come back from dinner. Could he have just doubled his dose?

Deciding that, if he had, he'd much rather die where someone might find him than alone in his hotel room, he ventured out into the hallway, keeping a hand on the wall all the way to the elevators.

A laughing couple with giant frozen drinks passed him on his route, the male frowning. "Woah, you alright buddy?"

"I'm fine," he managed, holding himself up with some effort as he brushed past them and pressed the elevator button.

"Some people just can't handle Vegas," the man remarked under his breath, prompting a snicker out of the female wrapped in his arm as they made their way around the corner.

Chris looked at the screen of his phone, unlocking it and laboriously navigating the out-of-focus icons until he opened up his text chain with Maria.

'Heading down. Think I took—

He paused. He'd had two beers over dinner. Maybe the mixture was intensifying the side effects of the medication. If that was the case, he'd be fine soon enough… Surely, two beers wouldn't cause the medication to kill him. And he didn't want to worry her… Not tonight.

Deleting what he'd started, he simply sent:

'See you soon. Can't wait.'

In the elevator, he leaned back against the handrail, seeing his pale reflection in the mirrors and cursing the medication for making him even less stable than he'd been before.

When he reached the lobby and the elevator doors opened, the world around him went completely black.

When his eyes opened again, he was sitting in one of the chairs in his room, Maria seething on the sofa opposite him in a pink-stained wedding dress, arms crossed over her chest while she tapped one foot impatiently against the carpeted floor.

Frowning, he sat up a little, only then noticing the red feathered boa wrapped around his neck. Spitting the feathers that had made it to his lips, he pulled it off himself, taking in the same stains all over his once white button-up shirt. "What the hell happened?"

She tilted her head sharply, glaring at him. "You tell me, superman."

"I don't know." And that was terrifying. Chris had never blacked out before and, given the way her eyes were piercing into his very soul, he assumed he hadn't simply passed out in front of the elevator doors. "The last thing I remember was getting in the elevator. How did I get back in the room?"

"Oh, your new friends brought you here," she said matter-of-factly, flipping her hair over her shoulder.

"What friends?"

"How the hell should I know? You called them all Al or Ally or A.J. or Alaina—*not Maria*—no, no, you wouldn't call *them* Maria, would you?"

He blinked. "I don't..." He noticed the sky outside the large windows was a dull grey. "What time is it?"

"6AM," she hissed. "Ask me what time I found you with your little friends... Ask me how many hours I walked in this stupid dress searching for you... how many times I called and texted you in a panic... thinking you were face down somewhere dead with your head split back open! Ask me how many people I gave your description to and begged to help me look for you. Ask me how many of those people saw this stupid dress and assumed you ran away!" She shot up from the sofa to pace. "Go ahead! Ask me!"

His entire face on fire, he felt his throat tighten. "Maria, I really don't remember anything. I took my pills and got a little dizzy, so I went—

"Three hours." She narrowed her eyes, slowly striding toward him. "*Three* hours I thought you were dead. I called Bud, and he told me you'd taken your pills while you were on the phone with him, and of course I panicked because I *watched* you take them before dinner, you idiot! Then I thought for sure you were dead. Started calling hospitals to see if someone had taken you to one.

But no, you weren't dead or in a hospital. While I was worrying myself sick about you, you were letting a group of half-naked women climb all over you at a club."

"A club?" He shook his head. "Maria, I texted you, got in the elevator, and then… I woke up here. That's all I remember."

"You were in a dance club at the Luxor. At the *Luxor*! Do you know how many people I had to question before coming across someone who'd spotted a group of women dragging you in there?"

He tried to remember something—*anything* resembling the accusation she'd just laid out. Slowly, a very blurry image of a dimly lit booth came to mind, a jumble of flashing lights and loud music, strange faces smiling down at him where he sank heavily into a seat, his body limp and paralyzed… He tried to recall how he'd ended up there after he'd left the elevator but came up short.

"I'm… I'm so sorry. It's no excuse for what I've obviously just put you through, but I'm telling you I have no memory of going to a club of my own free will!"

She stood directly in front of him, the knuckles of her fists white where she rested them against her hips. He could reach for her if he didn't think she might actually kill him if he did so.

"Don't you dare laugh. This isn't funny." She stomped her foot, and he removed all amusement from his features. She presented the stains down her white dress. "I rushed in there and found you mostly unconscious in a booth, an entire bachelorette party dancing on your lap. I was so relieved I'd found you, I couldn't even be mad when you threw up all over both of us. I knew you weren't yourself after taking those pills twice. You were out of it. And I felt so guilty about not being there to manage your meds that I was even willing to let go of the fact that you were calling those stupid women by *her* name. That is, until I took your hand and tried to pull you out of there… Do you remember what you said to me?"

He shook his head.

Her eyes watered, but her voice did not quiver. "You said *'Go away, Maria.'* You called them Al and Ally and A.J. and Alaina while you laughed and smiled at them, but you called *me* Maria and told me to go away."

"Oh, come on Maria, you can't really think that means anything? I wasn't myself! Obviously!"

Her nose twitched, and she took a deep breath. "I have been hurt by many men in my life... but you? This? It hurt more than any of them ever could."

"I didn't mean it. I swear. I was out of my mind. Whatever I was, whatever I said... I love *you*."

She growled. "Don't you dare use '*I love you*' to try to make this better! Those words mean nothing to me right now! You can't just say '*I love you*' and expect to erase the hell you've just put me through!"

"But I do love you, Maria, and I'm sorry."

She shook her head. "I really want to believe that, Kreese. I *need* to believe that because I love you with all my stupid heart. And maybe you did love me for a second before we changed everything... but you don't anymore. Not like you did... Not like I need you to. And I can't marry a man who hurts me this much. I won't do it..."

Abandoning all caution, he reached for her, pulling her close enough that he could wind his arms around her waist. "I'm an idiot. A complete fucking moron that I keep screwing things up with the one person in this world I don't want to screw things up with. Let me make this up to you? Let me prove you're wrong and I love you and I want to marry you more than I've ever wanted anything. Please?"

"No," she breathed, stepping out of his embrace to raise her chin. "You have hurt me too much to ever make this up."

He dropped down onto his knees on the floor at her feet, smiling up at her as he clasped his hands together. "I will worship you day and night, kiss your feet, live the rest of my life at your beck and call. I am nothing without you—the scum of the universe —and I know I'm not worthy of your forgiveness, but please don't leave me."

She crossed her arms over her chest, huffing audibly. "I'm not going to leave you, estúpido."

"Oh, thank—

"But only because I have nowhere else to go and I promised to find Liam," she added, fanning her fingers in front of her face to inspect her nails. "Get up off the floor and go wipe that glitter off your face. You look ridiculous."

"What about the wedding? I can buy you a new dress..."

She laughed haughtily. "I am not marrying you now, superman. After the night you just put me through? No. I might be crazy, but I am not *that* crazy. You will need to kiss my ass for the foreseeable future before I even consider marrying you again. Now go wash your face and pack your things. I will drive us the rest of the way."

Chapter Fifty One

As the month of wedding plans passed quickly, I'd taken every opportunity to venture off in search of Juan's hidden gold. There was something exhilarating in the solace of the hunt that made me feel emboldened; like this one little thing was exclusively mine and finding it would be an accomplishment I could wear proudly.

Pulling drawers and testing for loose floorboards inside each cabin, I found that my mind tended to drift off in exploration of the newly developed memories I hadn't previously allowed myself to visit.

Visiting them felt like a moot point. The moment I'd realized I was experiencing memories instead of dreams, I'd shut them out entirely, forcing them into the far recesses of my mind. There was no sense in analyzing a past I was hell-bent on putting back the way it was, and it was far easier to remember the events as they once were than to accept that I'd robbed Cecelia of her family and somehow benefited from it.

But, alone and undistracted while I searched the ship, I was unable to avoid them any longer, and they poured out behind my eyes beyond my control.

Without Owen, everything had been different. Cecelia had finished school, obtaining her bachelor's degree in veterinary medicine. She'd started her own clinic not far from our home and bought a condo fifteen minutes across town.

When we lost Evelyn, she practically moved in, consoling me round the clock so I didn't have the chance to shut out the world. She comforted Chris too, restoring our happiness with each other while being completely unaware we'd stolen hers.

Instead of melting down on my birthday and demolishing our dining room, I'd joined the family for dinner and cake. We'd talked about the loss—thanks to Cecelia—and then found a way to move beyond it together, ending the night with stories and laughter. Chris and I were almost entirely returned to the happy couple we'd once been after he'd gifted me the necklace later that night.

Of course Cecelia would make that possible. Cecelia had always been my rock growing up. She'd always found the right ways to pull me out of whatever funk I'd find myself in—whether it was a bad joke, some otherworldly bit of advice, or a simple punch to the gut—she was the one person that could lift me out of any rut. And when I thought about how much distance had been between us in the original timeline of my life, I was disappointed in myself. She built an amazing life, and I made myself an outsider to it; too caught up in the Alaina-show to allow myself inside.

'Lesson one in self-improvement, Alaina,' I told myself as I crawled beneath a bed I assumed was Juan Josef's to search for hidden compartments. 'Let yourself be present in the lives of the people you love. The person you want to be doesn't live exclusively in her own little world anymore.'

"Let that be a lesson to you as well," I said to the two babies lying on top of the mattress I had climbed under. "You two will always have each other. Don't ever let the bond you build slip away because you become too focused on your own lives. You'll hate yourself for it later."

Groaning, I eased myself out from beneath the bed, brushing off the layer of cobwebs and who-knows-what-else that coated my hair and arms as a result of being crammed in the small space. I sat up, balancing my arms over my knees and smiling at Zachary. "If you were a 1970s drug lord turned pirate, where would you hide your gold?"

Zachary squawked in response, his lifted face turning red and the small vein on his forehead becoming visible as he pushed out what remained of his morning meal.

"Seriously?" I rolled my eyes. "You *just* pooped."

He pushed harder, his face nearly purple with the effort.

"I'm running out of clean linens… and patience. It's not fair your father gets to have all the fun while I run back and forth changing *your* dirty diapers."

Unaffected by my confession, he clenched his fists and continued, a resounding *'pfft'* against the linen diaper adding insult to injury.

I chuckled as his face returned to its normal shade of pale pink. "You're such a jerk, but I love you all the same."

Rocking back to push myself off the floor, I gave up my treasure hunt, inserting them both back into the sling—one that was growing significantly heavier every day—and turning toward the door.

"You think he'd just *tell* me where the gold is?" I asked them as I returned to the hallway. "I mean… he's got no use for it now."

Cecelia trilled her lips in response, a cascade of drool and bubbles seeping down her perpetually liquid chin.

"You're right. Your father would never go for it. I *am* just a poor little helpless female who's fated to change diapers and sew pretty things, after all."

Zachary made a noise at that, and I frowned down at him. "Don't you even think about agreeing with me. I might be forced to raise you in this time, but you will grow up seeing women as your equal, not treating them like porcelain dolls."

Jim grinned from his seat between the two doors as I approached. "I see ye' ain't found it yet. I tell ye,' I can almost taste the sausage gravy now!"

"Arrogance doesn't look good on anybody," I said smartly, sauntering past him to place my palm on the handle of our door. Noting the lack of a second guard—namely one that tended to hover near the one presently standing watch, I turned back. "Where's Jack?"

Jim grinned. "Lilly put him to work movin' a couple chairs from the dining room out to the island for the big day."

I glanced over my shoulder and back. "So he'll be gone for a while?"

Jim crossed his ankle over his knee and leaned back. "Whatever kind of no good you're thinkin' about gettin' into, I want no part in it. I know that look."

I offered him my most innocent smile. "I was simply thinking I could peek inside that door you're guarding and ask one very innocent question."

"That's cheating," he assured me, folding his hands behind his head and balancing the chair on its two back legs. "Besides, I done asked him already and he ain't tellin.'"

I lifted an eyebrow, bending toward him so we couldn't be overheard through the thin walls. "Well, he wouldn't tell *you*, would he? He might, however, tell the one woman onboard that so closely resembles his long-lost and *most beloved* wife."

He snorted. "Woman, you're nuttier than a five-pound fruitcake. Ain't happenin.' Now go on wit' ye."

"Fine," I straightened. "We'll just live like peasants when we get out of here. Maybe I could sell my body to support—

"Oh quit. Ye' ain't pullin' the wool over my eyes that easy. Hoss would have my ass if I let ye' go in there and you damn well know it."

I scoffed. "*Hoss* doesn't have to know everything. I don't know all the details of what he's up to from one minute to the next."

"Woman, ye' ain't goin' in there."

"Why not?" I stomped, frustration getting the better of me. "You're not my handler and neither is Jack. If I want to go in there, I'll do what I damn well please."

"I'd like to see you try it." He grinned, lowering the front legs of his chair and placing both feet on the ground. "Come on then, try it. I ain't had me a good laugh in a while."

"How exactly do you intend to stop me?" I countered, examining the distance between myself and the door. I could possibly beat him to the handle, but if it was locked…

"Go for that handle, and we'll find out now, won't we?"

"Let her in," Juan Josef's voice drawled from the opposite side of the wall. "I'll behave."

Jim stiffened, an evident chill running down his spine. "Ye' got to be some kind of stupid to think I'd do any such thing!"

"You want to know where I hid the gold I stole from the English captain? I'll tell her. Let her in."

I raised an eyebrow, enthused by the offer but not quite dumb enough to buy it. "Tell me from here," I offered, knowing it was no use.

A deep, throaty laugh responded from the other side. "My dear, you are smarter than that. Come in. I am in chains and I cannot hurt you." He rattled them to support his claim. "Let me see your face and I will tell you what you wish to know."

Jim shook his head continuously from one side to the other.

"I don't believe you," I said, inching closer to the door to get a feel for his proximity to it. "Why would you offer up that kind of information?"

"Why wouldn't I?" He asked smoothly. "I've no desire for you or my sons to suffer while you embark on this journey to change our history. You'll need money to fund this endeavor and I *wish* to give it to you... Consider it my way of thanking you for keeping me alive; for adopting our mission as your own. Come in. Let me see your face."

"I won't go in all the way," I whispered, a little excited at the idea of being so close to finding the gold I'd spent nearly a month trying to find.

Jim held a finger to his lips, urging me to be quiet. "Ay Phil... I got a bullet in this gun with your name on it if you dare lie to me. Tell me right now, is Juan Josef in his chains?"

"Yeah," Phil called from further inside the room. "He's sitting on his bed."

I leaned into Jim's ear. "How far is the bed from the door?"

"About ten feet," he whispered back, then returned his addresses to Phil. "He got anything he could use as a weapon right now?"

"No."

Jim pursed his lips, lowering his voice. "Codeword for somethin' amiss is to use the word *'sir,'* but I don't like it... I don't trust him neither."

"You can check it out first," I said softly. "I'll stay in the doorway with the door open once you verify it's safe. If Juan Josef so much as stands up from the bed, I run out, we close the door and lock it back up. It was your idea to search for the gold... remember? What if it really is this easy?"

"You do know I'm a dead man if your husband finds out, right? If he kills me for this, that's on your conscience, not mine. And ye' ain't takin' them babies in there with you... And he probably ain't gonna' tell ye' nothin' anyways."

I glanced back at the double doors of our room. "Is Fetia in there?"

He sighed. "Yeah. But—"

I rushed into our room before he could change his mind, placed both babies in the cradle, waved an arm at Fetia, and said, "I'll be right back."

When I returned to the hallway, Jim had the pistol at the ready, his head wedged inside the door to inspect the room. "You so much as sneeze when she's in here, I'll kill you dead, you understand?"

I heard Juan Josef through the crack in the door. "I shall remain right where I am. You have my word."

"You too, Phil. I ain't past shootin' you just for lookin' at her." He opened the door wide enough that I could pass through, mumbling as I did, "this has got to be the dumbest thing I ever did."

I stood in the doorway, examining the room. They'd been generous with the shackles—each man had a length of chain that would allow for them to sleep comfortably as well as move at least five feet around their beds. I noted the distance between the two beds was enough that they could not reach each other. I also knew Chris had picked the locks on his own shackles once with relative ease. Phil had watched him do it, and I wasn't dumb enough to presume Juan Jr. wasn't capable of doing the same.

"There are those eyes," Juan Josef sang, remaining still at the edge of his bed. "Those eyes so full of life and the desire for adventure. I knew it was only a matter of time before you would come in search of it, my dear."

"Here I am, Juan," I said a little irritably. "A deal's a deal. You promised to tell me where to find your gold in exchange for seeing my face. You've seen my face."

As his eyes slowly scanned me from head to toe, I couldn't help but feel how little distance there was between us; couldn't help but imagine how quickly he could leap from that bed and get his hands on me. As a result, I also couldn't help but feel precisely like the poor little helpless female I was, the one who was indeed fated to change diapers and sew pretty things if she didn't learn a thing or two about how to properly defend herself.

"What's the rush?" He teased. "We have plenty of time... months before you will ever have a need for it. Why must you have it now when any one of those men might be tempted to take it away should your methods of keeping it concealed prove less effective than mine? Do you know how long those men have searched for it? All the while, I have kept it safely hidden. You think you can hide it so well as I? You think you will be safe if any of them find it in your possession?"

"I have had a year on that island to find plenty of places to hide things. I'll be just fine, thank you."

He laughed. "My word, Alaina, you are so much like Gloria sometimes, it is hard to remain convinced you are someone else. I will tell you where the gold is."

"Where is it?"

He smiled. "It is here. With me, of course."

"In this room?" I huffed. "You expect me to believe you brought it up here with you when they moved you?"

"It is here... how it got here and worrying about whether you believe me is not part of the deal I made. I agreed only to tell you where it is and I have."

I scanned the room. "Where?"

He grinned playfully. "What would be the fun in that, my dear? I have told you where to find it, but the exact hiding spot?" He made a *'tsk'* sound. "That is up to you to find."

Behind me, in the hall, Jim snorted mockingly.

"Thanks," I managed, spinning on my heel. The sound of clanging chains made me leap out of the room, and it was only at the perturbed expression on Jim's face that I looked back to see Juan had simply laid down in his bed; the movement creating a rattle in his chains.

Poor helpless female, indeed.

"Enjoy yourself in there, did ye?" Jim snickered as he closed the door and placed the key in the lock. "I like my eggs over easy, just so ye' know."

Remembering I needed to change Zachary, I turned away. "This isn't over, Jim," I promised. "I still intend to find it first."

Chapter Fifty Two

I watched as Jack balanced Zachary on his thighs where his knees were bent up in the bed. The two of them, looking more like each other every day, stared at each other, Jack matching every facial expression Zachary made.

"Do you remember on the island when I asked you to teach me to fight?" I asked, sliding into the bed beside him to hold Cecelia similarly in my lap.

Turning his head against the headboard, he frowned. "Yes…"

"I'm still waiting."

He ran his thumb over Cecelia's chin—a futile attempt to remove the drool that permanently lived there. "Who are you planning to beat up?"

I shrugged. "No one in particular, but I'd like to have the knowledge that I could defend myself if I needed to. I don't like feeling helpless and I don't like being treated like I'm helpless, either. We have time while we're stuck here waiting, and I want you to teach me everything you know."

He grinned, poking my upper arm. "If you're planning to beat up a man, we'll need to start with these."

I gasped. "Are you implying I am flabby and out of shape?"

"I'm implying that you'll need upper body strength to defend yourself. Learning to fight is about more than throwing a punch. If you're serious, we'll need to start with strength training."

I pursed my lips. "What about pressure points? Aren't there places I could take a man out even with my flabby, out of shape arms?"

He shook his head. "There are points that would disable a man if you struck him hard enough in them. I can show you those... but you'll still need core and upper body strength."

"I can hit hard once or twice; long enough to disable and run. I don't need to strength train for that."

"Okay, fine." He laid Zachary on his belly on the bed and stood. "Come here."

Grinning, I laid Cecelia beside her brother and joined him at the foot of the bed.

"First *pressure* point," he teased, taking my hand to slide it slowly down his inner thigh, "is here. Either the groin or the sciatic nerve just beneath it on the inner thigh. Hit a man here, and he'll go into shock; rendered momentarily dizzy with the intensity of the pain it'll cause. Ram your knee into it as hard as you can."

"I already know how to knee someone in the groin," I said, smiling proudly.

"Alright then, do it. I want you to ram your knee into *me*—into the spot I just showed you."

"Seriously?" I asked, looking around the empty room. We'd left the dining room early after Zachary had decided to throw a fit mid-meal. I imagined the others were just starting on the banana cream pie Bruce had obsessed over. "What if I hurt you?"

He hid a smile. "You wanted me to teach you to fight. This is your first lesson. I *want* you to hurt me. I'll enjoy it, trust me."

"Okay fine, *masochist*." I positioned my legs into a stance that would cater to kneeing him in my favorite place. As I turned to raise my knee, he wrapped both arms tightly around me, spinning me round so my back was stapled to his chest. The target was also pinned against my back, and it became evident he was *indeed* enjoying himself. I wriggled and attempted to work my way out of his grip, but he only held me tighter, chuckling deep inside his throat.

"This is why your mother needs strength training," he said to our little audience on the bed. "A man's instinct is to grab and hold. You need to be able to hurt me from here." He squeezed me tighter, taking my hand in his to place it against his jaw. "Second place is here. From this position, you should be able to head-butt me hard in the jaw. If you do it right, you could knock me out. Try it."

"But I don't want to knock you out," I pouted.

"You're not going to do it right, and I'm not daft enough to let you knock me out if you did. Whip your head back and try to catch my lower jaw."

"It's your funeral," I joked, launching my head backward as instructed, only for him to move out of the way and dig his teeth softly into my shoulder.

"Even if I didn't know what you were about to do, I could've seen that coming from a mile away. A part of strength training is working on your breathing... knowing how to use your breath to enforce your attack. As it stands, your breathing gives you away. Also, you're slow."

I attempted to elbow him in the ribs... unsuccessfully.

"But there's one spot you could do some damage—even though you're slow and weak and your breathing is all wrong."

I rolled my eyes. "You know, I wouldn't have asked if I'd known you were just going to tease me the whole time."

"I'm sorry," he chuckled, burying his face against the nape of my neck. "Have I hurt your feelings?"

"Tell me about this spot so I can damage you, smartass."

"The shin. If you drive the heel of your—

I didn't wait for further instruction, and proudly kicked him in the shin with my heel mid-sentence.

As he stumbled backward in a barrage of obscenities, I immediately regretted that decision.

"Oh my God!" I spun around to grab his arm while he bounced on one foot, his face twisted in a miserable grimace. "I'm so sorry! I didn't think I'd actually hurt you! I thought you'd move! I'm sorry!"

He teetered back onto the edge of the bed and rubbed his injured leg. "Jerk," he grumbled, working hard not to smile. "This was all just an excuse so you could beat me, wasn't it? I don't need to take your abuse. I am a strong and independent man."

Curling my arms around his neck, I stuck out my lower lip. "My poor baby. I guess my breathing didn't give me away that time, huh?"

In one quick motion, I was on the floor, my arms and legs pinned as he hovered above me. "What you gonna' do now, you little badass?"

"On *you*?" I chewed my lip. "I can think of a few things that'd disable you pretty quickly."

"I'm serious," he said softly, his face changing from playful to concerned as he loosened the grip on my wrists to run his thumbs over them. "This is how... how he did it?"

Understanding what he meant, my mood changed too, and I nodded.

"Fight me off."

Swallowing the knot that threatened to hitch my breath, I met his eyes. "Show me how."

"I should've shown you how a long time ago," he laid a kiss on my forehead. "We'll do it slow a few times until you get it, okay? And starting tomorrow, you're going to work out with me first thing so you have the strength to do this for real if you ever need to. Got it?"

"Got it." I would deal with strength training so long as it meant I wouldn't be this helpless anymore. As soon as he'd said the words, I remembered being in the same position beneath Phil, and I would not let anyone disable me the way he had.

"The first part includes three moves that you'll need to be able to do at the same time. You buck your hips as hard as you can upward and forward. The goal there is to launch my body toward your face. At the same time, you slide your arms hard and fast—don't lift them—but sweep them out and down toward your hips kinda' like you were making a snow angel. It's not natural movement for me given my trajectory, and it should force me to let go of your wrists to save myself from face planting. Lastly, you turn your face to one side to prevent my body from landing on top of it. Got it?"

"I think so."

"We'll go slow a few times. Let you get used to the motion until it's second nature to do the three at the same time."

Not being coordinated, it took more than *a few* times for me to grasp the series of motions, but I eventually got the hang of it. I immediately understood why I needed the strength training. Just that little bit of effort made my thighs burn.

"Alright," he said, repositioning his hands over my wrists. "Now, for the second set. It's important you don't stall in any way. I could recover quickly from the first move and be on alert for it a second time. You only get one shot to catch me off guard."

I nodded.

"This time, when my hips come off yours and your wrists are free, I want you to immediately hug my midsection, tucking your face tightly against my ribs. This will keep me trapped in the position with my hands on the ground behind your head. If I move them, I'll fall over, and my initial instinct will be to stay upright. Try that."

We did the motion. I bucked him forward, slid my arms down, and raised up to clasp my arms tightly around his midsection. Indeed, he was trapped, and I was in control. Suddenly I felt excited, enough so that I was actually looking forward to working out the next morning.

"From there," he said, "use your arms to climb up for better leverage, hook your arm under one of mine, and roll. When you hook the arm, you'll throw off my balance, and even though I'm bigger, you'll be able to roll on top of me with ease."

This move proved more difficult, but after several more attempts than it should've taken, I mastered it. Straddling him and out of breath after doing it for the twentieth time, I grinned. "Now what?"

"The jaw. Drive your elbow or your palm up into the jaw with everything you got, then get up and run while I'm disoriented.

We'll work on the proper way to do that tomorrow. I do believe you've worn me out tonight."

I wiggled happily against him. "Where'd you learn this?"

He brushed the hair from my face. "I told you my mother had me in a million classes when I was a kid. Jiu jitsu was one of the ones I actually enjoyed. Although…" He slid his hands down my sides to still my hips. "I think I enjoy it much more now."

I bent forward to lay a grateful kiss against his lips. "Can we do it one more time?"

Scanning my face, he nodded, smoothing his thumb over my cheek. "We can do it as many times as you need to in order to feel confident."

"Thank you," I said as he slowly rolled us back into the starting position. "I know it's just one move, but… you have no idea how much stronger I feel because of it."

"I'll never let you—

"Christ almighty," Jim spat, leaning against the door frame. "Cain't leave you two alone for two minutes without ye' gettin' tangled up and batter dipping the corn dog. Have ye' no shame? The dang babies are watching!"

I giggled. "It's not what it looks like this time. Jack's teaching me jiu jitsu."

"S'at what ye' callin' it now?" He muttered, making his way into the room to plop down on the sofa and toe off his boots.

"Ooh, fun," Lilly clapped, kneeling at the side of us. "I took a self-defense class in New York. Is this the trap and roll?"

"It is," Jack said, a hint of surprise in his voice as he observed her. "You know how to do it?"

"Oh yeah," she winked. "And then some. There was a little while there where I almost wanted someone to attack me just so I could use my super deadly skills.

I chuckled. "I think I'd like to see that!"

"I'll show you!" She patted the ground beside her. "Jimmy, come here and pin me down."

Jim tilted his head to one side. "What the hell was in that fish? Have ye' all lost your damn minds?" He motioned to Izzy. "There's children present!"

Jack rolled off me and I sat up beside him, watching as Lilly scowled at her soon-to-be husband. "I want to show Lainey my jiu jitsu move. Come over here right now and pin me down!"

Exhaling heavily, he rolled his eyes and joined us on the floor. "Ye' know," he complained as she laid down. "Every day yuns are stuck here, you get more looney than the day before." He crawled over her. "Now what?"

"Pin me! Hold my wrists down like you're gonna' attack me."

He twisted his lips to one side. "You gonna' hurt my nutsack in some way if I do this? It won't bode well for your plans to have *four* children if you do."

"I'm not gonna touch your nuts, you big chicken! Just do it."

Jim looked at me. "You remember earlier when I said that thing we did was the stupidest thing I ever done? I'm 'bout to outdo myself."

The moment he pinned her wrists, she executed the move perfectly, completely catching him off guard as she bucked, grabbed, and rolled him onto his back, ending with a different motion that left her forearm firmly pressed against his throat while both his arms were pinned beneath her legs.

I looked over at Jack and laughed. "Maybe I should've asked Lilly to teach me to fight."

She grinned, releasing her hold on Jim. "If you two are going to be practicing fighting, I want in." She stuck her tongue out at Jim. "And maybe you should too. You're slower than a month of Sundays."

He laughed at the southern idiom, attempting to get up and finding himself pinned once again. "Ye' know, I always knew I was gonna' marry a woman that could beat my ass. Ye' shoulda' showed me this sooner. We gonna' have some fun now."

Chapter Fifty Three

Chris

Las Vegas had been a disaster. So had the almost five-hour drive that followed. Maria, looking miniature in the driver's seat of his father's 1-ton pickup, refused to speak to him, despite his relentless attempts to strike up conversation. At one point, she'd connected her phone to the truck's bluetooth speaker and made a call, speaking exclusively in Spanish with a woman on the other end, both of them howling with laughter for nearly an hour of the trip.

When he'd asked who she'd been talking to, she simply said "my friend," and those were the only two words she spoke to him.

He'd cursed himself for not taking Spanish in school. Throughout her conversation, she'd glance at him mid-sentence and the deeper voice on the other end of the phone would burst into uncontrollable laughter. He knew she'd been mocking him, but he deserved every second of it.

The tension between them was momentarily forgotten when they'd pulled into the drive of Bud's Santa Monica home.

Tucked into the rolling hills and surrounded by lush green trees, the house was an architectural marvel of windows and wood; all of it built as if it had grown up out of the landscape instead of erected atop it.

The interior was like something out of a movie. Floor to ceiling windows lined every room of the house, interweaved with gorgeous sandstone and rich wood bead-board ceilings. The lighting and decor was put together in such a way, he couldn't help feeling instantly at peace the moment he'd stepped foot inside.

Maria, too, had relaxed the shoulders that had been otherwise stiff since he'd woken up without memory of his actions, and although she remained silent, she didn't shy away from exploring the house alongside him.

On the main floor, they perused through a large kitchen, living room, and a sunroom with wood slated doors that opened on three sides and overlooked an infinity pool. Down the hall, they passed through a guest bedroom that was the size of an entire house, and a bathroom-sauna combo that would've made her drool if she wasn't working so hard to give him the silent treatment.

Upstairs, they found three more bedrooms, each with floor to ceiling windows and sliding doors that led out to an immaculately decorated balcony that served as the roof to the larger first floor.

The whole home overlooked the hillside, the sunset pink and purple where it was visible over the ocean through the leaves of the trees.

For the two weeks that followed, he made every attempt to please her, determined to set things right with such a romantic backdrop surrounding them in which to do it. In the mornings, he'd venture down to the kitchen and, once he figured out how to use it, he'd make her a latte in Bud's absolutely glorious built-in machine. He would bring it up to her in bed and then massage and kiss her feet as promised while she silently sipped it.

When she showered, he warmed her robe in the dryer. When she was dressed, he cooked her breakfast. When she then curled up daily with a laptop to check on Melissa's Instagram or look into Izzy's family, he rubbed her shoulders.

He'd underestimated Maria's ability to hold a grudge. She was stubborn and unrelenting; speaking little more than a few words to him each day. More often than not, those words were, *'it's time to take your pills.'*

But Maria wasn't a silent person. She loved to talk, and she did plenty of it with the woman she'd called from the truck. Every day, sometimes several times a day, she'd have the phone pressed to her ear, swaggering through the house speaking Spanish and roaring with laughter while she tidied rooms that were spotless.

He'd gone to see Bud's friend, Dr. Evans, dropping Maria off to shop on his way, and the doctor had assured him his injury was healing nicely. He'd adjusted his medications, eliminating the narcotic and suggesting Tylenol for breakthrough pain. The new mixture was much more tolerable, and he felt almost fully himself after only a few days of taking them.

He'd spoken to Bud that morning and was delighted to hear he'd sent a friend to Irvine to bump into Anna's sister, Melissa, and while she didn't have specifics as to Anna's ex-husband's involvement, she'd learned that Liam was living with Melissa as her adopted son.

He was even more delighted to learn that Bud would be joining them in two days with the bulk of his research. He was excited to have someone else to talk to—someone that would actually talk back. They were getting close to their September departure date, and with Bud in the house, they could actually discuss their plans without feeling wary about who might be listening in.

"Oye, my friend is coming to visit today," Maria informed him, sliding around him at the kitchen island to make her third latte of the day.

"Are you going to tell me this mysterious friend's name?"

Pressing a button, the milk frother hissed loudly as she turned back to him with a smirk. "No."

"Oh, come on, Maria, can we please stop this now? I've apologized a thousand times. I've done everything I can do to get you to forgive me. Tell me what to do so we can move past this."

She turned back to the machine, moving her cup to the double spouts that would pour out espresso once the built-in grinder prepared the beans. "What, you think you can just rip my heart out of my chest and then say a few nice words or make me breakfast for a few days and I'll just forgive you? Like it wasn't the worst day of my life? No. That is not how it works."

"Then tell me how it works," he pleaded, moving behind her to curl his arms around her waist. "I miss you. And every day that you ignore me is the worst day of *my* life."

For a fleeting moment, she laid her head back against his shoulder, but, thinking better of it, she shrugged him off. "No. I am not done being mad at you. You have no idea what I went through in Las Vegas and I don't care if my pain is making you have a bad day. Go away."

Not to be deterred so easily, he squeezed her tighter, kissing her shoulder where her shirt had slid off it. "In every single relationship I've ever had, I always prided myself on saying the right things—doing the right things… well, most of the time, anyway. My mother always joked that I was born a romantic. But with you, I can't seem to do anything right. I'm always screwing up. And you're the single person I don't want to screw up for."

Again she shrugged him off and he let go, hovering close as she removed her cup and spooned sugar into it. "I don't want you to say and do all the right things, estúpido. Nobody wants a man that tries so hard to be perfect. Honestly, it's exhausting watching you try to be this person you think I want."

"Then tell me what you want."

She rolled her eyes, turning toward him as she sipped her latte. "You really are this stupid, eh? You think I fell in love with some perfect man? You think that moody person who told me exactly how much I annoyed him, put me in my place when I was being an asshole, and made every mistake possible while we were traveling with Captain Cook was perfect? That man was honest. That man didn't spend every second of the day trying to be something he wasn't, or second guessing everything he did, or apologizing round the clock for feelings he had no control over. He owned what he was. That's the man I love. That's who I want. Not this…" she waved a hand in the air to cover the expanse of him. "…whatever the hell this is."

He closed the gap between them, pinning her to the counter as he pulled the coffee mug from her hands. "Fine, you want honesty?" He set the cup on the counter. "I'm done with this." He wound his fingers into her hair, not giving her the opportunity to mouth off again before he covered her lips with his own.

He owned what he was, prying her lips apart and tasting the sweetened coffee that still lingered on her tongue. She tilted her head to him, inviting him for more as a soft moan escaped her. He pressed into her, showing her just how much he'd missed her as he reacquainted their mouths, his hands roaming rampant over her arms, hips, face, and hair. Pulling only his lips away, he breathed, "forgive me."

It wasn't a question.

Before she could respond, the intercom buzzed to indicate someone was at the front gate. She began to push him away, but he held her there.

"Forgive me."

While it didn't reach her lips, there was definitely a smile in her eyes. "I'll consider it," she said smartly, placing both hands on his chest and pushing again. "Now go away. My friend is here."

She hurried off to the living room, leaving him alone in the kitchen, taking efforts to settle the excitement the kiss had incited. Moments later, he heard their warm Spanish greeting at the front door, words spoken entirely too fast to attempt to decipher and long drawn out sighs as they undoubtedly embraced each other.

"¿Quieres café con leche?" Maria asked, their footsteps moving toward the kitchen.

"Sí," the lower female voice responded, followed by a faster cascade of words that he assumed, by the tone, was an exhausted account of her travels.

He spun toward the coffee machine and began to make a cup for Maria's guest; he knew very little Spanish, but he knew café con leche meant a fancy latte from Bud's machine.

Their chatter filled the kitchen as they took their seats at the table. Not turning toward them, he waited until the coffee was done, giving them time to continue whatever conversation they'd immediately dived into, and simply asked, "you want sugar?"

"Dios mío, María," the woman reprimanded. "You poor man. She still hasn't forgiven you? You know, she never will if you keep kissing her ass."

He turned then, nearly dropping the coffee mug as he took in her face. She had dark hair and olive skin, but the eyes, nose, and the way—

He did drop the mug then, the coffee splashing all over his legs as the mug shattered against the tile. Clasped around the woman's neck was the very same necklace he'd given Alaina five years ago, and he couldn't move, couldn't breathe... couldn't take his eyes off the face that looked so much like the woman he'd given it to.

"Oh my God," Maria hissed, jumping out of her seat to grab a towel from the sink. "What's gotten into you?"

The woman hurried to kneel beside Maria, carefully collecting the remnants of the shattered mug. All the while, he gaped at her.

Standing with a handful of porcelain shards cupped in her hands, she smiled at him. "I'm sorry. Maria has no manners. I am Dahlia. It's so nice to finally meet you."

"Dahlia?" He echoed, barely able to move his lips as she turned to deposit the broken mug into the trash can. "As in—

Dahlia spun around quickly and pressed a finger to her lips, her eyes a warning to say no more. "You know, I have never been to a California beach before. I see it is just down the hill from here. Maybe we could go for a walk? After being so long on an airplane and in the car, I could use some fresh air."

She moved her hands to mimic a pen writing on paper, her eyes urging them both to remain quiet.

"Oh yes," Maria countered, digging through the kitchen drawers until she was able to produce a small yellow notepad and pen. "We have been here for weeks now and Kreese has never taken me down there."

"No wonder she is still angry with you," Dahlia said, bending over the notepad to scribble the words: *'Agent parked in a van down the hill. Don't talk in here.'*

He was definitely being creepy, but he couldn't help it. He stared at Dahlia all the way to the beach as she recounted how Maria had contacted her and an immediate friendship had blossomed. She laughed as she explained how she'd immediately felt connected to her and couldn't wait to fly out to visit them.

Once they'd removed their shoes and were out of distance of spying ears, she shifted her tone. "When I was a teenager, despite my stepfather warning me not to, I made the mistake of telling my school counselor about what happened on the ocean that day. I was put in an institution; told I was delusional. It took my stepfather months to get me back home." She met Chris's eyes. "Maria told me you considered telling the detectives the truth. I'm warning you that if you do, they will do the same to you, or worse."

"You two talked about this? *Over the phone?*"

"Mi amore," Maria laughed, "If we would not talk in the house, we certainly weren't going to talk about this over the phone. Dahlia lives in Chicago. We met there while you were in the hospital."

"Why didn't you tell me?" He asked, crossing his arms over his chest.

Maria raised an eyebrow. "I was going to, but then you pissed me off... So... surprise, I found Dahlia."

Dahlia snickered, deciding upon a place in the sand and motioning for them to take a seat. "You two can rip each other's throats out later... First, I will tell you everything you want to know about what happened to us, then I want you to tell me everything about what you saw on the other side."

Chris nodded, digging his heels into the damp sand as he waited for her to begin.

"My father was a bad man. I didn't learn this until I was older, but I always had a feeling there was something wrong. We lived too well in comparison to the other children in Columbia, and people did not look him in the eyes when they spoke to him. Even as a small child, I knew this was not natural." She gazed out at the ocean.

"He was a drug lord, and his crimes cost him greatly. When he got caught, he flew me, my mother, my cousin, my uncle, and my two brothers out on a private jet to Kauai. We thought we were on vacation. It was beautiful. We hiked and swam and saw the most gorgeous waterfalls. But then my stepfather showed up. He was a DEA agent and had fallen in love with my mother while undercover. My father had beat her and he came to take us all away from him. My father had other plans. He didn't care who might be too close when he pulled out his gun and started shooting. My mother got caught in the crossfire and was killed right in front of us. Her death and my stepfather's bullet wound were all that was needed to call in reinforcements. My father and uncle loaded us onto his yacht and fled. The DEA followed. For days... Until that night."

She shuddered. "I was terrified. Devastated about seeing my mother killed. I could not sleep or eat or speak. My uncle held me and my cousin on a sofa on the back deck, trying to rock us to sleep and get us to stop crying. My father had taken my brothers to the control room to try to get my oldest brother to calm down separately. He'd seen her die too, and he loved her the most—even though she wasn't his real mother."

"Anyway, we were going so fast... and I remember the lightning hitting us all of a sudden. It came out of nowhere and it covered us, the ocean rising with it in a swirling tunnel of light. I was being pulled with it—the whole seventy foot yacht was being pulled upward into it, and I remember it rising off the water. It was my uncle that saved me. He jumped off the boat with me and my cousin still in his arms. We went from light to darkness, and I watched the whole thing get sucked up into that spinning light and disappear across the sky."

Maria frowned. "So it would've taken you too if he hadn't jumped off?"

"Sí. It was pulling us all. But when we landed in the water, the light was above us. It happened so fast… almost less than a second, but I remember it all in slow motion. And then my stepfather was there, pulling us into his boat. He'd seen it too…"

"You keep saying stepfather," Chris said. "Did your mother divorce your father?"

She shook her head. "No. I call him that because it's what he would've been if she had lived. He raised me afterward."

"Let me guess," Maria leaned back on her hands. "His name is Richard Albrecht?"

Dahlia nodded slowly. "Yes. How did you know that?"

"There are some things we should probably tell you now," Maria said, ignoring Chris's warning gaze that should've stopped her from saying more. "We met your father and your brothers on the other side."

"They're alive then?" The ghost of a smile washed over Dahlia's features—one that closely resembled Alaina's. "I knew it! The first time you reached out to me and I realized you were one of the survivors, I knew you had seen them; that you had lived to come back through that lightning. Everyone said I was crazy all these years, but I knew, deep down, I could feel them still. Tell me about them—about my brothers."

Maria, leaving out only the details of Richard Albrecht's ancestry and Juan Josef's plans to murder him, gave a detailed account of their experiences with Juan Josef and his two sons. She painted Dario and Juan Jr. as perfect gentlemen, refraining from mentioning their knowledge of their father's torturous treatment of them and their involvement in taking them captive.

Trusting Dahlia entirely with their secrets, she explained time travel, their encounters with Cook and the islands, and she even told her about Alaina and what the necklace really was.

Dahlia was beaming by the time Maria had finished answering all her questions.

Chris rubbed his jaw where he'd held it clenched the entire time. He had no intention of giving away so much, and yet, Maria had trusted Dahlia enough to offer it freely. Maria didn't trust anyone so easily, and he supposed, if she had that much faith Dahlia wouldn't use the information against them, he should too. Straightening his back, he turned his attention to their new ally. "We thought that only a certain number could go through... there's only ever been us, your family, and a man whose journals we found to serve as evidence of anyone going through. In the two instances where they went in September, only three crossed over; in your case, you and your uncle and cousin were left behind. In another case, nearly twenty men were left. I'd hoped you could shed light on your experience. Do you think it would've taken you had you not jumped? If so, that throws our whole theory of three out."

Dahlia nodded. "Oh yes. It was taking us, too. I could feel it. But it happened so fast, like the blink of an eye. The storm that took the boat disappeared into thin air, leaving us all there trying to figure out what we'd just watched happen. Maybe that's why some get left behind... Maybe it only takes whoever it can hit in that split second it shows up. Our boat was going fast, and it was like the trajectory of it was catching up as the lightning moved with us. Your plane too was moving faster than a 1920s boat could move... maybe that's why so many were taken with you?"

He twisted his lips as he considered it. He was no physicist, but there might be something behind the speed of the plane or yacht and the lightning... he felt their original hypothesis crumbling.

"And you're going to go back for your friends?" She asked. "Is that why you wanted to ask me about what happened? To see if it's possible for them all to come back through?"

"Sí," Maria said. "There are children with them and we are afraid to be separated."

"And you will go next month? In September?"

Maria nodded. "We hope so. Assuming we can avoid the detectives for a few more weeks."

Dahlia sighed. "I can help you. I could talk to my stepfather. Even though he retired, he is still connected to those agencies. I could see if he could get them to stall the investigation for a few weeks."

"No," Chris insisted. "We've already said too much in telling you. Telling anyone else anything might put us even further in the spotlight. We only have a few weeks to get through before we can get on the water."

"The detectives do not know me… if they have heard Maria and I talking on the phone, they will think we are long-time friends. They will not be watching me as closely as they watch you. I could hang around, tell you who is where. Warn you if I am approached and tell you what kind of questions they ask me."

Maria smiled. "We could use the help, eh superman? We didn't know about the van down the street. It's a good thing I am not talking to you, otherwise they would've known precisely when we were planning to leave and where we were planning on going. Did you get a look at who was in the van?"

Dahlia hid a smile. "Of course I did, mi amiga."

"Was one of them a giant bald black man?"

"No, I only saw a woman with blond hair."

Chris frowned. Detective Morris didn't have blond hair. He wondered if she, too, was staked out somewhere else. Perhaps listening just outside of Bud's condo in New York? And was Haywood in the van or with Detective Morris?

Blowing out the breath he'd been holding, he frowned. "Why are you so willing to help us?"

Dahlia curled an arm around Maria's shoulders, grinning. "When I met Maria in Chicago, I loved her instantly. We joked and gossiped for hours over lunch. But I had seen her face on the news and I knew all about the missing flight 89. I knew it was no coincidence she sought me out. And when I asked her directly if she knew about the storm, she answered me honestly. And when I asked her if she would take me with you if you ever returned to it, she promised she would."

Chapter Fifty Four

"I hate you," Lilly said through gritted teeth as she held herself in the same plank position I was attempting to remain in.

Jack chuckled as he paced around us on the deck. "You two are the ones that wanted to train. *Isn't that right, baby girl?*"

"Stop using the baby voice with her," I reprimanded, eyeing him where he bounced Cecelia happily against his shoulder while Lilly and I trembled in a plank that felt like it would never end. "You're supposed to talk to them in a normal voice. The baby talk throws them off."

"Red, I have been talking to babies in this voice my whole life. Not a single one of them came out damaged as a result of it. Straighten your legs. Both of you."

"I really, *really* hate him," Lilly noted under her breath, her arms shaking violently beneath her reddened face.

She said that every day.

We'd immediately gone to work strength training in the early mornings with Jack after our first night trying out self-defense moves. For an hour each day, we suffered through push-ups, sit-ups, planks, lunges, squats, and, my least favorite, lifting bags of flour or buckets of water until our arms were liquified.

Unlike squeezing a workout in during the 21st century, there was no plopping down on a sofa with a bag of chips as a reward when we were through. Instead, we maintained our usual daily workload of fishing, gathering fruit and water, mending the ship, or helping care for the livestock. When we weren't doing those things, we were catering to Lilly's increasingly over-the-top wedding plans.

In a few days, the wedding would take place, and none of us could wait for it to be over. The beach we looked out at from the ship's deck had been transformed into a monument to Lillian Renaud... and we were all exhausted from building it.

The idea of an arbor was one we all thought would be as simple as a few lashed pieces of bamboo. We were wrong. Lilly's "arbor" was a pergola. Four tall and thick bamboo posts supported a truss of bamboo beams, from which draped white and pink fabric curtains.

Lilly wanted pink—*blush* pink. And since we didn't have pink fabric, we created it through hours and hours of dipping white into boiling hot water and guava until the cloth came out the right shade. The entire massive structure was then draped with the fabric and framed with the island flowers.

An aisle made of white fabric, the same from my own wedding, led down the beach, flanked on each side by dining room chairs—also decorated with pink and white drapery and bouquets of flowers.

"Downward dog," Jack commanded, pulling me from my thoughts and back to the blistering heat of the morning.

Lilly groaned beside me as she pushed back onto her straightened legs.

I wondered if Jack wasn't being a bit extreme with his training methods partially as payback for Lilly's much more extreme wedding demands. He'd practically built the pergola himself and complained just as frequently as she did during our workouts.

"I thought we were going to practice fight moves," she grunted, walking her hands back a little. "I only signed up for this so I could kick your ass."

"I'll show you how to kick my ass soon enough," Jack mused, "but only once you two are in shape enough to be able to make it through the added hour I intend to tack on in the mornings to run through the moves... Plank."

"If I kill him," she whispered, teetering awkwardly down into plank, "would you really miss him that much?"

I focused on my breathing, which was difficult when she made me laugh so frequently, and I managed to hold the plank with less shaking this time. "Probably."

Unlike Lilly, who just wanted to punch people and look good in her wedding dress, I *wanted* the extra hour. I wanted the muscles I could already feel developing throughout my body; the strength to stand my own ground and be able to fight back if ever I needed to. I enjoyed the burn in my arms, abs, and legs, and couldn't wait to learn more.

"Alright, lower down," Jack winked at me as he sniffed Cecelia's diaper and winced. "That's enough for today. Go ahead and do your cool down stretches while I take care of this."

"I'll take her," Magna said, rising up from the bistro table where she and Fetia would always watch our torture.

"Oh, good." Lilly grinned, sitting up to bend over her outstretched leg. "I wanted to talk to you, Jackie."

"Nope," Jack said, handing Cecelia off and leaning against the table to check on Zachary where he was growling happily at the wooden rattle Jim had carved him, his little fist wound tightly around its handle. "You can call me just about anything but that."

Lilly pouted. "Fine. Jimmy and I have been talking, and since the wedding is only a few days away, we want to have a little joint bachelorette-bachelor party tonight. We could all use a night to cut loose after all the hard work we've been doing. And since we don't have strippers or dance clubs, *I* was thinking we could have a little drunken talent show. You could all be our entertainment. It'll be fun and Kyle already volunteered to stand guard tonight. What do you think?"

He crossed his ankles and smirked. "You want to know what I think about the idea of a drunken talent show for your amusement?"

She nodded innocently.

"I *think* we still haven't figured out who put that knife in our bed the last time we cut loose, and I *think* the last thing I could possibly be interested in doing as a means to cut loose would be to put on a talent show for you, Princess."

"Oh, come on Jackie," she hid a laugh, "Kyle and Michael will keep a close watch for any threats and I was planning to get Juan Jr. and Dario more liquored up than all of us with some old school drinking games. It could be a good test to see if they let anything slip. Besides, I was hoping you might do a bit of... ballet, perhaps."

I punched her shoulder, cringing at the glare he then delivered me.

"You can do whatever you'd like," he said coolly, "but count me out of your drunken shenanigans. And you," he focused his narrowed eyes on me, "you're doing three extra sets of squats and curls tomorrow."

My mouth dropping open in fake outrage, I dramatically drew in a breath. "How dare you use my own workouts as punishment?"

He lifted an eyebrow. "Oh, that's not the only punishment I intend to deliver."

"Gross," Lilly snorted, reaching for the foot on her opposite leg. "Tell you what, Jack, I'll do three extra sets of squats and curls with her and I won't complain even once if you contribute one small thing to my talent show."

"Do you have any idea how cheesy it is to want to throw a talent show? That's the best you could come up with for a joint bachelor party? We're not twelve-year-olds."

She sat up, curling her legs in to press her heels together. "A *drunken* talent show, Jack. Keyword: drunken. And I don't want just any talent. I want super secret hidden talents on display when we're all too wasted to do them."

"How is that fun for anyone but you?" He asked, crossing his arms over his chest.

"Aren't you curious what Alaina's secret hidden talent might be?"

He winked. "I already know *all* about her hidden talents."

"Do you?" I countered, tilting my head to one side. "I might argue that there are a few you have yet to witness."

"Is that so?"

Lifting my chin proudly, I smirked. "I guess you'll never know if you don't take part."

"Jim will hate this idea, you know that. The last thing he'd want for a bachelor party is some cheesy talent show…"

"You don't know Jimmy the way I do," she grinned. "He's going to love it."

Jack was a pushover. At least, he was when it came to Jim. After dinner and once Fetia and Magna had taken all three children down and put them to bed, Jim had talked Jack into joining us all in the dining room to kick off Lilly's *shenanigans*.

Lilly was a fan of drinking games—namely beer pong—and was desperate to play it at her bachelorette party. With a shortage of ping-pong balls available in the 18th century, she'd instead picked several small and unripened guava sprouts, all of them the perfect size for tossing into tankards of ale.

"So," she explained to Dario, standing at one side of the dining room table, "the object of the game is simple. You and your partner each get a throw. If your ball makes it into one of their cups, they have to drink the contents of the cup. Same going this way. For each cup they drink, they remove it from the table. If you clear their side before they clear yours, then they have to drink whatever's left on your end of the table as well. Make sense?"

Juan Jr. chuckled. "Aye, the object is to get pissed quick. We've got it."

"Good," she flashed her teeth. "You're up first against Jack and Jimmy." She grinned as she joined Jack, Bruce, and I where we stood at the halfway point of the table. "You'd better be good Jackie."

"Don't call me Jackie," he grumbled, making his way to the opposite end of the table beside Jim. "And this isn't my first rodeo, sweetheart."

It was, however, Dario and Juan Jr.'s. Their first throw yielded no results, both of them overthrowing their targets and cursing each other.

Jim closed one eye as he aimed his little green ball. "Oh, y'all are in trouble if that's the best ye' got!" He tossed and a delightful *'plop'* resounded from one of the tankards on the opposite side. Jack successfully sank his as well, and we all laughed as Juan Jr. and Dario chugged their drinks.

"It's fun, right?" Lilly encouraged them.

"Indeed," Juan Jr. breathed when he lowered his mug, wiping his mouth with the back of his arm as he focused on properly aiming the ball for the second round. Face sharp with intense determination, Juan Jr. likely wasn't accustomed to losing. He caught on quickly and his ball sank in the frontmost tankard.

By the end of the first game, my cheeks were on fire and my stomach ached from laughing. Jim, a natural trash-talker, had not held anything back. Juan Jr. and Dario, as the game progressed and their side of the table grew several cups emptier, had adopted a few of the modern day sayings. Dario couldn't stop himself from shouting *'in your face'* in his perfectly proper English nearly every time his ball made it into a target.

Jack and Jim won, but just barely. Juan Jr. insisted on a rematch, and Lilly and I welcomed it, both of us secretly wanting to see the foursome sloppy drunk when it came time to show off their talents. She, Bruce, and I sipped our ale while we observed from the halfway point.

Three games later, the lot of them—*and us*—were sufficiently *'pissed.'* Jim had an arm curled tightly around Jack's neck, raising his tankard high. "My single days is just about done gentlemen. I will be a rooster no more!"

"A rooster?" Dario laughed, holding himself up with a hand on the table to prevent him from sinking on his bent legs.

"Ye' know. Rooster one day, a feather duster the next," Jim explained, finishing off the ale in his mug and closing one eye to inspect it for any lasting drops. "Whatcha' wanna do now, Princess?"

Lilly giggled. "Well, that's my surprise, Jimmy. I've planned a drunken talent show on the deck. Everybody has to show off one hidden talent."

Jim groaned. "That sounds just God awful. Let's go skinny dippin' instead."

Jack nodded in agreement, his eyes glossed over already.

"Come on, Jimmy," she pouted, "this'll be fun. Trust me. If it's not, we'll abandon it and go skinny dipping, I promise."

Rolling his head back on his shoulders, he let out a long exhale. "Fine. Is there whiskey up there?"

"Of course!" She assured him. "Let's go!"

"I'll meet you up there," Bruce said between us. "I wanna go check on everyone first. Make sure nothing is amiss. I'll check on the babies, too."

"Thank you," I said softly while Lilly ushered us out of the dining room. "Have you got a secret talent to show off?"

He grinned. "You'll see."

On the top deck, the men immediately rushed to the bistro table where the bottles of whiskey and wine were waiting. They each poured themselves glasses while I took in Lilly's craftsmanship.

She'd scattered pillows on the deck for seats and, using one of the lower masts, she'd draped fabric in the style of a curtain as a stage in front of them. She'd then lined lanterns in a row to create more stage-like lighting. I admired her enthusiasm. Lilly didn't do anything small… Even if this was to be a disaster.

She hurried to the gramophone and wound its handle, placing a Sam Cooke record on its surface. Dancing back to where I'd taken a seat on the pillows with a bottle of wine, she grinned happily. "Lainey, this is going to be amazing."

I raised a doubtful eyebrow, peering past her to where Jack, Jim, Juan, and Dario were gulping whiskey and avoiding looking in our direction. "I don't know, Lill. They don't look like they're up for showing off their hidden skills."

"Oh, they will be… It's a bachelor party after all…" She took the wine bottle from me and sipped heavily from it. "Jimmy, baby, come here. You wanna know what I'll give you if you go first?"

"What's that, Sugar?" He asked fondly, swaggering over to the pillows to kneel down clumsily in front of her.

She leaned in and whispered something apparently filthy in his ear, prompting an immature sounding giggle to escape him. "You swear?"

She nodded. "Mmhmm."

"Alright, hang on," he kissed her quickly. "I gotta go get somethin.'"

Abandoning his whiskey on the floorboards beside us, he rushed to the stairwell and disappeared.

Jack, Juan Jr., and Dario, the whiskey bottles in hand, made their way to the pillows and got comfortable while we waited.

"Is this what you do in the future?" Dario hiccuped. "Get pigeon-eyed and make fools of yourselves?"

Jack suppressed a burp. "Pretty much."

"I love it," Dario added, bursting into laughter.

Jim, panting, returned at the edge of the stairwell, gripping the railing tightly while he caught his breath. "Alright. Get ready to have your minds blown." He pointed at Lilly and blew a kiss as he straightened.

Making his way to the stage, he shuffled the cards he'd retrieved from the dining room. "You swore," he reminded Lilly. "I'm gonna' hold you to that. Hoss, think of a card."

Jack hiccuped. "Done."

"Ye' sure? You know the exact card you're thinkin' of? Can ye' see it in your mind?"

"Yep. I go-ot it."

Jim grinned, shuffling the cards again. He cut the deck, pulling it up to show the eight of diamonds. "Behold. Your card."

Jack frowned. "That's not my card."

"It ain't?" Jim asked, still holding it up.

"Nope."

Jim pursed his lips and looked down at the cards. He let the eight of diamonds fall, exposing the jack of clubs. "How 'bout now?"

Jack snickered. "Nope."

Jim sighed, letting the jack fall to show the three of hearts. "This one?"

Jack bent over with laughter. "Do you even know this card trick, or are you just going to show me cards until you get it right?"

Jim smiled. "Never done a card trick in my life."

Lilly laughed loudly. "Ladies and gentlemen, the great Jim Jackson!"

He bowed dramatically, folding one arm against his stomach as the other flowed outward and we all cheered loudly.

"See," Lilly drawled, leaning into me. "I told you this would be awesome."

"You was supposed to go with the first one ye' summbitch," Jim sneered in Jack's direction, collapsing onto the pillows beside Lilly. "Some best man you turned out to be!"

Lilly smacked his arm.

"I never said I'd do it good, I just said I'd go first. Ay precious, you're up."

Dario shook his head. "Why me?"

Jim laid back against Lilly's lap, balancing his whiskey glass on his stomach. "Cause it's my bachelor party, and I said so. Go on. Entertain us with your talents."

Dario rolled his eyes. "So I just go up there and make an ass out of myself like you did?"

"Ooh," Jack howled. "Look who bites back!"

Dario laughed to himself as he made his way to the stage.

Jim sat up and leaned into me. "Bet ye' he sings."

I chuckled. "What makes you think he's going to sing?"

He shrugged. "Just got a feelin' is all... I bet if we had some Diana Ross or Donna Summer, he'd be all over that."

"Dario's not gay," I assured him. "And that's a very narrow-minded stereotype."

"Woman, that boy's gay as your aunt Edna's Easter bonnet. I ain't sayin' there's somethin' wrong with it. I'm just statin' the truth."

I watched as Dario took the stage, shaking my head. "Nu Uh."

"Yeah huh," he grinned, then shouted out, "Come on, precious, show us what ye' got."

On the stage, Dario pulled off his shirt, revealing a surprisingly sculpted upper body. Gay or not, he was lovely to look at. Lilly apparently agreed as she cupped her hands over her mouth and cat-called, "*Hello* Dario! Ow! Ow!"

The forgotten fiancé beside her merely snarled.

Dario blew Lilly a kiss the same way Jim had, then immediately pinwheeled into a handstand.

"Well, I coulda' did that!" Jim heckled. "You didn't tell me cartwheels counted as talent."

In response, Dario slowly spread his legs into a V and, in an impressive show of strength, raised one hand off the floor.

"Damn!" Lilly shouted, clapping. "Bet you can't do that, smart-ass!"

Dario held the one-handed stand steady for far longer than should've been humanly possible for how much they'd drank during beer pong, then swung his legs over, stood and bowed.

We all clapped and cheered loudly.

Jim took a swig of his whiskey as Dario pulled his shirt back on and joined us. "Ye' know, there'd be no question about who's the most gifted if we woulda' just gone skinny dippin' like I said!" He laid back down against Lilly's lap.

Dario gave Jim a wicked smile. "You sure about that?"

"Who's next?" Lilly asked, effectively neutralizing the pissing contest that could've gone on for hours.

"I am," Bruce called from the stairwell. "And Jimmy, this one's for the rooster, baby."

The deck ignited with screaming laughter as Bruce emerged from the shadows, a grass skirt around his waist and two coconuts affixed to his chest, his large belly exposed and jiggling beneath them. He wore a floral tiara around the crown of his head and, with his arms flowing at his sides, did his very best impression of a belly dance to the tune of *'Twistin' the night away.'*

He flowed hilariously through hip movements as the song progressed, coming close to spread his arms and shake his coconuts in Jim's direction before wiggling back to the stairwell and disappearing into the shadows.

"Christ Almighty," Jim panted between laughter, wiping tears from both eyes. "I done seen it all now."

The drinks continued to flow late into the night. I juggled—for a moment. Lilly did a backflip. Juan Jr. did a *real* card trick, and Jack hoped none of us would notice he hadn't taken the stage as longer gaps grew between performances to allow for conversation.

But even when he was cutting loose, Jack was working. Without hesitation, he took an opening in the casual dialogue around us while Juan Jr. had ventured off to relieve his bladder. "Who do *you* think put that knife in our bed?"

Dario, eyes nearly closed and tipping over, responded, "Probably my father."

"You think he got out of his room?"

Dario hiccuped loudly. "He built the ship his-self. If anyone would know how to sneak around it, it would be him."

I exchanged looks with Lilly. "You don't think anyone's helping him?" She asked.

Dario shook his head. "You killed the ones that were loyal to him, and my brother has plans of his own. He did it himself."

"Shutupnow," Jim coughed as Juan Jr. made his way back toward us. "Hoss, it's your turn."

And Jack, the big, strong man that had murdered a man with his bare hands, took to the stage and did a perfect pirouette.

Chapter Fifty Five

Chris

Bud sipped his coffee, glancing nervously through the patio doors where Maria and Dahlia were still at the kitchen table finishing their breakfasts. "Everything's ready. We've got enough fuel, food, and water to get us to the coordinates and to the island once we're through. What are we going to do about Dahlia?"

Chris shook his head, sinking down into one of the plush patio chairs. "We can't take her with us, you and I both know that, but how we're going to lose her when those two are attached at the hip is beyond me. Maria won't go back on her word, even though she knows Dahlia jeopardizes everything we're working so hard for." He tapped on the binder in his lap. "Even though she knows bringing her puts everything at risk."

Returning with a thick binder full of research, Bud and Chris—outside of earshot of Maria, Dahlia, or anyone listening in the van down the road—had worked out three different options to cater to three different scenarios.

The first and simplest was that they would bring everyone home. As long as Cecelia remained in the 21st century, her descendants would never make it to Juan Josef and therefore, he'd have no reason to flee to the coordinates. No one else would have to die, and those that had as a result of their encounters with Juan Josef, would be brought back to life... theoretically.

The second option, *Plan B*, was to pursue a Spanish naval officer named Juan Francisco de la Bodega. Plan B could only be used if Juan Josef didn't know his own lineage and if Jack and Alaina had somehow been detained in a way that would prevent their return through time. Juan Francisco was the great great great-great-grandfather of Juan Josef—but could be explained as Richard Albrecht's instead if needed. In 1775, he hadn't yet had the opportunity to sire children and, while killing him would also kill Dahlia, Dario, and Juan Jr., they'd still be able to save all the same lives in doing so. There was also the added benefit of his location during those years being in close proximity to the location of the man they'd need to pursue if they had to resort to Plan C.

Plan C went along with Juan Josef's original mission to take out Richard Albrecht's ancestor and eliminate the events that led Juan Josef to flee to the past in the first place. The ancestor's name was George Thomas Bennet. George was a British officer in the sixty-third infantry and served the crown during the revolutionary war. It wasn't clear where the sixty-third infantry was in 1775, only that they were in America, and finding him would be a daunting task. Finding Juan Francisco de la Bodega would be much easier.

The problem with all that was there was no plan that would bode well for Dahlia. In every instance, she'd either lose her life or her stepfather's, and bringing her along would only serve to complicate things. Getting attached to her was not something they could afford to do with their backs against the wall, even despite all she'd done to help them.

In the few weeks she'd spent in California, Dahlia had been vital to keeping the detectives subdued. As suspected, the moment she'd returned to her hotel the first night, Detective Haywood had approached her. She'd played the role of the unsuspecting friend more than willing to help with their investigation, and had met with Detective Haywood several times to answer questions or plant the narrative that there was nothing she could find that would indicate there was any merit to his claims.

She'd returned each time to fill them in on the questions asked, and it seemed like the plane hijacking theory Detective Haywood was clinging to was slipping out of his grasp. She got the notion that he was growing desperate, possibly getting flack from his superiors after six months without a single lead to support it.

"You've talked to Maria about it, then?" Bud asked, sliding into the chair beside him. "She understands we're talking about more than just jeopardizing a simple mission? That we're responsible for the lives of Anna, Jack, Zachary, and all those men on the beach as well as their descendants, including Owen and Maddy? Not to mention Lilly, Jim, Bruce, Kyle, and Izzy... She understands Dahlia puts *everyone* at risk?"

Chris sighed. "She didn't plan to get attached to Dahlia, but she is. It's weighing on her that what we plan to do could kill her. And now she's got this ridiculous notion that since I can remember both versions of my life—changed and unchanged—but Cecelia doesn't remember Owen, somehow my involvement in the past prevented my timeline from completely altering. She thinks taking Dahlia with us will magically allow her to continue living, even if we erase her heritage."

Bud frowned. "Are you willing to chance that?"

"No. Even without the risks to the mission itself, we still aren't sure the theory of three *isn't* correct. Just because Dahlia felt herself being pulled doesn't mean she would've gone through. She can't go with us. We can't risk anyone getting left behind."

"We're leaving tomorrow," Bud reminded him. "How are we going to lose her between now and then?"

Chris crossed his ankle over his knee. "You said everything's ready, right? We could leave today instead... while she's meeting with Haywood."

In the hopes it might turn the detectives' heads long enough for them to slip away on Bud's yacht the following morning, they'd planned for Dahlia to go straight to Detective Haywood after breakfast. Shaken, she was to inform him that she overheard Bud tell Chris he'd *'left the money in his condo in the safe'* and that he'd *'sent the combination to them this morning.'* Given that

Detective Haywood was at the end of his rope with the case, he might rush to New York himself at the promise of any potential evidence. At least, they hoped she would.

"And Maria?" Bud looked back toward the patio doors.

Chris's shoulders tensed as he considered how livid Maria would be if they forced her hand. They'd finally mended what he'd broken in Las Vegas, although she continued to shoot down any further talks of getting married, and he knew this kind of betrayal could very well be the end of them. "She'll have to find a way to live with it."

Bud balanced his elbows on his knees, draping his head. "I know you love her, son, but... if we're coming back... maybe it might be best to—"

"I'm not leaving her," Chris insisted. "Even if the detectives weren't a threat, I wouldn't leave her."

"You're right, I shouldn't have suggested it." Bud adjusted his tone. "I have gifts to take back with us. Money in the form of old coins, gold, and jewels should any of them need to stay. I've got a few history books, medical journals, a solar panel and a few things for Kyle, Izzy, and the babies... We could tell Maria we're going to load them onto the yacht and make a walkthrough. She'll want to see it, anyway. If you can get her below deck and keep her occupied long enough for me to pull out of the docks..."

"I can do that." His words were short. Bud's suggestion they throw Maria to the wolves had left a mark. Of course, she would get attached to Dahlia. No one in the group they were working so hard to save had ever really been nice to her; they certainly had never accepted her. Not Lilly or Alaina or Anna or Magna had ever once taken the time to get to know her. Dahlia, on the other hand, had loved her immediately—been the best friend she'd always dreamt of having. How could he blame her for wanting to save that? And how would he ever forgive himself once he'd robbed her of it?

"We should get going." Bud stood, finishing off his coffee and taking one last look around them. "I'll start loading the gifts into the truck now." He moved to step toward the house but stopped short. "I'm sorry for suggesting it. I know things haven't exactly worked out the way you intended in this time… with her… and I'm even more sorry that what we're about to do is only going to make matters worse."

Chris knew the Renaud family was one of the wealthiest families in the world, but knowing it and seeing it first-hand were two very different things.

Standing on the dock, looking up at Bud's massive three story yacht, made it that much more evident how abundantly wealthy he actually was in comparison to the rest of them. Chris had never seen anything like it, nor had Maria, based on the way her mouth fell open beside him.

"It's bigger than any house I ever lived in!" She announced breathlessly. "When we come back, can I live in this?"

Bud chuckled. "Unfortunately, she won't be coming back with us… unless we can figure out a way to power the engines that doesn't require fuel."

Maria shook her head slowly, her eyes remaining fixed on the shiny white beast. "Such a beautiful thing to leave behind…"

"It can be replaced, dear. The people we intend to save with it can't be." Bud motioned for her to step up onto the main deck before filling his arms with boxes they'd brought to the dock with them. "Let's get these unloaded, then you can pick whichever bedroom you want. There are plenty."

Chris loaded his arms with boxes as well, his heart stinging as Maria hopped happily onto the deck to begin exploring. "Where do you want these?"

"Straight through here." Bud motioned ahead of him to the tinted glass doors on one side of the stairs. "There are staterooms in the lower foyer we can toss them in."

Bud led the way, pressing a button for the doors to glide open while Chris lingered behind, watching as Maria marveled at the built-in bar, her fingers dancing along the smooth marble countertop. "Dahlia is going to flip out when she sees this!"

She was definitely never going to forgive him.

Crossing through the open doors, Maria gasped behind him as she took in the immaculate living area. Inlaid marble and rich walnut floors glistened beneath ivory and beige furnishings. Decadent artwork hung on the few patches of wall that weren't covered in windows.

Just beyond that was a formal dining area with ten tufted fabric seats, flanked by sliding glass doors that led out to another deck.

Bud headed down a narrow hallway, adjusting his boxes as he took a left turn and headed down a flight of winding stairs. Maria and Chris followed lest they get lost.

"Ay Dios mío," Maria breathed once they'd descended to a foyer surrounded by open bedroom doors on all sides. "How many bedrooms are on this thing?"

"Too many," Bud grumbled, turning into one of the rooms and juggling the contents of his arms to one side in order to pull open a large cedar closet. He stacked his boxes neatly inside. "I always thought this was far too excessive, but it's the boat Lilly wanted."

"This is *Lilly's* yacht?" Maria scoffed from a room across the foyer she'd ventured into.

"Mostly," Bud chuckled. "No one else really uses it."

Dropping his boxes into the closet, Chris hurried out to join Maria, unable to stop himself from laughing out loud at the bedroom that rivaled the luxury of the one he'd once worked so hard to build. A massive bed sat between two side tables, a TV mounted on the wall across from it, and its own private bathroom, complete with a shower big enough for four.

Bud leaned against the doorframe. "I thought I'd offer the two of you the master stateroom. It's far more spacious than this. Come, I'll give you a tour."

Back up the stairs, he led them further along the main deck's hallway. "The galley," he said, dipping through a door to his left.

Chris whistled as he turned a circle inside the spacious wood kitchen, complete with a top of the line refrigerator, subzero freezer, stove, oven, microwave, dishwasher, sink, and… a fully stocked wine fridge. "Wow," he marveled. "Maybe we *should* find a way to make fuel. I'd live on this and never leave."

Maria nodded, opening a door beside the pantry. "Maybe I should be nicer to Lilly… What's down here?"

"That's the crew galley," Bud informed her. "Mostly bunk beds and storage. Come, I'll show you the master stateroom."

The master state room might've been bigger than Chris's entire childhood home. It housed a desk, a kingsize bed, a sectional sofa, a cedar closet he could've comfortably slept in, and built-in dressers. To one side, it opened up to a bathroom that not only had a standing shower but also a two person circular tub with jets.

"We'll take it," Maria chuckled, turning in the bathroom mirror to admire herself for a moment before joining them in the center of the room.

Bud forced a smile and Chris could see his own guilt sitting heavily beneath it. "Come check out the sky lounge and then you two can come back here and get settled in, maybe unload some of your things into the dressers and closets."

Maria chewed her lip. "Do you think we have time? Dahlia's supposed to meet us at the house at two…"

Bud placed a hand on the small of her back and motioned for her to lead the way back out. "I left it unlocked for her. I was thinking we might take her out for a spin once before we set out, just to make sure everything's in order. Don't want to find out we've got an engine problem in the middle of the Pacific."

"Should I call her and let her know we'll be late?"

"It's still early," Bud assured her. "And she should be meeting with Detective Haywood. Let's not give ourselves away."

Bud led them back out to the deck and up another flight of stairs, where a second lounge area with a sectional sofa and bar looked out onto a large outdoor dining space.

Down another hallway, he showed them a complex pilot house, also furnished with a sofa and bar, then led them out to the bridge and bow, all lined with loungers and pillows.

"Would you like to see the best part?" He asked when they'd returned to the sky lounge.

"There's more?" Maria asked, raising an eyebrow.

Bud nodded and pointed to the set of stairs on her right. "The sun deck is the whole reason Lilly had to have it."

Maria went ahead of them and Chris put a hand on Bud's shoulder. "I don't know if I can do this to her," he said softly. "It doesn't feel right to trick her."

"Then tell her the truth," Bud said. "Tell her we're leaving and we're not taking Dahlia. She knows all the reasons why. Give her the choice to either leave or come with us."

Above them, she shrieked. "OH MY GOD."

Chris ran up the stairs, taking them two at a time, and found her standing in front of a built-in hot tub on the deck, laughing wildly as she stuck her hand inside the steaming water.

"Who lives like this?" She grinned.

"Maria," he placed a hand over hers. "I have to tell you something."

She turned, balancing her elbows against the edges of the hot tub. "We're leaving without Dahlia?"

He nodded. "I'm sorry."

She exhaled heavily. "I figured we were when I saw that Bud was bringing the binder with him. I left her a note to say I was sorry."

"You're not angry with me?"

She shook her head, dipping her fingers into the water behind her. "I am not stupid, mi amore. As much as I love having a friend, I know why we cannot take her; why I cannot love her. I have known all along we would go without her. I am just glad I got to know her for a while. You thought I would be angry at you for this?"

He let out a long breath, feeling relieved that she wasn't. "I thought you'd hate me for it."

She smirked. "Well, I'm not exactly thrilled that you and Bud thought you would fool me so easily, but no, I do not hate you for it. We are leaving now?"

"Yes."

As if on cue, the engines started.

She hummed, turning back to face the hot tub. "Will we come back, you and me? There is nothing in that research that dictates whether or not we have to."

"Do *you* want to come back, Maria?"

She shook her head. "No."

"Why?"

She looked up at him and smiled. "Because look at this yacht. It is too much. This life… all the noise… all the technology and decor and expensive things… it is too many things that could get in the way of the only thing we need… Each other."

Chapter Fifty Six

"Before we go back," Jack started, tying the last bouquet of flowers to the pergola as the sun set behind us. "We need to talk to you both about tomorrow."

I looked at Lilly, her brow instantly furrowing at the direness of his tone in reference to her wedding day. "About what?"

Jim leaned against one of the posts. "Sugar, ye' gonna' wanna' sit down for a minute." He motioned to the chairs lined up before us.

Her eyes widened. "If you're calling the wedding off, James Lee Jackson, I swear to—

"I ain't callin' off nothin,' ye' paranoid pain in my ass. We just gotta' talk to ye' about somethin' is all. Now, sit your scrawny ass down and listen."

Cautiously, she pulled me toward the sitting area, and her suspicious frown remained on her face as we each took a seat.

Jim snagged the two chairs that were positioned at the side of ours, spinning them so we could face each other.

"I *just* got those spaced out the way I like!" Lilly growled.

"Well, I'll put 'em back woman! They're just chairs! You're drivin' me nuts with all the—" He held up a hand to silence the impending argument he was bout to initiate. "Now ain't the time to be fussin' about no chairs. We got bigger things to discuss. Come on and tell 'em, Hoss."

"Tell us what?" Lilly asked, crossing her arms over her chest.

Jack sat down beside Jim, balancing his elbows on his knees to lean in closer. "Jim and I have had this theory, and if we're right, we all need to be ready tomorrow."

I straightened. "About the knife? Did you find something in the room you had Juan Josef held in downstairs?"

"No. But I think Dario planted a seed to pull us off his scent... like the gold... to keep us distracted and searching for some secret passage or hiding place instead of looking at what's really going on."

Lilly narrowed her eyes at Jim. "And what's really going on?"

Jim put a hand on her knee. "We've known each other for almost two years now. And we become thick as thieves in just that little amount of time. There ain't nothin' we wouldn't do for each other. Right?"

"Right..." she said slowly.

Jack cleared his throat. "These men have been together far longer than that. And the fact that not a single one has questioned where Juan Josef is, why we're the ones giving the orders, or so much as breathed a word about typhoid is suspicious. Isn't it?"

"I suppose," she tilted her head to one side. "But what's this got to do with my—*our* wedding?"

"We killed a lot of their men," Jack continued, "and I don't think for a second that Juan Jr. or Dario have kept it a secret what we did with that poison. I haven't seen a single crewman go out to collect fruit and come back with sea mango. We think that Juan and Dario, along with the remaining crew, have been biding their time, playing along, until it's the right moment to take the control back. They only need what Bud, Chris, and Maria will have to offer. There's nothing they need the rest of us for. We think tomorrow would serve as the right moment."

"Why?" Lilly demanded. "If they wanted to ambush us and take back over, they could've done it the minute Chris and grandpa went through that storm. Why would they wait for my—*our* wedding?"

Jim clicked his tongue. "Because they're outgunned. We got all the weapons and even if they outnumbered us with two of ours up on that summit, we could still easily take 'em out."

Jack nodded. "They're watching us… finding out our weaknesses… waiting for the right opportunity to catch us with our guard down. We think the knife in our bed was a warning from someone who wanted to tell us to keep our guard up."

"I hadn't thought of that…" I said, a little breathlessly.

"We did," Jim assured me. "We been talkin' about this for a while now… watchin' them the same way they been watchin' us."

"If it were me," Jack said, focusing on Lilly, "tomorrow would be the day I attacked. This wedding is all we've been talking about and planning for months. They'll think most of us will be unarmed during the festivities—like we were during the last wedding. But we won't be. That's why we worked on daggers and pistols during training yesterday. I want us all armed to the teeth."

Lilly looked around at the gorgeous wedding venue we'd constructed on the beach. "So our wedding day is going to be a war zone?"

Jim shook his head, pulling her hands into his and running his thumbs over her fingers. "Not if I can help it, Sugar. See, they'll think we're gonna' leave men at Juan Josef's door to stand guard while the rest of us are on this beach… just like last time. And that's exactly who I'd attack first if it were me planning a siege. I'd take out the guard, steal his weapons and use 'em weapons against us when we come back to the ship… while we're still on the sloop."

Lilly swallowed as Jack took over. "But we're not leaving a guard on the ship. We're not leaving *anyone* on the ship. We'll insist the crew joins us, and we'll bring the prisoners as well."

"Juan Josef… and Phil… at our wedding?" She pulled her hands out of Jim's to glare at him. "How long have you two been talking about this?"

Jim smiled apologetically. "A while. I wanted to tell ye' sooner, but I knew ye' wouldn't react well, and I didn't want no one overhearin' ye' complain about it when we're plannin' to catch them in the act."

"We needed them to think we were entirely distracted with this wedding," Jack assured her. "And when they are forced to attend and realize they're surrounded by watching eyes and all of us armed, either Juan Jr. or Dario is going to have to signal the others to stand down. The signal is all I need to confirm we're right."

"And if you're right?" Lilly asked. "Then what?"

"Then nothin' Sugar," Jim squeezed both her knees, "not tomorrow anyway. You and me will have a perfect wedding. We're gonna' make damn sure they all see we're ready for 'em tomorrow and they ain't gonna' do squat to disturb your perfect day but signal each other off. We're tellin' ye' now so you know why we're expectin' ye' to strap on daggers and pistols in the mornin.' And I didn't want ye' to lose your mind when ye' walk down that aisle and see 'em prisoners sittin' there beside Kyle and Bruce."

"And let's say they signal," she said, pursing her lips, "what happens the day *after* tomorrow?"

Jim grinned. "Then we dump their asses on this island and steal away on the ship. Kyle, Michael, Jacob and I was right there workin' alongside 'em when we sailed off the first time. We know what needs done; won't be easy, but we'll make it work. We'll go back to Tahiti and wait the additional three months there."

"And if they don't call it off?" I asked. "If they try to attack us, anyway?"

Jack let out a long breath. "Then you and Lilly and Fetia take the children and run for the cave while we... handle it."

I could see Lilly struggling to keep her emotions at bay. Her lower lip twitched, but she didn't break. "You really think they've been planning this all along? Dario and Juan Jr.?"

Jack shrugged. "I hope I'm wrong... but it's what I'd do if it were me in their situation."

Lilly chewed her lip, staring at the flower covered pergola against the red sunset before us. "This isn't how I want our wedding to go."

"Ain't nobody gonna' do nothin,' it'll still be perfect for ye.'"

"No, I mean... I don't want to walk down the aisle and be thinking about anything but the man I'm walking toward. I don't want a gun or a dagger strapped to my leg, worrying about whether I'm going to have to use them... or if someone's signaling something..."

"Ye' don't need to worry about none of that, darlin,'" Jim slid out of his seat to kneel in the sand before her. "You let me and Hoss worry about everything."

She placed both hands on his shoulders. "Jimmy, I don't want you worrying about that either. All this?" She waved her arm in presentation of the decor. "I wanted to make it perfect for *you.*"

"Baby girl, I got all the perfect in the world I need sittin' right here in front of me. Now, if this ain't what ye' want... we don't gotta' do none of it. We could call the whole thing off—

"No! We're not calling it off..." She softened, combing her fingers through the back of his hair. "We're not calling it off. Jack, will you promise me one thing?"

"Anything," he said.

"When it comes time for us to say our vows, you do all the worrying for both of us?"

"Of course I will."

"And after we're married," she focused her attention back to Jim, "you don't ever keep secrets from me again."

Jim knitted his brows. "I's just doin' it to—

"I know why you kept this from me, but never again, okay?"

"Never again."

She sighed. "Now, fix the chairs back the way they were and let's go pretend we actually want to be at dinner with Juan Jr. and Dario."

Chapter Fifty Seven

Chris

"How far are we from the coordinates?" Chris asked, looking out the windows of the pilothouse from his co-pilot seat beside Bud. The ocean was still, and the night sky was blanketed with stars. The only sounds around them were the hum of the boat's engine and the soft fizz of its bow cutting through the gentle waves.

They'd been on the ocean for several days, and because they'd left a day earlier than planned, they were able to cruise at a speed that allowed them to preserve more fuel. It was just past midnight on September 3rd. They'd be going through the storm soon.

"About an hour," Bud said quietly, mindful of Maria's sleeping body on the sofa behind them. "Once we get close, we'll need to stay together. Don't wanna chance anyone getting left behind. You brought the lifejackets up?"

Chris smiled. "Maria's using them as pillows at the moment."

Bud let out a laugh that morphed into a yawn. "And the lifeboat?"

"Inflated on the bow and tied to the rail. You want me to take over for a bit?"

"No," Bud stretched his arms over his head. "If the storm on that side is anything like the first one, I'm gonna wanna be in control to navigate us through those waves. I could, however, use a cup of coffee if you don't mind going down and putting on a pot? It's gonna' be a long night for all of us and, once we're there, I don't want anyone leaving this room."

"I can do that." Chris stood, cracking his back as he stretched. Turning toward the door, he smiled at Maria where she was curled up comfortably against the lifejackets, the book she'd been reading still open in her lifeless hand.

She'd found a case of books—*smut,* she'd informed him—he could only assume belonged to Lilly in the master stateroom. She'd devoured three in the time they'd spent on the ocean and had made a habit out of reading the more graphic scenes aloud in bed once she'd realized that doing so made him blush.

Gently prying the book from her fingers, he placed it down on its open pages to keep her place, then pulled the thin throw blanket up over her shoulders.

He stood staring at her for a moment, considering what she'd said about not wanting to come back, and he wondered why that comment had excited him. He should want to go back to his own time; to his family; to the life he was familiar with... but he didn't.

He'd enjoyed swinging a sword, building homes in Tahiti with raw materials, and navigating the ocean with Captain Cook. The idea of returning to the 21st century; working a job and coming home to a perfectly manicured house; grocery shopping instead of hunting or fishing... none of that appealed to him now.

Shoving his hands in his pockets, he strolled down the hallway, taking in the lavish furnishings of the sky lounge. He'd once wanted this... to be so successful he could live in such a way... a way people would be envious of. Not anymore.

The moment he stepped out on deck, the salty air hit him and he felt like he could breathe easier away from so much... unnecessary clutter.

Where would they go if they stayed? He could seek out Captain Cook... or another world traveler. Or he could buy his own ship. Bud brought no small amount of money for anyone who decided to stay behind. With his own ship, he'd have no trouble with a superstitious crew thinking Maria's presence onboard was bad luck. Perhaps, since Juan Josef would have no further need of it, he'd simply take his ship... or maybe he could salvage the yacht... add sails and remove the heavier engines... he could keep the solar panels and some of the... unnecessary clutter...

'Captain Christopher Grace...'

He chuckled to himself as he made his way down the stairs to the aft deck. He kinda' liked the sound of that.

Imagining himself at the helm of a ship, Maria beside him, and an infinite ocean around them, he was smiling when he crossed through the dining area and flipped on the hallway lights.

That smile faded, though, when he thought he heard footsteps on the stairs that led down to the crew quarters off the galley.

He froze in his tracks, watching the doorway for signs of movement. After a solid minute, he slowly inched forward until he was standing in the galley doorway.

The door to the stairs was closed—*as it always was*—and the kitchen appeared undisturbed, only the small backlights under the cabinets left on.

Could his injury be flaring back up? He'd been weaned off the meds a few weeks ago and had missed his last appointment. Was he hearing things again so soon?

He flipped the galley light on, plucking a knife from the butcher block and turning toward the door to the stairs. Likely as it was that he was imagining things, he couldn't let the sound go ignored.

He opened the door, peering down the dimly lit stairs with his spine stiff. "Someone down there?" He called.

Silence.

Slowly, he crept down the narrow steps, keeping his back against the wall and holding the knife tightly over his chest. "If someone's down here, speak up..."

More silence..

The lights were off in the crew galley, blackness meeting the bottom of the stairs when he turned the corner. He felt around for a switch, gripping the knife's handle even tighter until he found it.

Flipping the light on, he scanned the small space as the light slowly swelled to illuminate it. He'd never been down here. To his left was a small kitchen with a built-in nook, and on each side, a labyrinth of doors.

"Someone down here?" He asked again, beginning to feel a bit ridiculous.

He opened one door to reveal a set of bunks built into storage bins. He opened the next to a small bathroom. Returning to the kitchenette, he moved to the second set of doors and opened the first. When he flipped the light on, he found himself staring down the barrel of a gun, the wide brown eyes of Detective Haywood just beyond it.

"Drop the knife," Haywood commanded him.

He did, letting it clang against the pristine wood floorboards beneath him while his heart beat out of his chest.

"What are you doing here?" Haywood hissed, keeping his voice down should anyone be in the galley to overhear. "Where is it that you're going?"

This couldn't be happening. They couldn't afford to have Detective Haywood here... They were an hour away from the coordinates. There was no time to turn back, and nowhere to get rid of him. If only three could go through...

"I said, what are you doing here?" Detective Haywood repeated, still aiming his gun at Chris's forehead. "Where are you going?"

Feeling a bit emboldened, Chris frowned. "Do... do you have a search warrant for this boat?"

The detective didn't respond, and Chris noticed several beads of sweat were coating the man's brow and smooth head. His eyes had deep, dark bags beneath them, and his shoulders were taut. He must've been hiding down here for days with very little food and water... Dahlia had said he'd seemed desperate, but this seemed... illegal.

"If you don't have a warrant, then I'm afraid I have to ask you, what are *you* doing here?"

Someone else answered that question. A female… "He was *trying* to stop me."

Stepping out from behind Detective Haywood's massive body, her arms loaded with water bottles and bags of chips, Cecelia glared at him.

"Cece?" He took a step back and blinked heavily. "How—why—what are you doing here? You can't be here! Neither of you!"

She let the contents of her arms spill out onto the bunk beside her. "Why not, Chris? What the hell is going on? Where is my sister?!"

Realization washing over him, he tilted his head to one side. "You were in the van…"

"Yes."

He looked at the detective. "And you put her up to this? To spying on us?"

Detective Haywood shook his head, slowly lowering his gun but keeping it drawn. "No. I warned her several times to go home and let me handle the investigation. When she snuck on this boat, I thought she might get herself killed. I had no choice but to try to stop her. Next thing I know, we were moving. Where are you going? Are Lillian and Alberta Renaud in trouble? Is your wife in trouble? Tell me what's going on."

"You *both* are in trouble," Chris warned. "You can't be here."

Cecelia crossed her arms over her chest. "Why?"

"I can't tell you why." He ran a hand hard through his hair.

"Then tell me this," she said, moving in front of the detective. "Is A.J. alive?"

He sighed. It was too late to turn around, and he couldn't very well toss them off the boat. They were days away from land in the Pacific… to send them off on the lifeboat would potentially be sentencing them to death. Help wouldn't reach them if they called for it from here… Could it?

She stomped her foot. "Is my sister alive, Chris?!"

Chris ignored her, meeting Detective Haywood's eyes. "Do you have backup nearby?"

Haywood raised an eyebrow. "I can call for it if you tell me what's going on."

"How soon can they get here?"

Detective Haywood tilted his head to one side. "A few hours."

Groaning, Chris let his head fall back on his shoulders. "It'll be too late...."

Cecelia pushed him hard. "Is my sister alive?"

"Yes," he snarled, turning back toward the kitchen, "and neither of you is going to understand what you've just put yourselves in the middle of." He pulled at his hair. "You're not supposed to be here, Cece. Your mother..." He growled, thinking about what Sophia would go through when her youngest daughter didn't return home. Both her children vanished... and him a suspect in both of their disappearances. "How did you end up here? How did you know where I was?"

"Wait... She's really alive?" Cece's eyes watered. "Where are we going? Is she there? Is she alright? Please, tell me what's going on."

"Yes, she's really alive. Come on," he motioned defeatedly toward the stairs. "You can put the gun away, detective. No one's going to hurt either of you. We'll explain everything."

He'd made a stop in the galley, giving Cecelia and Detective Haywood an opportunity to raid the fridge while he brewed a pot of coffee.

Cecelia couldn't stop asking about Alaina—even with a mouthful of ham sandwich—and even though his answer to each was consistently, "I'll explain when we get to the pilothouse." For the ten minutes it took to make the coffee, she'd asked at least a hundred unanswered questions while Detective Haywood watched him warily.

If he'd thought to grab his phone off the control desk, he could've sent Bud a text to warn him about their guests. Unfortunately, Bud would have to learn the same way he had, and they'd need to figure out what to say to them on the fly. Telling them they were about to travel through time wouldn't be something either of them would believe. But keeping that information from them didn't seem right either.

They could be given a choice. Haywood could call for reinforcements. They could put them on a lifeboat and leave them for help to find. They didn't have to go through...

He loaded up a caddy with the coffee carafe, several mugs, sugar, and creamer, and led the way up to the sky lounge, down the hall, and into the pilothouse.

Maria was still asleep where he'd left her, and Bud sat in his captain's chair with his eyes on the controls.

"Bud," Chris said loud enough to stir Maria and cause Bud to spin around in his seat. "We have company."

He watched both Bud and Maria go wide-eyed as Cecelia and Detective Haywood followed him inside.

"Jesus," Bud breathed, slowly shaking his head. "You two aren't supposed to be here."

"We need to know what's going on," Cecelia insisted. "I *need* to know where my sister is."

"Bud, this is Cecelia." Chris informed him. "Alaina's sister. She's been following us. You've met Detective Haywood."

Bud nodded, narrowing his eyes at the detective. "I could sue you for stepping on my boat without a warrant, you know... you *don't* have a warrant, do you?"

Haywood shook his head. "No, but from the looks of things, I believe I was certainly onto something. Will one of you please tell me where we're going?"

Chris cut in, keeping his attention on Bud. "I think we should tell them the truth... I don't know that we have any other choice. And then we give them the option to either come with us or take that life boat out and wait for backup."

"Tell us what?" Cecelia asked, hugging herself.

Maria sat up, extending one blanketed arm in invitation for Cecelia to join her on the sofa.

Cecelia refused to move.

Bud exhaled audibly. "We can't afford to lose the lifeboat. If that storm takes this boat... We'll need it. But it's too late to turn back..." He looked at Cecelia where she stood trembling, and ran a hand over his face. "They're not going to believe it... you know that."

"Believe what?" Detective Haywood asked, peering out the windows at the clear night skies surrounding them. "What storm?"

"The same storm that took down our plane," Chris explained, "and made it impossible for you to find any trace of it."

"I don't understand," Cecelia inched closer, perching on the arm of the sofa.

Detective Haywood carefully positioned himself ahead of her, his patience clearly dwindling. "Neither do I. Explain."

"You know who I am, detective?" Bud asked. "I imagine you've gathered quite a bit of background on me during this investigation."

"I have."

"Then you'll know I'm a man that stands by my word. I don't fabricate or have any cause to deceive you." He stood from the control desk and poured himself a cup of coffee. "I'm going to tell you what happened to us, and it's going to sound unbelievable. It'll sound so unbelievable, in fact, that you're going to demand we turn this boat around. And I can't do that. I'm not stupid enough to think I could convince you to disarm yourself, so I need *your* word you won't use that gun to attempt to force this boat in any direction other than the one it's headed in. So long as I can remain on course, you'll be able to see the truth for yourself soon enough."

Haywood considered it for a moment, flexing the fingers on each of his hands. "So long as you do not pose a threat to the lives of those onboard or the lives of anyone in the direction you are heading, you have my word that my weapon will remain holstered."

"Good," Bud said, taking another sip of his coffee and sitting back down in his captain's chair. "Flight 89 hit a storm that came out of nowhere. There was not a cloud in the sky or a storm in the forecast. There was no warning. As soon as it appeared, it disappeared."

Bud spun the chair forward, pulling a sticky note from the display before turning back to extend it to him.

Haywood took the little yellow paper and frowned at the writing on its surface.

"The top number," Bud continued, "are the exact coordinates where the lightning hit the plane, splitting it in two. The second number is where we ended up on the ocean in a raft, nearly two thousand miles Southeast of where the plane was struck."

"Two thousand miles?" Haywood squinted at the paper. "How's that possible?"

"It's not," Bud assured him, "neither is the fact that, in addition to being two thousand miles off-course, we were also two hundred, forty-four years in the past."

Detective Haywood laughed out loud. "You're telling me that lightning hit your airplane and sucked you through time? That's the story you're going with? You're right. I don't believe that for a second."

Bud smiled. "I know that. The rest of our people are on an island not far from those bottom coordinates. That's where we're heading. You'll see for yourself. Once the lightning hits, these coordinates," he pointed at his navigation, "will change drastically. And when we pull up to that island, you'll find the rest of the first-class passengers, and they will corroborate this story. *If* you decide you want to go through with us."

"My sister is there?" Cecelia asked. "In the past? On this island?"

"She is," Chris assured her. "But—"

"Then, of course, I want to go through with you."

Chris shook his head. "There's one more thing you need to know before you make that call, Cece. There are only two times a year we've been able to determine you can cross through. September and March. We're still not entirely sure how it works; how many can actually go through it, or what happens to the ones that don't. We *do* know that six months there is equal to a year here. If you decide to go, you're gone for at least a year... And your mother has already lost one daughter. I know it sounds crazy, but it *is* the truth, and we're getting very close to that storm now."

Detective Haywood rolled his eyes. "Okay, the joke's over. Whatever it is you're trying to deter us from seeing with this elaborate story, it's not going to work. Mr. Renaud, I gotta' ask you. Are you and your family in trouble? We can work together here. No one has to know you talked to the police, if that's what you're afraid of. Give me a name and I can get your family to safety in a discreet manner."

Bud spun in his seat to prop both legs up on the desk, holding his coffee near his lips. "My family will be safe once I get to them with the information I have come back to collect. You'll see."

"There is a wedding ring on your finger, detective," Maria said, curling her legs up on the sofa. "If you are adamant about remaining on this boat, I suggest you call to say goodbye." She looked at Cecelia. "And you too. Tell the ones you love that you will be gone for a year. If we are lying to you, you can tell them it was a mistake... if we are telling the truth, they won't think you are dead like everyone thought we were."

Detective Haywood looked down at the silver band on his finger. "Ma'am, if you're in trouble—

"Ay dios mío," she huffed. "I am curled up in a blanket on a fifteen million dollar yacht. I am fine, I promise. But you will not be if you go through that storm without saying goodbye."

"This is insane. You're *all* insane." Haywood paced to the doorway. "You got anything stronger to drink than coffee?"

Bud grinned. "The bar down that hallway is fully stocked. Help yourself to whatever you'd like. But hurry back. We have to remain together when we get to the storm."

While Detective Haywood sauntered off, grumbling his disbelief under his breath, Cecelia remained on the edge of the sofa. "My phone died days ago. Can I borrow one of yours?"

Chris reached into his pocket.

"Not yours," she said, biting her lower lip. "Mom won't answer for you."

"Here," Maria offered up her own.

Cautiously, Cecelia took it, glancing between the three of them. "She's alive... but you two are... still together?"

Chris nodded. "Alaina can explain what happened when you see her. It's not my place."

"She *left* you?" Disbelief covered her features.

"Again," he said evenly, "it's not my place. What happened between us has bias on both our accounts. As her sister, I'd prefer you heard hers over mine."

"And you've met my sister?" She looked at Maria. "She... approves of this?"

Maria smiled warmly. "Sí. She gave him her ring so he could give it to me."

Cecelia turned her attention to the phone, dialing a number and holding it to her ear while staring at Maria skeptically.

"Mom?" she said softly, rising off the sofa to stand at the windows and look out. "I know it's late... no, I'm fine. I just—I said I'm fine, will you let me talk?... I'm in California. Listen, I know where Alaina is... Ma, let me talk... I'm going to sail out and get her, but I won't have reception. I could be gone for a while... a *long* while. And you're not gonna' hear from me. It could be a year. Trust me. I don't want you to worry. I promise, I'm fine. And she is too... No... Ma, stop. That's all I can say right now... Because that's all I can say... I just wanted to tell you I love you and I will be back so don't panic... I have to go... I know, but you gotta trust that I know what I'm doing... No... I really can't say. Just... Promise not to worry and I promise I'll bring her back... Okay... I gotta go... I love you, too."

She hung up the phone and held it against her chest, her eyes watering when she turned back toward them. "What happens next?"

Chapter Fifty Eight

Lilly stood at the floor-length mirror as I tied her stays, unusually silent, given it was the day she'd been waiting for her whole life.

"You alright?" I asked.

She nodded, frowning at her reflection.

"Are you worrying about the crew?"

"No," she said softly.

"Are you getting cold feet?"

"No."

There was a far off look in her eyes as she inspected herself in the mirror. One that I'd rarely ever seen from her.

"Do you want to tell me what's wrong, or shall I continue guessing?"

She sighed. "Am I good enough for him?"

Stifling the urge to laugh at the fact that a billionaire heiress was asking *me* if she was good enough, I shook my head. "Lil, you can't be serious with that question."

She turned to face me, her jaw set. "Why not? Because I come from money and should just assume he's the one that's making out on this deal? That's not what I'm asking, Lainey, and you know that. I'm asking if I deserve someone like him. Am I *good* enough?"

Brushing her dark hair over her shoulders, I smiled. "Lilly, I've never met two people more deserving of each other in my life. Of course you're good enough, and so is he. You're two of the best people I've ever met."

She looked down at her toes, flexing them against the wood floorboards. "*He's* the best person I've ever met. And he's always been good... He did everything to take care of his mom, changed his whole life when he found out June was pregnant so he could support them all... and even after she abandoned him, he sent Chris to give her everything he had to his name. Me? I have been pampered and spoiled and rotten all my life. You know I never once gave anything away to someone who needed it? I never volunteered for charity work or offered money to a homeless person on the street. The only goodness I have in me is because of him... Is that enough?"

"Lilly, that's not even remotely true." I took her hands in mine. "You have this light in you that illuminates all of us. We crashed into the ocean and ended up stranded on an island in a different century. Where we all would've otherwise been depressed out of our minds, you made it possible for us to smile; to laugh; to *live*. You shined, Lilly, and brought us all out of darkness. You talked me off a ledge so many times without even knowing you'd done it. Just that playfulness and passion for life you have... it was contagious. To say nothing of the fact that you stitched my head without even knowing my name or took Izzy in as your own and have been an amazing mother figure to her. There's still time for you to volunteer and donate, but don't think because you haven't yet that you're not good. You are the best of us. And you're marrying your equal. Of course you're good enough."

She let out the breath she was holding, and her arms exploded around me, squeezing tightly. "I love you so much, Lainey. Thank you. I don't know what I'd do without you here."

I smiled against her shoulder, winding my arms around her tiny waist. "I love you too, Lil."

There was a knock at the door.

"Ay, I ain't supposed to see ye,'" Jim called from the other side, "but I just wanted to make sure ye' didn't run off before I go put this monkey suit on."

She sniffled against me and laughed. "I already told you I'm not running anywhere, Jimmy."

"Good," he said, "cause I got somethin' ye' asked me to hold on to until today… Figured ye' might want it this mornin.'"

Lilly pulled out of my arms and her eyes went wide. "Gramma's letter… I almost forgot…" She looked toward the closed door. "Give it to Lainey and don't you dare try to peek in here!"

I smiled, spinning on my heel to crack the door open. "Jim," I said in greeting, grinning at him where he stood with the folded letter between his hands.

"Freckles." He extended the letter to me. "She ain't changed her mind about me yet?"

I shook my head. "No, sorry. I think you'll have to wear the monkey suit after all."

He snorted. "You tell her I'll wear that damn suit every day of my life if it'd make her happy."

"You can tell her yourself in a few hours." I glanced at the paper now in my hand. "Did you read it?"

He shook his head. "No. Thought about it… Lordt knows I could use a bit of that woman's wisdom… but it wasn't written for me, so I'll have to settle for what little wisdom I can get from Hoss and Bruce before I walk down the aisle. You take care of her now."

I kissed his cheek. "I will. See you soon."

He bowed hilariously and turned back down the hallway.

Back inside the room, Lilly sank onto the edge of the bed beside Izzy and the babies, staring wide-eyed at the folded letter between my fingers.

I offered it to her. "Do you need a minute? I can go hang out with Kyle outside the door…"

She looked at me as if I'd grown hair out of my eyeballs. "No. I need you to sit here beside me and hold my hand while you read it to me."

"You sure? It might be personal."

"You're my sister, remember?" She searched my eyes. "There's nothing too personal for me to share with you." She patted a spot on the bed beside her. "Come and read it to me."

I sat down beside her, unfolding the letter as she laid her head against my shoulder.

Written in pencil on the paper we'd used to give Izzy her lessons, Bertie's handwriting was flawless and graceful in its looping cursive. It was hard to imagine she'd been dying while she wrote it.

I took a deep breath. Lilly did too. "You ready?"

"Yes."

I held the letter out so she could see the words as I read them.

My dearest Lilly,

On the day you read this, do not wish I could be there with you, for I already am. There is no heaven that could keep me from watching you walk down that aisle today. So, as you read my words, know I am sitting beside you, and my darling girl, I am so proud of you.

While I write this, you sit beside me, sewing a dress for Izzy. And how I wish you could see the woman I've watched you grow into on this island.

I used to worry about who you might become without your mother there to guide you. Where your father was overly ambitious, she was spontaneous and free. She had the heart of a saint and could make even a man like your father come out of his shell just to dance with her. She was kind to everyone who crossed paths with her, and she could smile at a stranger and his entire face would light up in reflection of it. But to watch her love... that's what I worried about you missing. She held nothing back.

The day your father married her, he told me that the way she loved him brought tears to his eyes. He said he could just be looking at her and feel the urge to cry from how powerful that love hit him. She loved you the same way. I witnessed it and my own eyes watered.

And I've realized during these months I've spent beside you on this island, I was wrong to worry. You have grown up to be just like her and I can only assume that is because she's been there to guide you all along.

You won't need any advice from me if you love with the same vehemence she did. But, since I must pass on my grandmotherly wisdom to someone, I will give it to you anyway.

Your grandfather and I have had an amazing life together. But not every single day was a perfect one. There's no such thing as perfection when you share a life with someone else. The key to your marriage will be to always remember the word: share. So, here are the six things I learned about sharing my life with someone else.

1: Do not set expectations for each other. Those novels you read like to make references to two souls becoming one. Do not expect that. You are two people, and you will always be two distinct personalities, even after this day. You will have different thoughts and opinions, and those won't always align. But remember, you share your marriage, and therefore you have to make room in it for each other. If either of you tries to take up the whole space by expecting the other to adopt your exact same thoughts and opinions, your marriage will not work.

2: You're going to argue. Argument is healthy, and given your warrior personality, you may argue more frequently than others. That's okay. Don't compare your relationship to any one else's. But choose which battles are worth standing your ground and which ones are okay to give away. Let him win from time to time. You might be right, but winning isn't always the most important thing.

3: Let him have his bad days. Yes, he will have bad days too, and he may not always be able to express why. Your life may be shared with him, but neither of you will ever be able to read each others' minds. When he is down, don't be afraid to ask him what he needs, and when you are down, do not shy away from telling him what you need.

4: Everyone loves being told they're doing a good job. When he achieves or gives something, however big or small, don't ever forget to give him praise for it. Men need to feel empowered and appreciated. Always make sure he knows you support him in the life you share together.

5: Be honest always about how you feel. Never hide yourself from your husband. It's up to both of you to hold each other up and if you hide yourself, you'll sink. When you are sad, let him know what is making you sad. When you are angry, let him know exactly what has made you that way. When you are happy, let him know why you are happy. Share. Always.

6: But most importantly, enjoy every second you can. Your time together is not infinite and it will be over before you know it. Love with that unyielding passion you have inside you every day, even on the bad ones. I know you will. And I know you are going to have a wonderful life together as a result.

Now, go and have your perfect day. I am with you and I'm marveling at how beautiful you are. When you see your grandfather, straighten his collar since he has never learned to do it properly himself, and tell that old goat I'm with him too and to have some fun for my amusement.

I love you, my darling girl. And I look forward to the day, a long long time from now, when you come to sit beside me here and tell me all about the amazing life you've lived.

Until then, I'll come down from time to time to sit beside you when I'm needed.

Live like you mean to. And love the life you live.

-Gramma."

Chapter Fifty Nine

On the top deck, the crew begrudgingly loaded themselves into the sloops after we'd informed them that they all had been invited to attend the event. Kyle, Jim, and Abraham had gone ahead of the rest of us, escorting Phil and Juan Josef to their seats on the beach.

Jack, Jacob, and Bruce remained with us, all of them wearing swords, daggers, and pistols around their hips. Where I'd imagined the men being armed might take away from the aesthetic of a wedding, the weapons actually made them look more regal.

We made sure the crew saw when I pulled up the hem of my dress and adjusted the pistol strapped to my thigh. Fetia did the same. Jack's eyes remained upon Juan Jr. and Dario throughout.

We asked them to join us on our sloop, and, if there was truth to Jack and Jim's theory, neither of them showed any evidence of it as we lowered down and rowed to the shore.

"You look positively exquisite," Dario said to Lilly. "If I thought you might agree to it, I daresay I should be tempted to steal Jim's place at the altar."

Lilly blushed and hid a smile, but her attention was centered on the beach ahead. Jim was at the altar and his gaze was equally focused on our sloop and the stunning creature in white at the front of it.

She really did look exquisite. She'd rolled her hair in bamboo the night before and wore it partially up and loose. Long, silken chestnut curls laid between her exposed shoulder blades with white island flowers weaved in.

The dress was a masterpiece. It was simple, elegant, and timeless. She'd made the bodice out of two overlapping cuts of white fabric. The frontmost had been folded and bunched to create angled lines that wound from the off-the-shoulder sleeves down around her ribcage. From there, the skirts flowed out, reaching to the ground in a stunning ball gown silhouette.

She was beaming at the front of the boat. I could've sworn there was a glow coming off her. Cupping her hands around her mouth, she called out, "You're not supposed to look yet!"

"Too late!" Jim shouted back, his voice bouncing off the water. "I done seen ye,' and I ain't lookin' nowhere else!"

She grinned. "Lainey, you might have to hold me down to keep me from sprinting up there the minute we get to shore. Where in the world did he get that jacket?"

Jack squinted at the beach. "I have no idea."

I chuckled, glancing at Juan Jr. for any type of signal to the men on the sloop beside us.

He was straight faced and unreadable as he rowed us steadily. If he'd spoken at all since we'd come out onto the deck, I hadn't heard it. That wasn't entirely out of character for Juan Jr., but he seemed somehow stiffer than usual.

I adjusted the babies in my arms as I nudged his foot with my own. "Are you alright?"

He nodded once. "Of course. What makes you ask?"

I smiled. "You haven't said a word about how beautiful Lilly looks today."

He frowned, then turned his attention to Lilly, who was entirely unconcerned with anything but our proximity to the beach. "My apologies. Lilly, you are radiant."

"Thank you," she said giddily, not looking back as we made our way into the shallows. "For the love of God, please row faster!"

Dario, seated beside me, leaned in to my shoulder. "She does realize it's about to rain, doesn't she?"

I looked up at the sky. Caught up in either Lilly's excitement or our own show of displaying our weaponry, I don't think any of us noticed the dark clouds that were growing rapidly over the ocean and heading in our direction.

This was not a part of the plan. Lillian Renaud didn't spend three months sewing and dyeing and decorating only to have a monsoon wash her out. My heart ached as I looked out at the wall of water pouring from those clouds, threatening to wash away her perfect wedding venue, and I prayed it would miss our island.

I nudged Jack with my elbow and pointed.

"I saw," he murmured. "Think we'll beat it?"

"Maybe? If we go now."

We could hurry things. She wouldn't have the island reception she wanted, but she might have time to get their vows in before the worst of it hit. Maybe I could return to the ship and set up some kind of reception area in the big room.

Hopping out of the boat, Jack towed us the rest of the way to shore, quickly lifting Lilly, then Izzy and Fetia, then Magna, then me out to place us on the dry sand.

Fetia and Magna took the children and made their way to the back row of seats, where they could see the crew and make a run for the tree line if anything should go amiss.

Thankfully, Jack had the foresight to construct the pergola near enough to our island shelter that it was within reach should the sky decide to open up on us.

Bruce, noticing the clouds, ushered Juan Jr., Dario, and the crew hastily to the remaining seats before pulling the violin from its case and looking to us for his cue to begin.

"Lill," I curled my arm around her left arm as Jack did the same to her right, neither of us having the heart to point out the rapidly approaching storm. "You ready?"

Her eyes focused straight ahead, she grinned and nodded, holding her bouquet at her waist. "Yes. Please walk fast."

I laughed at that, knowing her impatience had nothing to do with the rain.

I nodded to Bruce, and he began to play. Two steps in, I felt the first drop of rain land on my eyelash. Ahead of us, Jim's face was turning shades of red as he smiled exclusively at Lilly and wiped his eyes.

He was wearing a long black frock, suited for the century with its two inches of gold embroidery framing the collar, lapels, and hem, over a white shirt and black pants, a sword hanging at his hip. He looked positively perfect under the blush and white pergola, and I couldn't help but tear up a little at the sight of the moisture in his eyes as we grew nearer.

I glanced at Kyle and Michael where they were watching the crew and the prisoners. Phil and Juan Josef were secured between them, their arms tied discreetly in their laps.

I then looked to my left at Jacob where he was diligently focused on the crew seated ahead of him. No signs of alarm... yet.

On the sixth step, another drop of rain kissed my arm, then another on the crown of my head.

I peeked at Lilly for signs of a meltdown, and I wasn't entirely sure she'd noticed, even with the few droplets that had landed on her forehead. Her eyes had reddened to match Jim's, and she was laughing as she stared ahead.

We hurried our pace as the gap between droplets became shorter, and we delivered her to the altar, quickly taking our places at each side.

Gazing out at the congregation, I noticed Magna and Fetia already up with the babies and Izzy, inching toward the cover of the island shelter. Magna signaled that all was well, using Izzy's signs to say, *'No trouble. Rain.'*

We would all use Izzy's signs today. If anything looked off, we'd tell each other with the language we'd made for her.

Dario and Juan Jr. had been strategically placed in seats at the front of the group, and both Jack and I watched for any movement of their arms or faces that might serve as a signal. Both faced forward, backs straight against their seats.

Abraham took his place under the pergola, the blush and white fabrics starting to quiver as the wind gradually picked up.

"We're going to have to make this faster than usual if we want to beat the rain. Where I would normally pray, I will ask you all to say a silent prayer in your hearts throughout this ceremony to bless this marriage. Let us begin."

Jim sniffled loudly, and he placed his thumb and pointer finger over his eyes to clear them.

Lilly leaned into him as Abraham, with no time to chastise her for touching out of turn, began, speaking each word rapidly.

"The vows you are about to take are to be made in the presence of God, who is judge of all and knows all the secrets of our hearts; therefore if either of you knows a reason why you may not lawfully marry, you must declare it now."

With no argument, and with the drizzle creating a layer of moisture on our skin, he spoke even faster. "Face each other."

Lilly tossed me her bouquet, and I awkwardly managed to catch it while she turned and took Jim's hands.

Fully facing my direction, Jim's eyes were bright red, his face mangled with tears. "Christ almighty," he whispered—loud enough the whole congregation likely heard him. "Ye' got me comin' apart just lookin' at ye.'"

"Jim," Abraham said, blinking heavily as the drizzle turned into a steady shower, droplets of it sliding down his pointed nose, "will you take this woman to be your wife? Will you love her, comfort her, honor and protect her, and, forsaking all others, be faithful to her as long as you both shall live?"

"Hell yes," he managed, half-sobbing as he did so. "I will."

Out of the corner of my eye, I noticed some of the crew were slowly making their way to the island shelter as the rain picked up even more.

"And Lillian, will you take this man to be your husband? Will you love him, comfort him, honor and protect him, and, forsaking all others, be faithful to him as long as you both shall live?"

"Hell yes I will," she giggled, her perfect hair officially soaked and plastered to her face. Jim reached out to smooth it back for her, and she held her hand over his on her cheek.

"Jim and Lilly," Abraham shouted over the wind. "I now invite you to join hands and make your vows, in the presence of God and his people."

He didn't wait for them to obey, but continued quickly while the storm began to break apart the flowers framing the pergola so they fell along with the rain in a shower over us.

"Jim, repeat after me..."

Remembering our own version of the same words, I looked past them to Jack. He was smiling, likely remembering the very thing I was, but his eyes remained on the crew as more of them hurried to the cover of the shelter.

"I, James Lee Jackson, take you, Lillian Farah Renaud, to be my wife, to have and to hold from this day forward; for better, for worse, for richer, for poorer, in sickness and in health, to love and to cherish, till death us do part."

Lilly took her time reciting the same, her face alight with her amusement as thunder cracked above us and the downpour officially spilled out onto us.

Everyone but the five of us ran for cover.

"The rings?" Abraham said, removing his glasses where they'd become useless against the moisture on their surface.

Jack handed the rings to each of them.

"Again, please say a prayer to yourselves. Jim, place the ring on the fourth finger of Lillian's left hand and repeat after me..."

He did as instructed, reciting the words: "Lilly, I give you this ring as a sign of our marriage. With my body I honor you, all that I am I give to you, and all that I have I share with you, from this day to the last of my days."

Lilly, unhurriedly, did the same.

Consistent loud thunder rumbling over us, Abraham shouted in order to be heard over it. "In the presence of God, and before this congregation, Jim and Lilly have given their consent and made their marriage vows to each other. They have declared their marriage by the joining of hands and by the giving and receiving of rings. I therefore proclaim that they are husband and wife. Those whom God has joined together let no one put asunder. Jim, you may now kiss your wife."

At that, Abraham bolted to join the rest of the congregation beneath the shelter. Lilly and Jim, both laughing, fell naturally into a kiss, both of them reaching for the others' cheeks as they did so.

Shivering, Jack pulled me with him to the shelter and we watched, huddled together and soaked, as Jim and Lilly remained inside the unraveling pergola, lips pressed together and lost in their own world.

Chapter Sixty

The storm was unrelenting. It offered a break only long enough for the entirety of the party to drag their chairs to the sloops and navigate back to the ship.

Safely onboard, we returned the seats to the dining room and lit the fireplace inside, all of us soaked through and trembling as the crew gradually ventured off to their quarters on the decks below in search of dry clothing.

Jim and Lilly hadn't let go of one another from the moment they'd been pronounced husband and wife. They stood closest to the fire, his arms wrapped around her tiny body where she rested her back against his chest, smiles covering both their faces, even when the thunder roared outside and the monsoon returned.

"I'm sorry, Lill," I offered. "If you want, Jack and I can take the gramophone down to the big room, decorate it a bit, and turn it into something resembling the reception you had in mind."

Still grinning, she shook her head, the ends of her hair dripping down her collarbone and causing her teeth to chatter. "N-Nothing I could've ever d-dreamed up can top w-what today was. It was p-perfect." She smoothed both palms over Jim's arms where he'd removed the jacket and rolled up his sleeves. "And I d-don't want any more d-decorations. We can eat and d-dance and laugh j-just fine w-without them."

"You're freezin' Sugar." Jim moved his hands rapidly up and down her bare arms to warm her. "Let's all go down and change 'for we catch our death."

She looked down at her soaked dress where the skirts were now cemented against her body, a thick layer of wet sand coating the bottom six inches. Sighing audibly, she nodded. "I w-wanted to d-dance with you in this dress…"

He chuckled, pulling her tightly against him to rest his chin against the crook of her neck. "Darlin,' there won't never be a time, far as I'm concerned, where I can look at ye' without seein' ye' walk toward me in it. Ye'll be wearin' this dress in my mind… always."

"G-good," she shivered. "Cause if I d-don't take it off soon, I m-might die."

"What do you want us to do with them?" Kyle asked, tilting his head to Juan Josef and Phil where they stood between him and Bruce, soaked thoroughly in their restraints.

Jack stepped forward, handing Cecelia to Magna. "I'll take them down and get them back in their chains. We'll move the party to the big room so we can all stand watch." His attention shifted to Juan Jr., who was still somber and stiff, his eyes seeming to be watching every one of us closely. "Will you two be joining us?"

Juan Jr. bowed his head to Lilly. "If it is your wish, my dear, we would be happy to celebrate with you and your husband."

Lilly giggled, snuggling closer in Jim's arms. "My *husband*… Yes, w-we w-would like that very much."

Dario smiled brightly. "Then my brother and I will give you ample time to change out of your wet clothing and meet you in your room."

There was something off between the two brothers. I noticed Juan Jr.'s shoulders tense when Dario spoke. Perhaps there was something to Jack's theory, and perhaps the two of them weren't aligned on whatever the plan was to take back control of the ship. Jack saw it too, and I was very much aware of how closely he was inspecting Juan Jr. as we all made our way down the hall.

Inside the big room, Jim and I went straight to work on pulling the pins from Lily's dress. She snickered at our soaked reflections where she stood facing the mirror, her dark eyeliner caked down both cheeks. "I can't feel my face."

Behind us, Kyle and Michael were hurriedly working to light the fireplace.

"Fire's comin' Sugar," Jim plucked a pin from the bodice.

"No," she laughed, "I mean from smiling. I don't think I've ever been happier in my life."

Jim grinned, shaking his head as his eyes met hers in the mirror. "Sweetheart, that makes two of us. Although, I still ain't sure we shouldn't have sent you through time to get *your* head examined."

An hour later, all of us changed into warm, dry clothing and a fire roaring in the stone fireplace, Juan Jr. and Dario filled the doorframe where it was propped open. Dario held the gramophone, and Juan Jr. carried two crates of records stacked on top of one another.

"Where would you like these?" Dario asked, struggling to keep the gramophone upright.

I waved to a small table beneath the bay window. "Over there's fine."

"Georgie is helping Bruce prepare to bring the food up," Dario said, depositing the contents of his arms on the table and sighing with relief as he rubbed both biceps. "Would you prefer to dine in the great cabin?"

Lilly shook her head, waving to the small dinette set in the corner of the room with one hand as she held a glass of wine in the other. "No. There's plenty of space in here."

Again, I noticed a stiffening in Juan Jr.'s shoulders. I took a seat on one of the sofas, grateful for the feel of the pistol still strapped to my thigh beneath my skirts.

Lilly sauntered over to the window, thumbing through the case of records. "What do we want to listen—

She froze, leaning over the record player to peer out the window. "Jimmy... Jack... you better come look at this."

We all moved to the window to look out toward our island. In the dimming twilight, high up on the summit, an orange flame had erupted, burning violently as it fought against the rain.

"Uati," Michael said under his breath. "That sign for Uati."

"We don't know that yet," I assured him, my heartbeat quickening. "And even if it is," I looked toward Dario, "we have cannons to fight them off before they can reach us."

"We can see out from the dining room," Kyle announced, already bolting down the corridor toward the stairwell.

As everyone hurried to follow him, Jack cursed under his breath while I bent over the cradle to collect our children.

"We can't afford to separate from each other," he said. "Someone needs to guard that door." His eyes darted from the window to the hall. "But the threat is not gone... they could use this..."

"I can stay with you."

He shook his head, pulling Cecelia against his shoulder. "I'd prefer it if you stayed with the larger group."

"Then you come with us, too. He's locked in there, Jack. Even if he got out, we have the weapons. Leave it. We need to stay together, especially if you're right."

Again, he looked out the window and back down the hall before inspecting me and our children.

"You're right." He motioned for me to lead the way. "Let's go before anyone has a chance to realize we've just given them an opening."

Rushing up the stairs, we quickly made our way into the dining room. Everyone, Dario and Juan Jr. included, was stapled against the windows staring out.

"What is it?" I asked, glancing back over my shoulder for signs of anyone who might creep up behind me. Finding only Bruce and the kitchen aid Geogie strolling our way with steaming trays of food, I turned back.

"Come see for yourself," Lilly said, waving me to her side.

Mindful of Juan Jr. and Dario, I joined her at the window, and I had to blink several times as I caught sight of the unnaturally bright lights moving quickly over the water toward us.

"It's grandpa!" Lilly said excitedly.

"How?" I pressed my forehead against the glass, as if doing so could somehow offer me a better look through the thick wall of rain that fell between us and the approaching lights.

"It's been three months," Jack said just behind me. "Six months there..."

They weren't supposed to come back so soon. Had something gone wrong? Was Chris alright? My pulse quickened as I squinted to see better.

No one moved as the light grew closer. Only when it was near enough to make out the shape of the massive yacht did Lilly spin away from the windows and sprint out the doors.

Everyone followed... everyone but me and Jack. Unwilling to expose the babies to the downpour, we held Zachary and Cecelia tightly, gazing out the window as the yacht pulled up at the side of the ship.

"Do you think they're alright?" I asked. "Something has to be wrong if they came back so soon... right? Can you see anything? Is Chris on there?"

"I can't—"

A loud crack pulled my attention from the window, and I spun around in time to watch in horror as Jack collapsed with Cecelia onto the floor and Georgie, discarding his club, ripped the pistol from his hip.

A stream of blood leaked out onto the boards around Jack's head and Cecelia broke out into a loud, bellowing cry in his lifeless arms.

Georgie cocked the pistol, aiming it at Jack while he grinned at me. "You didn't think we'd actually let you live, did you? After you murdered our men?"

"Not yet, Georgie," Juan Jr. instructed, pinning me against the windowsill with his full weight before I'd even had a chance to react to what was happening. "I want him to watch."

Zachary smashed against my shoulder between us, he let out a cry to match his sister's.

"Please," I begged, looking up to meet his cold expression. "Please don't do this."

"Lock the door, Walter," he commanded over his shoulder, not looking away from me.

"Juan, please, this isn't who you are." I looked down at my screaming child on the floor, watching as Jack's eyes slowly blinked back to consciousness when Georgie reached down to remove his sword from its hilt.

Juan Jr. extended one hand toward Georgie, a wordless demand that resulted in the pistol being placed inside it. "I am like my father in two ways, Alaina," he assured me, holding the pistol against my temple as his other hand bunched into my skirts and pulled them upward.

"The first is that I am willing to do whatever it takes to protect the ones I love." His hand slid up my thigh, and pinned as I was with a child in my arms, there was no way for me to defend myself. "There is no amount of time I wouldn't wait to right the wrongs my enemies have delivered me. And I am a far worse monster than he when it comes to righting those wrongs."

I closed my eyes as I felt him dislodge the pistol strapped to my leg. The cool metal skimmed against my inner thigh, forcing me to cringe as he took his time removing it.

"The second," he said, his breath moving to my ear as his hips cemented me to the window frame. "Is that I loved my mother more than anyone in the world."

At that, he spun around, and two shots were fired, one from each pistol.

Deafened by the blast, I held my eyes tightly shut, terrified to look at where I was certain those two shots had landed.

But as the reverberation of the shots faded and my hearing returned, I realized Cecelia was still screaming... and Jack was coughing… and slowly I found the strength to open my eyes to find Georgie and Walter on the ground, Juan Jr. still holding both smoking pistols steadily at where they'd once been standing.

Juan Jr. turned back toward us as I dropped to my knees beside Jack. "Are you hurt?"

Jack slid up to prop his back against the wall, allowing me the opportunity to pull Cecelia into my arms and inspect her for injury.

"We're alright," Jack said, holding the side of his head. "The others…"

"Are safe, I assure you," Juan Jr. said, kneeling before us to look over Cecelia. "She is not harmed?"

"No," I managed, swallowing the burn that was lodged in my throat.

Juan Jr. placed both pistols on the floor between us. "I give you my word, no one else will make an attempt on your life. Not once I'm able to detain my brother." He rocked back on his haunches. "He was too young to understand what our father was, and he is too easily influenced by the promise of his favor. I am sorry I was unable to stop him."

"*I* don't understand," I breathed, bouncing both babies to quiet them. "Why would you do this for us?"

He met my eyes and forced a smile. "You wear my mother's necklace and you resemble her. You are a part of her in some way." He looked down at the babies in my arms. "I intend to be returned to her someday soon… Knowing I shall retain the memories of this life, I am anxious to right the wrong my father delivered when I watched *his* bullet take her from me. I have begged for his life so that when he is returned to her—when he is within reach of the life he so desperately wishes to get back to—it can be my hands that strip it away from him."

Someone pounded on the doors. "Ay!" Jim shouted, beating heavily on the wood. "What's goin' on in there? Open this Got damn door right now!"

Juan Jr. stood, leaving the pistols where they were, and crossed over to the double doors to pull them open. "They're safe," he began to say, but was pushed aside by Jim and Kyle where they barreled into the room.

"We're alright," Jack said, wincing a little at the gash on his head. "Where's Dario?"

"He's on deck lowerin' a sloop to bring our people up." He frowned at the blood on Jack's head. "What in the Sam Hill happened? I thought I heard gunfire."

Juan Jr. remained at the doors, peering out. "I shall go up and retrieve my brother, along with a few of *my* men. We'll secure him in the room with my father and stand watch while you are reunited with your people. We can decide what to do with him after."

At that, he disappeared down the corridor.

Jack removed his palm from the wound, peering down at his blood-soaked hand. "I'll explain later. Did you get a look at who was on the boat? Is Chris with them? Everything alright?"

Jim nodded, meeting my eyes. "Yeah, he's down there with Maria and Bud both. They got two others with 'em too. One of 'em is askin' for her sister... A.J."

Chapter Sixty One

Everything went numb. At some point, I handed the babies to Jim and Jack and my legs moved me out of the dining room, down the hall, up the stairs and along the deck.

I didn't feel the rain pouring over me, didn't remember what had just happened in the dining room, didn't notice Juan Jr. hauling Dario off at the side of me as I stood staring down at the sloop while it was hoisted toward me.

Cece was there... My sister—my rock and my best friend— was there, almost within my reach. I could see her bright blonde hair as the sloop passed the lights of a window, and my knees trembled beneath me.

Everything burned. My eyes, my throat, my heart... And as the sloop came close enough I could see her face, I had to grip the railing to keep myself upright.

"A.J.," was all she said, and I broke at the sound of her voice. Warm tears blended with the cold rain on my cheeks and spilled down my jaw.

Gasping for air, I reached for her as she leapt onto the rail and I pulled her, both of us tumbling back onto the wood floorboards as we sobbed and held each other tightly.

I couldn't let go. Nor could she.

People moved around us, their feet splashing against the puddles that had formed on deck, their voices greeting one another in some world I wasn't a part of, and I squeezed her against me, unable to form words. Incoherent sounds emitted from us both as we found our way to a sitting position and rocked in each other's arms.

I pulled back long enough to cup her face between my hands, taking in the hazel eyes that were an exact reflection of mine. I scanned her face, unsure if I was dreaming, and pulled her back into my embrace just to feel her there for a moment longer.

"How are you here?" I asked, pulling back again to hold her by her shoulders.

Tears spilled from her eyes as she scanned my face the same way I was attempting to memorize hers. "I snuck onto the boat. I thought he killed you."

"Chris?" I laughed, unable to stop touching her.

She nodded. "What happened? Why aren't you and Chris together? The lightning, is it real? No, wait... How are you?"

I laughed at the onslaught of questions. Cecelia had never been able to master organizing her thoughts and tended to jump from one to the next, all within the same breath. "I'm good. There's so much I need to tell you... And so many people I need you to meet." Realization dawning on me, I remembered the condition I'd left Jack in. I gripped her hand and pulled her with me to stand. "Come on, I'll take you to them."

Winding my arms around her waist, I led her to the cover of the stairwell, and smiled as I observed Chris, Maria, and Bud leading the way, their arms loaded with boxes.

Chris winked over his shoulder at me. "Better than a boat full of photos?"

I nodded, barely able to speak as I pressed my cheek against my sister's. "So much better."

As we came upon the first landing, so did Jack and Jim, each of them holding one of the babies. The blood had been cleaned off Jack's face and a strip of Jim's shirt was now wound around his head. My heart leapt as I watched my sister's eyes meet his.

"You're Jack Volmer," she said, awestruck. "My sister was obsessed with you when we were teenagers."

He winked at me. "I'm pretty sure she still is."

"Cece, Jack is my husband. And these are our children."

She let go of me then, her eyes wide as she spun to face me. "Your *what* and your *who*?!"

I laughed out loud. "This one," I turned her toward the wiggling body in Jim's arms, "is Zachary William Volmer. And this one," I grinned, "is Cecelia Bertie Volmer. They're twins."

I smiled up at Jack while Cecelia admired her namesake in his arms. "Jack, this is Cecelia."

He nodded, the corners of his lips curling upward. "I've heard a lot about you. It's nice to meet you." He held Cecelia out. "Would you like to hold her?"

Tears once again spilling down her cheeks, Cece sniffled. "Uh huh."

As he placed our daughter in her arms, Kyle, a large box balanced on his arm, grunted while he made his way down the steps to the landing. "Bud brought gifts. And this guy." He tilted his head back toward the intimidatingly large bald man behind him on the stairs.

"...hi?" I said awkwardly. "And you are?"

"My name is Detective Haywood," he said in a thick baritone I felt all the way to my toes. "I've got questions for all of you."

"And we'll answer them," Bud assured him from where he'd paused on the second set of stairs leading to our room, "after we've had a chance to reconnect. Come on, let's get these boxes unloaded first."

Cecelia cooing over the baby in her arms, we followed, and I stopped short when we reached our room to give proper thanks to Juan Jr. where he stood with one of his men outside the doors.

"Your brother is..."

He bowed his head. "Locked away and no longer a threat to you. You are safe."

Over the past several hours, I'd witnessed a beautiful wedding, watched my husband and child be attacked, found an unexpected ally in Juan Jr., and had been reunited with a sister I never thought I'd see again. The emotions welling inside me boiled over at the word *'safe,'* and I was unable to stop from launching myself into his arms. "Thank you."

He awkwardly lowered a hand onto my back, stroking softly. "It is nothing. Go and be with your people. I will not let anyone get past me."

Sniffling, I took a step back from him. "You may think it's nothing…" I glanced to the room that housed my family—*Safe.* "…but it is everything to me."

"Are you coming?" Cece asked softly, appearing in the doorway with Cecelia still cradled in her arms.

Eyes watering, I nodded. "Juan, this is my sister, Cecelia."

He bowed to her, his eyes lingering on her face when he'd straightened. "Delighted to meet you, madam."

She smiled thoughtfully. "You're not joining us?"

I pursed my lips and looked up at him. "Would you like to come inside, Juan?"

"No. My place is to watch over you from here."

Cece's eyebrows shot up to her forehead. "Are we in danger?"

He shook his head. "Not any longer."

Inside, wedged between Cecelia and Jack on the sofa, I watched with a full heart as Bud stood before the stack of boxes in the center of the room. "We have a lot to discuss," he said, smiling, "but before we are forced to make such heavy decisions… I brought gifts for everyone."

He opened the first and peered around the room. "Bruce…"

Bruce stepped forward from where he'd been lingering behind the far sofa. "You brought me something?"

Bud laughed. "Of course I did. I said I had gifts for *everyone*, didn't I?" He pulled out a caddy full of spices. "Thought you might like a few extra ingredients out here."

Bruce took the caddy, inspecting its contents before clutching it tightly to his chest. "Thank you. And the rest of you will be thanking him in the morning!"

"You're welcome," Bud returned to the box. "For Zachary and Cecelia... and momma."

He handed me a box and my cheeks burned from smiling when I opened it to find bottles, a manual breast pump, pacifiers, a nasal aspirator, nail clippers, a thermometer, two rattles, and two stuffed bunnies. "Oh my God, Bud. This is amazing. Thank you!"

I laid the bunnies against each of their chests, where they were both balanced on Cecelia's legs. Zachary immediately curled his fingers around one of the ears and tugged it to his lips.

"The breast pump was Maria's idea," Bud informed me. "I brought medicine too. Tylenol and antibiotics. They're in that zipper bag in there."

Digging back inside the box while I explored the contents of the zipper bag, he pulled out a long, white package. "Lilly," he said softly, caressing the surface of the box. "Have you and Jim gotten married yet?"

Sitting on Jim's lap on one of the wingback chairs, she and Jim exchanged smiles. "Technically, grandpa, you crashed our wedding reception. We got married this afternoon."

His eyes lit up, then he frowned down at the box in his hands. "Well then, I don't suppose you'll need this, but it's yours all the same."

She climbed out of Jim's lap and took the box, flipping the lid and hobbling backward. "Is this... is this gramma's wedding dress?"

Bud nodded. "She wanted you to have it one day. I wish I could've gotten it to you sooner."

"No, this is perfect!" She pulled the bodice up against her chest. "Mine's ruined and we haven't had our first dance yet! I didn't want my first dance with my husband to be in a t-shirt and shorts! Thank you!"

"That's not all," Bud said, stopping her as she prepared to haul the dress off to the changing screen. "You made a few requests, remember?"

She sucked in air dramatically. "You didn't…"

"I did," he assured her, discarding the first box to unfold the edges of the second. "Tampons, pads, chocolate, and potato chips… and there's ice cream on the yacht."

Dropping the edges of the dress, she jumped up and coiled her arms around his neck. "You wonderful, beautiful man." She noisily kissed his cheek over and over. "I love you so very much."

He chuckled as she dragged the box to one side and fished out a candy bar. "Lainey? Izzy?" She held out the familiar brown and silver package and my mouth watered as she tossed it in my direction. Izzy nearly face-planted as she rushed from her chair to snag hers greedily from Lilly's hands. "Hey," Lilly said, tilting Izzy's chin up to face her. Signing and speaking simultaneously, Lilly shifted from spoiled granddaughter to mother-figure in the blink of an eye. "What do you say?"

Izzy turned to Bud, and he grinned as she vocalized, "Thang ooh."

Bud signed back. "I have something else for you."

Hypnotized by the candy wrapper she was unraveling, she didn't even notice the collection of stuffed animals and books he pulled from the next box, stacking them neatly on the rug in front of her. "I got a book on sign language too," he said to the rest of us, waiting patiently for her to finish unwrapping the bar and take a bite. When she looked up mid-chew, she squealed and attempted to pile every single fluffy animal into her arms at once.

Bud tossed the empty box to one side and pulled the next. As he did so, I noticed Lilly had swiftly disappeared along with the dress.

Bud peeked inside the box before him, then slid it off to the side. "This one's full of books on 18th century history. Everything we might need to know if…" he waved a hand in dismissal. "We'll worry about that later."

He dug into a new box. "Alaina..." He pulled out a small speaker and an iPod. I cupped them in my hands as if they might break. "Thank you!"

He winked. "And I brought a solar panel strong enough to charge both of those so you won't have to worry about conserving the battery. Chris helped me load it up with music you love. There are a few things on there for you too, Jim."

A natural Santa Claus, he'd picked the perfect gifts for each of us. For Jim, a crossbow, for Magna, a photo album full of pictures he'd found from her daughter's Instagram account. For Fetia, he brought a ring to symbolize her marriage to Kyle, and for Jack, he brought several books on off-the-grid living, chalked full of diagrams for setting up sewage, running water, wind power, and things we might need if we settled here. He gave Michael a pocket knife, and Jacob a new leather-bound sketchbook since he'd filled the one he'd had.

Pulling the final box, he looked at Kyle. "For you, my boy, I had this made special... now, if you don't like it or don't want it, you won't offend me whatsoever, but..." he presented a black oblong package and flipped open the lid to reveal a prosthetic arm, fitted for a loss above the elbow.

Kyle's mouth dropped open as he slowly drew his hand out to touch the lifelike arm inside. "How does... can I... can I try it now?"

"Of course you can!" Bud beamed. "Now, the solar panel only can do so much, so I couldn't get one of the fancier ones, but this one's got a sensor here that'll allow you to grip and release. That'll be easy enough to keep charged. Here, I'll show you how it goes on..."

As the two of them huddled together over the arm, I observed the detective fidgeting on the sofa across from me as he examined the expanse of the room. "Detective Haywood, was it?"

"Yes ma'am."

I smiled. "You got a first name we can call you by?"

"Terrence," he said flatly.

"Did you know you were going through time? You seem a little... shocked."

He smoothed a hand over his bald head. "I... didn't believe it... Not sure I believe it now... but this room... this ship... How am I ever going to explain this?"

Chris laughed. "Welcome to our world, Terrence. No one will ever believe you and there is no amount of fabricating you can do to cover it up. Someone like you will see right through the lies."

"How's your head?" I asked, cursing myself for not asking sooner. "And did you two get married?"

"My head's good. And no..." he exchanged smiles with Maria. "I tried to marry her a few times but..."

"But that world got in the way," she finished for him.

Cecelia squeezed my hand as she looked out at the two of them. "I suppose I owe you both an apology."

"For what?" I asked.

She bit her lower lip and frowned. "I was very cold to them both after I found your ring." She leaned to one side, holding the babies in place while she fished something out of her pocket. "Here." She tossed the ring to Maria. "I'm sorry. That belongs to you."

Maria inspected the ring and smiled as she slid it onto her finger. "Thank you."

"Oh," Chris leaned to one side, digging something out of his own pocket. "That reminds me..." He handed a small piece of paper to Jim. "What you asked for."

Jim took the paper, his arm remaining frozen in the air between them. "Ye' found her?"

"Yes."

Slowly, he retracted his arm and looked at whatever was written on the paper's surface. He nodded slowly, wiping his eyes as his lips formed a smile. "And you gave them the key?"

"I did," Chris said. "And if I never run into her again in my life, it'll be too soon."

"Who? June?" Lilly asked, reappearing from behind the dressing screen in a stunning lace ballgown she seemed born to wear.

Jim grinned as she spun a circle. "I got a son, darlin.' You got a stepson out there in the world... And that *idiot* mother of his named him Boley."

"*Boley?*" She smirked.

"First name Beau," he corrected. "Middle name Lee..." He shook his head. "That poor child is gonna' have a hell of a time with a name like that in school. 'Specially if he looks anything like me. He won't stand a chance."

Chapter Sixty Two

With the boxes cleared out of the way, Lilly decided our plans could wait until after her wedding reception was over. She'd snagged the iPod and the speaker and she and Jim scrolled through the library I had yet to look at, arguing over what song they would dance to.

"How 'bout this one?" He asked.

"*That's* the song you want to dance to?" She scoffed, taking the iPod from him. "On our *wedding day*? To remember me always if I *die*? A song about a *one-night stand*?"

"That ain't what it's—

He hummed a melody, mumbling the words under his breath. "Alright, maybe it is, pick somethin' else."

"So," Cecelia leaned into me, "you and Jack? When you and Chris left, you seemed so happy... what happened?"

Sighing, I looked out at Jack and Chris where they stood together looking over the pages of Jack's book and discussing wind power.

"Cece," I turned to face her. "Chris and I were only happy in the version of our lives you can remember. We killed a bunch of men on the beach—

"*You* killed somebody?" She sat up and glared at me.

"Our group, I mean. We were taken captive, and we poisoned them..." I waved my hand in dismissal. "We'll get into the details later. When they died, Chris and I got new memories... but we can still remember the original. You were married to a man named Owen, and you had a beautiful baby girl named Madison. You had this amazing life in Minnesota. You owned a campground together. And your life there... well, you didn't get to come and play therapist to me and Chris after we lost Evelyn. And Chris and I... we just couldn't get through it on our own. We ruined our marriage in the original timeline. One of those men we killed had to be connected to Owen. And that's what changed our memories. I'm doing everything I can to reverse what we did so you can have them back."

She frowned. "I don't understand. One: how in the world would you reverse what you've already done? And two, what makes you think I would ever want a life where I'm separated from you on a *campground* in Minnesota?"

"You were happy."

She huffed. "I'm happy now."

I laid my hand over hers in her lap. "Not like that, you're not. And changing it... well, the man you met in the hallway? His father is the one that took us captive. It was his men we poisoned. He crossed through the storm in 1977. If we can kill the ancestor of the man that brought him to the storm, we'll undo it and you'll have Owen and Maddy back."

She shook her head. "A.J., I don't want anyone to have to kill anybody to give me a life I'm not interested in."

"Trust me, you're interested in that life. You just don't remember it."

"Why don't you leave me to decide what I want for my life? Don't answer that... I don't want to talk about my life right now. I've spent the last three and a half years searching for you. I want to know about *your* life. About you and Jack... tell me everything."

I did. Curled up together on the sofa with the babies in our arms, I told her about everything that had happened since the plane crashed. I told her about the early days, mourning Chris, the summit, falling in love, the panic around being pregnant on the island, Jack leaving to find help, Anna, Captain Cook, giving birth, the wedding… everything,

When I'd finished, she scanned the people surrounding us to put faces to the names in the account I'd just laid out for her.

Maria stood with her hand on Fetia's stomach, laughing as she felt it kick. Bud held Izzy in his lap, flipping through the pages of the sign language book and trying out new signs while she squeezed a plush elephant against her cheek. Bruce and Magna were looking through her new photo album, Magna pointing to various pictures and offering backstory. Chris, Jack, and Kyle were walking through their own accounts of our time together with Terrence. And Lilly and Jim were still arguing over their song choice.

Cece hummed in a sigh. "I called mom when Chris told me where we were going. I told her I was coming to get you, and she wanted me to tell you that she loves you." She tugged on one of Zachary's toes. "She'd lose her mind over these two, you know."

"I know. God, I miss her. What I wouldn't give to see her dote over my babies the way she did yours. If you could remember Maddy, you'd know she lost her mind over her too."

"Let's not talk about a life I don't know tonight, okay?" She laid her head on my shoulder. "Because the fact that there's a whole other version of my life I don't know about makes me very uncomfortable… like… what the hell does that make me? A replacement? A fragment of what I was in the other version? Am I even real? Are you? I don't want to think about that tonight. Let's just enjoy each other for now."

"For the love of God, woman," Jim groaned, stealing our attention, "just pick one! I'm gonna' keel over dead before ye' find something."

"Okay, fine," Lilly spun to hide the iPod from view. "Go stand over there and wait. I'll do this the same way Jack did."

"As long as ye' do it before we all grow wrinkles," he teased, walking to the bit of open floor between the bed and the seating area to do his best impression of a shy and waiting female.

"Oh, I think I love those two already," Cece whispered, curling her legs up beneath her.

I grinned. "Good. I can't wait for you and her to get to know each other."

Lilly pressed play, and I was a little surprised to hear the familiar opening notes to Billy Joel's *'Just the way you are.'* A very fitting song for the two of them, but a surprise at it being *her* choice.

She curled naturally into his arms, and he led her gently, lacking his usual stiff arms and legs. I tilted my head to one side, watching as his movement aired on the side of graceful.

I peered across the room at Jack and waited for his gaze to meet mine. I raised an eyebrow, and he grinned, crossing over to us to kneel on the floor at my feet.

"You taught Jim how to dance?" I asked.

He nodded, glancing proudly back at them. "I did. And it was just as awkward as you could imagine it might be."

"When?" I chuckled, imagining the two of them hidden away in a room on the ship practicing.

"Why do you think we've been going hunting so often lately?"

I snorted. "I would've paid good money to catch you two in the act."

He bounced his eyebrows. "How much? For the right price, I'll whisk him right into a waltz here and now. I'm pretty poor and desperate these days."

"Not anymore, you're not," Cecelia said, touching his shoulder with her forefinger as if she were attempting to determine if the same Jack Volmer that hung on posters in *both* our bedrooms was really kneeling before us. "Bud and Chris brought a whole trove of gold with them. That's what drew the detective's attention. Bud came back and immediately started withdrawing large amounts of cash from his accounts. He thought you all had been taken hostage."

I laughed at that. "That would've been much simpler, eh?"

Jack squeezed my calf. "But not nearly as interesting. Cece, would you like to dance?"

"With Jack Volmer?" She swooned dramatically. "I would absolutely love to."

She laid Cecelia on her belly on the sofa and placed her hand in his, laughing as he led her out to the area that was serving as our dance floor.

Kyle, grinning from ear to ear across from me, adjusted his new prosthetic arm so it was coiled around Fetia's back, then took her hand in his and swayed gracefully to the dance floor.

Bud tapped Jim's shoulder so he could cut in and Jim relinquished his position happily, turning to motion for Izzy to join him in her place.

I watched with burning eyes and cheeks as Magna and Bruce and Chris and Maria also fell into dance.

I loved them all, and we were safe.

Whatever we were about to face, and wherever we might end up, the path before us no longer seemed so insurmountable with these people surrounding me. Whatever we were, be it replacements of our original selves or just remnants on the tides of time, we were together, and there was nothing else I cared to be.

Chapter Sixty Three

The following morning, we took breakfast in the great cabin so we could discuss the group's findings without Juan Josef in the room next-door to potentially overhear our plans.

Cece took a seat to my left at the table, Zachary in one arm while the hand of her other squeezed mine where she refused to let it go—neither of us had let go of the other since she'd come on deck, we'd even slept in each other's arms.

Jack sat to my right; Lilly, Jim, and Izzy taking their usual places across from us while Bruce, Magna, Kyle, and Fetia took the remaining seats.

Bud sat at the head of the table gripping a binder as he waited for us all to settle into our seats, Chris and Maria waiting at the opposite end while Terrence paced near the windows.

"There are three options we need to discuss," Bud said, opening the binder and silencing the chatter around us as he did so. "On these pages, I've got the lineage for each and every one of you, as well as Richard Albrecht and Juan Josef. Chris and I have spent hours poring over these reports to ensure that, should we go with plans B or C, it will not affect any one of us. We should run through them as a group to be certain there's no chance of overlap if we don't go along with plan A."

"What's plan A?" Lilly asked, daintily spreading jam on a piece of bread for Izzy.

"The simplest one," Bud assured her, handing me a quarter-inch report with my name on it. "Alaina and Jack just need to go to the future and never come back through the storm."

"That sounds simple enough," Cece said, leaning into my shoulder as I flipped through the opening pages.

I frowned when I landed on a tree map.

At the top of the map were my and Jack's names, followed by Cecelia and Zachary, then a list of descendants that led all the way down to Dario and Dahlia. "So Dario is my… great great great—however-many-great grandchild?"

Bud nodded. That explained why Dario had initially seemed familiar.

I returned to the top to scan the page more carefully. "Jack and I are—

My heart stopped as I read the death year beneath Jack's name. 1775…

I snapped the report closed, terrified that if I looked at it too long, it might actually become true.

1775….

All the warmth that had filled my heart from the wedding and Cecelia's appearance was suddenly replaced by ice that spread across my veins.

1775 was only a few weeks away…

"What?" Jack asked, reaching for the report only for me to pull it off the table and clutch it to my chest.

He laughed nervously, "Red, what's wrong?"

My mouth was suddenly too dry and all I could do was stare up at him, bargaining in my heart with God or whoever would listen for his life.

"Does it say when or how?" I asked no one in particular, continuing to stare at my husband's face; memorizing every curve.

"No," Bud said softly, "just the year."

Jack reached for the report again, frowning. "When or how, what? Let me see it."

I hugged the papers tighter, smashing them against my chest. "We'll go home. That's the plan. If we go home, we stop all of it…

You and I are Gloria's ancestors, so... they won't come here if she doesn't exist. That's what we wanted. We'll stay here on this island until March and then we'll go home."

"What are you trying to hide?" He asked, tugging the report until it slid free of my grip. "And why is everyone looking at me like that?"

Chris, Bud, and Maria were all staring at him the same way I was... as if he might disappear any moment.

He flipped the booklet open until he reached the tree map, and I held my breath while he scanned its contents. He read the page from top to bottom again and again, his brows knitting tighter together with each new sweep of his eyes across the page.

"It doesn't mean anything," I said, looking at Bud and Chris for confirmation. "If we stay on this island, and then go straight to the storm, you'll be fine."

"What in the hell are yuns talkin' about?" Jim asked. "Will somebody fill in the rest of us?"

Jack shook his head, still staring at the report. "Says here that I die in 1775... and Zachary will die in 1779."

At that, my heart stopped beating. I hadn't read anything past the date beneath Jack's name—hadn't even considered my children would go on to do anything but live long and happy lives. The idea that I could lose my son within four years made the room start to spin around me.

"So why the hell would there need to be a plan B or C then?" Jim asked. "Let's go home. Hell, since yuns came back three months sooner than we thought, we only got three more months to wait till' March. I'm pretty dang sure we can keep ye' alive for three months... even if we gotta' wrap ye' up in plastic."

Every bone in my body was ice, and my words reflected the chill. "We can't take any chances. No more prisoners. No more strangers. We kill the ones we're holding. If going back home changes everything anyway, it's not like they'll stay dead."

"Well," Chris pursed his lips, "one of them would."

"Two," Maria cut in. "If Gloria doesn't exist, then Dario *and Dahlia* will both die."

"I don't care," I assured her. "Not if it's a matter of my husband and child's lives versus theirs."

She wanted to say more. She opened her mouth as if to speak, but stopped herself.

She'd mentioned the night before that she'd met Dahlia. We'd asked how it was possible that more than three had made it through and she ran us through Dahlia's experience and explanation.

"And that man in the hall?" Cecelia asked. "The one watching over us... will he die too?"

"No," Chris said before I could even process the question or the sorrowful tone of voice she'd used to ask it. "Gloria was not his birthmother. His timeline should go unaltered."

"What about right now, though?" Lilly asked, inspecting Jack. "I know Juan Jr. helped us, but... does that mean we can fully trust him? If Jack's supposed to die in 1775, shouldn't we eliminate *all* possible threats? Separate ourselves from everyone who is not a part of this group? Including the rest of the men *as well as* Jacob and Michael?"

"Jacob and Michael aren't a threat," Kyle informed her. "Neither is Juan Jr. You can't seriously be thinking about killing them after everything we've all been through together. What if going back doesn't change anything?"

"Look, none of us has any idea how any of this works," Chris noted, running a hand over his face. "All we know is that Jack's got a death year on that paper that's fast approaching, and we need to get them home. I don't want to kill anybody either. What if we stock up the ship and the yacht and leave them on the island instead?"

"Is there enough fuel on the yacht to get there?" Lilly asked.

"To get to the coordinates, yes," Bud said, flipping through the other reports in the binder, "but beyond that, we'll be running on fumes. We'll have to tether it to the ship when we get close to the coordinates. Can't leave it to idle if we're hoping to use it to go through."

"How long can you keep the freezers running?" Jack asked. "Three months is a long time. We'll need to stock up on as much fruit and algae as we can. None of us can afford to go without the vitamins. Especially Fetia."

"If we only ran those on the solar panels," Bud said, "we could keep them running the whole time we're out there."

Kyle stood, crossing his new prosthetic arm beneath his other over his chest as he paced. "Let's say this works… we go out there and sit on the ocean for months… Then we sail into the storm… Will we even come out the other side or will we wake up in Tahiti… in the moments before we ever crossed paths with him? Wouldn't it work that way?"

I shrugged. "I don't think so. Chris and I didn't wake up in our old lives when we changed our own timelines… we just got new memories of the things that happened."

I caught the hint of a smile from Chris in acknowledgment of the shared changes.

"Yes, but… Anna." Kyle said, turning to look out the window. "She's in the ground. Will she wake up in the dirt with new memories and us gone? That can't be right… Can it?"

"We'll go get her," Bruce announced, rising from his seat. "We'll dig her up and put her in one of the rooms on the lower decks just to be safe." He moved for the door, but stopped short, turning back to us on his good leg. "For the record, I don't think we should leave Juan Josef *or* his sons alive. By going home, we prevent Gloria—the single person they all seem to care about—from being born. If the effects of our traveling through time aren't immediate, leaving them alive could give them the opportunity to escape the island and seek out Renauds, Jacksons, or Dietrichs the same way they did Albrechts. I don't know that I'm willing to live my life with that kind of dark cloud hanging over it."

Kyle huffed. "I don't know that *I'm* willing to live with the murder of innocent men hanging over mine. What we do with Juan Josef and Dario is of no concern to me, but Juan Jr… Jacob? Michael? We can't just kill them or leave them here to die."

"We have time to think about it," Lilly said, leaning against Jim's shoulder and taking a deep breath. "We need to stock up before we ship out, so we'll all use that time to think about what the right thing to do is, then we'll put it to a vote. Okay?"

Jack nodded. "Okay." He slid the report across the table to Bud. "That binder needs to be put someplace safe. In the wrong hands, it could be a death sentence to us all."

"I intend to burn it," Bud assured him, "the moment we sail out and know we're home free. Until then, I'll put it in a safe on the yacht."

"Good," Jack stood, offering Lilly and Jim an apologetic smile. "I'm sorry to cut your honeymoon short, but we should get started now. I'd like to try to catch a boar or two or three to take with us. I know you said the pigs should be safe to eat now, but I'd feel better if we caught a few more... Maybe we just shoot them with that new crossbow of yours and freeze the meat... And Red," he turned toward me, "you and Lilly are the best spear fishermen among us. Maybe you two can take Maria and Cece down to the beach and see about catching some grouper and crab to keep frozen?"

I nodded.

Magna cleared her throat. "Fetia and I can keep the babies with us. We'll get started on mending the bird cage so we can take some of the Kolea with us."

"Good," he said, turning to Kyle. "You think you can help Bruce with Anna?"

"Of course." He flexed the fingers on his prosthetic as proof, then nodded his head toward Terrence where he was leaning silently against the far wall. "What about him?"

Terrence cracked his knuckles where his fingers were curled into fists at his sides. "What *about* me?"

"Well," Kyle said simply, "are you helping us or not? And can we trust you?"

"Trust me?" He asked, pushing himself off the wall to stand near the edge of the table. "You are the ones talking about killing ancestors and altering history... time travel and folks coming back from the dead... I wouldn't even know where to *start* to help you."

"You don't believe us?" I asked.

He took a deep breath. "I honestly don't know what I believe. This ship…" He looked around the immaculately decorated room. "If this ship wasn't here, I'd swear every single one of you needed to be institutionalized. But…. This…" He moved his palm over the intricate woodwork framing the door. "It's too real—too much— too many old things that don't look old… and if that means we really are in 1775, well, there's not a whole lot of places a black man can go and feel safe… I'd much rather spend whatever time I'm stuck here on a ship in the middle of the ocean than risk running into the wrong people." He sighed. "I suppose I'll help fish if you've got a line and a hook."

Chapter Sixty Four

We returned to the ship late after a day spent hunting, fishing, and foraging; all of us so fatigued, we barely made it down the corridor before collectively collapsing into our beds.

Lilly, Maria, and I had caught five grouper while Cecelia roamed the beach collecting coconuts. We cleaned, filleted, and wrapped the fish in paper to be frozen, then proceeded to the opposite side of the island to harvest as much spaghetti algae as we could.

Cecelia had a nasty sunburn spread over her face, shoulders, and arms—similar to one I'd gotten during my first fishing trip on the island. She didn't complain, but the moment she got to the room, she laid down on one of the sofas and was out cold.

Jack, Jim, and Chris had managed to kill a boar. We'd all helped gut and butcher it—all but Terrence, who'd nearly vomited as we did so.

Juan Jr. had been curious, so we told him we were stocking the ship to prepare for our journey to the colonies in search of the Albrecht ancestor. For as much as I hated lying to a man who'd just saved our lives, I hated the death date beneath Jack's name even more.

My limbs were heavy as I climbed into bed beside Jack.

Exhausted and slightly sunburnt himself, he'd removed his shirt and promptly passed out on his stomach in the bed, his face turned to one side with both arms curled up beneath his pillow. In the light of the single candle still burning at the side of the bed, I admired his sleeping face. How peaceful he looked with his lips slightly parted against the pillow; his brow relaxed and his shoulders rising and falling with his deep breaths. I couldn't lose him... not ever.

And I wasn't going to. We were going home and we would never ever go anywhere near that spot on the ocean again.

Home.

For the first time since we'd discussed it, I considered what it'd be like to see my mother again... To watch her hold my children in her arms and spoil them with the type of affection she kept reserved solely for her own blood.

I considered what it might mean to meet Jack's mother and sister; to put faces to the stories he'd told so many nights on the summit and in the cave.

I smiled as I pictured our island family gathered around a large table for dinner, wineglasses clinking and stories about our time here being shared.

There'd be no Juan Josef... no made up identities or lies... no struggle to find food or a home or a place free of war... Just us... in a world we knew... with each other. I'd never thought of myself fitting into that world, but I fit into that image. With a family surrounding me, I couldn't wait to go home.

And as images of that family dinner played out behind my eyes, I surrendered to my fatigue, drifting away to join them in a dream.

"Are you kiddin' me?!" Jim shouted, forcing both Jack and I to sit up suddenly in the bed. "Hoss, get out here!"

Both babies began to cry, and I hurried to the cradle while Jack rushed out into the hall.

I held Zachary against my shoulder, bouncing him gently, as Cece showed up at my side to take Cecelia into her arms. "What's going on?" She whispered, yawning.

"Not sure," I said, creeping to the doorway to peer out.

The door beside ours was open, and both men were inside.

"What's going on in there?" I called. "Everything okay? Jack? You alright?"

"No," he said in a far-off voice. "They're gone."

I pushed into the room to find the bed unbolted from the wall, pulled back to reveal a small opening large enough to fit a person.

My heart sank. I'd searched the ship for secret compartments when attempting to find the stolen gold, but I'd never thought to unbolt the bed frames. I realized, as I peered into the opening to find it led around a corner, this was the reason Juan Josef had stabbed Phil and Eli. I knew, if I returned to the room we'd originally kept him held in, we'd find a similar passageway behind the bed there—possibly one in every room of the ship. He'd never been our captive. He'd used captivity as an excuse to spy on us.

Juan Jr. sat on the edge of the bed with his head hung low, a few papers in his hand, and a small chest of gold at his feet.

"They can't be far…" Lilly assured them once she'd inspected the passage for herself. "They've got to be on the island or—

"They ain't on the island, sugar." Jim motioned to the window. "They're gone."

"They stole the boat?!" she shrieked. "Are you kidding?"

"That's not the worst of it," Jack said, pulling the papers from Juan Jr.

He handed them to me, and Lilly hovered at my shoulder while I read the sharp cursive lettering on the first page.

'I told you nothing on this ship goes unheard. The knife is now at your throats.'

Beneath the letter was a page from Bud's binder. At the top was the name: George Thomas Bennet—Richard Albrecht's ancestor, and a single selection in the ensuing paragraphs was circled: December 9, 1775, Great Bridge, Virginia.

The message was clear. Juan Josef would not let Gloria go— would not let Jack and I simply return home to erase all that had happened. If we didn't pursue the Albrecht ancestor; if we didn't show up in Great Bridge on December 9th, he had the means to kill us all...

CPSIA information can be obtained
at www.ICGtesting.com
Printed in the USA
BVHW071014280622
640817BV00012B/517